SHALLOWS OF NIGHT

Second in the
SUNSET WARRIOR TRILOGY

...in which Ronin, Bladesman, sails a sea of ice with
Borros, called Magic Man; discovers an exotic city on
a continent undreamed of; and surrenders willingly to
the temptress Kiri in his quest to decipher the scroll that
is Man's last and only hope...

ERIC VAN LUSTBADER

*The bestselling author of THE NINJA is unequalled as a
creator of worlds dark with violence, bright with erotic
possibility, and shimmering with magic and grandeur. This
three volume series is the first paperback publication of his
sensational SUNSET WARRIOR TRILOGY.*

Berkley books by Eric Van Lustbader

BENEATH AN OPAL MOON

THE SUNSET WARRIOR CYCLE

THE SUNSET WARRIOR
SHALLOWS OF NIGHT
DAI-SAN

ERIC VAN LUSTBADER

SHALLOWS OF NIGHT

SECOND IN THE SUNSET WARRIOR TRILOGY

BERKLEY BOOKS, NEW YORK

This Berkley book contains the complete
text of the original hardcover edition.
It has been completely reset in a typeface
designed for easy reading and was printed
from new film.

SHALLOWS OF NIGHT

A Berkley Book / published by arrangement with
Doubleday & Company, Inc.

PRINTING HISTORY
Doubleday edition published 1978
Berkley edition / December 1980
Seventh printing / July 1986

ISBN: 0-425-09964-4

A BERKLEY BOOK ® TM 757,375
Berkley Books are published by The Berkley Publishing Group,
200 Madison Avenue, New York, NY 10016.
The name "BERKLEY" and the stylized "B" with design
are trademarks belonging to Berkley Publishing Corporation.

PRINTED IN THE UNITED STATES OF AMERICA

For all the heroes

Contents

There is no journey's end.

—Bujun saying

ONE

·Ice·

Soaring through frigid mists and roiling clouds, he stretches fully his long wings upon the unpredictable currents. Streamers of silvered plumage, running bilaterally across his wings and cresting his majestic questing head, ripple and blur in the wind. He banks and dips. There is a moaning in his ears. His large liquid eyes stare unblinkingly ahead at the immense eye of the setting sun, its face a broad and flattened disk, wider at the sides as if caught in a vise of immeasurable proportions. Then thick ribbons of cloud of a metallic gray ride before it like the ghostly remnants of a once vast, victorious army, reaving it.

He banks again, deftly avoiding a treacherous downdraft, and turns his incurious gaze beneath him, through the layers of cloud and mist, to the painful twisting of the earth far below.

High peaks beaten by age and scraped by merciless weather, crowned in bitter frost, sealed in pearl and emerald ice, thrust their humped backs in snaking lines against the whipping winds which, forever swirling, gather layers of fine powdery snow from the mountains' slopes, turning them into rising sheets, hurling them forward, like giants striding across the barren land.

He floats over sheer gorges, frosted thickly in gleaming sheets of periwinkle ice, plumes of loose snow drifting along their flanks like smoke from a funeral pyre. His keen eyes trace the vertiginous descent from dancing ice crystaled green-turquoise-magenta in

11

the dying light to the violent violet of their yawning and uneasy depths: precipitous chasms sliced out of the land as cleanly as if by a cruel blade of immense size. Powerful wings flutter as out of these depths now is heard the agonized groaning of shifting rock. Ozone and sulpher fill the air as the earth shudders and trembles. Shards of ice shear off in the dense clusters with infinite slowness, hanging impossibly in mid-air, crumbling in layers until, with an abrupt and complete swiftness, they explode silently into vast spurts of hyalescent spray high in the sky that turn to rainbow arcs as they catch the last oblique rays of watery light.

He wheels in the colored, suddenly solid air, unperturbed.

Everywhere is ice and draperies of snow with only the occasional tired fist of granite or twisted schist rising like ancient tombstones in an alien desert, useless punctuation on a blank and crumbling page.

Against this inimical icescape nothing moves.

The bird banks and glides in the sky, his black-irised eyes scanning the dreadful sameness of the land. Into the setting sun he flies, his majestic plumage stained a dilute scarlet and, glancing once more earthward, he sees a dark and tiny shadow limned before the glare of the ice. Muscles respond to the brain's command and the wings dip, their silver plumage losing for a moment the scarlet wash, turning a rich lustrous gray, as he heads southward for a closer look.

Resolution of image comes far too swiftly, for the shadow is huge. Abruptly it moves and, startled, the bird wheels away from the edge of the steep precipice along which he has been flying and, flapping his wings in alarm, speeds westward, rising, gaining the high currents, diminishing into the light of the lowering sun.

Transfixed, Ronin stands at the verge of the high

ice ledge staring southward, oblivious to the receding speck in the sky.

Motionless, his body tall and muscular, he appears more a statue erected to the countless legions who, throughout the myriad ages, have fought across the changing faces of this land. For here once grew lush verdant forests of giant fern and slender willow spreading their fans of feathered leaves, building dense jungles of crowding greenery and thick tangles of vines through which cocoa warriors crept and crouched, sweating, listening methodically to the shrill cries of startlingly colored birds, readying the leap, an uncoiling blur, tan and brown shadow, flickering in the filtering light, the quick silent slash, the gout of bright blood beading the foliage, the dying body of the enemy. And in another age—earlier or later, one cannot be sure—here swelled and sucked fifteen fathoms of green water alive with the riotous growth of the sea. High-booted feet tramped the stained tarred decks of wide-beamed wooden ships, long oars extending from their high curving sides, beating through air and water in hypnotic rhythm. Hoarse shouts filled the sky heavy with brine and heat as helmed and bearded warriors prepared themselves for battle.

Layers of hard snow encrust the slippery ice of the precipice upon which he stands, feet apart and planted firmly in the frost. Unconsciously he clenches his left hand, which is covered by a strange scaled gauntlet, dull and unreflective. The wind gusts, screaming in his ears, and rushes by him, unheeded, sucked in by the crevices and piled hillocks of the plateau tumbling at his back. The air is dry and chill. The staggering sight at which he gazes longingly resonates in his mind with the supravivid impact of an ecstatic dream. And for this time, the event of the recent past mercifully dim.

For what lies before and below him, just past the

beetling lip of the high ledge, is a cyclopean sea of ice. Desolate. Limitless. Awesome and electrifying.

"An overwhelming sight," said the voice quite near and behind him. And he turned slowly, as if in a dream, to behold Borros, the Magic Man.

"The true wonder is that we have been denied this sight for all of our lives." A thin and weary smile curled Borros' lips.

Wind whipped loose snow against their legs as they stood atop the ice plateau, strange creatures garbed in the one-piece foil suits they had found on the highest Level of the Freehold before each, in his own time and his own way, breached the last metal defense of their subterranean world, cracking the outer hatch, buried in drifting snow. The suits were extremely light, skin tight along chest and arms, with filled pockets of hardware and food concentrates, vacuum-sealed, immune to the ravages of time, even a small supply of mineral-enriched fluid to refresh themselves. These pockets ran around the suits' waists and down the outside of each leg, somehow increasing the warmth of the garments.

Ronin stared at Borros, seeing him now as if for the first time, the focus of reality at last forced upon him, and all the raw hate that he had held in abeyance for these long moments flooded back on an inexorable tide. Caught in the slipstream of sewage; shook himself, as if the motion would somehow cleanse him. He knew that he carried now within his depths an anger and a sorrow, that thus was bound to him irrevocably a hideous strength.

The Magic Man had misunderstood the gesture and he grasped Ronin's shoulder.

"Surely you are not cold?"

His fingers moved along the foil to a fold at the back on Ronin's neck. "Look here." And he pulled gently upward, the metallic skin stretching to cover

14

Ronin's head, leaving only his eyes and mouth exposed. Borros wrestled his own hood into place.

Borros turned to stare behind them, peering across the rubble of the frozen waste to the hidden Freehold, the tiny access hatch leading down and down to the world inside, a world at war now, factions struggling for desperate power.

"Do not think me a fool," the Magic Man said urgently. "But we must flee from here at once."

Tears call to Ronin and the mountains melting as he ceases to feel the bite of the wind at his eyes and lips. The sky colorless and the earth with no substance. His feet leaden. His heart pounding as it hit him searingly like the aftershock of a deep wound, the rent cauterized but the nerves still in dysfunction. At first there was no feeling at all. Numb. The body protecting itself. But there is a limit. His consciousness narrowed because he was struggling against it now. All his loves, all his friends, all the people. Gone in a wink of an eye. Just a flutter of time, the space to pull two breaths and lives are snuffed like tapers at first Spell. K'reen and Stahlig and Nirren and G'fand and—the Salamander, the center of it all, still down there, alive, alive. . . .

"—now."

Slowly, it seemed to him, he became aware of a plucking at his sleeve.

"Ronin, please, we must be off." He heard the words as if from a great distance. They hung in front of him like lamps, separate and solid, one after another, turning on some unseen axis, their sheen . . .

"Chill take it! Ronin, we must go now! Before pursuit from below can be organized."

Then the meaning had penetrated and he started as if from a deep slumber.

"Yes," he said hoarsely, turned to look at Borros. "Yes, of course we must be off." His colorless eyes were clear now, their gaze sharp and quick. "But which way?"

"There," said the Magic Man. And he lifted his arm in a sweeping gesture outward, over the lip of the precipice to the enormous expanse of the darkling ice sea.

There was nought but the crying of the freezing wind. The ancient rock at his face, rippling, studded with ice in pockets and rivulets, slipped away above him centimeter by centimeter. The sound was like the wailing of the damned. Striations made a constantly changing pattern that held his attention as he searched for foot and handholds. Following Borros down the immense face of the cliff toward the ice sea far, far below, he felt all too distinctly the void at his back. The magnitude of its emptiness beckoned to him, the wind its siren call, ululating hypnotically. Relax, let go, feel the gentle parting of warm flesh from cold stone, to fall backward, slowly, effortlessly onto the comforting cushion of the wind, turning, to be borne away, tumbling, into the void. . . .

An ending he did not wish.

"What, over the edge?" he had said.

A peculiar animation had come to the Magic Man's face, a keen anticipation. "Yes. Yes! Do you not see?" As if he had waited all his life for this kinetic moment. "It is the only way down to the ice sea. Our way lies south. South into the land of men."

And so Ronin had walked with Borros through the crusty snow and treacherous ice to the very edge, entirely free at last of the ties that bind every man at one time to home. Masterless but not directionless.

They went carefully along the lip for perhaps a thousand meters and then Borros slipped over the side. Without a backward glance Ronin too quit the plateau.

Ronin became aware that Borros had stopped below him. He called down but the fluting of the wind made communication impossible at this distance. Carefully he lowered himself to the other's side.

"The way below is blocked," Borros said in his ear.

Ronin peered down through the intermittent showers of snow. Indeed, directly below them a fresh fall of snow and ice crystals layered the cliff face and it was impossible to determine the nature of the footing. Suicidal to attempt the descent by touch alone, yet it was imperative that they move onward.

Ronin swung his gaze to their right where his peripheral vision has registered a dark area along the rock wall. Now, motioning with his head, he led the Magic Man toward its smudgy outline.

They inched along the narrow ledge upon which they had stopped their descent and soon the dark area took on definition. As Ronin had hoped, it was a cave of some considerable size and within its mouth they found a semblance of shelter from the wind and the cold.

Borros sighed deeply as he pulled off his hood. His hairless skull, faintly gleaming in the dim light, seemed peculiarly fitting for this foreign and forbidding place; its singular saffron color could almost have passed for the patina of age.

Ronin went away from the rough rock walls to the lip of the cave. Below him the cliff dropped precipitously. Beneath the heavy fall of new snow clinging to the rock with an almost sentient tenacity there must be a way down to the ice sea. He could just make out a sliver of its surface sparkling in the lowering light. But from what he could see, there was no way of knowing, therefore no practical way down. Laterally there was only the mean ledge along which they had come. Farther to the right it disappeared into the rock face only meters from where he stood. He kicked at the snow, left plumes arcing out into the wind as he returned to the twilight of the cave.

Borros was agitated. "What are we to do?" he asked Ronin as he stalked back and forth. "We must continue the descent. Already men from the Freehold will be searching for us."

Ronin's mouth moved into the semblance of a brief, chill smile. "Do you really believe that they would allow anyone onto the Surface? They must think that we shall perish out here."

The Magic Man's eyes darted from the cave's opening to Ronin's face, back again. "You do not know Freidal. Or Security. My escape—" His eyes flicked back to the cave's mouth. "He will kill me if he catches me." His gaze passed across Ronin's face again like clouds across the face of the sun. "You also. If he finds me, he finds you."

"No one is after us," Ronin said flatly.

Borros pulled his hood up over his bald skull. "You are wrong but it makes no difference. Even if Freidal was not coming after us, we would still have no choice. We must descend to the ice sea. We cannot survive long here."

"Better to die on the way down than here in the cave," Ronin said sardonically.

Borros shrugged. "Are you coming?"

He did not answer immediately but walked away from the light, into the cave's dank interior, smelling the acrid odor of raw minerals and rock dust, hearing the whistling of the wind diminish. Yet there was sound.

Far back in the cave he dimly heard the Magic Man's strident call but he ignored it. He listened intently, moving purposefully, his pulse quickening. And now he was sure. Excitedly he put his arms out, hands floating through the blackness, feeling along the wall like a blind man's.

He heard Borros calling thinly again, a forlorn and lonely sound, and he went slowly forward so as not to miss it. As last he stopped, his fingers running over the metalwork he had been searching for and his heart soared because he knew now that there was after all a way down to the ice sea. He called out to Borros.

What he had thought was the soughing of the wind had in fact been the distant sound of rushing water. The wind had been in his ears for so long that it was not until he moved farther back into the cave that he had been able to pick up the subtle tonal alteration. Even so, had he not made the long descent from the Freehold to the City of Ten Thousand Paths—the flicker of G'fand's smiling face frozen in his mind's eye, dissolving into the bloody wreck of the Scholar's corpse flung along the dusty cobbles of the ancient street, eyes bulging, throat torn out by the nameless towering thing that Ronin had tried twice to kill and failed, inhuman eyes like crescent moons, a chill more deadly than a coffin of ice and a power—he never would have recognized the new sound as a torrent of water pitching headlong over smooth rock down and down in a frantic cascade. He and G'fand had encountered the immense waterfall on their way to the City of Ten Thousand Paths and its reverberations had been with them for many kilometers. It was the same sound now, merely muffled by distance.

"Borros," Ronin called again.

They were obviously far from the cataract yet the presence of the sound was a clear indication that this cave was perhaps more than just that. Ronin believed now that they were in the outermost reaches of a tunnel. He thought of Bonneduce the Last, the small, lame man, and his companion, Hynd, a creature that was more than an animal. He and G'fand had encountered the pair in the City of Ten Thousand Paths. Bonneduce the Last had assured them that he and

19

Hynd dwelled on the Surface but had given no indication of how they had come to the City. Could this have been his entrance and egress? Ronin was certain that it was. Given that, the cave must contain a means to descend to the ice sea.

His hand wrapped around the haft.

Borros came up then.

"I have found something," Ronin told him. "Do you have tinder?"

The Magic Man reached into one of his pockets, produced tinder and flint. Together they lit the torch.

The flame, tiny at first, sizzled pale yellow and smoked on the damp material so that they choked and, coughing, were forced to turn their heads away. The orange light leapt and quivered and, wiping the water from their eyes, they were for the first time able to see the rough and gritty walls, black ice gleaming like obsidian in the shadowed hollows, the surface streaked ocher and green silver and pink by the exposed minerals.

Everything they needed was there, hanging by the metalwork of the torch's niche. Long coils of rope of a peculiar material not thick but, as Ronin pulled on them, obviously more than strong enough. Beneath the ropes, small metal hammers with long heads and with these bags filled with metal spikes of unfamiliar manufacture, flattened and broader at the end through which was punched a circular hole large enough for the rope to pass through.

"And so," said Ronin, "we descend the cliff after all."

His head whipped up and his nostrils dilated as the smell came to him. They had worked hard, on their knees driving the spikes into the rock floor of the cave just inside the mouth. They had inserted the ropes and tied double knots, leaning back and pulling hard to test the fastness of their handiwork. The small bags they had tied to their suits; the hammers dangled from their wrists by short thongs. Wrapping the ropes about their waists, they had walked to the lip of the cave. Ronin let the rope drop and his fist went to the hilt of his sword.

Before, it had been a stench when the monstrous thing came for them from out of the black shadows through the dry dust and golden dimness, its fearsome visage dominated by the glowing eyes and the curved, wicked beak. His stomach heaved at the thought of its invulnerability, the desperation of his attack as G'fand lay mutilated. The smell was like a living thing then. Now it was far off but, he surmised, reachable; it was getting stronger. He let the anger and fear mingle within him until it became rage. Adrenalin rushed through his body and he clenched his hand within the gauntlet left for him by Bonneduce the Last, cunningly made from the giant claw of one of the hideous creatures. How many of them were there? he wondered fleetingly. He began to withdraw his sword.

And felt the hand on his shoulder, heard the voice crying urgently at his side, "What are you doing? You fool, we must go now! There is no time to lose!" His hand tightened on the sword hilt. "Ronin, we must reach the ice sea!"

Instinctively he knew that Borros was correct. Their survival must come first. His battle would have to wait. And perhaps that was for the best. He wanted to be able to pick the time and the place when he would next meet the creature. But more importantly he needed more information about it if he was to have a real chance of killing it and surviving.

He let go the sword and picked up the rope, securing it once more about his waist. He nodded wordlessly to the Magic Man and they crunched backward through the snow. On the ledge the wind bit into the

21

exposed areas of their faces as they went over the edge.

He hung suspended, dangling, the rope biting cruelly into his ankle. Momentum, he thought as warily they circled him, knowing their advantage but fearing him still. He had no weapon and of course that was the point. Because, as he had once told G'fand, learning the art of Combat meant much more than being taught to wield a sword.

His body, near naked and slick with the sweat of exertion and heat, swung along its brief orbit. Keep the body relaxed, the Salamander had told him. Work within as small a space as you feel you can allow without sacrificing the momentum provided by the orbit of the swing. You understand, Ronin, that once inertia takes over you are finished because an opponent will gut you in the time it takes you to overcome it.

Other students in the special Combat class presided over by the Salamander had attempted the *cruol*, that length of rope suspended from the ceiling to which one was tied head down a meter off the floor. Four students attacked with wooden staffs the length of a man's body. No one had survived for long. However, none of the students had been trained by the Salamander as extensively as had Ronin. And none had his skill.

Because it was so terribly difficult, the *cruol* was now used almost exclusively for punishment. Yet up here on the Salamander's Level it had other uses.

He kept the momentum going, consciously feeding the adrenalin flowing through his body, knowing he would need all that he could produce in the coming moments. A staff came at him, whistling through the air. He twisted his shoulders and felt a burning down his back at the narrowness of the miss. The students

22

fanned out, swinging at him again and again. He used his forearms to block the staffs, while gradually increasing the length of his arcs. Less and less, they found the need to advance toward him in order to make contact; they were too intent on the attack to take notice.

He swung, waiting for a peak, and for a lateral cut. He saw one coming from the left and he knew that it would be close because he was just at the peak of his arc and the student's blow had to be fast or he would lose the advantage of the momentum. But the staff came at him with tremendous force and it was all right because now he was beginning to arc away from the oncoming staff, his momentum picking up, and now, instead of blocking the blow, he reached for the blurred weapon, his tightening fingers slipping along its length in the slick sweat running off him. Palms burning with the friction, a blow from another staff numbing the muscles along his back. Ignore the pain. Concentrate. He used his mounting momentum and, twisting his wrists at the last instant, wrenched the staff from the startled student.

He was moving to his right with great speed now and, taking advantage of the direction of his swing, slammed the staff into the collarbone of a student on that side. He crumpled to the floor as Ronin began to reverse his arc and caught a second adversary in the mid-section so that the student doubled over, retching and gagging.

There was only one now because the one Ronin had disarmed was forbidden to interfere once he had lost his weapon. This one was wary. He would not be trapped as his fellows had been. Ronin noted that he was concentrating on Ronin's weapon. Then he attacked, swinging at the base of Ronin's staff, seeking to bruise his hands. The blows were rapid-fire so that, for every one Ronin blocked, one slammed into his knuckles. They soon turned red and the first spattering of blood appeared as the skin split and tore. The student pressed his advantage, moving in, the bright blood fascinating and irresistible. His concentration narrowed.

It was then that Ronin used his free leg, slamming the sole of his boot against the side of the student's head. The man staggered, off balance. The blow had not been hard enough to knock him down because Ronin lacked the leverage, but it was enough. The staff sang through the air, catching the student on the neck. He gasped hollowly, his face turning white and his mouth hinged open as he fell. There was only the sound of forced breathing then as Ronin dropped his staff, relaxing his body, turning slowly again in his brief orbit.

Suspended in whiteness, his breath fogging the frigid air, descending hand over hand, Borros slightly above him a meter away, Ronin recalled well the lesson of the *cruol*. But now the context had altered, small patterns interlaced with other patterns until, as one steps back to view the configuration, an overall image begins to emerge, different, unexpected.

"My dear boy, of course they hate you."

The voice was rich and vibrant but with more than a hint of effete coyness that was as disarming as it was spurious.

"It is quite understandable, really."

The Salamander, the Senseii, the Weaponsmaster of the Freehold, stood in the doorway of Ronin's spartan cubicle. Not much time had passed since they had cut Ronin down and told him to return to his room.

Ronin moved to stand up but a curt motion, a flash of the Salamander's wide wrist, stopped him.

"Sit, my dear boy, by all means. You have certainly

earned the privilege." The voice flowed thickly, honeyed the air.

The Salamander, an immense figure, was garbed informally in crimson shirt, hung in layers which cunningly concealed the extent of his true bulk, jet-black leggings and high boots of the same color polished to glossy perfection. His rich black hair was swept back along his skull like the wings of some awesome predatory bird. His thick brows and high cheekbones managed in some unfathomable fashion to accentuate the large onyx eyes, oval, and as hard and opaque as stone.

He moved into the room and it seemed to shrink in size, a diminishing and insignificant background in his presence. He stared unblinkingly at Ronin.

"You are not happy here, my dear boy." It was not a question. "Perhaps this is because you feel that you have no friends."

"Yes," Ronin said unknowingly. "All the students hate me."

The Salamander looked at Ronin with a veiled gaze and smiled without warmth.

"But of course that is true and that should please you greatly. It does me." Ronin's face was blank with surprise but the Salamander ignored that. "You are the best, my dear boy; without question the very best student that I have trained. And now no one can touch you, not student, not Bladesman. Oh yes"—he laughed at the expression on Ronin's face—"that is quite true. You are as far above them as I am above you." His laughter took on a manic quality.

Ronin was acutely aware of the compliment. It puzzled rather than delighted him. The reaction was quite inexplicable.

The Salamander's fist clenched and his rings caught the light in brief explosions of color. He bent forward slightly, his voice less oratorical now, more personal.

"They hate you, my dear boy, because you are better than they, you have the talent that they wish they possessed, and they will not rest until they best you in Combat." His laugh was a bark of emotion. "Good! For that too serves my purpose. My Bladesmen must be the best in the Freehold." He touched his chest, a dramatic gesture he nevertheless managed to imbue with a certain grandeur. "Am I not alone of all the Saardin, Senseii? It is honor. What do the other Saardin know of that?" His voice lowered in volume and gained in intensity. "They know only to bicker among themselves, vying for power." He threw his head back and his eyes squeezed shut, then flew open, impaling Ronin with their implacable gaze. "They do not understand the meaning of the word 'power.'" He stopped abruptly, realizing that he had revealed more than he had intended. "It is honor," he said then, "that must be upheld always." He stepped closer to Ronin. "You must understand this totally."

He came and sat on the thin bed.

"But you, my dear boy"—a heavy bejeweled hand stroked softly Ronin's arm—"you also serve my purpose. I have labored long and hard to make you a Badesman unmatched by any bound to the Saardin of the Freehold. Tomorrow you will enter the Square of Combat for the last time as a student." His voice held a quivering note of triumph which he did not bother to conceal. "You will stun the Instructors who will be there to judge you and then, when you have emerged from Combat a Bladesman, the Freehold's finest Bladesman, while the Instructors and the Saardin are still babbling to each other of your skill, then you will return here to be my Chondrin."

A stillness eddied in the room, as absolute as a vacuum. For a time it ruled and then, quite slowly, it seemed to Ronin, the tiny background sounds of the Level returned to his ears, drifting male voices, the

26

comforting slap of boot soles against the wooden floor, the distant metal clangor of Combat practice, sounds which had comprised the environmental context of his life for so long. Changed now, these noises came to him as harsh and brittle and without meaning, as if, of a sudden, he found himself in an alien world, wondering just how long he had been there. And looking into the glittery, obsidian eyes so close to his, he saw nothing whatsoever.

They dropped silently into the void, from time to time using hammer and spike to gain footholds along the sheer face of the cliff, or to circumnavigate an otherwise impassable section. It seemed that they had descended for hours, through the mist and the small snowfalls like choking dust storms flung against them by fierce updrafts. They paused neither to rest nor to eat, gulping handfuls of snow occasionally to slake their thirst, to keep them going.

Borros' urgency had become infectious. For Ronin it was perhaps the stench of the monstrous creature, still crawling in his nostrils, which had finally severed the twanging chord of his grief, once as raw and painful as an exposed nerve, and which now allowed him to focus on the reason for this journey. He had gone to the City of Ten Thousand Paths on Borro's urgings. The Magic Man was convinced that a terrifying menace was threatening to engulf the world of man. Perhaps Ronin only half believed him when he first journeyed forth but after encountering Bonneduce the Last and Hynd, after the battles with the thing that killed G'fand, he felt within him a peculiar kind of personal confirmation of what Borros had told him. And the journey had been successful. The Magic Man had sent him on a quest for an ancient scroll, which Ronin had found in the house of dor-Sefrith, purportedly the most famed and feared sorcerer of the legendary isle of Ama-no-mori, now no more than mounds of cracked stone and masonry beneath some far-off sea, Ronin mused. Pity. But I have the scroll now and, as Borros has told me, it is the key to stopping this inhuman menace. He smiled to himself. Despite Freidal's efforts, despite the Salamander's attempted interference. Only I have the scroll. He glanced at the thin face, drawn and haggard with fatigue, the yellow tinge sickly in the failing light. I have yet to tell him. That should bring a smile. And when we find out what it says, we shall return.

Ronin indeed returned from the Square of Combat a Bladesman. He had, as the Salamander had correctly predicted, stunned the Instructors and the Saardin, who had never before seen his like in skill and speed in Combat. Their excited talk sickened him. Yet in one important decision the Salamander would be proven wrong.

Ronin returned Upshaft to the Senseii's Level not in the least elated. He had had no doubts as to his ability and therefore felt no trepidation when it came time for his Trial. On the contrary he felt that the Salamander had dawdled over him, procrastinating, postponing again and again his Trial date. In his own mind, he had been ready many sign ago. Now it seemed to him that the date itself meant more to the Salamander than the Trial itself.

The Salamander was waiting for him in the Hall of Combat. His enormous figure was draped in ceremonial robes of jet. His hair was newly coifed and oiled and the fan that he could wield as dexterously and as fatally as a sword or dagger protruded from his wide scarlet sash. He wore a sword on his left hip, sheathed in a formal scabbard of openwork silver with an ebon tip, intricately carved in the shape of a rampant lizard on a bed of black flame.

On either side of him, dwarfed by his bulk, stood two of his Bladesmen. One held the bands which went obliquely from left shoulder to right hip across the tunic of each Chondrin. These bands were differing colors to identify which Saardin the Chondrin was bound to. The Bladesmen held black on black bands, the Salamander's colors.

The moment Ronin saw the bands, his decision was made. He knew quite clearly what he should do, what he had after all been trained for. He stopped before the Salamander and bowed stiffly, his face a mask, thinking, I know too what I must do. There was a great sadness within him. The Salamander inclined his head solemnly. He was more to Ronin than Combat Instructor, Senseii, Saardin. Yet still Ronin would have no man his master; would have no one now impose his will upon him, that time was surely passed forever. Free at last, he would not enslave himself within the complex political labyrinth of the Freehold society. He had his strength and power; he required nothing more.

"Now you are Bladesman," the Salamander said formally. Was there a trace of pride in his voice? Oh, surely not from the Salamander. "You are henceforth my vassal. You obey my commands; are subject to my disciplines, my ordinances, and my will. No other may command your arm or your mind so long as I shall live. In return, you have my protection, the power of my office as Saardin and my power as Senseii of the Freehold. In honor I offer you the bands of the Salamander, Saardin, Senseii of the Freehold, as my Chondrin, to advise, to defend, to command my Bladesmen, to obey me."

The Bladesman holding the bands stepped forward.

"Do you accept the bands of Chondrin and by so doing pledge your arm and your mind to me?"

"Salamander," said Ronin hoarsely, "I cannot."

"Not much more to go," Borros said over the crying of the wind. Ronin looked down. The mist and snow had thinned enough for him to see that several hundred meters below them the cliff face ceased its precipitous plunge earthward and became a widening slope upon which they could likely walk downward the rest of the way to the ice sea.

The expanse was lit now by the wan silver light of the moon, its mottled face hanging large and hungry in a sky of trembling cloud. Ronin stared at the oval, then back again to the ice sea still far below them.

And still they descended, though weariness gripped them like a tightening vise.

In the end it would be his face that stood out in Ronin's memory. For just an instant, a sliver so brief that perhaps only Ronin could have caught it, the seemingly impenetrable façade of the decadent and rather bored Weaponsmaster, refined and honed for so many years, appeared to crack and, like the onrush of a spring waterfall, sending rainbows into the light, a score of emotions seemed to dart across his visage. So quickly were they covered that Ronin could not even be sure. Had he seen sadness, shock, anger, hurt? All of them, Ronin surmised. He had been too wrapped up in what he had to do to understand then the larger pattern.

"You cannot!" bellowed the Salamander. "Cannot? What are you saying, you cannot? You will! You must! It cannot be any other way!" Still impaling Ronin with his furious gaze, he reached out, clutched at the Chondrin's bands, waved them at Ronin. "You mock this trust! Just as you mock me!" His face was red and spittle flew from the glistening surfaces of his wet lips. He crumpled the bands and threw them in Ronin's face. Ronin felt unable to move or to speak.

The huge face quivered before him. "You cannot?

You do not even understand the meaning of those words." He raised a huge fist. "I saw in you what no one else could, what you yourself were blind to. It was *my* vision which created you, *my* ideas which molded you into the Freehold's finest Bladesman." His voice had risen in volume and force; now his entire frame shook as if within him a fierce storm raged. "I trained you, accepted you, offer you the highest honor!" He advanced on Ronin. "And you spit in my face!" The voice was a shriek now, echoing off the high walls. Abruptly he swiped with the back of his hand, the motion so swift that Ronin could not have reacted if he had wanted to. But he had not wanted to; he knew with a chilling finality that if he moved at all he was a dead man.

The blow caught him full on the face, the rings scouring his cheek. It was a gesture of disdain and that hurt him more than the enormous force of the blow, more than the cuts opening up the skin of his face. Those would heal eventually.

"You do not understand. You know nothing of honor!" The Salamander hurled the words out as if they were somehow tainted. Then he hit Ronin again, and a third time with his hand now a clenched fist, crying out in rage because Ronin would not fall, would not retreat, would not retaliate. "How dare you! How dare you!" A litany of humiliation. Pounding at Ronin. Now his Bladesmen attempted to restrain him. He shook them off like droplets of water.

"Get away from me!" he screamed. "Get out of here! Get out!" And they scrambled obediently from his presence.

Still he beat Ronin, howling "Aaahhh!" beyond coherent speech now, staggering, irrational, inhuman.

He reached thick fingers into his sash, grasped the fan, about to draw it forth, spread its lethal edge, a supple guillotine. Then he stopped, his breathing hard and irregular.

"No," he gasped. "No. That would be too easy." His hand came away empty and, turning, he lurched out the door.

Ronin stood in the center of the Hall of Combat, hearing the susurration of his harsh breathing like the pounding of wild surf upon a desolate shore, his head and torso aflame with throbbing pain he only dimly felt, and thought, Now we are both shamed.

"What now?" Borros called to him.

They twisted in the air. Some twenty meters below them beckoned the lower slopes of the cliff. But they were, literally, at the end of their ropes.

"We are short," said the Magic Man. He kicked at the rock face to stop his twisting; it only made it worse.

"Quit that," Ronin said. "Relax your body."

"I have no strength left," Borros called pitifully, "I am exhausted."

"Then save your breath," Ronin said reasonably. He peered down again. In the uncertain light, as dense clouds rode across the moon's pale face, he could just make out the blanket of new snow covering the upper slope. But how deep was it? he asked himself. He took the small hammer off his wrist and let it go. It hit the snow and disappeared. He unhooked the bag of spikes and dropped that too. It hit the snow near the spot where the hammer went in and disappeared. Only one thing left to do, he thought. And let go the rope.

He heard a scream and it confused him momentarily and then he was into it, under it, its weight upon him, and he could not breathe and the blackness was a suffocating mass around him, above him but he pushed up, straining and clawing, and broke the surface, inhaling the chilled air in great lungfuls. He felt ice and rock beneath his feet.

The scream came again and he knew that it was Borros.

"All right, Borros," he shouted, cupping his hands by his mouth. "I am in the snow below you. Can you hear me?"

The sobbing of the wind.

"Yes."

"Let yourself drop. The snow will cushion your fall."

"I am afraid."

"Close your eyes and let go the rope."

"Ronin—"

"Chill take you! Do it!"

He heard the crunch against the crisp top layer of snow and was already moving, using sound as well as sight, as fast as he could to the spot. But the deep snow pulled at him and he panted, thinking of the Magic Man's exhaustion, knowing that he would have to pull him free very quickly or he would suffocate.

The undulating expanse of snow was albescent in the moonlight. He waded through it, tired himself, and stumbled, face in the snow, and instinctively pushed up with his hands, sinking deeper into it. Then his brain began to function again and he pushed this time with his feet and knees against the ice and then he was up. He located the darkness of the hole, went to it and dug down hard, shoveling desperately with his fingers, feeling at last the body like a dead weight, and hauled upward now with all his strength, hauling at a weight that seemed inordinately heavy, feeling time slip away beneath him, willing his fingers not to slip.

Borros came up slowly, like an ancient galleon buried beneath a sea reluctant to part with its prize, and as soon as his head came into the open Ronin

33

slapped it. The Magic Man coughed and sputtered and half-melted ice drooled from his slowly working lips. Ronin picked him up.

"All right," Borros whispered, so softly that it could have been the moaning of the wind. "I am"—he choked, caught himself, then inhaled his first deep breath—"quite all right."

Ronin shoveled snow with his arms, making a shallow depression along the lee of the slope just below the sheer face of the cliff, an implacable wall lifting black shadows, it seemed, into the reaches of the tremulous sky. Deep enough for them to huddle, taking respite from the constant bite of wind and frost while they rested. Borros attempted to rake out several small packets from within his suit but his hands were shaking badly and Ronin had to lift them out, feed Borros as he fed himself.

Across the trackless slope they went dazedly, down, ever down, the wind blowing the drifting snow into their faces mingled with sharp-edged ice crystals as the temperature plummeted. Their lips were frosted and their eyebrows and lashes rimed with ice. Beneath their hoods, their cheeks were already numb. Still they moved painfully onward and when Borros fell Ronin bent and lifted him, the weight as nothing now. He half dragged him, stumbling, along the downward slope, through the drag of the heavy snow, deaf from the wind and then blind in the night, animal instinct alone lifting one foot after another onward, onward. . . .

His first thought was the warmth and he recalled a fire leaping and logs crackling and the cheery orange glow. He tried to move closer to the warmth and could not budge. Through a thick haze he understood that something was wrong. One side of his face was warm and— With a start he realized where he was,

34

that he was face down in the snow. With infinite slowness he lifted himself centimeter by centimeter until he was sitting up. He touched the side of his face eventually and discovered that it was numb.

Even then, when it occurred to him within the context of reality that they might die, he would not give in to it. He went to his hands and knees, saw Borros lying beside him. He was facing the way they had come, away in the distance the solid rock of the awesome, towering cliff down which they had made their descent.

He tried to stand and slipped, sliding downward along his belly. It took him several moments to realize. Then he looked down, oblivious suddenly to the freezing cold and the harsh bite of the wind. He reached out with his hands, felt the ground.

Smooth.

"Borros," he called in a cracked and dry voice.

Smooth and flat and hard.

"Borros!"

And he turned his face, then his body, until he was facing southward and he beheld the enormous glowing expanse of the ice sea.

"We are here!"

Heat fled up his arms from his finger tips into his shoulders. The image of the flame, dancing lazily from behind the small grating, was hypnotic. The gentle bumping, the soft creaking, a soporific. Across from him, Borros was already asleep, his utter fatigue taking him. Ronin felt the swift motion under him, knew sleep was almost here. Almost.

They had lurched, insensate, down the final series of low slopes, to the very edge of the ice sea, without knowing it. There at its banks they had collapsed.

At first Ronin had believed Borros delirious when he had revived him and the Magic Man had told him at last the secret of survival upon the ice sea. Impossible. But already Ronin was learning to ignore that word, for he had been through so many seemingly impossible situations, seen so many startling sights, been forced to readjust to many of the concepts he had originally been taught, this was but a momentary reaction. And too it was their only hope of survival upon the world's forbidding surface; he lost no time in useless queries, he began the search.

It was easier than he could have imagined. Barely a thousand meters from where they had fallen, he found the small headland that Borros had assured him would be there. Mounded in snow many times higher than any area near it, it jutted out into the ice sea. And feverishly now he began to dig.

Moonlight, pale and glittery against the smooth surface of the platinum ice, revealed to him what Borros had told him he would unearth.

Even so it came as a shock, a current like lightning racing through his body momentarily thawing the chill. He began to dig harder now that the outlines had been uncovered and at last he was through and he turned and brought the Magic Man, a muscular arm across his back for support, so that they could both see it together.

The mist had risen, diffusing the monochrome light, but above the moon was riding free, its intermittent cloud cover racing westward. Of this fact they were oblivious as they stood, captivated by the image which loomed before them.

It was sleek. Long and curving, raised on slender runners.

"A felucca," Borros breathed almost reverently. "They did not lie." There were tears standing in the corners of his eyes. "For years I read and dreamed and, when I was sure, I promised myself that one day—" He shook his head and the tears flipped to the piled snow of the promontory. "But now I see that I was not so sure after all, a doubt remained. Until this moment. Oh, Ronin, look at it!"

It was a ship. An ice ship.

Slowly they went on board, explored the high prow and the sweep of its beam all the way to the low stern; they strode along the smooth deck, ran frozen fingers across the top of the low cabin aft rising just above the gunwale.

They went below, finding narrow berths with blankets along the hull, and a black metal oblong in the center of the cabin. Ronin took tinder and flint and, on Borros' instructions, opened the small hinged grate in the front and sparked a flame. The fire came instantly to the interior and Ronin, closing the grate, was too grateful for the warmth to inquire about the fuel source.

He put Borros on a bunk, listened to him talk for a short time, then went on deck. He took the mast from its storage rack along the port sheer-strake and set it in its place just astern of midships. He set the yard, low down on the mast. Then he went over the side and hacked at the metal chocks holding the runners in place. When they were freed, he went aboard and unfurled the high sweeping lateen sail.

Coming down the low slopes, the wind had been off the sea, into their faces. At some point it had turned and, picking up velocity, was now whipping almost due south. Ronin, setting the last of the rigging, thought, Now there is nothing more to do. Borros assures me that we need not stand lookout this night, that there is clear sailing. Does he really know, I wonder?

At that moment there came a powerful lurch and, as the sail caught the wind, the vessel, now standing clear on its runway of ice, was launched upon the ice sea.

Ronin, fatigued and unprepared, fell to the deck. Moving cautiously to the stern, he hauled hard on the wheel and lashed it tight as Borros had instructed him. They flew along the ice due south, the stiff wind billowing the sail, pushing them. He stared ahead for a moment, but the moon had disappeared behind racing clouds and new mist was settling in. Nothing more to do. With a final glance at the fastness of the rigging, he went below.

Sleep.

"Tomorrow night."

A small squat lamp hanging from a beam in the cabin's low ceiling had been lit. It swung with the ship's motion, shadows fleeing across the bulkheads.

"What?" he said thickly.

Through round crystal portals set in either bulkhead he saw that it was still dark out. It was warm and comfortable here and he closed his eyes, sighing.

"We slept through the night," said Borros from his berth across the cabin, "and all of the next day." He smiled wearily. "I got up once and it was near sunset, that is how I know. I went on deck and found that the wind had changed slightly. We were running more to the west than I wanted, as close as I could tell—the sun sets only roughly in the west—so I reset the wheel." He stood up carefully. He looked thin and gaunt. "Hungry?" Ronin opened his eyes.

They ate voraciously from the stores on ship; concentrates with unsatisfying flavors, but they filled the belly. Abruptly he remembered the frostbite of his face but, lifting a hand, he could feel no burn or discomfort.

"The ancients anticipated that possibility also," said the Magic Man. "You will find a packet of the unguent in one of the pockets of your suit. When I woke yesterday, I fixed us both up at the same time." He smiled almost apologetically. "I did not see the need to wake you." He lay back on his bunk, as if the talk had weakened him.

"Are you all right?" Ronin asked.

The Magic Man lifted a slender hand. "Only—it will take me somewhat more time than you to recover." His lips turned up again in a watery smile. "The disadvantages of age, you understand."

Ronin turned away. "I have a surprise for you," he said.

"Ah, good. But first you must tell me of your journey to the City of Ten Thousand Paths." Ronin looked back at him in time to see the sorrow and regret in his eyes. He shook his head ruefully. "I am so sorry, Ronin. I sent you on a madman's quest, an impossible—"

"But—"

"They told me about G'fand—"

"Ah." His heart felt as cold as ice. "Did they?"

"Yes." He grimaced. "It was part of my treatment. Freidal had already subjected me to such prolonged physical torture"—unconsciously his thin fingers sought his forehead, where before Ronin had seen the terrifying marks of the Dehn spots—"in trying to pry out of me all that I knew of the Surface, that he felt it was time to change tactics. I knew all along that I had sent you down to the City of Ten Thousand Paths and he could have stopped you at any time—"

"He wanted to see what I would return with, since he could not break you."

But Borros was not listening; he was remembering. "He was so clever, Chill take him! He came in and told them to stop; gave me water and let me rest. Told me that I had been through it all and had not given in; that it was useless for him to try any more. He—he said that he admired me"—his voice turned to a tremulous fluting—"that as soon as I had recovered, I

39

was free to go." He passed a frail hand across his eyes as if the gesture would blot out the nightmare that played in his mind and which, compulsively now, spewed from his mouth.

" 'Oh, by the way,' he said, as if it were the last thing on his mind, 'we have taken Ronin into custody. He has just returned to the Freehold after making an unauthorized exit. We have asked him quite politely where he went, after all it is a Security matter. The safety of the Freehold is at stake; if he can egress, others may gain entrance. So you understand that we must find out where he went and why. It is a matter of utmost importance.' Freidal sighed. 'But so far he has been most reluctant to accommodate us. He refuses, Borros, to do his duty to the Freehold. You understand what must be done now.' I did indeed; he meant to use the Dehn on you. 'His disrespectful actions leave me no choice. Oh yes,' he said then, 'I almost forgot. The young man who accompanied him—a scholar, I believe—G'fand—was killed. Unfortunate, but scholars are hardly essential to the stability of the Freehold.' "

Borros shifted uncomfortably on his berth but found no surcease. His eyes were still turned inward. "Freidal was furious that I did not crumble then, as he had hoped, so he"—the Magic Man's thin frame shuddered—"he had Stahlig brought in. He had his daggam drag Stahlig in front of me. Someone held my head so that I could not turn away; they hit me when I tried to shut my eyes." He lifted his head, the narrow skull shining like ancient bone, his eyes lusterless. "When Stahlig looked at me—I have never seen such terror written upon the face of a human being." He let go a suspiration then, and it all came out. "Freidal said to him: 'What is it that you fear most, Stahlig? The loss of your feet? Would you care to crawl through the Freehold on your knees? Perhaps your eyes. Do you fear blindness? No? I could break your back then; leave you alive, alive and immobile.' And seeing the look in Stahlig's eyes, he continued: 'That would be most fitting, would it not? Your friend Ronin left my man Marcsh with a broken back. But you know that; you treated Marcsh. You will be totally helpless; to be fed and wiped like a baby.' "

The wind, muffled somewhat by the cabin's bulkheads, moaned mournfully, momentarily drowning out the soft scraping sounds of the runners gliding swiftly over the ice, as if it too was witness to the horror that the Magic Man had conjured.

Borris put his head in his hands. "In the end," he whispered so softly that it was like a ghost's breath, "Stahlig died of fright."

There was silence for a time save for the moaning and occasional creak of the fittings abovedecks. Ronin lay back on his berth and tried to think of nothing, but his brain was on fire and he got up and went silently up the short vertical companionway.

The small ship shot through the mists of night ever southward. Ronin, on deck, could see nought but the blurred shadows of the ribboning ice as it sped by beneath the vessel. It was a quarter wind which now propelled them and he busied himself learning the fundamentals of tacking into it, working hard at the rigging to keep them on course.

He went aft and freed the wheel, steering manually for a time, letting the vibrations flow from his hands into his body borne away on an imaginary tide. The endless gentle soughing of the runners peeling a thin film of ice below stood by him like a spectral companion.

The wind strained the sail. Already the weather was changing, the air wetter, denser than before and, because of it, the cold seemed fiercer, creeping beneath

41

the skin into flesh and bone. At length Ronin lashed the wheel to and, taking a last deep breath, went below.

Borros lay on his berth staring blankly upward.

"The surprise, Borros," Ronin said gently. "I have not told you what it is."

"Uhm."

"Do you remember why you sent me to the City of Ten Thousand Paths?"

"Of course, but—" He sat up so suddenly that he barely missed hitting his head on a beam. Color had returned to his yellow face. "You cannot mean—" At last there was a light kindling his eyes. "But Freidal had you and—"

"And the Salamander also; his men took me from Security." A wintry smile broke out on Ronin's face.

The Magic Man's mouth opened soundlessly.

"And?"

Ronin laughed then, for the first time in many cycles. "And? And? Freidal found nothing, though he was justifiably curious about this"—he lifted his strange gauntlet—"and the Salamander lacked the time to find anything—"

"Are you telling me that you actually found the scroll? Ronin, you have it?" Borros came excitedly across to him.

Ronin withdrew his sword, grasped the hilt, and twisted it three times. It came away in his hand. From within its hollowed-out recesses Ronin gently pulled forth the scroll of dor-Sefrith. He handed it to the Magic Man, who delicately opened it and stared, breathing, "You *have* found it. Oh, Ronin—!"

He gave Borros several moments before he said, "Now you must tell me what it says and why it is so important."

Borros looked up at him, the flame from the swinging lamp reflecting in his eyes, turning them colorless.

"But you see, Ronin," he said in a tired voice, "I do not know."

There was a time—he could actually force himself to remember that far back in the dim and cloudy past, though he rarely wished to—when Stahlig, the Medicine Man, was not a part of his life.

He had fallen down half a flight of stairs, choked with rubble and debris. Exploring. As he had come to a landing, something had shot across his path, tiny nails clicking industriously, and he had lost his balance, tumbling down the Stairwell.

He might not have been hurt at all if it had been clear. But he had fetched up against a fallen girder, twisted and red, his leg slamming into its side where it lay slashed through a rent in the outer wall. Perhaps he passed out from the pain. Eventually, he got to the Medicine Man on the next Level, limping and crawling because no one was about to help him.

His left leg was broken but he was young and strong and Stahlig knew his business. It was a clean break and with the white end protruding through the torn flesh appeared worse than it in fact was. The bones knit perfectly but that became secondary to him. Stahlig talked to him while he went about setting the leg. That was what interested him, intrigued him, what, ultimately, caused him to return to Stahlig's med rooms whenever he was able. The Medicine Man had no reason to treat Ronin in a special way, yet he did, recognizing somewhere within him a potential others would not.

The two became friends and the reason did not matter at all, at least to either of them. That did not mean that it did not go unnoticed in some quarters of the Freehold, noted, written down, filed away for future use.

We accepted each other, Ronin thought as the ship

43

rocked beneath him. And now you have joined so many others who have known me and because of it have died.

Outside, the wind was rising, plucking at the rigging in mournful melody.

"You do not know?" echoed Ronin without emotion. "What have you done to me?"

Borros put the scroll back into its hiding place in the hilt of Ronin's sword. He rubbed his eyes.

"Sit," he said, and put his hand on Ronin's shoulder. "Sit and I will tell you all that I *do* know."

In ancient times, when the world spun faster upon its axis and the sun burned with energy in the sky, when multitudes of people roamed the surface of all the planet and, beneath their feet, the land turned from dirt and high grass plains as they walked, to fields of rowed food plants green and golden in the sunshine, to arid deserts smeared with low-growing flowers of many hues, to steep windswept steppes and mountain ranges blue with haze, when high-prowed ships from many nations plied the seas in search of trade with new lands, then Ronin, then we were known by another name. We were scientists and then our work was highly empirical, our theorems coming almost exclusively from the forebrain. Are you familiar with the word 'empirical'? Ah, good. Methodology was our watchword, this strict catholicism a firm and supportive base for our work.

But times changed radically and the world of the ancients was disappearing. In that interim period, the world was seized by a progression of natural cataclysms. The continents broke apart and fell away to be replaced by others, rising steamily from beneath the boiling seas. As you may well imagine, many people died but, perhaps more importantly, at the same time the laws that had heretofore governed the world of the ancients were overthrown and destroyed. Others came into being.

The inconceivable had occurred; by what means it is impossible to say, nor is it entirely germane to this account. Still, whatever formal records of that time ever existed are lost now—what remains are but fragments pertaining to the world as it was before.

Naturally, among the living were numerous scientists, yet so tied were they to the bedrock of their empiricism that, though it was clear to many others that the world had irrevocably changed so that the old methodology now worked only sporadically, the scientists refused to listen.

Certain members of these others, born to the new order of things, were able to make, because they had not been trained in the traditional ways of man, the great leap forward in thinking. These then became great mages, as they explored new methods, discovering alchemical, then sorcerous pathways, shining like beacons in the night. So they grew in power, at length banishing the scientists whom they scorned and ridiculed as they threw them down. Then they took upon themselves the mantle of overlords and in so doing lost sight of the original goals of their creation. Irresponsibly, they began to vie with each other for territory and power.

The inevitable holocaust of their quarreling spread throughout the world. The destruction was ghastly; its extent blossoming to unthinkable heights. Many people went underground. The City of Ten Thousand Paths came into being in this way. It was an attempt to form a peaceful society composed of members of all the surviving nations.

But among the populace of the City of Ten Thousand Paths were both mages and scientists, and they were ever at war. It is said that of all the mages only dor-Sefrith of Ama-no-mori remained unmoved and

45

uninvolved though both sides desperately sought his considerable power.

From the time of the holocaust onward, there was of course an attrition of knowledge and each succeeding generation learned less and, eventually, when even dor-Sefrith's long neutrality ceased to maintain the uneasy peace, factions broke away, tunneling upward through the mineral-rich rock to form our eventual home, the Freehold, only residues of each side's knowledge remained.

We became the Magic Men, not-scientists, not-mages, struggling with but scraps of the methodology of both, learning languages long dead, convoluted equations which we neither understood nor would likely work under our present laws. And even if we grasped the tatters of the ancient concepts, even if we were somehow able to piece together the scattered information to make a coherent whole, we lacked the resources—our Neers so ill-trained that they could not even repair the essential machinery of the Freehold, let alone building for us the machines we would require—to accomplish anything.

Most of the Magic Men languished until enterprising Saardin began to see that we had a limited usefulness in the Freehold's power struggle. Then, one by one, the Saardin sought us out for affiliation. It was the end for us. From noble beginnings, we had been reduced to the lowest level, devising projects for the Saardin to increase their power.

I turned my back on them and for many sign would not even step onto their Levels. I spent my time with the remnants of the scholars, on the twenty-seventh Level, studying as best I could the lore of the ancient world, so that I might regain for myself some semblance of my heritage.

But the more I read, the more convinced I became

that we were a dying race, strangling in our own mingled blood, indolent, inbred, incestuous.

"G'fand felt the same way," Borros concluded.

"You knew G'fand?" Ronin asked.

"Oh, yes. He helped me quite a bit in deciphering many of the ancient codices. There were revelations each cycle, but everything was in fragments and too often we were only tantalized by the pieces we had managed to decode, discovering afterwards that they were isolated passages, their beginnings and endings lost."

"I remember," said Ronin, "that when we arrived in the City he would stop at every corner to read the glyphs carved into the buildings."

The Magic Man nodded. "Yes. I can imagine his excitement. Such a storehouse of knowledge." He reached into a cupboard under his berth and pulled out food concentrates. He offered some to Ronin, who shook his head, then sat and munched thoughtfully for a time.

"One day," he said—his voice had a thin far-off quality now—"we came across a rent manuscript. It was frightfully old and so desiccated that it took us more than three cycles to carefully clean it enough so that we could begin to read the glyphs and restore the missing characters. Then G'fand set about deciphering it and I lost interest as I was involved in a project of my own at the time. Several cycles later he came to me saying that he could make no headway at all; the glyphs were totally alien to him; they bore no resemblance to any language he had studied.

"I laughed. 'Well, what can I do?' I said. 'You are a far better translator than I.' 'I do not know,' he said, 'but come take a look in any case.'

"The glyphs which were so baffling to him jumped out at me with such vividness that I had to conceal my surprise, and for once I was grateful for my peculiar

47

training. For this codex was written in one of the forgotten—and I had supposed useless—languages which I had learned as a child.

"The codex foretold of a drastic shift in the presumably immutable laws of our world. 'When the foundations of our science are thrown down, then will man tremble before the true power. Conceit is his undoing and he will not heed the coming of his doom until it crushes him. The Dolman, a sorcerous creature of terrifying power beyond man's ken, will come against mankind. The shifting of the laws presages his invasion. Indeed it is his invitation. First his legions, then the Makkon, then The Dolman himself will come to claim the world. With that, annihilation.' "

The wind outside had picked up in intensity, buffeting the ship as it sped across the ice sea. Yet the sound seemed remote to them, unreal, frozen in sticky time. Neither one said anything for a while. Then Borros roused himself and, listening for a moment, made a motion upward.

"The sail."

If they had left it up any longer it would likely have been torn to shreds. As it was, they managed to reef it just in time. The wind, blowing frantically out of the northwest quarter, tore at their faces, forcing them to gasp for breath and turn their heads from its might. They were blind in the pit of night and only by guesswork did they surmise their direction.

Below, they blew into their cupped hands and shoved them near the fire, trying to warm their faces. Ronin prepared food for himself and before he had eaten his fill Borros was already asleep on his berth. He stretched out and stared at the swinging lamp, thinking long about The Dolman.

He must have dozed, for when he next looked about the cabin the ports were illuminated by a thin milky glow.

"Dawn," breathed Borros, and sat up. "The sun rises. Soon we can unfurl the sail."

On deck they got their first real glimpse of the ice sea since setting sail. Ronin saw now why Borros had not been concerned about keeping watch at night. In all directions the ice flew away from them flat and seamless and dark. No high ridges, no steep protrusions marred its surface. And there was a limitless horizon which in all directions held no sight of land.

In the east, the gray clouds had taken on a pale saffron color as the sun began its quotidian trek across the heavens. The wind came in gusts and Borros was obliged to go aft to reset their course.

Ronin stared southward, watching the shredded clouds pile and tumble, blown across the sky by the high winds aloft. Are there really people out there? he asked himself. Would they look like Bonneduçe the Last? He shrugged and busied himself with the rigging, tightening knots which had loosened during the night.

The air became heavier still, leaden despite the strength of the wind, and there was a slight pressure in his ears. He took special care, moving along the rocking deck, remembering his slip the first night and, peering into the wind, he spied the purple and black thunderheads massed just above the horizon on the northwest quadrant that heralded the coming storm.

A shout twisted his head aft, but he could see nothing amiss. He made his way toward Borros, who was already pointing northward.

"What is it?" Ronin asked, coming up to him.

"A ship." Borros clutched at the wheel. "Following us."

Ronin peered aft but could still discern nothing on the expanse of the ice sea.

"Obscured now by the mist."

"Borros, are you certain—"

"This ship's sister," the Magic Man hissed. "Yes, Chill take it! I did see it."

Ronin turned away, twisted Borros with him. He stared hard into the old man's face and tried to ignore the terror squirming like a serpent there.

"Forget it," he said reasonably. "You are still fatigued. You saw what your imagination wished for you to see. You have been through so much but it is over now. Freidal cannot threaten you now. You are free."

Borros glanced briefly sternward, into the building mist.

"Let us pray so."

All the day the wind strengthened, a gale now whose great gusts shifted from one quarter to another, hurling them southward at ever increasing speed. It seemed to Ronin, as he worked the rigging, that their runners barely touched the ice, so swiftly did they fly across the frozen wastes. From time to time he caught Borros gazing aft, but he said nothing, keeping his thoughts to himself.

He marveled at the workmanship of the craft. He watched the small storm sail which they had unfurled when they came on deck at first light. Buffeted by the strong winds, stretched to its limit, it yet would not tear. It was constructed of a different fabric than the woven canvas of the main, lighter, more supple.

For much of the time the pair did not speak. It was essential that the wheel and the sail be manned at all times now because of the sudden unpredictability of the winds. Ronin worked the sail because that took more strength. He spent most of the time hauling on the rigging and staring ahead, one arm about the wooden mast, feeling it tremble, listening to the rhythmic creaking of the fittings, the soughing of the runners against the ice, the desolate call of the wind.

He thought then of nothing; the future would be as

it would be. But a peculiar warmth stole over him in those solitary moments against the varnished wood, counterbalancing the pull of the ropes, and he absorbed the transmission of their quivering strength, their pliancy the key to survival upon the ice sea. A bond was slowly forming of which he was not yet perhaps fully aware, as it had inevitably with many men, throughout many ages, on seas too numerous to count. It was an instinct rooted perhaps in some ancestral memories, if such things indeed existed on that world and in that time. It was what allowed him to feel the changing of the wind on his face and pull or slacken the rope immediately so that they continually maintained their course. It was what caused him to pick up a thousand different subtleties of sailing in so short a time.

Just past midday the winds ceased their gusting and steadied enough for the pair to decide to lash wheel and storm sail long enough to go below for food and rest.

While they ate, he told Borros the details of the events which had transpired in the City of Ten Thousand Paths. When he recounted the creature's attack, the Magic Man exclaimed, the sound exploding through his lips. He coughed and swallowed convulsively. Then he had Ronin describe the creature again as best he could.

"The Makkon," he said then, his face drained of color and looking more than ever like a skull. "The creatures that are not animal, the four Reavers of The Dolman." He quivered involuntarily. "If that is truly what you encountered, then The Dolman is closer than I had suspected." His eyes closed. "Is there still time? Oh, Chill, there must be! *There must be!*" He looked up. "Ronin, we must make all haste southward. Nothing must stop us, nothing, do you understand?"

"Calm yourself, Borros," Ronin said gently. "Nothing shall stop us."

Late in the afternoon the day darkened prematurely and the violent storm which they had been attempting to outrun began to overtake them with an inexorable fury.

The wind shrilled in the rigging like the screams at the gates of the damned and Ronin went to reef the storm sail.

"No!" bellowed Borros, the gale causing his voice to sound muffled. "Leave it up! We must make all speed no matter the risk!"

Ronin looked to the sky. The racing purple-black clouds, thick now and lowering menacingly from the west, were gathering themselves. Within them, the storm.

"We may turn over if it does not come down!" He yelled into the wind, the words blown from his mouth like crisp leaves.

Borros' face was mottled in fear.

"I have seen the sister ship again! She is closer! Ronin, she stalks us!" His eyes bulged. "I will not be caught!"

Ronin began to reef the storm sail.

"You have only seen what you want to see; no one is following us. I want to survive this storm!"

Moments later, slender fingers grasped his arm, tugging feebly. He turned and looked into Borros' rolling eyes, saw the line of sweat freezing along the Magic Man's forehead.

"Please. Please. The ship comes after us. If we slow, it will surely overtake us." Borros' voice came out in puffs of steam on the chill, dense air. "Do you see? I cannot go back. I can take no more. Freidal had done what—"

Ronin touched him gently. "Return to the wheel

and guide us," he said softly. "The storm sail will stay up."

Gratefully Borros went again aft and Ronin retied the knots, vowing to reef the storm sail at the first sign of the gale's full force.

So they raced onward, riding before the gathering wind.

TWO

·*Aegir*·

He has turned from the west, away from the murder of the sun at the grasping hands of the ice plateaus. Frightened now, he flees before the turmoil of the vast sky. He feels, just behind him, the intense excitation of the storm as it bursts open and he is engulfed now by the fierce bite of the high winds, the pressure of the roiling banks of dark cloud, the kinetic scrape of leaping lightning.

Of these elements he is not afraid as he soars upward in a futile attempt to fly above the storm. He had ridden out many a gale, safe on the shifting wind currents, the whirling flurries of snow, the hard pellets of ice affecting him not at all.

The fear is of another kind and he is frantic to escape. His silver plumage a blur, he dips now, the air this high too thin for even his avian lungs, and desperately he tries to find a swift current to take him away from the feel of the living thing behind him, its frozen breath on his spread tail feathers, a pulsing caress of death. For it rolls on at his back, alive and malignant and indefatigable; something beyond life, beneath life. Coming.

He flies like a bolt into lurid purple cloud, out again, his flesh alive with crawling sensation. He tries to call out in his terror, cannot. Down and down he plummets until he sees the surface of the ice sea, dull and flat and comforting. It rushes by beneath him.

It was useless, and worse than that, suicidal. Through the curtains of blinding snow, dense and dark and turbulent, blotting out all else from sight and hearing, Ronin went aft, mindful of the slick layer of ice already forming on the deck.

It had hit with an electric jolt, one moment behind them, the next surrounding them in a frenetic shroud, dancing, swirling, driving. The gale was far too strong; even with both of them gripping the wheel, the ship was being hurled about as if it had abruptly lost all weight. Better by far for them to be belowdecks. He was especially concerned that Borros could be blown overboard.

He skidded once as the ship lurched to port, tilted, trembling in the howling winds, and righted itself. Slowly he unwound his freezing fingers from the rigging and moved now as a mountaineer would, using handholds at every step.

Borros, obsessed now by the thought of the pursuing ship, clung maniacally to the wheel, his blanched face a frozen mask, lips pulled back in a grimace of fear. And Romin, coming alongside him, was reminded of the visage of the newly dead. Clawlike, Borros' fingers were white bones against the wood. Ronin yelled at him, but his voice was drowned in the mounting shriek of the gale. He seized the Magic Man, chopping at his frail wrists to force him to let go of the wheel, and dragged him, lurching and sliding, to the cabin, thrusting him down the companionway. Then he turned and lashed the wheel firmly in place, went forward and slid along the icy deck, fetching up against the starboard sheer-strake. On hands and knees against the fury of the storm, he crawled to the mast and, pulling himself to his feet, reefed the flapping storm sail. He choked in the crush of whipping hail and frozen snow as it beat at his face and shoulders. He secured it to the yard, doubling the knots.

Only then did he go below.

Borros sat on the cabin's deck shivering in a small pool of water. Ronin sank wordlessly to his berth and thought that perhaps it was after all too much. Too many new situations arising each minute and neither of them yet fully acclimated to the surface. For Ronin, it was not so bad; he was young and strong, with a warrior's body and adaptability. But just as importantly his mind was open and flexible. He could accept. He knew that from his journey to the City of Ten Thousand Paths.

But for Borros, huddled pathetically upon the wooden deck, more concerned with an imaginary ship carrying his all too real tormentor than he was with the realities of the storm hurling itself at their craft, it could not be the same.

The howling outside increased and the ship shuddered and swayed dangerously as it sped within the storm. We live or we die and that is the sum of it, Ronin thought. But, Chill take it, I will not die!

Borros had gotten up and was making his way drunkenly up the companionway to the secured hatch. Ronin caught him.

"What are you doing?"

"The sail," said the Magic Man, his voice almost a whine. "I must be sure—that it is up."

"It *is* up."

He squirmed in Ronin's grasp. "I must see for myself. Freidal comes behind us. We must make all speed. If he catches us, he will destroy us."

Ronin whipped him around so that he could look into the tired eyes. They were clouded with panic and shock. It is too much for him, Ronin thought for the second time.

"Borros, forget Freidal, forget the sister ship. Even if it is following us, the storm will protect us. He cannot find us in this." The eyes looked blankly back at

57

him, then they turned toward the hatch. Ronin shook him, finally out of patience.

"Fool! The storm is our enemy! There is death out there. It is the sail which will destroy us in this wind!"

"Then you have taken it down!" It was the irrational wail of a disillusioned child.

"Yes, Chill take you, I had no other choice! If I had not, we would be on our side now breaking up."

Frantically Borros clawed at Ronin. "Let me go! I must put it up! He will overtake us if I do not!"

Ronin hit him then, a swift blow at the side of the neck, breaking the nerve synapses and blood flow for just an instant, and the Magic Man collapsed, eyes rolling up, his body folding onto the companionway. Ronin put him on his berth and turned away disgusted.

The ship groaned under the onslaught and the hanging lamp swung crazily on its short chain, splashing the bulkheads with bursts of sullen light and geometric shadows.

After a time Ronin reached up and extinguished the flame.

He lay listening to the howling darkness, feeling the felucca shudder and lurch under him, smelling the thin trail of smoke from the doused lamp. The gale tore through the rigging, moaning as if alive, spattering hail against the hull in furious bursts.

The darkness deepened and the sounds modulated subtly downward in pitch, becoming muffled as if heard through layers of viscous fluid. Yet other aspects of the sounds, unnoticed until now, were supraclear. Then the volume altered, increasing and decreasing in a slow rhythm that was comforting. The sounds lengthened, as if stretched out of their original shape by the swell.

He was deep, deep, and the towers of the world

rose above him in cyclopean grandeur, steep walls of hard volcanic rock with thick-knuckled ridges of darkly gleaming stone as obdurate as obsidian. Pale fronds and spreading algae partially obscured their faces. The foundations, hewn and sculpted during an age so ancient that Time was but an abstract concept and Law was unknown. An age of great upheaval and movement, when the world was forming and crying out like an infant; when red and yellow molten rock spewed forth in sizzling rivers from the innards of the earth, crawling down new rock edifices, boiling into the violent seas; when land masses arose, glistening and foamy, in the middle of the oceans; when cliffs slid like cataracts into churning waters white with slate and pumice. In an age when all was beginning.

A shadow; he is not alone.

In the awesome canyons of the foundations of the world he feels a presence, diffuse and elemental

Large it is; unutterably immense so that he does not know whether it moves or is at rest. Perhaps it has features; perhaps it is acephalous or again quite shapeless. There is no way of discerning. Its sides pulse with energy, the source it seems to him of the oceans' very tides. He glides silently over the slippery mountains of its body, a metonymical terrain without end. And he wonders. But in the absolute silence no answers are forthcoming.

He awoke with an enormous thirst and a need to urinate. He ventured on deck. The storm was still raging but the sky appeared somewhat lighter. Dawn, he thought, or just after; impossible to tell in this weather. He relieved himself, then bent and stuffed snow into his mouth, returning to the cabin, shivering.

Borros was still asleep, which was just as well, Ronin thought, since he would wake with a headache.

Ronin crossed to his berth and, leaning across it,

ran his hand experimentally along the outer bulkhead. The craft was obviously built as well as it was designed. He could detect no sign of weakening and, satisfied that it was withstanding the gale's fury, he sat and ate a spare breakfast.

Borros groaned and rolled over but he did not wake up. Ronin saw the blue bruise along his neck. He crossed the cabin and bent over the frail figure. He saw then that the Magic Man was shivering.

Quickly he turned Borros onto his back. He was hot and the skin had a dry, taut look about it. The eyes came open slowly. They were enlarged and abnormally bright.

Ronin reached under the berth and pulled out a woven blanket. He stripped the spare frame of its suit and found that the material was dry but the flesh underneath was damp from the residues of melted snow and fever sweat. The suit was superbly designed to keep out the cold and the damp but conversely, if the body was wet, the material would not allow it to dry.

The body shook with the force of the fever and Ronin, covering Borros with the blanket, cursed himself for a fool. He should have realized sooner that their enormous differences in physical stamina and mental adaptability would result in the Magic Man's eventual collapse. Because he had been the one to continually urge them onward, Ronin had ignored the signs of utter exhaustion on the other's face. How much did Freidal's terrible probings take out of him? Ronin wondered.

Outside the storm smote the ship in monotonous abandon. From time to time Ronin attempted to cool the Magic Man's face with water. The bare skull, gleaming waxily in the diffuse light of the waning day, seemed a constant reminder of his vulnerability. At sunset the fever appeared stronger. Borros had slept fitfully, eating not at all. Now he was delirious and

60

Ronin felt certain that if it did not break soon Borros would die.

There was nothing he could do and his helplessness vexed him. He had searched the cabin in an attempt to find medicine, but he soon realized that there was no way of knowing what the potions and powders he found were meant for. The wrong choice could kill the Magic Man more effectively than any fever could. So he had left what he had found in the cupboard below the berth, unused, unknown. Borros moaned and the gale shrieked in the rigging.

Abruptly he heard a sharp grinding noise and was sent tumbling as the ship lurched. The motion has changed, he thought as he regained his feet. And then: Chill take it, we have hit something!

It was true. He felt now the slender felucca sliding over the ice at a precarious, oblique angle. If I do not right the ship, our momentum combined with its mass will topple us.

Pulling on his hood, he raced up the companionway, through the hatch, and out into the blinding storm. Needles of ice struck at him and the high winds tore at his torso. Over the screech of the gale he heard a rhythmic heavy flapping and, shading his eyes, peered across the deck. A long strip of rigging had worked loose and was whipping itself against the hull. There was no visibility.

He went aft with the ship trembling as it sped on its oblique and unnatural course. Slowly, he felt the felucca turning broadside into the gale. We shall break up for certain then, he thought. Hand over hand he continued aft, stepping cautiously through the calf-high mixture of ice and snow covering the deck.

A gust of wind tilted the ship and his grip loosened in the slippery iced rigging. He stumbled and skidded along the ice and as his momentum built he knew that he was going over the side. He struggled to regain his balance on the heaving deck, could not, and desperately reached out for the gunwale with his gauntleted hand. He saw with intense clarity the scales of the Makkon hide slide, frictionless, along the slickly iced wood. He tightened his grip, feeling the might of the wind against his body slamming him against the sheer-strake, and he was tossed upward as if weightless over the side, into the howling storm, almost gone, the dark and featureless ice unraveling in a blur below him so close now. His breath caught in his throat and his mouth clogged with flying ice dust. A fire running along his arm and into his chest as the wind pulled at him, moaning and crying, and he twisted in its fierce grip. And through a haze he thought, Now, now or it will surely claim me.

Calm at the core.

Momentum, he thought. And used it. With the gale tearing at him, he used the last of his strength, concentrating it into his gauntleted hand, exerting the pressure, the scales now biting through the ice, gripping finally. And still the wind battered him.

But now he had a pivot and, using it, he no longer resisted the powerful tug of the storm, but rather relaxed into it, letting it swing his body. At the height of the arc, he pushed. Up came his feet, his legs, his torso and he lunged at the gunwale with his boots, feeling them slide along the icy top. Then he had one boot over and he hooked his leg until the second was over the gunwale, and he was aboard, climbing carefully onto the deck.

He slid gasping along the sheer-strake of the stern, recalling what he had seen as he swung aboard. Just to port of the stern was a long gash in the hull. What did we hit? he wondered.

The thought was thrust aside as he scrambled for the wheel, realizing that he had lost precious time because they were still moving broadside. The rope holding the wheel on course had snapped. He gripped the curved wood and leaned against it with all his might. He took deep breaths, seeking to restore his energy, his lungs on fire, and his exhalations made harsh plumes of smoke before him. The wind howled in his face and the felucca juddered as he strove to right its course. He pushed from his feet, hauling at the wheel, using the mass of his body, and heard at last the agonized squeal of metal against ice as the runners fought friction and the storm to turn. Muscles jumped and contracted along his arms and back and thighs.

The craft was frozen in her arc; it no longer swung to starboard. But she was still sliding obliquely and he knew that he could not push the wheel farther, that there was only one chance now before a fierce gust caught the hull across the beam and turned her full broadside to the storm.

Quickly he found another piece of rope and lashed the wheel in place. Then hand over hand he went forward to the mast. His hands moved deftly over the knots, unfurling the storm sail. He pulled at the yard, plucked at the rigging, strung the storm sail.

An ice shower flung itself upon him, heavy clusters, black and jagged as exploded metal, slamming him to his knees, boot soles slithering in the ice. The rigging flew from his hands and the felucca leaped forward, shivering, as the storm sail took the wind.

He tried to get up, sliding in the ice as the gale tore at the ship, and did not attempt it again. Instead he sat, back braced against the port sheer-strake, boot soles buttressed by the base of the mast. He had regained the rigging and was hauling now, hauling to shift the yard into the proper angle.

He became one with the craft. All the creakings and moanings of joints under stress, the trembling of the hull, the incredible singing tension of the mast as it gave in to the wind and thus derived its sleek power,

63

all these were now extensions of his arms and hands and fingers as he fought for the life of the ship.

And slowly the crosstree swayed, moving centimeter by centimeter toward the needed position. It was not a steady process because the storm railed against him, shifted by gusts at odd moments so that he had to be extremely sensitive to the currents.

At first, so minutely that he was not even aware of it, the stern began to swing to port. He thought then that he might fall from exhaustion before he saw any change at all and in that suspended instant of time felt the shift. Like the first long pull of potent wine, a sense of overwhelming exhilaration warmed his chest and new strength flowed into his rigid arms.

At length he lashed the rigging in place and went aft to reset the wheel. Once at the stern, he had time to peer over the side at the gash in the hull. Curious, he thought, the damage is high up. If we had hit a rock outcropping, the mark would have been lower down. What could we have hit? He took another quick look and judged that the damage was not serious. Still, we cannot afford to let that happen again.

Day was done. The purple had deepened, drowning the gray cast of the long afternoon. And now darkness fell with a completeness that was awesome. Still the storm raged and all about him was the dizzying swirl of ice and snow. Just before he went below, he went forward and reefed the storm sail, securing the yard. He was of two minds about it but in the end he felt that it was safer to run the storm without the sail.

"You must tell me."

"Wait, my friend. Wait."

"Borros, too many have already been slain over this. I must have answers."

Dawn, almost. Faint pearled light an incipient glow at the cabin's thick ports. During the night the fever had broken and since then Borros had been breathing easier, the rattle gone from his lungs and throat, the inhalations deeper and more regular. When he awakened after the fever's cresting, he had drunk the warm liquid that Ronin had prepared, gulping greedily and asking for more.

"Later," Ronin said.

Borros lay back for a time, his energy spent, and drifted off into a deep sleep that his body demanded. Just before dawn he had awakened once more, appearing stronger. His eyes were clear and the color of his face was near normal.

"How long?"

"A cycle. A day and a night."

He ran a thin hand across his face. "Can I have something to drink, do you think?"

"Of course." Ronin offered him a bowl. "Not too much."

The whine and whistle of the wind, the muffled patter of ice crystals against the hull.

"You know," said Borros after a time, "I have for so long dreamed of the Surface, imagined what it would be like—in every detail, I mean—wished to be free of the Freehold for so long—and then for my time with Freidal I wished just to die up here—that is why I told him nothing, because I knew that if I did I would die in that hole—and that terrified me more than anything, even"— He shuddered and his eyes closed. He looked bleakly at Ronin. "Can you understand?"

Ronin nooded. "Yes. I think I can."

They had begun talking and, inevitably, the subject of the scroll arose.

"Answers, Borros."

"Yes, my boy, quite. But I can only tell you what I know." He sighed deeply. "The scroll is a key of some sort. The writings spoke of it as a door to the only pathway that could possibly stop The Dolman. He is destined, it said, to return to the world. First the shift in the laws, then the Makkon and the gathering of his legions and, finally, when the four Makkon are all there, they will summon The Dolman. They are his guardians, his outriders, his messengers, his reavers. Of all the creatures at his command, only the Makkon communicate with him directly. Once the four are here, their power multiplies. That is all the writings told me."

"And where are we bound?"

"Ah, that I can answer with more certainty. We go south; to the continent of man. There I trust we will find those who can translate the scroll of dor-Sefrith."

"And if not?"

"If not, Ronin, then The Dolman shall indeed claim the world and man shall cease to exist."

Ronin thought for a time. At length he said, "Borros, tell me something. If we hit a protrusion of the ice's surface, it would scrape us low on the hull, correct?"

The Magic Man looked puzzled. "Well, yes, I suppose so. It is hardly likely that the weather would allow any high ice formations to develop. Why?"

"No reason," said Ronin, turning away. "No reason at all."

It was dusk when it came. They had been so long with the background static of the storm that at first they thought that they were going deaf and it was not until the white noise filled their ears completely that they realized what it was. The gale had spent itself, leaving only the uncertain silence of the ice sea.

Ronin helped Borros don his foil suit and together they went on deck. To the east, banks of dark cloud gravid with moisture and lightning scudded against the sky and overhead rolled remnants of thunderheads, the last flutterings of torn banners; but to the west the air was clear, the long horizon virtually unbroken, colored by a sliver of sun, lowering like a swollen ember in a banked fire. The sky was the color of cold ash, tinged magenta and pink about the sun's arc. And then it was gone, night stealing over them so swiftly that it seemed as if the sun had never been there at all. Ronin held the image of the sunset in his memory, his heart lightened after so many days of seamless gray and claustrophobic white.

They set about clearing the deck of the debris of the storm. But Borros was still weak and he was forced to stop, moving aft to see to the wheel and their course. While he did this, Ronin stowed the storm sail and set about erecting the larger mainsail to block and tackle along the yard and mast. When he unfurled it, it immediately caught the stiff breeze, billowing out. They shot forward as if fired from a bow. Blue ice flew at the bow.

"Ronin!"

A cry of desperation.

And he knew what it was before he turned his head aft; had known from the moment he had been in the process of swinging back aboard during the gale and had seen it high up on the hull. Too high for any ice, he thought. We did not hit a protrusion. Something hit us. He turned his head and then saw it.

Borros cried out again. Both of them stared sternward. In their wake, in the clearing weather, in the silvered light of the sleeping sun, reflected off the ice, was silhouetted the unmistakable shape of a lateen sail.

"You see!"

Limmed for a moment, before it winked out with the wisps of light, it appeared to have a sinister cast.

"I told you!"

No time for that now. It was indeed a sister ship to

67

their felucca, now perhaps half a kilometer behind them and closing. Could they have lightened the craft somehow? thought Ronin. And how did they find us in all of the vast ice sea? True, they knew our exact starting point; knew that we would head due south. Yet still it disturbed him. He gazed at the spot where last the sail had been. The storm, he mused. The storm should have made this impossible. It blew us about; it blew them about surely. How could they now be so close; what were the chances . . . ? He shrugged resignedly and gave it up. No matter the reason, they are just behind us now.

The Magic Man was clever. Whatever other reading he had done, he had somehow managed to learn a good deal about sailing. That knowledge stood him in good stead now. With the sister ship giving chase, he steered them with the wind so that, with Ronin using his muscle to keep the yard at the proper angle, they caught each gust, using it to its fullest advantage, making top speed. It was all they could do. Here on the limitless expanse of the ice sea, with not even a hint of land on the horizon, evasive maneuvers were useless. But that we do not seem to be doing, thought Ronin as he ran the line through its block so that the yard swung several centimeters to starboard.

"We can outrun them," Borros called from his position aft at the wheel.

Ronin thought not. How is Freidal managing to sail that ship? he asked himself. Even with his daggam; they have no knowledge of ships? But it was merely another question that had no answer. In any case, he thought savagely, I do not believe I wish to outrun them; I have a score to settle with Freidal. I care not for what Borros said.

"It is not death so much," said Borros, "that I fear. It is all that shall come before it." The fear haunted his eyes, making them appear bulged and glassy. "You are but one Bladesman; they will cut you down and make you live through it as I have. And I," he said heavily, "will have to endure it once again." His thin lips quivered. "I cannot, I cannot."

Unwilling, Borros went below. The night was but half gone but he had almost fallen to the deck and he had no choice, his body betraying him despite the overwhelming fear in his mind.

"Go to sleep," Ronin had urged him as he helped him to the cabin's companionway. "You are safe."

The Magic Man looked at him sardonically.

"You are like all your kind," he said sharply. "Every Bladesman thinks himself invincible; until he feels the life streaming out of him."

Now in the silence of the night, Ronin stood against the trembling mast, oblivious to the delicate shhhing of the runners against the ice, the tiny sounds of the fittings. He stared ahead into the darkness, deep as obsidian, black as basalt, his mind a theater.

Freidal, you madman, you defend death. The Freehold is no more. The Saardin scheme for greater power, a power as hollow as this vessel. The lower Levels are in chaos, the workers mad and destitute. And you are pledge to uphold the laws of this place.

Freidal, you slayer, you destroyed Stahlig, slowly, joyously crushing the life from him, the terror mounting until the laboring heart burst. You have destroyed Borros too; he still lives but he is not the same man; he lives in total fear of your retribution. And you wanted to destroy me; I saw it in your face, etched as clearly as a stylus shapes warm wax, when you captured me after my return from the City of Ten Thousand Paths. You had already sent your minions after me: on the Stairwell with K'reen, my beloved, my sister; in the Square of Combat with Marcsh. Now you come for us again. Well. I will not run, for it is time we met, you and I, in Combat.

In the pale wash of first light, the sky a feathered shell of mother-of-pearl, Ronin leaned hard on the wheel.

Sunrise flew to starboard as the bow swung round, describing the beginning of its long arc, and shortly it pointed directly at the sail of their sister ship.

Prepare yourself now, Ronin called silently to Freidal. Time has almost run down.

They closed with terrifying swiftness, Ronin guiding his craft from out of the southeast quarter. The contours of the other ship bloomed abruptly from harmless toy size in the strengthening light. The day was overcast, with layers of stratified cloud, white in the sunrise. A strange light fell across the scene, oblique and somehow harsh as the sun crept over the horizon, so that every edge had a sword-blade shadow and all shapes turned angular.

He could discern now dark figures on the deck of the sister ship, dark robes fluttering thickly, white faces staring intently at him. Then there was the briefest flash of cold light, thin as a bolt, and his gaze swung to the tall slender figure at the bow. He knew even without the coalescence of features that it was Freidal. The Security Saardin's false eye had caught the light of the rising sun as it broke momentarily from the gray cloud cover, reflecting it back at him.

Ronin swung farther into the quarter, turning, feeling the adrenalin rising in him now that he was sure that it was Freidal who pursued them, turning until he ran parallel to the other felucca. They sped now across the ice sea linked together more surely than if they were physically one vessel.

Ronin watched, outwardly impassive, as Freidal went slowly aft until he was near midship. The right eye, the real eye glared at him.

"Of course you were behind this," Freidal called across the frozen expanse as the ships drifted closer. "I have come for you, sir; you and the Magic Man. He willfully escaped my custody." Ronin's eyes roved the other ship. How many? "You were taken from me but I still have many questions to ask you." Certainly two daggam. Were there more below? "The Surface is forbidden to all of the Freehold. I am charged with your return." They will be the best Bladesmen under his command; he will not underestimate me now. "The Saardin wish to question you." Discount the scribe, writing tablet strapped to his wrist, stylus scratching across its face, recording for Freidal. "Unfortunately, neither of you shall survive the journey back. I am no longer concerned with where you were or what you were doing." His good eye blinked and burned. "My daggam are sacrosanct; no one attacks them without being charged with the consequences. You broke Marcsh's back. Now you will pay. Death without honor awaits you, sir!"

Ronin heard a shout aboard ship, saw Borros' head and shoulders emerging from the cabin's hatch.

"Oh, Frost, they have caught us!"

Ronin was fed up. "Get below," he yelled. "And stay there until I come for you!"

The Magic Man stared at the tall figure of the Security Saardin, so close now over the narrowing slice of ice, transfixed with terror at the glowering visage.

"You shall die now, sir!" Freidal called.

"Get below!" Ronin shouted once more and the figure disappeared. The hatch slammed shut.

The twin ships raced on before the wind, and now Freidal motioned to the daggam and they lifted cables with black metal hooks, swung them over their heads, hurled them toward him. They hit the deck and they hauled on the cables, the hooks scraping across the

71

deck until they bit into the wood of the sheer-strake and held.

Now the feluccas were fairly touching and, securing the cables, the daggam leapt to the gunwales. Ronin lashed the wheel in place as they came aboard. Freidal stood silently, his false eye a milky round; the scribe was immobile, stylus poised.

They were tall, with wide shoulders and long arms. They had brutal faces, feral but not unintelligent; one narrow and hatchetlike, the other with a nose wide across the flat planes of his cheeks. Triple brass-hilted daggers were scabbarded in oblique rows across their chests; long swords hung at their hips.

For Ronin it was a moment of delicious hunger, these last still instants before Combat, when the power surged like a flood within him, controlled and channeled. He licked his lips and drew his blade. They advanced upon him. Now the waiting was at an end.

Over the ice they fled, the white spray of their swift passage rainbowed the light, the ships rocking, locked together in an embrace only death could now sunder.

They were a team. They swung at him from different angles, but at the same instant, seeking to confuse him. The blades caught the rising sunlight and, because he was watching their descent, he was blinded momentarily, his eyes watering, and it was instinct that guided his parry, the sword up and twisting broadside on. He got one but missed the other and it sheared into his shoulder, no help for it now. The nerves numbed themselves and the blood began to flow. The daggam grinned and came on.

Everything, said the Salamander, *every thing* that occurs during Combat may be used to your own advantage if you but know how. A strong arm but holds the sword; the mind is the force which guides it. They were more confident now, seeing how easily he was cut, and they swung at him in tandem, with co-ordinated precision, chopping and slashing, moving him backward in an attempt to cut off the number of angles through which he could attack them. They passed the bulk of the cabin as they moved forward along the ship. Let your opponent make the first moves if you are unsure of his skills; in his actions will you find victory.

And so they battered him as he catalogued their offensive strategies, attacking occasionally to gauge their defenses. They were excellent Bladesmen, with unorthodox styles, and he lacked the space to effectively attack them together.

At midship, he split them, using the yard as a barrier. It was done most swiftly, for they were not stupid and they would counter almost immediately. Almost. He had one chance only and he went in fast at hatchet-face, slashing a two-handed stroke that slit the daggam's midsection just under the ribs. His innards glistened wetly as they poured upon the deck. The mouth opened in silent protest, so quick had been the blow, and the tongue protruded, quivering. The eyes bulged as the body collapsed, hot blood pumping, congealing on the frigid deck.

But now the second daggam hurled himself under the temporary barrier of the yard, furious at being separated from his partner. Ronin parried his first attack, moving away from the center of the ship, toward the gunwale across which the hooks had been thrown. The second daggam had glanced briefly at his fallen companion and, noting this, Ronin kept his blows low so that the flat-faced daggam would assume that he was attacking the same spot now. Their blades hammered at each other, sparks flying as they scraped together, then snapped apart, only to clash again in mid-air. Ronin parried again and then, instead of the oblique strike he had been attacking with, swung his

73

blade in a horizontal arc. Too late the daggam brought his own sword up and the flat-faced head, severed now at the neck, flew from the jerking body and landed not a meter from where Freidal stood on the other ship. Ronin heaved at the corpse with its curtaining fount of blood, sent it overboard as he sprinted, gaining his ship's gunwale. He leaped, landing with his soles firmly on the deck of Freidal's vessel.

The rigging vibrated, singing dolefully in the breeze as the Security Saardin turned to face him, the tight cap of his blue-black hair gleaming, his long lean face swiveling like that of a predator's. His hand at his chest; a blur, and if Ronin had had to look, he would have been dead. But he was already turning as the blur came at him, whispering past where he had just stood. And he was off across the deck, sword up, knees bent, searching with his peripheral vision for other daggam. He passed the scribe, solitary and unmoving, stylus poised until words rather than weapons filled the air. His cloak flapped sullenly in the wind; otherwise he could have been carved from rock.

"Ah, sir, you have come to me at last." Stylus in motion, then he was off, circling in a shallow arc so that he could see the entire length of the ship. "The corps are unleashed first." The voice emotionless. "A basic rule of warfare." Past the creaking mast, the straining sail. "Soften the enemy with a preliminary attack." Mind the yard, swinging. "Deplete his energy with the soldiers." Past coils of rope, lashed kegs, the spare mast as on his own craft fixed to the port sheer-strake. "Then come the elite." Slick patches of ice near the starboard gunwale. "To finish the task." *Shhhhhh*, the runners peeling the ice below. "An admirable plan, sir, do you not agree?"

The face closer than expected, white, the thin-lipped mouth, long and cruel, pulled back into a sneer. "Not too much trouble to kill a traitor!" The two remaining daggers caught the light as they lay nakedly strapped to his chest. Freidal, Saardin and Chondrin in one man. "The Freehold cannot tolerate your kind. You are a disease that must be cleansed. You see, I cannot allow you to return to the Freehold." At last he drew his great sword. "Now I will crush you; with great care and equal skill, paying attention to the finer points." He twisted sideways until just his right shoulder was presented, leaving Ronin the smallest target to attack. "Of pain." He advanced obliquely. "And fear."

The first was a downward thrust twisting at the last moment; the second a horizontal slash of enormous power coming from the opposite direction. Ronin parried them both and then Friedal had a dagger in his left hand, holding it before him, point tilted upward.

The scribe observed them impassively as they moved slowly along the deck in a strange and deadly dance. They were just forward of midship when Ronin's booted foot hit something on the deck and he stumbled. At that moment, his eyes still on Freidal's face, he saw the barest flicker of the Saardin's good eye and instead of struggling to regain his footing he relaxed his body and fell to the deck. He heard the angry whine as the dagger buried itself in the wood of the sheer-strake above his head.

Now there was but one yet it would be enough and he had to close immediately before Freidal got to it and he sprang at the tall figure looming over him. The ship shuddered in a heavy gust of wind and the Saardin, shifting to compensate, avoided the full brunt of the blow of Ronin's gauntleted fist. It scraped along his cheek, missing the bone which it would have otherwise shattered, dragging shards of skin as it flayed the flesh, split the corner of his mouth at the end of the arc. His head snapped back, recoiling as Ronin

75

flew by, momentum carrying him into the port gunwale, striking him in the ribs, forcing the breath out of him. He gasped and tried not to double over. Freidal swiped at the blood whipping from his torn face in long droplets and swung a two-handed blow. A haze had descended over Ronin and with only his hearing now, not even fully comprehending what was occurring, he threw up his mailed fist, the scaled hide of the monstrous Makkon his only defense now. The blade hit the gauntlet and its hard peculiar surface rippled with movement. It absorbed much of the force of the blow and the sword slid against the scales as if they were oiled, glanced off, the killing blow turned aside, and it sliced into Ronin's already wounded shoulder. The pain woke him and he pivoted off the gunwale, blood whirling like a crimson scarf about him and, renewing his grip upon the hilt of his sword, staggered away from the sheer-strake while Freidal stared in disbelief at the dull hide of the gauntlet.

His bloody face twisted in fury and he came in low and fast and their blades rang like angry thunder as they met. Ronin kept close to him and now the Saardin attempted to retreat as if he was being forced to give way under Ronin's attack. But Ronin knew it for a ruse, knew that he wished only for room to throw the last dagger. Ronin drove into him, crowding him back against the mast. Freidal gripped the gleaming hilt of the dagger and Ronin's gauntlet closed over it. Their blades locked, scraping edge against edge down their long lengths. Freidal shook himself, twisting lithely, and tore free of Ronin's grasp to withdraw the dagger. They moved at once, as if provoked by the same impulse. The dagger's bright blade came at him and it could not be avoided because Freidal was not throwing it as Ronin had assumed he would, but slashing, and Ronin's momentum took him toward it. Freidal had aimed for the neck and missed, the point hitting Ronin's collarbone, abrading the flesh. And then Ronin was past him, a dark blur, his sword held now in a reverse grip so that the blade trailed behind him. Plant the feet, breathe in with a long suck, swing the mass of his frame, pushing from his ankles, the sword like living lightning striking backward at the Saardin, who was just turning to face Ronin, the point ramming into his mouth. A bubbling scream choked off. A twist of the blade and Ronin was pivoting, his sword raised above his head for another blow. It was white in the light, darkened near the tip by red rivulets.

Freidal writhed upon the deck, the lower half of his face covered by his hands and arms. Blood was everywhere. Then he was still and Ronin looked up, awaiting more daggam. The deck was clear save for the scribe. He stood watching Ronin approach.

"You have written your last line."

The stylus dipped to the surface of the tablet, scrabbled there. Ronin left him, went aft, and threw open the cabin's hatch. Down the companionway and into the cabin. No one.

Across the deck and leapt for the gunwale and, crouching there momentarily, turned. Below him, blurred ice like marble. Freidal was where he had fallen. The scribe had not moved. Ronin scanned for the last time his impassive face, then with one long stride he was aboard his own felucca. With a mighty sweeping stroke, he severed the cables holding the ships as one. They parted and, helmless, the sister felucca gradually swept away to port, into the east, growing smaller and smaller, a memory now to some.

Borros did not believe him of course, but that was to be expected; it did not concern him.

"He is dead," said Ronin as he moved about the cabin. "Believe it or no, as you will."

The sun was setting dully behind curtains of blank cloud, colorless, featureless; a deflating end to another day. Just before he went below, Ronin had peered into the west, thought he had seen the outlines of land, but he could not be certain. As it turned out, it did not much matter.

"We still have far to go," Borros said somewhat brusquely when Ronin gave him the news. "And I do not believe that he is dead."

"Perhaps you would have us turn around and make sure," Ronin said acidly.

"If we but had the time, I would insist on it," the Magic Man replied obstinately, "so that I could kick his head in."

"Of course you would. Now."

"I do not regret," he said with a trace of self-righteousness, "that I lack your zeal for Combat."

Ronin sat on his berth and, having found a piece of material, began to clean the blade of his sword.

"My zeal for Combat, as you put it, is all the protection you presently have."

"From the vengeance of the Freehold. Their power is severly limited now that we are on the Surface."

One edge at a time, upward from the thick middle to the tapered tip.

"You would not have said that this morning."

"Ronin, you do not yet comprehend. We have been locked away for generations, progress checked, choking on your own detritus." A nerve in Borros' face began to spasm. "You are as much a product of that as is Freidal. You are proud to be a Bladesman," the voice dry and pedanic, "an artificial life style created by the Freehold." His hand described a sweeping gesture. "It is totally useless here."

"It has not been so far."

"Yes, by all means mock me. What I mean is that we shall soon reach the continent of man. It will be a civilized society. Man has already learned the bitter lessons of the sorcerous wars—"

Ronin stood up.

"What is it you fear, old man?"

"I?" The gray eyes blazed momentarily. "I fear that sword you wield and the arm which wields it. I must speak plainly. I fear that your presence may jeopardize our contact with civilization. I am a man of science and knowledge; I have studied much. They will listen to me but you—you are a barbarian to them. The blood instinct runs strong in you and the chances are quite good that you will misinterpret a movement or a gesture and someone will die."

"You know me not at all, then."

"I know only that you are a Bladesman and that is sufficient. You are all alike; you know how to do only one thing."

"Tell me," said Ronin, mounting the companionway, "how you would have fared on the Surface without me." And went up into the night.

Its tremulous light spilled like wan petals onto the ice sea, over the flying ship's deck, across Ronin's hunched shoulders. He opened his eyes—lashes, brows, stubble of beard rimed with frost—to the pinks and saffron yellows dimly streaking the south. Still sleep-fogged, still feeling the dream-warmth of K'reen's smooth, supple-muscled body sleekly trembling beneath him, still inhaling the perfume of her hair, tumbling, the last parting of a forest dark before him, he turned his head to behold the ripening spray of red-orange-gold in the east as the sun rose behind low lacquered clouds on the horizon. Above him the vault was cloudless, immense, cerulean and translucent, for the first time open to him.

For long moments he sat transfixed. Then he rose and stretched his knotted muscles, warming them with motion. He crossed to the starboard sheer-strake and watched the land unravel itself perhaps four kilometers away. He withdrew a poignard from his belt and thoughtfully scraped at his whiskers while contemplating the view; it was good to see land again after so much time in the center of nothingness. He breathed deeply. The air was fresh and bright, sparkling with a chill brittleness that was not unpleasant, all the more enjoyable after the oppressiveness of the storm.

"Land at last," Borros said from behind him.

Ronin turned.

"Here."

He sheathed the poignard, took the food the Magic Man offered him. The old man appeared to be somehow smaller in the light of the new day, as if his ordeal on the surface had actually shriveled him. Ronin thought he could see new lines scored in the taut, yellow-tinged face, under the slender almond eyes, at the corners of the downturned mouth. He was peering at the oblate sun which, having quit its low cloud cover, was rising with the lassitude of age.

"We are farther south than I could have hoped."

"But we still have ice," said Ronin, pointing to the low humped shore, covered completely with ice and snow.

"Yes, well, that is to be expected for a while. But the storm propelled us far beyond what would have been possible otherwise. Can you feel that the temperature rises? It does so exceedingly slowly yet there is already a difference. And the ice too, I believe, has been affected. See there, the difference in color; its thickness diminishes."

The wind had slackened somewhat and they ran gently across the ice sea, an occasional gust billowing the sail. Ronin sat against the port sheer-strake, honing the double edges of his sword, feeling the heady beat of the strengthening sunshine.

Borros was near midship, checking the spare mast and yard and clearing the last residue of ice and frozen snow from the deck.

A calmness had crept over them both during the day, a liquid lassitude, dreamy in its warm stillness, which they both welcomed as respite from the kineticism of their journey since descending the ice plateau. Now they were content to drift through the long afternoon without speaking or even thinking.

They ate a cold supper below and then returned to the deck just before sunset. To starboard the cliffs of ice and snow had given way grudgingly to less forbidding rock faces of scarlet and gray. Snow was still plentiful, but for the first time the land appeared to be able to lift itself from beneath the white carpet. Farther off, seeming flat in the dusky haze of evening, a strong line of mountains marched across the horizon, deep violet, snow-capped, jagged and indomitable, wreathed in mists of mauve and lavender. Abruptly the sun broke onto their summits, light like shards across their peaks, and they lapsed all at once into black paper silhouette with a backdrop of crimson.

Ronin heard it just as the top edge of the swollen sun disappeared behind the mountains. He was near midship and immediately ran to the port gunwale. Borros was at the bow, searching for a spare block to replace one that had cracked during the gale. It was a sound that Ronin did not comprehend, for it had no analogue in his life. It was a dream-sound, as if the world was being split.

It came again. Louder. Longer. Two sounds simultaneously: a deep rumbling roar that vibrated the ship; a high screaming that set the teeth on edge. Borros' head came up.

Then Ronin saw in the lowering light a dark jagged

81

line growing in the ice off the port quarter in front of them. The ice lifted and, in a sledge-hammer blast, flew apart. Chunks of ice were hurled into the air, raining over them. The craft lurched and Ronin reached for the gunwale, hanging on.

He stared awe-struck as, through the widening rent in the sea, a black shape was rising, monstrous and swaying. It rose over them now, blotting out the sapphire twilight, and in a sudden flash of movement Ronin glimpsed a huge eye, baleful and alien, beneath it a narrow ugly jaw. And then it was past him, swooping onto the high stem of the felucca. Shivers ran through the frame and Ronin was hurled into the mast. The runners screeched as the vessel was thrown obliquely across the ice, then shuddered to a halt with an enormous squeal of protest. The deck splintered as the thing lashed itself against the bow for a second time. Fabric tore and Borros screamed. Ronin staggered to his feet and, drawing his sword, scrambled forward, its tip stained crimson in the last of the light.

He heard a violent hissing and inhaled a fetid stench, rotting flesh, slime, and salt and other odors he could not define. It was above him and he felt the chill of the sea depths and the drip of stinking water. Thickets of slimed weed dropped against his face and shoulders. He was in total darkness. Felt rather than saw its presence close to him off the port side and he swung the sword in a vicious two-handed blow. The keen edge cut into scaly hide, into strange flesh. A high keening sound came to his ears as he swung again and again into the thing's side.

It heaved itself away and he caught another glimpse of that terrifying eye, double-lidded, green with black-rimmed iris. He turned and nearly vomited as he confronted the gaping maw of the creature; the stench was overpowering. The jaws were all teeth, enormous and triangular, green with scum and bits of decayed flesh. The head lunged forward and he leaped away, hearing the horrendous snap of the closing mouth.

The head came up and he saw its visage, nightmarish, a great saurian face with a long narrow snout and underslung jaw, blazing filmy eyes on either side of the swaying head and, farther back, rows of crescent slits fluttering along the glistening hide. Then the sight was blotted out as the snout came for him, propelled by a sinuous neck that was the beginning of its great body. Salt spray and seaweed flew at him and he was forced to duck behind the insecure protection of the mast and flapping sail. Too late he realized his mistake. The thing threw itself after him with complete abandon, slicing into the mast and, with a snap and a splintering sound, it collapsed among a forest of shroud and rigging.

The ship rocked under him as he fought his way clear of the clinging tangle to see the dripping jaws hovering over the cowering form of the Magic Man. Ronin raced forward, knowing that he was too far away. His right hand was a blur in the night air as the poignard flew at the thing's head, burying itself just behind the right eye. The terrible head shot forward with incredible acceleration, jaws agape. They snapped shut with a hideous metallic popping. Borros screamed and a geyser of blood and torn viscera showered the air, misting over Ronin as he drove his blade point first into the unblinking eye.

Had he not been as strong, the creature would have jerked the heavy hilt from his hands; but it was his sword and he would not let it go. He was whipped about as the thing writhed in agony. He tried to pull the sword free of the bone into which it had been thrust—an outcropping of skull beneath the destroyed eye. With a grinding sound, he at last pulled it free and dropped to the deck. The saurian head, green viscous blood oozing from the gaping eye socket, quested vainly for its tormentor. Ronin, crawling along the deck, barely missed a blind swipe of the jaws; human blood spattered over him in the thing's wake. Then it reared up and crashed into the ship. The port gunwale near the bow splintered and flew into the air.

It was imperative now that he get to the creature before it tore the ship apart. He had to get it to see him and he moved around so that its good eye stared directly at him. He stood and the head ceased its writhing. It shot at him with alarming speed and he swung at the snout. The blow glanced off the thick scaly hide and he was nearly decapitated by the snapping jaws. He would not attempt that again. But there must be a way.

He turned, searching, and spied the lower half of the mast, the top splintered and sharp. He sheathed his sword and ran aft, the great head following. He ducked another swipe and heaved at the mast. Slowly it pulled up from its mounting. A searing pain scoured his back and he was flung to the deck. Nausea assailed him and his back was on fire. He shook his head and his nostrils dilated at the stench; the head was returning to finish him. Now, he thought through the red haze threatening to engulf him in unconsciousness.

He regained his feet and hauled again on the mast, feeling the thing closing again. Agony shot through him and then he had it and turned to see the glistening jaws. He rammed the broken mast into the gaping maw at an almost vertical angle. The jaws snapped shut and the mast, braced against the lower jaw, slammed its upper end through the roof of the creature's mouth, through the soft palate and into the brain. The head rose into the night, spurting upward, a scaly fountain, crying.

And then it was gone, slithering back beneath the ice, dying or already dead, drifting languorously down and down with only the cracked surface of the ice sea, the blood and slime coating the deck of the felucca to mark its passage.

Ronin, on his knees, fell forward to the deck, forehead against the coldness. He panted, gulping at the air, clearing now after the creature's descent, then crawled painfully forward.

Borros lay in a pool of blood and rent flesh. His legs were gone and the lower half of his torso was a pulpy mass without recognizable form. Ronin stared blankly. Dead.

Onward, he thought. Onward.

But they were motionless on the ice sea. He tried to stand. A wave of dizziness and pain caught him and his knees buckled. He clung to the port gunwale and waited. Moments later, he was able to stand and, putting the pain into the back of his mind, he went carefully over the side and along the ice until he came to the leading edge of the runners. Chunks of ice, thrown up by the ascent of the creature, blocked the ship's way. He moved off cautiously to port, to the gaping rent in the ice, went down on hands and knees. Too dark to see anything but he listened. A gentle lapping came to him, echoing and distant. Water! The ice was thinning. He raised his head, peering southward. Out there. An end to the ice sea? The beginnings at last of civilization? Men.

And then what? he asked himself. He shook his head like a wounded animal. First things first.

He climbed painfully aboard the stalled ship, went forward and lifted the ruined body of the Magic Man. Down to the black ice, to the slippery edge of the obsidian pit. Home at last, thought Ronin. It slid easily from his arms, a pale, smeary flash in the starlight before it disappeared. Just for a moment the splash broke the rhythmic wash of the subcutaneous waves.

He worked for what seemed an interminable time,

clearing the rubble from in front of the runners. His back burned and he was sweating and trembling by the time he had finished.

He went aboard and sat on the deck trying to regain his breath. Moments passed like centuries and he crawled along the length of the ship beneath the cold carpet of stars and in the platinum luminescence broke out the spare mast, fitting it carefully into its mounting, then attached the yard. Ran the rigging through block and tackle while the breeze sighed about him. He attached the sail and went down to his knees, a blackness in his brain, a buzzing in his ears. He pushed himself up and, sitting, raised the sail, lashed the ropes to. It was almost dead calm and the canvas flapped uselessly. He did not care; tried to make it to the warmth of the cabin but fell in a stupor of shock and exhaustion before he could take two staggering steps.

The pain inside him grew and he weakened. Sometime during the long night a strong wind sprang up and the boat lurched uncertainly, then slithered forward, picking up speed. He awoke toward dawn but the movement of the vessel lulled him back to a feverish sleep.

It was night again when he next opened his eyes. He lay unmoving for long moments, his mind attempting to retrace the events of the journey. It was too much. At length his hands went to the pockets of his foil suit but the last of his food was gone. His teeth rattled as a dull bassy booming broke upon him. It took some time for the sound to penetrate, then he flopped over and crawled slowly across the deck.

There was a fitful glow to starboard, flickering smears of reds and oranges lighting the sky. It appeared to him that in the distance a mountain was on fire, belching ruby smoke, casting burning effluvia into the obsidian night. He squinted, fascinated, convinced that he was dreaming. A dense pressure came to his ears. Great chunks of dark soapy stone were hurled high into the air and liquid fire, saffron, pale green, violet, shot from the summit of the mountain, igniting the air as it rose, then cascading downward to the earth. Blue flame, ghostly and luminescent, wrote itself inscrutably upon the tumultuous darkness while the land seemed to shiver and shift in a great upheaval. A roaring vibrated his body, filling him with the incandescence of energy. The entire world was kinetic. He imagined that he heard a mournful wail and the mountain seemed to bleed as rock, white and yellow and crimson, poured steaming and thick down its side, and forests of vapor rolled ponderously into the dulled sky. Then the night and all it held was obscured by a blackness darker even than sleep and Ronin began to choke on the soft dust.

The ship sped southward away, away from the trembling land, the red and onyx sky, over the thinning ice and, when once more the oblate sun cracked the horizon, still steeped in clouds glowing amber from its light, the morning was less chill, promising a day cool, not cold.

Still Ronin lay upon the maimed deck, delirious, the tatters of his foil suit fluttering over his gouged back. Perhaps it was better thus: that he did not see the vast chunks of ice shearing off with great cracks like barks of thunder, floating now out onto the dark green water.

The ship hit the last thin sheet of ice with a noise that was part groan, part splinter. The crust disintegrated under the weight, and at last the ship was afloat. The bow dipped precariously, then righted itself, the stem coming up in a shower. The cascade streamed over the gunwale running aft, eddying around the prone form lying on the deck.

He awoke briefly, snorting salt water from his nostrils, lifting himself weakly, grasping the gunwale, peered over the side. Water! his numbed brain screamed. Water! But he could not think why that was so important. He lifted his head and the sun blinded him. He looked again at the water, blue-green, sun-dazzled golden, and then beneath the surface at—what?

A shadow? Its immense bulk flickered deep beneath the waves without outline or contour. He stared at it for what seemed a long time. Then all that winked back at him were the green waves, tipped with reflected light, chopped into ten thousand minute crescents bobbing and dancing. What? Then he passed out, his body falling limply to the salt-slick deck.

The day turned chill as billowing clouds, dark and gravid, passed before the face of the sun, blotting out its warmth. The sea changed color, becoming slate gray; and now here and there whitecaps appeared. A heavy, gusty wind sprang up from the northeast and tore at the sail. Moments later, in the gathering gloom, the squall hit with full fury. The seas rose and the ship, unmanned, began to founder. She was turned beam on by the wind, into the troughs of the oncoming waves whose high crests now swept incessantly over the felucca. She began to take on water as she lay heavily in the crashing seas. Rain came in sheets and the day turned gray-green, dark and featureless, filled with the hiss and drum of the downpour.

The ship was sinking and nothing could save her. The wind hit her just as a wave crested broadside and she began to break up. The rain slackened but the wind intensified, as if it knew that the vessel was in the throes of going under.

The deck beneath Ronin's body buckled and collapsed and he was washed unceremoniously into the turbulent sea. He awoke in the water, gasping and choking for air as the sea filled his mouth and throat. He rose to the surface, hearing the grinding roar of the splitting ship all around him. Disoriented, heavy with the weight of his sword, he went under, clutched for a floating piece of the mast, missed, regained the surface, lungs bursting, back a glyph of agony as the salt drenched his wounds, reached again for the mast, felt its slippery length for only an instant before it rolled away from him. He tried to go after it but he had no strength and he knew with a peculiar calmness that he was drowning and there was nothing he could do about it. He went down into the cold green depths, watching the light recede from him, taking with him in his lungs a fast-diminishing piece of the sky.

THREE

·Sha'angh'sei·

Even when Rikkagin T'ien looked him full in the face, he was never sure what the stubby man was thinking.

"Tea?"

As now.

"Please."

What rules him? Ronin wondered not for the first time. Rikkagin T'ien was solid, built low to the ground. His wide shoulders, muscular arms, and short legs made him seem almost other-wordly. Then there was the fact that he was hairless.

"So pleasant to relax every now and then, so?" He lifted the small pot, lacquered in a multicolored wheel pattern. "You must excuse the lack of a lady," he continued as he delicately turned the small cups. "It is most unseemly for a rikkagin to perform this function." He poured the honey-colored liquid. It steamed the air. He tilted his head. "However war causes us to make do with so many things that we would normally find abhorrent." He shrugged as if talking to an old friend. His yellowish skin gleamed in the low lamplight, his wide oval head with its small ears, black almond eyes, and smiling mouth seemed almost regal in this atmosphere. The distant sounds of the ship wafted around them like a fragrance, dominated by the rhythmic singing. Rikkagin T'ien ceremoniously presented Ronin with a filled cup. He smiled dazzlingly and sipped at his own cup. He sighed broadly.

"Tea," he said, "is truly the gift of the gods." Then his face fell. This made him appear oddly childlike.

"How strange that your people are ignorant of its existence." He sipped once more from his cup. "How tragic."

They sat cross-legged on opposite sides of a low wooden table lacquered in squares of green and gray.

"You are comfortable in your new clothes?"

Ronin put a hand to his loose shirt, looked at his light pants.

"Yes," he said. "Very. But this material is new to me."

"Ah, it is silk. Cool in the heat, warm when it is cold." Rikkagin T'ien sipped again at his tea. "Some things are changeless, so?" He placed his cup precisely in the center of a green square. "Now that you are at your ease, please tell me again where you are from and why you are here."

Something pulled on his feet. His descent was checked. He was cradled, the sea washing over him. Then he rose toward the rippling emerald pool of light, rising from the depths, from the awful liquid silence, from the buoyancy of death, into the clean sweet air, the churning of the waves. Gripped again by gravity, he coughed and retched sea water, his lungs working like bellows, automatically, independent of his brain, which was still fogged, in the coruscating quietude of the ocean, not yet ready to accept the return to life. Then he rose into the air, a gasping, wounded phoenix.

"So," Rikkagin T'ien said, nodding. "A Bladesman you call yourself." He stared hard at Ronin; at his face, at the muscles along his arms, at the deep chest. "A soldier you are, a tactician. Well. You are ill and the injury to your back is quite serious. My physician informs me that you will carry those scars for the rest of your life." He stood up, planted his bare feet wide apart, bending his knees slightly. Three men came into the room, swiftly, silently, all armed, and if he had made a move to summon them, Ronin had not seen it. "Yet a soldier knows one thing. He knows how to fight, so?" He beckoned Ronin to stand. "Come," he said in a light tone that held no overtones, no rancor. "Come against me."

A song in his brain. A song. It dominated his senses, filling the air with a smoky tang, washing over him like the sea. It was a singsong tide of voices, rhythmic, sleepy, and muscular at the same time.

Slowly, numbly he turned over. Dazed. He had been drowning, tumbling gracefully down, twisting on the currents. He stretched out his arms. And now?

He was looking down through the slimy web of a net within which he lay. Below him, the swell and suck of the sea against long wooden planks. Curved. His eyes traveled upward and a word forced itself into his brain. A ship, he thought dizzily.

Drenched and dripping, he swung perhaps thirty meters above the water. Above him, the ship rose another forty meters. Its immense side sloped outward near the botton. The hull was painted a deep green from the gunwale until almost fifteen meters from the sea. From there down it was red. From the side of the vessel myriad square ports had been cut and from these jutted long slender staffs, it seemed to Ronin, cleaving the water at an oblique angle. A forest of staffs; on separate levels. Two? Three? Staring upward, the sun struck his eyes and he vomited the last of the sea water before he passed out.

" 'Rikkagin,' " said Rikkagin T'ien, after Ronin had for the first time told him the story of the Freehold, "is a title not dissimilar to that of Saardin, so?"

That had surprised Ronin because at no time since

he had been brought aboard had he ever been disarmed, even when he was in the presence of Rikkagin T'ien. Slowly he had come to realize that this was because they did not fear him.

Rikkagin T'ien beckoned to him and these thoughts flew through his mind like doves fleeing before a chill wind. What the little man said to him was true; he was not yet fit. Much of his strength had been sapped by his ordeal and it would be many days before he returned to good health. Yet he was a Bladesman and T'ien was again correct: he would have to prove himself.

He stood and Rikkagin T'ien bowed to him, a curious solemn gesture which he had sense enough to return. Two of the men came forward and, stooping, removed the low table from between them.

Slowly Rikkagin T'ien withdrew his sword, the light gleaming along the single slightly curved edge. Ronin withdrew his blade.

"Ah," said Rikkagin T'ien as if he had been holding his breath.

Heat. He sensed it even before he opened his eyes. The polyglot odors hit him then: sweat and briny salt, tacky tar baking in the sun and aromatic pitch, fresh fish flopping in the warmth. The singing was in his ears and the deck rolled gently under him to its thudding tempo. Heat. Against his chest and cheek.

He was stretched out on the deck. The burning along his back had somehow lessened. He sensed movement around him. A shadow crossed his face and the heat lessened. He tried to rise. A hand, gentle, firm, stopped him and he obeyed, understanding now that someone was working on his back. He felt weak and drained, not even sure, if he were pressed, what reserves of energy remained within him. The situation was unclear. He had no idea where he was. On a ship.

Just a ship. With that came the thought of the mast of the felucca. Bend, he told himself. Bend or you will break. Thus he willed himself to relax in the midst of the unknown. Thus did he survive.

He closed his eyes and let the breath flow out of him completely until his lungs sucked in the air of their own accord. He repeated this, cleansing his respiratory system and energizing himself by oxygenating his blood. His eyes opened. He stared at Rikkagin T'ien. He forced all speculation from his mind.

The curving sword was a blur, flashing upward, and simultaneously Rikkagin T'ien screamed. Ronin parried the blow. Just. The intense sound had surprised him. The clang of the blades echoed off the cabin's bulkheads. The rikkagin whirled and his sword hummed in the air again, the force of the blow stinging Ronin's wrists.

Back burning anew, Ronin lifted his blade; it was as heavy as a drowned corpse. Pain flared in his chest, making him gasp, and his guard dropped. Through the veil of agony, he saw Rikkagin T'ien advancing and, sweat rolling down his head and torso, he attempted to defend himself. Slowly, his sword came up, trembling. The end, he thought.

But instead of striking, Rikkagin T'ien stood as still as a statue, lowered his sword, sheathed it. The deck whirled, seeming to rise toward Ronin, and then he was in the powerful arms of the two men who had stepped behind him. They set him gently on a mat of rushes, carefully sheathed his sword.

Rikkagin T'ien's oval face hovered in Ronin's line of vision. He smiled reassuringly. Ronin struggled to rise.

"Stay still now," said T'ien. "I have found out what I needed to know." He shrugged, a totally pragmatic gesture, free of any theatricality. "Do not regret your pain, Bladesman." His face was a great yellow moon planted in the sky. "You see, we saw your boat break up and your story was most convincing, especially with the evidence of your back. But still"—the moon waned before his eyes, blood pounded in his temples—"we are at war and I must tell you that my enemies would do anything to discover my plans. Please do not think me melodramatic; it is quite true. And frankly the distinct possibility arose that you were in their employ." Pain was rippling through his chest, making breathing a labor. The moon smiled benevolently in the cloudless sky. "Rest now; you have proven your story; you are who you claim to be. Only a lifetime of training would have allowed you to come against me with three broken ribs." The moon wavered and broke apart. He strained to see it. "Now my physician is here. He will give you a liquid. Swallow it. He must set the ribs." Then the moon went out and he was falling, falling.

The passage of the days and nights were as puffs of smoke to him, blooming briefly, evaporating on a jasmine wind as if they had never existed; they were replaced by others, an ephemeral progression blending into a canvas of tonal colors, snatches of sounds, watery whispers of almost heard words. Most of the time he slept deeply, dreamlessly.

When at last he sat up he felt the constriction of the bandages fastened tightly across his chest. Immediately, one of the men in the cabin went out. The other leaned forward and poured tea from a clay pot into a small cup set on a lacquered tray. He held it for Ronin, who sipped gratefully until his thirst was slaked. He sat back and regarded the sailor. He had a sharp aquiline nose and a wide thin mouth. His deepset eyes were blue. He wore an open shirt and widelegged trousers. A scabbarded sword hung from his right hip. The cabin's door opened and the physician entered.

"Ah," he exclaimed, smiling, "you have had tea already. Good." He knelt and pushed Ronin gently down onto his back, his fingers moving deftly over the contours of the bandages. He was yellow-skinned as was T'ien, with almond eyes and a wide nose. He clucked to himself, then looked at Ronin. "It was a very bad fracture, yes. You were hit with great force." He shook his head as the fingers continued their probing travels. Ronin winced once and the physician said, "Ah," quite softly.

"He is better, so?" said Rikkagin T'ien from close by. Ronin had not seen him enter.

"Oh my, yes," nodded the physician. "Very. The ribs are knitting faster than I had anticipated. A very fine body. As for the back"—he shrugged almost apologetically—"it will heal but the scars are forever." His face brightened. "Still, not so bad, eh?"

"So," said Rikkagin T'ien, addressing Ronin. "When you feel fit enough, you will come on deck. Then we talk." He turned and left.

"Give him as much tea as he wants. And rice cakes," instructed the physician before departing. And Ronin was left with the men. Soon he drifted off to sleep.

A dense and smoky tangle, it climbed into the hills. It spread upward and outward from the wide harbor, the shores of the yellow and muddy sea, in a jungle of one- and two-story buildings of wood, dark paint, brown brick. In many places they seemed set so close together that he could not tell where one ended and another began.

"Sha'angh'sei," said Rikkagin T'ien.

Ronin could discern movement along the vast front of docks and wharves thrusting out into the slowly

97

lapping waves. Dark masses milled like ants over an earthen mound; they were still too distant for him to pick out individuals. A peculiar haze hovered over the immense city, a component of its clutter and sprawl, obscuring its loftier reaches so that he had no clear idea how high the houses extended.

"Welcome to the continent of man." There was a harsh edge to the laugh.

Ronin tore his eyes away from the domination of the city and looked at the man who stood on the deck beside Rikkagin T'ien. He was tall and muscular with cerulean eyes and short-cropped thick blond hair. An ivory bar was run through the lobe of one ear. He wore a light-colored, loose-fitting shirt of silk tucked into tight black leggings. A long curving sword hung in a battered leather scabbard on one hip. A wicked dirk of extraordinary length, its hilt studded with rough-cut emeralds, a rather nonchalant statement of their value, was stuck into his sky-blue waist sash. T'ien had introduced him as his second in command: Tuolin.

"It was I who fished you out of the sea," said the blond man. "It was reflex, really. Most of the men believed you already drowned; you were under a long time."

Ronin shook his head. "I recall sinking, holding my breath, then darkness and a beating silence and then—"

Rikkagin T'ien called out an order and half a dozen men sprang from the deck, racing up the rigging lines. He turned back, observing them both.

"What happened to your back?" asked Tuolin.

"Have you been north?"

Tuolin shook his head, no.

"On the ice sea," said Ronin softly, "far enough south so that the water was already coming up on the ice, thinning it, a—some kind of creature broke

98

through the crust and attacked us." Tuolin's eyes narrowed; he glanced quickly at T'ien, back to Ronin again.

"What kind of creature?"

Ronin shrugged. "I cannot truthfully say. The world, it seems, is filled with strange and monstrous things. In any event, the light was almost gone. It took us totally by surprise. There was no time for anything save death. The men in the rigging had reached the highest yards and they began to furl the topsails, using darting rapid motions. "It tore my friend in two; ate his legs."

They stood like three statues on the high poop deck, near the stern of the ship. A soft breeze brushed their faces, the tentative touch of a reunited lover.

"You must understand," Rikkagin T'ien said, "that death means little to us here in Sha'angh'sei; it is our way of life." He peered up briefly. The men were returning down the rigging. "War, Ronin. That is all we have known; all we shall ever know. Death waits for us behind every doorway, beneath every bed, down every dark alley of Sha'angh'sei." The ship began to slow as the command was given for the rowers to slacken their pace. "We would have it no other way."

"We have lost the ability to mourn for our dead," said Tuolin regretfully. "Still, I would very much like to know more of this creature of the ice sea."

"I am sure there is little more I can tell you," said Ronin. "However, I am most curious about this craft's mode of travel. It I could see—"

"The rowers?" said Tuolin. "I hardly think that you—"

"Tuolin," interrupted Rikkagin T'ien, "I do not think that under the circumstances we have much choice. It is a simple exchange of information." His eyes sparkled. "By all means, lead us down to the rowers."

99

Tuolin's face had set into hard lines and ridges and Ronin wondered what he was missing in this dialogue. He understood only that he dare not interrupt.

It seemed as if there was no air and one had to take short breaths because of the concentrated stench but over all it was cleaner than he would have expected. The men sat along low wooden benches, three to each oar. They were naked to the waist and the ridges of their working muscles along shoulders and backs glistened in the low light. They moved in perfect unison to the cadence of a drum and the rhythmic singing. Three tiers of men along three quarters of the length of the ship. He stopped counting at one hundred. They were dark-haired and swarthy, thick-boned and short, fair-skinned and fair-haired, yellow-hued and almond-eyed; a jumble of humanity, inhabitants of the continent of man.

"You can plainly see," said T'ien expansively, "that we refuse to rely solely on the inconsistencies of the weather. Canvas is fine when the wind is up, other-wise—" He shrugged.

They walked slowly down a narrow central aisle between the oarsmen.

"They are continually manned," T'ien continued. "The men work in shifts."

"They do not mind this work?" asked Ronin.

"Mind?" said Tuolin incredulously. "They are sol-diers, bound to Rikkagin T'ien. It is their duty. Just as it is their duty to fight and die if need be for the rikkagin's safety." He snorted. "Where is this man from that he does not understand this? He cannot be civilized, surely."

Rikkagin T'ien smiled somewhat absently as if he were enjoying some private jest. "He comes from a long way off, Tuolin. Do not judge him so harshly." Tuolin's eyes blazed and for just an instant Ronin believed that he was going to turn on his rikkagin.

"Teach him if he does not understand our ways," said T'ien placidly.

"Yes," said Tuolin, the cold light receding from his eyes, "patience is its own reward, is it not so?"

T'ien walked on and they followed, a pace or so behind.

"You see," said Tuolin, "we carry with us many moral obligations which we are taught to honor virtually from birth." A dark blur at the corner of Ronin's vision. "To be bound to a rikkagin has many benefits." Oblique approach, ballooning. "One eats well, one is clothed, one has money, one is trained——" And Tuolin had seen it too because even now he was moving, the long dirk no longer in his waist sash. There was a scream, disturbing the heavy air like a sudden breeze parting a velvet curtain, and the figure was upon them. Tuolin leapt forward, his dirk flashing in a savage thrust. The body, long and thin, sweat-coated, wielded a curving single-edged sword. The face was pinched, the mouth screaming, lips pulled back from rotted stumps of teeth in a rictus, the eyes glassy and bulging fanatically. Then the figure was spitted on the blond man's blurred weapon. The legs kicked violently and then the eyes rolled as the blade ripped through the naked chest, spewing forth blood and bone fragments. The man's sword clattered uselessly to the wooden boards. Rikkagin T'ien watched impassively as Tuolin withdrew the dirk and with a deft economy of motion slit the man's throat. Ronin noted that T'ien had not even drawn his sword.

Now the rikkagin sighed and without looking at either of them said, "It is best if we return abovedecks." And stepped nimbly over the crumpled corpse.

Sha'angh'sei loomed over them as they maneuvered the sea lanes clogged with vessels large and small and eased into the port. The ship plowed slowly through the thick sea, yellow-brown and clinging, past square-rigged fishing craft and high-sterned cargo vessels. Off to starboard, Ronin thought he could just discern the broad mouth of a river spilling into the sea.

He stood on a high poop drinking in the city while all about him was movement as men raced through the catwalk rigging, reefing the last of the unfurled sail, securing yards and lines, the forest of oars high in the air, dripping and shining, as the rowers prepared to ship them. It lay before him in the inky twilight like a vast fat jewel, dusky and dim with age, smoldering with fitful movement, heaving itself from the spume and effluvia of the land.

The low buildings closest to him appeared to be built on a delta and he looked again for the river's mouth for confirmation but it was lost behind the thick clumps of buildings. Beyond the flat of the delta the city rose like the arched spine of a frightened animal and many of the dwellings in this area seemed to need the aid of wooden columns sunk into the hillside, which supported their jutting balconies, fluted and columnated, dark hardwoods gleaming in the smeary glow as lamps and torches were abruptly lit throughout the city as if by some prearranged signal. The deepening haze, sapphire and mauve, softened the flicker of the flames so that the individual sources blended and blurred and the city seemed to glow with an ethereal incandescence.

Ronin's pulse quickened. By chance he had come to Sha'angh'sei, and it was obviously a major port on the continent of man. Here, he felt confident, he would find someone who could unlock the riddle of the scroll of dor-Sefrith. The wash of light reached out for him as the ship maneuvered toward the waiting warf. Perhaps, he mused, Rikkagin T'ien will know of someone.

Men swarmed along the long arm of the wharf in

anticipation of their arrival and Ronin, observing the frenzy of activity, felt the muscles of his stomach contract momentarily as his spirits soared. The continent of man: Borros had been correct all along. So many people here, such a teeming world; even now, though it was before his eyes, it was a shock; so long talked of, it was a dream world that had been an integral ingredient of the fantasy that had kept them alive with a goal as they flew across the featureless platinum ice for endless days and nights with nothing but the cutting wind and cold as their reality. This dream had kept Borros alive until the end, Ronin was sure; his body had been beaten and, save for this land beckoning him on, Borros' mind would have let go in the midst of Freidal's torture within the confines of the Freehold. And now: now I step upon the cluttered foreshore of the continent of man. A dream no more.

There came a brief command and the ship touched the creaking timbers of the long wharf.

There was an electric hum, the live-wire abrasive intensity of rushing bodies, the cacophonous atonality of voices raised in argument, laughter, command, the chunky slap of cargo continually being loaded onto ships ready to sail to other ports, unloaded from just-docked vessels, the brief slam of working doorways, the beckoning cries of vendors, the lilt of hoarse monotonous work songs, the crisp cadence of soldiers' booted feet, the clangor of arms, the tolling of far-off bells, a whiff of mysterious chanting, and beneath it all, the heavy wash of the yellow sea lapping at the belly of the city, caressing it, washing its soil, eating its bedrock.

He stood on the wharf, an alien island in an ocean of moving bodies. The debarking soldiers passed him in formation, elbowing aside the scurrying workers, bare-chested and barefooted, tattered pants rolled up their legs, sweat streaming down their laden backs, some bent double under their immense loads, others in pairs trotting with crates of food-stuffs suspended from bamboo poles supported on their shoulders. Overseers screaming their instructions, orders being barked, sellers frantically hawking their wares, bodies coming against him like breakers, sounds like waves beating upon the shores of his ears, engulfing him. He breathed deeply and his nostrils flared to the steamy air laden with the fragrances of man, the pungency of fresh spices and syrupy oils, the mingling of exotic perfumes and thick sweat, the briny scent of the sea, rich with the myriad animal flavors of life and death.

Tuolin found him eventually.

"The rikkagin will see you tomorrow in the morning." Caftans of silk and cotton, tight blouses over firm breasts, long earrings clashing softly. "He is most anxious to speak with you at length." Gold rings glinting, a wooden leg with a worn shoe stuck on the end, colored skirts swirling, armbands dully shining, flash of yellow feathers. "Now he has many preparations to make and we could both use food and drink." Carts bumping, green eyes flashing, strange two-wheeled carriages pulled by toiling runners, dark hair floating in the soft scented breeze, music skirling. "Especially drink, eh?" Faces hidden by veils, faces covered with long beards, greased and curling, the savory mouth-watering perfume of roasting meat, a black and terribly empty eyeless socket, laughter, mouths gaping wide, black teeth, eyes crinkling, flash of dirk. "And afterward, a very special place, Ronin. Oh yes."

Along the sweep of the wharf the crowd thinned momentarily and Ronin was transfixed by a constellation of bobbing lights along the waterfront. Low, wide boats, some with makeshift shelters, most without, rocked gently on the evening tide. Lanterns were hung, illuminating the occupants. Families crowded the vessels, men, women, scrambling children and screaming infants, old ones still as statues, all assembled now for the meal at day's end; sitting with cracked shallow bowls of rice close to their faces, eating with long sticks, throats working as if they were famished.

"Home for many people," said Tuolin. "Generations have worked on land and have lived on the tasstans." Bodies closed over the view in an unwashed tide, blotting out all but the sea lanterns' mobile glow reflecting off the restless water. They began walking again. "There is no room for them in Sha'angh'sei." Shouts and the sounds of running feet. "There never was."

"Yet they work here, do they not?"

"Oh yes." A scuffle beside them; coarse curses, receding, drowned in the sea of bodies. "There is always work from dawn until dusk; for a copper coin which the merchants take at the end of the day, for the mildewed rice that they must eat. There is always work in Sha'angh'sei for a strong back, day or night. But nowhere to live." Tuolin laughed abruptly and clapped Ronin on the back. "But no more talk now. I have been too long from this city." He guided them skillfully through the jostling throng, moving at an increasing pace.

"Come," he called as he moved ahead. "We go to Iron Street."

Night lights flared along every street they took; black iron lanterns, wrought in openwork grills, the flames within licking smokily at the darkness. The packed streets were cobbled, lined with buildings variously assigned as apartments or shops without any discernible pattern. Men, thin and fat, lolled in open doorways, picking at their teeth or smoking pipes with long curving stems and tiny bowls, squatting against grimy wooden and chipped brick walls, talking or dozing. Off these thoroughfares were ubiquitous narrow twisting alleys, blacker than the night, down which people would sometimes wander, disappearing within instants, leaving behind only a dissipating breath of sweet smoke.

They passed many soldiers, of differing types and obviously bound to various rikkagin. They seemed to be the only people in these noisome streets not in a hurry. Ronin was pleased to be able to walk; it gave him a chance to test his body. His back had ceased to pain him days ago and the wound in his shoulder was almost healed but he knew his ribs needed more time to mend. His chest was stiff and sore but most of the sharp pain had left him and this exercise was invigorating, not tiring.

On Iron Street, two men threw a set of five dice against the side of a wall, talking softly to each other, intent on the faces of the cubes. A woman in filthy clothes sat in the dust of the street, a bawling baby in the crook of one arm. She held a grimy hand, nails torn and black with dirt, palm upward.

"Please," she called in a pitifully weak voice. "Please."

Her sad eyes caught Ronin's and they were filled with pain.

"Ignore her," Tuolin said, noting the direction of Ronin's gaze.

"But surely you can spare something for her."

Tuolin shook his head.

"Please," the woman called.

"The baby is crying," said Ronin. "It is hungry."

Swiftly Tuolin crossed the crowded street and, thrusting aside the folds of the woman's robe, grasped the hidden wrist and Ronin saw that she held a dirk which she had been digging into the baby to make it cry. Her almond eyes flashed angrily and she wrenched her wrist from his grip, lunging at him with the blade's point. Tuolin stepped back out of harm's way and they resumed their walk along Iron Street.

"A lesson of Sha'angh'sei," he said.

Ronin glanced back through the crowds of people. The woman sat, palm outstretched, the other hand hidden. Her lips moved; her eyes searched the passing faces. The baby cried.

"War is the reason Sha'angh'sei was built and it was built in a day."

"Surely you are not serious."

"Perhaps I exaggerate just a bit."

"How long?"

"To build the city?"

"No. How long has the war been on?"

"It is endless. I do not remember. No one can."

"Who is fighting whom?"

"Everyone against everybody."

"That is not an answer."

"Yet it is the truth."

They were sitting in a low-ceilinged tavern, at a plank table located along the back wall which ran almost the entire width of the establishment. A wide wooden stairway to the second story took up the remainder of the wall.

The air was thick with smoke and grease and burning tallow. Before them lay platters of broiled meat and steamed fish, raw vegetables and the inevitable rice. Cups of a clear rice wine, hot and potent, were constantly refilled as they ate using the long sticks. The men aboard ship had taught Ronin how to use these peculiar eating utensils.

"All the races of man are here, I think," said Tuolin between mouthfuls, "in differing strengths. And they have never gotten along."

"Borros, the man I traveled with over the ice sea,

107

believed that the sorcerous wars had ended all conflict."

Tuolin smiled as he swallowed but his eyes showed that he was not amused; they were as coldly blue as ice. "Man will never learn, Ronin. He is eternally at war with himself." He shrugged. "There is no help for it, I am afraid."

Six soldiers in dusty uniforms came into the tavern, pulling up chairs around a table near the door. They ordered wine and began to drink, laughing loudly and pounding on the table. Their long swords scraped against the floor boards.

"This city is composed of factions," said Tuolin, "all of them mistrusting the others because the war allows you to make much money if you are shrewd."

In the far corner two cloaked men, tall and light-haired, sat with arms around a pair of sloe-eyed women, slight, with high-cheekboned, flat-nosed faces, long black hair falling sleekly to the middle of their backs.

"The city is filled with many, many hongs—merchants—who are rich and fat from the war."

"They live here?"

One of the couples was kissing now, a long and passionate embrace.

"Hardly," Tuolin snorted. He gulped at his wine. "They live on the upper reaches." He refilled his cup. "In the walled city."

"Another city?"

"Yes and no." He took more meat with his sticks. "It is still Sha'angh'sei."

Along the opposite wall a woman with long eyes and a curiously simian face whispered to three men in dark cloaks. She wore her shiny hair piled upon her narrow head and long earrings of a green stone spun as she moved her head.

"What about the war?"

108

"It is everywhere. It is why we returned to Sha'-angh'sei. An army of bandits have massed to the north and west." Three children ran in from the street, thin and filthy and hollow-eyed. The tavernmaster called to them as they clattered up the stairs. He shouted and the tallest one returned and laid a number of dull coins in the man's hand. The tavernmaster slapped the boy so hard that his frame shook. The boy dug a dirty hand into a pocket and extracted several more coins, then he ran up the stairs after the others. "The hongs are paying us to protect their interests before the bandits become a nuisance by descending on the city itself."

Even to Ronin, so short a time with these people, it seemed an implausible story; however, he could not guess why Tuolin should lie to him.

"Then you will be leaving Sha'angh'sei?" he asked.

The simian-faced woman was gesturing now with narrow bony hands. Her long nails were lacquered green and, Ronin saw with some surprise, her teeth were black.

"Yes. The day after tomorrow. It is a three-day march to Kamado, the fortress in the north."

One of the men got up and walked out. The remaining two resumed talking to the simian-faced woman with increased animation. Her teeth gleamed darkly.

Ronin was about to say something but Tuolin's hand on his arm stopped him. He followed the blond man's gaze.

Two men stood in the doorway. They wore dark baggy pants and black cloaks over silk shirts. They were almond-eyed with flat wide faces. Their long hair was waxed and bound in queues. An errant gust of wind plucked at their cloaks and Ronin caught a glimpse of short-hafted axes thrust into their sashes.

"Keep still," whispered Tuolin, his eyes drifting

109

slowly away from the tall figures. His voice carried a peculiar note, of fear perhaps? He looked at Ronin and said in a more normal tone, "The rikkagin will require you at a specific hour tomorrow. Until that time, he requested me to be your guide around the city." Ronin stared at him. "Sha'angh'sei is a most complex and at times bewildering city. The rikkagin does not wish for you to get lost."

The men were still in the doorway, their black eyes sweeping the room. The tavernmaster glanced up from serving a table and, wiping his hands on his apron, hurried across the room. He drew from some inner pocket a small leather sack which he handed to one of the men. The other said something to him and laughed. The tavernmaster bowed. Then the two were gone without a sound.

"Who were they?" asked Ronin.

"The Greens," said Tuolin as if that were all the answer needed. He drained the last of his wine. "I have had my fill of this place. What say you, Ronin, shall we move on?"

Tuolin paid for their meal. The green stone earrings of the simian-faced woman danced as she spoke.

Outside in the fragrant air, there seemed less people about than earlier in the evening. Tuolin looked both ways along the street, then he seemed to relax, stretching.

"Now," he said, "the evening begins."

The gold plaque said "Tenchō." It was fixed with golden spikes to the brown brickwork to the left of the high yellow double doors at the head of a curving iron stairway on Okan Street.

Twice he had caught Tuolin glancing behind them as if he thought they were being followed. However, it seemed quite impossible to tell among all the bodies darting in every direction.

Tuolin knocked on the yellow doors and after a moment they opened inward.

"Matsu," he breathed, smiling.

She stood between the two armed men, her slender frame appearing smaller for their presence. She had an oval face with long almond eyes and thick black hair which she wore straight and loose so that one eye was continually blanketed by its cascade. She wore a silver robe with a high neck and flaring sleeves, embroidered with gray doves. Her skin was very white; her lips were unpainted. The oval lapis pin at her throat was the only relief from the black, gray, and white.

She smiled at Tuolin, then gazed for a long moment at Ronin. Then she murmured to the guards, who relaxed somewhat.

She led them wordlessly through a narrow foyer. Strips of thin carpeting covered the wooden floors; a tall gold-framed mirror briefly discolored the small procession. They went through open doors on the left from which yellow light wavered and danced.

They were in a wide, deep room with blond wood paneling along the walls to a height of an average man's waist. Above this, the walls were painted a muted yellow. The high ceiling was bone white. From its center hung an immense oval lamp constructed of faceted topaz; perhaps five hundred crystals had been cunningly mounted so that the lamp's myriad small flames, set in its center, shone through the facets. It was this singular light which gave the room its tawny aspect.

Scattered about the lacquered wooden floor were small intimate couches and groups of plush chairs upon which sat the most diverse assortment of women that Ronin had ever seen. Some were with men, drinking and smoking, others were in small groups talking languidly among themselves, turning their exquisite faces to the prowling men like petals of a flower following the path of the sun. Young girls in quilted jackets and wide silk pants of pastel colors moved between these groups, ships in the indeterminate voids separating these trembling constellations.

Matsu left them, crossing the room to a group of two men and a woman. After several moments the woman detached herself and approached them. She wore a floor-length saffron silk dress, slit up one side so that with every step she took Ronin could see the length of one naked leg. The dress was embroidered in patterns of fantastic flowers in the palest green. Like Matsu's, the dress was wide-sleeved and high-necked and this style managed somehow to highlight her figure.

But it was her face that was most extraordinary. She had long dark eyes, the upper lids dusky and sensual without seeming to be painted. Her face was narrow at the chin, accentuating her high cheekbones. Her lips were painted deep scarlet; glossy, half opened. Her hair was so violently dark that it appeared blue-black; she wore it very long and brushed to fall delicately across her left shoulder and breast.

She smiled with small white teeth and lifted her hands, pressing them together.

"Ah, Tuolin," she said. "How good it is to see you again." Her voice had the tonality of a bell, far away, lilting. She dropped her hands. They were small and white with delicate fingers and long nails lacquered yellow. She wore topaz earrings in the shape of a flower.

Her head turned slowly and she gazed at Ronin and at that precise moment he had the peculiar sensation of seeing double.

"Kiri, this is Ronin," said Tuolin. "He is a warrior from a land far to the north. This is his first night in Sha'angh'sei."

"And you brought him here," she said with a musical laugh. "How very flattering."

A young girl in a light blue quilted jacket and pants came up to them.

"Liy will take you to bathe. And when you return, you shall decide." The dark eyes regarded him.

The girl led them across the room of topaz light, through a wide teakwood door into a short passageway of rough-hewn stone. The contrast was absolute.

They went down a narrow stairway lit by smoky braziers set high up along the walls. The stone steps were damp and somewhere, not far off, Ronin could discern the soft slap of water. The stairs gave out into a wide room with rock walls and a low wooden ceiling, lamplit, warm. Into one wall had been hewn an immense fireplace within which hung an equally enormous cauldron steaming as the fire boiled its contents.

The room itself was dominated by two large square wooden tubs set upon raised wooden slats; one of the tubs was half filled with water. Four women, dark-haired, almond-eyed, naked to the waist, stood as if waiting for their arrival. Water steamed and gurgled.

"Come on," Tuolin called happily, stripping off his dirty sea clothes and hanging his weapons on one of a line of wooden pegs set into one wall. Ronin followed suit and the women directed them to the empty tub. As they climbed in, the women drew up buckets of hot water, filling the tub. Then they climbed in and, taking soft brushes and fragrant soap, began to wash each man thoroughly.

Tuolin snorted and blew water from his mouth.

"Well, Ronin, what do you think of this? Was home ever so pleasant?"

The hands were soft and gentle and the hot soapy water against his skin felt delicious. The women murmured to each other when they saw his back, the scars long and livid and newly healed, and they took great care in cleansing this part of him so that he felt no discomfort, only pleasure. They stroked his chest, gently massaging his muscles almost as if they knew of his recently broken ribs. They murmured to him and he and Tuolin moved, creators now of their own waves, commanders of tides and currents, to the second tub to which clean hot water was added. Two of the women began to clean the first tub while the other two gathered up the pair's dirty clothes and went out.

Ronin lay back, stretching out his legs, letting the heat slowly soak into his body. Gradually, his muscles loosened and much of the tension drained out of him. He closed his eyes.

How unexpected this all was. How utterly different were the circumstances than what Borros had pictured. How— Abruptly the realization came that he had had no idea of where he might be headed or even if he could survive when he had ascended onto the surface from the Freehold's forbidden access hatch. He had followed Borros blindly, not caring, wanting to escape from the Freehold as much as he had wanted to solve the mystery of the scroll of dor-Sefrith. The heat climbed into him like the presence of a naked woman close beside him.

And with that the barriers which he had so painstakingly erected folded in upon themselves and he thought of her. Oh, K'reen, how you must have been tortured. He destroyed you day by day with the poison he fed you. The lies!

The water rippled and Ronin looked up, into the present. One of the women had climbed in beside Toulin.

"Do you want the other one? It is perfectly all right but you must ask."

Ronin smiled wanly. "Not just now. The water is enough."

The blond man shrugged and splashed the woman, using his cupped hand. She giggled.

Strange. The Freehold seems like so long ago; as distant as another lifetime. But she does not. She is still with me and there is nothing, Chill take him, that the Salamander can do about that.

He glanced at his great sword, swinging a small arc, brushed by one of the women as she slipped out of the room. Within it was the scroll and perhaps, if Borros was right about this, the key to man's survival. And he could no longer doubt the Magic Man. He had already grappled with the Makkon; felt its awesome power. And instinctively he had known that such a creature was not of this world; it held its own kind of monsters.

Of this he was certain: at least one Makkon was already here. If the scroll has not been deciphered by the time the four converge, they will summon The Dolman and mankind will surely be doomed.

"Ready?" asked Tuolin.

They both stood up, dripping.

"Let me look at you."

The scarlet lips opened. The tiny pink tongue brushed the even white teeth.

She laughed. "She is always so clever about these things."

He wore a silk robe of a color that could have been light green or brown or blue or any one of a dozen colors. Yet it was none of these but perhaps a subtle blend to cause the finished cloth to appear colorless. Along the body and arms were fierce dragons, rampant, eyes seething, taloned limbs seeking, embroidered in gilt thread so that their hides seemed molten. Tuolin was clothed in a robe of deep blue with white herons on front and back.

"Ah, Tuolin, you must have brought me a remarkable man." Kiri directed her eyes to Ronin's. "You know, I will not say this to all who come to Tenchō, but Matsu chooses the robes to fit each person who enters here. She is rarely wrong in her matching."

"And what does this mean, then?" asked Ronin, glancing down at the glittering dragons.

"Why, I am sure I do not know yet," she said with a small smile. "I have never seen that particular pattern before."

She turned to Tuolin then and took his arm. Her perfume came to Ronin, rich and subtle, musky and light. The three of them strolled across the room of topaz light, stopping momentarily as one of the girls offered them tea and rice wine, and Kiri introduced them one by one to the women who were not already engaged with men. All were beautiful; all were different. They smiled and stroked the air with their ornamental paper fans. At length, Tuolin made his choice, a tall slender woman with light eyes and hair and a generous mouth.

Kiri nodded and turned to Ronin.

"And you," she said softly. "Whom do you wish?"

Ronin looked again at all the women, the jutting landscape of femaleness, and he came back to her black dusky eyes.

"It is you," he said slowly, "that I wish."

When the organism does not comprehend, sight and sound become meaningless. The light-haired woman therefore looked strange to him as she opened her mouth wide and emited a sound.

She gasped, then half giggled, stifling it with a swallow as the three others stood quite still watching her. Around them the movements continued, the languid flutters of a fan, the flashes of naked legs, the sweet smell of smoke curling, the steaming of hot tea and spiced rice wine, like the slow immense wheel of the stars.

There came then the chink of a cup being set down on a lacquered tray, as separate and distinct a sound as a crack of thunder of a rainwashed night.

Tuolin said: "But that is im—"

Kiri's delicately upraised hand halted him in midsentence.

"He is," she said, "from another land. That is what you told me, Tuolin, yes?" The yellow nails were like slender torches in the light. "I asked and he replied as he wished." Now she was gazing into Ronin's eyes but she spoke to the blond man. "You have selected Sa, as *you* wished. Take her then."

"But—"

"Think no more upon it, lest your harmony be broken and this house become worthless. I take no offense." The yellow nails moved fractionally, spilling light. "I shall take care of Ronin. And he shall take care of me."

"What happened?" asked Ronin after Tuolin and Sa had departed.

She took his arm and laughed softly. They began to walk in the room of topaz light. "Death," she said lightly and without any trace of coyness. "It is death to ask for me, foreigner."

A tiny girl in a pink quilted jacket came up to them to offer rice wine.

"Please," Kiri said and he handed her a cup, took one for himself. He sipped at the wine; it was quite different from the rice wine of the tavern. The spices added a tang and sweetness that he appreciated.

"I will choose another then."

There was muted laughter and the sinuous rustle of fabric against scented skin. The sweet smoke was heavier now.

"Is that what you wish?"

117

"No."

"You told me what you desired."

He stopped and looked at her. "Yes, but—"

"Hmmm?" The scarlet lips opened and curled in a smile.

"I wish also to abide by the rules of your people."

She urged him to begin walking again.

"The one thing you must remember about Sha'angh'sei, the only thing worth remembering is that there are no laws here."

"But you just told me—"

"That it is death to ask for me, yes."

The yellow nails traced the gilt dragons of his robe, over flaring nostrils, open mouth, and snake tongue, down the serpentine body, across the rampant claws, following the sinuous tail.

"But everything is yours for the taking. The factions of this city bind themselves in codes and unwritten rules." Her eyes were huge and mysterious; he felt the pressure of her nails through the cloth. Her voice was a whisper now: "Who dwells in Sha'angh'sei but the dominators and the dominated?" He drew toward her. "Yet law is unknown here."

It was less dense in the room of topaz light as the couples began to disperse. The girls were cleaning up in perfect silence and soon its tawny splendor was left to them alone.

"No," she said, and when she shook her head her hair was like a forest in the night, "you are not from Sha'angh'sei or anywhere close. You are totally untouched by the city."

"Is that so important?"

"Yes," she whispered. "Oh yes."

"Tell me again why you have come to Sha'angh'sei."

"You have heard it before."

"Yes, but this time I wish Tuolin to hear it."

"I had never heard of the city until you told me of it."

"Of course," he said, not unkindly.

Rikkagin T'ien sat cross-legged behind a green lacquered table on which stood a fired clay teapot, a cup showing the dregs of many fillings in its bottom, an inkwell, and a quill pen. He put aside the sheaf of rice papers upon which he had been writing a vertical list of figures.

"Begin, please."

Ronin told the story of the scroll of dor-Sefrith, the gathering of the Makkon, the coming of The Dolman.

There was silence in the room when he had finished. Yellow light streamed obliquely through the leaded glass panes beyond which, one story below, lay Double Bass Street where the rikkagin and his men were quartered and from which they would depart at dawn tomorrow for the long march to Kamado.

He saw T'ien glancing at Tuolin, who stood, hands clasped behind him, facing away from the windows. With the light at his back, his face was in deep shadow. It occurred to him then that they did not believe him; that, despite Rikkatin T'ien's words to the contrary, they perhaps thought him still an enemy. Nevertheless, I must ask.

"Perhaps you could help."

"What?" T'ien had been pulled from some deep thought. "Help in what way?"

"By deciphering the scroll."

The rikkagin smiled somewhat sadly. "I am afraid that is quite impossible."

"Perhaps the Council could aid him," said Tuolin.

Rikkagin T'ien looked bewildered for a moment and he stared at the blond man as if he were a statue which had just spoken. Then he said, "Yes, now that you have brought it up, that might be the answer." He seemed lost in thought again.

"You see," said Tuolin, "the city is governed by a Municipal Council: nine members with the major factions represented and the minor ones currying favors through taels of silver and other commodities. If any in this city possess the knowledge you seek, they would."

"Where does the Council meet?"

"In the walled city, on the mountain above us. But you will have to wait until tomorrow; I do not believe there is a Council session today. Is that not correct, Rikkagin?" Tuolin smiled.

"Hmm? Oh yes, quite so," T'ien said, but his mind still seemed preoccupied with other matters.

In the small silence, the soft clatter of the rikkagin's men attending to their preparations drifted lazily through the open windows.

There came a knock on the door and Tuolin crossed the room before T'ien had a chance to say anything. A soldier bowed his way in, handing Tuolin a slip of folded rice paper. The blond man opened it and read its contents, his brows furrowing in concentration or anxiety. He shook his head at the soldier, who immediately departed. Then Tuolin crossed the room and laid the paper open in front of the rikkagin. While T'ien read it, he said, "I am afraid that a number of last-minute administrative problems have arisen and they will require the attention of the rikkagin and myself for the remainder of the day. Please feel free to see the city but we should like it if you would return here and take the evening meal with us." The smile came again.

T'ien looked up. "Ask one of the men downstairs for directions. They have been instructed to give you a bag of coins. You cannot get anything in Sha'angh'sei without paying for it."

Outside, he turned left and then right, walking down a street of some incline. The day was overcast and a yellow mist was still rising. He caught himself thinking of T'ien and Tuolin. Again he had the feeling that he had missed something vital in their exchange, yet the answer remained elusive. He shrugged and put the problem out of his mind.

He came to a broad avenue after several minutes and the noise of the city welled up at him. Rows of stalls lined the crowded street. One sold fowl. They were hung by their necks, cooked and varnished with a shiny vermilion sauce so that they looked wooden and unreal. As he watched, people stopped, putting down a few coins. The stall's owner brought out bowls of rice and sticks and commenced to cut up pieces of the cooked bird into the rice. The people ate standing up. For another coin they received a small cup of green tea to wash down the meal.

Elsewhere, a tailor of leather worked, making boots and cloaks. And at a busy intersection a fat man with a thin drooping mustache sat within a square metal cage, lending money at the day's going rate, which, Ronin surmised, was somewhat higher than yesterday's.

He heard the cadence of boots and a group of soldiers tramped by, moving disdainfully through the clouds of people.

He walked the city's twisting fluid streets, caught up in the rapid pulse, repeating and changing, flashes of color, a riot of sound, aromatic spices drifting across his meandering path.

He observed transactions of all kinds, handled in quick sharp movements; he watched people who seemed to do nothing but watch other people, standing by shopwindows or sitting along the sides of buildings.

He was staring at a line of six barrel-chested birds

121

on a thick wooden perch, preening their long saffron feathers, when it came to him, strained through the myriad sounds of the city, yet perfectly clear as it gyred in the wind. Following his ears, the sound pulling him in like a net, through the turnings of broken streets and dank alleyways until at length he stood before a stone wall and listened to the tolling of the bells, coloring the air. An ancient wooden door was set into the stone wall. Without thinking, he opened it and went through.

The tonal wash of the city faded as he crossed the threshold and he heard the bells more clearly now although their source seemed still far away.

Across a sudden background of misty silence he heard a horn sound once.

The bells tolled sweetly once again, in the garden neat, precise, beautiful. Glistening flowers of white and yellow and pink were arranged amid rocks and furry moss and feathery ferns in exquisite patterns.

Water burbled and farther on he found a tiny waterfall and a pool filled with small fat fish with long silver fins fanning the green water like veils. He walked on a path paved with brilliant white gravel.

The bells ceased and the horn sounded again. A quiet chanting began, lilting, pleasing to the ear, drifting somnolently on the still air. Ronin strained his ears but could discern no sound from the city without the stone wall.

In the center of the garden was a large metal urn, of brass perhaps. Beside it sat an ancient man in brown robes. His wrinkled face was serene, his eyes were closed. His sparse hair was white, his beard long and wispy. He sat still as stone.

Ronin reached out and touched the bulging metal sides and felt—nothing. So pure a nothingness that it was tangible. An immutable space yawned, years falling like dry leaves, centuries passing like silent

122

drops of rain, eons emerging, merging, sundered. And an immense quietude entered him: the thunder of eternity.

He was shaken.

He found that he had closed his eyes. When he opened them, the bells were tolling again, high in the air. He went on stiff legs through a wooden doorway and it was as if a gust of melody had transported him to another world. The air was humid with incense, the light was dim and brown as if it were ancient. Stone walls and marble pillars, a ceiling indistinguishable in the gloom.

In the distance, masses of squat yellow candles were lit, the tiny flames swaying like a chorus of dancers preparing for a performance. The incense and the tallow caused the air to take on a third dimension. Thus he moved now, feeling like the fish in the pond outside, as slowly as through water. The centuries hung upon him as taels of silver, dense and beautiful.

Then from somewhere he thought he heard a coughing, low and questioning. An animal presence. Perhaps a voice, so distant that he heard but the echo, said, *Find him*. Soft pad of paws, a scratching as gentle as the rustling of autumn foliage. *You must find him*. Echoes echoing. Away.

He looked dreamily about him. The chanting came again, pellucid, peaceful, scenting the air. Shafts of tawny light fell obliquely through the high narrow windows, lacquering the store floor and the reed mats. He was alone.

He thought of the bronze urn and the man who sat so still beside it.

He was there when Ronin returned to the exquisite garden. Eyes closed. A statue. The fish swam lazily. The water gurgled throatily. The bells were silent.

He approached the stone wall, went through the wooden door, and as he closed it behind him the discordant noises of the city, frantic and desperate, descended upon him like a horde of locusts in the heat of summer.

He walked randomly, still half dazed, until he realized by the waning light that the day was almost done. He asked a corpulent merchant lolling indolently in the doorway to his store, waiting impatiently for customers, gap-toothed and sweaty, for directions back to the rikkagin's quarters. The man looked at him, his clothes, the sword at his hip, the bag of coins in his belt.

"You go to dinner, gentleman?" His breath was foul.

"Yes, but—"

"A goose perhaps. Or a fine fresh-slaughtered pig for your host." His voice took on a wheedling tone. "A magnificent gift, very generous and at a most modest price. Twenty coppers only."

"Please tell me where—"

The merchant's brow wrinkled. "If you are thinking of Farrah's, his meat is not one tenth as fine as mine." He clasped his fat hands as if in anguish. "And the prices he charges! I should inform the Greens."

"Double Bass Street, is it near here?"

"I would, you know, but I am not a vengeful person, ask anyone on Brown Bear Road. An honest businessman only. I mind my own affairs. Do not ask me, as many do, what goes on around the corner or"—he rolled his eyes—"upstairs. If I told you—"

"Please," said Ronin. "Double Bass Street. How far?"

"If they want to do those vile things, well, who am I to say—"

Ronin left him, walking blindly down the street.

"Go to Farrah's then, as you planned all along," the fat merchant called after him in his high whine. "You deserve each other!"

He passed up a carpet shop along Three Peaks Street. It was crowded with customers and an army of clerks who all looked as if they were related. Next door was an apothecary, its huge stone jar hanging above the doorway on ancient creaking chains, a dusty window filled with small colored packets, phials of gritty-looking powders, liquids in tall tubular jars. In the center of this display was a lidded clear glass bowl filled with a slightly yellowish liquid suspended in which was a root in the singular shape of a man. It was dusky orange-brown and had many threadlike tendrils. The thing stirred his curiosity and he went inside the shop.

It was long and narrow, dusty and tired-looking. A high wood and glass case ran the length of the shop's right wall. Within it lay neat piles of containered liquids and stacks of cartoned powders, a hundred and one items, he supposed, for headaches and stomach pains, muscle pulls and swollen feet. The proprietor stood behind a counter along the back wall.

He was small and old and stooped as if he carried his years about with him as a tangible burden. He was a sad man, with almond eyes and yellow skin as thin as rice paper, almost translucent. Long strands of hair hung down from the point of his chin, otherwise he was hairless. He was measuring out portions of a sapphire powder upon clean white squares of rice paper.

He looked up as Ronin approached.

"Yes?"

"Am I near Double Bass Street?"

"Well now, that depends." The gnarled yellow hands continued their work.

"On what?"

"On which way you go, naturally." He stoppered the container of powder, put it carefully away on one of a series of shelves behind him that ran all the way to the ceiling. He turned back. "If you cut through the

125

alley there to Blue Mountain Road, well then, you are but five minutes away." He began to pour each mound of powder into blue glass phials. "However, if you were to walk farther down Three Peaks Street until you reached the Nanking it would be infinitely safer." He had two of them filled now. "Longer but safer." His head nodded. "Yet"—he looked up at Ronin—"you did not come in here merely to ask me the way to Double Bass Street." He pointed with one crooked finger. "Anyone out there could have told you just as well. No, I believe you came in to inquire after the root."

Ronin did not hide his surprise. "How could you have known?"

All the phials were filled now. One by one, he stoppered them.

"You are not the first, by any means. It is not there for decoration, though many passers-by think so."

Ronin was fed up.

"Will you tell me?"

"The root," he said, lining the phials up on a shelf, "is ancient. And as with all things ancient, it has a history. Oh yes! Not a very pleasant one I am afraid." His nostrils dilated and he shifted several times. "Come closer." He nodded. "Yes. It was you, then, who was at the temple." He closed his eyes for just a moment. "There is a lingering trace of incense."

"But what—?"

"I heard the horn sounding, after all."

"The horn?"

" 'A visitor,' it said. 'A visitor.' "

"What foolishness. It was merely a Sha'angh'sei temple."

The old man smiled oddly and Ronin saw that his teeth were lacquered black, shiny and square-cut. He thought of the simian-faced woman in the tavern:

126

what mysteries had she been selling, and for what price?

"Ah no." The old man shook his head. "The temple was here long before Sha'angh'sei came into being. The city grew up around it. It is the temple of another folk, being gone from this continent before the beginnings of man." He shrugged deferentially. "Some say so, at least."

"But there was a man in the garden of the temple."

The smile was released again, oblique and inferential.

"Then perhaps what they say is not the truth. You know people often tell you only what they wish you to know." The old man put a hand to his head as if it pained him. "Such as the house on Double Bass Street."

Ronin stared at him. "What?"

"Take the Nanking."

"But that is the longer way, so you said."

"It does not matter. There is no use in your going there."

A crawling along the back of his neck.

"Why not?"

"Because," said the old man flatly, "there is no one inside."

Ronin went out the door fast without bothering to close it, weaving through the throngs of bodies, his eyes searching ahead for the alley leading to Blue Mountain Road. He almost overran it, so narrow and dark it was. The braziers and lanterns of the city were just being lit, luminescing the deep purple haze that seemed to cover Sha'angh'sei each evening.

Three Peaks Street was still dusky with the lingering dregs of afternoon so that he did not have to pause in the gloom of the alley for his night vision to become effective.

The darkness deepened and he knew at once there was trouble. There should have been at least a glow from the lanterns of Blue Mountain Road, even from around this turning just before him. He slipped his sword free. Silent and deadly now, he advanced along one dank wall, went around the bend.

The smell of raw fish, putrefying; human excrement. There were hard, scraping noises. Panting. A grunt. He froze and listened intently. More that one person; more than two. That was as exact a determination as he could make. But that was all right because the adrenalin was pumping through him; his sword had been sheathed far too long. Now he ached for battle. He did not care how many men awaited him. He advanced.

Whites of eyes peered up at him as he approached at a run and he counted quickly and precisely because he knew there was little time and he had to prepare his entire body. The battle lust would not impede him because his training automatically took care of the organism. Six.

A man lay on the ground, the six over him. Brief glint of a curved blade, heavy, twisting, then the image was gone from his sight, lost in the night. But something lingered and he reviewed it because it might be important. The glint was not silvered, but black on white, wet-looking. Red is black in dim light. Blood.

He heard the faint whirring and let that guide him because he knew now what it was and they would not expect that.

Speed.

He thrust in a blur and there was a piercing scream. A chink on the stone as the ax hit the paving. He had deliberately aimed low, to open the soft viscera of the stomach and intestines to make a mess. He lifted the blade as he withdrew, flicking it, so that a fountain of

128

black blood and wet organs spewed forth as the man collapsed.

He was already moving forward with a two-handed thrust as the second man leapt for him and the blade whistled in the air as it clove the man from shoulder to belly. The corpse danced drunkenly, dead before it hit the ground, twitching still.

The fever mounted and it seemed as if everything around him slowed as his own speed increased. He saw the ax peripherally and knew that he could not get the sword up in time because of the angle, so he let it fall and allowed the crescent blade to come at him, gleaming, whispering scythelike. At the last instant his gauntleted hand came up, closed over the blade. The hide of the Makkon absorbed the force of the blow. There was a gasp and he saw the whites of his opponent's eyes all the way around as they opened in fear and surprise.

He laughed then, and it boomed through the close corridor of the alley, echoing menacingly off the wood and brick walls, dank and covered with slime.

The sound of running feet, the breathless air fanned, muttered voices, cursing, and the lights of Blue Mountain Road at last glowed at the far end of the alley. Ronin rubbed the scales of the gauntlet as he retrieved his sword, sheathing it.

Hc turned then to the man who lay twisted on the ground. He bent on one knee, searching for the pulse at his throat.

The man coughed. He was dark-haired with almond eyes but there was a strange cast to his face that, even in this dim and uncertain light, looked vaguely familiar to Ronin. He was clad in a tight-fitting suit of dull black cloth.

"Uk—uk—uk."

Blood came out of his mouth, black and wet in the night. His hand reached up convulsively and clutched at his neck. He coughed once more, blood and something more. Then he died.

Ronin stood up, then impulsively he bent again and opened the man's clenched hand. A slender silver necklace with something on it. He took it from the dead man for no reason at all and slipped it into his boot. Then he went down the alley and out into the confusion and flaring light of Blue Mountain Road.

Silence.

The night still and calm.

The old man had been right. There was no one at Rikkagin T'ien's quarters, not T'ien, not Tuolin, not a soldier, not a porter.

Ronin turned on the step and surveyed the street. He was absolutely alone. They had all gone. To Kamado, he assumed. Early. Not a good sign. Perhaps the situation to the north had deteriorated. If they had told him the truth; and he was not at all sure now that they had.

Abruptly, he remembered the strange root. In his haste to get here, he had not had the time to hear its history. He shrugged. Well, it was too late now, the shop would be closed. He could stop by tomorrow before he went up the mountain to the walled city to see the Council. And in any event he was hungry. He had not eaten since the morning and then only rice and tea. He went down the steps of Rikkagin T'ien's house and along the street in search of a tavern.

"Someone will come for you."

"But—"

"No instructions."

"All right. And the payment?"

"Now. In taels of silver."

"Just a moment—"

"You wish to be there? You wish to see it?"

"Yes, but—"

130

"Then you will do as I say."

The simian-faced woman was wrapped in a green cloak. A hairless man sat by her side tonight, narrow-skulled, flat-faced, a bright ring through his nose. He smoked a pipe with a long stem, curved downward slightly, and a small bowl. The simian-faced woman was speaking to a man with russet hair and light eyes. His skin was milk white and he sat in a peculiar position as if he could not bend one leg.

"It is too much," said the man with the russet hair. The other man was impassive, pulling on his pipe.

The woman leaned forward and Ronin could see the sheen of her black lacquered teeth. "Think of what the silver will buy you. The Seercus is not an everyday occurrence." She laughed tautly. "And I need not remind you of the restrictions. Consider yourself fortunate." The odd head nodded, up, down. "Most fortunate."

They were sitting at a corner table, near enough to Ronin so that he had no difficulty in hearing their conversation over the steamy noise of the tavern.

It was a large, smoky room off the Nanking, one of Sha'angh'sei's main roads. Low wooden beams crossed the ceiling; the air was thick with wax and grease. It was, in short, like every tavern in the city.

Ronin pushed away his rice bowl, lifted his sticks, and put a last morsel of broiled meat into his mouth. He reached for the rice wine.

"Perhaps I can get a better price elsewhere," said the man with russet hair, but there was little conviction in his voice.

The simian-faced woman laughed, a soft silvery tinkle, surprising in its delicacy. "Oh yes, by all means. And the Greens will—"

"No, no," said the man quickly. "You misunderstand. Here." He reached out a leather pouch from beneath his cloak, counted out forty silver pieces.

The woman stared at him solemnly, did not look down at the taels. The hairless man swept them off the table, his yellow hand a blur in the light for only a moment.

"And ten more," said the woman evenly.

The man with the russet hair started.

"Ten—but you gave me a price—"

"For this ten, I will not inform the Greens."

She laughed as the man reopened the pouch.

"The Seercus," she whispered.

The hairless man took the coins. He pulled again on his pipe. There was a cloud of smoke. They got up and left.

The man with the russet hair ran a shaking hand over his face, reached for the small flagon of wine on his table. Drops beaded the wood as he poured.

Two men came in and sat down at Ronin's table. The proprietor wandered over and they ordered steamed fish and wine; Ronin asked for another flagon of wine.

"And how were the fields, now that you've seen them firsthand?" asked one.

"The poppies are not good." This one had a large nose, red-veined and wide-nostriled.

"Ah, the Reds again. This time we must enlist the Greens to—"

"Not the Reds." He was still brushing the silt of travel from his gray cloak.

"Eh?" He looked suspiciously at the other. "This is not another of your tricks, is it? You know I agree that what the Greens ask is enormous, but we stand to lose much more if the harvest is ruined. I should well think that you would understand that by now."

"No, I tell the truth."

"Well, what then?"

The proprietor came over with a tray laden with

food and wine and they remained silent until he had served them and drifted away.

The man with the large nose sighed and poured himself wine. "I wish I knew. Truly." The fish looked at them from the center of the table. He picked one up with his sticks, bit into the head. "The Reds in the north have, I believe, split apart."

The other laughed uneasily, pouring wine. "I hardly think that is possible."

"Still, that is what I have heard." He began to shovel rice into his mouth with his lips close to the rim of the bowl. "Every day, more kubaru disappear and the crops themselves are not producing as they should."

"Well, if they are not being properly attended—"

"I am afraid that is only part of it." He took a gulp of wine, perhaps to steady his nerves. "It is as if the land itself has changed, become less fertile—" He began to cough thickly.

"Are you ill?"

"No, a chill only. The weather is much colder than it should be at this time of year."

At first Ronin had been listening peripherally. He wanted to understand this complex city. To do so he had to understand its inhabitants better. Listening in on conversations seemed as good a way as any to start. It was another reason why he had chosen to go to a tavern instead of visiting one of the many street stalls selling an infinite variety of foods. But his rather casual eavesdropping became more intent the further on this conversation went. Perhaps this was the beginning; perhaps he had less time than he had thought. If so, it was more imperative than ever for him to gain admittance to the Council of Sha'angh'sei; to find someone who could decipher the scroll of dor-Sefrith.

Now the merchants talked of other matters, prices and the fluctuating market. Ronin paid for his meal and left. In the Nanking, he asked a boy for the way to Okan Road and had to pay for the information.

She was not there and so he waited.

It was already late. He asked for rice wine and it was brought to him by the tiny girl in the pink quilted jacket. He remembered her.

"How old are you?" he asked as he savored the spices.

She lowered her painted eyelids.

"Eleven, sir." So low he had to strain to hear her.

He opened his mouth again and she ran off.

"He tried to relax, opening his ears to the soft sounds of silk brushing satin thighs, liquid pouring, low talking that was almost like the murmuring swell of the sea. The tawny light. He closed his eyes to slits, hearing in his mind a horn sounding, far off and alone. A gentle laugh intruded. A giggle, stifled. Perfumes drifting upon the languid air. A hint of sweet smoke from somewhere and he thought of the poppy fields. "There is much fear in the north," the merchant with the large nose had said. Why?

"Ronin."

He opened his eyes.

It was Matsu. Skin white as bone; eyes like olives. Her body small and supple.

"She will be very late." Black hair drifting over one eye. "Please let me take you upstairs."

She offered him her hand. Firm and warm. He stood up, rubbed her palm with his fingers. He towered over her as they went up the broad polished wood staircase to the second story. Yet he felt her support, strong and comforting. One arm was around her slender shoulders. He stroked her cheek as they rose. The yellow light grew brighter as they ascended toward the great crystal lamp. The tiny flames shivered, sparking pinpoints of light across their faces.

He peered down, drunk with wine and fatigue, at the grand, deserted room with its golden couches and low lacquered tables. Even the serving girls had gone to bed by now. The room was spotlessly clean, not a stained teacup lay about, not a spill of wine, not an ash-laden pipe remained.

The tawny light streamed down endlessly, it seemed, until Matsu shut the door of the room. She did not light the small lamp on the black lacquered table next to the wide bed. The room had a high domed ceiling and across the patterned walls flowers were tossed and dripping in a summer rainfall. The curtains had not yet been drawn and through the window he could see that the moon was up, pale and ghostly but perfectly clear in the night sky.

He sat on the bed and stared out the window at the pulsing carpet of pinpoints, blue-white like rare gems and startlingly close. Matsu knelt and pulled off his boots. A part of the sky was lighter, as if a translucent scarf had been laid over the blackness of the night; a bridge of light formed by the closeness of the stars within its width. She removed his clothes and he donned the dragon robe which she held out for him.

She put him under the covers and then came into the bed, her naked body trembling from the cool of the night sweeping in from the open window, her soft skin raised in gooseflesh, and he put her head in the hollow of his shoulder, stroking her hair, his thoughts over the hills and far away.

She smoked a little, the sweet smell engulfing them as she inhaled deeply with a quiet hiss. Sounds drifted up to them from the city that never slept. A dog barked, far off, and rhythmic singing wafted up from along the waterfront. Something metallic clattered on the cobbles close by and feet pounded briefly. A hoarse shout. The rattle of a cart and someone whistling tunelessly. Matsu's eyes glazed and the cold pipe fell from her open fingers spread like the petals of a small white flower on the dark covers.

She was asleep against him, close and warm now, her shallow rhythmic breathing a soporific. At last he relaxed. Carefully, he put the pipe away. The moon was huge in the black glittering square of the window, flat and thin as rice paper. Then a cloud rode across its face and his eyes closed. He dreamed of a field of poppies shivering in a chill wind.

It was still dark when she woke him.

"She will not come tonight."

The moon was down but the sky had not yet begun to lighten.

"It is all right."

"Do you want me to stay?" Her voice was tiny, like a child's.

He watched her at the side of the bed, the light silk robe clinging to her firm slender body.

"Yes," he said. "Stay with me."

A sinuous rustle as the robe slithered off her and she climbed into bed. Black and white.

There was silence for a time and he listened to the leaves trembling in the trees on Okan Road. Footsteps and muffled voices briefly heard. Matsu pulled the covers closer around them.

"Cold."

Ronin felt her lithe body against him and held her close.

After a time, she spoke again. "Do you know Tuolin well?"

Ronin turned his head to look at her.

"Not well, no."

She shrugged. "It does not matter. He will die at Kamado."

He lifted himself on one elbow and stared at her.

"What are you saying?"

136

"He told Sa many things in the shallows of night. I have heard many others. Tales of evil."

"What," he asked, "have you heard?"

"The rikkagin's armies no longer fight the Reds in the north. I have heard that they fight side by side now: the lawless and the law."

"Against whom?" But he already knew.

"Others," she said, giving the word a strange overtone, as if that were not the word she wished to use. "Creatures. Men who are not men."

"Who told you this?"

"Does it matter?"

"Perhaps very much."

"My friend's husband is a soldier with Rikkagin Hsien-Do. So is his son. They spent much time in the north, near Kamado. They returned three days ago." She clutched at him and he felt the shivers in her frame, thought of the green leaves on the trees outside. "My friend's husband is blind now. They had to carry the son back to Sha'angh'sei. His back is broken." Her voice came in little gusts now. "They did not fight the Reds; they did not fight bandits. They fought—something else." Another shudder went through her frame. "Even the Greens are talking among themselves about the situation in the north."

There was a thin line of the faintest gray now, visible only if he looked away because at night vision is better around the periphery. He held onto the shaking body and, from the corner of his eye, watched the line of gray widen with agonizing slowness, bringing the burden of another day.

She was still sobbing so he said, "Who are the Greens?" Because he wanted to stop her; and because he wanted to know.

"The Greens." She sniffed. "You must have seen some of them."

Two men in black in the tavern's doorway, axes at their sides, demanding payment.

"I am not sure."

"They are," she said, "the law."

He was surprised. "I had assumed that the rikkagin were the law."

She shook her head, her hair fanning his cheek, and the last of the tears fell from her cheeks onto the darkness of his arm as it lay along the covers.

"No," she said quietly, calmer now. "You must understand that the rikkagin are not native to Sha'angh'sei, or this land. Oh, they are the reason that it has grown and become—the way it is. But many are from far away. They brought their legions here to fight for the wealth of the land, the poppy fields, the silk farms, the silver, and more. They twisted the land and its people to their own ends." She sighed a little as if she were not used to speaking so much. She moved her head against his chest; he inhaled her fragrance, clean and sweet. Her feet twined with his, their soles rubbing together. Friction warmth.

"But this is a most ancient land," she said. "Here there are still many who have not forgotten the ways of their ancestors, handed down carefully from father to son and daughter. A legacy more precious to us than land or silver, even after the coming of the rikkagin, the turning of the hongs."

Her hand sought his, lightly, a feathery touch, yet it conveyed to him an intimacy most singular. "The Greens and the Reds have been at war for all time, or so it is told; from the moment of their births there was enmity. Now each seeks to gain each other's territory."

"What is the nature of the enmity?" he asked.

"I cannot tell you."

"You mean you will not?"

Her eyes flicked at his face, surprised. "No. I do not know. I doubt if they do themselves now."

On the Okan Road, the sky was pearling the rooftops of Sha'angh'sei. A fine rain began to fall, sighing among the trees, misting through the window, blown on a gentle morning breeze. A sea horn sounded in the distance, muffled and melancholy.

She kissed his broad chest as she opened his robe, the dragons writhing. "They are," she whispered, "the terrorists of tradition." And she offered up her mouth, moist and panting.

It was the angle that made it so dreadful.

Matsu choked and turned her head away and he held her as her body convulsed.

There was nothing there and that was why the head was at such an inhuman angle; he could imagine her shock. She seemed steadier now and she turned, needing to look once more, to help dispel the shock. The head remained attached to the shoulders only by a sheet of skin glinting readly in the dismal light.

The scream had burst in on them like a thief in the night and he had unsheathed his sword and was out the door before it had entirely died away, the gilt dragons fluttering in his wake. There was noise on the wide landing from behind myraid closed doors; movement as the sleepers awoke. The scream tried to force itself out again, like a caged animal, but it was choked off and he heard instead a liquid gurgling.

He raced down the hall, toward the head of the staircase. A dull thud, leaden with finality, and he knew he had just passed the door. Matsu was coming after him, tying the sash of her robe, closing the gap now because he had stopped. Raising his sword, he opened the door, slamming it wide with his shoulder, and leaped into the room.

He saw the window first because it was directly in

his line of sight and because he knew it was the room's only other egress. It was open to its fullest extent. On one side, the curtains were completely gone, on the other, the tatters fluttered uselessly. There was an increasing clatter from the hall but he ignored it. He inhaled the stench.

She was on the bed, her head at an impossible angle because everything had been torn out: throat, larynx, neck musculature. Just the frayed skin and a great pool of blood. He looked at last at her face. Sa.

He took Matsu outside into the hall, though he had to force her, because there was nothing either of them could do. He closed the door behind them.

"I have never," said Matsu, "seen such a death."

The hall was crowded now, mainly with women; the men preferred their anonymity.

"Has anyone seen Kiri?" Ronin asked them. No one had.

He took Matsu back to the room of dancing, crying flowers and once there began to dress. She pulled her robe tighter about her; peach marsh with pale green ferns.

"The Greens?" he asked because he wanted to be absolutely certain.

She shook her head, hair like a thick mist, fanning out. "No, the Greens use axes and"—she shuddered—"not that."

He buckled on his belt and went to her, drawing her up to him. Her pale hands were like ice.

"It is most important that I go out; and I must go now. Do you understand?" Because her eyes were clouded like the sky on the dawn of a stormy day. "Will you be all right?" His fingers gripped her shoulders. "You will stay with the guards?" He wanted to make certain.

She looked up into his colorless eyes now. "Yes," she said and he believed her. "Kiri will soon return."

"Tell her I was here."

The ghost of a smile.

"Yes," she nodded. "I will."

The door closed softly behind him.

It was a disquieting day: overcast, rain falling more heavily now, pattering against the roofs of the street stall, and he pulled his cloak about him. It was somewhat lighter directly overhead but dark clouds scudded across the sky in the distance.

The weather had not diminished the crowds, however. Oiled rice-paper umbrellas and thick cloaks to keep out the dampness were much in evidence.

He paused at a stand on Blessant Street, for rice and tea and to inquire after the surest route to the walled city. But there was a crawling in the pit of his stomach and he found that he had little appetite. He drank his green tea and listened to the forlorn drip of the rain on the stand's meager canopy.

He took Blessant Street as far as King Knife Street, which wound around in such circuitous fashion that several times he believed that he was headed away from the incline of the mountain.

Once he saw a beggar, sprawled in the street, filthy, unmoving. It was only after he had passed the body that he realized there was no life in him. Death was ignored in Sha'angh'sei, as T'ien had told him; at least most forms. Which brought him back to Sa's death.

He had known before he asked Matsu that it had not been the doing of the Greens. The stench was still in his nostrils. But that was a time factor; even if he had been later, the smell dissipated, he would have known by the way she was killed. It was the same manner in which G'fand had died in the City of Ten Thousand Paths. The Makkon.

But why had it killed Sa? He felt that it was important for him to know, but the answer eluded him.

As King Knife Street began to wind upward, the old dustworn shops thinned and gaps between buildings became more frequent. At first these were mere dirt alleyways into which filth and refuse had been dumped. But gradually, as he continued to ascend, they were filled with wild grass and thickets of fir trees, tall and willowy, their slender dark green tips swaying in the swirling rain.

As the incline increased so the aspect of the houses he passed was transformed. There was more brickwork in evidence here, in good repair and ornately crafted. Different styles of architecture made their presence felt.

The road was well paved now but fairly free of people and it occurred to him that here, on the way to the walled city, was the only area of Sha'angh'sei he had been to so far that was not jammed with people.

It was eerily silent. At once he missed the hubbub and jostle of the throngs, the thick swirl of commingling scents, the filth, the life and the death, the vast mysterious panoply of humanity.

In the absence of the teeming crowds, he was struck by the artificiality of the houses and he recalled Matsu's words, *They twisted the land*. For this seemed an entirely different Sha'angh'sei, at once cleaner and crasser. It seemed to him that here, among the columnated houses, with their plaster and wrought-iron scalloping, the natural tones and inclinations of the land had been pushed back, held at bay along the foothills, and that here the brand of the legions of rikkagin from faraway lands, squatting, growing fat from the wealth of Sha'angh'sei's land, was very apparent.

He topped the last rise of King Knife Street and went into the chill shadow of the walled city. The wall itself was some six and a half meters high, constructed of enormous yellow stone blocks joined so cunningly that he could barely distinguish the joints. Heavy metal doors stood open to the inward side but a latticed metal grillwork gate barred the entrance.

Men in purple quilted jackets and wide black leggings stood just inside the gate. They all were armed with curved single-edged swords and short-hafted throwing axes. They were almond-eyed and their long greased hair was bound in queues.

A thickset man with a flat face and wide nose came and opened the gate.

"Why do you come to the walled city?" asked the man. "You are a new compredore, perhaps?"

Another man drifted over in a cloud of sweet smoke. He took the pipe out of his mouth and regarded Ronin with heavy-lidded eyes.

"No, I seek an audience with the Municipal Council."

The flat-faced man guffawed and walked away.

"They will not see you," said the second man, pulling at his pipe.

"Why not? It is most urgent that I see them."

Smoke swirled in the air and the man turned languidly, pointing at the trees of the walled city running in thick rows away from them, lining the quiet avenues; the large, stately buildings, flat-roofed, terraced, with carefully sculptured gardened fronts.

"Here the fat hongs and sleek functionaires of Sha'angh'sei live and build their fortunes, unseen and, for a price, safe."

"From what?"

The black eyes studied Ronin with unwavering intensity.

"From Sha'angh'sei," he said.

He sucked at his pipe but it had gone out. He knocked the bowl against the wall, began to refill it from a leather packet within his quilted jacket.

"No one sees the Municipal Council, my friend." His eyes were unnaturally bright. "At all."

The rain beat down. The avenues were slick with wet, gleaming dully. The trees rustled in the wind, flinging moisture, and somewhere a bird sang sweetly, enfolded within brown branches and green leaves.

"Where is the Council building?"

The man with the dark eyes sighed. "Take the avenue to the left. Second turning." He moved into the shelter of an overhang.

The echoes of marble. The soft sighing. The prolonged susurration of whispering. The quiet click of boot soles.

The hall was cold and columnless and empty of ornamentation. Its only furniture was low, wide, backless benches of the same pink and black marble.

The hall echoed to his footsteps as he crossed the polished floor. Ahead of him, the desk.

He passed people sitting humped on the benches. There was a peculiar air about them, as if most of them had been here for so long that they had forgotten their purpose in coming. Expectancy had perished a long time ago.

The desk too was of marble, curved and thick, a heavy shield for the woman who sat behind its imposing façade. Although she had the black hair and almond eyes of the people of the Sha'angh'sei area, her face was nevertheless less delicate, with a more pronounced bone structure so that he knew that she had other blood in her. She had light eyes and a square chin which she knew gave her the appearance of strength. She spoke accordingly.

"Yes, sir. State your business, please." She had before her a long list of names and was in the process of drawing a line through the third name from the top with her quill.

"I seek an audience with the Municipal Council of Sha'angh'sei."

The quill dipped into the inkwell. "Yes?" Scratch.

"I come on a matter of the utmost urgency."

She looked up then.

"Is that so?" She smiled charmingly with small white teeth. "I am afraid it will do you no good."

"I am sure that when the Council hears—"

"Pardon me, but you do not seem to understand." She wore a tightly cut green and gold quilted jacket that showed off her jutting breasts and narrow waist in a way that was severe and, because of it, sensual. Her startling sapphire nails plucked at the jacket. "One must make an appointment to see the Council." She brandished the list in front of her. "It will be many days."

"I do not think you appreciate the gravity of the situation," said Ronin, but already he was feeling rather foolish.

The woman sighed and pursed her lips.

"Sir, everyone who seeks audience with the Council is on an urgent mission."

"But—"

"Sir, you are in the Municipal Building of Sha'angh'sei, the seat of government for not only this vast city but the enormous area of land in the surrounding vicinity. Maintainence is a most complex and problem-filled task. Can you understand that?" She leaned forward, her face intent. A strand of hair came loose from its binding, stroking the side of her face as she spoke. "In the event that you do not, let me tell you that this city must feed and house not only its numerous inhabitants but also many of the outlying communities. We also must take care of the constant flood of refugees from the north." She threw her shoulders back as if it were an act of defiance; it had a double effect. She knows her job, he thought. "Sir, through the port of Sha'angh'sei comes the bulk of the raw materials to sustain much of the continent of

145

man. It is more than a full-time task in these evil times to keep this city running." She finally swept a hand up, flash of deep blue, tugging the wayward strand over her ear. "Now you can appreciate why we cannot allow the Council to be errantly disturbed. Why, if everyone who came to this building were allowed an immediate audience, I cannot imagine how this city would function." She took a deep breath, leaning back in her chair. Her breasts arched at him, an unsubtle offering of consolation.

Ronin leaned over and stared into her eyes.

"I must see the Council today. Now."

He did not expect her to be intimidated and she was not. She clicked her sapphire nails and two men appeared armed with axes and curving dirks.

"Would you care to have me add your name to the list?" she asked sweetly, her eyes never leaving his. They laughed.

"All right," Ronin said, and gave it to her.

"Yes," she said, the quill moving. Then she sat back and her pink tongue strayed for a moment between her lips. "That is most sensible."

The rain was heavier and they were all within the roof's brown overhang, squatting around a brick pit. Flames crackled and sparked. They were drinking rice wine when he came up. The man with the dark eyes peered at him through the smoke of his pipe; the others ignored him.

Ronin came unbidden out of the rain, shook the water off his cloak.

"The Council would not see me."

"Yes," said the man, "a predictable course." He shrugged his shoulders. "Lamentable but what can one do?"

Ronin squatted beside the man. No one offered him wine. "What I want," he said, "is a way in."

146

The man with the flat face looked over at him. "Throw him outside, T'ung," he said to the man with the dark eyes. "Why waste your time?"

"Because he is not from Sha'angh'sei?" said T'ung. "Because he is not civilized?" He turned to Ronin. "What would you give me as payment?" The flat-faced man grunted knowingly.

Ronin lifted the bag of coins at his waist, letting the fat chink of the coppers speak for him.

T'ung eyed the pouch and screwed up his mouth. "Mmm, much too small, I am afraid." His face assumed a sad expression. "Not nearly enough."

"What, then, would you want?"

"What else have you?"

Ronin looked at him.

"Nothing."

"That is most unfortunate." He sucked on his pipe, blew smoke lazily. It held on the humid air, a translucent pattern, a mysterious glyph.

"Wait. Perhaps there is something." He dug in his boot. "A chain of silver."

Ronin drew out the dead man's chain. The silver blossom gleamed in the diffuse light. He handed it to T'ung.

The rain dripped dolefully, pattering against the overhang, making the leaves on the trees dance to its rhythm. T'ung sat very still, staring at the silver blossom. It flamed orange as he twisted it and it caught the firelight. Slowly he put down his pipe.

"Where," he said softly, "did you get this?"

"What?"

A brief flash in darkness.

"Tell me."

Black blood. The scythe blade blooming silver as it swung at him in the alley.

"I want an answer." The voice turned harsh and grating. Heads turned. The flat-faced man rose.

147

Too late, Ronin thought savagely. He stood up, staring at the scythe-bladed ax hung at T'ung's side. Greens.

The flat-faced man saw the silver blossom and his hand went to the haft of his ax. T'ung stood and the others, alerted now, dropped their cups and pipes and came toward him.

Ronin backed away, thinking furiously, Chill take me for a fool! Those were Greens in the alley.

T'ung was between him and the open gateway beyond which teeming Sha'angh'sei beckoned like a sweet reward.

T'ung clutched at the chain and withdrew his ax. And the others came on.

"Kill him now," said the flat-faced man.

He crouched in the tangle, panting, taking deep breaths, swallowing to get the saliva back into his mouth. He listened for the sounds he knew would come, magnified by the rain. But all he heard was the rustle-drip of the soaking foliage. The sky was all but gone. The rain beat against him, running down his face. He blinked, lifted one hand across his forehead to clear his vision. He heard the sounds then.

The right arm had decided him. It was out and up, about to begin the ax's deadly descent. They had been expecting him to use his sword and to retreat defensively. He did neither. He launched himself headlong at T'ung, lifting his forearm and knocking the ax blade aside as he smashed into the body. Taken by surprise, T'ung crashed into the wall and the way was clear.

Then he was through the gate and running in an erratic zigzag through the rain, acutely aware of the axes at his back, knowing that they could be thrown as well as swung.

Boots pounded behind him and he heard the flat-faced man screaming and, farther behind, T'ung's voice, curiously calm and remote.

He heard the panting coming closer; the flat-faced man was gaining on him because he ran in a straight line, did not have to dodge.

He turned then, planting his feet and withdrawing his sword in one motion. The flat-faced man was quick and agile but he was angry and that would help. Ronin swung first and his foot slipped on the wet paving. Idiot!

Grinning now, the flat-faced man dodged the blow, came on, and the blade of his ax was a blur in the rain. Ronin was moving away when it bit into his arm with a searing white heat. Ignore. He swung his own blade in a reverse arc and the Green, not used to double-bladed weapons, was slow to react. Ronin's blade caught him beneath the arm, sinking deep into the socket. He cried out, his body jerked, and the bloody ax fell from his trembling fingers. His gaping mouth filled with water. Ronin wrenched at the hilt to free it and the arm came off. The flat-faced man shrieked and folded like a paper doll. Rain washed at the running blood. The others were coming now and Ronin took off down King Knife Street.

Through the beat of the rain he heard the boots and the echoing shouts; he kept his body low and the sounds were amplified. Then voices came to him on the wind: queries, shouts of anger. He risked some movement in order to get a visual fix. Led by T'ung, the Greens fanned out, searching for him. One was coming directly toward him.

In the end, the cart had saved him. It swerved out of a walkway blind to King Knife Street and he almost ran the owner down but there was just enough time and he missed it. It was now, however, directly in the path of his pursuers. The delay was brief but sufficient. Around the next turning, rows of houses and an explosive tangle of wild greenery, within which he promptly lost himself.

Still and calm, he remained behind his house of trees and tall ferns. Drip, drip. The rain beading and streaking the leaves. They quivered before his face. A bird fluttered in the branches above him. Crunch. The sound very close indeed and he felt the presence, separated only by the tenuous curtain of greenery. He held his breath. Perhaps—no, the branches low down swayed and began to part and he had no choice. Silently he put down his sword, then turned away from its mirrored surface, his reflection distorted by the moisture.

After a time, with Ronin's forearm jammed against his windpipe, the Green's eyes rolled up and he collapsed without a sound, his face white and pasty. Ronin crouched, listening. Still. The pinging of the rain. He dragged the Green behind a dense section of foliage, went back to where he had left his sword. He wiped it down and sheathed it, then crouched again behind the sheltering leaves until he was certain that they had gone back to the gate.

The rain had ceased by the time the shops of Sha'angh'sei built themselves around him once again on the cluttered level ground of the lower reaches of the city. Through the filth of the milling throng he pushed himself, his left arm soaked in blood and the pain a constant thing now that he attempted to clamp down on.

He passed a large group of people, wide straw hats, torn and uneven, feet bare and black with the muck of the streets, all carrying sacks and hurriedly tied bundles. Soldiers were directing them to a building farther along the street.

"Refugees," said a soldier in response to Ronin's question. "Refugees from the fighting in the north."

"Is it worse?"

"I do not see how it could be," the soldier sighed. "This way," he called sharply to a straggling few, staggering in exhaustion. One of them, a frail figure, fell into a puddle of brackish water. No one paid the slightest attention.

Ronin moved toward the still form.

"He is beyond help," said the soldier.

Ronin knelt and turned the body over, wiping the black mud from the gaunt face. The mouth was slack, the eyes closed. It was a woman, young and still beautiful despite the ravages of near starvation. Ronin pushed back her stiff wide-brimmed hat, felt along the side of her neck. He opened her mouth wide and breathed into it, slowly, deeply.

The soldier sauntered over. Most of the refugees had been herded inside now.

"Save it," he said, taking a large bite out of a tightly rolled brown stick. "She is gone."

"No," said Ronin. "There is life within her still."

The soldier laughed, a dark and evil sound. "She is less than worthless." He hawked and spit. "Unless you lack the coppers for a woman. Still she seems a poor—"

But Ronin had risen, turned, hand on sword hilt. Jaw set, muscles rigid, staring into the soldier's eyes. He said something, his voice like the whistle of a steel blade as it strikes.

There was a long moment when he saw the soldier weighing it in his mind. He looked for his comrades, found none.

"All right," said the soldier. "Do whatever you wish. It is no concern of mine. Let the Greens handle it." He turned away, heading toward the building into which the refugees had gone.

She was taking shallow breaths now but her eyes were still closed and clearly she was seriously hurt or ill, perhaps both. He could not leave her here and, since he had been on his way to the apothecary's, he hoisted the frail form carefully onto his massive shoulder and disappeared into the hurrying masses of humanity.

The enormous jar hung suspended, creaking on its chains in the lowering light, the metal burnished. The dust seemed thicker in the shop, as if he were returning here after a century instead of merely a day.

"Ah," exclaimed the old man without much surprise. "So you went through the alley after all." His long chin whiskers trembled with the movement of his mouth.

Ronin went down the narrow aisle, put the woman onto a stool. The apothecary came around from behind his counter. He wore a wide-sleeved yellow silk robe and strange shoes which seemed but wooden platforms for his feet. He glanced at Ronin, then looked at the huddled figure.

"She is not from Sha'angh'sei—"

"Yes, I can see that." The hands moved deftly.

"She is from the north, the soldier told me. Fleeing the fighting."

The old head shook from side to side. He touched her face, then went behind the counter, reached out packets of powders, red, gray, gold, mixed them with a milky liquid. He pushed the contents across to Ronin.

"Get her to drink that." He turned. "You will take her with you?"

"Yes, I cannot leave her. I am sure that they will take care of her at Tenchō."

Something inexplicable came into the apothecary's eyes and he nodded.

Ronin pressed the hinge of her jaw and the mouth gaped open. She was still unconscious. He cradled the back of her head, mindful of the angle, and let the thick liquid dribble into her lips. Half of it went down her neck and he had to depress her tongue to prevent her choking, but he got a fair amount in her.

The apothecary returned from the musty interior of the shop and began to work on Ronin's arm, laying a square greasy pad along the wound, then wrapping it in white cloth. Over this he poured a clear liquid which seeped into the cloth and thence into the wound. For a moment the pain was exquisitely sharp. Then, almost immediately, it was gone.

There was time now, he thought.

"Tell me about the root."

The apothecary poured more liquid, wiped at the seepage.

"It is said that it was found by a warrior." The voice was dry and dusty like the wind of the ages. "The greatest warrior of a people now long dead. The warrior was out riding, for he was bored. His skill was so great that none could stand against him, so that that thing which he desired most—the conquest of a powerful foe—was denied him." He wrapped the shoulder in dry bandages.

"As evening drew nigh," the apothecary continued, "he came upon a glade in the high forest of his land. No other thing grew near it and a pale new moon, already lambent in the sky, illuminated the root. The glade was quite large and as he dismounted he found that cracked and weathered stone slabs were set in the earth, as if this place were an ancient burial place, but of what people he could not imagine, for time had long ago beaten the writing on the stones."

Dust swirled in the shop, as if a wind from an unmentionable quarter had sprung up.

"The warrior went to the root and pulled it from the soil. He found that he was suddenly ravenous and

153

he cut a piece of the root and ate it." The apothecary was putting the last of the packets away.

Ronin stared at him.

"The warrior, so the tale goes, became more than man."

"A god?"

"Perhaps." The apothecary shrugged. "If you wish. It is but a myth."

"Not a pleasant one, you told me."

"Yes, that is true." The old man's eyes blinked, looked huge. "The warrior indeed became more than man but in so doing he became a danger to the old laws because now surely there was none to stand against him. So was unleashed upon him a terrible foe. The Dolman."

The vertigo was so severe that he thought for an instant that the tiled floor of the shop had become a river. He worked to control his breathing. Somewhere the echo of laughter.

"What was The Dolman?" It sounded like someone else's voice, faraway and indistinct.

"The ancient of ancients," said the apothecary softly. "The primeval fears of man. The terrors of a child alone and afraid at night. Nightmare given free reign, embodied now, substantive."

A dry wind at the core of his being, plucking.

"It does not seem possible." Merely a whisper in the aged dust.

"It is a most monstrous creation."

"Where did it come from?"

"Perhaps the root?"

"Then where is the root from?"

"The gods themselves cannot know—"

"She wishes to see you."

"Good, she has returned then."

"She asks for you to wait for her."

He regarded Matsu in the tawny light. The slender face, with the planes and angles of a man-made structure. Small, wide-lipped mouth, large black eyes as soft as velvet dusk at the waterside. She wore a robe of pastel blue with brown cicadas embroidered across the body and wide sleeves. It was edged in deep gilt with a sash of the same color. He thought—

"Wait for her here, please." She studied the floor at his feet.

"Will you stay with me tonight?"

"I cannot." The voice barely a whisper. He tried to find her eyes. "Yung will see that you have wine."

She bowed to him, a curiously formal gesture.

"Matsu?"

She went away from him, across the room of tawny light, through the buzzing conversations, the opulent silks, the exquisite bodies, the perfect faces.

These people are still a mystery to me, after all, he thought.

He found an empty chair and sat wearily. Almost immediately, tiny Yung in her pink quilted jacket appeared with a lacquered tray with a wine pot and cups. She knelt at his side and poured the wine, handed him the cup.

He sipped and she left. He savored its warmth down the length of his throat, tasting all the spices, and he was reminded that he had not had a full meal that day.

Afterward, the apothecary had returned to the woman while Ronin withdrew his sword. He removed the hilt and produced the scroll of dor-Sefrith. Once again he studied its glyph-covered face. So many times. It stared at him blankly.

He turned. Evidently the old man had found a wound on the woman. He had tied a poultice in place on the inside of her thigh.

"Do not change the bandages even if they should

155

become dirty. There is medicine underneath." Then he saw the scroll and began to shake his head.

"Do you know what this is?"

He looked away. "I cannot aid you in this."

"You have not even looked at it." Ronin thrust the scroll toward him.

"It does not matter."

Ronin's eyes blazed. "Chill take you, it does! You know of The Dolman, you alone of all the people I have met in Sha'angh'sei. You know that he exists so you must know that he is coming once again to the world of man."

The old tired eyes stared at him without expression.

Desperately Ronin said, "His minions are even now prowling the streets of the city. The Makkon killed this morning."

A faint tremor began at the corner of the old man's mouth and he appeared about to crumble from misery and pain.

"Why do you speak to me of such things?" he asked in a cracked voice made thin by fear and something else. "There is not a day in my life that I have not suffered and I have seen many days; I wish now but an end to the suffering."

"Do you wish the death of mankind?" Ronin cried, suddenly furious. "By not speaking of what you may know, you become an ally of The Dolman."

"A new age is dawning. Man must look after himself."

"Are you not a man?"

"I am unable to help you by reading that scroll."

"Tell me then who can."

"Perhaps no one, any more. But I can tell you this. The Dolman does in fact come and this time the world may be ground into the utter oblivion that is The Dolman's victory. It is the destroyer of all life, warrior, wielding a power beyond imagining. Already its strengthening forces are marshaling themselves in the north. Ah, I see that you have suspected this. Good. Now go. Take the woman and care for her well. Remember what I have told you. I have done all that I may for now."

Yet what was he to do now? The Council of Sha'angh'sei would not see him for many days and he could not now return to the walled city because the Greens would never allow him through the gate. Kiri was his only hope. She knew many people, a large number of them extremely influential, for through the saffron doors of Tenchō flowed nightly the cream of Sha'angh'sei society and business; Tenchō was for the wealthy and the powerful. Among these were, no doubt, several officials of the Council itself. There leverage could be applied, if she would consent to aid him. He had to ask her now. Time was fast growing short. With each passing day the chill shadow of The Dolman reached farther into the continent of man as his legions consolidated their strength.

Thus he waited for her, as she had bidden, sprawled in the plush chair, his scabbarded sword scraping the polished floor, drinking the clear wine—Yung had already come and gone twice more—his mind drifting, his eyes watching. The women passing were colored reeds, pastel and slender, bending, robes sweeping in perfect folds and rustling in the gentle wind, fans and long lashes fluttering like nervous insects in the oblique rays of the sun at day's humid end as it dazzles the still water. Placid oval faces, helmets of flowing hair, the fabulous blossoms of impossible flowers, mysterious and erotic.

Two willowy girls in matching quilted jackets came for him then and led him off to be bathed and dressed and he knew that tonight would be special.

"Am I not worth the wait?" she said without coyness.

She was dressed in a formal robe of rich purple silk, like a plum sunset with threads of the palest dove gray woven into a pattern of opening flowers.

Her lips and long nails were purple and she wore an amethyst pin in the shape of a fantastic winged animal in her hair. Her extraordinary black eyes danced with diamond-point lights.

Still, she looked subtly different.

They had bathed him and dressed him in black silk pants and wide-sleeved shirt laced with platinum thread which glittered in the light. When he was ready, they had led him to a small room and she had come in.

"Are you hungry?" she asked now.

"Yes, very."

She laughed and it was like hot sun glancing off a naked blade. "Well, come then, my strong man, and remember well what you have said."

Out into the Sha'angh'sei night they went, of moist wispy fog, lavender and blue, of a thousand eyes and ten thousand knives and one million running feet.

Down the wide sweeping stairs and into a square covered carriage Kiri called a ricksha. They climbed in and the barefooted kubaru lifted his poles and set off without a word, the ride much smoother than Ronin would have imagined because it contained a peculiar rocking motion tied to the runner's gait that he found soothing.

The blazing streets of the city, aflame with the swinging lanterns and the crush of people, the smells of broiling food and boiling rice, fresh shellfish and spiced wine flowed past them in a rippling without end, a vast variegated canvas upon which it seemed all the events of the ages of man must be painted in subtle colors too potent to be real.

He breathed the musk of her perfume and stared into her eyes when he could tear his vision away from the flashing city. They were so huge that he imagined that an entire universe resided within their depths. Platinum flecks shivering and he saw with a start that her eyes were not black but the deepest shade of violet that he had ever seen.

Upward they climbed, away from the crawling delta of the port, onto higher reaches of the city where silver taels made room for spired houses, ornate balconies, sculpted stone walls, and landscaped greenery.

Trees whispered their mysterious messages and the night deepened as the intense light from the multitude of lamps drifted silently away from them, down the mountainside, the fast receding shore of an incandescent isle, remote now and unreal, just choppy splashes on the dense ocean of the night.

Just the panting of the jogging kubaru's breath, the slap-slap of his feet, soles burnished like leather, the intermittent tiny sounds of the nocturnal insects, an owl hooting high up in a tree.

Once he thought about telling her but the pale oval of her face caused his words to catch in his throat and he said nothing, but watched the platinum motes.

The ricksha stopped before a two-storied house of dark brick and carved hardwood, columnated, flamboyant. Slender lamps like torches stood on either side of the wide yellow-metal-bound doors.

Ronin stepped out of the ricksha and turned. Kiri came into his arms. Together, they walked up the stone steps. The doors opened inward as they approached. A rather overly dramatic welcome, Ronin thought.

Two tall men stood before them. They were clad in black cotton shirts and leggings, armed with short single-edged swords which hung unscabbarded on thick brass chains at their sides. They had eyes like

159

slits, mouths thin-lipped and wide, their faces peculiarly canine. They bowed to Kiri and stepped impassively away from the doors, allowing them entrance. They stared curiously at Ronin as he passed them.

They were in a towering hallway the height of the entire structure. The whole of its far end was taken up by a forked staircase curving upward to the second story. To the left were two closed doors. To the right opened sliding doors of oiled fragrant wood through which they entered a large room, warmly furnished with satin-cushioned chairs and plush settees without legs. The floor was covered with an enormous rug of dark swirling patterns. The pale green walls were edged in gilt. The room was windowless.

There were perhaps ten people arranged about the room; less than half were women. A tall slender man turned as they entered and a curiously white smile split his long face. He came toward them. He had round eyes of a pale blue and thick graying hair which he contrived to wear very long. Unbound and brushed, it framed his face in such a way as to give him a startlingly leonine appearance. He was dressed in a formal Sha'angh'sei suit, leggings and loose shirt, in a shadow pattern of gilt on gilt.

"Ah, Kiri."

The voice was deep, well modulated. He smiled again and Ronin saw the semicircular arc of raised white flesh beginning at the left corner of the mouth and terminating at the side of his nose, which at some earlier time had had its left nostril sheared off.

"Llowan," said Kiri, "this is Ronin, a warrior from the north."

The man turned his ice eyes on Ronin and bowed formally.

"I am most pleased that Kiri brought you."

"Llowan is the city's bundsman. He oversees the transactions of all the harbor hongs, collecting for

160

Sha'angh'sei, duties on each shipment coming in and departing the port."

Again that strange smile, unnaturally extended by the livid scar.

"You honor me, lady." Then to both of them: "You must have some wine. Hara," he called to a servant, who served them a sparkling white wine in stemmed crystal glasses.

"Are you really from another civilization?" asked Llowan, leading them into the vortex of figures, beginning the introductions over Ronin's reply, then, coaxed into a peripheral conversation, leaving Kiri to continue, names tumbling like leaves in an autumn wind, and he concentrated then on the faces.

"Rikkagin," said the large man with no chin and tiny eyes like broiled insects, "one is becoming quite alarmed by the tales being told of the fighting in the north."

They were sitting on silk pillows on the bare floor around a low table made of a wood with grain like a stormy sea, polished to a high gloss upon which were laid out glazed pots of hot wine and bowls of various small foods such as pieces of fish, battered and dipped in hot oil, steamed vegetables, small sticky sweetmeats.

"What of it?" said the rikkagin in a tone of voice clearly indicating that he had no wish to discuss the matter. He was a wide-shouldered man with a ruddy complexion vanguarded by a wide red-veined nose. He had a thick gray beard stained yellow around his red lips. "This is a city of tales, Chi'en. Most of them, as I am sure you are well aware, are utterly false."

"Yet these persist," said Chi'en, his yellow jowls quivering. He reclined on the pillows, an ornate fan waving at the side of his sad face.

"Tales to frighten hongs such as yourself are easy

161

to create," the rikkagin said with some disdain. "Do not be an old lady."

The large man bristled. "But the fighting is not—"

"My dear sir." The rikkagin was frowning now, his thick brows beetling like thunderheads. "Without the war Sha'angh'sei would still be a muddy swamp with primitive paper houses collapsing in the first high wind and you would be in the rice paddies with your wife earning just enough to survive. It will come as no great news to any of us here that the war is what has made us rich. Without it—"

"You speak of war," said a thin, dour man with dark eyes and close-cropped hair, "as if it were an object to hold in one's hand and use as one pleases." Ronin thought for a moment, recalled his name: Mantu, a priest of the House of Canton. "Yet war is death for thousands and mutilation, starvation, and suffering for countless others."

"How would you know?" interjected a high-cheekboned woman, another hong. "You who have never ventured forth from the sanctity of your region of Sha'angh'sei."

"I am not required to do so," the priest said acidly. "I have quite enough on my hands with the refugees that daily stream into the city from the north seeking sanctuary and solace at the House."

"Your piousness sickens me, Mantu," said the rikkagin. "Where would the Canton House be without the war? Without the great suffering who would come to fill your cathedral?"

"Tradition would—"

"Do not talk of your tradition."

The voice was harsh and heads turned. The man was slender and muscular, with a bony face dominated by eyes like slatted windows, black as night. He had dark curling hair and a long drooping mustache that gave him a sinister appearance. He alone at the table wore plain clothes and a traveling cloak. "Your people came to this land before the rikkagin but as surely as they preached the faith of Canton you took from my people as much as the soldiers. The House of Canton. My tongue grows thick with rage whenever I am forced to utter that hideous name. Yours is not the religion of Sha'angh'sei.

"Po," said Llowan kindly, "your people are traders, nomads from the west."

The slatted eyes flashed like dark lightning. "You delude yourself if you believe that there is a difference. Are not my eyes the same as Chi'en's? Is not my skin the same color as Li Su's? They were wealthy hongs of Sha'angh'sei just as their parents were before them. They are from the south, their origins far from my people, is that what you would have me believe? Yes?" His fist hammered the table and the sound was like the crash of hammer onto anvil in the green and gilt room. "I tell you no! Ours is a land of unlimited wealth yet my people eat half bowls of rice and, if they are fortunate, week-old fish heads which they find discarded on garbage heaps. And all the while they toil to distill the fruit of the poppy for the lords of Sha'angh'sei."

"The tradition of the Canton House is without reproach," said Mantu somewhat didactically. "It has stood for many years—"

"Growing fat like the rikkagin and hongs from the sweat of our labor," sneered Po.

"You obviously do not understand the Canton teachings and, like most men, you are misdirected," Mantu said. "All men crave permanence." He lifted his arms. "Hence they acquire many things as if in these possessions they may truly find the belief that they will not die." The arms folded in on themselves, somehow communicating pity without condescension. "Yet all life is transient, and man, in desiring permanence, is inevitably defeated and thus suffers; and in his suffering, makes those around him suffer."

"Philosophy is all well and good for those with time on their hands," said Chi'en irritably, "but I am more concerned with what I have been hearing, Rikkagin, that the war has changed."

"Oh, out with it," said the rikkagin in exasperation, wiping at his beard. "If we must listen to your prattle, best get it over with."

Chi'en ignored this outburst. "The tales," he said quite carefully, "filtering into Sha'angh'sei are that the soldiers in the north no longer fight men."

There was a small uncomfortable silence in the room then, as if an uninvited and unwelcome guest had arrived unexpectedly with news they all dreaded yet wished to hear.

"A tale to be believed by fools," said the rikkagin disgustedly. "Come then, tell us, Chi'en, what these beings 'other than men' are like. No doubt you have detailed descriptions for us."

The large man's jowls quivered and his eyes blinked several times in surprise. "No, I have told you all that I have heard."

The rikkagin grunted and leaned forward to snag a piece of fried fish with his sticks. He sighed rather contentedly. "Yes, it is always most enlightening to hear how the truth is twisted to serve the needs of the individual—"

Po laughed at this, a short discomforting sound like the abrupt cracking of a dry twig in a forest when one had been certain that no one else was around.

The rikkagin looked down his nose at Po and continued. "The Reds have enlisted the aid of a savage tribe, a northern people who, it seems, are much addicted to the fruit of the poppy. From what I understand, they extract the syrup, freeze it, and then chew it."

"What?" exclaimed Li Su. "Uncured and uncut? It cannot be! The effect would be—"

"Most extraordinary," said Llowan with his white lopsided smile. "I believe we are all agreed on that point, Godaigo."

"Quite a frightening habit, I agree," said the rikkagin.

"I did not say that," replied Llowan, and they all laughed.

Godaigo wiped his red lips on a silk cloth provided by the host. "Be that as it may, it is this unusual lever that the Reds are using to induce the tribe to join with them against us." He put his hands up. "And I admit that until reinforcements are in place we will be rather inconvenienced. But that is all."

"Still the tales exist," interjected Mantu. "It would be most appropriate if they were true."

"What are you saying?" said the rikkagin.

"I am telling you quite plainly that I would welcome the veracity of these tales because it would likely mean an end to the war. That is, after all, what the House of Canton seeks."

"The House seeks dominion over the continent of man," said Po harshly. "And in that it shall surely fail."

"We seek dominion over no one; you speak out of ignorance."

"Just their souls."

The priest smiled benignly. "Life, my dear Po, is soulless. The essence of each man survives death to be placed in, one hopes, a more worthy body, until the final Nothingness is achieved."

"Their minds, then."

Mantu smiled and shrugged. "Shall we debate semantics, trader?"

"Well," said Llowan, clapping his hands for the servants and seeking to head off another dispute, "I believe that it is time that we get down to the serious business of the evening. I trust everyone has brought that which they need." The white grin.

The servants first filled everyone's glass with a cold clear wine, "to clear one's palate," as Llowan told them. Then they ladled out a rich steaming soup of fish stock into large enameled bowls.

Following this, new glasses were brought into which was poured a sparkling wine while several dishes of spiced raw shellfish were put before the guests.

Ronin was still thinking of what the priest had said when the servants staggered in with huge platters of meat of a bewildering assortment. Each platter had half the meat shorn in thick slabs from the white carcasses. With this was served more of the clear sparkling wine.

"Mantu," Ronin said. "This Nothingness you spoke of. What is it precisely?"

The priest turned to Ronin, seeming glad for the interest. "It is the state to which all men must aspire—"

"Women also?"

Mantu was not sure whether he was being mocked.

"Certainly. Theologians use the word 'man' as a shortening for 'mankind.' " His small mouth glistened with grease. "Nothingness is, in essence, the total extinguishing of the ego."

Ronin was somewhat surprised. "Do you mean that the individuality of each person must be surrendered?"

"Is that so valuable a possession?" asked Mantu. "It is, in the end, no different than land, a house, taels of silver, a work of art or"—he looked at Ronin—"a sword."

"But those are all physical."

"Yes, but all possessions are indistinguishable and

166

must be surrendered before the Nothingness so that wholeness may be attained."

"And what then?"

"Why, then perfection," said the priest, somewhat nonplussed.

"But I do not believe that man was meant for perfection."

Llowan laughed and pounded the table.

"He has you, Mantu."

The priest did not join in the general good humor.

The animated conversations continued as the servants silently removed the dishes only to replace them with fresh ones onto which they heaped portions of steamed and fried rice diced with meats and vegetables. No sooner had this course been devoured by the guests than gleaming tureens piled with whole boiled langoustes were served with cups of rice wine.

Ronin thought then of Kiri's earlier remark and he saw that she was smiling slyly at him. Yes, I was famished, but this—

He cracked into the thin carapace. She had spent most of her time in conversation with Llowan and Li Su and he began to wonder why she had brought him here. He felt now that he was jealous of her soft whisperings and gentle touches because they were directed toward their host. He gulped at his rice wine.

Perhaps she did not own poppy fields or trade in the silver market yet she was a powerful woman, the city's leading merchant of a commodity at times more precious than either smoke or metal or silk for that matter. Was she really privy to the secrets of Sha'angh'sei? If so, she was his only way now into the Council. Yet, even as he thought again on these matters, he felt the ebbing of the urgency. As he stared at her awesome beauty, imperfect and therefore terribly thrilling, as he felt the radiance of her aura, the only imperative was his desire to master her.

167

The langoustes, empty red and green exoskeletons languishing now in their own congealing liquids, bits of white and pink flesh still clinging to their edges, were slowly carted away.

Hot scented cloths were brought for face and hands and then bowls of pudding, dark and creamy, custard, yellow and fluffy, trays of pastries stuffed with candied fruits were put before each guest.

"A warrior Llowan called you," said Po, leaning over so that Ronin could hear him more clearly. "My folk were such once upon a time."

Ronin bit into a pastry, washed it down with more wine. He was not really interested in what this trader had to say; he could think of but one thing.

"What happened?"

"Very unprofitable." The black eyes regarded him like those of a dangerous reptile squatting beneath a rock, suddenly magnified, unknowable in the brief moments before—

Ronin realized belatedly that he was being baited. He dipped two fingers into a pudding, cool and spicy. It did not seem to matter.

"Perhaps they were not then sufficiently adept."

The dark eyes widened, staring madly for an instant, and Ronin's fingers closed around the hilt of his sword. Then the face relaxed and, like a thunderstorm after a long drought, Po began to laugh.

"Oh yes," he gasped, gulping at his wine. "I might even get to like you." He bit into a pastry. "But tell me, how did my people fail as warriors?"

"They do not rule this land," said Ronin softly.

The smile was gone and the face before him now seemed incapable of expressing any happiness. The mouth opened.

"Yes, warrior. I cannot argue with that." He sighed. "Yet they had no choice, a small tribe from the west." He shook his head. "We lacked the numbers."

"There are many tribes in this land?"

"Many, yes, scattered on the land."

"The unification of many into one might have been a beginning."

The ebon eyes peered at him with keen interest now. "Do you imagine such a task to be a simple one? Words! But it takes—" He was choked with emotion, boiling inside, an unleashed storm, and his hand clutched whitely at his glass. His voice but a sibilant whisper now, controlled and venomous. "But there was no one. We cried out to our gods for help, sacrificed our children, rent ourselves in desperation, and how were we answered?" The unpleasant smile returned. "*They* came. The foreign priests and then the rikkagin and by then it was too late; enslavement seemed almost pleasant by comparison."

The salad arrived in great bowls, accompanied by wedges of yellow cheese and thick slices of a heavy bread made from grain.

"Yes, it is too late now," Mantu observed, "because you failed to keep what could have been yours. It is ours now and it serves you ill to blame others for your own shortcomings."

"Silence, you!" cried Po.

"You see," said the priest blandly, turning to Ronin. "An illustration of the Canton teachings. Man's craving causes suffering to all about him."

"Words!" Po spat.

"My dear fellow." Llowan raised a hand warningly. "You really must learn to control—"

But the trader was already on his feet, swaying. A tall dark creature of the night.

"For too long have the outlanders plundered our land, twisted the ideologies of our people with taels of silver. Too late, is it?" He laughed. "Now! Now the time of retribution draws nigh! Now come the days of darkness and all foreigners shall taste defeat before

169

they are ground into the mud of the Sha'angh'sei delta!" His cloak swirled like the wings of an avian predator as he pivoted and strode from the room. In a moment they heard the door slam.

"A bitter man," said Mantu out of the silence.

"I trust we can all forget that unfortunate outburst," said Llowan.

But Ronin was watching the rikkagin and he did not like the look in the other's eyes.

Llowan clapped his hands and, with that, the last course was brought. Oranges, peeled and soaked in wine, figs, white raisins, and an assortment of nuts.

When, at length, the last of the dishes had been cleared away, pipes were distributed, bone-white with long stems and small bowls. Tiny open lamps were set beside each guest and Llowan commenced to carve chunks from a block of a brownish substance.

They began to smoke and it seemed to Ronin that after a time the light in the room grew dim and diffuse and there were more women around the table than before. He took little of the smoke himself but watched the others relax as they inhaled deeply. The air became thick and sweet. Kiri shared a pipe with Llowan as they continued to whisper together. He leaned over, inhaling her perfume, anger welling within him. He gripped her cool wrist and she turned as he pulled, falling into his arms because he was expecting resistance and there was none.

Her purple lips were at his throat and he felt the press of her breasts as she murmured, "Let us not overstay."

He felt only surprise as he watched her kiss Llowan gently on the lips.

He was rising dreamily, holding her lithe form as they moved off the soft cushions and through the sweet smoke, across the room, speaking to no one, their departure unnoticed, past the guards and out the

170

doors into the chill startling night. He breathed deeply, freeing his lungs of the cloying scent, clearing his head. And the sweating back and jogging feet took them down the mountainside, away from the tall firs and thickets of gardened foliage filled with the chirruping of cicadas, away from the round shining faces, lips slick with gravy and bubbling wine and lust, away from the gilt and the guards bought with precious metals.

He was silent.

She watched him for a short time as if wanting to imprint the outline of his profile on her mind.

"You are angry with me. Why should that be so? I have done nothing to you." The call of a whippoorwill.

"Why did you bring me?"

Light on her brows and cheek like a new moon.

"Must I have a reason?"

"Yes."

"I wished to be with you."

He laughed shortly and she shivered a little. "You spoke with Llowan all evening."

"What does that matter? I am with you."

He closed his eyes for a moment, sensing a tension springing up between them which was both unpleasant and vaguely comforting in its familiarity. *K'reen, why are you crying? You know I hate that.* Oh, you bloody fool!

Not again.

He opened his eyes, found her staring at him, the gathering lights slithering by them reflecting in her impossibly violet eyes. He smiled.

"Yes, it was foolish of me. My mind was filled with thoughts of other times. Let us forget it, yes?"

Her lips opened and she leaned toward him, the heat reaching out to him, her "Yes" a vibration in their mouths.

Into the clearing night with a fresh sea breeze blowing, into the blazing Sha'angh'sei delta, chittering with countless people, past stalls selling rice and frying fish, silks and cottons, knives and swords, past brutal brawling men, drunk and stinking, past women in pink and green parasols, white-faced, red-lipped, long-legged and beautiful, past wine vendors and money-changers hiding behind the protective barrier of their street-corner cages, past marching soldiers and screaming hongs, past thieves and pickpockets lurking in the blackness of the alleyways and drunken cripples living along the edges of the streets, past battling children and slinking dogs, past piles of refuse upon which dark figures slept and crawled, past rotting corpses kicked and stepped upon by the teeming crowd, onto the Nanking and halted now by the festival's milling throngs, the wide avenue a riot of color and frenzied motion.

They were confronted by a giant dragon, thrice colored, undulating to the movement of the crouched figures beneath its paper hide. It eyed them mock malevolently before turning aside and following the turning of the Nanking. Children in tattered clothes danced along its writhing flanks, urging it on. There was discordant music, percussive and staccato, and much shouting as the people accompanied its slow rippling passage.

Kiri, enfolded within his arms, put her lips to his ear so that she could be heard over the tumult.

"The festival of the Lamiae is this night reaching its zenith. This creature before us is the effigy of the Lamiae, the female serpent which lives in the sea at the edge of Sha'angh'sei. It is she who turns the waters yellow by the thrashing of her immense coils, thus lifting the silt from the sea's floor. The festival annually honors her who guards our dragon gates."

"This land is filled with legends."

"Yes," she said. "So it has been for all time."

They moved on, their kubaru seemingly tireless as they rocked gently through the endless tumbling streets filled with the sleeping and the dead, huddled families and vacant-eyed ancient men and women alone in the sputtering cracked darkness.

He smelled at last the sea as the blackness of the port quarter engulfed them, the streets slick with salt water and fish blood, the great warehouses windowless, gleaming in the silver light from the moon which had finally managed to slip its cloud cover, looming over them like vast mysterious stone monuments. The sea smell was very strong now and, when they stopped, Ronin thought that he could hear the lapping of the sea against the wooden wharves.

They slipped from the ricksha into a silent black building. He closed the door behind them and in pitch-darkness Kiri went away from him. He heard small sounds and, after a moment, a yellow flame flickered as she lit a lamp.

She led him through the rooms, four on this level.

"This is one of Llowan's harrtin," she said. "Where his produce is stored and where, normally, his compredore lives."

"Llowan is a hong also?"

She laughed lightly. "Oh yes. He is master of many poppy fields in the north." They stepped into another room. "Here," she said quietly, "are stored dreams enough for ten thousand lifetimes. Dreams of passion. Dreams of desperation."

"What?"

She started. "Nothing."

They moved on.

"Look here," she said. "The compredore's office. He is the go-between for Llowan and the stevedores and kubaru. He runs the day-to-day shipping and oversees the storing. A most lucrative position."

173

"And where is he this night?"

She turned to him and smiled. "At Tenchō, my warrior. At Tenchō."

The room on the second story stretched almost the entire length of the building. The far wall was constructed of a series of window doors, wooden and slatted, beyond which the spangled night beckoned.

To the left lay the expanse of an enormous bed, low, with many pillows, which took up most of the width of the room. To the right, rugs were strewn across the wooden floor boards. A massive writing desk took up a far corner. Above it was a large mirror set in a carved wooden frame. There were several low chairs made of a tough resilient reed.

Ronin went across the room and pulled at a window door. It opened, folding back on itself, and he was surprised to find that he could step out onto a wide veranda.

Below him the sea: dappled in platinum moonlight chopped to a shower of rippling shards by the undulating surface, so clear in the night that it might have been a molten pathway building itself, beckoning him to climb to the far reaches of the sky, to illimitable whirling shores. Dazzled now, he listened to the quietude composed of the gentle sea lapping at the wharves' stanchions, the creaking of the dark brooding ships at anchor, the stirrings of sleeping families on the galaxy of tasstans rocking on the waves, the splash of a fish. All these now familiar sounds made more searing to him the absolute alienness of the cosmography arched like bits of a shattered world above him.

He felt her presence behind him just before he felt the touch of her body as it pressed itself against his. Through his silk suit, seeped the warmth of her skin;

174

the contours of her breasts and thighs, at once soft and firm, defined themselves. The heat.

He turned and pressed his mouth against hers and her small tongue licked at him and the night beat on around them, the eternal lapping, the soft singing of the kubaru as they made ready for the sailings at first light, the distant cries of the festival of the Lamiae. His finger tips traced the indentation of her spine, descending slowly.

She drew him inside and the sea breeze followed them to the edges of the bed, soft and downy, upon which they tumbled as one.

Her hair whipped his face as he opened her robe and kissed the opalescent flesh. His thirst was enormous.

"Ah," she moaned. "Ahh."

And the tide took him.

Floating in the loss of tension.

The window doors all folded back now so that sea and sky were before them.

"You went to see the Council today." Her voice held a note of puzzlement.

"Yes, this afternoon."

"And fought the Greens. That was most foolish."

He sighed. "It could not be helped."

"Did you have to kill one?"

"I have killed more than one."

She made a sharp sound.

The moon had disappeared and they had had to re-light the lamp. He listened to the quiet splash of the sea for a while.

"They will come after you now."

"I am not afraid."

Her hand stoked his chest. "I do not want you to die."

He laughed. "Then I shall stay alive."

"The Greens are not to be taken lightly—"

"That was not my intention. I mean only that what has been done cannot be altered. I am a warrior. If Greens come for me, then I shall destroy them."

She stared at him, her eyes unreadable. He thought he could hear the plaintive cry of a sea bird far out on the water.

"Yes," she said at last, "I believe you would." Then, "I cannot imagine saying that to anyone else."

"Is that a compliment?"

She laughed then, a clear sparkling sound, and he reached for her hand in the night, feeling its warmth, the fingers twining in his.

She scraped a nail along his flesh. "Why did you seek out the Council?"

He told her.

"But you cannot mean that the tales are true?"

"That is just what I do mean, Kiri."

"But Godaigo—"

"The rikkagin was not at Tenchō this morning."

Her head twisted so that she could see him more fully. "What has Sa's death to do with tales of beings that are not men fighting our soldiers in the north? My men have already dispatched the murderers."

"Murderers?" Ronin said thickly. "Who?"

"Why, the last men with her, of course, but—"

"Kiri, she was not killed by men."

He felt her quiver and the skin along her arms was raised in gooseflesh. It might have been the strengthening wind.

"How could you know that?"

"Because," he said, "I have fought the creature that killed her. It destroyed a friend of mine in precisely the same manner."

He felt her pull away from him. "I cannot believe that; just as I cannot believe that the war is anything but what it has always been from a time long before you or I were born."

"Still, I ask you to aid me with the Council. I cannot see them without your assistance."

"Why do you believe that the Council can aid you?"

"Tuolin told me of the Council."

A cloud passed across her face, fleeting. She shrugged. "I cannot think why he did. The Council will be of little—"

Ronin gripped her shoulders.

"Kiri, I must see them!"

"There is no other way?"

"None."

She tousled his hair. "All right, my warrior. Tomorrow you will be within the Council chambers."

He drew her to him and kissed her hard, feeling her melt as her sinuous body began to writhe slowly against him. The unbound forest of her hair lifted in the wind, a tremulous bridge between their coiling muscles. The lamp sputtered and went out.

She reached under a pillow and her hand lifted, a signpost, long and white and slender, the nails as black as dried blood in the almost-light. Between thumb and forefinger a small black shape, between forefinger and middle finger, its mate. She put thumb and forefinger to her lips, inhaled, then reached out, the arm extending to him, her lips calling, calling in the werevoice of the sea bird flying lonely above the tossing waves. Fingers against his lips. A cold sensation.

"Eat this."

And after he had opened his mouth, "Do your trust me?"

But it was rhetorical and he felt no desire to reply.

The warmth suffused him, friction like a satin glove stroking yellow ivory.

177

Again and again her open lips, wet and shiny, spoke a kind of litany of sound and motion and form. Words were a distant concept, dim and unremembered, discarded within a far-off cave of bright light and animal smells.

The wind died and the air grew calm, ceasing its dancing. The darkness of night hung like a black velvet curtain, containing them. The atmosphere paused between breaths and he hung suspended, listening to the lapping of the waves, as clear and powerful as thunderclaps, rushing against his eardrums in time with the throbbing of his body.

And his body changed, filled now with a delicious warmth, a sexual ecstasy suffusing his feet, climbing upward through his legs and groin and torso and into his brain, and in that moment the strength of Kiri's body moving against his became an exquisite physical sensation. Sight, sound, touch, taste, and the visions in the theater of his mind became one while he was made aware of them as totally discrete inputs, savoring them independently and simultaneously, time stretching out before him like a new-found joyous friend, endless and concurrent. A conduit.

He plowed the heaving seas at the prow of a mighty ship filled with warriors bent on revenge, the feeling a taste at the back of the mouth, sweet and hot. He climbed the curving neck of the high prow, carved into the sinuous head of a dragon, brandished a long sword, screamed at the wind. He was the ship, feeling the heavy water washing over his flanks, his bow cleaving the seas, sending shivering spume into the bright air, leaving white spray in his wake. Man and vessel, he was both and more.

He plunged into the sea, yellow and turgid, and felt his legs grasp the slick scaly coils. He reached down and triumphantly brought the head up, ineffably exquisite, Kiri's deep violet eyes, dark as the depths of

178

the sea, platinum flecks like schools of flying fish, with soft seaweed hair and a face as white as snow. The coils writhed beneath him and he rode the Lamiae from out of the shallows of the Sha'angh'sei sea, past the creaming reefs, teeming with life, and out, away, away, on the great westerly currents, into the deep.

It was then that the cold terror came, a dread presence, and he was swept up like an animal in the vortex of a whirlwind. And for the first time he knew its name. From his core, which beat like an incandescent stone and which remained unmoving in the flux caused by that which he had eaten, came the sound: The Dolman. His entire being opened now and attuned, he felt it drawing near. And it was devastation; it was annihilation. A suprahuman observer, he saw the cinder of the world, blasted and lifeless, blown through the fabric of space by a firestorm of incalculable power. The terror gripped him in its fierce claw and he felt his chest contract until all the air was forced from his burning lungs. He struggled against the coming, feeling helpless. Hearing what he could not comprehend. *Thee*, howled The Dolman, the universe trembling. *Thee. Thee!*

He screamed and came off the bed, stumbling, crashing into the wall. The shutters shivered. He was drenched with sweat. Or sea water.

Kiri came after him, lovely and naked, ivory and charcoal, crouching beside him.

"It's all right," she said softly, mistaking his reaction. "I had forgotten that you are not used to the smoke; this was much more. I had thought to give you only pleasure."

He put his arms around her, felt the whip of the chill night wind racing in from the water. He looked out at the black sky and willed himself to breathe deeply, oxygenating his body.

"No, no, Kiri," he said his voice thin and strained.

"I felt it, more than seeing. Whatever you gave me created a—connection of some kind. I felt—The Dolman is close, very close." His voice was now a metallic whisper in the rising notes of the wind.

"And it comes for me."

She would not let them rest and he felt the rising terror within her, as deep as an undug wellspring, although he was calm now, the intensity still with him but a shell forming, replacing the aftershock that allowed normal thought.

They dressed and went out into the narrow shiny streets. It was the time of night when the moon was down and dawn had not yet begun to pull upon the last thread of darkness. It had begun to rain and the air was heavy with an acrid active smell.

They raced the downpour to the patiently waiting carriage and the kubaru took off at his steady rocking pace, across the marshy delta of the port and into the black back recesses of Sha'angh'sei.

Lightning wreathed the sky like the twisting branches of a great ancient tree and peals of thunder echoing off the buildings' walls caused the runner to break his stride now and then.

By the storm's pale flickering light he watched the lovely profile, the eyes pools of shadow, the cheekbones whitely limned, emphasizing the face's strength and sweep.

They were in what looked to be the most ancient section of the city now, traveling down narrow unpaved streets, earth churned to mud by the rain and the fleet passage of the kubaru's soles, slap-slap, slapslap, black water splashing in a bow wave, presaging their progress.

Small houses of board and reed grew here as if from the soil itself, dilapidated yet with a peculiar sorrowful dignity that was impossible to define. Perhaps

180

it was merely the congruence of meager dwelling to its surroundings that was sufficient to impart this feeling to him. Nevertheless, he understood without being told that he was seeing Sha'angh'sei as it must have been before the Canton priests and the round-eyed rikkagin had come to the land.

The ricksha halted unbidden before the towering columns of a stone temple, squat and thick, its face slick now with rain, cracked and half covered with climbing plants.

They went into the narrow street, following the kubaru through double doors of bamboo bound in black iron. He took them through a crowd of kubaru who milled about the entranceway and who, Ronin suspected, would turn away those who they did not wish to enter.

The gray stone floor, the arching stone walls, caught murmurings and mutterings, echoing them along their length and height like the desultory flame of a guttering candle. This temple had a completely different feel than the one Ronin had come upon in the midst of his wanderings.

"What is this place?" Ronin whispered.

Kiri turned her face toward his and he saw that she had produced a plum-colored silk scarf from somewhere and had wrapped this around her head as if she did not wish to be recognized, though who here would possibly know her he had no idea.

"Kay-Iro De," she said, using a word that was of the ancient tongue of the Sha'angh'sei people and which had no ready translation into modern speech. It meant variously sea-song, jade-serpent, and she-who-is-without-members, and it perhaps had more meanings of which no one spoke.

"I have told you that tonight is the culmination of the Festival of the Lamiae," she said softly, her violet eyes shining. "Yet tonight is more. Every seventh year on the last night of the festival comes the Seercus of Sha'angh'sei." A simian-faced woman wrapped in a green cloak, a hairless man by her side gathering in the taels, her clandestine whisperings.

It appeared now that the temple was immense as they followed their kubaru down a narrow, window-less hall that seemed endless. The dank stone walls, beaded with cold moisture, echoed their footsteps. At regular intervals, stone arches were built into the pas-sageway and from their apexes were hung iron bra-ziers casting a dim, fitful light. At length they reached a wide stairway down which they descended. He noted with some curiosity that the hall seemed to have no other egress at this end.

They went carefully downward, their way lit now by flaring torches set into scorched metal sconces, en-crusted with the detritus of the ages. Fifty steps and then a landing, peopled by kubaru who scrutinized all who passed. Down and down they went with the air becoming increasingly humid and chill, the stairs slick with moisture and slime, until he gave up counting the number of landings.

The atmosphere was thick with salt and phosphorus and sulphur by the time they reached the last landing and passed through the guard of the kubaru there. The runner motioned silently to them and they stooped, half crawling through a cramped passage-way, utterly dark, rough-cut from the living rock. Small creatures skittered past their feet in the wetness.

The tunnel gave onto a vast grotto lit by immense guttering torches, crackling and smoky in the damp air. Great natural columns of stone, flecked and streaked with minerals winking metallically in the light, rose up from the craggy floor into the dark reaches of the unseen ceiling.

There were so many people crowding the cavern that at first Ronin did not see that which actually dominated the place. Then, in some unfathomable shifting, the throng parted momentarily and he saw the pool.

He stepped closer, mesmerized. It was an immense oval stripped out of the floor of the cavern by some cataclysmic upheaval eons ago and the water that filled it was of the most remarkable color he had ever seen. Not a trace of blue or brown could be seen in its shifting depths, yet surely no water could exist without at least a hint of these shades. Yet the water into which he now gazed was the most extraordinary green, halfway between a forest of firs in deep summer and the translucence of the most exquisite jade. Its depth seemed limitless. Surely it led to the vast ocean beyond Sha'angh'sei's shores.

He thought again of the simian-faced woman and her hissed words, *the Seercus,* her inflection imparting to them a mysteriousness that Ronin had supposed was merely a part of her pitch. Now he found himself at the Seercus and he wondered.

Kabaru continually poured into the grotto from several low apertures in the walls similar to the one they had used. Almond-eyed, black shining hair pulled back into long queues, wearing loose suits of dark cotton and coarse silk. He felt that he was, at last, viewing the true Sha'angh'sei, naked in the arena of Kay-Iro De on this most sacred of nights. They were free now of the immense burden of the fields and of the war, of intruder and of time. The betrayals were held for this moment suspended. Ten thousand years had fallen away like so much dead skin to reveal—what? Soon the answer.

He heard chanting, far off and aloft, and the dimness gave grudging way to warm yellow light as the priests entered the grotto from some hidden doorway, carrying before them immense lanterns constructed from the whole skins of giant fish, dried, blown, and lacquered to stiffness. Various pigments had been used to cleverly reproduce and enhance the original aspect, heighten the character of each creature.

The priests wore swirling cloaks of sea-green which left their strong arms bare. They were long-skulled and yellow-skinned, hairless and quite young.

They set the fish lamps down in prescribed places and now he could see that towering over the pool, on the far shore, was a statue. It was of solid gold, carved most cunningly in the shape of an enormous dragon, its thick coils entwined about a regal throne of gold. But where he had expected a female head to be was carved a skull of semi-canine structure, with long grinning muzzle, sharp-toothed and flaring-nostriled above which large round eyes of sea-green jade sparked in the brighter light.

Kiri gripped his hand in hers and her breathing was heavy as she stared at the priests.

All were assembled now and kubaru were stationed at each entrance, he supposed to discourage intruders though in all the crowd he had not seen any glint of weaponry save his own.

One of the priests now gave a signal and incense was thrown into a wide brass brazier. Clouds of yellow steam rose into the black mists of the grotto and spices came to him on the moist air. A young boy appeared leading an animal that Ronin could not readily identify; perhaps it was a young boar. Squealing, the animal was laid out upon a stained stone slab and the chanting began again from the priests and this time it was echoed by the assembled: "Kay-Iro De. Kay-Iro De."

One of the priests reached inside his cloak and produced a knife with a hilt of yellow crystal. Lifting it high over his head, he spoke in the ancient tongue, words that neither Ronin nor, he suspected, Kiri could understand. Yet the meaning seemed clear and Ronin was not surprised when the gleaming blade flashed downward in a shallow arc and pierced the flesh of the animal. Hot blood spurted from the severed artery, spattering the robes of the priests. Dropping the knife, the priest reached his hand into the still trembling interior of the animal and pulled out the warm heart. This he tied with coarse thongs to the knife and cast it into the center of the sea pool while his fellow priests set about collecting the blood of the animal in a glazed yellow bowl. With the splash a kind of sighing went up from the multitude and the chanting began again.

The priests marched silently around the perimeter of the pool toward the golden dragon on the far side and, laying the bowl of blood at the foot of the throne, each in turn bent to dip his hands into the crimson liquid. One by one, then, they climbed the huge throne and daubed the blood onto the eyes of the dragon until it dripped down the muzzle, into the mouth, staining the teeth darkly and thence from the points into the deep green waters.

Now they returned and with them was a young girl in a white robe with silver fish embroidered on it. He felt Kiri against him now, warm and trembling, as they brought the girl before the multitude. She was white-faced and beautiful, tall and shapely with black almond eyes and dark hair that came down to her buttocks. She seemed very young.

Ceremoniously, the priests washed their hands and, at another signal, more incense was thrown into the braziers so that now a green cloud rose into the thick air. Ronin felt then the heat of the throng and the denseness of the atmosphere and he was obliged to take deeper breaths to get sufficient oxygen.

Their hands still wet, the priests donned masks of papier-mâché that caused them to take on the appearance of articulated fish, scales gleaming, gills starkly

185

delineated, round eyes staring unblinkingly. Slowly, they moved in a semicircle around the young girl and the chanting from the throng took on volume and urgency. With infinite slowness their hands lifted and unwound the robe from the girl.

Naked she was breath-taking, with wide hips and heavy breasts and firm thighs. In that electric instant, the priests' robes fell away and she collapsed to the floor of the grotto.

The chanting was all but a roar now and Ronin strained along with the others to see clearly as the priests followed the descent of the girl to the cavern's floor. For many moments the rhythmic movements of the muscular bodies moved to the cadence of the chanting. "Kay-Iro De, Kay-Iro De," and when the priests had finished they rose as one and servants of the temple clothed them once again and removed their fish masks. The girl lay whitely, her breasts heaving like waves upon an agitated sea, fists clenched between her legs. Kiri moaned softly next to him.

Up from a small side pool was drawn a flapping sea creature of some kind, black and sleek and gleaming. It was surely not a fish, for when the priests slew it, this time with a knife of purest green jade, the thing bled red blood as an air-breathing animal would. Again the priests caught the blood in a bowl and with it drew near the prone girl once more.

They grasped her arms and lifted her until she was standing, cradling her as they forced her head back and made her drink the warm blood. Choking and gagging, she drank and when it was all gone they took her to the far side of the sea pool and thrust her roughly upward onto the golden throne, so that her legs entwined with the metallic coils. She clung weakly to the dragon's slippery hide, her head hanging so that the face was concealed by the black forest of her tossed hair. And in no time her body convulsed and she vomited the red liquid so that it drenched the fierce head of the statue.

She shuddered and her grip upon the thing loosened and the priests' arms were retreating and, like the sticky spume that now dripped from the fanged mouth of the golden dragon, she slid inexorably from its slippery embrace into the cool green waters of the sea pool, into the bloodstained salt sea.

There was a collective gasp from the crowd and the chanting began once more from the mouths of the priests, "Kay-Iro De, Kay-Iro De."

The girl thrashed in the water, choking, seemingly not able to swim. Her head disappeared, then she surfaced again, mouth open in a silent scream and with a thrash, descended into the depths.

At that moment the waters of the pool appeared to swirl as if subject to a swiftly passing current, fierce and unnatural, and the air above the water seemed to shimmer as if from some terrible heat.

Tension stung the crowd like an incipient thunderstorm and they seemed caught between an urge to press forward and an instinctive fear to pull back. As a result, they milled about chaotically as the chanting of the priests rose to the howl of a tornado, the rock walls of the grotto hurling the sounds back upon their ears.

"Kay-Iro De. Kay-Iro De."

And now, though he could scarcely believe his eyes, a whirlpool was forming in the center of the sea pool and abruptly the green waters darkened. Emerald mists rose from the pool's sides and salt foam fountained from its core.

"Kay-Iro De. Kay-Iro De."

And the fountaining presaged the presence of something from deep within the sea. He saw the ill-defined shape, black and monstrous, through the imperfect lens of the water, staining the pool with its bulk.

"Kay-Iro De. Kay-Iro De."

And now it broke the water's surface, a reluctant, elastic barrier, into the molten atmosphere of the cavern, heavy with incense and freshly spilled blood, hot with the body warmth of the frenzied people. Foam flying from the tangled seaweed of its hair, black almond eyes huge and baleful.

"Kay-Iro De. Kay-Iro De."

Oh, surely not, thought Ronin. The black eyes within the human head surveyed the throng, the body arching upward so that within the green foam and white spray of its thrust could be seen thick, sinuous coils, scaly, encrusted with algae and yellow barnacles. And within those twisting coils, a glimpse of a white broken torso, slim legs.

With a crash like the collapse of a building, the thing shot straight down, merely a ripple, dark and remote now beneath the waves clapping at the sea pool's edges. And then nothing, only the trembling of the water, limpid and deep green once again.

For an instant, all sound ceased, and had it not been for the tiny slap-slap of the diminishing wavelets, Ronin might have believed that time itself had stopped.

Kiri, shuddering, gripped his arm.

"Look," she whispered hoarsely. "Look."

And his eyes lifted to the far side of the pool, at the immobile dragon. There, instead of the canine head darkly dripping blood, was the golden head of an exquisite woman with almond eyes carved of sea-green jade.

When he awoke, the sun was already past its zenith. He lay quite still for a moment, watching the bright whips of sunlight rippling like molten lead across the floor, listening to the close sounds of singing, hoarse shouts, the frenetic slap of jogging feet, the creaking

188

of ships being outfitted, the metallic grate and the splash as a ship weighed anchor.

For a moment he floated above the receding abyss of his unconscious where rose . . .

And sat up. Slatted wooden doors through which the salt breeze blew and light streamed and he knew then that he was in Llowan's harrtin, though why Kiri had brought him back here instead of to Tenchō he could not remember. He was alone in the room. He stood up and, naked to the waist, went out into the day.

The veranda too was empty yet still he felt the complex shreds of last night clinging to the edges as if they were real and fluttering in the wind.

He looked out at the sluggish sea, clogged with vessels large and small. It was a bright, clear day with thin high clouds near the lid of the sky and he squinted in the sunshine. Below him, the activity along the long wharves of Sha'angh'sei was fierce with loadings and unloadings, the compredores calling to the stevedores, who in turn shouted at the singing kubaru, jogging under the weight of bales and barrels filled with the wealth of the city, the foods and textiles of the continent of man.

His eyes moved from the white billowing sails studding the near waters to the yellow sea farther out and, like a wave pungent with salt and phosphorus washing over him, the events of last night flooded in on him.

Kay-Iro De. Kay-Iro De.

He shook his head. Perhaps it was only the aftermath of the substance which he had taken. What had Kiri called it? The tears of the Lamiae. Merely an illusion, rising and falling like the tide. Sun dancing on the restless water, shards of liquid gold. A memory elusive and vague, as if it were part of another lifetime, lapped at the edges of his consciousness. What? A shape, dark and vast and inconstant and . . .

189

He heard a sound behind him and turned, passed through the open shutters into the cool room to find Matsu, serene, lithe Matsu, standing in the center in a pale green silk robe edged in rust, leaves of the same color falling across its surface. She held a deep blue lacquered tray on which sat a clay pot glazed gray and red and several small cups painted in the same pattern.

"I have come to take you to the Council," she said, kneeling and setting the tray down before her. She lifted a slim arm. "Please. Sit. I have brought your breakfast." Her dark eyes stared up at him unblinkingly and for a moment his stomach contracted.

He ran a hand across his face and went to her, knelt, the tray a low barrier between them. He washed his face and hands from a large bowl of water which she handed him. She patted his face dry with a clean white cloth. He sat back.

"Matsu, where is——?"

"She has much to accomplish today and it is already afternoon."

"How is the woman I brought to Tenchō?"

She did not answer but concentrated on the ceremony of the tea, the turnings of the cup, the stirring, the pouring, all the precise movements that made it so special. He sat quietly and watched her deft hands.

At last the tea was steaming in the cup and she lifted it, an oblique offering, saying, after he had accepted it, "She has awakened. Her name is Moeru, she wrote it for me."

He sipped the tea and it tasted better because of the way she had served it to him.

"Has she still a fever?"

"I think not. The sweat no longer rolls off her and she is eating now."

"That is good." Her eyes hiding behind sooty lashes.

"She wished to remove the bandage."

"What bandage?"

"The one high up on her thigh. The dressing is dirty."

He put the cup down on the tray.

"Ah, no. The apothecary told me to leave it on. There is a healing poultice beneath the cloth."

"But she says that she has no pain there."

"Then the poultice is working."

There was silence for a time. He continued to sip his tea. Matsu watched him, her small white hands folded on her lap. Leaves rustled as she breathed. Smells of sweat and spices and fresh fish from the wharves. Shouts and hoarse laughter. Oval face like still water, strands of hair floating in the breeze, the perfect column of the neck, slender and ivoried.

"Your friend's husband," he asked. "How is he?"

"Ah," sighed Matsu, her head minutely in motion so that a wave of black hair fell over one eye, across her cheek. "It is most sad. He was knifed last night, fighting in a tavern."

"I am sorry."

She smiled wanly. "It is as well he died. The war had changed him. My friend no longer knew him. He brought only sorrow to those who loved him, even his son who lies paralyzed on a bed in my friend's house."

"I do not understand."

"His back is broken but he still has eyes with which to see. His father resented that." She shrugged. "As I said, it is perhaps better this way."

"Will you have some tea?"

Matsu shook her head. "It is for you."

Outside, the sun beat down out of a deep cerulean sky. They smelled the gutted fish drying in the heat, a hint of cinnamon, of cloves, of coriander, and Ronin's nostrils dilated for a moment as if recalling on their own a distant and odious scent.

Then they were in the ricksha, moving off down the narrow, baking streets, past the blind faces of the harrtin which Ronin now knew opened opulently their splendid verandas onto the bund—the wharves of Sha'angh'sei and the swelling yellow sea.

Deep within the jungle of the city, the kubaru runner stumbled and fell and the ricksha jerked to a halt. Although he had been talking to Matsu and his head had been turned away, the bright line of crimson along the runner's side caught the periphery of his vision and as the two men leaped onto the still rocking ricksha his sword was already withdrawn.

It was the wrong action in the confined space and the man who went for him had the advantage, the hilt of his filthy dirk slamming against the inside of Ronin's wrist with a quick flick, the sword clattering to the muddy street. A professional, Ronin thought, and he did the only thing he could do, grappling, tearing the momentum so that they both fell to the ground.

He inhaled the stench of the body and the foulness of the breath as the man slashed the dirk at his throat. Saw the yellowed stumps of teeth, holes in the gray gums, images flashing across his vision path as the head whipped and the shoulders twisted and the blade blurred into the soft earth just past his neck.

Elbows in and up, using the heavy bone structure, and the man's jaws clashed together with a crack as Ronin hit him. He had the good sense to scramble away then so that he could regain his advantage.

He let Ronin get up before he came toward him, confident because Ronin was unarmed. He was small but very powerful with broad shoulders and lean hips and thick muscular arms. He had a wide flat intelligent face, dark cunning eyes. He was bald save for a long queue of dirty blue-black hair. He was missing an ear.

He was clever and ignorant at the same time. He feinted, the blade of his dirk appearing to whip toward Ronin's neck, canting downward at the last instant, reaching to slit his stomach. Using the man's momentum, Ronin stepped into the thrust, grasping the extended arm, and leaned back, his hip and groin beneath the man's buttocks, a solid base as he planted his feet and stiffened the muscles of his legs. He lifted his right foot, slamming the sole of his boot down onto the stretched knee joint. Resistance was minimal. The kneecap shattered in a shower of white and pink and the vulnerable thighbone cracked as if it were a dry twig. The man screamed and collapsed and Ronin reached for his fallen dirk.

"Stop right there," said a voice.

Ronin turned and in that instant remembered the second man. He stood now several paces from Ronin with Matsu drawn to his side, his dirk at her throbbing white throat, so perfect, like ivory. The blade grazed her windpipe for emphasis. He stared into her eyes, saw in their darkness no fear. What then?

The second man shook his head sadly.

"You should not have done that." He was large, very tall, with a grizzled beard and long greasy hair. He had a high forehead and the eyes of an animal. Ronin froze. "What shall I tell his woman and her children? How will they eat? Now I will take your money and the woman." His feral eyes flicked at the man, broken and unconscious in the muddy earth, came back to Ronin. "She will fetch a high price at the Sha-rida." Matsu gasped in pain as the blade bit into her throat.

"Sha-rida?" said Ronin, edging closer, wanting to keep the man talking.

"Outlander. Fool to travel these streets in a ricksha.

193

The scent of your money precedes you." He smiled mockingly. "Yet I salute your foolishness because you are my living. Long may it last. Do not come closer," he snapped suddenly. His voice was now cold and hard. "The woman will be breathing through the hole in her throat. You are not that foolish, I trust." The man pulled Matsu in front of him and his blade caught the sunlight in a dazzle. "Now come, let us not drag out this encounter. Toss your money to the ground."

"All right," said Ronin. "Do not harm her." Because he was close enough now and Matsu was in the correct position. He had deliberately moved because he wanted her in front of the man, where he could look at her, read her expression. He needed that advantage. His sword was out of the question. She would die before he got halfway to where it lay.

His shoulders moved minutely, slumping in an attitude of defeat. Back within the depths of the Freehold and his Senseii, the Salamander was before him, saying, "Provide your foe with clues. He will be trained to look for the key to victory through the tiny betrayals of your body. So you must give him that which he wishes to find." These men were sufficiently adept.

His hands were at his belt, slowly unknotting the cord to his bag of coins. He stared at Matsu and she read what he wished her to know, written in his colorless eyes.

The bag hit the soft ground with a heavy chink and the gauntleted hand sped across the short space without warning. The hesitation, the merest split instant caused by Ronin's attitude of defeat and the visual and aural distraction of the bag of coins dropping, was sufficient. Ronin grasped the blade just as it commenced its inward stroke. He wrenched at it and the metal snapped. At the same time, Matsu twisted her body, swung her arm, and her fist hit his stomach.

194

Then she was away and Ronin was closing with the man.

He went for the throat and the man blocked him, turning as he did so, taking Ronin down. There was pressure against Ronin's windpipe and he had to force his breathing. The man's fist smashed into the side of his head and the grip tightened on his throat. He felt the urge to retch as his body rapidly used up the last of the oxygen in his stilled lungs. He fought to breathe, could not, and so turned his attention to bringing up his right hand. It was caught between their bodies and he worked at freeing it while he began to strangle on carbon dioxide. The man's attention narrowed as he increased the pressure and now the hand was free; bring it up, through the maze. Groping, he found the open spot on the side of the neck, jabbed with his thumb.

The man could not even scream and Ronin was up, his lungs heaving in great bursts of air. They were on their knees in the mud and slime and the man was recovering and there was no time to reconsider, the organism out to survive. Ronin's fist, sealed within the hide of the Makkon gauntlet, smashed into the lower end of the man's sternum. The bone cracked, splintered, the force of the fist plunging it upward into the heart. Blood and viscera fountained outward, drenching him as the face before him, drained and white, bobbed like a berserk marionette. The jaws snapped shut spasmodically, biting off the end of the lolling tongue.

Ronin stood and kicked at the body, looking around, but there was only Matsu staring at the ruined corpse.

She started then, looking at him. She went and got his sword and he sheathed it as she bent to pick up the bag of coins. Then she went to the slain kubaru and ripped off his damp shirt, returning to Ronin and wiping the pink foam from his face and chest and arms. She reached out and touched the strange scaled gauntlet, horny and unreflective, glistening now, beaded with dark fluids.

"What is that?" she whispered, stroking the hide.

"A present," Ronin said, watching the thin line of red across her throat where the dirk had crossed the delicate flesh. It stood out like a tear on a shadowed cheek. He licked his finger, wiped it along her neck. Her eyes closed and she shuddered. "It was given to me by a little man who walks with a limp, whose companion is a singular creature. It is made from the claw of the thing that killed Sa."

She seemed not to hear him. "I could not believe that any man could do what you have just done. Was it the gauntlet?" Her fingers dark now with the viscous liquids.

Ronin wiped her hand and the gauntlet on the sodden shirt, then threw it from him. He shrugged. "Perhaps, in part." He reached for her. "Now we must finish our journey. The Council awaits me."

The dark eyes lifted, looked at him strangely. Then she nodded and they set off through the labyrinthine streets, finding at length the Nanking and then, a short time later, a narrow winding road with no name that Ronin could see.

"I came a different way the last time."

"I have no doubt. But it is not prudent to take King Knife Street, is this not so?"

He laughed then. "Yes, Matsu, it would indeed not be wise. But what about the Greens at the gate?"

She smiled. "There are many entrances to the walled city."

The climb was steep this way. No houses lay along the road, only giant firs and lush green-leafed trees. The earth was thick with small plants and wild flowering bushes.

Soon the shadow of the great wall blotted out the warmth of the sun and they stood in the cool dimness while Matsu spoke in low tones to the Greens who guarded this gate. The metal door swung open and they went through. The Greens ignored them, returning to the absorption of their dice game.

Within the perfectly linear corridor of the carefully tended trees he asked her, "The Sha-rida, Matsu. What is it?"

She laughed nervously, the sound like shattering crystal in the quietude, and he heard the sighing of the trees before she said, "The Sha-rida is a tale told to frighten outlanders." But he saw the look on her face and did not quite believe her.

"Tell me then," he said lightly. "I am not easily frightened."

Her eyes swept his face and she tried a smile but did not quite make it.

"It is a market, a special kind of market, which, it is said, moves from night to night, through the black alleyways of Sha'angh'sei, opening only after the moon has left the sky."

"A flesh market," said Ronin. "Slave trade."

She shook her head. "No. There are many of those in the city. They conduct their business during the day."

"Well then?"

"It is true that the Sha-rida deals in human flesh, but only the most beautiful women and men, young and healthy."

"Toward what end?"

They walked in silence for a time. The cicadas were singing among the trees and birds called in staccato rhythm above their heads. The avenue stretched before them, white and empty, as if it were some giant's plaything abandoned now for some newer and more elaborate toy.

"Toward, it is said, a hideous death." Her voice was like the first touch of autumn's winds. "The buyers wish only to observe death and the act of dying, and the more they indulge themselves, the more bored they become and the more monstrous the forms of dying they conjure up." She looked at him. "Even in a city such as this, such a thing does not seem possible."

"It is only a tale."

"Yes," she said. "That is all."

Their footsteps shattered the silence of the hall and the still air eddied softly in their wake. The woman with the light eyes and jutting breasts was at her post behind the heavy marble desk. Two Greens, armed with axes and curving dirks, stood watch outside heavy wooden doors with iron rings in their centers.

"Yes?" she inquired, lifting her head. She did not seem to recognize Ronin. He was about to say something when Matsu squeezed his arm.

She spoke to the woman who said, "Ah," softly as she listened, her eyes on Ronin.

"Ah." Her lacquered nails scraping across the cool desk top like articulated insects. "No, I am afraid—" But Matsu cut into her prepared speech and they stared at each other now, a test of power that encompassed more than mere wills. The woman licked her lips with her bright tongue. "Well, I—" Matsu spoke at length and the woman's face came apart, a subtle thing which he observed with some wonderment. "Yes. Yes, of course." She signaled to the Greens who turned and, pulling on the iron rings, opened the doors.

At last, Ronin thought, as they went forward. An audience with the Municipal Council of Sha'angh'sei. They went into the Council chambers. He was already unscrewing the hilt of the sword. An answer to the long riddle. An end to the uncertainty. The way now open to defeat The Dolman and his hordes. The doors closed behind them. His hand stopped as it was about to pull forth the scroll of dor-Sefrith.

He whirled on Matsu.

"What insane jest is this?"

"There is no jest." Calm. The black eyes steady.

"Then surely this is the wrong chamber."

"You can see for yourself that this is the Council's chambers."

It was a high-ceilinged, windowless room dominated by an immense ornate table around which were placed at regular intervals high-backed wooden chairs, richly carved, regal. Save for the two of these, the chamber was empty.

"Why did you bring me on a day when the Council is not in session," he demanded.

"If it were not in session, the building would have been closed."

Ronin's temper broke and he shook her by the shoulders.

"Are they ghosts then that I cannot see them?"

"No," The voice as distinct in the room as a bird call in high summer. "It is quite simple."

His hands moved. "Matsu, I will break your neck—"

"The Municipal Council of Sha'angh'sei does not exist."

The dragon stared at him quizzically. From the chair, its golden eyes sparked in the last oblique rays of sunlight. Its head was erect but its body was distorted, foreshortened by the folds. Ronin crossed the room and, removing his shirt and weapons belt, donned the robe as Matsu had bidden him. The silk moved in the breeze from the open window and the dragons writhed.

Day was almost done. They had not spoken on the

journey back to Tenchō. Although he had been hungry and although they had passed many street stalls filled with a variety of fragrant foods, he had denied himself that pleasure, preferring not to delay the explanation. He had spent too long seeking an answer only to find other riddles.

He had raged at Matsu, threatening to tear the chambers apart, to destroy the Greens outside the door. She had merely stared at him and asked that he return to Tenchō with her. "The answer is there," was all that she had said and had waited him out.

Eventually he had given in. He had no choice.

Clouds were piling up to the west, darkening the lowering sun, turning it from orange to deep crimson, a half-seen oblate, bloated and veiled by the oncoming weather. Another storm approaches, Ronin thought, sliding the dragons over his torso. The silk felt cool on his flesh.

Matsu came to him beside the window and tied his sash in the formal manner. She had changed into a crimson formal robe, the color more vivid than was usual for her. Deep brown reeds on the body, the wide sleeves plain, bordered in deep red.

She studied him for a moment in the twilight, the fast-disappearing sun now a dusky ruby glowing between the buildings on Okan Road. And the strange light, burnished and intense, drew all the color from her face, causing her to appear pale, shadows building in layers around her eyes, across the hollows below her cheeks. The skin was perfectly drawn, not a line, not a blemish marred its satin surface. She stood quite still, all light and dark, and he felt compelled to reach out and touch the face to assure himself that it was indeed flesh and blood, warm and pliant, that he was not staring at some fantastically conceived and crafted mask. Her lashes dipped for an instant and her lips parted as if she were about to say something. Then her lids rose and her slim hand moved startlingly, passing through the light, then black shadow, as she reached down for his hand. And she managed somehow to turn that simple gesture into a tender caress as she led him wordlessly from the room, into the dim corridor, the great lamp not yet spilling its tawny light.

Down the curving stairs in a wide arc and into the rear of the house where he had never before ventured. They went out the back, swiftly silently, through a small wooden door with a large iron lock and, instead of the expected crowded street, Ronin found himself in a spacious garden, lush and green with the plumage of ripe foliage.

Amid the artful jungle of greenery stood a pair of four-legged creatures, saddled and harnessed. They snorted and pawed the earth as Ronin and Matsu neared them so that their attendants were obliged to pull on their bits and talk to them soothingly in meaningless words.

"These are not horses," said Ronin and Matsu smiled.

"No. They are luma. Steeds from the far north, very powerful and quite intelligent." She shrugged. "Horses are quite stupid. They are fine for warfare and that is where they are primarily used. In any event, the luma are quite rare." She lifted one arm. "This one is a present from Kiri."

The animal was a deep red-brown stallion with a thick red mane. It had a long tapering head with flaring nostrils and erect triangular ears. Its eyes, round and large, were a deep blue and, between them, thrusting from the thick skull, were three stubby yellow horns in a vertical row like a miniature trident. The luma had no tail but the lower reaches of its legs were streamered with silky red hair.

Slowly, Ronin approached it. One large blue eye

followed his progress with curiosity and, as Matsu had told him, intelligence and when he reached out to stroke its head it snorted and pushed its muzzle against his hand.

He mounted the luma and Matsu leapt onto her own, a gray mare with a pure white mane. He saw that a double slit in her robe allowed her to sit astride the luma without difficulty.

They rode out from the dense garden, the attendants opening thick iron gates, the luma's hoofs resounding against the cobbles and the close walls of the city's streets like pounding hammers, and blue-white sparks flew in their wake.

The dragons along his arms rippled in the wind, seeming to come alive dancing across his body to the music of their movement. Matsu, riding just ahead of him, cried out frequently, guiding her mount and warning the crowds clogging the streets. Dark figures scrambled hastily from their path, pointing and murmuring, their words jumbled and lost in the swift passage.

Into the dark labyrinth of the delta, the port area less jammed with people but with narrower, twisting streets. Then, all at once, they broke from the confinement of the alleys of the bund, purple and black and deep red in the last of the sun, a minute crescent now against the unmarred horizon as it heaved its bulk into the welcoming embrace of the singing sea.

Along the wooden boards of the bund they raced, the kubaru's songs a spice on the salt air. He inhaled the scents of the sea, pungent drying fish, the cloying sweetness of the poppy's syrup, and the violet faces of the harrtin with their wide verandas, impassively observing the end of another day, swept by them in majestic array.

Until, abruptly, they were alone on the sand, the curving, darkling beach stretching before them in exultant desolation, and Ronin's luma lifted its head in an unmistakable sound of pleasure and triumph, calling, galloping, galloping, the sea to the left now cinnabar solid in the last of the red light, and he felt a tremendous jolt of adrenalin, as if he were joining battle, and his heart thudded and, as his steed leapt over a dark dune, its crest as sinuous as a snake, he unsheathed his sword and lifted it toward the cold pinpoints of light just becoming visible and he thought, Let The Dolman come. I welcome now the Makkon's freezing embrace, for surely I am its nemesis. I am its slayer.

And he rode on into the deepening dusk with Matsu at his side, her shadowed face impassive, thinking her unfathomable thoughts.

When the hazy golden lights of Sha'angh'sei were but a smear behind them, Matsu broke off and called to him, into the singing wind rolling in off the turbulent sea, alive with green and blue phosphorescence.

"I must leave you here, Ronin. Ride on. The luma will take you unerringly."

"But what—"

She was gone, had already wheeled her mount, its hoofs but a whisper against the sand in the night, and he shrugged, dug his heels into the luma's flanks as she had instructed him, and it leapt forward. He concentrated on its power, the concordant rippling of its muscles, the thin film of sweat slickening its rich coat, and then it was slowing, snorting and bobbing its head as if telling him of something ahead.

He peered into the darkness and heard the luma's prancing steps before he saw its silhouette looming up before him. All at once he was close enough to see that it was of a deep saffron with a black mane.

Astride it sat Kiri. The lustrous violet eyes stared back at him. She flicked her head and he saw the unmistakable lines of her proud face. Her long dark hair was unbound, streaming in the wind. It was held back from her face by a narrow band of yellow topaz. She wore a pale yellow robe with golden flowers embroidered upon it in the most intricate pattern. It was different from all the others he had ever seen but he could not tell why.

"Kiri," he said almost breathlessly, the wind moaning between them, "I thank you for this present. It gives me great pleasure to ride."

She smiled. "It suits you well, the luma, and I am told that it welcomed you immediately; they are not easily tamed, the luma."

"Yes, but how in—"

"Come!" she called over the shifting sand, pulling on her reins. "Ride with me, my warrior."

And over the undulating dunes, by the shore of the crashing luminescent sea, they flew, chill white spray thrown up by the luma's flashing hoofs, sparkling their hair and faces. Her feet were bare, digging into the creature's flanks, spurring it on.

"Kiri," he called. "What of the Council? What trick have you played on me?"

She shook her head, hair like a vast fan. "No trick. Only the truth." Her pale face turned to him. "If I had told you, you would not have believed me." The sea crashed around them as they sped into the yellow surf. He could hear the jangle of the bits, the creak of their saddles very clear on the cold air. "The Council is an elaborate myth. It is best for the people to believe that a body rules their lives and governs the city. But the truth is that no such Council could exist here and survive. Sha'angh'sei would not tolerate it."

"You talk as if the city were alive."

She nodded. "There is no other place in all the world like it. Yes, a Council of the factions makes

204

sense here only as thought. In reality, they would tear each other apart."

"Who sees the people who wait for audience in the walled city?"

"They see me, when they see anyone at all."

He stared at her, back erect, hair billowing, eyes like wells out of time.

"You? But why? Do you lead a faction within Sha'angh'sei?"

She laughed then, deep and long, a delightful sound, the wind carrying her melodious voice into the reaches of the night.

"No, my warrior, not a faction."

Surf sprayed along the lumas' flanks so that they gleamed in the phosphorescence. She dug her heels into her mount and she sped ahead, over the sighing dunes, their white crests shifting, and he took the water route, cutting across a crescent cove, the sea flaring outward like wings in his wake. The stars seemed very close at that moment.

He broke from the surf, his steed's coat fire red now, as deeply crimson as a hurled torch, hearing her startling cry, "Not a faction, oh no. Only one can rule. Into one's hands is delivered the ultimate power." Her face a platinum and onyx helm in the cold light. "It is I, Ronin. I am the Empress of Sha'angh'sei."

The night was an expert shroud. Somewhere, water dripped dolefully. The lamps were unlit and no one came to relight them. A strident argument raged from an open window on the second story overhead. There was a slap and a brief cry. Silence. He crouched in a doorway, cloaked in shadow, still and watchful. A dog howled and he heard the pad of its paws. The sharp odor of sweat as two women reeled by, laughing, their robes held together by unsteady hands; the momentary glow of white skin. Then the street was quite deserted.

The gates opened at their approach and he inhaled the humid perfume of the green velvet garden, black now in the night, for only after they had dismounted and their glistening luma were led away, snorting and prancing, was a tiny torch lit.

The lushness was overwhelming after the barren beauty of the white sand and black sky. He breathed the jasmine air, listened to the myriad rustling all around him.

Yellow insects dancing in the torchlight as she moved toward him. The silence was startling and he put a hand out to stop her. After a moment the nocturnal noises commenced again.

She took his hand, her face a pale oval, wreathed by the trembling forest of her hair, and they walked across the grass, through a maze of hedges reaching far above their heads, past whispering firs, scented and jeweled with dew, to the other side of the garden. She dropped the torch and smothered the flame. They were in total darkness and the small sounds were suddenly amplified as vision went to nil. His pupils expanded. They stood before a blank stone building. A recessed door stood ajar and she bade him enter. He turned on the threshold.

"Kiri, why did Tuolin suggest I seek out the Council?"

She shrugged. "Perhaps he wished to give you hope."

"But there is no Council."

"I hardly think that Tuolin would know that."

"Are you sure?"

"Reasonably. Why?"

"I—do not know. For a moment I thought—"

"Yes?"

"Why should he leave so unexpectedly?"

"Soldiers are governed by their own time. He left because he was summoned early."

"Of course, You must be right."

He turned. They were in a black corridor.

"Walk straight ahead," she said from behind him. "There are no turnings."

Still he kept his eyes moving.

"The woman you brought in is much better. She is up and wanting to help the girls. Her recovery has been remarkably swift."

"What has she told you?"

"Nothing."

"Nothing at all?"

"She is mute."

"I would like to see her."

"Certainly. Matsu has told her about you. She wants to thank—"

He staggered and almost fell, the breath lost inside of him, sucked away. Before him was light, an abrupt end to the blackness, and what he saw was an immense hall built all of streaked marble, yellow and pink and black, the arched, gilt roof supported by twelve pillars, six on each side. The muraled walls were dusky in the light from golden braziers hung at intervals, watery and flowing in their depiction of strange, beautiful women and men, golden-skinned, sapphire-haired, tall and lithe. He blinked and forced his lungs to work.

"What is it?" Her hands on his shoulders.

"I have seen this place before." Voice thick and furry.

"Oh, but that is impossible. You—"

"I have been here before, Kiri—"

"Ronin—"

"Will be here again, I know that now. Believe me, I know this place. In the City of Ten Thousand Paths, in the house of dor-Sefrith, the great magus of Amano-mori—"

He had waited long enough. He went cautiously

across the street, from shadow to shadow, and when he stood beneath the stone jar his sword was out.

He went in quickly and silently, leading with his right shoulder to present the smallest target. The stench of the shop's supplies of potions and powders was heavily in the air and he knew even before he looked that the bottles and jars and phials were lying smashed on the floor, their mysterious contents spilled darkly, lying in small mounds and thick streaks, mingled in arcane combinations, drifting on the night wind.

He found the apothecary against the side of the counter in back, spread-eagled, the blade of an ax protruding like an obscene growth from the frail chest. Ronin tried to pull him down but the blade had gone entirely through him, impaling him to the wood. Ronin pulled at the haft and it came away, the body sliding limply down into the dry rivers of powders littering the floor.

Ronin stared at where the old man had hung. Along the wood were two dark streaks in the shape of an inverted V, as if he had been trying to write some message in his own blood as it gushed from him, life ebbing away.

The last hope gone now, the scroll useless and nothing to stop The Dolman, the death of man assured, and his blade was a silver arc and he felt the bite and heard the scream at the same instant. He hacked through both legs and an ax fell heavily to the floor. Creakings as of weight on the floor boards and there was movement all around him. He whirled and thrust obliquely, short and chopping, the blade biting deeply, then, reversing the momentum of his thrust, used the opposite edge to slice into another man's neck. Hot blood spurted at his face and he moved away from the bodies dancing frenziedly as they died.

They rushed him now, lunging for his sword arm,

and he swung, fingers dismembered, hands split like butchered meat, but there were far too many, they were taking no chances, and at length they had it and pulled him down to the airless floor. Forearms along his windpipe. He struggled but his hands and legs were pinioned and, lungs laboring, finding no oxygen, he began to tumble down an endless escarpment of sand into a black land where sickle-bladed axes grew like uncut wheat from crimson corpses.

"We are not greedy souls."

Tourmaline hung in the smoke.

"We are what we must be."

Red green brown, its facets winked dully in the pearled glow.

"What history decreed we become."

The blue haze, frozen, rose and fell like the swell and suck of the sea.

"Pawns."

There was a raucous burst of laughter bubbling like the release of water under pressure.

"Oh my. Oh my." Voice deep and heavy.

Tourmaline dancing in multicolored splendor, a miniature sun upon the convex surface.

"Yes. We are the result of an unforgiving past. Hurled this way and that by the necessities of our land. Did we arise before the need for us had arisen? Could we?"

Tourmaline sun shaking against its quivering sky.

He had fat cheeks and heavy jowls which wobbled when he laughed. Wide flat nose, cheekbones lost in flesh guarding long almond eyes of cobalt blue. No neck, his billiard head stuck to his massive shoulders and bare chest, deep green robe open to the waist. His mouth was small and delicate.

"We were formed from the minds of our gods, in

centuries too distant to calculate, for the protection of our people, to guard the wealth of the land."

He was sitting in a wicker chair, its high back curving up and out like the questing necks of some monstrous and headless creatures, mindless twins.

"To destroy the Reds!"

A massive arm lifted, fell to the wicker with a sharp snap.

"To undermine the power of the rikkagin. To take vengeance on all who come within our precincts seeking only wealth. Thieves and worse. Murderers."

The cobalt eyes shifted their focus.

"Our price is high, yes; and it is met every hour of every day and night within the borders of Sha'-angh'sei. We are paid to protect those who live like frightened ants within the walled city. Yet the walled city is ours if we so wished. The fat hongs deliver up to us the tariffs we request. The rikkagin, who grow rich on the war to the north, pay us taels of silver on the last day of each month—" The eyes flashed. "How I hate them! How I work to defeat them. It is not enough to take their money, no, not nearly. Infiltrate, am I not correct?"

There was a noise. The eyes peered down in front of him.

"Has he heard, do you think?"

He made a motion with his hand, a flicker of movement, and Ronin was drenched with sea water, chill and fecund with microscopic life. The salt burned in his wounds but it cleared his head. He groaned again.

"We wish you to be fully conscious." said the immense man.

Ronin broke his bleary gaze from the tourmaline around the man's neck. He was in a room whose walls were constructed of bamboo, coated in a clear lacquer so that they gleamed in the low lamplight. There were no windows but overhead a skylight was open to the clear night.

"You have caused us many deaths, brought grief to many women and their families." He sighed. "We are the Ching Pang. The Greens." His hand reached into his robe. Something sparkled in the air and dropped in front of Ronin. "There."

It was the silver necklace he had taken off the dead man in the alley and which T'ung had taken from him at the gate of the walled city. He stared at the tiny silver blossom, wiping the salt water from his eyes, and for an instant he fancied he heard the tolling of far-off bells, the muted call of a horn, seeing again the lazy fish in the perfect garden of that mysterious temple, lost now within the maze of Sha'angh'sei. Eternity.

"Tell us who you are. Who sent you to Sha'angh'sei?"

Ronin coughed, put his hand up to his throat. He swallowed experimentally.

"Not the Reds, surely. They know less of the sakura than we do."

"I know nothing of this necklace."

"That is a lie. You attacked Ching Pang in the alley, trying to save your friend."

"Who?"

"The man in black." The voice was patient, an uncle speaking to a mischievous child.

"I saw someone being attacked by many men. I went to help him." The immense man laughed.

"I have no doubt. Stupid to expose yourself to us so openly. You underestimate us. Why were you sent here?"

"I came to Sha'angh'sei to seek the answer to a riddle."

"Where did you come from?"

"The north."

"Liar. There are savages only to the north."

211

"I am not of this land."

"And the sakura."

"I do not know what you want."

The immense man looked with pity upon Ronin and then lifted his eyes.

"T'ung, it is time for you to do what you must do."

"Shall I kill him first?"

"No, but be content, that will come later."

"I want him."

"Yes, of course you do. But first you will take him with you."

"But—I—"

"Let him witness it."

They moved stealthily through the twisting, refuse-strewn alleys of the city, deep in shadows where no night lanterns shone, where the sweet smoke drifted through the air and the rattle of gaming dice was an intermittent atonal tattoo.

He went with four of them. T'ung and two other Greens garbed in deep blue, ax blades sheathed in black fabric so as not to reflect. They had with them a man with lusterless skin and bright burning eyes, whose body trembled with fear and who ceaselessly implored them to spare him. His hands were bound to a short bamboo pole behind him.

T'ung, ever by Ronin's side, had whispered to him, "If you attempt to cry out, I will stuff a rag in your mouth. This is Du-Sing's order. I would slit your belly now, if I could. But I am a patient man. My time will come when we return."

The shadows were endless as they moved silently through the replicating alleys in the night. A dog barked throatily. There was the sound of someone urinating against a wall close by, curiously distinct. They heard distant laughter, the thrumming of nocturnal hoofs, a tense and enervating noise. They walked through the litter of the tiny animals who screeched briefly at the disturbance.

"Where are we bound?" said Ronin, careful to keep his voice down.

T'ung smashed him just above his ear.

He called softly to the Green leading the way and they turned to the right, into a dimly lit street, residential, a fairly wealthy area.

They approached a house and one of the Greens produced a bowl of rice from beneath his cloak. The man's eyes bulged at the sight and the other Green was obliged to hold him.

Carefully, ritually, the first Green set the bowl of rice onto the street directly in front of the steps leading up to the front door. Then he rose, produced a pair of sticks, bent again, setting them beside the bowl. He turned and, bowing to T'ung, went and stood beside Ronin.

Swiftly T'ung moved to the side of the squirming man, slammed his fists into the hinges of his jaws so that they gaped open in reflex. His left hand moved into the mouth, the fingers expertly grasping the slippery tongue while the right hand flashed upward. The glint of naked metal. The man was about to gag and the blade had already slashed through his tongue. Blood spurted, black in the dimness of the street, and the man's head whipped about. Terrible guttural sounds issued from him like an animal pathetically attempting to mimic human speech.

Again the dagger rose and flashed forward and the man's head recoiled horribly and the mouth redoubled its efforts to scream. The Green gripped the dripping hair and the blade came up for the third ghastly time. Then the Green let go of the head and it bounced back and forth as if on a spring. The maimed face came up and stared sightlessly at Ronin, two black holes, wet and shiny, running with blood and ribbons of viscera.

T'ung nodded and the Green unsheathed his ax, arcing it down, severing the tendons at the backs of the man's knees, so that the body folded in on itself and he was forced to kneel in the dust of the street. He fell over into his own blood.

T'ung bent and arranged the tongue and eyeballs on their bed of rice as if they were savory delicacies to be consumed by the most discerning of gourmets. When he had finished, the Green placed the body of the man next to the bowl and sticks.

The Green who stood beside Ronin handed T'ung an immaculate yellow silk cloth as he came up. T'ung wiped his hands.

"He knew many things," he said to Ronin when he was quite close. He handed the cloth back. "But he said them to the wrong people."

He shoved Ronin and they all vanished into the alley from which they had moments before emerged and were swallowed up by the Sha'angh'sei night.

"You see how unfortunate it is," said Du-Sing. "We who are the protectors of Sha'angh'sei must rule it by fear. It is an imperative of this city, a given rule, if you will, which we view simply as another fact of our existence. There are no two ways about it. Fear cuts through all boundaries. If you say to a kubaru, 'Tell us what we wish to know or we shall be forced to cut off your foot,' why then he will respond because, without his foot, he cannot work the poppy fields and thus feed his family. Similarly, if you say to rikkagin, 'Tell us or we shall cut off your sword hand,' what do you imagine his answer will be?" He laughed, his fat face jiggling.

Then Du-Sing's face took on a sorrowful edge. "It is the hongs and the rikkagin and the Canton priests spewing their soulless filth who rob the people of Sha'angh'sei. Yet it is the Ching Pang which gains the reputation of thieves, murderers, and evil men." His fat hands clapped together. "Nothing could be further from the truth!"

"Is that justification for what T'ung and these others just did?" asked Ronin.

"Justification?" cried Du-Sing. "We require no justification here. We do what must be done. No one else will do it. And this city must survive. Through us it does." He settled himself more comfortably in his wicker chair. "You were shown that as a moral lesson. You are drawing breath now under our sufferance." He drew out the silver necklace. "Where is yours?" he snapped suddenly.

"I have only seen that one," replied Ronin.

"Did you bury it, perhaps?"

"I have only seen that one."

"Is your mission in Sha'angh'sei the same as the other's?"

"I never heard of this city until I was fished out of the water."

"Is that where you met the man?"

"I never saw him before—"

"There are many ways to induce the truth from you and T'ung knows them all. I need not remind you how eager he is to have you all to himself."

"The truth has already been spoken."

"Spoken like a true hero," said Du-Sing sarcastically. "Are you so stupid as to believe that we lack the skills to break you?"

"No. You will eventually find a way and then I shall be forced to tell you a lie so that you will kill me."

"The truth is all that we require."

Ronin laughed shortly. "That and my life. I am not

a kubaru or a fat hong whom your threats can affect. I am not of this city. I do not hold you or the Ching Pang in reverential awe as all do in Sah'angh'sei. You are nothing to me." He stared at the deep blue eyes, which had not blinked for the longest time. "And besides, this is all academic. Tomorrow's handwriting is already on the wall. All your carefully built networks of power will be for nought if The Dolman cannot be stopped."

T'ung stirred behind him. "Such foolishness is—"

A flicker of Du-Sing's heavy hand stopped him. The blue eyes blinked and within the instant Ronin thought he could detect a hint of some emotion quite foreign to Du-Sing flickering uncertainly in those depths.

"He knows of the Bujun," said T'ung. "I know it. He can tell us—"

"Silence!" roared Du-Sing. "Fool! Do you wish your tongue ripped from your mouth?" He made a great effort to calm himself. "Have Chei send in four men," he said after a time.

T'ung went to the door and spoke softly to a Green standing just outside. When he returned, Du-Sing looked up at him and said: "Now give him his sword."

Ripple like liquid silver. One, then two in the lamplight. Cold and hard and honed. Whistle of curved blades swinging through the air, the hot pungency of sweat and animal fear. Ripple along the periphery of his vision. Light squirting across the double edges of his long blade causing his heart to soar, the adrenalin pumping again, the brain thinking in rapid-fire bursts. Double. Thrust and reverse.

They did not understand, their style was different and adaptation takes time. He did not give it to them. A blade scythed upward at him and he deflected it out and away, reversing simultaneously, his own blade biting into the flesh of the Green behind him on the vicious downswipe. The man cried out as the blood spurted from his side. He stumbled and fell.

Ronin whirled as he felt an ax nick his shoulder, ripping into his robe. His sword thrust forward, scraping along the curving blade, and blue sparks flew. He parried two more blows before lunging in under an oblique swipe, thrusting with the point, spitting a Green through the mid-section. The man went to his knees as Ronin withdrew, his shaking hands clutching at the ooze, trying vainly to stem the flow. The stench of death thickened the air.

He was out of position now and the second man slammed his blade against Ronin's sword and it all but flew from his hands. The ax came at him again and he went to his knees in parrying the jarring blow. His sword flashed again and again but he could not regain his feet, so profuse were the slashes raining upon him. He waited patiently for an opening and when it came, an instant when his opponent reached back to deliver the killing blow which would break through Ronin's defense he used his blade vertically, driving upward with all his strength. He caught the man under the chin, the tip biting deep. He jammed it in, through the throat and into the brain. The body jerked, arms flying out wildly as if the man were attempting to fly. The mouth gaped open and bits of pink and gray spattered out. The corpse convulsed as if trying to throw off a tremendous weight and the ax skittered along the floor.

Ronin ripped his sword through the head and dropped, rolling across the room until his back was against a lacquered bamboo wall. The fourth man moved toward him but T'ung caught him by the arm and, staring at Ronin, said, "He is mine. Stay away."

T'ung advanced on Ronin then, crouching, his gleaming ax blade swinging. He came in low, aiming

217

for the knees, wanting to cripple first and then kill, and Ronin got his own blade down barely in time. As it was, the sickle came away with skin and a film of blood.

T'ung feinted right, came in on the left. The blow was deceptively sluggish and he got in behind Ronin's guard, the crescent of sharp metal rushing toward the collarbone. Ronin was in no position to block the attack so he swatted at the ax with his gauntleted hand.

The blade made contact and T'ung's eyes widened as, instead of slicing through flesh into bone, it was deflected harmlessly.

Ronin saw the look and immediately dropped his sword, lunging for T'ung with the gauntlet. Light spun off the scales as his hand went in. He slammed the right arm to get the ax out of the way and his fist hammered at T'ung's windpipe. The eyes bulged, the tongue came out in reflex and the ax dropped.

T'ung tried to get his hands inside Ronin's arms so that he would have the leverage but Ronin would not let him. The gauntlet, balled into a fist, slammed into T'ung's face and his cheekbone shattered. He screamed and his head twisted. His hands scrabbled along the floor for his ax. The remaining Green moved to give it to him but stopped at a motion from Du-Sing. Again Ronin smote him, visions of the dark alley and the pleading and teeth cracked under the force of the blow, the lower jaw smashed and hanging, eyeless sockets like the gates of hell and a mouth that could not speak, and he drove in again with a kind of black joy and the nose a pulpy mass spread over the crimson face.

Then he was rolling off and grasping the hilt of his sword all in one motion, moving in on the last Green, the balanced weight in his right hand like holding lightning.

And now he moved in, the blade a humming instrument of destruction, hacking at his opponent with the blood singing in his ears and his vision pulsing with the power welling up, shooting through his arms, his skin gleaming with sweat and sea salt, rippling as if a serpent reared beneath his skin.

Terrified, the Green retreated, and then he stumbled, his ax coming up centimeters to the right of where it should have been, and Ronin's blurred blade, pulsing platinum along its length, screamed downward and clove his head in two. The body leapt into the humid air like a speared fish and he whirled, the blur a halo of death surrounding him.

One step, two, the corpse jerked as if it were still alive and as it crumpled to the slick floor Ronin scooped up the fallen silver necklace. He raced for the door and, picking up momentum, crashed into the Green just outside, sending him flying.

Chei came through the door, ax over his head.

Du-Sing made a brief gesture. "Leave him." And then, after a moment, "Close the door and come here."

Chei went through the carnage, stepping carefully across the outflung corpses, thinking of the dangerous man. Crimson dripped along the shining bamboo, beading like bright tears of pain.

Du-Sing rubbed at his eyes with his thick hand, waiting for Chei's return.

"Summon a runner," he said slowly, "and an escort of three Ching Pang. Our best. You will go with them." He stared at the man in front of him. "I wish you to take a message to Lui Wu."

"But, Du-Sing, you cannot mean that you will now—"

"Yes. That is precisely what I mean to do. I am contacting the taipan of the Hung Pang."

"The Reds," breathed Chei, and there was only

wonderment on his face as he gazed upon the cold blue eyes of Du-Sing.

He was not running from the Greens. It was not in his nature and, too, he felt that somehow they were not a danger to him now. Not after what he had seen in Du-Sing's eyes. The man knew of The Dolman, or at least that the war to the north was no longer what it had been for so many centuries.

Nonetheless, he ran through the torpid Sha'angh'sei night, down back streets filled with slumbering families and roaming yellow dogs, skin ribboned with jutting ribs, through the wider thoroughfares where nocturnal revelers staggered and moaned and vomited, sodden with drink and lust and the smoke of the city's notorious pleasure houses, coughing and shaking as with a fever, kissing, pressed together against filthy brick and wood walls, fighting with bleeding fists and crusty knives, locked within the penultimate stages of arguments whose beginnings had already been forgotten. A woman screamed somewhere in the jasmine night, a piercing shriek abruptly cut off, and at last he knew that it did not matter where the sound came from.

And he ran on, his lungs on fire, his legs pumping on their own, desperation sweeping over him as he headed toward Okan Road. His mind was filled with a succession of minute details, words and events and hints which he had absorbed but which had been floating in the back of his mind. Separately, they were meaningless, yet as pieces of a whole they held a terrifying imperative. Oh, Kiri, like a song in his dazzled brain, as he slipped through the crowded labyrinth of streets.

And at last Sha'angh'sei came alive for him, a glowing throbbing entity with a corporeal existence of its own. As he rushed through its sinuous entrails, filled with naked thighs and almond eyes, thrusting breasts and canted hips passing him by, pouting lips, drowsing children and petty thieves sharing the same oblique bars of shadows, comfortable in the blackness, he felt its presence like a lover's body, hot and moist, exciting and frightening, possessive and insatiable, and the mingling of triumph and terror was overwhelming within him.

The Okan Road was perfectly silent in the unlight of predawn, the tall trees still and calm, the night sounds of the city seemingly far away, as if they belonged to another time, some dimly perceived future perhaps, voices chiming in the slow changing of the centuries.

Up the gracefully curving stairway he flew, reaching the top and pounding on the massive yellow doors When they opened, he clutched at the wide-eyed woman, panting, "Kiri, where is she?"

She recognized him of course and stayed the guards who would otherwise have attempted to restrain him, taking him to the room of tawny light and then leaving him hurriedly.

He prowled among the settees and tables, searching anxiously for some wine, but as usual it had all been put away. He turned as the woman came down the staircase.

"She will be with you."

Relief flooded him and he allowed himself to relax somewhat and he opened up his breathing to oxygenate his system.

Then she was on the stairs, slender and lithe, black hair falling around her, and for a moment she seemed to be someone else. Then he gazed into her violet eyes, platinum flecks swimming in their depths.

"What has happened to you?" She came down the

stairs quickly, with an economy of movement. "Are you hurt?"

He glanced down at his torn and bloody robe.

"Hurt? No, I do not think so." He looked up. "Do you know Du-Sing?"

She stared at him. "Where have you heard that name?"

"Greens were waiting for me at the apothecary's. They took me to him."

"Yet you are not dead." She looked surprised. "He thought you had information. But what kind—"

Ronin sighed. "In the alley that evening, when I fought the Greens, remember, I told you—"

She waved a hand, flowing lavender along her nails. "Yes, go on."

"I took a silver chain from around the dead man's neck. It was an impulse only. That was the basis of my altercation with the Greens at the walled city."

"You showed it to them."

"Like a fool. Trying to buy my way into seeing the Council."

"It would be funny if it was not so serious."

"Yes, well—"

"What is the chain's importance?"

"It holds a silver flower. The 'sakura,' Du-Sing called it."

"I—"

He held up a hand. "I will show it to you when there is more time. Right now I must see the woman I brought to you. Moeru."

"But it is so late. I do not want to wake her."

"Kiri—"

She smiled. "All right, but then you must tell me what Du-Sing wanted. And about the man in the alley—"

"Come on," he said.

She led the way upstairs into one of the rooms

222

along the dim corridor. They went in and she lit the lamp on the wooden table beside the wide bed.

She was quite beautiful, he saw now. Stripped of the filth and mud and pain, dusky face in repose, with days and nights of food and rest behind her, Moeru was lovely. Her long oval eyes and wide mouth gave her face the openness of innocence, a child asleep in a distant land.

Kiri bent over her. Her eyes came open and she stared at Ronin. He saw the wild open sea.

"This is the man who saved you, Moeru. Matsu told you about him."

The woman nodded and reached out a slim hand. They had cut and polished her ragged nails and they had already begun to grow shiny and translucent with clear lacquer. She touched his hand, stroked the back of it. He watched her mouth, but the coral lips did not move. Mute from birth, he thought.

"Moeru, I must ask you to do something for me. It is very important. Will you do it?"

She nodded.

"Pull down the bedcovers," he said.

Kiri watched him silently.

Moeru did as she was told. She was naked. Skin like burnished gold. Perhaps a trace of olive. Her body was as beautiful as her face, firm and rounded and sensual.

"Has the bandage been changed?"

"You asked Matsu that it not be," Kiri said.

"Moeru, I will take the bandage off now."

The long blue-green eyes regarded him placidly. She opened her legs.

Ronin reached between them, fingers on her warm thigh. A muscle jumped under her skin at the contact. He pulled carefully at the dirty fabric, a bulge against her inner thigh. He looked at her legs. Apart, they formed the configuration of an inverted V. He lifted the bandage from her thigh. Beneath it, nestled within the cloth, was the man-shaped root.

Moeru stroked her thigh where the bandage had come off, then covered herself.

"She had no wound under the poultice, Ronin," said Kiri.

"Yes, I know. The old apothecary used that as a ruse to hide this." He showed her the root.

"What is it?"

"The root of all good," he said with a laugh. "Or of all evil."

The scream came then, filled with terror and something more, and he bolted out the door with Kiri just behind him. Down the hall he ran, his ears questing ahead for sounds of scuffling. Then he smelled the stench and felt even through the closed door the unutterable cold.

He stopped.

"No," moaned Kiri. "Oh no."

And he did not understand until he had flung the door open and was already within the room. Then the enormity of his error hit him and cursed aloud and, brandishing his sword, slammed the door shut behind him. Kiri pounded on it from the other side. He ignored her, concentrating on the thing in front of him.

It was over three meters in height with thick powerful legs, short, twisted, hoofed. Its upper limbs were much longer, with six-fingered hands tipped by curved talons.

Its head was monstrous. Baleful alien eyes, the orange pupils no more than vertical slits below which protruded obscenely a short curving beak opening and closing spastically. The creature pulsed unsteadily, its outline ebbing and flowing. A tail whipped behind it.

It turned to look at him and a short eerie cry broke from its beak. It threw the remains of what must once

224

have been a man at him, a broken pink and white husk.

Ronin moved easily out of the way but it had Matsu and his stomach contracted again because he should have known. He had been with Matsu, not Kiri, that night when the Makkon came to Tenchō and killed Sa. *Thee,* The Dolman had called in his mind. *Thee.* Thus had he raced to return to Tenchō, less concerned with Du-Sing and the Greens than he was with the revelation that the Makkon had been searching for him that night and that it would surely return soon. He had thought only of Kiri, with whom he had been so much lately, and now he saw the look in Matsu's eyes and his heart cried out in sudden pain.

His lips moved, calling softly her name.

The Makkon cried out again and its taloned fist slammed into her hip and she screamed in pain as her pelvis cracked and white bone pushed itself through her soft flesh.

"Matsu."

Ronin rushed the Makkon now, nauseated by its awful stench, his unprotected face already beginning to numb from its unearthly chill. He yelled reflexively as the pain raced through him, his blade sliding off its scaly hide.

The hideous beak opened and a peculiar sound filled the room, a dreadful laughter, and the thing brushed Ronin aside with a lightning motion, moving toward the open window and the werelight of pre-dawn.

The whistle came then, high-pitched and piercing, echoing in his mind, and the Makkon fell silent. The sound came again, insistent now. The Makkon screamed in fury, wrenched at Matsu's arm, ripping it from its socket, and as Ronin advanced, still dazed from the mighty blow, the thing reached up and slowly, deliberately, tore her throat out, all the pale flesh of her body running red now, and the Makkon threw her at him finally as it went swiftly out the window.

Ronin staggered as she came into his arms. Too late, he thought numbly, why did I not think of the gauntlet? He stared down at her crimson corpse, oblivious to the renewed pounding at the door, did not even turn around when it splintered and flew open.

He knelt in the center of the room, a cold wind blowing over him, cradling all that was left of Matsu. Only when a shadow dropped across his face did he look up to behold Kiri in breastplate of deep yellow lacquered leather, high polished boots, and light leather leggings.

She went straight to the window and looked out. She gasped as she saw through the dawn's deep haze the hideous orange beacons, pulsing, the snapping beak with its thick gray tongue.

The Makkon screamed again.

And Ronin, clutching the chill frame to him as if he could prevent the life from leaking from her, thought of the night he had held her close, feeling the delicious warmth seep into his body, listening to her speak as he watched the slow wheel of the stars in the glowing heavens. Again and again, bound upon a tortuous circlet. Are my feelings so well hidden? Ah, Chill take me.

Surely, he thought, I am a doomed man.

FOUR

·Hart of Darkness·

"Strange," she said, reining in her mount.

To their right the sky was pearled lavender, the sun still but a ghost ascending behind the morning's thick haze. To the north and west it was not yet light.

Their luma snorted and stamped at the earth, eager to be galloping before the wind again. Sha'angh'sei was a sprawl at their backs, a dirty smudge stretching, entangled, to the sea.

They were on a hill burned brown by the sun which overlooked the wide snaking river whose mouth Ronin had glimpsed when first he sailed into port aboard Rikkagin T'ien's ship. It was deep, turbulent in spots, quiet and sluggish in others. It ran out from the edge of the city at seaside almost due north. The Makkon was following its path and they it.

"What is it?" asked Ronin.

She turned to look at him, her long hair trailing across her face.

"The autumn wind is blowing," she said.

He felt the strong gusts, chill and damp, plucking at their cloaks, shivering the lines of tall slender pines.

"What of it?"

There was a curious cast to her face caused perhaps by the oblique light.

"It is," she said softly, "the season of high summer."

"You are going after it and I am coming with you."

He was about to say no but he saw across her visage the play of stormy emotions. She was beyond weeping, her face a white mask of hatred.

"I want to tell you something—" His chest hurt as if he had been struck down.

"There is no need." The sound of bitter tears, the clash of gleaming metal.

"I do not understand. You cannot know—"

"I can and I do." She turned to the window, the budding light strange and spectral still. "Matsu was more than sister to me. More than daughter."

"What then?"

"If I told you, you would think me mad."

They sped through the new day, the light quickening around them like molten metal, the winds of autumn whipping at their cloaks. Kiri's unbound hair swept behind her like the tail of some mythical creature, half animal, half human.

Over the bleak countryside they raced, past the long level fields of marshy plants in precise rows down which myriad kubaru women and men in wide-brimmed straw hats, skirts gathered and tied about their waists, waded, bent almost double as they plucked the raw rice. Along the shooting waters of the river as it sliced ever northward toward the death and destruction of the war, its banks wide and brown with mud and silt, precious minerals thrown up to nourish the far-flung fields.

After the Makkon they flew and Ronin, glancing at Kiri, the noble profile with its firm nose and high cheekbones, failed to notice the movement behind them, as a pursuing luma kept pace with them.

By midday the land had swallowed them and all vestiges of civilization, all habitation and settlement, seemed a thing of the past. The remnants of the alluvial delta which was the source of much of

Sha'angh'sei's material wealth had long since dropped away. The terrain became increasingly dry and rocky, undulating in ever higher waves, like a storm-tossed ocean.

There was little vegetation now. Brown and green plants, scraggy and deformed, grew here and there among the chunky rocks, hanging on tenaciously for whatever nourishment they could find. The earth was drier and coarser and ran before them in a gentle incline, rising higher the farther they got from the sea.

Once, to the east, they spied a long line of soldiers marching northward, a supply train of horses to the rear, horsemen to the front, kicking up long plumes of dust. They spurred their mounts onward and soon left the column far behind.

Sun still shone to the south but overhead and to the north billowing gray clouds were roiling.

"Tell me now what Du-Sing wished from you."

Ronin shrugged. "He wanted something that I could not give him. I know nothing of the sakura."

"And what of the man in the alley?"

"He had been struck by Greens, perhaps four of them, maybe more. I went to his aid."

"What did he look like?"

His head came around and he thought, Ah.

"Now why would you ask that?"

"It is a natural question."

He shook his head. "Not really."

She smiled. "All right. I have a reason. Will you tell me now?"

He contemplated her for a moment, watching her hair brush her cheeks. It reminded him of Matsu. Her hair would—

"He—did not look like the Sha'angh'sei people and he did not look like my people. But it was difficult to see because of the light—"

"His skin was yellow?"

"Yes."

"And his face?"

"Black eyes. High cheekbones."

"Let me see the chain." She took it, saw the silver blossom.

"Bujun." Her breath an explosive sound.

"The Green, T'ung, mentioned that word and would have gone on but Du-Sing cut him off."

"Yes, I imagine he would." She gave the necklace back to him. "The Bujun are the lost race of man, purportedly the greatest warriors and the elite magi during the ages when sorcerous elements formed the primal elements on the world. The sakura is their symbol. It is a flower which is said to grow only on their isle."

"What happened to them?"

"No one knows if they actually exist. The stories of the Bujun dropped away sometime during the sorcerous wars. Perhaps Ama-no-mori was destroyed—"

Ronin started.

"Their island is called Ama-no-mori?"

"The floating kingdom, yes."

"Kiri, the scroll I possess is written in the hand of dor-Sefrith, the most powerful magus of Ama-no-mori."

"Who told you this?"

"A Magic Man from the Freehold. He had been studying ancient codices which told of the scroll. It was confirmed later by a man I met in the City of Ten Thousand Paths, Bonneduce the Last. Dor-Sefrith is Bujun, there is no doubt."

"Then the man in the alley was Bujun also. They still live!" Her violet eyes flashed. "No wonder Du-Sing was so anxious to learn of your involvement. The presence of a Bujun in Sha'angh'sei indicates that their interest in the continent of man will cause the balance of power to change. He wishes the Ching Pang to stay ahead of the Hung Pang."

Ronin nodded.

"Yes, at first. Now I believe he has other concerns; the same as ours."

"What do you mean?"

"Du-Sing could have had me killed at any time, yet he did not. All right, it is obvious that he wanted information from me. But he is a shrewd man and at some point he realized that I knew nothing of the sakura—"

"Why should he believe that?"

"I do not think that he had a choice and he knew it. I told him the truth and he was aware the I would not break. I told him then about the coming of The Dolman. And he knew, Kiri!" He slapped the pomel of his saddle. "The fox knew! You know better than any save Du-Sing himself how extensive his network is. Every caste in Sha'angh'sei is involved with the Ching Pang. He has ten thousand cycs and cars within the city and without. He knows that the war in the north is no longer against the Reds; he understands the rikkagin's anxiety. They fight that which is non-human. You have already seen the Makkon and what it can do to human life. The traditional lines of enmity which have guided the fates of the Greens and the Reds, and thus Sha'angh'sei itself, have broken at last. The forces of The Dolman have come to the continent of man."

They had been traveling along a high platcau and this gave now onto a gorge of red rock and dry dust, their luma leaving a vapor trail drifting high above them as they descended. On the plateau behind them came the sky-blue luma, carrying its slim passenger.

They were well into the gorge now. Far to the right, atop a low bluff beyond the perimeter of the red defile, a last row of green pine trees swayed in the gathering wind. Above them, a flock of gray and brown birds flying high moved swiftly southward before the oncoming clouds. Ronin thought that he could hear them calling to each other in shrill cries of longing, but perhaps it was merely the wind shivering the lonely pines. The desolation of this land lent their presence the symbolic strength of eternal guards at the outpost of man.

They wended their way through the gorge, around huge boulders and stratified shelves of crimson shale until, at length, they found the way rising again onto another plateau.

They reined in and Ronin dismounted, stroking his steed's long neck as he went around it to look at the tracks. It danced impatiently as he knelt, fingers moving in the dust. Unmistakable. The hoofprints of any lesser creature would have been at least partially obliterated by the wind-swept dust. But the signs of the Makkon's passage could not be so easily obscured. At least if it wished to leave a deliberate trail. *Thee*. An echo in his mind. *Thee*.

"Are we gaining?"

He shrugged. "If it wants us to, then we will."

He leaped upon his luma and they took off over the plateau, riding easily, giving their mounts their heads so that they galloped full out. The creatures seemed indefatigable, happiest when they pushed themselves to their limit.

"I would choose the place of battle this time," he called to her over the rushing of the wind and the hard jangle of their riding gear.

"That may not be possible."

"I know that better than anyone."

They were aware that the sun was about to set only when the light abruptly began to fade. It had been diffuse for most of the day, gray and vitiated by the thick tumultuous cloud layers that now enveloped all the sky for as far in every direction as they could see.

The land was colorless and shadowless and they had had for some time the peculiar and disquieting sensation of traveling across an endless dreamscape, that they moved not in kilometers but rather in spirit farther and farther from the familiar world of man into the realm of another kind of life that was both more and less than they.

It was dark in the north already when they reached the far edge of the plateau and so rode downward into a vast valley completely engulfed in shadow. They had descended perhaps halfway when Kiri gasped and strained forward in her saddle. She pointed wordlessly ahead.

Below, rushing toward them as they sped over the rubble-strewn slope, was a field of waving flowers, as white as bleached bones. Then the sweet smell flooded over them like a sticky cataract and they were within the meadow.

"Poppies!" Kiri breathed.

The luma shook their heads and called to each other and they lifted high their legs, careful now because they could not see the earth.

It was a sea through which they plunged, rustling with an infectious insistence, white crests and blue troughs caused by the rippling of the blossoms as the wind swept across their illimitable faces.

At that moment the sun broke through a rent in the clouds at the edge of the sky to the west and the sea was stained a lurid purple. That same singular light illuminated before them a hulking shape, rising up as if from the floor of the ocean, a fearsome, apparition with lambent orange eyes.

Its outline pulsed as it waded heavily toward them, its long arms swinging, the talons cutting dark swaths in the purple sea. The luma screamed in fear and

233

reared, kicking out their forelegs. Their eyes rolled in their sockets and Kiri yelled to him, "Dismount! Dismount before it throws you!"

Into the waving poppies they dropped, up around their waists, Kiri's curving sword already out. He waved her back.

"Your blade will hurt it no more than did mine."

She did not glance at him.

"I must kill it." Voice like frost as she advanced on the Makkon.

Ronin grabbed at her, held her tightly, his face very near hers. She struggled in his embrace.

"Hear me, Kiri. I know how you feel. The Makkon slew my friend. I have fought it before. Mere metal and muscle are useless against it. It is not of this world and therefore not bound by its laws." Still she stared over his shoulder at the shambling monstrosity coming toward them. "Too many have already lost their lives. G'fand, Sa, then Matsu. You will not be the next."

Her violet eyes were glowing coals in the dusk as she looked at him at last.

"This is not a time for reason; that has fled for all time." With an effort she broke away from him but he still stood between her and the Makkon. "I am already half dead," she cried wildly. "Oblivion will be heaven if I can take that foul thing with me!"

She came at him and he hit her then, swiftly and compactly and without warning, striking her along the jaw. Just a ripple of movement. He caught her as she fell, thinking, At least you will not die, and gently laid her down in the purple poppies. They danced, whispering, above her still form.

"You cannot kill it," he said sadly. "And you also mean something to me."

The long sword was a heavy weight around his waist, threatening to pull him to the ocean's floor, and

234

he turned, watching the stumbling rush of the Makkon as he unbuckled the belt. The sword fell beside Kiri.

The creature screamed as it recognized him and he heard the luma away behind him calling nervously to each other as he went out to meet it, out from the shallows into the depths of the sighing sea, the strange blossoms caressing his legs, the rich sweet aroma mingled now with the choking stench of the thing.

He came in under the swift sweep of its arms, his gauntleted hand held before him like a shield. He leapt at the last instant so that his balled fist smashed into its cruelly curved beak. The Makkon howled and he thought that his eardrums had burst. They were hot and blood began to leak from them because of the vibrations but he had opened the beak and was fighting now for leverage, in order to force the gauntlet down its throat.

The howling increased in intensity and he was forced to close his eyes to the terrible slitted orbs which hung before his face like hateful crescent moons in an inimical alien sky.

But now as he struggled for purchase on the scaly hide, needles of pain shot through him like shards of broken glass and tears welled up in his eyes, coursing down his cheeks. The cold was so profound that his legs were already numb as they attempted to climb the alien musculature. He began to shake with the pain and his resolve weakened. The beak ground down against the gauntlet and unless he kept up the thrusting pressure it would slip out and he would be as good as dead. Slowly and purposefully it had stood there and torn out her throat, ripe flesh that he had kissed and stroked ruptured now and gouting red and bits of it flying in his face, the taste of her blood, salt and sticky with spume like sea water, and what are we anyway but salt and phosphorus and water like the ocean? And the hate burned at his core and its heat glowed and grew as he banked the fire with the images, forcing himself to remember the details, her blood in his mouth in an abrupt spray, and he yelled silently, bringing the killing power together within him, and he reached up with his arm, though the pain still shook him and water was in his eyes, forcing the gauntlet farther inside.

Then the Makkon's arms came up across his back, the talons seeking his flesh, trying to pry him from its maw. There was no longer air in his lungs and he subsisted from heartbeat to heartbeat, time taken, molded like putty in some monstrous claw, perverted and realigned so that it no longer bore any resemblance to the concept which ruled his world. His heart pounded and he was Outside, his stomach churning in nausea, his back aflame with pain, his legs hanging uselessly, a cripple, and still he persisted, though the numbness now lapped at his brain, an unstoppable crimson tide, and still he strove, long after his last inhalation, his lungs deflating, pulse surging vainly—And he took the last step, all thoughts but one gone, out into the deep.

From his hip, up through his massive shoulders and along his arm, as unyielding now as a forged metal blade, pushing solely by instinct, reasoning at an end, berserk at last, reduced to pure matter, elevated to pure matter. *Survival!* It bellowed through his brain like a firestorm, battering behind his blind eyes, and a warm rain now washing the lining of his body, emanating from his core, the central vortex of which he mercifully had no understanding, and blue lightning ringing the sky above him, gyring across the opening heavens, something feeding him now and, though he was past knowing it, the shaking fist enclosed within the sanctity of the Makkon gauntlet, scales bright with alien saliva, finally slipped past the spasmodically working tongue, breaching the roof of the creature's mouth, driving with inhuman power upward into its eye cavity.

The vibrations became intolerable and he burst apart then into ten thousand fragments, his hot red flesh drifting upon a cool wind which gusted upward in a tenacious spiral, the serpentine breaching the roiling lavender clouds, away, away . . .

First it was the sweetness and then the darkness.

Night had fallen.

He attempted to rise but he seemed incapable of any movement. All about him the susurrations of the poppies. Above him the nodding bell petals.

He rested, concentrating on his breathing, his mind turning over with curiosity each of his senses. Sight, sound, taste, smell, touch: life.

At length able to move his fingers, then his hand, finally his arm. He attempted to sit up. No movement. He explored, found that he could not feel his feet. It was his back then, where the Makkon had enwrapped him.

He called to Kiri but his voice was a quiet croak in the restless meadow. His throat was dry. He heard movement, above and behind him, and he called out again as loudly as he was able and there was a snort, hesitant, questioning. The sounds of the poppies parting, stalks whooshing, and he longed to look but could not.

A long head and wet muzzle were abruptly over him. His luma. Its blue eyes looked at him with intelligence and he whispered to it softly, wordlessly, a crooning singsong as he had heard its attendant talking to it in Kiri's jeweled garden. The luma moved closer, extending its muzzle. He heard its hoofs very close and felt the columns of its strong forelegs almost touching his head. It opened its wide mouth and licked at his face and then lower so that he could

237

drink its saliva. Then it rested its head against his while he spoke to it again, stroking the side of its head, reassuring it.

After a while he slept and the luma stood over him, watchful in the night, its wide nostrils flared for first scent, its triangular ears twitching to pick up any movement. Several times it called to the mare who stood some meters away, over Kiri's sleeping form.

The luma guarded them through the night. But no one came.

And only Ronin heard, deep within his being, below the dreams that played across his mind, the confused jumble of echoing voices, calling, calling in some desperation now, *Have you found him? You must find him. Yes, I will. But if he does not have it? We are truly lost then. Even if I find him, the Kai-feng still comes. There is little time then, even for us—*

Abruptly, borne on some desolate wind, the voices drop away from him.

The blue morning light woke him. Above him stood the roan luma, its coat a glowing red in the sun's first oblique rays. It shook its head and stamped the poppies beside him. The exhalations from its nostrils were white clouds in the chill air.

Ronin reached up, grabbing for the swinging stirrup, pulled himself hand over hand until he stood on his feet, testing his legs and back. The numbness was gone but his co-ordination was off and he leaned on the luma for a moment, gathering his strength. He walked with its help across the white and blue field to where the golden luma stood over Kiri.

She was still asleep deep within the rustling sea. A large purple bruise swelled along the left side of her forehead.

She awoke as he bent over her and he stepped quickly back, half expecting her to unsheathe her

238

blade and cross swords with him. She was, after all, the Empress of Sha'angh'sei and he had struck her. But she was quite calm.

She broke out food from her saddlebags, feeding the luma before she would eat herself. She offered some to Ronin.

"Against your strong advice, I rushed the Makkon," she said ruefully. "You did not hit me that hard. When I looked it already had you and I struck at it with my sword." She gave him a small smile then. "I did not believe you, I suppose. I thought, well, you are a warrior and—the rikkagin do not approve of women warriors; they are frightened, I think."

Coming against him in the metaled ellipse just below the crust of the surface, his equal perhaps as warrior, who knows, no one ever will now.

"Now you know I told you the truth."

"Oh, but yes!" She reached up and gingerly touched the bruise. "It slapped me, just a backhand swipe of its claw. I have never felt such power. I was flung a good distance away. That is all I remember."

Ronin chewed on his food. "I wounded it," he said.

"But how?"

He lifted the gauntlet so that the strange scales caught the light of dawn.

"With this! Its own hide." He laughed then. "Thank you, Bonneduce the Last, wherever you may now be. A better gift you could not have left me."

He went to pick up his sword and as he buckled the belt around his waist she said, "What now? Where has it gone?"

"Impossible to say. Too much time has already passed for us to attempt to continue to pursue it. Do you know of Kamado?"

"Of course."

"Can you guide us there?"

"It lies north, along the river. I do not think that we shall have a problem finding it."

They rode hard due north, keeping the snaking river on their left, and it was not long before they encountered soldiers streaming northward in long lines, columns bristling with weaponry and machines of war.

They joined this caravan for the last part of their journey, riding swiftly by the soldiers' sides.

Flags fluttered in the wind, the men in leather jerkins and metal helms, armed with long curving swords and bright, finely tipped lances. There were archers, their immense longbows strung vertically on their backs, and cavalry, acting as outriders and scouts, protecting the column's flanks. Metal clanged and jangled and the wooden carts, laden with food and spare arms, creaked under their heavy loads.

They moved up gradually until they reached the horsemen of the rikkagin's retinue who directed them to their commander. He was a sharp-faced man with a long queue and many scars along his desiccated cheeks.

"Are you bound for Kamado?" asked Ronin.

"All are bound for Kamado these days," said the rikkagin darkly. "Or away from it."

"Do you know the Rikkagin T'ien?"

"By name only. There are many rikkagin."

"I have heard that he is at Kamado."

The rikkagin nodded. "Yes. That is my understanding also. You may ride along with my men, if you wish."

"Thank you."

They rode in silence for a time, listening to the wind and the creaking of leather, the clop-clop of hoofs in the dust, the clash of metal.

"You have been to Kamado before?" asked Kiri.

The rikkagin turned his bleak gaze upon her.

"Too often, lady. We were not due back there for

240

another fortnight but the enemy grows stronger each day and we must return now. From whence they come, I cannot say. Nor can anyone else, though we have made strenuous efforts to find out."

"You have learned nothing?" said Kiri.

"Nothing at all," answered the rikkagin. "For none of our scouts have returned."

They caught sight of Kamado just past midday, its dun-colored walls, thick and high and crenellated, dominating the huge hill on which it had been built long ago. The wide river crashed along the left of the fortress and, to the north, it was possible to make out the verdant splash of a forest.

It was truly cold now and the sky had been lowering as they moved farther north. A fine rain had sprung up a short time before but it was freezing, turned to sleet by the unnatural weather, and it hammered now against the soldier's helms, caked the mounts' hides.

They had broken the crest of a rise and, across the last gentle valley the yellow outline of the great fort had come into sight, rising like a spectral city in the wilderness of the bleak landscape.

The stone walls rose upward, an extension of the dusty hill, wider at the bottom. It was roughly circular, with newer extensions to the east and west, rectangular bulges which gave it a peculiar look.

Massive metal-bound doors faced them, guarded by wide outcroppings of the walls along which soldiers constantly patrolled. To the west, the hill dropped away, sweeping down to the water. A wooden bridge with two stone pillars spanned the river at that point. On the far shore, a multitude of tents and pavilions could be seen among which strode many soldiers, some leading horses. Cooking fires were already being started in several places.

The rikkagin halted the column and sent a rider ahead to inform the citadel of their arrival. The man spurred his mount up the slope of the hill, through the thickening sleet, calling out to the guards on the ramparts.

After a brief time he turned in his saddle and signaled the rikkagin who, spurring his horse forward, ordered the column to move out.

With an enormous clash of arms and booted feet, the soldiers marched to the war, trudging in a tired procession through the huge gates of burnished bronze, dwarfed by the towering walls, into the dark and dismal depths of Kamado, the stone citadel.

It was a city unto itself, constructed expressly for the agonies of war; not petty raids or vengeful strikes but centuries of sustained conflict. There was no way of determining this by observing it from outside, where all that was visible were the awesome stone fortifications four and a half meters thick so that men could walk atop the walls, safe behind the stone crenellations. And perhaps this was artfulness also, for it gave no hint at all of the citadel's interior.

Kamado was so vast and so complex in construction that, seated atop his luma just inside the southern postern, Ronin could not discern the far northern limits of the fortress.

Long two-story buildings formed the immediate southern area of the citadel. The walls facing outward were windowless and constructed of stone so that they could not burn should any invader choose to rain liquid fire into Kamado's streets. They were blank, featureless, save for the stains and scars of the years.

However, their appearance changed as one went between them, down the angustate streets. Their inward faces were of wood, with wide beams carved in the shapes of the ancient gods of war, fierce women in

242

high curving helms, attended by dwarfs with curling beards and rings in their noses, from whom the warriors of yore sought advice and favors to assure victory.

Certainly, from this evidence alone, Kamado predated the building of Sha'angh'sei which, Ronin had been told, had sprung up largely because of the rikkagin from other lands. Who then had constructed this fantastic monument to battle? Surely not the Sha'angh'sei people.

All about them as their luma danced gingerly down the dirt streets, the corps of the conflict were to be seen preparing themselves for battle. Grinding wheels sharpened axes and scimitar-bladed swords in a shimmering cascade of cold blue sparks, archers stringing their bows, fletchers gluing feathers to thin wooden shafts that would soon, in their diligent hands, become arrows. Soldiers doubling as stable hands fed and watered horses, wiping at their lathered flanks. Men trotted by them, relief for the soldiers manning the battlements. Up narrow stone stairways they clambered, reaching at last the topmost ramparts.

All about them too were the wounded, a pain-filled world of blood and bandages, of the one-armed and the one-legged, of the eyeless and the scarred. They lay, backs against the wooden pillars or curled in the dust in front of their lost gods of war, who looked down upon them, arrogant and uncaring. Perhaps their rikkagin had not gone before these deities with sufficient humility, perhaps their sacrifices were not great enough, or, more likely, the time of their power had long since been swept from the face of the world. Alone and forgotten, they yet looked out mutely on a domain no longer theirs.

Ronin stopped before one group of wounded men and asked for directions to Rikkagin T'ien's quarters.

They moved on, through inner gates and circular

243

courtyards, along straight avenues and around stone buildings, and at length dismounted before a wooden-fronted barracks. They turned, hearing voices and the heavy tramp of boots.

He saw Tuolin first, his blond hair and height unmistakable in the crowd of soldiers.

"All right, bring him out here."

A group of soldiers with drawn swords emerged from the barracks. Ronin strained to see whom they held prisoner. Slowly, he drifted toward the men, circling to get a better angle. He stopped short.

The man the soldiers escorted, hands bound behind his back, was Rikkagin T'ien. Light gleamed along his hairless head. He stared straight ahead.

At Tuolin's command, T'ien and his guards halted.

"You are Ching Pang, do you deny this?"

"No." Eyes straight ahead.

"You are a spy."

"I am Ching Pang, that is all."

"All?" echoed Tuolin sardonically. "The Ching Pang wish us destroyed."

"We wish only for the freedom of the Sha'angh'sei people."

"And what would they do with this freedom?" Tuolin said contemptuously. "Return to the mud and bamboo hovels of their ancestors?"

"Our ancestors were great once. Greater than your people ever dreamed of becoming."

Tuolin turned abruptly away and, as if that were a signal, the soldiers surrounding T'ien slashed at him simultaneously and in an instant he was but so much dead meat.

"I do not understand this," Ronin said to Kiri. "Rikkagin T'ien a Green?"

"What are you talking about?" She glanced at him. "The Rikkagin T'ien comes toward us now."

"That is Tuolin."

"Yes," she nodded. "And Rikkagin T'ien." She noted the look of puzzlement on his face. "All rikkagin take a second name at the end of their training."

"Then who was the man Tuolin just had executed?"

"Lei'in, the rikkagin's chief adviser." She seemed amused. "And a Ching Pang; Tuolin must be furious."

Ronin was about to tell her of the ruse T'ien had used on him but thought better of it. He wanted to think it through himself now. He recalled the events aboard the rikkagin's vessel. He had not been disarmed when he was brought aboard; he had been kept at ease. When they judged him well enough, he had been interviewed by Lei'in masquerading as the rikkagin. He had been tested. Only then had he been allowed abovedecks into Tuolin's presence. Yes, it made perfect sense now; war breeds its own form of paranoia. It all fitted now, the assassination attempt on the ship, his night out with Tuolin.

The big blond man had seen them now and he seemed unsure whether to scowl or smile, finally opted for a neutral look.

"Did you find the Council of assistance?" he asked Ronin.

"I—never got to see them." Ronin remembered Kiri's warning that Tuolin did not know.

"What a pity," he said without much conviction. He turned to Kiri. "I almost did not recognize you." He glanced down at the sword scabbarded at her left hip. "Can you actually use that or is it for show?"

"What do you think?" Kiri said.

"I think I prefer to see you at Tenchō," Tuolin said quite calmly. "I distrust women on the battlefield."

"Oh, why is that?" She was struggling to control her anger.

"They never seem to know which way to go."

"I do not understand you at all."

He shrugged. "There is nothing to understand. Fighting should be left to those who can do it best. End of discussion."

He turned his attention back to Ronin as if she did not exist. "Why are you here?" He began to walk toward the barracks and they went with him.

"That depends."

"Oh, on what?"

"On whether you think you can trust me yet."

Tuolin threw his head back and laughed.

"Yes, I see." He wiped at his eyes. "I think we can safely say that your time of trial is at an end."

They went up the wooden steps and into the interior. It was dim and cool. The low ceilings were beamed and dark with smoke residue. The furniture was sparse and utilitarian. In the main room of the first story a fire burned on a large stone hearth.

Tuolin led them through this space, filled with soldiers, into a smaller back room, windowless, with a desk of scarred wood, several hard chairs, and a low cabinet against the back wall. At some time previous, the doors had been removed. The rikkagin sat down behind the desk and reached into the cabinet. He offered them cold wine, which they drank.

Ronin wondered briefly about the rikkagin's changed attitude toward Kiri, then put it out of his mind.

"Sa was killed, then Matsu, by a creature whom I had fought in my own land. It came north out of Sha'angh'sei. It was waiting for me in the poppy fields half a day's ride south of here." He paused. "You do not seem surprised."

"My friend, many things have transpired since first we met. I have seen many sights, battled foes I could not have dreamed of in my worst nightmares." He gestured at the walls. "We fight non-men." He sighed

"Not many here remember the things spawned by the sorcerous wars."

"I do not think that these creatures are connected with that time."

Tuolin drained his cup and poured himself more wine without offering them more. He waved the cup. "No matter. These men are not cowards; for most, fighting is all they know. But they are used to foes who bleed when they are cut; give them an enemy that they can see and kill. But this—" The wine sloshed over the cup's rim and onto the desk. He ignored it. "We are losing this battle."

Ronin leaned forward. "Tuolin, this creature, the Makkon, is an emissary of The Dolman. Do you remember? I told you—" The rikkagin waved his cup at him. "There are four Makkon and it is imperative that I kill at least one before they can all gather."

"Why?"

"Because when the four come together they will summon The Dolman and then, I fear, it will be too late for all of us."

"You have already fought one of these—Makkon?"

"Yes, more than once. But this last time I was able to injure it. With this—" He held up the scaled gauntlet. "Tuolin, it cannot be harmed with ordinary weapons. But this is made of its own hide. I hurt it but it almost killed me."

The rikkagin ran a hand over his eyes and Ronin became aware of the new lines of fatigue etched into his face.

"The Makkon is likely here then."

"I must find it," said Ronin.

"All right." Tuolin pulled at the ivory bar which pierced one ear lobe. "We must cross to the field encampment. There we will be most likely to find news of your Makkon.

"I am pleased that you believe me."

247

The big man sighed. "I have spent too much time with the dead and dying not to," he said wearily.

The dusty streets of Kamado were filled with the din of hoarse shouting, the clang of iron against heated iron, the snort and stamp of war horses, the moans of the injured, the tramp of booted feet.

They went out through the southern postern, escorted by soldiers as far as the bridge.

Dark thunderheads were piling up in the northwest, writhing their way rapidly southward. The wind had died and the air was leaden and chill. The moist land steamed whitely.

They moved as swiftly as they could across the wooden planks, hands gripping the rope sides. Ronin peered down into the frothy depths, catching an occasional glimpse of glistening black rocks and sleek leaping fish.

To the south, the land was brown and barren, as if blasted by intense heat. Off to their right, almost due north, lay the encampment with its rows of tents and bright pavilions, lines of tethered horses and bright flickering fires, like silent insects, around which the shadows of the soldiers darted.

The encampment was on the near edge of an undulating meadow of high green grass perhaps a third of a kilometer wide, beyond which began the first low bushes and wide trees of the forest Ronin had seen as they approached the fortress. Now, as they neared the far shore, he could see that the forest was immensely thick, the tree trunks so tall and the numerous branches so heavily foliaged that it appeared to be a solid wall of green.

Soldiers met them as they stepped off the bridge. Tuolin ordered them to take them to Rikkagin Wo's pavilion. They went into the high grass. Fireflies swept the twilight with minute arcs of cool light. The meadow rustled in the wind and cicadas chirruped. Everything was steeped in deep blue except the far-off forest, cloaked in black shadows, pooling and impenetrable.

The pavilion was striped bright yellow and blue, its canvas walls quiescent now as what little breeze there was died. Lamps were being lit throughout the encampment. Wood smoke and charcoaled meat were the dominant scents which came to them.

Within, it was warm and bright from a multitude of lamps. Shadows danced along the insubstantial walls as soldiers went to and fro, preparing for battle. An almost constant stream of runners came and went, depositing and receiving coded messages on slips of rice paper.

Tuolin led them a seemingly circuitous path through the disciplined confusion toward a tall man who broke abruptly into their field of vision. He had dark hair which he wore long and loose and a thin pinched mouth. His chin thrust forward. He turned and gazed at Tuolin as they approached.

"Ah, T'ien, has Hui arrived with his troops?"

"Yes, just before sunset."

"Good. We need every man."

Rikkagin Wo took a slip of paper from a runner, went a few paces away, nearer a light and farther from them. He read the message, went to his desk, and wrote several characters with his quill. He gave the slip back to the runner, who left.

He turned back to Tuolin. "We lost another patrol this afternoon."

"Where?"

"Due north. In the forest."

"How many?"

"Thirteen. Only one came back." Wo looked disgusted. "And he is no good to us. Raving like a lunatic."

"What did he say?"

Wo took another message. He did not look up. "I cannot remember. Ask Le'ehu, if you wish. I would not bother myself."

Tuolin, with Ronin's urgings, sought out a heavy squat individual with his black hair in a queue, fat cheeks and long glittering eyes.

"Le'ehu drew them to the side, against the canvas, where few passed close to them.

"He is gone now, the last soldier." He paused, his eyes on Ronin and Kiri.

Tuolin patted his arm. "Go on, these two will not pass on what you say."

"All right, it is just that"—he rubbed at his upper lip, which had begun to sweat—"I killed him, you know, in the end." The glittery eyes glanced quickly around. "I mean he was dying anyway and he pleaded with me. He could not bear to live another moment, after what he had seen—"

"What attacked the patrol?" asked Ronin.

Le'ehu looked startled. "How—how did you know? How did he know, T'ien?"

"Know what?" asked Tuolin.

"He knew a 'what' attacked the patrol."

"Did the man describe it?" asked the blond man patiently.

"Yes, curse him. I will not sleep this night. It was huge with great claws and a nightmare face. It ripped out their throats, he said."

"The Makkon," Ronin said and Tuolin nodded.

"In the forest?"

"Yes." The man tried to swallow. "Over the meadow's ridge, perhaps a kilometer into that cursed place—"

They were silent, waiting for him to continue. Le'ehu stared over their shoulders at the fluttering shadows along the far side of the pavilion.

250

"What else?" Tuolin said very gently.

"It was not of that creature that he talked before he died." The words came out of him reluctantly now, as if by saying this aloud he might conjure up terrifying creatures. "Something came in that thing's wake."

"Another one?" asked Ronin.

Le'ehu's head snapped around. "Another—? Oh no. No, it was, I do not know, something else. There was whirling fog, he said, and blood raining in the melee. He caught a glimpse only—"

"And," prompted Tuolin.

Le'ehu swallowed again.

"Rikkagin—he said it was the Hart—"

"Oh, come on," Tuolin snorted.

"Rikkagin, he bade me kill him," the squat man said miserably. "I do not think that otherwise—"

"The Hart is but legend, Le'ehu, a foul—"

"What legend?" asked Ronin.

"The tale is told," said Tuolin, "of the Hart. He is half man and half beast."

"That is all?"

Tuolin stared at Le'ehu, who winced at his words. "Some say that he is evil incarnate. And others suggest that he was once a whole man, transmogrified, forced now to serve a sorcerous liege, fighting those who are really his kin."

"Whatever is truth," said the squat man, "that soldier believed that he saw it"—he turned his head—"out there. In the forest."

Ronin turned to Tuolin.

"I care not for legends. The Makkon is my only concern. At first light I must go into the wood and destroy it—"

Le'ehu's eyes bulged. "Surely you must be mad. The Hart—"

"Be silent," snapped Tuolin. "We are confronted with enough real monstrosities without you fabricating nightmares." He swung his gaze toward Ronin and his tone softened. "You cannot mean to go alone. I will accompany you."

Ronin shook his head.

"You will not be able to help. I require two men who know this area. When I find it I will send them away."

The big man put a hand on his shoulder.

"My friend, I have done many things for you. Fished you out of the sea when you were half dead, introduced you to Tenchō. It is time now to repay me. I want to see this Makkon for myself." His grip tightened. "I must know the enemy, can you understand that?"

Ronin searched the cerulean eyes and nodded. "Yes, that is something that I can accept."

Le'ehu stared from one to the other, backing off.

"You are both mad! You—"

A stifled yell. The clash of metal against metal.

They all turned at the sounds. Boots pounded outside and there came now confused shouts.

"Quickly," Tuolin said. "Outside."

The heavy darkness of the massive forest seemed to have pervaded the meadow. The fireflies were gone. Above the waving grass now rolled an oncoming tide of black shadows.

They came swiftly and silently, without the telltale gleam of metal. Somehow they had pierced the perimeter of the encampment without an alarm being sounded.

They were like tree trunks, dark, with wide shoulders and thick legs. Their long beards and wiry hair were greased and plaited. Their faces were moon-shaped and perfectly flat as if evolution had decreed to their ancestors that the protrusions of nose and cheeks and forehead were superfluous. They seemed more animated creatures from the wall paintings in

Kiri's palace than true men. Yet they were real enough, brandishing wide scimitars of an unreflective metal that was almost black with bell-shaped fist guards.

Behind them loomed other shadows, coalescing slowly in the dark, impossibly tall and bony, their skin pallid gray, their faces desiccated and fleshless, their skulls gleaming in their nakedness. These creatures strode behind their fellow warriors, swinging heavy short chains ending in fanged iron spheres. Ronin caught the sound of their brief hissing arcs in the close air.

Tuolin unsheathed his sword as did Ronin and Kiri. All about them were confusion and disarray as soldiers scrambled for their weapons. Fires guttered and flickered out as if by a strong wind, although the air was calm.

Mist rolled in, sweeping through the meadow and into the encampment, and there was a choking stench as the enemy advanced, the first wave already past the hapless outer patrols. The scimitars swung darkly in whooshing arcs, cleaving a hideous harvest in this sorcerous high summer.

Still within the long grass, the gaunt warriors whirled their chains, the deadly globes hissing in the night like locusts, crushing flesh and bone indiscriminately, and the groans of the dying mingled with the wet slap and crunch of the reaving.

Ronin leapt forward with a cry and his blade swept to and fro in mighty two-handed slashes, ripping into the torsos of those wide men closest to him. They squealed and backed into each other, bewildered, and he stepped into their midst, using oblique blows now, slicing into the juncture of neck and collarbone of one warrior, withdrawing his sword and, in the same motion, decapitating another.

Beside him came Tuolin and Kiri, hacking at the

warriors as if they were wild foliage. He concentrated, moving slowly forward, his blade singing its fiery song of death, gleaming, running with blood. He hammered at them without letup, his heart thudding in his chest, his arms electric with the power of the destruction he was reaping, no longer conscious of the peripheral sights and sounds of the night; he was intent, content as he hammered at them, severing bodies which convulsed and spurted their liquids hotly about his swaying form. His muscles rippled and glistened with a fine film of sweat, beaded with sprays of his enemies' blood and entrails, and he grinned in savage delight. He clove a warrior from shoulder to ribcage on a forward swing, slashed into the mid-section of another on his backward arc.

Near him, Kiri was nearly disemboweled as she watched horrified and fascinated. She parried at the last instant and turned her face away from him, working at her own task.

At their backs, they heard Rikkagin Wo's voice lifted in sharp command. Men ran everywhere, attempting to form themselves into defense lines, but it seemed useless; the warriors moved inexorably forward. The mist rolled past them and over the soldiers, burning their calves with cold. And more of the gaunt warriors appeared as their shorter compatriots fell beneath the swords of the soldiers. These were destroying the rikkagin's men with terrifying expertise. They carried round iron shields, in addition to their weapons, which seemed much too heavy for any man to wield effectively yet these warded off most of the soldiers' blows while, with their other hands, the fanged spheres described their tight orbits, exploding with terrible impact.

Ronin felt himself ingulfed in a dark tide, no longer an individual, another piece of floating flotsam carried along by the undertow. He fought and the warriors fell before his blurred blade like wheat before a scythe but always there were others to take the place of the fallen, as if in each individual's death two more were created.

Onward he waded, the footing unsure and gluey with the innards of the fallen as he made his laborious way out into the meadow to meet the gaunt death-head warriors. Tuolin and Kiri were just behind him. The rikkagin's great blade lifted and fell and in his left hand was the emerald-hilted dirk with which he slashed and parried. For her part, the Empress was using her sword with consummate skill. Her breast-plate was shiny, sodden with blood and splattered gore, her black hair had slipped its bonds and now whirled about her, a dark mantle.

With an enormous swipe that ripped apart a barrel chest, Ronin went through the outer fringes of the wide warriors and for the first time in many moments there was space around him. The still air was alive with the harsh whisper of the globes. The last of the soldiers went down, his head smashed open like a ripe fruit, and he peered into the roiling night at the grinning faces, as white now in the guttering firelight as the pallid poppies. Their sunken eyes were featureless holes with no discernible trace of iris or pupil; their heads turned on their spindly spines as they looked about them.

Ronin lifted his blade and went in quickly, driving it down in a blur, through the collarbone of one of the warriors. The neck was severed and the head flew from the bony shoulders. There was no blood but a shower of gray dust which plumed momentarily, spitting shards of vertebrae from its periphery. The de-capitated torso came at him, its arm still lifted, the fanged globe whirring, and he was obliged to duck the blow that came. A hissing passed over him as he crouched and the creature, shuddering now, stumbled on its nerveless legs and collapsed.

At that moment he felt a titanic wrench and his blade went spinning to the sodden ground. He lurched forward and almost fell on top of the gaunt corpse. He turned, saw another deathhead warrior whipping back the globe that had slammed into his sword. It advanced upon him, the deadly sphere a menacing blur.

The creature leaned back and the globe came at him with such speed that its fangs grazed his cheek even as he jerked away. He risked a glance downward, saw that he was too far from his sword to risk lunging for it and the gaunt warrior was circling so that he was now between Ronin and the weapon.

Ronin turned his body sideways, waited for the next swing, counting to himself so that the timing would be perfect. The globe glistened as it came at him and he was away, counting again to be certain of the rhythm. He timed his dive to coincide with the peak of its arc away from him to give himself the maximum amount of time.

He hit the ground and rolled onto the warrior he had just slain, his fingers scrabbling along the moist earth for the chain and globe. The long grass made it difficult to locate but his peripheral vision had picked up where it had fallen when the warrior fell and now he had it and he was rolling. He regained his feet and went down immediately to avoid the globe.

Whir. The other's weapon was circling again and he swung his own globe, gaining momentum, but the fangs loomed at him without warning and he had time but to throw up his globe reflexively. The chains clashed, momentum taking the globes and whipping them around as the chain entwined.

The gaunt warrior pulled viciously and Ronin, caught off balance, was jerked forward, slamming into his adversary. The skeletal figure bent and the head

256

darted toward him, the mouth opening impossibly wide. Filed yellow teeth, long and ragged, snapped hideously at his face and he writhed away just in time. The clashing jaws pursued him as he attempted to disengage himself. But to break free now was to lose his only weapon. Snap, snap. The neck, long and willowy, brought the fangs at him again and again.

Still holding onto the chain, Ronin brought his left hand up and, balling the Makkon gauntlet into a fist, he smashed upward into the working mouth. Shards of fractured teeth rained upon them both and Ronin punched once more and the thing let go his weapon, bringing his shield up with both hands.

Ronin whirled the spiked globe and aimed it. The bony skull caved in, the entire left side crushed, and the thing went down on its bony knees. Ronin hit it again and the warrior keeled over as its knees splintered and the bones in its legs cracked.

Ronin ran for his sword then, dropping the chain and globe and, grasping it, turned back into the fray. The soldiers were dying under the assault of the deathhead warriors.

He heard Tuolin's shout and, looking around, he located the tall rikkagin. He moved off in this direction, dodging hissing spheres. He saw Kiri fighting at Tuolin's side.

"We cannot hold against them, Ronin," he panted as he hacked at a skeletal figure. "The encampment is routed, I fear. We must find Wo and marshal the remaining men in a retreat to Kamado."

Ronin looked about them. The gaunt warriors were advancing steadily and were now within the perimeter of the pavilions. The moans of the dying were in his ears as he retreated with Tuolin and Kiri back to the pavilions, slashing at their foes with each step. Firelight blazed up briefly and he saw a tent bursting into flames. There were screams from soldiers trapped inside.

The night was streaked with yellow and orange and heat danced in waves, alternating with the chill. The earth steamed whitely until they could no longer see their boots. Kiri slipped and fell over a body, her head cracked against a skull, and when she lifted her face, her forehead was black and shiny with blood. Ronin lifted her, her hand grasping his arm, and they went on, through the narrow dark lanes between the canvas walls, ducking flames, hacking at the wide warriors who blocked their way. The ground was muddy with viscous liquids and soft things squished under the soles of their boots. More pavilions began to smoke and crackle with flame.

Just ahead of them, the green canvas wall of a pavilion bulged and ripped open, three men tumbling through, slashing at each other. A wide warrior hit the ground at a bad angle and his neck snapped. At the same instant a deathhead warrior swung his globe, smashing the breastbone of the soldier, who moaned and folded in upon himself.

Ronin's blade struck off the head of the gaunt warrior and the skeleton body crashed backward into the pavilion's interior.

They went on, Tuolin leading them now, searching through the frenzy for the yellow and blue pavilion, picking their way through the grisly litter stewn across the earth like stinking loam.

It was already in flames when they reached it, sheets of orange sparks cracking open the night. They swept aside the burning walls and went in, finding Rikkagin Wo armless, his shoulder sockets crimson. White bones protruded pinkly. One side of his head was a pool of blood and pulpy matter. His face was untouched.

Tuolin took them out of the burning pavilion. A

shower of bright sparks fell along their shoulders. Outside, the night had heated up. Flames crackled everywhere. They ran into a pack of the wide warriors and slew them. They backed away from Ronin and he went after them, back into the torched pavilions, and Tuolin was obliged to take him by the shoulder and turn him around. More of the deathhead warriors were arriving.

"We have lost the field this night, Ronin," he said. "We must return to the fortress."

They went out of the encampment, the earth once again firm beneath their feet, along the black and deserted road leading to the bridge. Blood rolled off them like black rain. They were numb and sick at heart. Onto the bridge, the screams and crunchings following them like living creatures. No other sound could be heard. No insect trilled; no bird called to its mate.

A wind had sprung up from the northwest, chilling, plucking at their sodden cloaks, twanging the ropes on the bridge. Below them, the water whooshed by, pale, ribboning in the gloom, swirling against the black rocks.

It was quieter now and the night lit up as they passed a stand of tall firs and the illumination of the flames reached them again. And Ronin was singing all at once at the shadows looming grayly between them and the sanctuary of Kamado. They had been waiting for retreating soldiers, standing in the shadows midway across the bridge. Only the flickering firelight had betrayed them and the night was abruptly filled again with the hiss and whir of the fanged globes. One gaunt warrior swung into Tuolin's side before he had a chance to react. Ronin heard his sharp exhalation like a dull explosion as he swung in a short oblique arc, severing the chain. The rikkagin clutched at his bleeding side, leaning on the guide ropes along the bridge's edge. His legs began to buckle and blood oozed through his fingers.

Kiri moved in front of the big man, slashing within the guard of a warrior, her blade sinking into its narrow chest. Its head weaved on its long neck and it threw its shield at her. It slammed into her shoulder as she attempted to twist away, caroming over the side of the bridge, its flight a dull booming in their ears. She staggered and her guard came down and the wounded warrior launched his globe.

Two of the warriors pressed Ronin back, attempting to split him off from the other two, but he counterattacked, his blade blurring whitely, lashing out at the two globes filling the air around him like flying creatures.

Tuolin was panting, his face a pale mask of pain. He tried to lift his blade. Sweat broke out on his face with the effort.

Near him, Kiri pressed her attack, rolling to avoid the warrior's blow, leaping up and slamming her boots into its stomach. She swung at him, two-handed, her feet wide apart and planted firmly, swinging up, from the hip, the power traveling into her shoulders, along her arms, the momentum flashing the blade in the night. It clove into the warrior's skull, down from the cranium into the blackness of its eye, crashing at length into the roof of its mouth. The skull flew apart like a shell, the bone fragments whirring and pattering around her. The body folded and went down heavily.

She turned then, eyes flashing, and in one long beautiful sweep of her sword cut through the torso of one of Ronin's foes. The head swiveled even as she began to withdraw the blade and the gnashing mouth reached for her. Startled, she stepped back and almost fell off the slickened verge of the bridge. The teeth clashed together as the torso fell at her feet.

Ronin swept aside the whistling sphere, timing it

perfectly so that he deflected its flight back into the warrior's face. As it jerked desperately away from the oncoming globe, its head whipped directly into the path of Ronin's extended blade, flying apart in a gray flurry of bone and dust.

Another deathhead came at Kiri and she calmly cut its legs under it. Ronin saw her wince with the blow. With a second swipe, she sent the collapsing body over the brink, a bony blur cartwheeling out of sight. But she was spent now, the blow from the heavy iron shield taking its toll, and she stood, gasping, leaning on her sword while her thighs trembled with fatigue.

Ronin heard a grunt and swung around. The last of the gaunt warriors had taken his severed chain and had wrapped it around Tuolin's neck, the silvered links biting into his flesh. The inconstant light of the flames played over their struggling bodies, the one wiry and stooped now, yellow as old bone, the other twisting in pain, dark with running blood. The rikkagin's eyes bulged and his empty hands scrabbled uselessly at the metal links tightening about his throat. Blood pooled at his feet.

Ronin leapt at the thing, grasping its wide shoulders, attempting to wrest it away from Tuolin. The head swiveled and the jaws gaped, snapping at him. He raised his sword but he lacked the room to use it and he could not step away and attack the warrior for fear of cutting the big man.

The creature's head snaked forward while he was thus debating and caught the blade in its mouth, the teeth gripping it so that Ronin could not pull it away. Still the warrior heaved on the chain and Tuolin sagged, choking on his own exhalations as his lungs vainly strove for air. His knees buckled and the death-head warrior pulled mightily on the chain, the grinding sound of the links tightening unnaturally loud in the night.

Only Ronin's left hand was free, his right was trapped on the hilt of his blade and he dared not let go. He brought the hand up, using the thumb at his opponent's neck, pressing in through the small space under his horizontal sword. Just above the base of the neck, he located the triangular soft spot and lunged inward, puncturing the throat. Fetid gas swirled at him and he gasped, turning his head away, ripping upward along the stalklike neck with his thumb. The long teeth rattled against the smooth metal of his blade and the grip of the powerful jaws loosened as the thing tried to regain its breath. He drove inward then, using the full weight of his body through his right hand, and the keen edge of his blade swept before him, unstoppable, shearing through the warrior's skull.

Ronin slammed the corpse aside, working frantically on the chain still tightly bound around Tuolin's throat. The bony hands refused to relinquish their hold on the links, though the body was half slumped over the side of the bridge. And Ronin pried at the fingers, staring into the rikkagin's pinched face. His skin had a blue tinge around the eyes.

Kiri was there, then, using a small curved knife to slash at the clenched bones, shearing through the knuckles until one by one they came apart. With a harsh grate, the links slid back slowly as Ronin forced the chain from around the big man's neck. He caught him as he fell.

It had begun to snow, the large white flakes sheeting down obliquely, dusting the corpses on the bridge, their faces white masks already, sparkling in the flickering glow from the encampment. They hissed in the flames and Kiri shuddered, thinking of the spinning fanged globes.

She turned, holding her left arm to her side, tucked

in, using her hipbone as support for the weight to ease the pain in her shoulder.

Ronin sheathed his sword and scooped Tuolin into his arms.

"Now, Kiri," he called, pushing her before him. They sprinted across the remaining expanse of the bridge and onto the high road stretching uphill to Kamado.

They were met by soldiers who escorted them to the towering walls, calling to the guards at the postern. The metal-bound gates creaked open just enough for them to slip through. Then they swung shut with an echoing clang.

There was an immediate tumult around them. Ronin delivered up the rikkagin into the hands of his men, his neck torn and black with terrible marks, his shirt and leggings dripping blood; they bore him away to his barracks. Ronin followed, his arm around Kiri as she struggled against unconsciousness. He declined the soldiers' aid but when he stumbled they took her from him and two of them lifted her up the barracks steps and through the entrance. Ronin sank down on the steep steps, too weary to go any farther.

After a time a man came out of the barracks and sat down beside him.

"He almost died."

He was tall and wide-shouldered, with graying hair and a full but close-cut beard. His nose was long and curving; his eyes were black.

"T'ien's own physician is inside if you need attention."

"I am tired," said Ronin. "That is all."

"Perhaps he had better see you anyway."

He called for the physician, who came out and grunted when he saw Ronin. He was the one from aboard Tuolin's ship. While he worked, the other said, "Good for us that he did not die, eh?" Then, more softly, "What is your name?"

"Ronin."

"I am Rikkagin Aerant."

"Ronin leaned his head against the wooden banister. The ancient gods of war, carved into the columns, looked blankly out at the darkness.

"You saved his life."

"What?" There was a stinging along his shoulders.

"Tuolin told me that you saved—"

"Do you always call him by his other name?"

"We are brothers."

Ronin turned his head. "You hardly look it." The physician finished tying the bandages. He went back inside.

"We had different fathers."

"I see." He thought of nothing.

"I can help you."

Ronin ran a hand over his face. "How?"

"Tell me what happened."

Rikkagin Aerant nodded his head as Ronin related the events in the encampment.

"Best that Wo is dead, truly. His mind was closed to this war; he was so used to fighting Reds and the northern tribes that he could not see that the war had changed."

"How could he explain the warriors who do not bleed?"

Rikkagin Aerant shrugged. "The military mind can rationalize any situation. He lacked imagination." He brushed at his leggings. "Pity. He was a fine leader."

"He was unprepared for that attack."

"Yes. I would dearly like to know how they got through the perimeter so easily."

"Tuolin told you—"

His face was bright in the torchlight. "Yes. I have seen this thing which you have fought."

"You told Wo?"

Rikkagin Aerant laughed shortly. "I told no one but Tuolin and even he——" His eyes were like cool crystal, they were open and keenly intelligent. "You know, even brothers do not love each other all the time."

"He wanted to go with me."

"He will not have that now." Several sentries ran by, their boots echoing against the wooden walls. The snow had ceased for the moment, but the sky was low and the air felt heavy and damp. "It is best that way."

"Do you wish to go?"

Rikkagin Aerant turned his head away. A dog barked along the next block of barracks. "I do not know. But it does not matter. I am needed here. I will send you two Reds. They were born in this region."

"All right."

He stood up, his eyes dark and unreadable as he stared down at Ronin.

"Perhaps you will return."

He went off down the muddy street.

Snow fell quietly along the rampants, dampening the scrape of the guard's high boots against the stone. It pattered about him, obscurring the last dying embers sparking in the ashes of the encampment, a wan carpet humped along the earth, hiding the bodies of the fallen combatants.

It was still in Kamado save for the crunch of an occasional group of soldiers on patrol. Soft voices floated up to him for a moment then were gone in the hissing of the snow. He pulled his cloak closer about his shoulders. The pain there was lessening. He willed his mind to be blank, not wanting to anticipate.

He saw Kiri walking along the ramparts, searching for him. He called wordlessly to her.

"How is your shoulder?" he asked.

265

"Better." She sat beside him. "The bone was knocked out of the socket. He is very good." She meant the physician.

He nodded into the night.

She put a hand along his arm, ran it upward. "There is a room in the barracks."

"I do not think so."

"I will return to Sha'angh'sei at dawn. I must talk to Du-Sing. The Greens and Reds must unite now."

"Yes."

"And you must go into the forest at first light." Her breath ran in warm white puffs against the side of his face. "Why not?"

He looked into her face. "You have changed."

He did not know what he expected to see there but he was surprised. She looked humiliated, her cheeks flushing pink.

"Of course. Matsu is dead. I am half a person now, not fit to be with." She got up and went away from him, along the white escarpment of the high rampart, disappearing down the steep stairs.

Dawn was a blood-red smear, burning coldly through a long rent in the massed gray clouds, pink-edged and pearled now in the east where the bloated oblate disk of the sun rose with agonizing deliberation.

He watched the light come into the world, atop the southern rampart where he had stayed all the long night. The snow had stopped falling just before first light and this day seemed somehow more natural than the last.

Ronin stood up, breathing deeply the chill air, and stretched his cramped muscles. He peered southward along the barren trail, completely white now. Higher up the snow was pink. He could pick out no imprints and the sparse foliage and his angle of elevation made it clear to him that the way was clear back to Sha'-angh'sei.

He went down to the barracks. Two short men with long queues and black almond eyes waited patiently for him. A soldier came down the steps with a steaming cup of tea. He took it gratefully and sipped it, savoring its warmth and spice. He declined the bowl of rice.

Kiri was already at the stables. She saddled her luma silently, running her hand constantly down its flanks. His luma snorted and beat its hoofs against the earth as he came in. Straw floated through the air.

She mounted the animal and it pranced in its desire to be away. She pulled hard on the reins to keep it in check. It called to the roan, a plaintive farewell touched with the exultation of the wind and the road, and Kiri pulled again on the reins.

She took the luma out from the stable, Ronin at her side. They went along the quiet streets, the mount's clop-clop muffled by the carpet of snow. The luma's head bobbed as it sniffed the cold air, plumes of smoke shooting from its wide nostrils. Its ears twitched and Kiri spoke to it softly, a singsong litany.

At the southern postern she drew up and he pulled her down to him, kissing her cheek.

"Kill it," she said in his ear with a sob. "Kill it before I return."

And she dug her boot heels into the luma's flanks, rattling the reins, and it leaped through the parted gates, a saffron streak, out from the citadel, onto the long white road home.

The silence was like a clap of thunder, lapping at his eardrums with an unnatural proximity. Deep in the forest, the snowfall was but a light dusting because of the canopy of thick branches overhead. He was stuck by their austere beauty, frosted white across their interlacing upper surfaces, the spreading undersides a deep green shading into black among the blue shadows.

The quietude was extraordinary. If he ceased to move, he could hear the hissing of his own breath and, somewhat farther away, the inhalations and exhalations of the two Reds.

With a shivery rustle, a miniature snowslide fell from a branch and Ronin instinctively looked up. The wide green bough with its sweet-smelling needles bobbed and a flash of deep scarlet flew off in a flutter.

They were in a minute clearing but even so the sky was entirely obscured. Within the tall stands of pines, beds of fragrant brown needles cushioned the forest floor. The frozen earth was hard near the ancient twisting oaks with their entwining networks of branches and the profusion of oval leaves.

They moved deeper into the forest, Ronin carefully imitating the Red's slow, deliberate movements, creating a minimum of disturbance. The way was so entangled that more often than not they were forced to go single file, turning their bodies sideways in order to move through the narrow gap between the trees.

He became aware that they were on an incline and, as the way became steeper, granite outcroppings began to appear. Soon they crested the rise and the forest floor fell away from them. Off to their left, they could make out the clatter of a stream. Black birds flew among the laden branches, calling in shrill staccato cries, sending occasional showers of powdery snow onto the earth about them. There was little underbrush, only green moss and a grayish-blue lichen which clung to the rock faces.

They saw no tracks that morning and Yuan, one of the Reds, sent his companion off on a tangent.

"Perhaps we will have better luck this way," he said to Ronin.

They went ever north, the forest unchanging in its denseness. Once Yuan halted and pointed to their right. Ronin saw a red fox, long tail sweeping the ground as it ran from them.

Just past noon the Red signaled to him and, crouching, he moved from tree to tree as silently as he was able until he was next to the kneeling man.

Yuan whispered in his ear and Ronin looked through a stand of thick oak. There was movement and he inched closer, changing his angle of vision. On the other side of the trees were perhaps a dozen of the gaunt deathhead warriors, shields on arms, fanged globes swaying at their hips as they marched. Beside them strode a score or more men with straight black hair combed back into a queue. They had black almond eyes. They were armed with the single-edged curving swords and short-hafted axes identical to Yuan's. Another man came into view and he started. Eyes like stones magnified in still water, long drooping mustache. He would not forget that face. Po, the embittered trader who had walked out of Llowan's dinner party.

Ronin touched Yuan on the shoulder and they moved back from the oaks.

"Who are the men with the tall ones?" Ronin asked softly.

"Reds."

"Why are they with the enemy?"

"They hate the Greens. That is an old hate. The tall ones promise them power in Sha'angh'sei where the Greens are supreme in exchange for their aid here in the north."

"They would battle their own kind; join forces with those that are not men?"

"Power is strange, is it not?" said Yuan.

"Yet they will die along with us, if this enemy is victorious."

The other stared at him. "Do you think that you could convince them of this?"

Ronin thought of Po's outburst. He shook his head.

The afternoon waned as they searched vainly for any trace of the Makkon. Near dusk they gave it up and Yuan led them back to the clearing where they had arranged to rendezvous with the other Red.

"We can only trust that Li had better luck," said Yuan.

The clearing was darkling when they arrived, the snow blue, the shadows bluer still. Across the small open space a tree loomed in the dusk, lumped and misshapen. Yuan went and stood in front of the tree. Ronin went slowly after him, his eyes raking the shadows.

At perhaps the height of five meters from the forest's floor a branch had been torn from the tree, leaving a long ragged stump like a spear. Upon this makeshift stake Li had been impaled through back and breastbone, as if he had been hurled there by a titanic force.

Without a word Yuan unsheathed his sword and swung it over his head, shearing through the branch behind Li. He fell heavily to the ground, his legs crumpled under him, his eyes open, staring wildly. The snow was dark where he half sat, back against the old tree trunk.

The ground was too hard to bury him so they moved north, making camp shortly. Yuan gathered dry wood and set about making a smokeless fire.

Ronin took the first watch. The pale firelight danced against the blue expanse of snow and black trees. Shadows ran to and fro. Just outside the ring of light, he heard the small skitterings and soft susurrations of the nocturnal animals.

If he leaned to his right he could just make out the crescent moon and its attendant star, bits of glittering

270

platinum, cool and remote, through a tiny gap in the forest's canopy.

Something howled, a snow wolf perhaps, and the forest chitterings ceased momentarily. But the sound did not come again and gradually the tiny myriad sounds sprang up once more. An owl hooted and, unseen, a bird flapped its wings above his head.

Near the end of his watch it began to snow, a fine dusting filtering down upon him and Yuan through the maze of branches, leaves, and needles.

He woke the Red, who stretched, yawned, and went to put more wood on the dying fire.

Ronin fell asleep instantly, a long dreamless flight until the blackness gave way to a flickering crimson and it seemed to him that the sky dripped blood. He heard low voices, far away yet so close that the individual words seemed to reverberate upon his eardrums. *Not yet? There can be no more delay. You know as well as I what must transpire before I can find him. Yes. All right. I am already in place; the vessel is prepared. I will get him there, be assured of that. I am assured of nothing now; time flows past too quickly: the Kai-feng comes. But we are Outside. Yes, but we must depend on those who are not; our time is ending.* He fell away from it and opened his eyes. He heard the soughing of the branches in the wind, a whippoorwill's mournful call. He turned his head. The fire crackled, the embers glowing orange and white. Yuan sat, arms around his knees to keep out the cold, staring out into the forest's shadows.

Ronin closed his eyes and went back to sleep.

The chill blue light of dawn woke him. He remembered the voices and for an instant, disoriented, thought that two men had been by the fireside.

The fire was out, the ashes gray and cold. Yuan sat in the same position, staring into the trees. Ronin crossed to him, reached out a hand, and paused. He

271

crouched down. The Red was dead. There was a black hole through his heart. Something had gone swiftly through him from chest to back. He might have been gored by a wild animal. He had not moved during the night.

Ronin went away from the campsite, swiftly and without a sound, moving north, farther into the forest. His spine tingled.

Snow began to fall again, harder now, deadening sound and limiting what visibility there was in that maze.

A wind arose, plucking at his cloak and swirling the snow into his face. He thought then that he heard a horn sound, plaintive and far off.

Mist steamed from the forest's floor, pearled and thick. Now all sound, all sense of direction was blotted out. His boots were silent along the ground but he heard the hammering of his heart. Oblique bars of gray light slanted down, illuminating the translucence of the mist, and abruptly he was lost in wilderness of smoke and vague shadows.

The minute sounds of the forest were gone now and with them the small comfort of being with other living creatures. He felt cut off, as if he no longer trod the world of man.

The snow fell silently, mingling with the syrupy mist. He went cautiously forward with one hand held before him like a blind man to guide him around the tree trunks which loomed in his path, visible only at the last moment.

His sense of time slipped away. He no longer knew whether he had been marching for hours or days whether the sun shone above the roof of his world or whether it had set.

He opened his mouth, letting the snow melt and slake his thirst. With that, he was suddenly aware of his hunger. He began to search the forest for game but he saw nothing. No animal, no fruit-bearing bush or tree. His hunger grew, gnawing at him. He pushed on.

At length he stumbled over an exposed root and he knew numbly that he must rest. Exhausted, he sat with his back against the trunk of an old pine. Its scent was all around him. The brown needles were soft beneath him. His head nodded on his chest but the hunger would not let him sleep.

It seemed darker now, the diffuse light flickering at the periphery of his vision. He became aware of a bulge under his belt. Half asleep, he fumbled with his fingers, found something. It was spongy. Food. He looked down at it but the uncertain light made it impossible to see. He took a bite, then another, chewing thoughtfully. It tasted slightly bitter. It was only when he had finished that the mist seemed to clear from his mind and he knew that he had eaten the strange man-shaped root from the apothecary's in Sha'angh'sei. An immense urn, fish swimming lazily, gossamer fins waving in the current, the feel of the curving side—Eternity. He shrugged. He felt a renewed strength already. All he needed was—

At that moment he thought he heard a distant call, like a shout of triumph, and he stood up, about to move in that direction, when he heard a more immediate sound behind him. He turned.

The mist was thicker now, the pearl gray glistening in rainbows at the edges of his vision.

He faced a shadow, distinct from those of the trees, within a line of vast ancient oaks, within the deep blue of their shade. He took a step forward, sure now that the Makkon had found him. His hand went to the hilt of his sword by force of habit. It would do him no good against the creature.

The figure stepped out from the shadows, a minute snowfall fluttering about its shoulders as a branch was

273

disturbed by the movement of its head. Shivering, the branch turned from white to deep green.

The sound of Ronin's sword unsheathing was an unnaturally sharp rasp, its volume shattering, for he looked upon a visage so strange as to drive all thought of the Makkon from his mind.

Ronin stared at the Hart.

He was over four meters tall, with wide shoulders and long, slender arms, thick-thighed legs. He was dressed in leggings of the deepest black, a peculiar, dense shade that was difficult to focus on. He wore a mail shirt lacquered the same color, dull and unreflective. A cloak swirled out behind him to the forest's floor. He had a massive black metal belt strapped across his waist and from it hung two scabbarded swords, one so long that it almost scraped the earth, the other shorter than the traditional Sha'angh'sei weapon. Ronin stared at these for long moments, wondering why they were so familiar. He was certain that he had never seen their like before and still—

His eyes were drawn irresistibly to the head yet with a reluctance that he found confusing. He was not afraid of death but he was terrified now. There was shivering inside himself, not at all a physical thing, as if someone was plucking the cords of his nerves at the core of his being and there was a terrible laughter from somewhere within him, a chill and ghastly rending. His stomach contracted.

The immense head emerged into the uncertain illumination of the mist. Shadows fluttered behind it. It was dominated by a long muzzle with wide wet flaring nostrils and, below them, a huge mouth with large square-cut teeth. The swiveling ears were triangular, furry and, beside them, growing out from the canted forehead, were two enormous antlers, curved and treed.

The entire head was covered in deep black fur, rich

and glossy. His gaze moved along the pelt until he looked into the Hart's eyes. They were not round like an animal's but rather oval, the intelligent eyes of man. They were piercing, pigmented with a cold color that had no analogue on this world.

The Hart opened his lips and something screamed through Ronin's brain so that his knees buckled and he dropped his blade, falling before the creature. There was maniacal laughter and beyond that a horrified voice was screaming *Get up! Get up and slay the beast, for beast is all it is!* But his arms would not respond and his fingers were numb as they clutched the soft pine needles of the forest's floor. *Destroy him before he destroys you!* He tried to vomit but nothing would come up. His head bent to the snow, the cold like flame against his forehead as the Hart moved farther out from the cerulean shadows. His high boots crunched the snow, echoing among the trees. The wind rose steadily, howling through the maze of branches like a hateful child. Ronin felt rooted to the earth, another tree in the forest, gravity sucking at him.

One strange horny hand moving to his side, the Hart withdrew the long sword, its blade a deep black onyx, translucent, forged by ancient anvil. There was a sighing as the leaves trembled, whispering his name: *Setsoru.*

The Hart came to rest before Ronin's kneeling form and, reaching down with his free hand, he gripped the hair, pulling the head back so that he stared into Ronin's face. The immense sword was held high, flashing through the mist which curled about them. And then the Hart looked down. He stared into Ronin's colorless eyes. The animal lips pulled back in a snarl and his own eyes rolled in their sockets. The antlers shook the snow from the branches overhead.

Hatred and fear swam in his visage and the onyx blade trembled.

No! the Hart screamed. The wind howled. There was a voice in Ronin's mind; his ears heard only the gathering wind.

And in that instant of hesitation, when both figures, locked together, seemed incapable of movement or cohesive thought, there came a fierce growl and a frantic blur of lithe motion. From out of the swirling mist streaked a shape, huge jaws agape and slathering forepaws extended. Their curving talons raked at the Hart's throat. Still distracted, his face a hate-filled mask, he could do little more than throw up his free arm to ward off the unexpected attack. But the creature held on tenaciously, the jaws snapping, the claws raking at the exposed pelt again and again. The body thrashed powerfully.

The Hart's mouth opened and from it emerged a terrifying scream of rage and confusion which echoed in Ronin's mind like a crack of thunder. He gave one last swipe at the creature with the hilt of his sword and, with amazing swiftness, he bounded into the maze of pines and oak, vanishing instantly.

The attacker was still now, sitting calmly in a bed of pine needles near Ronin's prostrate form, licking quietly at its forepaws.

You have found him then.

As you knew I would. The attacker's head lifted. He was perhaps two meters long, a four-legged animal with a tough scaly hide along his muscular body and powerful legs. He had a furred head with a long wicked-looking snout filled with sharp teeth. His eyes were red and quite intelligent. His wire-thin tail whipped back and forth, rustling the needles.

Hynd, did you . . . ?

Yes. The intelligent eyes looked at Ronin. *The luma is waiting at the edge of the forest.*

Excellent. Is she still there?

Yes. She will come. Is that good?

It is what must be. The disembodied voice somehow conveyed a shrug. *The Makkon is being otherwise occupied but I do not know for how long.*

I understand.

The creature stuck his snout down and began to push at Ronin's head, directing the cool snow onto his face.

He awoke, blinking, seeing before the green and white trees or the glint of his fallen sword the friendly face of Hynd. Hynd, the cruel-visaged but wondrous companion to Bonneduce the Last, the mysterious small man whom he had encountered in the City of Ten Thousand Paths, who had made him a gift of the Makkon gauntlet.

He sat up, still half dazed. The pearled mist was receding. Golden sunlight streamed down in fluttering bars through the forest's canopy. He rose and, sheathing his blade, allowed Hynd to lead him through the tangle of trees. The forest's floor became less rocky and softer as the ancient oaks gave gradual way to stands of willowy pine and blue spruce. Unerringly, Hynd led him to the eastern fringes of the forest. They broke through the last stand of trees, pushing aside the smaller ground foliage which formed the verge, and Ronin saw his luma, its coat glowing crimson in the light. He saw the sky, a rich blue, evening already in the east.

Beside his luma stood another, smaller, its coat sky blue. Astride this sat Moeru. He went to her, Hynd loping easily at his side. She smiled and touched his face with her small pale hand. Her long black hair whipped about her, covering one eye. Just like—

"Moeru, how did you get here?"

She looked down at him, drew in the dust coating her saddle two dots, moving, one behind: riders.

He gripped the quilting of her riding jacket.

"Why did you follow us?"

She laid a finger along his collarbone, tracing down the contours of his chest. Her clear nail scraped against the fabric.

Abruptly, he felt a wave of dizziness and he leaned his head against the cool leather of her saddle. The riders disappeared. He felt her hand on his neck, stroking. His head cleared. She wiped the dirt from his forehead, licking her fingers.

Ronin felt a pulling at his pants leg and he looked down. Hynd growled. He knelt, stroking the strange plated hide.

"It was you I heard searching for me?"

Hynd coughed softly. He swung his snout at Ronin's luma.

"Where do you take me, then?" It was a rhetorical question.

He stood up, went to his steed. He paused with one foot in the stirrup. "What of the Makkon, Hynd? I must slay it or we are all doomed."

The creature growled again, low in his throat.

"I must follow you, I know." He glanced down at Hynd. "And how did you find me, I wonder?" There was no answer.

He swung up across the saddle and gathered in the reins. The luma snorted and reared, calling, and Hynd loped up an incline heading east. Ronin pulled on the reins and his luma wheeled. He dug his heels into its flanks and took off, Moeru beside him, into the darkling east, away from the forest of bowing pines.

The land gradually fell away from them as dusk gave way to night. They galloped along a winding path, the terrain now filled with outcrops of rock against which dense scrub foliage flourished in wild abandon. Yellow blossoms studded the earth in great patches.

Abruptly, they were struggling up a steep incline and he soon realized that they were winding their way up the slopes of a mountain. The flowers disappeared as the way became increasingly precipitous. Here and there the black outline of a stately pine broke the skyline, but the farther they climbed the sparser the trees became until all flora was gone.

The night sky was filled with dense turbulent clouds with vaguely phosphorescent undersides sliding through disturbing hues. Ronin watched them pile and shape themselves as he felt the luma's powerful musculature working under him in fluid cadence and coordination.

Through the chill darkness they swept, the animals tirelessly galloping at full speed. The luma rejoiced in their kinetic flight, perhaps drawing energy from the journey itself, for it seemed to Ronin that the farther they went the stronger the mounts became. They were guided by Hynd's bounding body, calling to him or to each other.

It began to snow in cold driving bursts, the wind like a cruel knife, ripping at body and face, shoving them, moaning through the boulder-strewn mountain pass along which they continued to climb. The air became frigid and the snow turned to hail, pattering onto them, bouncing off the granite, the frozen earth, matting the luma's coats, ringing like metal off Hynd's armor plate.

Once Ronin glanced behind him. The plain from which they had ascended was still visible and he saw the spread of fat flames streaking the velvet of the night and he heard deep rumblings that were impossible to fathom. And it seemed to him that he saw the dark shadows of moving men, marching to a deep drumbeat, and the arcane structures of a full array of the machines of war, inventions to kill and maim, mutilate and cripple. It was raining fire, the continent of man shaking with the movements of war. Breath left him and, his eyes half closed, he dug his boot heels into his steed's flanks, following the lithe form of Hynd as he loped easily ahead. Then immense projecting rocks blotted out both sight and sound as they raced around a turning, adrift among the restless sleeting clouds.

His eyes flew open at the sound of a high shriek beside him. He drew up, calling to Hynd, who was already doubling back. He peered into the gloom, saw Moeru on the ground pinned beneath her luma.

He dismounted and went to her. The luma cried out and he saw that its left foreleg was broken. He bent down and carefully pulled her free; she seemed unhurt. He withdrew his blade and swiftly cut the luma's throat.

Sheathing his sword, he mounted his roan and, leaning over, drew Moeru's slim form up behind him. She wrapped her arms around him. He felt her warmth, the press of her breasts, the quickness of pulse at the back of his neck, the rhythm of her breathing.

All through the night they climbed the mountain and, as the coming sun commenced to stain the eastern horizon, they reached the summit. Ronin reined in for a moment to take in the mounting light. The mountain's eastern slopes were spread out before them, leading far below onto a plateau of geometric fields and meadows, dotted with the deep green of several forests, which descended gradually to the sea, sparking and glistening as the red sun inched over the horizon. It lacquered the sea crimson, flat and shining like burnished metal.

Then they were making their zigzag way down the mountainside and by dusk they were on the verge of the plateau. They raced across the undulating carpet of grass. There was no trace of snow here and the sky was clear, a deep blue, dark already near the eastern horizon where the sun was first to come and first to leave.

Hynd led them a winding path as the grasslands gave way to cultivated fields, sodden and deserted rice paddies on the edges of which stood ramshackle wooden houses on stilts, roofed with paper, tiny lanterns hanging from their front doors like glossy insect eyes in the gathering darkness.

Several times Hynd guided them into the shallows of the dripping paddies, the water sloshing around them until they stood perfectly still, Ronin stroking his luma's neck so that it would not call out, as distant rumblings became the urgent thunder of many horses' hoofs, scattering clods of dirt and grass as they passed in long lines.

At length the rice fields ceased and they flew past groves of trees hissing in the night. They were on dry land again, picking up speed, Hynd's instincts superb.

And now they ran with the wind, due east, the land flat with only low brush to break the monotony. Hynd bounded forward as if sensing that the end of their journey was near. The luma snorted and took off after him and Ronin, drunk with the speed and the repetitive rhythmic movement of the long ride, still not recovered from his singular encounter in the forest, held on now, allowing his mount to take him, no longer contemplating the journey's end, Moeru's cheek a gentle weight on his shoulder, no longer caring whither he went, wishing only for it to end now or for it never to end, numb, spent.

Thus, led by the strange hybrid that was part crocodile, part rodent, and something far more, riding a sweat-streaked crimson steed, with a woman he barely knew clinging to his back, he rode into the small port town of Khiyan, exhausted and bleary-eyed, half starved, his lips puffy from thirst and his face black with travel, past startled early risers, for it was just before dawn. They pounded down the slick cobbled streets, past wooden houses with slanting roofs and stone chimneys from which thin trails of smoke were already rising into the cool salt air of morning.

Gulls wheeled in the sky, skimming low off the water, crying into the sunrise. And at last Hynd led them onto the waterfront, to a tavern with a swinging wooden sign hanging above its open double doors, its black lettering too worn by wind and rain to make out. The crescent webbing of fishing nets was strung along one wall.

At the side of the door stood a short man with white hair held back from his face by a worn leather band, a grizzled beard, and deep green eyes set wide apart on his lined tanned face. He was dressed plainly in a creased leather jerkin over which was hung a chain mail vest. He wore brown leggings and low boots of a soft leather. He came away from the door to greet them when they drew up. He had a discernible limp when he walked.

"Ah, Ronin," said Bonneduce the Last. "How good it is to see you again."

"The continent of man is under siege from all sides now."

"But Kamado is the main thrust."

"Yes. I believe that the Kai-feng will be won or lost there."

"I have heard that word before—"

"It is the last battle of mankind."

"But the key is the Makkon. To destroy one is to stop The Dolman from appearing on the world." He gulped down a piece of meat, poured more wine for

Moeru. "Why then did you have Hynd take me away from it?"

"Because," Bonneduce the Last said slowly, "you cannot yet defeat the Makkon. If it had got to you in the forest, it would surely have destroyed you."

"How do you know?"

"How did I know that it would slay G'fand in the City of Ten Thousand Paths? The Bones."

"You knew, yet you let us go?"

"You would not have let me stop you."

They sat in the dim interior of the tavern, near the front windows and the open doors which faced the wide wharves of Khiyan. Tall ships with square-rigged sails as white as snow lay at anchor, their fittings creaking. Longboats laden with men and stores made their way across the short expanse of water from dockside to the lee of the ships. Two fishermen passed by the doorway, began to take down the nets from the side of the tavern. There was laughter. The owner of the tavern went out from behind his bar and stood talking to the fishermen.

Within the tavern, the stone hearth along one wall was spitting flames upward into the lower reaches of the blackened chimney but it was still too early for the place to have become smoky. The wood rafters were dark with an accumulation of charcoal and cooking fat.

Bonneduce the Last had granted Ronin three hours of sleep in a small room on the second floor with leaded windows overlooking the docks and a high goose-down bed onto which he fell without a sound and not even the harsh cries of the sailors along the short embankment outside disturbed his slumber. The little man had shown Moeru to the adjoining room. She was up before Ronin, gently shaking his shoulder to wake him when she heard Bonneduce the Last's limping step on the stairway.

"Where are they?" Ronin asked suddenly.

Bonneduce the Last reached into his leather jerkin with a thin smile and produced the seven geometric shapes, carved, so the little man had told him, of the teeth of the legendary giant crocodile. Strange glyphs were etched into every face. The Bones.

"What do they tell you?"

"The Kai-feng has commenced, Ronin. All are now committed to playing out their parts in the last struggle. Even Hynd and I."

"Even?"

The little man's face darkened. "By this battle will mankind stand or fall. A new age is dawning, Ronin, and no one can say what it will bring."

"Not even the Bones." It was not a question.

"No man, no being, may know the balance of power now." Hynd stirred at his feet. His forepaws twitched. Ronin glaced down at him. Perhaps he dreamed, as Ronin had, of grasslands flying by under his feet, racing with the Hart, transmogrified, his great treed antlers now a gleaming helm. "Thus, with all the glistening lines to the future severed, are the blind forces arrayed. Thus is the struggle for power made complex, thus is the winning worth the suffering: thus"—he reached down and stroked Hynd's plated back—"I know no more of this battle's ending than do you."

Thoughts of the Kai-feng and the Hart, inexplicably intertwined, filled Ronin's mind. Then he put these questions aside, raised his gauntleted fist.

"I have cause to thank you. Your gift has aided me often."

Bonneduce the Last smiled. "I am pleased then."

From somewhere, Ronin thought he heard a sonorous ticking like that he had heard in the little man's house in the City of Ten Thousand Paths. He poured more wine.

"You must tell me how Hynd found me."

"Yes, of course. I thought you knew. It was the root."

"You mean eating it?"

Bonneduce the Last nodded. "Once you had possession of it, it was only a matter of time before you ate it—"

"But how could you know—"

"Circumstances." He rubbed at his short leg. "In any event, our connection is now stronger and that is important—"

"But—"

"You did not question the Makkon gauntlet," Bonneduce the Last said carefully. "Do not question this. It was the penultimate step in the ending of the Old Cycle." He held up a hand as Ronin was about to voice another query. "There is no time now. Three of the Makkon are already come to the continent of man and the fourth is very near."

"What of the scroll?"

"I was just about to tell you," the little man said sharply. "You must sail," he said, "for Ama-no-mori."

There was silence for a time. Across the room the flames licked along the huge logs in the hearth and, with a soft crash, the bottom one split, eaten through. Sparks sailed upward. Outside, along the docks, the calls and songs of the sailors outfitting their ships for their sea runs seemed dim and remote. The sunlight streamed down in molten bars, warm as honey, far away.

Ronin stared at the seamed face.

"You know where the isle lies?"

The little man nodded. "I have plotted your course. The knowledge you seek, the knowledge which mankind needs, no longer exists on the continent of man."

"The Bujun—" said Ronin.

"Yes."

The air was warm and gentle as the air of summer should be. The aged sun seemed to burn stronger here. Yet it was not possible to forget the strife destroying the continent of man beyond the blue hazy slopes of the mountain in the west.

Ronin's face was grim as he strode along the foreshore and out onto the docks. Bonneduce the Last and Hynd loped along. He held Moeru by the hand.

The little man pointed and, shading his eyes from the sun, Ronin followed his hand outward and saw the two-masted vessel lying off the shore. Its square sails were unfurling and men climbed its rigging, preparing to weigh anchor.

"The *Kioku*," said Bonneduce the Last. "Your ship."

"Mine?" Ronin stared.

"You are its captain. The crew is already picked and on board." He put his hand on Ronin's shoulder. "You sail on the tide. Now."

Along the quay, a longboat had heaved to and its crew waited patiently as it rocked in the gentle swells. Ronin let go of Moeru's hand.

"Take care of her."

But Bonneduce the Last shook his head.

"She sails with you, Ronin."

He looked from the little man to the woman beside him. Perhaps it was the light, but he thought that her eyes were different, not at all like the eyes of the people of Sha'angh'sei. Within them, some far-off, storm-tossed sea.

"Yes. Perhaps it is better this way."

Bonneduce the Last glanced out to sea.

"It is the only way."

They climbed down to the longboat and sat in the midship seats, facing the bow.

"I wish you could come," Ronin called out.

The little man's hand scratched at the fur along Hynd's neck.

"We have much to do and other places to go. I trust your journey will be successful."

"Will I see you again?" Ronin called. But the longboat had already pulled away from the dock and the wind swept the little man's reply away into the dazzling sunlight. And they moved out from the shores of the continent of man.

The *Kioku* weighed anchor as soon as the longboat had delivered up its passengers and had been hoisted aboard. The white sails billowing in the freshening wind, the ship headed into the morning sun.

Ronin stood on the high poop deck at *Kioku's* stern watching the creaming water wash along the sleek flanks of his ship as it headed out into the deep, toward Ama no mori, toward an uncertain and enigmatic future. *Thus, with all the glistening lines to the future severed, are the blind forces arrayed.* Even the Bones useless now. Moeru stood by his side as the last gulls wheeled about the masts of the ship before sheering off and returning landward.

And so entranced was he by the enormous vista of the swelling open seas, by the anticipation of at last seeing the mysterious fabled isle of Ama-no-mori, the end to his long and arduous journey, that he failed to recognize or even notice the visage of his first mate, now hideously disfigured and scarred about his twisted mouth, which had no lips, no jaw. Had he taken more care he would have seen within that bizarre mask of pale white flesh the writhing of controlled loathing burning like cold flames in the black eyes so well known to him. But his mind, filled with new and arcane visions, was very far indeed from the unguided ship arcing away from him on the vast uncharted ice

287

sea so long ago; far from the Saardin he thought dead, who now stared balefully up at him from the *Kioku's* gleaming foredeck, contemplating his terrible agonizing revenge.

THE MANOR
OF DEATH

Bernard Knight

POCKET
BOOKS

LONDON • NEW YORK • TORONTO • SYDNEY

First published in Great Britain by Simon & Schuster UK Ltd, 2008

This edition published by Pocket Books, 2008

An imprint of Simon & Schuster UK Ltd

A CBS COMPANY

1 3 5 7 9 10 8 6 4 2

Simon & Schuster UK Ltd
Africa House
64–78 Kingsway
London WC2B 6AH

www.simonsays.co.uk

Simon & Schuster Australia
Sydney

A CIP catalogue record for this book is
available from the British Library

ISBN: 978-1-4165-2594-3

Typeset by Rowland Phototypesetting Ltd,
Bury St Edmunds, Suffolk

Printed and bound in Great Britain by
CPI Cox & Wyman Ltd, Reading, Berks

acknowledgments

I would like to thank Dr John Morgan Guy of the University of Wales, Lampeter for his help on medieval religious matters and Mr Ted Gosling, the Secretary of the Axe Valley Heritage Association, for his advice about Axmouth and Seaton in ancient times – and to Gillian Holmes and Kate Lyall Grant for performing their usual editorial wonders.

Professor Bernard Knight, CBE, became a Home Office pathologist in 1965 and was appointed Professor of Forensic Pathology, University of Wales College of Medicine, in 1980. During his forty-year career with the Home Office, he performed over 25,000 autopsies and was involved in many high profile cases.

Bernard Knight is the author of twenty-two novels, a biography and numerous popular and academic non-fiction books. *The Manor of Death* is the twelfth novel in the Crowner John Series, following *The Noble Outlaw, The Elixir of Death, Figure of Hate, The Witch Hunter, Fear in the Forest, The Grim Reaper, The Tinner's Corpse, The Awful Secret, The Poisoned Chalice, Crowner's Quest,* and *The Sanctuary Seeker.*

Also by Bernard Knight

AUTHOR'S NOTE

Much of this story takes place in Axmouth in South Devon – not to be confused with Exmouth, a dozen miles to the west. Now a small and picturesque village, in former times Axmouth was one of the most important ports in the west of England, being situated on the then wide tidal estuary of the River Axe. One of the few natural harbours on that steep and rocky coast, it was an important Roman port, attested by their settlements in the vicinity. In fact, the Fosse Way, the great Roman road to Lincoln, began at Axmouth, with a spur to Exeter.

In medieval times this port along the lower banks of the Axe was of prime importance for the shipment of tin, stone and especially wool, the last being England's most valuable export, accounting for the 'Woolsack' still being the seat of the Lord Chancellor when presiding over the House of Lords. Unfortunately, in the fourteenth century the wide entrance to the estuary began to be blocked by a huge pebble bank and, in spite of many efforts over hundreds of years to remove it, the harbour became unusable. The size of the estuary as seen today is only a vestige of how it would have appeared in Crowner John's time, when it extended several miles inland and was up to half a mile wide. The present village would have been far larger, and recent excavations have revealed the foundations of many more buildings.

The 'Keepers of the Peace' described in the story were the forerunners of the present Justices of the Peace, first introduced in 1195 by Hubert Walter, the Chief Justiciar to Richard the Lionheart, a year after he revived the office of coroner. Richard's castle of Château Gaillard, where some of the action takes place, was the finest example of military architecture in Europe, its ruins still standing above the Seine today. Unfortunately, he did not live to see its completion.

One of the problems of writing a long series, of which this is the twelfth, is that regular readers will have become familiar with the background and main characters and may become impatient with repeated explanations in each book. However, new readers need to be 'brought up to speed' to appreciate some of the historical aspects, so a Glossary is offered with an explanation of some medieval terms, especially those relating to the functions of the coroner, one of the oldest legal offices in England.

Any attempt to use 'olde worlde' dialogue in a historical novel of this period is as inaccurate as it is futile, for in late-twelfth-century Devon most people would have spoken Early Middle English, which would be incomprehensible to us today. Many others would have spoken a Celtic tongue similar to Welsh, Breton and Cornish, and the ruling classes used Norman-French – while the language of the Church and virtually all writing was Latin.

Almost all the names of people and places are authentic, the former being either real historical characters or taken from the Exeter Crown Pleas Roll of 1238. Unfortunately, though the sheriffs and senior churchmen are known, history does not record the names of the Devon coroners until the thirteenth century, so Sir John de Wolfe has to be a product of the author's imagination.

The only money in circulation would have been the silver penny, apart from a few foreign gold coins known as 'bezants'. The average wage of a working man was about two pence per day, and coins were cut into halves and quarters for small purchases. A 'pound' was 240 pence and a 'mark' was 160 pence, but these were nominal accounting terms, not actual coinage.

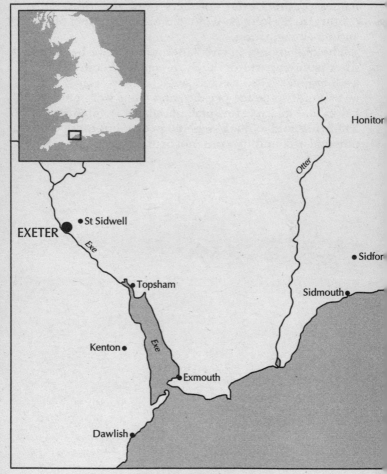

Map 1: Exeter and surrounding area.

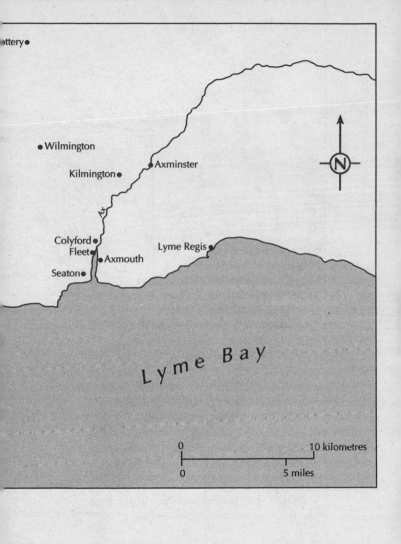

ttery•

• Wilmington

Kilmington•   •Axminster

Colyford•
Fleet•   •Axmouth
Seaton•

Lyme Regis•

Lyme Bay

0   10 kilometres

0   5 miles

N

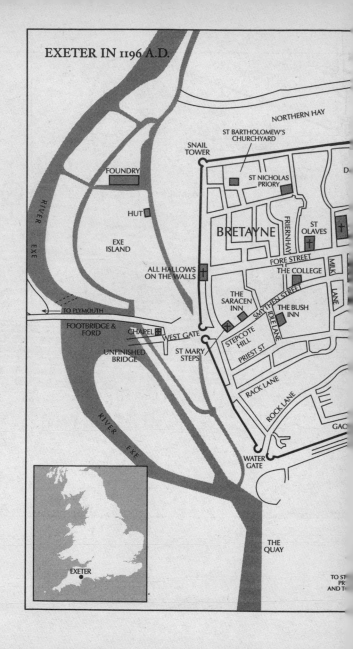

EXETER IN 1196 A.D.

RIVER EXE

NORTHERN HAY

ST BARTHOLOMEW'S
CHURCHYARD

SNAIL
TOWER

FOUNDRY

ST NICHOLAS
PRIORY

HUT

EXE
ISLAND

BRETAYNE

FRIERNHAY

ST
OLAVES

ALL HALLOWS
ON THE WALLS

FORE STREET

THE COLLEGE

MILK
LANE

TO PLYMOUTH

THE
SARACEN
INN

SMYTHEN STREET

THE BUSH
INN

IDLE LANE

FOOTBRIDGE &
FORD

CHAPEL

WEST GATE

STEPCOTE
HILL

UNFINISHED
BRIDGE

ST MARY
STEPS

PRIEST ST

RACK LANE

RIVER EXE

ROCK LANE

GAO

WATER
GATE

THE
QUAY

EXETER

TO ST
PR
AND T

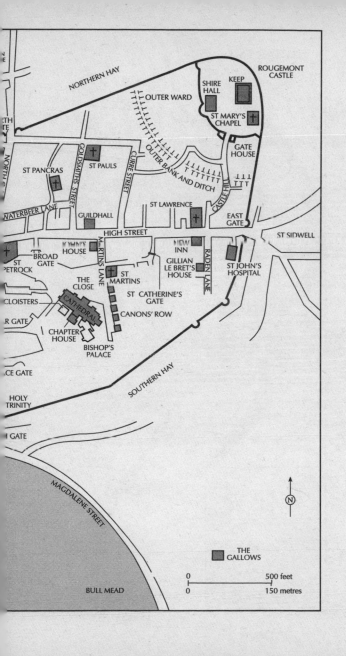

NORTHERN HAY

ROUGEMONT CASTLE

SHIRE HALL

KEEP

ST MARY'S CHAPEL

OUTER WARD

ST PANCRAS

ST PAULS

GOLDSMITHS STREET

CURRE STREET

OUTER BANK AND DITCH

GATE HOUSE

CASTLE HILL

WATERBEER LANE

GUILDHALL

ST LAWRENCE

EAST GATE

ST SIDWELL

HIGH STREET

JOHN'S HOUSE

BROAD GATE

MARTINS LANE

NEW INN

RADEN LANE

ST PETROCK

ST MARTINS

GILLIAN LE BRET'S HOUSE

ST JOHN'S HOSPITAL

THE CLOSE

CLOISTERS

CATHEDRAL

ST CATHERINE'S GATE

CANONS' ROW

R GATE

CHAPTER HOUSE

BISHOP'S PALACE

CE GATE

SOUTHERN HAY

HOLY TRINITY

GATE

MAGDALENE STREET

N

THE GALLOWS

| 0 | 500 feet |
| 0 | 150 metres |

BULL MEAD

GLOSSARY

ABJURING THE REALM
A sanctuary seeker, if he confessed his crime to the coroner, could abjure the realm of England, never to return. He had to dress in sackcloth and carry a crude wooden cross, then walk to a port nominated by the coroner and take the first ship abroad. If none was available, he had to wade out up to his knees in every tide to show his willingness to leave. Many abjurers absconded *en route* and became outlaws; others were killed by the angry families of their victims.

ALE
A weak drink brewed before the advent of hops. The name derived from an 'ale', a village celebration where much drinking took place. The words 'wassail' and 'bridal' are derived from this.

AMERCEMENTS
Arbitrary fines imposed on a person or community by a law officer for some breach of the complex regulations of the law. Where a fine was imposed by a coroner, he would record the amercement, but the collection of the money would normally be ordered by the royal justices when they visited at the **Eyre** (q.v.).

APPROVER
A criminal who attempted to save himself by implicating his accomplices. His confession had to be recorded by the coroner.

ASSART
An area where forest has been cut down to increase the amount of arable land.

ATTACHMENT
An order made by a law officer, including a coroner, to ensure that a person appeared at a court hearing. It resembled a bail bond or surety, distraining upon a person's money or goods, which would be forfeit if he failed to appear.

BAILEY
Originally the defended area around a castle keep, as in 'motte and bailey', but later also applied to the yard of a dwelling.

BAILIFF
An overseer of a manor or estate, directing the farming and other work. He would have manor reeves under him and be responsible either directly to his lord or to the steward.

BONDSMAN
An unfree person in the feudal system. Several categories, including villein, serf, cottar, etc.

BURGAGE
A plot of land, usually comprising a house and garden, in a town or city. Long and narrow at right angles to the street, it was often the property of a burgess.

BURGESS
A freeman of substance in a town or borough, usually a merchant or craftsman. A group of burgesses ran the town administration; and in 1195 they elected two portreeves (later a mayor) to lead them in Exeter.

CANON
A senior priest in a cathedral, deriving his living from the grant of a parish or land providing an income (a prebend). Exeter Cathedral, a secular not a monastic establishment, had twenty-four canons.

CHAPTER
The administrative body of a cathedral, composed of the canons (prebendaries). They met daily to conduct business in the chapter house, so-called because a chapter of the Gospels or of the Rule of St Benedict was read before each session.

COB
A plaster made of straw, clay, dung and horsehair which was applied to panels of willow or hazel withies, which filled the spaces between the frames of a house. Small cottages might be constructed entirely of cob.

COG
The common sea-going vessel of the 12th century, developed from the Norse longship, but broader and higher. With a single mast and square sail, it had no rudder but a steering oar on the 'steerboard' side. Partly decked with a hold, it was converted to a fighting ship by adding raised 'fore-castles' and 'after-castles' at bow and stern where bowmen and other soldiers could stand.

COIF
A close-fitting cap or helmet, usually of linen or felt, covering the ears and tied under the chin: worn by men and women.

CONSTABLE
A senior commander, usually the custodian of a castle, which in Exeter belonged to the king. The word was also used of a watchman who patrolled the streets to keep order.

CORONER
Though there are a couple of mentions of a coroner in late Saxon times, the office of coroner really began in September 1194, when the royal justices at their session in Rochester, Kent, proclaimed in a single sentence the launch of the system that has lasted for over 800 years. They said, 'In every county of the King's realm shall be elected three knights and one clerk, to keep the pleas of the Crown.'

The reasons for the establishment of coroners were mainly financial: the aim was to sweep as much money as possible into the royal treasury. Richard the Lion-heart was a spendthrift, using huge sums to finance his expedition to the Third Crusade and for his wars against the French. Kidnapped on his way home from the Holy Land, he was held for well over a year in prisons in Austria and Germany, and a huge ransom was needed to free him. To raise this money, his Chief Justiciar, Hubert Walter, who was also Archbishop of Canterbury, introduced all sorts of measures to extort money from the population of England.

Hubert revived the office of coroner, which was intended to collect money by a variety of means relating to the administration of the law. One of these was by investigating and holding inquests into all deaths that were not obviously natural, as well as into serious assaults, rapes, house fires, discoveries of buried treasure, wrecks of the sea and catches of the royal fish (whale and sturgeon). Coroners also took confessions from criminals and fugitives seeking sanctuary in churches, organised **abjurations of the realm** (q.v.), recorded the statements of **approvers** (q.v.) who wished to turn King's Evidence, attended executions to seize the goods of felons, and organised the ritual of **ordeals** (q.v.) and trial by battle.

As the Normans had inherited a multiple system of county and manorial courts from the Saxons, the coroner also worked to sweep more lucrative business into the new Royal Courts. This gave him the title of Keeper of the Pleas of the Crown, from the original Latin of which (*custos placitorum coronas*) the word 'coroner' is derived.

Although the coroner was not allowed to try cases (this was later again specifically forbidden by Magna Carta), he had to create a record of all legal events to present to the royal justices when they came on their infrequent visits to the **Eyre** (q.v.). The actual recording on the 'coroner's rolls' was done by his clerk, as the coroners, like the vast majority of people, were illiterate. Reading and writing were almost wholly confined to those in holy orders, of whom there were many grades besides the actual priests.

It was difficult to find knights to take on the job of coroner, as it was unpaid and the appointee had to have a large private income: at least £20 a year. This was supposed to make him immune from corruption, which was common among the sheriffs. Indeed, one reason for the introduction of coroners was to keep a check on sheriffs, who were the king's representatives in each county.

COVER-CHIEF

More correctly 'couvre-chef', a linen head cover flowing down the back and shoulders, worn by women and held in place by a band around the forehead. Called a head-rail in Saxon times.

CURFEW

The prohibition of open fires in towns after dark, for fear of starting conflagrations. The word is derived from 'couvre-feu', describing the extinguishing or banking down of fires at night. During the curfew, the city gates were closed from dusk to dawn. A thirteenth-century mayor of Exeter was hanged for failing to ensure this.

DESTRIER

A sturdy warhorse able to carry the weight of an armoured knight. Destriers were not the huge beasts often portrayed in historical art; they were rather short-legged, the rider's feet being not that far from the ground.

EYRE

A sitting of the King's Justices, introduced by Henry II in 1166, which moved around the country in circuits. There were two types, the 'Eyre of Assize', which was the forerunner of the later Assize Court, which was supposed to visit each county town regularly to try serious cases. The other was the General Eyre, which came at long intervals to scrutinise the administration of each county.

FARM

The taxes from a county, collected in coin on behalf of the sheriff and taken by him personally every six months to the royal treasury at London or Winchester. The sum was fixed annually by the king or his ministers: if the sheriff could extract more from the county, he could retain the excess, which made the office of sheriff much sought after.

FRANKPLEDGE
A system of law enforcement introduced by the Normans, where groups (tithings) of ten households were formed to enforce mutual good behaviour amongst each group.

FREEMAN
A person other than a bondsman of the feudal system. The villeins, serfs and slaves were not free, though the distinction did not necessarily mean a different level of affluence.

FLETCHING
The feathered flights on the end of an arrow made by a fletcher. On crossbow bolts, the fletching was usually of leather.

GAOL DELIVERY
As the circulation of the King's Justices at the Eyre of Assize was so slow, with years between each visit, the counties were visited more often by lower judges, called Commissioners of Gaol Delivery, in order to clear the overcrowded prisons of those held on remand.

GUILDS
Trade or merchant associations set up for mutual protection. Merchant guilds mainly functioned to ward off foreign competition and to set prices. Trade guilds were organisations for the many crafts and manufactures, controlling conditions of work, the quality of goods and the welfare of workers and their families.

HALL
Most houses, as opposed to tofts (cottages), had a single room, the 'hall' which occupied most of, or even all the building. Then 'solars' were added (q.v.) and extra side-rooms in larger homes. Outhouses in the yard or bailey provided kitchens, wash-houses, brew-sheds and privies.

HAUBERK
A long chain-mail tunic with long sleeves to protect the wearer from neck to calf, usually slit to enable riding a horse.

HUNDRED
A sub-division of an English county, introduced by Alfred the Great. The origin of the name is uncertain but was either an area occupied by a hundred households or a hundred hides of land.

JOHN LACKLAND
A sarcastic nickname for Prince John, Count of Mortain. The name came from the refusal of his father King Henry II to endow him with significant territory. When his brother Richard came to the throne in 1189, he gave much land to John, including Devon and Cornwall.

JUSTICES
The king's judges, originally members of his royal court, but later chosen from barons, senior priests and administrators. They sat in the various law courts, such as the Eyre of Assize or as Commissioners of Gaol Delivery. From 1195 onwards, Keepers of the Peace, later to become Justices of the Peace, were recruited from knights and local worthies to deal with lesser offences.

KEEPERS OF THE PEACE
In 1195, the Chief Justiciar of England, Archbishop of Canterbury Hubert Walter, followed up his revival of the office of coroner the previous year, by establishing law officers to assist in keeping the peace in the counties. With no police force, the old methods of keeping order by the local feudal methods, such as frankpledge (q.v.) could not cope with increasing lawlessness and outlawry, so he appointed knights, of whom there was a surplus after the end of the Third Crusade, to try to supervise and assist the sheriffs and Hundred sergeants and bailiffs. There were few at first, confined to the worst trouble spots, but in 1265 under Henry III, the Statute of Winchester made them more widespread. Then in 1361, an Act of Edward III formally appointed 'Justices of the Peace', who still deal with the bulk of criminal cases to this day.

KIRTLE
A ladies' floor-length gown. Many variations of style and fit, especially of the sleeves, existed in the fashion-conscious medieval period.

LEMAN
A man's mistress or concubine.

MANOR-REEVE
A villein in a manor elected by his unfree fellows to represent them. He organised their daily labours and was in turn responsible to the lord's bailiff or steward.

MANTLE
A cloak, either circular with a hole for the head, or open-fronted with the top being closed either by a large brooch on the shoulder or by a top corner being pulled through a ring sewn to the opposite shoulder.

MATINS

The first of nine offices of the religious day, originally observed at midnight or in the early hours.

NECK VERSE

If a man claimed 'benefit of Clergy' to obtain immunity from the secular courts on the grounds that he was in Holy Orders, he had to prove that he was literate, but this was commonly done by reciting a short passage from the Bible, usually the Psalms. This became known as 'the neck verse', as might save him from a hanging.

ORDEAL

A test of guilt or innocence, such as walking over nine red-hot ploughshares with bare feet or picking a stone from a barrel of boiling water. If burns appeared within a certain time, the person was judged guilty and hanged. There was also the Ordeal of Battle where a legal dispute was settled by combat. For women, submersion in water was the ordeal: the guilty floated. Ordeals were forbidden by the Lateran Council in 1215.

OUTLAW

A man who did not submit to legal processes. Usually an escaped felon or suspect, a runaway sanctuary seeker or abjurer, he was declared 'outlaw' – by a writ of exigent – if he did not answer to a summons on four consecutive sessions of the county court. An outlaw was legally dead, with no rights whatsoever, and could be legally slain on the spot by anyone. If caught by a law officer, he was hanged. A female could not be outlawed, but was declared 'waif', which was very similar.

OUTREMER

Literally 'over the sea', the term was used to refer to the countries in the Levant, especially the Holy Land.

PELISSE
An outer garment worn by both men and women with a fur lining for winter wear. The fur could be sable, rabbit, marten, cat, et cetera.

POSSE
The *posse comitatus*, introduced by Henry II, was the title given to a band of men raised by a sheriff to hunt felons or enemies of the realm across the county.

PREBENDARY
The canon of a cathedral, deriving an income from his prebend, a tract of land granted to him (see canon).

PRESENTMENT
At coroner's inquests, a corpse was presumed to be that of a Norman, unless the locals could prove 'Englishry' by presenting such evidence from the family. If they could not, a 'murdrum' fine was imposed on the community by the coroner, on the assumption that Normans were murdered by the Saxons they had conquered in 1066. Murdrum fines became a cynical device to extort money, persisting for several hundred years after the Conquest, by which time it was virtually impossible to differentiate the two races.

QUIRE
The area within a church between the nave and the presbytery and altar, which gave rise to the name 'choir'. The quire was usually separated from the nave by a carved rood screen at the chancel arch, bearing a large crucifix above it.

SANCTUARY
An ancient act of mercy: a fugitive from justice could claim forty days' respite if he gained the safety of a church or even its environs. After that time, unless he

confessed to the coroner, he was shut in and starved to death. If he confessed, he could **abjure the realm** (q.v.).

SERGEANT
The term was used in several ways, denoting *inter alia* an administrative/legal officer in a county Hundred, or a military rank of a senior man-at-arms.

SECONDARIES
Young men aspiring to become priests and under twenty-four years of age. They assisted canons and vicars in their duties in the cathedral.

SHERIFF
The 'shire reeve', the king's representative in each county, responsible for law and order and the collection of taxes. The office was eagerly sought after as it was lucrative; both barons and senior churchmen bought the office from the king at high premiums, some holding several shrievalties at the same time. Sheriffs were notorious for dishonesty and embezzlement – in 1170, the Lionheart's father, Henry II, sacked all his sheriffs and heavily fined many for malpractice. The sheriff in the earlier Crowner John books, Richard de Revelle, though fictional, was named after the actual Sheriff of Devon in 1194–95. He was appointed early in 1194, then lost office for reasons unknown; he returned to office later in the year, but was dismissed again the following year.

SOLAR
A room built on to the main hall of a castle or house for the use of the lord or owner, usually for the use of the lady during the daytime and often as a bedroom at night.

TRENCHER
A thick slice of coarse bread, often deliberately stale, used instead of a plate to hold cooked food. Especially after feasts, the trenchers were given to the poor and beggars waiting ouside the hall.

UMBLE PIE
The umbles were the less desirable parts of venison, such as the offal. Especially at Christmas, they were given by a lord to the poorer people to make 'umble pie', from which the expression 'to eat humble pie' arose as an indicator of subservient status.

VICAR
A priest employed by a more senior cleric, such as a canon, to carry out some of his religious duties, and especially to attend the many daily services in the cathedral. Such a priest was often called a 'vicar-choral' because of his participation in chanted services.

WIMPLE
A linen or silk cloth worn by women to cover the neck and upper chest, the upper ends being pinned to their hair to frame the face.

WOLF'S HEAD
An outlaw was said to be 'as the wolf's head', for like a wolf, he could be beheaded with impunity and a bounty of five shillings could be claimed from the sheriff.

PROLOGUE

April 1196

A brisk south-westerly wind sent the two ships scudding up the Channel, almost midway between the Cotentin peninsula in Normandy and the coast of Devon. Both landfalls were far out of sight, which was just as well, given the bloody acts that were soon to take place.

The smaller vessel was faster than the heavy-laden cog, which was hauling a cargo from Barfleur up towards King Richard's new harbour at Portsmouth. The shipmaster was desperately trying to coax every knot from his ungainly craft, and the single sail bellied out so tightly that he feared that some of the stitched repairs in the fabric would tear apart. Every few moments he would look fearfully over his shoulder as he leant on the single long oar pivoted over the steerboard quarter. His heart chilled as with every glance he saw the lighter craft remorselessly overhauling the *Blackbird*. The other cog, though almost as squat and cumbersome, had a larger sail and a slightly less bulbous hull.

His four crewmen, powerless to do anything further to speed their ship, stared helplessly astern at what they feared would be their nemesis, for the men they could see on the deck were more than twice their number. As

1

they came nearer, the desperate men on the *Blackbird*
saw that two of the pursuing crew had crossbows ready
strung, and the others brandished long knives, maces
or short spears. The only one unarmed was a youth,
who watched with horror as they drew alongside and,
with ferocious yells, all except the steersman leapt
across the bulwarks and lashed the two vessels together
with ropes.

Within a couple of minutes all the *Blackbird*'s crew
were either lying dead on the deck in pools of their
own blood or had been thrown overboard to drown in
the choppy waters. The steersman of the pirate vessel
abandoned his oar to rush across to join his shipmates
– on the way, he gave the youth a buffet across the head
and yelled at him as he passed.

'Come on, you yellow-livered pansy, there's cargo to
be shifted! Haven't you seen corpses before?'

Reluctantly, the lad followed him, but as soon as he
had clambered over on to the other boat, he retched
at the sight of two men lying with their throats cut
and then vomited his breakfast on to the pitching deck.
Another man grabbed him and threw him towards
the single hatch, where the pirates were ripping off
the loose planks that covered the hold. Gagging and
keeping his eyes off the dead men nearby, he scrabbled
at the boards and then toiled with the others in trans-
ferring the kegs of wine and dried fruit and the bales
of Flemish cloth across to their own ship. As soon
as everything had been pillaged, he heard the sound of
axes smashing through the hull down below, and soon
they all hurried back across the bulwarks to cast off the
ropes before the doomed vessel could drag their own
ship down with her.

Within a few moments the *Blackbird* rolled over and
sank, taking the remaining corpses with her. Crossing
himself, the young man sobbed out some prayers to
himself and stayed hunched miserably in a corner

against the forecastle, as the marauding cog turned north and clawed her way across the wind towards the distant shores of England.

CHAPTER ONE

In which Crowner John rides to Axmouth

Spring was in the air, but Sir John de Wolfe was oblivious to the primroses along the verges and the singing of little birds in the bushes. He had a boil coming on his backside, and riding a horse was the last thing he needed today.

'You need to see an apothecary, master,' chided Thomas de Peyne, his diminutive clerk. 'A good clay poultice would draw out the poison.'

'Or I could lance it with the point of my dagger!' offered Gwyn, his unsympathetic henchman, who rode on his other side as the three trotted along the road eastwards from Exeter.

The gaunt coroner scowled at his two assistants, not deigning to answer their helpful advice. He was too concerned about taking the weight off his bottom by pressing his feet down into the stirrups – hardly the best way to cover the twenty miles to Axmouth. Before they had left soon after dawn, his housekeeper Mary had given him a folded pad of soft wool to slip inside his breeches, which helped a little. But now, as they entered the hamlet of Sidford some two hours later, he felt the need for a rest and some refreshment.

Gwyn of Polruan, a giant with unruly ginger hair

and a drooping moustache of the same hue, had an insatiable appetite for food and drink, which led him unerringly towards one of the thatched cottages that clustered around the packhorse bridge that spanned the little River Sid. A bedraggled bush hanging over the low doorway indicated it was an alehouse, and soon a snivelling youth had led their horses around the back to be fed and watered, while the coroner's trio went inside to seek some victuals.

The building was old and decrepit, patches of the lime-and-horsehair plaster crumbling from the panels of hazel withies that filled the spaces between the timber frames of the single room. The floor was of beaten earth with a sparse covering of mouldy rushes, the only furniture being two rough tables with benches on each side and a few rickety stools. The coroner carefully lowered himself on to a bench, so that the offending part of his anatomy overhung the back.

The Saxon ale-wife who ran the establishment was civil enough, glad of the custom of a Norman knight and a priest, though she looked askance at the wild-looking redhead in his scuffed leather jerkin. At their request, she filled two clay pots with ale from a five-gallon crock in the corner and poured Thomas a smaller mug of cloudy cider from a large jug.

'I can give you good potage, sirs,' she offered. 'Got some rabbit in it, fresh trapped this morning. And there's new bread and cheese.'

'Must have been a bloody small rabbit!' grunted Gwyn a few moments later as he stirred through his bowl with a wooden spoon, trying to identify some shreds of meat amongst the thin gruel.

'It's been a hard winter. Many of these remote villages have very little left by this time of year,' rumbled de Wolfe. Though one of the toughest of men, he had grown up in a small village and had much sympathy for those who lived in manors whose land was poor or where their lords and bailiffs were incompetent managers. In bad years, many villagers starved to death because of poor husbandry.

Their conversation was muted until they had finished eating, even the fastidious Thomas devouring the plain fare without complaint. He looked as if he needed the food, being a pale, scrawny young man with a slight hump on his back. His appearance was not improved by his peaky face, a long sharp nose emphasising his receding chin. However, his poor looks were more than compensated for by an agile brain and a compendious knowledge of religion and history. Recently restored to the priesthood after being defrocked several years earlier following a false allegation of indecent assault, he now combined religious duties at Exeter Cathedral with invaluable assistance to the coroner as his very literate clerk.

Gwyn, the coroner's officer and bodyguard, sank the rest of his quart of ale in a single swallow and after a thunderous belch brought the conversation around to their present assignment. 'Are we sure that this is a killing, not just some body washed up on the beach?' he demanded. 'That messenger didn't seem all that sure of it.'

John de Wolfe shrugged, though even that gave him a twinge in his buttock. 'He was the clerk to this Keeper of the Peace, so maybe he can recognise a murder when he sees one,' he grunted.

Last evening, just before the city gates closed at curfew, a rider had entered Exeter and sought out the coroner, who was still in his chamber above the gatehouse of Rougemont Castle. He had been sent by his master to report the finding of a body in suspicious circumstances at the small harbour town of Axmouth, in the east of the county near the boundary with Dorset. Though seemingly vague about the details of the death, he was adamant that his employer, Sir Luke de Casewold, considered that the deceased had been murdered.

Gwyn reached out to tear off a chunk of coarse rye bread from the loaf on the table, the crust burnt black on top by a careless village baker. He used his dagger to hack off a slice of hard cheese from the lump provided by the landlady but paused with the food halfway to his mouth to ask a question. 'This Keeper of the Peace is some newfangled official, is he?'

Thomas, always the best informed about current affairs, looked scornfully at his big colleague. 'If you ignorant Cornishmen spent less time eating, drinking and gambling, you might know more about what's going on in the world!' His head stuck out of his shabby black cassock like a rabbit peering from its burrow. 'Just as the Chief Justiciar established coroners eighteen months ago, last December he carried out the king's orders to set up knights in every county to keep the peace – or try to, in this disorderly realm where people seem to have conveniently forgotten the Ten Commandments!' He crossed himself piously, as he did a score of times each day in a habit as compulsive as Gwyn scratching his armpits or his crotch.

John de Wolfe added to his clerk's explanation, forgetting his sore bottom for a moment. 'The bailiffs and serjeants of the Hundreds have been such a dismal failure at keeping law and order that the king decided to augment them with men made of sterner stuff. Now that the Crusade has ended, there are plenty of unemployed knights knocking about the countryside who could help the sheriffs to seek out and arrest wrongdoers.'

The Cornishman champed on his food for a moment, then washed it down with a mouthful of sour ale. 'I thought that was our job, Crowner?' he said.

De Wolfe grinned sardonically. 'Only because the last sheriff was a crook and the present one is bone idle! I'm supposed to present the evidence to the courts, not go out and catch the bloody criminals as well!'

Thomas's dark little eyes flicked from one man to the other. 'Do you know this new Keeper, Sir John? I'd never heard of him until now.'

The coroner shook his head, his black hair swinging over the back of his collar. Unlike most Norman gentry, he wore it long, instead of shaving his neck right up to leave a thick mop on top of the head.

'He's from this eastern edge of Devon, a foreign land to me!' De Wolfe came from Stoke-in-Teignhead, down towards Torbay. 'He was never in Ireland nor the Holy Land with us, Gwyn, though I think he fought in France.'

Draining his pot, he stood up and slapped a penny on the table in payment for their refreshment. 'Time we went. I'd like to get back to Exeter tonight; I've not seen Nesta for a few days, you know. She gets irritable if I leave her too long.'

Gwyn smirked. He had a great fondness for de Wolfe's mistress but was constantly amused by their bickering.

De Wolfe grunted a farewell to the ale-wife and ducked his head under the low lintel to lead them into the road outside. Both he and Gwyn were six feet tall, though he was as lean and spare as his officer was massively built. A slight stoop and his habit of always dressing in black or grey made him look like some predatory crow. His great hooked nose, black eyebrows and pugnacious chin combined to make most men step hurriedly aside when he bore down upon them.

When their horses were brought around, John climbed gingerly into his saddle, his old warhorse Odin waiting patiently while he arranged his posterior in the position of least discomfort.

'We're well over halfway, I reckon,' advised Gwyn as

they set off over the little bridge. 'I came up here many years ago to the harbour in Axmouth, when my father came to buy a new boat.'

Gwyn, who for almost twenty years had been de Wolfe's squire, bodyguard and now coroner's officer, had previously been a fisherman in his native village of Polruan, at the mouth of the Fowey river in Cornwall. He had followed his master to campaigns in Ireland, France and to the Third Crusade in Palestine, but now that they were both over forty, their fighting days seemed over.

It took them almost another two hours to pass through the village of Colyford, on the western side of the wide valley of the Axe. Across the vale, a barrier of green hills ran north and south, dividing Devon from Dorset and ending in an abrupt headland where the estuary opened into the sea. The tide was in and a great expanse of water lay below them, like a fjord reaching almost two miles inland, being up to half a mile wide. They trotted their horses down to the marshy ground, where the track became a crude causeway leading to a small bridge, where at this stage of the tide the water was lapping almost to the edges of the boards. The bank rose on the other side as they reached the lower slope of the ridge where there was a crossroads. When they stopped, the knowledgeable Thomas pointed up the road to their left, where the valley vanished northwards. 'That's a branch of the Fosse Way, built by the Romans,' he announced with the air of a pedagogue. 'Goes all the way to Lincoln!'

The coroner's officer was not impressed by his learning. 'Then we'll take the opposite direction, which with a bit of luck goes all the way to another alehouse!'

They turned down towards the sea and for a mile or so followed the well-beaten track to the large village of Axmouth, the high ridge close above them on their left. It was virtually a small town, straggled along the

edge of the estuary. It existed because the river provided one of the safest harbours along that coast, the
tide swelling the river twice a day to allow vessels to
beach themselves safely along both banks. It was one
of the busiest ports in the west of England, as well as
having an active fishing fleet, as did the smaller village
of Seaton on the opposite bank.

'A bigger place than I remember,' observed Gwyn as
they walked their steeds down the last furlong. Though
not actually fortified, it had a substantial wall around
the centre of the village, above which could be seen the
tower of a stone church. There were two solid gates,
which, like the wall, were higher than a man. One faced
them as they approached, the more distant one leading
out on to the quayside on the seaward side. Cottages,
shacks and storage huts straggled along the river bank,
showing that the place had expanded beyond the
confines of the walls. A small side valley cut into the hill
on their left, revealing more dwellings and barns.

'Looks as if we're expected, master,' observed
Thomas, pointing at a small group who were waiting
outside the landward gate, staring at the approaching
horsemen.

'That clerk must have told them we were on our way,'
said Gwyn. The man had left Exeter even earlier that
morning, and his rounsey would have been faster than
the plodding Odin or Thomas's pony.

As they came up to the gate, they saw the clerk,
Hugh Bogge, standing alongside another one of the
group, a man better dressed than the others. As they
approached, he left his fellows and came towards them,
his hand held up in greeting. John sat on his horse
and looked down at the man, who looked about his
own age. He was of average height, but an ale-belly was
beginning to push out a good-quality yellow tunic and a
surcoat of brown wool. His round, plump face carried a
prim, pursey mouth, and strands of straw-coloured hair

poked out from under his floppy cap of green velvet.

'Sir John de Wolfe, I presume?' he asked in a rather harsh voice. 'I am Sir Luke de Casewold, the Keeper of the Peace for the Hundreds of Axminster, Colyton and Axmouth.'

He said this in such a self-important manner that the coroner immediately began to dislike Luke de Casewold. However, he held his tongue and cautiously eased himself out of his saddle, feeling relief at being able to stand up. After John introduced himself, the Keeper turned and pointed at the silent group standing a little way off, looking uneasy and sheepish.

'These are people concerned, coroner. I know what the law demands and have made sure that the First Finder and anyone who might have any knowledge of this business have come before you.'

Again, he announced this in such a way as to give the impression that he was doing the coroner a great favour.

'And what exactly is this business?' grated de Wolfe. 'Your servant seemed to have little idea of it, apart from the fact that there is a corpse.'

Sir Luke rubbed his hands together almost gleefully, as if this was a special treat he had arranged for the king's coroner. 'Indeed there is, my friend! I will conduct you to it without delay.'

He made no effort to enquire whether de Wolfe and his assistants needed food, drink and rest after their long ride from the city, but at that moment there was a diversion. Through the open gate under its stone arch, two men came striding purposefully towards them. The first was a powerfully built man with coarse features and a rim of black beard around his fleshy face. He had a mouth like a rat-trap and cold deep-set eyes under brows as dark as the coroner's own. He marched straight up to de Wolfe, completely ignoring the Keeper.

'I am Edward Northcote, bailiff to the Prior of Loders, who holds this manor,' he snapped. 'If you are the coroner, then you have had a wasted journey. You were sent for without my knowledge or consent.'

Within minutes, John now had another person to dislike on sight. He was not disposed to be ordered about by some prior's servant.

'If there is a dead body lying here, then I will be the judge of that,' he growled. 'Unless it died of a sickness, with witnesses to testify to that, then it comes under my jurisdiction, as granted to me by the king and his Council!' He added the last part to give weight to his royal appointment.

The other man who had arrived with the bailiff now spoke up, in a more conciliatory tone. 'We realise that, Crowner, but wished to have saved you a fruitless journey from Exeter. No doubt this is just some poor seafarer washed up from God knows where.'

'Nonsense! The fellow was done to death violently, not drowned,' brayed Luke de Casewold, his podgy features red with anger at being contradicted by Elias Palmer, the portreeve, a rake-thin man with sparse greying hair and a long narrow face. He wore a long tunic down to his calves. It was of a nondescript buff colour and the front was spattered with ink stains. Most manors had a reeve to organise the farming activities, but in Axmouth it was different, as agriculture played a much smaller part in the village economy. Though it was not a chartered borough, it was important enough by virtue of its harbour to have some officials, and Palmer had been appointed as portreeve by the Priory of Loders, which lay some twenty miles away in Dorset, to supervise all trading in the town. The manor itself was in the charge of the prior's bailiff, the aggressive Edward Northcote, so between them they were the effective rulers of Axmouth.

The coroner held up his hand to quell the argument

13

developing between them and the Keeper of the Peace.

'I'm here now, so let's settle matters by letting me see the corpse,' he commanded. 'But tell me first the circumstances of its discovery.'

De Casewold turned and beckoned imperiously to someone in the group of onlookers. 'It's best coming from the First Finder, as is proper!' he brayed, again making John want to kick the man's rump for trying to tell a coroner his business. He was surprised when an elderly man in a long black robe, his grey hair shaved into a clerical tonsure, stepped forward. Completely toothless, his mouth had caved in, his sharp hooked nose pointing down at his chin.

'Here's one of your lot!' muttered Gwyn into Thomas's ear as the old priest came up to them. The clerk scowled at him for his habitual irreverence, then turned and smiled at the priest and murmured a greeting in Latin.

'This is Henry of Cumba, the parish priest of St Michael's there,' said Luke, waving a hand towards the church tower. 'It was he who found the body.'

Father Henry's lined face looked apprehensive as he confronted the forbidding figure of the coroner, and he spoke up in a quavering voice. 'I had an old hound, of which I was very fond, sir,' he began.

At this apparent irrelevance, John wondered if the aged priest's mind was wandering, but the old man soon made it clear.

'The poor beast died yesterday, mainly of old age, as I had had him more than a dozen years. Rather than cast his body on to the village midden, I thought I owed it to him to bury him decently, so took a spade and wrapped him in a sack.'

Gwyn, an ardent dog-lover, nodded his appreciation of the old man's humanity, as Henry carried on with his tale.

'I went outside the walls – through this very gate, in

fact – and sought a place to dig a hole, well beyond those cottages.' He pointed back up the sloping track down which the coroner had approached the village. 'Behind a hazel bush, I began to dig, as I saw a patch of soft earth which would be easier to shift, my old backbone not being as strong as it used to be.'

'Get to the point, man!' urged the Keeper irritably.

'Well, not more than a spade's depth down, I unearthed a foot, and a couple more strokes showed me a whole leg. I stopped digging and uttered a prayer or two to shrive the poor fellow, then went back to the village to tell someone.'

'What happened to the dog?' asked Gwyn.

'Oh, I buried him first, twenty paces away,' the priest reassured him.

The bailiff and portreeve were becoming impatient with this long-winded tale from their rather vague old vicar. 'Why did you not come straight to me?' demanded Edward Northcote belligerently. 'We could have settled the matter quickly and you could have given the man a decent burial in your churchyard, without all this unnecessary fuss with the coroner.'

Henry of Cumba smiled weakly at the bailiff. 'I intended to seek you out – but I met the Keeper here as I entered the gate and told him instead.'

'Just as well I happened to be here on my weekly per-ambulation from Axminster,' said Luke de Casewold breezily. 'From what he told me, it was a clear case for the coroner, not one to be brushed aside for the sake of convenience.'

'Nonsense! You're just an interfering busybody!' shouted Northcote, his hard features twisted in anger.

Incensed by this insult, the Keeper once again went red in the face and rattled his sword in its scabbard. 'Have a care, bailiff! You are just a servant, albeit of a priory – but I am a knight of the realm and deserve respect from such as you! One of the reasons that our

15

blessed King Richard set up Keepers last year was because of the laxity and corruption of sergeants and bailiffs.'

Again, John de Wolfe stepped in to quell the developing fight – if he had had a bucket of water, he would have thrown it over them, as if they were two dogs snarling in the street. 'Enough of this! I wish to see the body, straight away. I trust it has not been moved?'

De Casewold shook himself, like an angry cockerel settling its feathers.

'Of course not, Crowner! I know the law: the cadaver must be left *in situ* until viewed by the coroner. Though I had the nearest householders to put up hurdles around it to keep off dogs and foxes overnight.'

They set off back up the track, the Keeper of the Peace marching ahead importantly with his clerk trailing behind him. They were followed by the coroner's party, then the locals, headed by the bailiff and portreeve.

As they passed the few small thatched huts that straggled up from the town, heads poked out from each doorway, peering at these strangers from distant Exeter. Everyone knew that the coroner had been called, but no one wished to become involved unless they were forced to, as any contact with the law was likely to prove inconvenient and expensive in terms of attachments and amercements.

As they walked, John turned and beckoned to the portreeve to catch him up. 'Why did you say this was only a sailor whose body happened to be washed up here?' he asked. 'He could hardly get himself washed into a grave behind a hazel bush,' he added sarcastically.

Elias Palmer looked confused and guilty at the same time, as the bailiff hurried to join them. 'I thought . . . I only meant . . .' he stuttered, until Northcote interrupted gruffly.

16

'He meant that someone must have found the corpse washed up along the high-tide mark and decided to hide it away to avoid trouble ... such as that from the coroner!' he said rudely. 'We all know that having a corpse on your manor means an inquest and no doubt amercements for some breach of the rules, which you law officers always manage to find!'

Though he did not admit it, John had to agree that often the inhabitants of one village would drag a dead body across the boundary into another manor to relieve themselves of the problems that a corpse always presented. He grunted, his usual means of expressing his disapproval.

'Then someone here must have had prior knowledge of the corpse – and kept it to himself. I'll have him amerced for that when I find out who it was!'

As he uttered this threat, the Keeper stopped ahead of them and gesticulated, jabbing his arm towards the undergrowth that fronted a wood that lay at the foot of the high ground that was a backdrop to the town. On the other side of the track, the ground dropped away to the edge of the estuary.

'In here, Crowner, a hundred paces further.'

He dived into a patch of bushes and small trees, all greening up with the new growth of an early spring. Trampling primroses and violets, the half-score men plunged into the scrub and stopped alongside de Casewold as his clerk pulled down one of the hurdles of woven hazel withies to reveal a shallow pit.

'Here he is, Sir John! Kept quite intact for you,' he said with the air of someone who was offering a valuable gift.

De Wolfe looked down at the hole, where the gritty soil had been thrown aside to reveal a man's body lying face down in the earth. It was clothed in a leather jerkin rather like Gwyn's and a pair of canvas breeches cut off at mid-calf, with no shoes or cap, the typical wear for a ship's crewman.

'Do we know who he is?' was John's first demand.

There was much shaking of heads and muttered denials. Everyone from Axmouth was anxious to keep their distance from any knowledge of this cadaver.

'I lifted his head to see his face when I came back with the Keeper,' said the old priest hesitantly. 'But he's not one of my flock, that's for sure.'

John looked across at Gwyn, who from long experience knew the routine they needed to go through now. The big Cornishman stepped down into the excavation and lifted the corpse as easily as if it was a bag of straw, turning it over on to its back. 'He's a young fellow; I doubt he's reached eighteen summers,' he reported, brushing soil from the face with his fingers.

The coroner stepped down to join him and they both bent over the dead youth, while Thomas de Peyne, whose task was to record the findings, fumbled in his large shoulder bag to make sure he had his pens, ink-flask and parchments. Gwyn muttered something to de Wolfe and pointed to the half-open eyes. John nodded and prised open the lids with fingers and thumbs to examine the whites.

'Spotted with blood!' he bellowed. He turned his head to glare at the bailiff and portreeve accusingly 'So much for your damned drowning!' He picked up a hand and wagged it as if shaking hands with the corpse, determining that there was no death stiffness. Staring at the pads of the fingers and the palm, he shouted again. 'Not a sign of washerwoman's skin. He's not been in the water for long, if at all!'

Meanwhile, Gwyn had been industriously brushing away the remaining dirt from the face and neck, finally cleaning it off with a grubby kerchief that he dragged from a pocket.

'Look at this, Crowner,' he muttered as he gave a last wipe with his rag. John shifted his gaze from the hands and saw that around the front of the neck across the prominence of the Adam's apple was a livid line the width of his little finger. It passed back under the angles of the jaw and disappeared behind the ears.

'Turn him back on to his face!' barked the coroner, and when his officer had done so they looked at the back of the neck. When the skin was wiped clean, they saw that the dark lines, which had chafed the skin into brownish grooves, crossed over each other at the nape of the neck.

'Looks like a thin rope, with a spiral pattern,' observed Gwyn.

Anticipating his master, he turned the body over yet again and they both studied the face. It was in good condition as far as decay was concerned, as though the weather was mild it was still typically April and together with being buried in cold earth no decomposition had yet set in. The face was puffy and reddish-blue with congested blood, especially the lips. More of the tiny pinpoint bleeding spots that John had seen in the eyes were clustered around the mouth and temples.

Experts in modes of death from two decades on the battlefield and eighteen months of dealing with the corpses of Devonshire, the coroner and his officer had no doubt how this young man had died. John looked up at the ring of expectant faces looking down into the grave.

'He was strangled by a rope, held by someone standing behind him!' grated de Wolfe. 'So much for your drowned sailor, portreeve! Keeper, you were right: this is murder!'

Sir Luke de Casewold smiled smugly. 'I knew it from the outset, though the earth prevented me from seeing that strangling mark. But what innocent death ends up in a hole behind a bush, eh?'

De Wolfe rose to his feet, feeling the twinge in his bottom that he had mercifully forgotten for the past few minutes. 'Have you a dead-house or somewhere where we can lay this poor fellow until I hold the inquest?' He directed his question at the whole group of onlookers, but it was the old priest who answered.

'We have a shed in the churchyard where we lay cadavers awaiting burial. Will that suffice, sir?'

Within minutes, a handcart was fetched from the quayside. It stank of fish but was good enough to transport the corpse past the gawping villagers back to St Michael's Church, a sturdy stone edifice that had replaced the earlier wooden chapel of Saxon times. When the body was safely parked in the ramshackle lean-to against the north wall of the building, with a couple of barley sacks thrown over it, John turned to face the men who had trailed behind the cart.

'Now I need to get some sense out of you all!' he rasped, glowering around them, some obviously not disposed to be particularly cooperative.

'What the hell do we know about it?' growled the bailiff. 'He's a stranger here. I've never set eyes upon him before.' Elias Palmer, the lanky portreeve, nodded his agreement, for he seemed to go along with anything Edward Northcote decreed.

'We need to know who he is, as soon as possible,' said de Casewold with an air of authority. 'The coroner here has to enquire into his death without delay.'

Again John was exasperated that the self-important Keeper seemed intent on doing his work for him. 'There are many issues to be settled, apart from his identity, though I admit that is of prior urgency.' He fixed his stony stare on the parish priest. 'Father Henry, you say he is not one of your flock from this village. Have you any other suggestions?'

The cleric rubbed his bald pate as if to stimulate his ancient brain. 'He was buried more than a mile from the river mouth, so is unlikely to have been washed up from the open sea.'

'He showed no signs of being in the water – at least not for more than an hour or two. And he certainly didn't drown!' snapped de Wolfe.

'It suggests that he is from the locality, if he's not a shipwrecked sailor,' mused the priest. 'Yet he wears a seaman's garb.'

Gwyn leant towards his master. 'If he's not from this port, what about those other havens nearby?' he whispered hoarsely.

John nodded at the suggestion. 'What about the village on the other side of the river, almost on the shore?'

The portreeve seemed anxious to keep in favour with all sides of the debate.

'Seaton, you mean, Crowner?' he asked eagerly. 'There are certainly ships and shipmen there, though most are fishermen. He could have come from there, I suppose.'

'And equally from Sidmouth or Budleigh – even from Lyme, in the next county!' countered Northcote, intent on being difficult.

De Wolfe next addressed the Keeper, determined to show him who was in charge here. 'I suggest, Sir Luke, that you send your clerk across the river to enquire if any man has gone missing from there in the past few days. The state of this corpse suggests that he has been dead less than a week, even though cold earth slows down the pace of corruption.'

De Casewold looked slightly affronted at being told what to do by a law officer he considered to be of equal status, but he made no protest and sent Hugh Bogge, with one of the villagers, to find his way across the water to Seaton.

'Meanwhile, I and my officer and clerk need some sustenance after the long ride from Exeter,' declared

21

the coroner. 'Where can we be fed and rested for an hour?'

Normally, a king's officer such as de Wolfe would claim hospitality from the local lord in his castle or manor house – or failing that in an abbey or priory. As Axmouth had none of these, it fell to the bailiff to grudgingly offer his own house for the purpose, rather than suggest one of the many taverns that catered mainly for seafarers. 'I can't offer much. I have no wife to cater for me, only an idle servant,' he warned.

John and his two companions followed him from the church back up the short street that lay within the walls to one of the better buildings in the village. Luke de Casewold attached himself to them without invitation, as did Elias Palmer.

Like most of the other cottages, the bailiff's house was built of cob plastered within stout oak frames, but it was in good condition, with fresh whitewash on the walls and new thatch on the roof. It consisted of one large room, the end partitioned off for his bed, a luxury indicative of his position in the community. In view of the mild weather, only a small fire glowed in the clay-lined pit, ringed with stones, in the centre of the floor. What little smoke there was wafted upwards to find its way out under the eaves, as there was no chimney. No cooking was done here, as there was a separate kitchen-hut behind the house, with a larger fire tended by his servant.

A table with benches and a few stools completed the furniture, except for another long table against the wall which bore tally-sticks and some parchments as well as quill pens and an ink-bottle. These caught Thomas's eye as he entered, as it was unusual to find anyone in a village who was literate, apart from the priest. Edward Northcote noticed the clerk's interest and gruffly explained.

'Elias, my portreeve, uses this room to make his

manifests, the lists of cargo going in and out of the port. He's the only man who can read and write, apart from the old priest.'

He waved them to the table, and his servant, a toothless old man with a bad limp, brought in clay cups and a pitcher of ale. While they waited for him to bring some food, John enquired about the port. 'I've not been here before. It seems a busy, thriving place.'

The portreeve hastened to broaden the coroner's knowledge, the pride in his voice being almost proprietorial. 'Axmouth has long been an important harbour, sir. We know that the Romans used it, but doubtless it was known before that.'

As usual, the erudite Thomas could not resist airing his own knowledge. 'Indeed it was! The classical writers tell of Phoenicians sailing here to collect tin, long before the birth of Our Saviour.' He paused to cross himself at the mention of the Holy Name.

The bailiff, his own pride in his little town not to be denied, nodded his agreement. 'It is one of the major ports of England, with its estuary safely tucked under the long headland behind the town. We rarely have fewer than half a score of vessels moored here during the sailing season.'

'What is their main trade, then?' asked John. His interest was not prompted by his role as coroner but as a partner in a wool-exporting business with Hugh de Relaga, one of the portreeves of Exeter. They used the wharves of that city to send their bales abroad, mainly to Flanders and the Rhine.

The portreeve answered him, a frown on his narrow face. 'On the outward voyages, fine limestone from the quarries of Beer, but mostly wool, Crowner, though this tax that King Richard has imposed has begun to stifle the trade.'

De Wolfe caught a warning glance pass from the bailiff to Elias Palmer and assumed it was a hint that it might be undiplomatic to criticise the monarch in front of two of his law officers.

'And what do they bring in to this place?' asked John.

The bailiff shrugged his big shoulders. 'All manner of goods, depending on where they come from. French wine from Barfleur or Bordeaux, dried fruit from France – and of course finished cloth from Flanders or the Rhine.'

John nodded. It was the same with the ships he and his partner employed, though much tin was also exported from Exeter, being one of the smelting and assay towns.

Their talk was interrupted by the old servant bringing in a board bearing a haunch of cold mutton, two loaves, butter and cheese. He set it on the table, and Northcote cut thick slices of meat with his dagger, laying them on the board for the others to take. The portreeve slashed the loaves into quarters, and each man started to eat, picking up the food with their fingers or with small eating knives from the pouches on their belts.

'I live simply,' growled Northcote. 'I have been a widower these past five years and live alone, apart from that old fellow in the kitchen.'

'You keep the records and accounts, bailiff?' ventured Thomas, nodding towards the other table with its parchments and writing materials.

'I am the prior's creature in that respect. He is insistent that everything is properly recorded.' Edward Northcote picked up another piece of mutton and held it before his lips before continuing. 'The portreeve here does most of the organising of the town's trade and deals with the shipmasters, and as I am unlettered he also scribes all the records.'

They fell silent as the rest of the food was devoured. Then the ale-pots were refilled and Sir John returned to the matter in hand.

'My officer and I will finish our examination of the body, then I wish to see that every effort is made to put a name to the victim.'

Luke de Casewold, who had been quiet for the duration of the meal, looked doubtful. 'I doubt my clerk will return this afternoon. By the time he crosses the river, makes his enquiries in Seaton and gets back again, you will not have time to return to Exeter tonight.'

Though the coroner would dearly have liked to get back to the city before the gates closed at the dusk curfew, he accepted that their horses would not relish a forced march after already covering twenty miles that morning. He resigned himself to a mattress in one of the inns, no hardship for such seasoned campaigners as Gwyn and himself, though Thomas would probably whine at the discomfort. He told de Casewold that he would stay over and hold an inquest in the morning, hoping that the corpse's identity would be established by then.

'For now, I will just spend an hour looking at the quayside and questioning some of the shipmen. If this poor lad was a sailor, they may know him.'

The coroner left the bailiff, the parish priest and portreeve together in the house and walked with his assistants and the Keeper of the Peace back to the church. Here Gwyn stripped the clothing from the corpse and, together with John, examined it closely from head to toe. The young man was slim but had plenty of muscle in his arms and legs. His dark hair was plastered to his scalp and forehead by the dampness of his makeshift grave, but there was nothing abnormal to be seen apart from the ligature mark around the neck and the clear signs of strangulation in the face. Gwyn searched the scanty clothing and found nothing useful. 'No belt or pouch, not a coin or badge to help us,' he muttered, as for the sake of decency he pulled the garments back over the corpse.

'How long would you say he's been dead?' ruminated de Wolfe. 'A few days?' He often had a contest with his officer, both reckoning themselves experts in all aspects of death.

'His death stiffness has passed off. It was cool in that grave, but I doubt he was croaked earlier than about Saturday.'

It was now Tuesday, and de Wolfe nodded his agreement. He turned to Thomas, who was hanging about outside the mortuary shed, still queasy about dead bodies even after a year and a half as coroner's clerk.

'There's nothing to write on your roll until we hold the inquest, so I suggest you find Father Henry again and see if he has any useful village gossip. You are usually good at wheedling information from your fellow clerics.' Thomas wandered off, not sure whether the coroner's remark was a compliment or a jibe.

When Gwyn had covered up the corpse again, still lying on the fish-barrow, they began walking towards the quayside. Luke de Casewold still strode alongside them, as John was unable to shake him off. He could hardly order a fellow law officer to go away, especially as this was an obvious murder on the Keeper's own territory. No one seemed quite clear how far the functions and powers of these new officials extended, as far as de Wolfe could make out; only a few knights had been appointed around the country on a somewhat random basis, depending on who could be persuaded to take on the job. Like the coroners, they were unpaid, with expenses doled out from the sheriff's funds, but no salary. The trio walked out through the other town gate, just beyond the church. Here the road turned sharply to the left and carried on along the water's edge, where, on their right, half a dozen ships were settling on to the mud as the tide receded. On the landward side, there was a narrow belt of land under the loom of the large ridge above the estuary. Here were more cottages and taverns, as well as barn-like buildings with thatched or stone-tiled roofs.

'These are storehouses for goods either brought in or waiting to be loaded on to the ships,' said Luke helpfully. 'Though that one is the fish market.'

He pointed to an open-fronted shed where a dozen men and women were gutting fish and dropping them into baskets. The estuary here was wide and open to the sea, and on the other side the villages of Seaton and Fleet also had small ships beached along their banks. Nearer the sea, which shimmered in the distance in the early-afternoon sun, John could see pebble and shingle banks around a tiny island set off the shore at Seaton.

As they walked, John saw that some parts of the water's edge had been strengthened by stone, forming wharves where the cogs could be tied up at high tide and supported when it dropped, so that loading and unloading could be carried on more easily. Elsewhere, at low tide, the vessels leant over a little on their keels, but still the crew and other labourers managed to hurry up and down planks laid to the shore with their sacks, bales and kegs. It was a busy scene, with some of the cargoes being stacked on the ground or loaded into the many ox-carts that trundled back and forth. Still more was being moved in and out of the warehouses on the other side of the track, and John was particularly interested in one that was half filled with bales of wool. Many of these were being carried across the road to a larger ship, to be stacked in the single hold that gaped in the middle of her deck.

The tall, gaunt figure of the king's coroner received many curious stares from both the porters and seamen. His hunched figure, dressed all in black, was an unusual sight on a harbour wharf, especially as he was accompanied by a ginger giant with a large sword. The Keeper of the Peace aroused no interest, as he had been a frequent and usually unwelcome visitor to Axmouth since his appointment.

They walked the length of the quayside and continued for almost half a mile down to where the estuary met the open sea, beneath the cliffs of the headland rising on their left. It was a calm day, and only low waves rippled in across the wide harbour mouth, petering out as they travelled upstream.

'This place would look mightily different in a westerly gale,' observed Gwyn, his maritime past making him a confident expert. 'But these vessels would be safe enough, especially if they moved further upriver if it got really rough.'

De Wolfe grunted. He was not much interested in the ships, but rather in their crews. 'That corpse must have been a seaman, dressed as he was,' he ruminated aloud. 'We should make some enquiries of some of these shipmasters.'

'Checking on gossip in the alehouses might be the quickest way,' suggested his officer, ever keen to find some excuse to enter a tavern. The only tavern John was keen to enter was the Bush in Exeter to see his mistress, but that was twenty miles away.

'You go, then, Gwyn; see what you can discover. I'll have words with a few of these shipmen and we'll meet in the village in an hour.'

With the Keeper still in tow, he loped back to the cog that was loading wool, as Gwyn vanished across the road to a shack that had a wilting bush hanging over the doorway. The blunt vessel was leaning a little towards him, but men were padding across from the storehouse over the road, each with a large bale of wool on his back, securely trussed with coarse twine.

As they clambered up the gangplank to the deck, a man in a russet tunic and green breeches stood at its foot, staring at each load and muttering to himself.

'Who's this fellow?' grunted de Wolfe.

'That's John Capie,' answered Luke de Casewold. 'He's the tally-man who reckons up the Customs dues – though I suspect that far more gets past him than he records!' he added cynically.

John looked more closely and saw that the sallow-faced Capie had a long cord in his hands, which had a multitude of knots tied along its length. As each man hurried past with his burden, his fingers moved on another knot, his lips moving as he counted.

The coroner nodded in understanding. Now he knew how his own export taxes were calculated on the quaysides of Exeter and Topsham. The lucrative wool business he shared with Hugh de Relaga would be even more lucrative if they could avoid the Customs dues that the king's Council had imposed upon England in order to pay for the Lionheart's adventures overseas. Like de Casewold, he had his suspicions that not all the tax due on the bales that sailed out of the River Exe was actually declared, but this was something he did not wish to know about.

He looked up at the rising stern of the vessel and saw a burly man with a bushy red beard standing on the afterdeck. With his hands planted firmly on his hips, his posture suggested that he was the man in charge, as he glared at the procession of seamen and stevedores as if daring them to slow their efforts.

'That must be the shipmaster. I'll get up there and have a word with him,' grunted de Wolfe. He fitted himself into a gap between two men lugging bales up the plank and strode up to the deck, the Keeper following behind the next porter.

The man with the beard scowled at him as he approached.

'What do you want, sir?' he growled, though his habitual bluster was tempered by his recognition that this was a man of substance. The sombre but good-quality clothing and the expensive sword that swung at his hip told of wealth and authority.

'I am Sir John de Wolfe, the king's coroner for this county. Have you heard of the finding of a man's body near the village today?'

Impressed as he was by the rank of this law officer, the shipmaster remained surly. 'I have too much work here to listen to gossip,' he grunted.

'News of a strangled youth is somewhat more than gossip,' snapped de Wolfe. 'And this fellow appeared to be a shipman. We need to know who he is, so have you any of your crew missing?'

Red Beard shook his head. 'Half my men were paid off when I arrived yesterday. God knows where they are now. We only had one young 'un; he had hair the colour of wheat straw, if that's any help.'

As the dead boy's hair was almost black, this ruled him out, if the sullen shipmaster was telling the truth. The coroner climbed back down to the quayside and strode along the river, calling at each vessel and asking similar questions at every one of them. He had little but reluctant answers and surly shakes of the head, which made him suspect that there was a conspiracy of silence amongst these seamen.

'Not a very helpful bunch, are they?' he growled to Luke de Casewold as they finally reached the gateway into the village.

'Sailors are a strange lot; they stick together against the world, just like tinners,' observed the Keeper, who seemed to possess a philosophical streak.

'I got the feeling that they were hiding something from me,' grumbled John.

'They're like that with all law officers,' said Luke reassuringly. 'On principle, they are reluctant to give us even a "good morning" if they can avoid it. Not that that's confined to shipmen; every damned man and woman in the hundred answers me grudgingly.

Everyone has a guilty conscience about something!'

'What have these seafarers got to hide, then?' demanded de Wolfe.

As they entered the village, de Casewold sniggered. 'They are all crooked, Crowner! Smuggling is their main sin, though I'd not put a little piracy past some of them.'

'I thought that tally-man down there was supposed to check all the goods. How does he operate, then?'

There was an alehouse just inside the town gate, on the left side of the track opposite the church. It was known by common usage as the Harbour Inn. Luke waved the coroner to a rough bench outside and yelled through the door for jars of ale. As they sat together in the sun, he explained the system that collected the dues from a busy port such as Axmouth.

'This fellow John Capie does his best to record all taxable goods that go out or come in from the harbour. Christ alone understands how he does it, mainly with knotted strings and notched tally-sticks, for he can neither read nor write.'

A slattern brought out two quart pots of ale, which tasted better than it looked, though John pined for the good stuff brewed by Nesta in the Bush back home. He drank and listened while the Keeper carried on with his explanation. 'Capie then goes twice a day to Elias Palmer, who writes down what Capie calculates has been loaded or discharged from each of the ships.'

'But he can't be at every ship all the time,' objected John.

'That's very true, though he checks the goods in the warehouses as well, trying to get some idea of what is being moved in and out of the port.'

De Wolfe saw Gwyn approaching in the distance and gulped down the rest of his ale, confident that he would need another jug as soon as the Cornishman arrived.

31

'This system seems wide open to error and abuse, if you ask me!' he growled. 'How does he actually get the money paid?'

'That's Elias Palmer's job. He charges both a manor tax and a county tax, squeezing it from whoever owns the wool or wine or whatever the goods happen to be. The first levy goes to the Priory of Loders, who own the village, then the royal tax goes to the sheriff as part of the county farm.'

Gwyn of Polruan stamped up the last few yards to the Harbour Inn and dropped heavily on to the bench.

'Waste of bloody time! Nobody knows a thing – or so they say!' he reported. 'Wouldn't tell us if they did, by their attitude! Something strange about this village, I reckon. As if they are keeping some big secret.'

Luke de Casewold nodded sagely. 'I've felt the same ever since I started coming down here as Keeper,' he asserted. 'The whole damned place is up to something, I can feel it in my bones!' He drained his ale-jar and stood up. 'I'm going to get to the bottom of it, too, whatever the cost! I was appointed to keep the peace – and that includes anything that's to the detriment of our good King Richard.'

John de Wolfe was as ardent a supporter of the Coeur de Lion as any man in England, but he felt strangely embarrassed at this over-pretentious loyalty. The fellow had been in office only a few months and here he was declaring that he was going to root out the king's enemies in a flea-bitten seaport like Axmouth. He had better watch his step, thought John. Edward Northcote, the Prior of Loders and some of those tough-looking shipmasters would not take kindly to this popinjay interfering in their affairs.

Almost immediately he felt guilty, for was he not himself a king's officer, sworn to uphold the law and justice in all their forms? Maybe he was influenced by his own dealings in wool and other commodities in his

partnership in Exeter to be sufficiently condemnatory
of any sharp practices elsewhere. As he pondered this
potential conflict of interests, there was a distant shout
from beyond the town gate. The three of them turned
and saw that Hugh Bogge, the clerk to the Keeper,
was coming up from the river bank, where there was a
landing for the small boat that ferried people across
the estuary to Seaton. Behind him waddled the figure
of a woman, dressed in black with a dark shawl over her
head in spite of the warmth of the day.

'It looks as if he's found someone,' said Luke smugly.

The clerk marched up to them, having the same self-
important air as his master. Bogge was a short, rotund
fellow with a moon face and pasty complexion. His
mousy hair was shorn into a tonsure, and his stained
black cassock was clinched at the waist with a wide
leather belt, through which a large sheathed dagger
was thrust, somewhat incongruously for a man in minor
holy orders. The woman, who looked old but may
not have been more than fifty, plodded up behind him,
her lined face telling of a hard life and little expecta-
tion of it becoming better. She looked warily at these
men from Exeter and Axminster, for law officers never
heralded anything other than trouble and sadness.

'This is Edith Makerel, a widow of Seaton,'
announced Hugh Bogge, displaying the old lady with
an almost proprietorial air. De Wolfe rose from his
bench and gave her a curt nod, while Gwyn gently took
her arm and shepherded her to his seat.

'Edith had already reported the disappearance of
her son Simon to the reeve in Seaton,' continued the
clerk. 'He was a shipman who returned from his last
voyage a week ago. On Saturday he went out of their
cottage, which is down near the beach – and that's the
last she ever saw of him.'

Widow Makerel sat looking up at the men, her eyes
red-rimmed with old tears. She had a piece of rag in

her hands, and her fingers continually tore at it as she spoke.

'He was not really a shipman, sirs. The lad wanted to become a clerk, but I could not afford for him to go and learn his letters. He said he would earn enough in a few years to do that and had been apprenticed to a baker in Seaton, but it burnt down a month ago and he had to seek work elsewhere. Since his father was drowned at the fishing, my two sons are our only support. The other one labours in the quarries in Beer. I did not want my boys to suffer the fate of my husband, but Simon was determined to go.'

'So he went to sea recently, madam?' asked John politely. 'But he returned home safely some days ago?'

She nodded, still shredding the rag between her fingers. 'It was but his second voyage, sir. He hated it, but it earned the few pence we sorely needed. In fact, he came back last Thursday with more than we expected. He flung it down on the table and refused to say where it came from. I knew something was very wrong.' She began to sob, and again it was Gwyn who tried to console her. The big, shambling officer placed an arm around her shoulders as he bent over her. 'We need you to look at a body, Edith. Only you can help us in this. Come with us now, across to the church.'

As they all slowly crossed the village street to the church of St Michael, Luke de Casewold murmured to his clerk: 'How did you find her, Hugh?'

'I went around the few ships on that side of the river, but none could – or would – tell me anything. Then I found the reeve of Seaton and he said that Widow Makerel had been searching for her son Simon. I went to see her and it seemed likely that a dark-haired youth of eighteen might be the one we seek.'

In the churchyard, before the procession reached the mortuary shed, Thomas de Peyne and the parish priest, Henry of Cumba, appeared from the ornately carved arch which was the entrance to the church. Hugh Bogge briefly explained to them what was happening, and now the two priests took over from Gwyn as supporters of Edith Makerel. They guided her under the lean-to roof and the identification was short and dramatic.

With a howl, the poor woman fell upon the body as Thomas uncovered the face and lay sobbing across the odorous fish-cart. Her pathetic cries of 'My son, my poor son!' left no doubt as to the identity of the corpse.

An admitted coward in the face of emotional crises, John backed away and left the two priests with the distraught woman. As he walked back to the gate of the churchyard with the Keeper of the Peace and his clerk, he pondered the possible significance of what they had heard.

'Why strangle some young deckhand?' he muttered. 'He was hardly likely to have a heavy purse upon him that could be stolen.'

'What about this money that his mother said he gave her?' asked Luke. 'She seemed surprised and a little suspicious of where it came from. And why did she say there was something amiss with the lad when he returned from the voyage?'

De Wolfe turned to Hugh Bogge as they reached the village street. 'Do you know what vessel he was sailing on? Is it one of those still along the quayside there?'

'No, I asked the widow. She said this was the second voyage her son had made on a cog called *The Tiger*. He was due to sail on her again for Calais yesterday, but of course he went missing.'

'Damnation! I needed to have called her crew to my inquest tomorrow.' The coroner was irritated that nothing seemed to be going smoothly with this case. 'Is there no one else who knew the boy?'

'There is his brother – and his mother said he has a girl in Seaton whom he hoped to marry.'

'Get them to the inquest in the morning – I will hold it in the churchyard at the tenth hour. My own officer can roust out the rest to form a jury; the bailiff, the portreeve, the priest and a dozen villagers will suffice.'

De Wolfe looked at the Harbour Inn across the road. 'This looks the best tavern in the place. I need to find us a good meal and a mattress each for the night.'

CHAPTER TWO

In which the coroner holds an inquest

Soon after dawn, John de Wolfe roused himself from his bed, which had been a hessian bag stuffed with straw. The accommodation for guests in Axmouth's premier inn was a barn-like building at the back of the tavern, where the upper floor was reached by a ladder. On the bare boards, a dozen such mattresses were spread out, the management providing a coarse blanket as an added luxury, under which the lodgers slept in their clothes, minus boots and headgear. The coroner stood up and looked around the loft in the pale morning light, which squeezed in through several slits in the walls. He saw four or five other men huddled on their pallets, as well as Thomas and Gwyn, the latter snoring like a grampus.

Pulling on his boots, he prodded his officer and clerk with a toecap and, when he was sure that they were groaning themselves awake, went down to the floor below. Here, several other men, all shipmen by their clothing, sat on benches at a long trestle table, slurping gruel from wooden bowls and eating fresh barley bread cut from several loaves lying on the scrubbed boards.

At the end of the room, a boy was stirring the oatmeal in a large pot hanging from a tripod over a fire.

When de Wolfe dropped heavily on a bench and grunted a vague greeting to the ruffian next to him, the lad brought him a bowl of porridge and a spoon carved from a cow's horn. Then a young girl, no more than eight years old, came around the table with a large jug to top up the crude clay pots with watered ale.

As he finished his gruel, which had the consistency of back-yard mud that had been trampled by pigs in wet weather, he reached for the nearest loaf and cut off an inch-thick slice with his dagger. There was half a cheese next to the loaf, and at the risk of blunting his blade he hacked off a large piece and began chewing while he cleared his mind of sleep.

By now, Thomas and Gwyn had tumbled down the ladder and started on their own frugal breakfast.

'We hold this inquest and then ride for home, Crowner?' asked the Cornishman hopefully.

John grunted. 'Doubt we'll learn much from it, but we have to start somewhere. I need to talk to the bailiff and the portreeve first.'

'A pity that vessel, *The Tiger*, sailed on Sunday,' observed Thomas, his narrow face twisted in distaste at the sour porridge. 'I feel someone aboard her might be the miscreant. After all, the lad lived across in Seaton, but his body was hidden on this side of the river, so he was almost certainly slain here.'

'Well, they bloody have gone, so there's no use regretting it.'

A man sitting opposite joined in. 'They'll be back, as that cog belongs here, she's not just a visitor to the Axe.' He was a beefy mariner, with a short tunic which looked as if it had been made from a spare sail.

'When is she likely to return?' demanded de Wolfe.

The sailor shrugged. 'They've gone to Calais, but it doesn't mean they'll sail straight back. They might find a cargo for the Rhine or back down to St-Malo. Could be ten days, could be a month.'

The man next to him sniggered. 'Depends on who they meet out in the Channel!' He was a foxy little fellow with a bad squint. The first shipman glared at him, and John had the impression that he had kicked Foxy hard on the leg under the table, as the smaller man jerked and winced.

'Who's the shipmaster – and who owns the vessel?' asked Gwyn.

'The master is Martin Rof, who lives in this vill. As to the owner, I've no knowledge; you'll have to ask Northcote or Elias Palmer.'

He rose rather abruptly, leaving half his bread on the table, as if he was unwilling to answer any more questions. As he left, he gestured sharply at the squinting man, who followed him sheepishly out of the door.

'What was all that about?' growled Gwyn. 'I say again, there's something odd about this place.'

The coroner turned to his clerk. 'Thomas, did you learn anything from your ecclesiastical friend yesterday?'

His clerk confessed that Henry of Cumba had nothing solid to tell him, though Thomas had sensed that all was not well in the town of Axmouth.

'It was clear that the Prior of Loders had a strong grip on the place and dictated much of what was done there,' mused the clerk. 'The parish priest is but a vicar employed by the priory for parish duties. This bailiff Edward Northcote seems an iron-handed master and acts more like a manor-lord than a servant of the priory.'

'What about the portreeve?' asked John.

De Peyne's humped shoulder shrugged under his thin cassock. 'It's clear that he is under the thumb of Northcote, though the pair of them seem to rule everything that goes on in Axmouth. Yet I had the notion that Father Henry suspects that Elias Palmer has his own intrigues, even though he appears to defer to the bailiff in everything.'

Thomas had coaxed little else out of the parish priest, and when they had finished eating John paid the ale-wife a few pennies and they went into the main street.

'Get as much of a jury as you can scrape together, Gwyn,' ordered the coroner. 'With that damned ship gone, we must make do with the widow, the lad's doxy, the First Finder and a few villagers and shipmen. If they are reluctant, wave your sword at them and threaten them with the name of the Lionheart!'

Gwyn ambled off towards the quayside and John led Thomas back up through the village to the bailiff's dwelling. It was a bright morning, spring being now well advanced. Birds were stealing straw from the thatched roofs of the cottages to build their nests, and the sun was drying the mud that rutted the road through the town. Inside Northcote's house, they found him leaning over the portreeve, as the latter inscribed a parchment on a table against the inner wall. Suddenly conscious that Thomas de Peyne was able to read, Elias blew rapidly on his wet ink and took a large pebble off the foot of the document, so that the parchment rolled itself up, out of sight of prying eyes.

'Just recording the tally of a cargo of wine unloaded yesterday,' he piped unconvincingly. 'There'll be dues to pay on that, by merchants in Taunton and Bristol.'

De Wolfe had no interest in Customs tax; he had a corpse to investigate. 'I will need you both at my inquest this morning. I will hold it across the cadaver in the churchyard, around the tenth hour. I want to get home to Exeter as soon as possible.'

Edward Northcote scowled at him. 'I have no time to waste on such matters. What has the slaying of some youth from Seaton to do with me?'

John's black eyebrows rose up his forehead. 'Are you not the bailiff of this vill?' he demanded. 'It is *you* who should be helping *me* in this tragedy. You are responsible for law and order here, on behalf of the sheriff! No wonder the Chief Justiciar has appointed Keepers such as de Casewold, if the bailiffs will not shift themselves to do their duty!'

'De Casewold! A self-important nonentity, running around bleating about justice yet unable to do a thing,' sneered Northcote. 'He has no power, no authority apart from his own rasping voice!'

The coroner gestured impatiently. 'I'm not here to bandy words with you, bailiff! I want to know about the vessel that the dead youth sailed upon.' He did not bother to ask if Northcote and Elias had heard that the lad's identity had been discovered, as he was well aware that those two would be fully informed within minutes of everything that went on in Axmouth.

The bailiff scowled at him suspiciously, an attitude that seemed almost permanent with him. 'Simon Makerel was a shipman upon the vessel. What else is there to know?'

'The cog herself, damn you,' snapped de Wolfe irritably. 'I know her name and that of the shipmaster, Martin Rof. But who owned her, where had she been on the last voyage and where has she gone now?'

It was the portreeve who answered this. He rolled up his parchment and stood it on end on the table before getting up from his stool.

'*The Tiger* belongs to Robert de Helion, a manor-lord who lives in Exeter, though his lands are scattered about this county and that of Dorset.'

De Wolfe knew of de Helion, but he had no closer acquaintance with him. He knew he was a rich merchant as well as a landowner but had no idea he ran ships as well. 'And what about this cog, when will she be back?'

He received the same reply as the one he had got on the quayside.

'She came in here last week from Barfleur with wine and dried fruit – and has taken wool and some tin over to Calais. Who can tell when she will return? It depends on what cargoes the master can find across the Channel.'

The coroner glowered at the pair before him, which seemed to leave them quite unperturbed. 'Is there anything else I should know about this vessel or her master?'

The bailiff and portreeve looked at each other, then Northcote shook his head. 'I don't know what you mean, Crowner. What is there to say about a merchant ship? They come in here by the dozen.'

'Their crewmen don't end up strangled by the dozen!' retorted John.

Edward Northcote shrugged dismissively. 'This is a seaport; sailors are rough, heavy-drinking men. They get into brawls over women and money all the time and not a few end up dead, one way or the other.'

The coroner made a rude noise. 'This was a youth on his second voyage, a lad who was mild-mannered, wanting to become a clerk. Is it likely that such as he would end up strangled and buried in a hidden grave?'

Northcote stared stonily at de Wolfe. 'That's for you to discover, sir. You catch the killer and I'll judge him in the Hundred court.'

John stuck his head forward aggressively, like a large black vulture. 'You'll do no such thing! When the man who did this is caught, he'll go before the king's justices in Exeter.'

He swung around to leave, but at the door he threw a parting command over his shoulder. 'You'll both be in the churchyard at the tenth hour – or I'll attach you in the sum of five marks!'

*

The inquest was as unrewarding as de Wolfe had expected, but it had to be done, partly to allow the widow to have her son's body returned for reburial across in Seaton. A motley crowd assembled on the green patch around St Michael's, with most of the population of Axmouth who were not otherwise occupied staring over the low wall at these unusual proceedings, the first inquest ever to be held in the village.

Gwyn had rounded up a score of men from both the village and the ships berthed along the strand, bullying them into a straggling half-circle facing the east end of the church. The corpse was wheeled out on its fish-cart and placed in the centre, as Gwyn bellowed out his summons for 'all good men of the county who have anything to do with the king's coroner touching the death of Simon Makerel to stand forth and give their attendance'.

De Wolfe's menacing black-clad figure hovered alongside the cadaver, while Thomas sat nearby on an empty keg brought from the tavern opposite. He had a board across his knees to support ink and parchment, so that he could record the proceedings, sparse though they were. On his other side, somewhat to John's annoyance, Luke de Casewold stood as if he was also involved in conducting the enquiry. The Keeper of the Peace had insisted on riding the five miles from his home near Axminster especially to attend the inquest.

Henry of Cumba was called as the First Finder, and John accepted that the parish priest had fulfilled his legal duty by immediately informing the portreeve and bailiff of his discovery of the corpse. Strictly speaking, he should have raised the hue and cry by knocking up the four nearest households to search for the killer, but as the body had obviously been buried for days and the whole village had rapidly turned out to gossip about the event, de Wolfe refrained from imposing a fine.

Next, the bailiff grudgingly admitted that he had been informed of the death by the priest and had gone with the portreeve to confirm that there was indeed a body behind the hazel bush. Then the Keeper stood forward, even before de Wolfe could ask him, to deliver a self-important and long-winded description of how he had heard of the discovery and had sent his clerk hurrying to Exeter to notify the coroner.

Edith Makerel, the widow from Seaton, was this morning supported by her remaining son and a young woman who John took to be the girlfriend of the dead Simon. Between them, they gently moved the weeping mother forward, where she haltingly confirmed that the body was indeed that of her son.

'He was a good lad, kind to me and gentle, as one would expect for one who wanted to take holy orders,' she said between sobs. 'He should never have gone to sea. The life and the men he was with were too rough for his temperament.'

The coroner, as always uncomfortable with any show of emotion, particularly from women, tried to get her to enlarge on her comment that Simon had been worried or unhappy after returning from his voyage, but she was unable to be more specific. John tried another approach.

'If your son was of a religious nature, might he not have confided something to a priest?'

Edith wiped her eyes with the back of her hand. 'He was a diligent attender at Seaton church, sir, and respected the priest there very much. He might have done, I suppose, but he said nothing about it to me.'

John bent down to Thomas and muttered into his ear: 'We should have got the priest from Seaton over here. Would you be able to get anything out of him if you went over there?'

Thomas, though always anxious to help, looked dubious. 'If it was said in the confessional, he would not divulge it even to me. It seems an unlikely path to follow, master.'

De Wolfe grunted his acceptance of his clerk's opinion and carried on with some questions, but they led nowhere. The brother of the dead man, a sallow fellow probably six years older than Simon, had little to offer.

'As our mother has said, my brother seemed distant in his mind when he returned from his voyage. And he had money, which was unusual.'

Simon's girlfriend, a plain pudding of a wench about sixteen years of age, was equally unhelpful. De Wolfe gained the impression that she was more a dog-like follower of the sailor than his choice of a future mate – which fitted with his ambition to one day enter holy orders.

Then John called the portreeve, mainly to justify his insistence that Elias Palmer must attend the inquest, but, apart from confirming his view of the body and the name of the cog and her master that Simon Makerel had sailed upon, it was a futile exercise.

After scowling around the blank faces of the jurors, he asked if anyone had anything they wished to say that might be relevant, but there was a stony silence. Then Luke de Casewold, to John's smouldering annoyance, spoke up in his harsh, piercing voice.

'Come, someone must know something! This is a small port. Everyone always knows each other's business.' He smacked his palms together, like a school-master warning his pupils. 'Speak up, or it will go badly with you!'

His threatening exhortation fell on deaf ears. Though there was some muted grumbling and men looked sullenly at each other, no one volunteered a single word. The coroner, though regretting the lack of any progress, was secretly pleased that this interloper's brashness had failed so abjectly.

The last act in this fruitless performance was the exhibition of the body to the jury, which was demanded by the law. Gwyn pulled down the sheet that covered the head and neck, and the score of village men and mariners filed past, as de Wolfe pointed out the marks on the neck, which had become more livid and prominent with the passage of time.

'There seems nothing more to be said, then,' he concluded. 'No verdict can be reached on such thin evidence, so this inquest is adjourned until some later day. That will probably depend upon when the vessel, *The Tiger*, returns to this harbour.'

He stopped and cleared his throat as he looked at the grieving mother. 'In the meantime, the body of Simon Makerel may be restored to his family for burial.'

Gwyn stood and bellowed out that 'all good men may now depart and take their ease', and the crowd melted away, a substantial proportion going in the direction of the Harbour Inn and other alehouses.

Thomas packed away his writing materials into the capacious shoulder bag that he always carried, and the coroner's trio prepared to ride back to Exeter.

'We'll take food in the next village,' rumbled John as they collected their horses from the stables of the tavern. 'The sooner I'm out of this place, the better I'll be suited.'

He grunted a farewell to the bailiff and portreeve, who seemed indifferent to whether he stayed or not. The Keeper was a little more outgoing at their departure and came up to John's side as he settled himself carefully in Odin's saddle so as to minimise the soreness of his backside. The boil had subsided a little, but it still gave him considerable discomfort.

'Sir John, it was a pleasure to work with you,' brayed de Casewold. 'I look forward to meeting you again when you return to hold the full inquest. I will keep you informed about the return of that cog and her crew.'

The coroner scowled at him. 'I have already charged the bailiff with that task,' he snapped ungraciously. 'About time the damned fellow did his duty. I'll be having words with the sheriff about his lack of enthusiasm for his job!'

Luke gave a wide smile. It was clear that there was animosity between him and Edward Northcote. 'I will keep my ear to the ground, coroner. There is something going on under the surface in this town and I'll not rest until I get to the bottom of it!'

Though he disliked the Keeper, John felt a little uneasy at the prospect of one lone man meddling too deeply in a place where there seemed to be a tyrant in charge. 'Take care how you proceed. I don't want to visit here again to deal with another corpse!' he advised.

De Casewold sniggered through his little rosebud of a mouth. He tapped the hilt of his sword. 'I can look after myself, thank you. Keeping the peace was the task our royal master gave me and I'll carry it out regardless of peril!'

With these brave words, he strutted away with a final wave to the brooding figure on the massive grey stallion.

They reached Exeter late in the afternoon, and de Wolfe was heartily thankful to see the great twin towers of the cathedral rising above the walls as they approached. His buttock and left leg ached from the long ride, and he resolved to visit an apothecary the next day if the boil did not improve considerably overnight. Gwyn left them outside the East Gate to go to his cottage in St Sidwell's, while Thomas continued to jog behind the coroner into the city. They rode along High Street until they reached Martin's Lane, a narrow alley that was one of the many entrances into the cathedral Close. Here, John bade him a gruff farewell as the little clerk carried on to the lower town, where he shared a room with a vicar-choral at a lodging in Priest Street.

With a sigh, de Wolfe hauled Odin's head around into the lane and rode the few yards to the livery stable where his lumbering horse had his home. After delivering the animal to Andrew the farrier, John crossed to his house opposite, one of two high, narrow buildings that stood in the short alley. Built of timber, its front was blank apart from a small shuttered window and a heavy front door. He pushed this open and entered a small vestibule, where boots and cloaks were discarded. On the left, a passage ran around the side of the house to the back yard, and on the right was another door that led into the hall, which occupied most of the building.

As he lowered himself gingerly on to a bench to pull off his riding boots, there was a patter of feet and a large brown dog appeared from the passage to greet him with a wagging tail and a lolling wet tongue. As he fondled the ears of his old hound Brutus, other footsteps approached and his cook-maid Mary came into the vestibule. A handsome dark-haired woman in her late twenties, she now stood with her hands on her hips, regarding her master with an assumed severity that masked her concern.

'How's your arse now, Sir Coroner?' she demanded bluntly.

'A kiss would improve it, no doubt,' he replied, standing up and pushing his feet into a pair of soft house shoes. He stepped towards her, obviously intending to put his words into deeds, but the maid moved back and jerked a warning thumb towards the door into the hall.

'She's in there and in a strange mood, so tread carefully!'

John groaned. 'My dear wife is always in a strange mood. What's the trouble this time?'

Mary picked up his riding boots to take them away to clean off the mud. 'Her brother called today, the first time we've seen him since he slunk off in disgrace. There was a lot of shouting and he left in a temper.'

Richard de Revelle, his brother-in-law, had been sheriff of Devon until the previous year, when largely at John's instigation he had been ejected by the king's judges for malpractice and suspected treachery. He had been in further trouble since then and had been lying low in one of his distant manors, so John was surprised to hear that he had appeared again in Exeter, though he had recently bought a town house in Northgate Street.

'I'll bring you a meal within the hour, then afterwards you had better let me attend to that boil of yours,' declared Mary.

As she left for her kitchen-hut in the yard, John reflected that exposing his nether regions to her would be no embarrassment for either of them, as they had enjoyed many a tumble in the past. Then Matilda had got herself a French maid, Lucille, who was too fond of carrying tales to make it safe for them to continue dallying in the wash-house or kitchen.

With a heavy heart at the prospect of his wife's sombre mood, he pushed open the hall door and went around the screens inside that helped to reduce the draughts in that gloomy chamber. The hall went right up to the bare beams supporting the shingled roof, the dark aged timber of the walls relieved only by some dusty tapestries portraying scenes from the Scriptures. The only modern feature was the large stone hearth that filled much of the inner wall, which John had copied from some he had seen in Brittany. Most houses still had a firepit in the centre of the floor, the smoke having to find its way out under the eaves, after half-choking and blinding the occupants. The conical chimney that rose above the fireplace to the roof was a recent innovation, like the flagstones beneath his feet. Matilda's elevated ambitions had insisted on these, instead of the usual floor of beaten earth covered in rushes or bracken.

He loped towards the hearth, where a small fire of beech logs burnt in spite of the pleasant weather. His wife was sitting in a high-backed wooden seat with a cowled top, holding a pewter cup in one hand and a rosary in the other. Her fingers were slowly clicking the beads and her lips were moving silently, but she did not look up as he entered.

John went to a side table and poured himself a cup of red wine from a pottery flask, then lowered himself gently into a similar chair on the opposite side of the hearth.

'I am back, wife. This suppuration on my body is giving me no small discomfort.'

Matilda slowly looked up and the clicking of her rosary stopped. Her heavy features regarded him dully, but she said nothing. He wondered again if her mind was failing, and his pity was mixed with a curiosity as to whether his marriage could be annulled if she lost her wits completely.

'I have spent the night on a hard floor in an alehouse in Axmouth – and much of the rest of the time on Odin's back,' he said, trying to strike some spark of reaction from his wife. She often upbraided him for spending so much time away from her, attending to his coroner's duties over half the county – which he resented, as it was she who had made him accept the appointment in the first place, as a stepping stone to her ambitions to climb higher in the hierarchy of Devon society.

His attempt at conversation failed, for her small dark eyes under their hooded lids swivelled back to regard the burning logs in the grate, and her fingers resumed their relentless manipulation of the holy beads. They sat in silence, and John moodily stared at her stocky body, swathed in its long kirtle of brown wool under a surcoat of dark red velvet. Her head was swathed in a white linen cover-chief that was draped around her face, even her neck being hidden by a wimple of the same material. They had been married for seventeen years, though until the last three he had barely spent a total of six months at home, being away with Gwyn at campaigns in Ireland, France and the Holy Land. They had been thrust together by their respective parents in a union that disposed of the least attractive of the de Revelle daughters and, in the case of John's father, struck a useful bargain between a younger son with no land and a woman from a rich family. De Wolfe did not hate her, in spite of the endless animosity that she generated between them. He just wished that she did not exist – or at least not as his wife.

Making one last effort, he told her of his exploits at the coast. 'We had a strangled youth at Axmouth. Buried and then unearthed by the parish priest.'

The mere mention of something religious seemed to trigger a reaction in Matilda, who spent part of every day on her knees, either in the nearby cathedral or at St Olave's Church in Fore Street. Apart from her considerable interest in food and drink, attending places of worship seemed to fill the rest of her life. Her head came up and she seemed to focus on her husband for the first time.

'A priest? How came that to be?' Her voice was rough, as if her throat was sore.

De Wolfe explained the circumstance, emphasising the religious connections. 'The town is part of a manor owned by the Priory of Loders. It seems the prior keeps a firm grip on the place through his bailiff and portreeve.'

Matilda nodded, looking almost animated compared with her former torpor. 'Loders is a daughter house of Montebourg Abbey in Normandy,' she announced as if she was preaching a sermon. 'Richard de Redvers, a former sheriff of Devon, gave it to the abbey many years ago.'

'Well, it looks as if they are reaping a good profit from it, for it's one of the busiest ports along this coast,' grunted John. 'The new Keeper of the Peace, a knight called Luke de Casewold, suspects that some of their business is not strictly honest. But that's none of my concern unless it's connected with the death of this poor lad.'

Once the mention of priests had passed, Matilda lost interest and went back to clicking her beads and staring into the fire. It was only the arrival of Mary with a large tray bearing their supper that brought her out of her gloomy reverie. She rose to her feet and took her well-padded body over to the long oak table that sat in the centre of the hall, with benches on each side and a chair at each end. Dropping heavily into one of these, she waited until the cook-maid had set a thick trencher of yesterday's bread in front of her, then laid two grilled trout upon it. A wooden bowl of boiled cabbage and another of fried onions appeared alongside, before Mary went to the other end of the table and gave the same to her master. Then she returned with a large jug of ale and filled earthenware cups before vanishing to the back yard to get the next course.

Matilda took her small eating knife from a pouch on her girdle and attacked the trout, muttering that it was fish again and not even a Friday!

John tucked in, as he was hungry after a day in the saddle and Mary was a cook to be treasured. Most people ate the main meal of the day at around noon and had very little afterwards, but Matilda, always keen to adopt new fashions that she could brag about to her friends at St Olave's, insisted on eating in the early evening – though this did not stop her healthy appetite from also being exercised at midday.

They ate in silence, which was the usual state of affairs in their household, as John was usually out of favour for one reason or another. A fresh loaf appeared, with yellow butter and a slab of cheese, and when Mary had cleared away the debris of the fish she brought two platters of dried fruit, imported from France.

When they had finished and gone back to their chairs near the fire, John sensed that his wife was even more depressed than usual. He tried again to strike up a conversation, and because of the guilt that she was always able to engender in him tried to discover what was troubling her today. Since de Revelle had been exposed as an embezzler and a coward, her former adoration for her elder brother had turned into a disillusion that had soured her life, but today she seemed worse than usual.

'I hear that Richard has visited you, Matilda?' he began, trying to keep his voice as neutral as possible and not to display the dislike and contempt he felt for his brother-in-law.

'What do you care about that?' she whispered throatily, turning her square face towards him. 'Though I admit that he has gone from bad to worse, it was you who hounded him out of office and even out of the city!'

As John had saved Richard's life twice – and probably bent the law sufficiently to save him from the hangman's noose – he felt aggrieved that Matilda should unfailingly put the blame on him for the retribution that was inevitably to fall upon the former sheriff. He tried to ignore it once again, though it was difficult, given de Wolfe's irascible nature.

'Did he have any particular reason for calling today?'

'Does a man need a reason to visit his sister?' she snapped. Then she turned her head away and John was surprised to glimpse tears forming in her eyes. Matilda was a hard, unforgiving woman, whose only emotion was usually anger. To see her on the verge of weeping over her wayward brother touched a nerve in his generally unsympathetic character, tapping the guilt that she never allowed him to forget. He got up and placed an arm around her shoulder, though she sat as rigid as a plank under his unfamiliar gesture.

'Give it time, Matilda,' he muttered gruffly. 'It has been only a short while since that affair over the Arundells.* If Richard lays low in his manor and keeps his nose out of public affairs, the matter will gradually be forgotten.'

'But I won't forget, will I?' she snapped with a vehemence that surprised him. 'I will go through the rest of my life with the knowledge of his perfidy – and I will always be pointed out by others as the sister of that man Richard de Revelle!'

There was no answer to that, and with a sigh John went to the side table and poured them each a cup of Anjou wine. Matilda accepted it wordlessly, never one to refuse a drink, whatever her mood. He sat down and, with the faithful Brutus dribbling on to his knee, quietly sipped his wine until the silence became too oppressive even for him to endure. Desperate to strike up some sort of dialogue, he searched his mind for some innocuous topic.

'It seems that the vessel that this strangled youth sailed upon was owned by a rich merchant from this city,' he began, knowing of his wife's fascination with, and compendious knowledge of, all the wealthy and titled families in this part of Devon. 'I've heard his name, but know nothing of him,' he said artfully.

* See *The Noble Outlaw.*

Matilda took the bait and slowly turned her face towards him. 'Who was it, then?'

'Robert de Helion, a manor-lord from Barnstaple way, I believe.'

She shook her head reprovingly. 'It's Bridport, not Barnstaple. He keeps a town house near the East Gate.' She sniffed in a superior way. 'I sometimes glimpse his wife in the cathedral, though she usually attends St Lawrence's Church, which is almost next door.' Matilda gave the impression that anyone who did not patronise St Olave's was akin to a pagan.

'Is he a rich man, d'you know?'

'He is reputed to be very rich. By the way his wife dresses, he must be both affluent and generous.' Again she managed to convey a hint that her own husband was both poor and miserly. John ignored this and persisted in tapping his wife's knowledge of Exeter's elite.

'I am told he runs three cogs from Axmouth and some from Dartmouth. It is strange that Hugh de Relaga and myself have not run across him, being in the same line of business.'

He realised too late that he was entering dangerous territory here, as recently his partnership with de Relaga had been enlarged by taking in Hilda of Dawlish, one of John's former mistresses. Her ship-master husband had been killed and his three ships had been absorbed into their wool-exporting venture. Matilda immediately pounced on the matter.

'No doubt you are too interested in your new partner to notice much about your business!' she growled. However, the temptation to air her knowledge over-came her jealous indignation. 'He has several sources of income, apart from his manor and his ships. I hear he owns both a tannery in Crediton and a fulling mill on Exe Island.' She scowled at John. 'If you would only take more interest in civic affairs and cultivate the burgesses and nobility more, you could be far more prominent in county affairs than just a corpse-prodder!'

De Wolfe felt an angry reply boiling in his breast at this unfairness. He had had King Richard's direct nomination for the post of coroner and was the second most important law officer in the county, after the sheriff. To be called a 'corpse-prodder' by the woman who had cajoled him into the appointment was outrageous, but he managed to hold his tongue long enough to down the rest of his wine, stand up and march to the door.

'I have to go up to Rougemont to see if there are any more reports of corpses for me to prod!' he growled sarcastically. A moment later the street door shut with a bang, leaving Brutus staring after him, disappointed that he was not getting his expected walk down to the Bush Inn.

chapter three

In which Crowner John seeks out an old flame

The early-April evening was waning by the time the coroner made his way along High Street and up Castle Hill to Rougemont, the fortress built by William the Bastard following the Saxon revolt two years after the battle at Hastings. It was in the angle of the old Roman walls, at the highest point of the ridge on which the city was built, and the ruddy colour of the local sandstone gave it its name. Two sets of defences arced around the castle: a wide ditch and rampart enclosing the outer ward, where soldiers and their families lived, then an inner castellated wall high on a bank, guarded by a dry moat and a tall gatehouse. It was on the upper floor of this that the coroner had his chamber, the most inhospitable room in Rougemont, grudgingly allotted by his brother-in-law when he was sheriff.

This evening, as dusk was drawing in, de Wolfe did not bother to toil up the narrow winding staircase, as both his clerk and his officer would not be there until morning. Instead, he called in at the guardroom inside the arched entrance and spoke to Gabriel, the gnarled sergeant of the men-at-arms who formed the garrison at Rougemont. They were old friends, having shared a battle years before in Ireland, when old King Henry was trying to curb the ambitions of his unruly barons who were carving out their own empire there. Always ready to gossip, Gabriel produced a jug of cider and some mugs. Pushing two young soldiers off a bench, the only furniture in the bleak cell, he waved John to a seat and they spent half an hour discussing old campaigns, the state of the nation and the price of wool, until the sergeant remembered that he had a message for the coroner.

'A fellow came in at around noon from Kenton, sent by the reeve there. It seems their miller has got himself killed in his own pond and they want a coroner to attend.'

Deaths in water mills were common, both from drowning in the millstreams and from being caught up in the ponderous machinery that ground the grain. Children and millers were by far the most frequent victims, and John had dealt with a dozen such accidents since he had become coroner in 1194. He swallowed his cider and stood up. 'It will have to keep until tomorrow. I'll take a ride down there unless my rump prevents me from sitting on a horse.'

It occurred to him that Kenton, a small village a few miles south of Exeter on the west side of the river, was over halfway to Dawlish on the coast. With a little mental gymnastics in respect of his conscience, he decided that it might be useful to speak to one of his own shipmasters there to see if he had any knowledge of the situation in Axmouth and the vessels that sailed from there. The fact that Hilda also lived in Dawlish could be viewed as irrelevant, though it would be churlish of him to visit the port without calling upon her! He went out into the passage of the gatehouse, where a bored sentinel stood under the raised portcullis just above the drawbridge over the ditch.

'Do you know if the sheriff is still here?' he asked the youth. The young man-at-arms stood to attention, greatly in awe of this menacing knight, whose reputation amongst the soldiery bordered on the fabulous. A Crusader and actually part of the Lionheart's escort when he was captured in Austria, de Wolfe was known in the army as 'Black John', both from his appearance and from his temper when displeased.

'He went out about a hour past, Crowner,' answered the guard respectfully. 'I think he went to his house in North Street.'

The sheriff, Henry de Furnellis, had a manor near Crediton but also kept a dwelling in the city, shunning the dreary quarters provided for him in the castle keep, a two-storeyed building on the further side of the inner ward.

De Wolfe had intended to tell de Furnellis about the murder in Axmouth, as nominally the sheriff was responsible for all law and order issues in the county. However, Henry was unenthusiastic about his duties, as he was only a stopgap sheriff, appointed quickly after the sudden removal of de Revelle. He was content to leave the pursuit of crime to the coroner, while he devoted himself to the administration of Devon's finances.

Dusk was falling and John decided to go back home and get Mary to minister to the sore on his bottom. By then, Matilda would be in bed in her solar at the back of the house, and he would be free to give Brutus his cherished walk, undoubtedly in the direction of Idle Lane and the Bush Inn.

Later that evening, as John de Wolfe was sitting in the alehouse with an arm around his Welsh mistress, a ragged man was trudging along the highway in the extreme east of the county. Dusk had long faded into night, but an almost full moon lit his way along the deserted track between the villages of Kilmington and Wilmington. He held a long staff in one hand, the other easing the nagging pressure of one of the shoulder straps that supported a shapeless backpack.

The pedlar, who rejoiced in the name of Setricus Segar, was tired, weary and hungry. He had not a single penny in his pouch, for he had sold nothing in Widworthy that day, the goodwives being unimpressed by his crumpled selection of ribbons or his slightly rusted sewing needles.

Once a moderately successful chapman, going around the countryside selling a whole range of household goods, he had gradually degenerated into little more than a beggar, thanks to his drinking habits. It was true that he had reason for this decline, as his wife and child had died of smallpox five years before and soon afterwards his dwelling in Chard had burnt down, leaving him destitute.

Nowadays he usually stole to keep him in a little food and more ale, as well as to buy the meagre stock of haberdashery which was his excuse for wandering the roads between towns and villages. Tonight he expected to sleep under a bush, which was his bedroom more often than not – but if tomorrow he could get as far as Exeter, he could cadge a meal and a mattress in one of the priories.

Though the day had been mild, the clear moonlit sky made the night cold, and he shivered under the threadbare cloak that he wore over his torn fustian tunic. He had rags tied around his feet to secure the detached soles of his worn shoes and a dirty pointed cap sat on his even dirtier hair, the tassel flopping on his shoulder as he tramped wearily along. Though he was not yet forty, he looked a score of years older, his lined face sallow and haggard under a week's worth of stubble.

The countryside was infested with outlaws and cutthroats, but one advantage of being so obviously destitute was that he was unlikely to be robbed. However, when he heard a distant noise behind him, his sense of self-preservation made him stop and cup a hand to his ear. Somewhere a wagon was moving and it was not long before he could hear the squeaking of wheels and the snorting of oxen as they toiled up the long slope of this stretch of the Honiton road. When he glimpsed the canvas hood in the moonlight, Setricus melted into the undergrowth at the side of the rutted track, where rank weeds gave way to bushes before the tall trees of the forest began.

He crouched behind the new leaves of an elder thicket and waited. Soon the two grunting draught animals came in sight, dragging the covered wagon with its pair of solid, creaking wheels. Two men sat on the driving-board, one idly flicking the oxen with a long switch, though they took not the slightest notice of him. As they came level with the pedlar, he made a sudden decision, got up and hurried out into the road.

'Hey, brothers, can I sit on your tailboard? My poor feet are worn down to my ankles!' he whined.

Startled by this apparition, the man on his side roared with alarm and raised a knobbed cudgel that he had lying alongside him.

'Clear off, whoever you are! Come closer and I'll brain you!' he yelled.

Setricus Segar continued to trot alongside the cart but kept out of range of the club that the driver's mate was waving at him.

'I'm but a poor chapman, travelling to Honiton,' he pleaded. 'All I want is a lift on the back of your wagon.'

'He said, bugger off!' shouted the driver, joining the fray. 'If you're some scout for a bunch of outlaws, tell 'em we've got another two armed men inside.'

'Do I look like a trail robber, with this damned pack on my back?' persisted the pedlar. 'Any Christian man would give me aid. It costs you nothing to be charitable.'

For answer, the man with the cudgel hopped down

from his seat behind the shafts and began raining blows on Segar, who screamed and sheltered his head with his arms, then blundered back into the brambles and scrub at the side of the track. The guard followed him for a few paces, cursing and blaspheming as he gave him a valedictory few whacks on the shoulders. Then he gave up the chase and ran back to catch up with the wagon, clambering back on to the driving-board.

Setricus cowered in the long grass and nettles until the creaking vehicle had passed out of sight. Then he stood up and stumbled back into the roadway, shaking a fist after his assailants.

'You miserable bastards, may you rot in hell!' he shouted, but not loud enough to provoke the man to return with his club. He began walking again, his shoulders and neck aching from the blows they had suffered. The next village could not be far off now. Wilmington was the last hamlet before the small town of Honiton, not that he would be able to stop at either at this time of night, with not a single coin to buy a pallet in an alehouse loft. As he walked he began to wonder why a covered wagon with an armed guard would be travelling at dead of night along the highway. He wished he knew what was in the back of the cart, for as well as being as curious as a cat, there was always the chance of being able to steal something worthwhile.

Setricus toiled on, stumbling now and then in some deeper rut than usual, though the pale moonlight revealed the road fairly well. If it had been cloudy or if the moon had not risen, it would be impossible to walk at night and he would have had to curl up under a tree unless he could find a barn that was not guarded by dogs.

The road ran from Axminster to Honiton, where it joined the high road from Exeter eastwards to Ilminster, Salisbury and eventually London. Setricus had never been further than Yeovil on that road and now had no ambition other than to get near Honiton tonight, find some niche to sleep in until the morning and make an early start on an empty stomach towards Exeter. He optimistically hoped to make some sales in the city, if he could sneak in through the gates past the porters and then avoid the constables seeking unlicensed hawkers.

As he plodded over a rise, he could see the roofs and church tower of Wilmington in its hollow below. One faint flickering light was visible – he presumed from either a candle or a horn lantern – but otherwise the place looked dead, as was normal in the countryside, where folk went to bed with the dusk and rose with the dawn. When he got down to the hamlet, he was intrigued to see that the light was coming from the open door of the alehouse and that several figures were moving in front of it, their shapes silhouetted against the flames from a log fire in the middle of the room. Even more interesting was the presence of the covered wagon just outside the tavern.

After the blows he had suffered, he approached cautiously, keeping out of the moonlight in the shadow of a hedge on the other side of the road. The rags on his feet muffled any sound, and he sidled along until he was opposite the cart. He stopped and watched what was happening outside the inn. The two men who had been on the footboard were carrying small kegs into the low thatched building whose whitewashed walls stood out starkly in the harsh moonlight. At the door, a fat man was watching them, presumably the landlord. The pedlar waited as about half a dozen of the firkins were taken inside. Then about the same number of flat bales were transferred from the back of the wagon, before he saw the driver pulling down the canvas cover and lashing it to cleats on the tailboard. At the alehouse door, the man who had beaten him was in close conversation with the innkeeper, and though

Setricus could make out none of their muttering he distinctly heard the clinking of coins.

The two men climbed back on to the cart and the inn door was quietly closed as the oxen jerked into life and the vehicle rumbled away out of the village. The pedlar followed it at a safe distance and for a quarter of an hour he trailed behind, wondering what manner of delivery needed to be made after dark in the depths of the countryside. He guessed that their boast that there were more armed men in the back was a bluff, as there had been no sign of them when they stopped at the tavern.

Assuming that they were going to Honiton, he stepped out quite boldly a couple of hundred paces behind, there being no chance that his soft footfalls could be heard over the rumble and squeak of the solid cartwheels. Suddenly, however, the wagon began to make a sharp turn off the highway, and Setricus scurried into the shadow of the bushes in case they looked back the way they had come. He saw that they had pulled into a space alongside a small toft, a solitary dwelling of cob-plastered wattle, with a thatched roof that even in the pale moonlight looked ragged and grass-grown. A rickety fence marked off a neglected plot of land, but there was no sign of man or beast.

The driver and his aggressive companion got down and untied the two oxen from the shafts, releasing them from the yokes across their shoulders. With a smack on their rumps, they drove the animals through a gate into the compound around the cottage, then vanished around the back. There were some noises within for a few minutes, but no light appeared through the roughly shuttered window-opening and soon all was quiet.

Setricus waited for many more minutes, then surmised that the men had taken to their beds. By the look of the place, these would probably be merely bags of hay or a pile of bracken on the floor – though he would dearly have liked the same comfort himself.

Setricus was gripped by a fervent desire to know what was left in the back of the wagon, especially if he could steal some of it. He shrugged off his pack into the hedge and quietly sidled up to the back of the cart. Undoing one of the thongs that secured the flap at the rear, he raised himself on tiptoe and peered over the tailboard. In the poor light, all he could see were some more kegs and bales, all of which were too large for him to carry away. There seemed to be some smaller objects on the floor between them and, determined to purloin something for his trouble, he undid the rest of the lashings and pulled out one of the wooden pegs that held the tailboard in place. He had expected the other end to be fixed in a similar fashion, so that he could ease the planks downwards when he removed the second pin – but this happened to be missing, and without warning the heavy tailboard dropped with a crash!

Frozen with terror, Setricus stood immobile for a moment before he could get his legs in motion – but he was too late. Seconds after, there was a roar from behind the house and the two men appeared just as the pedlar started to run for the roadway, all too visible in the bright moonlight.

'It's that bloody spy we met on the road!' roared the cart driver. 'He'll not get away to tell tales this time!'

Soon after dawn next morning, John de Wolfe was again on the road with his officer. He had broken his fast on his usual gruel with honey, then bread, cheese and watered ale in Mary's kitchen-shed in the back yard, where she cooked and slept with Brutus for company. Matilda was still snoring when he left her on the large mattress on the floor of the solar, an extra room built out on stilts at the back of the house. It was reached by a wooden stairway, under which her French maid Lucille lived in what was little more than a large box. Mary had again dressed his boil and padded it inside his breeches with a wad of linen, so that he was able to sit in the saddle without too much discomfort. John had been afraid that he would have to visit Richard Lustcote, the most experienced apothecary in Exeter, to have it lanced, but it seemed to have stayed brawny, without any sign of pus accumulating under the skin.

He rode down to the West Gate, where he had arranged to meet Gwyn, having left a message at Rougemont the previous evening. Thomas was performing his duties at the cathedral, where he had a stipend to say prayers and Masses each day for a rich merchant who had left money for a priest to intercede in perpetuity to ease the passage of his soul from purgatory to heaven. If needed urgently by the coroner, the little clerk could hand over this task to someone else, but today John felt that he could do without Thomas, who was such a poor horseman that he was a liability when they were in a hurry or needed to travel a long distance.

With the Cornishman alongside on his big brown mare, they waded the river alongside the flimsy footbridge, as it was low tide. The new stone bridge was still only half-finished after many years, the builders having run out of money again, but unless it was high tide or the Exe was in spate from heavy rain on Exmoor, the crossing could be made with only the horses' bellies getting wet. On the other side they trotted through several villages, then turned off the main highway that led to Buckfast Abbey and distant Plymouth. This side road went down towards the coast, and a few miles further on was their first destination, the hamlet of Kenton, which lay between the flat lands bordering the estuary and the Haldon Hills behind. De Wolfe knew it well, as it was on the road from Exeter to his home manor, Stoke-in-Teignhead, ten miles further on towards Torbay. His mother, sister and elder brother still lived there, and if there was time he resolved to visit them later that day.

The mill in Kenton was a stone structure with a roof of wooden shingles, built alongside a stream that had been channelled into a narrow leat to increase the speed of the flow. After emerging from below the wheel, the water spread into a large pool, and it was here that the body of the miller had been found the previous day.

When the coroner and his officer arrived and dismounted outside the upper entrance to the mill, they were met by a small deputation consisting of the manor-reeve and the bailiff, for the place had no local lord, being part of the royal demesne, owned by the Crown. The parish priest, incumbent of All Saints', was also there, as well as several members of the dead man's family, but it was the bailiff, Adam Lida, who did all the talking. He was an earnest fellow of about thirty, with close-cropped blond hair and a mournful expression on his narrow face.

'The body is lying in the mill here, Crowner,' he explained, leading the way through the low doorway into the grinding room. Here, the two large stones were still and silent, the water having been diverted from the wheel by sluices. Amongst the spilt corn and bags of flour lay the corpse of a fat man, partly covered by a couple of sacks.

'We couldn't leave him floating in the pool until you came, sir,' said Adam. 'But I thought it best to keep the cadaver as close by as possible.'

De Wolfe grunted, but the bailiff could not tell if this was disapproval for moving the body from the scene of death or a commendation for not taking it very far. 'When was he last seen alive?' demanded John.

'The previous night, sir. It would seem that he was pretty far gone in his cups. The reeve here saw him leave the alehouse at the end of the evening and he was staggering then.'

De Wolfe nodded impatiently. 'Let's have a look at him, then.'

It sounded a familiar story, a drunk weaving his way home and falling into deep water while his wits were befuddled. The reeve confirmed the story and Adam Lida added that Alfred Miller was a heavy drinker, worse since the death of his wife several years earlier.

Gwyn and the coroner went into their well-worn routine, squatting on each side of the corpse, as the Cornishman pulled off the sacks. Outside the door, the family and a dozen villagers crowded together to peer inside as the law officers began their examination.

'He's been in water a good few hours,' grunted Gwyn as he lifted a stiff arm and peered at the hand. The skin of the fingertips was wrinkled and soft from saturation with water.

Alfred Miller had a belly the size of a woman about to go into childbirth, and John pulled up the short tunic to prod it with a forefinger. 'Must be an ale-belly, for it's not the swelling of corruption. Anyway, he's not been long enough in the water to start rotting.' He looked carefully at the eyes and felt the scalp for injuries, but found nothing suspicious under the shock of blond hair that suggested his Saxon ancestry.

'When we pulled him out yesterday morning, he had froth coming out of his nose and mouth, like the head on a brew-vat,' said the reeve helpfully.

De Wolfe glanced at Gwyn and his henchman nodded. Then Gwyn placed one of his massive hands on the middle of the dead man's chest and pressed hard. There was a gurgling hiss as the miller gave his last breath and a plume of pinkish froth issued from his nostrils and some watery fluid leaked out between his clenched teeth.

The coroner nodded in satisfaction. 'Drowned right enough! Let's make sure he's got no injuries. No reason why a wounded man can't drown as well.'

Gwyn pulled off the man's belt and then struggled to pull up his tunic to the armpits. Then they pulled down his hose, two separate legs of brown wool held up to his waistband by laces. There were no cuts or bruises anywhere. Satisfied, John motioned to Gwyn to replace the clothing.

Standing up, he turned to Adam Lida. 'There seems to be no problem here, bailiff. I will hold a short inquest straight away and get it over with.'

The proceedings took a very few minutes. The man who had found the body was called, then the reeve to say that he had seen Alfred Miller drunk on the night he had died. No one else had anything to add, so de Wolfe caused the jury to parade past the corpse and view the 'washerwoman's skin' on the hands.

When they lined up again, the coroner addressed them in tones that brooked no dissent. 'You know better than I that this poor fellow was too fond of his ale and that when last seen he was in a drunken state. There are no injuries upon the body, and he has clearly drowned.' He glared around the stoical faces. 'I doubt that you will be able to come to anything but the conclusion that Alfred Miller fell into his own millpond. It seems unlikely that he went into the stream above the wheel, as he has no scratches or bruises from being dragged under the paddles, common though that is in other cases.'

John jabbed a finger at the reeve, who stood in the middle of the jury, and abruptly appointed him foreman. 'Decide a verdict amongst yourselves now.' He almost added, 'And be quick about it!', but it was not necessary, as after a hurried muttering and nodding of heads the reeve announced that they were satisfied that it was an accidental drowning.

The family came to claim the body for burial, the priest delivered his scrap of parchment with the few names written upon it, and within minutes John and Gwyn were astride their horses and trotting southwards out of the village.

Four miles beyond Kenton, they came into Dawlish, where the coast rose from the flat estuary of the Exe into the undulating cliffs that stretched down to the River Teign and onwards to Torbay. Dawlish was a large village that depended mainly on fishing, but a few small merchant vessels were based there, beaching in the mouth of Dawlish Water, a stream that issued from the hills behind. Three of these cogs had belonged to Hilda's husband, Thorgils the Boatman, but he had been savagely murdered with all his crew a few months earlier.* Hilda was the daughter of the manor-reeve of Holcombe, a couple of miles further down the coast – and Holcombe was the other manor owned by the de Wolfe family, in addition to Stoke-in-Teignhead. Though Hilda was more than half a decade younger than John's forty-one years, they had known each other since their youth – and by her teens they had been lovers, which had continued intermittently until he went off to the French wars and then the Crusade. Given the social gulf between the son of a manor-lord and the daughter of his Saxon reeve, Hilda had no prospect of becoming his wife, so she had married Thorgils, a widower more than twenty years older. Thorgils had become rich and had built himself a fine new stone house in the village. Though it was hardly a love match, he was amiable and kind to her, and when he died she was genuinely grieved. Until the last year

* See *The Elixir of Death.*

or so, John had sometimes visited Hilda when her husband was away at sea, but his increasing devotion to Nesta had brought that to an end.

Ostensibly, John was coming to Dawlish today to question the masters of these cogs to see if they had any knowledge of the ships sailing out of Axmouth – but he knew only too well that his main motive was to call upon Hilda. John told himself that his interest was solely to enquire after her health and happiness following her bereavement – but a little devil sitting upon his shoulder kept reminding him of her blonde beauty and passionate nature. He wondered whether it was possible to be in love with two women at the same time. His conscience was robust enough to assure him that even if tempted he was stout enough to resist – but that small devilish voice whispered that such temptation would be very welcome.

Gwyn plodded alongside his master, well aware of the reason for de Wolfe's thoughtful silence. They had been through this routine before, usually when travelling to and from John's home further down the coast. They would look into the little river as they passed through Dawlish to see if Thorgils' cog was there – and if not, Gwyn would tactfully adjourn to an alehouse for an hour or so while John went off on some unspecified errand, which both of them well knew meant a visit to Thorgils' fine house. Now, of course, Hilda was a widow and such subterfuge was not needed, but in fact, since the shipman's death, John had called upon her only twice and had not seduced her for a year or more, much as he was tempted. He had been faithful to Nesta all that time, a record for fidelity where John de Wolfe was concerned.

When they reached the village, the tide was full in, preventing them from fording the stream that emptied into the sea across the beach. They had to ride up the right bank until it was shallow enough for them to cross, but this gave them an opportunity to see that several merchant vessels were bobbing at their moorings.

'That's one of Thorgils' cogs,' said Gwyn, forgetting for a moment that it was now partly his master's. 'I remember the look of her from when they came down to Salcombe to salvage the ship he died on.'

They trotted back down the other side of the stream and reined in alongside the vessel, which John remembered was called the *St Radegund*. Several men were working on the rigging of the single square sail, and two others were hammering at deck planks around the gaping hold in the centre.

'Is your shipmaster aboard?' yelled Gwyn.

Several of the men looked up, and one recognised the forbidding figure of the coroner astride his old destrier. He rapidly hissed to his companions that their employer was visiting, then walked to the bulwark and called across the narrow strip of water, which was beginning to run out on the ebb tide.

'Sir John, good day to you! Roger Watts has gone to say farewell to Mistress Hilda, as we sail for Exeter tonight to load your wool for Calais.'

De Wolfe felt a pleasant glow of ownership as he heard this and waved a hand at the shipman, calling a few words of encouragement. Sailing the Channel was always a hazardous occupation, with not only winds, fog and tide to contend with but the ever-present threat of pirates and privateers, who came from as far away as the North African coast and even Turkey.

'Gwyn, I must talk to Roger Watts to see if he has any knowledge about Axmouth. Get yourself to a tavern and find something to eat and drink. I've no doubt you can manage that!' His attempt at unfamiliar jocularity was born of pleasure at having a legitimate excuse to visit Hilda at her house, sufficient to assuage his conscience in regard to Nesta.

Gwyn grinned at this transparent subterfuge and ambled away towards the Anchor alehouse a few yards away. Dawlish was little more than one main street along the track that led from Kenton to Teignmouth, with a few houses on a short lane that went at right angles to the stream, behind the high street. Here, Thorgils had built his mansion, a substantial stone dwelling of two storeys, easily the largest building in the village. It had two pillars in front joined by a shallow arch over a front door and the roof was of stone tiles, rather than thatch or wooden shingles. There was even a chimney, the whole house being a copy of one in the main street of Dol, in Brittany.

John strode boldly up to the door and rapped loudly upon it, so different from the rather furtive visits he used to make when Hilda was a wife rather than a widow. It was opened by her frail little maid Alice, who was always in awe of this great dark man who came to call upon her mistress.

'I believe one of our shipmasters is here, Alice,' he boomed.

The girl, who could have been no more than twelve, bobbed her knee. 'Yes, sir. Master Watts has called and is upstairs.' The maid invited him in, leading him along a passage and up an open staircase to Hilda's solar, one of two rooms on the upper floor – a luxury indeed, even in the grander houses of Exeter.

The master of the *St Radegund* was sitting on a bench in the window, whose shutters were flung wide to give a view of the sea over the roofs of the low buildings in the main street. Roger Watts was a short, burly man of forty, with a red weather-beaten face. He rose as soon as his employer came in and touched a finger to his forehead in salute. 'A welcome surprise, Sir John!' he exclaimed. 'I was just about to leave to see how my repairs are coming along,' he added tactfully, glancing at Hilda.

The widow sat in a leather-backed chair facing the window, but she also rose as de Wolfe came in. Dressed in a pale blue kirtle of fine wool, she was tall and slim, a blonde beauty looking much younger than her thirty-five years. In the house, she wore no head veil and her waist-length hair was braided into two honey-coloured plaits that hung down over her bosom, the ends encased in silver tubes. A silken rope was wound twice around her waist, with tassels dangling from the long free ends. She glided across the room, her hands held out in welcome. John took them briefly and looked longingly into her blue eyes, but in deference to the presence of the sea-captain he did not hold her close and kiss her, as he would have done if they were alone – though on previous visits since she lost Thorgils, the little maid had crouched determinedly in a corner to act as chaperone.

'John, I am so happy to see you! Sit yourself down, please. Alice, get wine and pastries for us all.'

Roger Watts edged towards the doorway and prepared to say his farewells, but John stopped him with an upraised hand.

'Though I am always delighted to see Mistress Hilda, it is you that I really came to see, Roger.' He managed to give a covert wink to Hilda as he said this, before parking his tender backside on the padded bench and motioning Watts to be seated again.

There was a short interlude of pleasantries about each other's health, in which John avoided mentioning his present embarrassing disability. Then the maid returned with cups, a wine flask and a platter of thin pasties filled with chopped meat. As they ate and sipped the red wine, John explained his mission.

'I have had to deal with an unusual murder in Axmouth. The victim was a young shipman, strangled and buried outside the village. We have no idea who is responsible, but the whole affair is mysterious and the

Keeper of the Peace over there thinks that there is some evil business afoot.'

He explained that the lad had been a crew member of *The Tiger*, but the cog had sailed away and until she came back he had no means of pursuing the investigation. 'You are one of the most experienced shipmasters along this coast, Roger. Is there anything you can tell me about Axmouth or this vessel that might help me?'

Watts drank some of his wine, frowning in concentration. 'Axmouth! A strange place, that!' he said ruminatively. 'I rarely moor in that river, as Exeter, Topsham and Dartmouth are my main ports of call. But sometimes I do pick up cargo there.'

De Wolfe fixed him with a steely glare. 'Why a strange place?'

'It's run by the bailiff and his lapdog, Elias the reeve. That Edward Northcote is an arrogant dictator, running everything in the name of the priory that owns the manor, but I think he has a major stake in it himself.'

This was in complete accord with what John had observed.

'Is there anything illegal going on there, d'you know?' he asked bluntly.

Roger Watts shrugged. 'I'd wager my own anchor that more goods get smuggled in than those on which the king's Customs are paid,' he said. 'There's a fellow there supposed to keep tally, John Capie by name, but he can't cope with the volume of ships that come in and out – and, anyway, every tally-man I've ever known was wide open to bribes.'

Hilda had kept silent all the while, feeling that she had no call to interrupt men's business even if she was a ship owner herself. But now she spoke up.

'It's common knowledge that everyone tries to avoid these harsh taxes if they can. I realise that you are a loyal officer of the king, John, but you must know that people increasingly resent these crushing dues, just to finance wars which they feel are none of their business.'

De Wolfe felt uncomfortable at this turn in the conversation. His own appointment as coroner was mainly to raise money for the Lionheart's treasury, in order to pay for the huge ransom that Henry of Germany demanded for his release over two years earlier. The fines, amercements, surrendered bail money, the seized property of hanged felons and fees for cases that he swept into the royal courts were all grist to the Exchequer's mill in Winchester. King Richard was now engaged in an apparently endless war against Philip of France and was squeezing all he could from England to pay for it. The Church had been bled dry, their silver plate and chalices taken and some of their huge wool output from the larger monasteries confiscated. Along with tin, wool was the staple product of the country and every bale exported was supposed to be taxed for the benefit of the Crown.

Another reason for John's discomfort was the knowledge that undoubtedly some of his own wool sent across to the Continent evaded the Customs duty by various means. No doubt Roger Watts was well aware of this and so was Hugh de Relaga. John steadfastly did not want to know what went on and depended on Hugh not to tell him! He tried to steer the conversation into another channel.

'What about this vessel *The Tiger*?' he asked. 'I gather her master is Martin Rof. Tell me about him and the ship's owner.'

Under this interrogation, Roger Watts was beginning to wish that he had not chosen this morning to call upon Mistress Hilda, but the coroner's expression told him that he could not prevaricate.

'Martin Rof is a rough diamond, sure enough!' he

began, nervously studying his wine cup. 'A good sea-man, but a hard master to his crew. Like most of us, he sails from all the ports along this coast, but mainly Axmouth, where he lives. His cog *The Tiger* is well known on both sides of the Channel.'

This told de Wolfe nothing he wanted to know. 'But what about the man himself? Is he honest and to be trusted?'

Roger Watts gave a hollow laugh. 'Who can tell that, Sir John? I hope I am honest, though I admit I do not shed tears if the tally-man happens to forget a few casks or bales now and then. Martin Rof has a reputation for being even more forgetful about paying his Customs dues, but few would hold that against him.'

Aware of his own vulnerability in that regard, John did not pursue the issue. 'Is anything else known about him? This lad who was slain was a member of his crew, though admittedly the killing occurred after the cog berthed in Axmouth.'

Roger shrugged. 'Knowing nothing of the matter, I can't venture to say. But why would he be involved in the death of one of his own men? I admit I've some-times wanted to slay some useless sod in my crew, but I've never actually done it!'

He tried to inject some levity into the talk, but it fell flat with de Wolfe.

'The Keeper mentioned piracy along these coasts,' growled the coroner. 'What do you know of that?'

Again Roger Watts looked uncomfortable, not that he had any fear of being branded a pirate himself, but seafarers – like tinners – stuck together and were reluctant to tell tales to law officers.

'There is no doubt that attacks and pillaging and killing go on out at sea,' he admitted, squirming a little on his bench. 'But these are almost all down to bastards from either Brittany or the French coast, some of whom claim to be at war with England.'

Hilda, who had been listening attentively, broke in again. 'I recall Thorgils saying that vessels from the far south – Spain and even the Middle Sea – used to come ravaging into the Channel and as far as the Severn Sea. He told me how he had once outsailed an oared galley that must have come from the Barbary Coast.'

John nodded. 'I remember that story of his,' he said gently. 'He was always one for a good tale. You must miss his company, Hilda.'

She inclined her head but smiled sadly. 'He was a good and kind man. He did not deserve the fate that took him from me. Like all wives of shipmen, I always expected to hear of his loss from storm and shipwreck, but not murder!'

'That was piracy, by foreign devils,' agreed de Wolfe. 'But I have heard of some home-grown pirates in these waters. Is that so, Roger?'

The shipmaster decided he could stall no longer. 'It is, unfortunately. The men from Lyme have the worst reputation, but Dorset was always a barbarous place. Though most of us are concerned only with the safe delivery of our cargoes, some vessels prey on others, may God rot their souls on Judgment Day!'

'Is it known who indulge themselves in this murderous business?' demanded the coroner.

Roger Watts shook his head. 'Who is to know what goes on once out of sight of land?' he said warily. 'It is legal and indeed to be commended if an English ship attacks a Frenchie, given that there is a state of war between us most of the time. Those bastards are quick enough to pillage our vessels.'

'Yet there are widows and fatherless children in this port for whom English shipmen are said to be responsible!' cut in Hilda, her lovely face set with concern. She was well known for her generosity to the families of men lost at sea.

'We certainly hear tales that suggest that is true,'

answered Watts. 'But how can it be proven? A pirate must kill every crewman on the stricken ship if he is to avoid retribution. And the vessel must be scuttled after the cargo is seized, to remove all traces of the crime.'

De Wolfe scowled at this apparent impasse. 'Do the rumours of piracy involve Axmouth?' he snapped. 'And does this Martin Rof's name ever crop up in discussion of the problem?'

Roger shrugged hopelessly. This was a conversation in which he would rather not take part. 'I've heard nothing, Crowner – but any man who bandies about the name of a supposed pirate is asking for a sudden death!'

John fixed him with his brooding eyes. 'And a sudden death is exactly what I am concerned about in Axmouth!' he growled.

After the master of the *St Radegund* had thankfully made his escape from the coroner's interrogation, John was left alone with Hilda. The little maid Alice had hung about the doorway but was sent packing by her mistress, who felt she needed no chaperone now, especially with a man with whom she had lain intermittently since they were youngsters rolling in the hayloft in Holcombe.

As soon as Alice had gone downstairs, he took Hilda into his arms and kissed her languorously, somehow being able to assure himself that this was merely brotherly affection. Eventually, she managed to draw breath and pushed him away gently, sitting down again on her chair and pointing him to the bench.

'And how is Nesta?' she asked pointedly, though with a smile that told him she was teasing. Mentally throwing the little devil of temptation from his shoulder, John said she was very well, though in fact he had seen little of his Welsh mistress these past few weeks, as a succession of deaths and court cases had kept him out of Exeter more than usual.

Evading the subject, though Hilda and Nesta had met a number of times and enjoyed each other's company, he made solicitous enquiries about Hilda's health and happiness.

Though he had cuckolded Thorgils for years, he had been very discreet about it and came to Hilda only when the older man was away on his voyages. He wondered now what the blonde beauty would do, as she was still comparatively young and, having inherited her husband's house, treasure chest and his three ships, was a rich enough widow to attract many suitors. Though her origins were humble enough, as the daughter of a manor-reeve, her marriage to a well-known and affluent ship owner now lifted her many rungs up the social ladder.

'I have no plans, John. I am content for now to live in this fine house. I attend the church diligently and spend much time with the families of those shipmen who died with Thorgils in the *Mary and Child Jesus*.'

The ship had been repaired after being wrecked and now formed part of the trio of vessels that Hilda had brought to John and Hugh de Relaga's partnership. De Wolfe was curiously relieved to hear that she was in no hurry to find a new husband, even though he had no thoughts of taking up with her again. At least, he firmly suppressed such thoughts, even though the nearness of such an attractive woman gnawed away at his self-control. They talked away pleasantly for some time, finishing the wine and pastries, until John reluctantly felt that he should drag Gwyn from the alehouse and make their way down to see his mother at Stoke-in-Teignhead. With a final hug and a long kiss, he broke away and, with a promise to see her again soon, left in a slight daze of amorous longing. As he loped back to the tavern, he had a rare moment of introspection, wondering how such a hard bastard as himself, veteran of years of campaigning, could become so soft and sentimental over women – or, to be more exact, two particular women.

CHAPTER FOUR

In which the coroner visits the Bush

John de Wolfe did not in fact get to see his family at their home manor that day. When he reached the alehouse, he found – wonder of wonders – Gwyn standing outside, staring at the small estuary where the stream poured out across the beach into the sea. The tide was now right out and the vessels were high and dry, tilted over slightly on their flat keels. He realised from the low water that he had been with Hilda much longer than he had anticipated.

'We could easily get across the ford at Teignmouth,' said his officer. 'But we'll not get back again! By the time you reach Stoke and have a decent talk to your kin there, the tide will be in full flood on the return journey. We'd never reach Exeter before curfew.'

There was no argument with this, as it would take too long to go up the Teign on the other bank to the first bridge and then find the inland road back to the city. Resignedly, John went with Gwyn to get their horses and soon they were back on the road. This time they avoided Kenton and went over the marshes to the ferry, where they and their horses were carried across the Exe to Topsham on what was little better than a large raft. They reached Exeter's South Gate much earlier than John had expected, and rode straight up to the castle, where de Wolfe decided to call on the sheriff and bring him up to date on events.

Henry de Furnellis was a veteran of even more wars than de Wolfe, a big man of sixty with a face like a sad hound, jowls hanging below his chin. He had been sheriff previously, as when Richard de Revelle was suspended two years earlier he had been appointed for a short time as a stopgap, until de Revelle was reinstated. After Richard's second dismissal, de Furnellis was again wheeled in, but he fervently hoped that it would be for a short time, as he wished to return to retirement at his manor near Crediton. Most of his time was occupied with sorting out the finances of the county, which was one of the sheriff's main responsibilities on behalf of the king. During his predecessor's shrievalty, de Revelle had deliberately obscured the true accounts, as part of his methodical embezzlement. The other prime task, the maintenance of law and order in Devon, Henry was content to leave to the coroner, even though it was not strictly his duty.

John found the grizzled knight in his chamber at the side of the large hall that occupied most of the lower floor of the keep. Below was the dismal undercroft, which was both the castle prison, storehouse and quarters for Stigand, the obese gaoler and torturer. Above the hall were various rooms for clerks and living accommodation for Ralph Morin, the garrison commander, for Rougemont had been a royal castle ever since it was built by William the Bastard after the 1068 rebellion.

Henry de Furnellis was listening to a long and boring explanation by his chief clerk Elphin about evasion of taxes by a manor-lord near Okehampton. He greeted John's arrival with relief and waved the sour-faced Elphin away to obtain a respite from the accounts. Inevitably, the wine flask and cups were produced and parchments pushed aside on the sheriff's large table to make room for them.

When John had lowered himself into a sling-backed leather chair opposite Henry, they chatted for a while, then he told him of the events of the past couple of days, concentrating on the strange goings-on along the River Axe.

'It's not only this murder, but the rumours of corrupt practices there,' concluded de Wolfe. 'Doubtless there's much evasion of the king's Customs, but the possibility of piracy is more serious.'

The sheriff ran a hand through his wiry grey hair and glanced shrewdly at the coroner. 'They're a strange lot over there, right on the edge of the county. A mile or two further and they'd be Dorset men, and you know what that means!'

It was a hoary old joke that those in the next county were all rogues and villains, most of them being not quite right in the head. It arose from the bad reputation of the shipmen of Lyme, who had often preyed upon both fishermen and ships from Devon.

'Who suggested that there might be piracy involved?' asked Henry, refilling their pewter wine cups.

'This new Keeper of the Peace, Luke de Casewold. He's a pain in the arse!' added John, suddenly aware that the phrase had personal relevance to himself, though thankfully his backside seemed to be improving by the hour.

The sheriff nodded, leaning back in his chair. 'Luke de Casewold, eh? I installed him in the post some months ago, on the strength of an Article of Eyre that came from the royal justices at the last session in Taunton. There are half a dozen of them now scattered around the county. There should be more, but no one wants to take on the job. Like you coroners, they are forbidden to take any salary, though I suspect they make up for it in other ways!'

'I doubt this fellow is corrupt; he's too keen to make his mark,' grunted John. 'Wants to chase every ne'er-do-well in Devon but has no one to back him up. The bailiffs and serjeants in those Hundreds over there don't seem keen to give him much help in keeping the peace.'

'What do you intend doing about it?' This confirmed John's impression that the sheriff had no inclination to stir himself out of his chamber to keep law and order, when he had a coroner stupid enough to do the job for him.

'Nothing can be done, unless some new information comes to hand,' he growled. 'I'm waiting for this cog *The Tiger* to return to Axmouth, so that I can talk to the shipmaster about the dead youth. I've not much hope of anything useful coming from it; these sailors will hardly give you a good morning, let alone confess to a murder.'

As Elphin came back into the room clutching a sheaf of parchments and looking accusingly at his master, Henry sighed. 'I'd better get back to work, John. Maybe de Casewold will turn something up. He seemed a ferreting kind of man, by what I recall of him.'

John threw down the last of his wine and stood up. 'He'd better watch his step over there, or he'll end up floating face down in the river,' he grumbled.

On leaving Rougemont, John walked to North Street through the back lanes of the city, intent on visiting an apothecary to make sure that his boil was really on the mend. Of the several men in Exeter who claimed proficiency in pharmacy, Richard Lustcote was the acknowledged leader, being warden of their guild and the longest-established apothecary in the city.

An avuncular man with greying hair, he kept premises on the ground floor of his house in North Street, where a journeyman and two apprentices were kept busy making potions, lotions and all manner of salves to sell to the more affluent citizens. The poorer majority were content to seek their medical care from local 'wise women' and from members of their family who claimed to possess some degree of familiarity with herbal remedies. There were no doctors in Exeter, the nearest thing to a physician being provided by the priories.

The coroner entered the aroma-reeking shop of the apothecary, its walls lined with shelves and compartments filled with dried herbs and packets of powders and salves. Lustcote sat at a table, decanting liquids into phials; in the room behind, several youths were rolling pills and pounding concoctions in a pestle and mortar. Richard was an old friend of John's, and after a brief explanation of his complaint the coroner was taken behind a curtain in a corner of the room to expose his nether regions to the apothecary.

After some gentle prodding and probing, accompanied by a muttered commentary to himself, Lustcote fetched a pottery jar of some green foul-smelling salve and applied it liberally to the brawny swelling on the coroner's buttock. Covering it with a pad of wool, he bound it in place with a long length of linen and presented the pot of ointment to his friend.

'Get someone to replace this each day under a new pad,' he advised. 'It's getting better slowly, so it'll not turn into a purulent abscess now. In a week it will be entirely gone.'

John pulled up his hose and lowered his grey tunic back to calf level, then looked at the pot suspiciously. 'What's in this stuff?' he asked.

'It's quite innocuous,' said Lustcote reassuringly. 'Strong sea salt to draw out the poison, together with pounded leaves of marshmallow, cabbage and a little myrrh.'

As John was fumbling in the scrip on his belt for the

two pence that was all that the apothecary requested for his fee, he asked him where he obtained all the raw materials for his medicaments.

'Most come from the fields and woods of the countryside,' replied Lustcote. 'I send my apprentices out to seek them, but others I buy from dealers whose trade it is to collect them. And of course some have to be imported. They can be very expensive, like the myrrh that's in that salve I gave you, which comes from Africa.'

John was intrigued by the notion that some exotic substance from the almost mythical continent of Africa could find its way to his left buttock. 'How in God's name do you get hold of such rare products?' he asked.

'There are some dealers who supply me at intervals – but I also give lists to certain merchants who have ships trading across the Channel. They bring me certain goods I need – I don't ask how they get hold of them.' He winked and tapped the side of his nose as if half-revealing some secret.

A small warning bell rang in John's head. 'Do these marvellous substances carry any levy or tax when they come into England?' he asked.

Richard shrugged. 'I don't ask. I just pay the price demanded. Merchants and ship owners in this city pass on the lists to their traders, and in the fullness of time the packages arrive.'

'And which merchants would be involved in this trade?' queried John, wearing what he hoped was a guileless expression.

Richard Lustcote began to wonder what earthly interest the coroner could have in the means by which he obtained his medicaments, but he had no reason to prevaricate. 'There are a few of them. Edward of Yeovil for one – and some come on the ships of Robert de Helion, whom I know quite well.'

This name cropping up again made de Wolfe decide

to call upon the merchant at some early opportunity. Though he had no idea if medical supplies carried any Customs duty under the new financial regime of Hubert Walter, the rather secretive manner of the apothecary made it worthwhile to enquire, as Luke de Casewold had seemed convinced that Axmouth was involved in some dubious business.

With his bottom now more comfortable, John bade his friend goodbye and walked back to Martin's Lane in the gathering dusk. After his supper, the usual silent meal opposite a morose Matilda, John sat for a while staring into the glowing logs of a small fire in the hearth. He had his customary cup of wine in one hand, the other fondling Brutus's ears as he squatted beside his master's knee. Predictably, it was not long before Matilda called for her maid Lucille and went off to her solar, to be undressed for bed after a long session on her knees in prayer.

John gave her another half-hour, then rose and, with his hound padding expectantly after him, took his sword and a short cloak from the vestibule and stepped out into the lane. When he turned right into the Close, the two great towers of the cathedral were dark silhouettes against the remaining pale light in the western sky, which was clear enough to give a chill to the evening. One of the bishop's proctors was lighting the pitch-brand that hung in an iron ring over Bear Gate on the other side of the wide burial ground that fronted the great church. John walked across towards it, past the imposing West Front of the building, Brutus ambling from place to place, cocking his leg against any projecting structure.

The Close was a warren of overgrown burial mounds, piles of rubbish and a few open grave-pits, ready for tomorrow's corpses. Beggars crouched in corners, and respectable citizens were loath to walk alone there at night, for fear of the cutpurses that often lurked in the darkness. John had no fear for himself, as it would be a very bold robber who would tackle this tall, formidable man with a sword at his belt and a large hound at his heels.

He strode the familiar path out into Southgate Street and then across to the smaller lanes that sloped down towards the western wall and the river beyond. Crossing Milk Lane, he went down Priest Street, where Thomas lodged, and then turned into the short lane that joined it to Smythen Street, where the iron workers had their forges. This lane had almost no buildings, as they had burnt down in a fire some years earlier, and the empty ground around the Bush Inn gave it its name of Idle Lane. The tavern, itself substantially rebuilt after a fire the previous year that had almost claimed the life of its landlady, was a whitewashed stone structure with a steep thatched roof that came down to head height. A low door flanked by two shuttered window-openings graced the front, with a large fenced yard at the back containing Nesta's brew-shed, kitchen, privy and pigsty.

De Wolfe bent his head to enter the low room that occupied all the ground floor, making for his favourite bench at a table near the central firepit. It was sheltered by a wattle hurdle from the draught from the front door and was so well known as the coroner's personal seat that anyone already sitting there would hastily move out of his way. Brutus slid under the table, aware that he would soon get a bone or some scraps from a platter, while John eased himself down on to Lustcote's new woollen pad. Almost immediately, a quart jar of best ale was set in front of him by the potboy. This was old Edwin, who had not been a boy for fifty years – an old soldier with a crippled foot and one eye, the other being a ghastly white globe in a scarred socket, the legacy of a spear-thrust in one of the Irish wars. The garrulous old fellow saluted John in semi-military style, calling him 'captain' by virtue of their being in the same campaign in France many years ago.

'The mistress is in the kitchen-shed, cap'n!' he croaked. 'Screaming at a new cook-maid who can't boil a bloody egg.'

Edwin was easily the most inquisitive man in the city of Exeter and had often fed John useful titbits of information gleaned from the hundreds of travellers who passed through the Bush. The coroner thought it might be worth trying to tap his store of gossip.

'Know anything about Axmouth, Edwin? I've got to deal with a killing over there.'

The haggard old man rubbed his chin, his dead eye rolling horribly.

'God's guts, Crowner, they're funny buggers over that side of the county!' he said, falling in with most people's opinion of the inhabitants of the Axe valley. 'Busy place, though, a lot of trade passing in and out of that river. I left from there in '73 on a voyage to St-Malo when we went to fight in Brittany for old King Henry.'

John was more interested in present problems than in ancient history.

'You must get shipmen in here sometimes. Have you heard of any ill-doings in that port, such as piracy or smuggling?'

Edwin gave a toothless grin as he gathered up empty ale-pots.

'Smuggling? Of course, who doesn't dodge the tally-man when he can? Goes against the grain to pay for something, then have to pay the bloody Exchequer as well . . . Begging your pardon, Crowner,' he added hurriedly as he realised that he was speaking to a senior officer sworn to uphold the law.

As this seemed an almost universal sentiment amongst the citizens, John let it pass. 'What about piracy?' he demanded.

Edwin considered this for a moment. 'Well, cap'n, there are rumours, but you get them from any port along the western coast. A few drunken shipmen have occasionally boasted how they outran some privateer – and there are whispered tales of ships never being heard of again and of corpses washed up with their throats cut.'

'But Axmouth in particular?' persisted the coroner.

The old man shrugged. 'Never recall anyone mentioning it, sir. As I said, they are a rough lot over there; they don't seem to have much to do with us here in the city.' He heard the back door bang and saw the landlady bustling towards them, so he made a show of wiping John's table with a rag to mop up the spilt ale. 'Here's the missus coming,' he muttered and moved away.

'What's that old rascal been gossiping about, John?' she asked briskly, then slid along the bench towards him and grasped his arm. 'And where have you been this past week, Sir Crowner?'

This was Nesta's half-bantering, half-sarcastic mode of addressing him when he had annoyed or neglected her. He slipped an arm around her shoulders and gave her a kiss, looking down at this pretty, auburn-haired woman of twenty-nine, his mistress for the past two years.

'I've been dealing with the villains of this county, of whom there are far too many,' he said lightly, for he knew that he had failed to visit her often enough lately. Cases seemed to come one after the other and, though they took little time to settle, the travelling around the second-largest county in England swallowed up the days and left him weary by the time he got back home. Thank God, recently they had managed to replace the coroner for the north of Devon, the first one having killed himself after a fall from his horse. For a long time, de Wolfe had had to deal with deaths and other incidents as far away as Barnstaple and Clovelly, the round trip taking several days.

'Have you eaten, John?' asked Nesta in a more conciliatory tone.

They spoke in Welsh, her native tongue and one that John had learnt at his mother's knee, as Enid de Wolfe was the daughter of a Cornish knight and a mother from Gwent, the same part of south-east Wales from which Nesta came. Even Gwyn could converse with them in that language, being a Cornishman from Polruan – a fact that annoyed Thomas when he was with them, as he was a dyed-in-the-wool English Norman, his father being a minor knight from Hampshire.

John assured Nesta that he had not long eaten, having been filled to capacity by Mary, who had boiled a whole pike and served it with turnips, onions and beans. As tomorrow was Friday, no doubt they would have the rest of the large coarse fish then, in some guise or other.

As the hazel eyes in the heart-shaped face looked up at him while he recounted his tales of visits to Axmouth and Kenton, he tried to erase the images of Hilda from his mind. A mildly guilty conscience made him omit any mention of the extension of his trip down to Dawlish, though he knew that Nesta had sufficient knowledge of geography to know that Kenton was almost within spitting distance of Hilda's village.

'That was what I was asking old Edwin,' he said, adroitly turning the conversation. 'He hears all the gossip, and I wondered if he knew anything sinister about Axmouth, for it seems an odd place.'

Nesta's high forehead, framed by the band of her white cover-chief, creased in thought and she pursed her rosebud lips. 'Wasn't there some scandal there a couple of years ago, about a bailiff beating a man to death? I seem to remember gossip about him being judged innocent.'

John shook his head. 'I recall nothing about that. It must have been before I was made coroner, surely?'

'Indeed, my Meredydd was still with me then, God rest his poor soul.'

This was Nesta's husband, an archer from Gwent. He had been with de Wolfe in several campaigns, and when he had ended his fighting days he had taken John's advice and spent his war booty in buying the Bush, bringing his wife down to Exeter from Wales. For a year or so they had worked hard to improve the tavern, then Meredydd died of a fever and left Nesta with serious debts. John had come to her rescue with a loan, and their friendship had blossomed into romance.

'Do you remember the name of this bailiff?' he asked, but Nesta had no more information and even Edwin, when he was asked later, could throw no more light on the matter. 'I'll have to make enquiries with the court clerks. Maybe they have records, unless this was in another county like Dorset.'

Their talk drifted on to other things, but de Wolfe had the feeling that his mistress was rather sad and preoccupied this evening. They had settled into a routine these past few months, where John came down to the alehouse several times a week and often they retired up the broad ladder at the back of the taproom. Here, Nesta had her little chamber, partitioned off from the large loft where rows of straw-filled hessian pallets provided accommodation for those who wanted a penny lodging for the night, which included ale and breakfast. In this small room they would make love in the comfort of her goose-feather bed, though it was rare that he could ever manage to stay all night, unless Matilda was staying with her cousin in Fore Street or, in former times, with her brother at one of his manors. This routine had slowed lately, mainly because of John's increased workload.

Tonight, she seemed listless and made no move to

suggest that they went up to the loft, claiming that she must keep going out to the yard to keep an eye on the new girl in the kitchen, who could not be trusted for long on her own. The food, and especially the ale, in the Bush was famed throughout the city, and much of Nesta's skill in making the business a success after her husband died was due to her reputation in this direction. Several times, she rose and left John at his table, returning after some time to complain about the stupidity of her new skivvy. Nesta was usually more tolerant than this, and eventually John pulled her to his shoulder and asked her if she was quite well.

'You seem out of sorts tonight, *cariad*,' he said affectionately. 'Is something bothering you?'

She sighed and reached out to take a sip from his ale-jar, which Edwin had recently refilled. 'Nothing new, John. I just feel that things are so hopeless for us. The weeks and months go by and nothing changes. Nothing can change, can it?'

John knew what she meant, for they had been through this many times before. He was a Norman knight, married to the sister of another Norman knight and a former sheriff. In addition, he was a senior law officer in the service of the king, who had personally nominated him. By contrast, she was a lowly ale-wife and a Welsh foreigner to boot. What chance could they ever have together, short of running away to Flanders or Scotland?

As always, de Wolfe had no answer for her. He squeezed her to him in a futile attempt at comfort and reassurance. 'We can go on as we are, my love,' he murmured. 'Nothing has changed, as you say. But we have managed like this for two years and more.'

'Yes, we have managed,' she said bitterly. 'But can we ever do more than just "manage"? You have to skulk down here in the evenings, pretending to take your hound for a walk. We can never be in public together like other folk. People nudge each other when they see us, with a sneer or a knowing look.'

This was a little unfair, as though every patron in the Bush knew of their landlady's liaison with the county coroner they all approved, and their prime feeling about it was one of mild jealousy at his luck in having such an attractive mistress.

'Do you want me to go, Nesta?' he asked, baffled at the situation. John de Wolfe and any sort of emotional crisis mixed as well as oil and water.

The offer instantly softened Nesta's mood. 'Of course not, you great oaf!' She snuggled closer, and several nearby patrons tactfully found some other direction in which to stare. 'I'm sorry, dear John. Maybe it's the time of the month. I get so sad sometimes, but take no notice.'

After her next foray to the kitchen-shed, de Wolfe decided that he had better make for home, as Nesta's remarks probably indicated that the loft would be out of bounds that evening. Finishing his ale, he went with her to the door, where a final good-night kiss saw him on his way to Martin's Lane.

The next day, Friday, was taken up with the county court, held in the Shire Hall, inside the inner ward of Rougemont. The central area of the castle, ringed with its defensive wall, held three buildings, the keep at the far side from the gatehouse, the small garrison church of St Mary and the courthouse. This was a bare stone box with a slated roof, as thatch would be vulnerable to fire arrows in the event of a siege. However, there had been no fighting here for over half a century, since the castle had held out for the Empress Matilda for three months in the civil war against King Stephen.

The coroner was required for a number of duties at the shire court, held frequently to settle a variety of criminal and civil cases. He had to call upon 'attached' persons to answer to their bail and, if they failed to appear for four successive courts, declare them outlaw. This particular day, he also had to present various other matters, including several appeals of felony and two criminals who wished to turn 'approver'. There were several forfeitures of the property of hanged felons to register and a number of other administrative tasks, some of which would have to be handed on to the higher court, the Eyre, when it eventually delivered four king's judges to Exeter to try the most serious cases.

The day passed, with Thomas de Peyne doing sterling work in producing documents and rolls and scribing new material for eventual presentation to the Justices in Eyre. At the end of it, John was content to go home to eat the rest of Mary's large pike for supper and doze with a jug of Loire wine. When his wife vanished to her devotions and her bed, he did not even have the will to get up and go down to the Bush. Ignoring Brutus's accusing eye, he slumped in his chair before the fire and let his mind wander over all his problems, professional and personal, until he finally fell asleep.

CHAPTER FIVE

In which Crowner John rides to Honiton

Next morning It was almost a replay of the previous Tuesday, as Hugh Bogge, the Keeper's clerk, again turned up at Rougemont soon after the eighth hour, having left Honiton as dawn lightened the eastern sky. His message was also similar, in that he came to summon the coroner to the scene of a violent death.

'Not a strangled young shipman this time,' he announced with morbid relish. 'A packman with his head stove in! But Sir Luke thinks there might be a connection between them.'

In spite of his three-hour ride, Bogge was quite willing to travel back with them after a bite to eat and a change of horse. By noon they had retraced the fourteen miles of relatively good road back to Honiton, even Thomas keeping up a decent pace on his new rounsey. De Wolfe and Gwyn had become so frustrated by his tardiness on the old broken-winded pony that John had dipped into the sheriff's expense fund and bought a dappled palfrey for the clerk.

They rode into the large village along its straight main street that was part of the Fosse Way, until Hugh Bogge led them down a side track that joined the road to Wilmington and Axminster, where the Keeper of the Peace lived. The cottages and shacks of Honiton petered out after a few hundred paces and, beyond a few strip-fields on either side, trees began again, patches of woodland at first, then denser forest beyond. Just where the last length of ploughed land gave way to a copse of beech and ash, John saw a cluster of people about twenty yards off the road.

'That's the place, Crowner,' said Hugh, his fat face almost glowing with excitement. He obviously relished being a Keeper's clerk, savouring the minor dramas that went with the job.

As they rode up and dismounted, they could see that Luke de Casewold was holding court amongst a handful of villagers. Some held a rake or hoe in their hands and seemed to have been working in the adjacent fields, where early oats and barley were showing green, as well as young bean and pea plants. After tying their horses' reins to convenient saplings, the four newcomers went along the edge of the trees to the group, and de Wolfe pushed his way past the yokels to confront the Keeper.

'A dead packman, your clerk said?' he growled by way of a greeting.

Luke de Casewold pointed down to a shallow depression in the ground, an old pit half-filled with moss and new nettles.

'Hardly merits being called a packman, though I'm told he was more respectable once upon a time.'

In the hole, partly obscured by the new spring weeds, was a body lying face up, his glassy eyes staring at the midday sun. A few bluebottles buzzed around the bloody fluid around the battered lips, and John could see that there were already yellow fly eggs on the eyelids. The face was badly bruised and one ear was half torn from the side of the head.

'You say you know who he is, then?' demanded the coroner.

'A well-known pedlar in these parts by the name of

Setricus Segar,' replied Luke. 'Tramps the roads of Dorset and Devon trying to earn the price of his ale, on which he seems to live instead of solid food.'

De Wolfe looked down at the pathetic figure crumpled in what was almost a ready-made grave. Hard as he was from years of fighting and killing, as well as the morbid tasks of a coroner, he could not but feel a twinge of pity for this wreck of a man having come to such a dismal end.

'Then it's unlikely that he was robbed for his purse, if he was as poor as you suggest,' he said. 'What about his pack or whatever he carried to sell his wares?'

Another man spoke up this time, introducing himself as Edgar, bailiff of Honiton. He was a tall, fair man of obvious Saxon blood, dressed in a short serge tunic and cross-gartered breeches. 'That's the odd thing, sir! His pack wasn't worth two bent pennies, just a few pins and needles and some creased cloths. But it was found untouched a mile from here, hidden under the hedge at the side of the road.'

'Is this how he was found?' John waved a hand at the cadaver.

'Indeed it was, Crowner,' said the bailiff. 'We know better in Honiton than to move a body before you are summoned,' he added virtuously. 'One of these men found him last evening when he was dumping weeds from the field.'

'Do we know when he was last seen alive?'

'A carter from Seaton said he saw Setricus in Wilmington the day before yesterday, trying to sell his wares.'

Gwyn, who had stepped into the hole and was testing the dead man's limbs, looked up. 'Stiff as a plank! With these fly eggs, but no maggots yet, I reckon he died the night before last, if he was seen the day before that.'

De Wolfe nodded at his officer. 'Have a good look at him, Gwyn. See how much of a battering he's suffered.'

Then he turned around beckoned Luke away from the ring of locals who were gawping down at Gwyn's examination.

'Why do you think there might be some connection with the death in Axmouth?' he muttered, out of hearing of the others.

De Casewold's chubby face was pink with excitement as he expounded his theory. Like his clerk, he obviously thrived on mysteries and violent intrigue.

'It was where the pack was found, John! It was hidden in the hedge just outside a ruined toft down the road. No one lives there, but there were signs that someone had been using it very recently. And there were cartwheel tracks in the track alongside the hovel, as well as fresh ox-droppings in the pasture.'

The coroner disliked this man using his Christian name so familiarly, but he concentrated on trying to extract some sense out of what he was telling him.

'What has that got to do with our corpse down on the Axe?' he growled.

The Keeper leant forward, as if imparting some great secret. The sour breath from his bad teeth made John move back sharply, but he listened intently to his deductions.

'I'm sure there are illicit goods coming into the harbour there – but they have to be shifted inland. The only way to move heavier stuff is by cart, probably at night so as not to make it too obvious.'

'So what has this to do with a dead pedlar?'

'Maybe he was too nosy – or tried to steal something from them. Why else would anyone want to beat a penniless drunk to death?'

John thought the notion unlikely but not impossible – and he had no better theory to offer. 'I'd better have a look at this place – a mile away, you say?'

De Casewold nodded, but just then Gwyn gave a shout.

'His head's been cracked like an egg, Crowner. Hit with something hard and heavy, I reckon.'

Even Thomas, who usually hung back when his big colleague was ministering to the dead, moved to the edge of the hole with Hugh Bogge to see what Gwyn had found. He saw a long gash in the greying hair of the scalp, as long as a man's hand.

'Surely that must be from a sword or big knife?' he quavered, a hand to his mouth.

Gwyn guffawed and poked his finger into the gash to feel the broken plates of bone grinding against each other. 'No, you don't need a sharp weapon for this! A good smack with a club or a bit of tree-branch will split the scalp as clean as a whistle!'

As Thomas cringed and moved back from the pit, the coroner joined his officer and between them they looked at the corpse in more detail. Pulling up the threadbare clothing, they found bruises all over the belly and chest, many fractured ribs being felt under the thin skin of the emaciated pedlar. When they had finished, John told the bailiff to have the corpse carried the short distance back into Honiton, where he would hold an inquest in the churchyard in a couple of hours. Leaving Gwyn and Hugh Bogge to organise a jury, he motioned to Thomas and they joined the Keeper in a short expedition to the ruined cottage. Their horses covered the distance in a few minutes and they alighted at a semi-ruined hovel set on its own in a half-acre of overgrown land.

'Probably was lived in by some free tradesman from the village,' observed de Casewold. 'Long abandoned, by the looks of it. Perhaps he died without sons.' The mouldy thatch had caved in in places, causing one end wall to partly collapse, where the rain had dissolved the cob, a mixture of clay, straw and manure. The Keeper pointed to fresh-looking ruts that led in from the road to the side of the cottage, and de

Wolfe saw for himself the ox-droppings on the rough grass nearby.

'Where's this pack of his?' he grunted.

'I left it inside. We can have a look around – perhaps they left something.'

What they had left were the ashes of a recent fire and a stink of urine. The three investigators got in by pushing down a decrepit door whose leather hinges had rotted through. Thomas pointed to a crust of bread on the floor.

'That can't have been there long, otherwise rats and mice would have devoured it.'

The pack belonging to Setricus Segar did not detain them long. It was a poor haversack of canvas, containing several leather rolls with pins and needles, a bundle of faded ribbons and some folded lengths of woollen and serge cloth.

'We are little the wiser, Keeper,' observed de Wolfe as they came back out into the sunlight. 'Does no one in Honiton know of this mysterious cart that travels by night?'

Luke shrugged. 'Those who know, won't tell! And when the cart appears by daylight, who is to mark it from a score of others that ply up and down the roads every day? This is the direct track from Axminster to Honiton and Exeter.'

As they jogged back towards the village, the coroner persisted in questioning Luke about his conviction that Axmouth was involved. 'Why do you think that they are shifting illegal merchandise from there?' he asked. 'No doubt most ports try to evade some of the duty due to the Exchequer, but is Axmouth any different from the rest?'

The Keeper looked slyly across at John. 'I'm sure that it's more than just dodging the tally-man now and then – though I know he's as bent as a shepherd's crook. I feel it in my bones that there are people with blood on their hands involved in some of this trade – and both this hawker and the lad from that cog were silenced to keep their mouths shut.'

Further questioning produced nothing in the way of proof, but de Casewold seemed adamant that some nefarious business was being run from the port on the estuary of the Axe. John wondered if some of the man's obsession was due to his personal dislike of Edward Northcote and the portreeve.

They stopped at one of Honiton's several taverns for a bowl of potage and some bread and meat, then John held his inquest, another futile exercise in which he cajoled a dozen bewildered locals to bring in a verdict of felonious killing by persons unknown. Disgruntled by the inevitable imposition of the murdrum fine at the next Eyre, as it was obvious that no presentment of Englishry could be made over the body of Setricus, the jury dispersed, grumbling at the iniquity of the village having to find five marks just because some bloody pedlar got himself killed on their territory.

As Thomas packed up his writing materials after inscribing the lacklustre proceedings on his rolls, de Wolfe had a last word with the Keeper of the Peace before they parted in opposite directions, Luke to his home in Axminster and John back to Exeter.

'What are you going to do about this notion you have concerning Axmouth?' he grunted.

De Casewold lowered his voice and looked around, though there was no one within twenty paces. 'I intend to find this damned cart – or one like it, travelling at night. If I can arrest the driver, I'll soon make the bastard talk!'

For a short fat man, well past his prime as a sword-wielding knight, Luke seemed very confident of his prowess as a thief-catcher, and de Wolfe, though he disliked the man, hoped that he was not going to do something foolhardy and put himself in danger. Unlike his own bodyguard Gwyn, the Keeper's clerk, Hugh Bogge, would be about as much use in a fight as a bladder of lard. Still, there was nothing that he could do about it, and with a perfunctory wave he wheeled his horse about and set off back to the city and the prospect of another dismal evening with his wife.

The following day was not only a Sunday but Palm Sunday, when Matilda began her orgy of devotions for the coming Holy Week with three attendances at the cathedral and one at the 'parish' church of St Olave's.

To be exact, there were no formal parishes in Exeter, but the twenty-seven churches served numerous small areas within the city walls, some catering for only a handful of households within their shadow. The cathedral was not meant to provide for the general public, apart from the great festivals, being a place where continuous worship of the Almighty was maintained by the priesthood at their nine services each day. Palm Sunday was one of the occasions when the great church of St Mary and St Peter put on a show, with a procession not only within the precincts but around the city itself.

John was not an enthusiastic churchgoer, but every few weeks and on the major religious festivals he stirred himself to accompany his wife, mainly out of a sense of duty and propriety. This day, he donned his best grey tunic and a short black cloak, both of them displaying the only colours he ever wore, to Matilda's eternal disgust. She would have preferred him to be more colourful, like the majority of upper-class citizens, but he was obdurate in his choice of clothes.

Matilda had already been to a service at Prime, before the eighth hour, but now urged him out of the house an hour later to watch the procession before Lauds and High Mass. A great winding serpent of figures came out of the West Front of the cathedral, bearing crosses and banners as incense was wafted about. The canons and vicars, the secondaries, choristers and the parish priests preceded the portreeves, burgesses and guild wardens as the cortege chanted and sang its way around the Close to the Palace Gate and out into the streets to perambulate the city.

When the procession finished its circuit, it came back into the cathedral to celebrate Lauds, Matilda and John joining the throng to enter the huge building. As they stood with hundreds of others on the bare flagstones of the great nave, watching and listening to the arcane performance of the quire and canons beyond the carved screen, Matilda nudged her husband with an elbow.

'That's the one you were asking about, over there with the wife wearing the red-velvet mantle'

John looked across a few heads and saw a tall dark-haired man dressed in an expensive green tunic under a long surcoat of cream wool. 'Who is he?' he muttered, not understanding what she was talking about.

'That's Robert de Helion, the manor-lord of Bridport and a very rich merchant,' she murmured impatiently. 'You said he was the owner of that ship you were concerned about.'

De Wolfe stared again, as this was the man he wanted to speak to about the cog *The Tiger*, which had not yet returned to Axmouth, as far as he was aware. He resolved to go and visit the man in the very near future, though Easter Week was a difficult time to conduct official business.

Soon, the service came to its climax with the High Mass, and before long John found himself outside again, on the steps at the West Front. He hung about awkwardly while his wife gossiped with her cronies, which seemed mainly an opportunity for them to show off their new clothes and their old husbands, if they were men of note or successful at commerce. Matilda had long ago given up trying to inveigle John into these huddles to display him as the king's coroner, and he stood silently on the margins, hunched like some large black crow in his sombre raiment. Eventually, the groups and cliques dispersed and they made their way home to Mary's dinner, before Matilda made off again to St Olave's for another round of kneeling and praying.

De Wolfe declined to suffer any more religion that day and, after taking Brutus down to Exe Island for a run around on the grassy mudflats, he came home and slept in front of his beloved hearth until Matilda returned in time for supper. To him, the inertia of the Sabbath was a boring interruption of the week's work, and as he nodded off into slumber he resolved to do all he could in the coming days to get to the bottom of the murderous problems in the east of the county.

When the new week began, the coroner's plans to pursue the Axmouth mystery were frustrated by new cases. First of all, he had to spend a full day in Crediton, investigating a house fire in which a man was killed by a falling beam when he tried to rescue his treasure chest. On Tuesday morning, after attending three hangings out at the gallows in Heavitree, he had a summons to ride to Totnes, where a felon awaiting execution had escaped with the connivance of the gaolers and had sought sanctuary in the nearest church. The fugitive had already spent twenty of his allotted forty days' grace sitting near the altar, to the annoyance of the priest, but now wished to abjure the realm. John had to ride down there with his officer and clerk and go through the ritual of confession, then send the man, arrayed in sackcloth and carrying a crude wooden cross, down to Dartmouth to catch the first ship that could take him out of England.

With insufficient daylight to ride back home that night, he claimed lodging in Totnes Castle, an impressive circular fortification perched above the town, before setting off next day. It was late on Wednesday afternoon when they arrived back in Exeter at the end of the twenty-five-mile journey, and after enduring a stony-faced Matilda, who always complained when he spent a night away, he felt too tired to stir himself after supper to tramp down to the Bush. Though his boil had subsided, the long ride had made it ache, so he was glad to crawl into his bed as soon as it grew dark, ignoring the snores of his wife on the other side of the wide mattress. He knew that this new series of absences from the tavern in Idle Lane would not endear him to Nesta and promised himself that he would get down there on the following day, come what may.

Maundy Thursday began wet and windy, and de Wolfe was glad that after checking with the guardroom at Rougemont no new deaths had been reported overnight. Neither were there any hangings due at the gallows-tree outside the walls on Magdalene Street, so after a pint of cider and some bread and cheese with his assistants in their dreary chamber in the gatehouse, John announced that he was off to track down Robert de Helion. Matilda had said that he had a town house near the East Gate. If he was that rich, no doubt it would be one of the city's bigger dwellings on the south side of High Street, possibly in Raden Lane. He took his cloak from a wooden peg driven between the rough stones of the bare wall and left Thomas to his scribing of duplicate rolls for the next Eyre. Gwyn no doubt would find himself a game of dice with his soldier friends in the garrison while the coroner went in search of information.

He went across the drawbridge and down the hill through the outer ward to reach High Street. Ignoring the fine but steady rain, he pushed through the shoppers thronging the booths along the edge of the now muddy road and went into a quieter lane on the opposite side of the main thoroughfare. Here were houses of varying styles, many now in stone, but the majority still timber, set in long burgage plots that ran at right angles to the narrow road. Few were thatched, as this was now frowned upon in the tightly packed cities where fire was an ever-present hazard, so slate or stone tiling were the usual roofing materials.

Halfway along, he saw a young servant girl throwing used floor-rushes out into the street, where they would soon be trodden into the mud. He enquired about Robert de Helion's dwelling and the flustered child called an older manservant, who directed him to a large house on the corner of a side lane opposite. It was stone-built and, though opening directly on to the road, had an imposing front door between two pillars, which reminded him of Hilda's house in Dawlish. Shuttered windows on each side were matched by a pair on an upper floor in the modern style, suggesting that the dwelling was fairly recent.

He knocked on the door with a fist and it was opened by a middle-aged servant wearing a red tunic with an embroidered crest across the front, an extravagance usually confined to the greater lords and barons. After John had announced his rank and office, he was told that Sir Robert was at home and would undoubtedly be willing to receive him. They stepped into a vestibule, from which two leather-flap doors led into the side rooms behind the lower windows. A wooden door straight ahead of them entered the hall, a lofty chamber occupying all the centre of the building. John was pleased to see that in spite of the grandeur of the place it still had a central firepit, unlike his own treasured hearth and chimney. The furnishings and tapestry wall-hangings were expensive, and a large dresser displayed a multitude of fine pewter and silver dishes.

Robert de Helion was sitting at a table to one side of the fire, a few smouldering logs dispelling the chill of early spring. He was surrounded by parchments, and a grey-haired clerk stood alongside his master, just as Elphin hovered over the sheriff back in Rougemont.

The merchant-knight stood up to greet de Wolfe, then motioned for him to sit on the other side of the table and waved at his emblazoned bottler to bring wine. The clerk stepped tactfully into the background and de Helion courteously enquired about the coroner's business with him. As the wineskin and goblets appeared, John took the opportunity to study Robert at close quarters, as he had seen him only at a distance in the cathedral. He was above average height, slim and erect, with a head of dark brown hair cut severely in the Norman style, the sides and back being shaved up to an abrupt ledge that ran horizontally around his head. The face was strong and brooding, with a passing resemblance to John's own, the big nose and long jaw being similar.

'I have come to make enquiries about one of your cogs, as well as the general situation in Axmouth,' he began after he had sipped the excellent wine.

De Helion looked puzzled. 'Is this not a strange task for a coroner, Sir John?' he asked. 'I thought that your duties were in the courts and investigating deaths?'

John nodded and explained more fully. 'I am looking into a murder in Axmouth, where the dead youth was a shipman on one of your cogs. I am told that you own *The Tiger*, is that not so?'

The manor-lord of Bridport still failed to comprehend. 'Indeed, that vessel does belong to me, along with about a dozen other ships! But I know nothing of the death of a crew member, though I suspect that fatal brawling and disputes are all too common amongst seamen.'

De Wolfe shook his head. 'This was no wharf-side

brawl. The lad was strangled, then his body buried to avoid detection. I have been waiting to question the shipmaster and crew, but the damned thing has vanished over the horizon.'

Robert turned his head to speak to his clerk. 'Stephen, do we know where *The Tiger* is and when she might return?'

'The vessel must be due back at any time, sir, according to Henry Crik. She went across to Rouen with tin and to fetch cloth back from Caen to Axmouth.'

De Helion swung back to the coroner. 'A short voyage. You should be able to speak to her master very soon.' He spoke again over his shoulder to Stephen. 'Remind me who he is, will you?'

'Martin Rof, sir. He used to sail mostly out of Dartmouth until last year.'

The ship owner nodded. 'That's why I don't recall him that well. I have cogs that use the Dart as well as the Axe and Exe. But I have little to do with the crews or their ships; that is the task of my agent Crik and others, like Elias Palmer in the case of Axmouth,' he added dismissively.

De Wolfe rubbed his bristly chin. 'Ah yes! Elias Palmer – and the bailiff Edward Northcote. I have heard rumours of irregular dealings down at Axmouth, which may not be unconnected with this killing.'

He stretched the truth for the sake of his investigation. 'Have you any reason to suspect that anyone in your employ down there might be involved in illegal or even criminal pursuits?'

De Helion stared at this gaunt, dark figure who had descended upon him without warning. 'I've no notion as to what you might mean, coroner,' he protested. 'What kind of crimes?'

'To put it bluntly, evasion of royal taxes on certain goods – and possibly the passing of pirated goods.'

Instead of looking shocked, Robert de Helion gave a

wry smile. 'Evasion of royal taxes? That's a polite way of saying "smuggling", I think. Sir John, many people consider these Customs dues an added imposition on an already overburdened population and if they can "evade" them, then good luck to them. I don't involve myself in any such schemes, but I fully understand those who will accidentally forget to show the tally-man every bale or keg.'

The coroner grunted: this was a sentiment that seemed to fall from everyone's lips. 'And piracy? Have you heard rumours of that? Our new Keeper of the Peace in that area seems convinced that the cargoes of some vanished ships end up deep inland – and that some get there through Axmouth.'

The expression on the ship owner's face hardened. 'That I cannot believe, but again I have no personal knowledge of these matters. Being a merchant and financier with fingers in many bowls, I do not involve myself in the daily running of my various enterprises. I pay agents and clerks to handle that, so how would I know what some of my shipmasters get up to when they are a dozen leagues from land?'

This was a neat disclaimer, but de Wolfe could find no reason to disbelieve what the other knight said.

'You mentioned the portreeve, Elias Palmer,' he persisted. 'Along with the bailiff, Edward Northcote, they seem to have the port of Axmouth very much under their thumbs. Have you any reason to think that they might be involved in some underhand business?'

Again Robert de Helion gave a sardonic smile. 'Axmouth is very much under a thumb – but it is the holy thumb of the Prior of Loders! We all know that the Church is as concerned with its worldly possessions as with its heavenly duties – did I not hear recently that now about one third of England belongs to them, rather than to the barons or even the king?'

He stopped to swallow some wine. 'And of the priests

and monks who are keen on their estates and their incomes, the Prior of Loders is amongst the keenest. He keeps his bailiff on a very short rein, and I warrant that he would know straight away if as little as one clipped penny went astray in the accounts kept by old Elias.'

For a man who claimed to be aloof from the daily running of his business, Robert seemed very well informed about the finances of Axmouth. Further questions produced nothing useful, and John sensed that the merchant was becoming impatient to return to his clerk's ministrations. Soon, he rose to leave and de Helion promised to send him word as soon as he knew that his ship *The Tiger* had returned to Axmouth.

As he strode back to Rougemont, John pondered over what he had learnt, which in truth was very little. He was not sure what to make of Robert – the man was rich and probably powerful in certain circles, though he seemed to have no political ambitions. No doubt the guilds had considerable respect for him, as he offered employment to many of their members, but he seemed to keep a very low profile amongst the county aristocracy. He had told John that he and his wife and family spent most of their time at his manor near Cullompton. His Exeter house seemed to be used mainly for conducting his business, though he had said that he also travelled regularly to Southampton, Plymouth and Dartmouth. The coroner had no grounds for thinking that any of de Helion's obvious wealth came from illegal sources, as a dozen ships, a fulling mill and God knows what other business enterprises would surely bring him in more than enough to maintain his lifestyle.

Disgruntled, he returned to his chamber, conscious that at every turn his efforts to discover who killed Simon Makerel seemed to run into the sand. Whether or not the irritating Luke de Casewold was right in trying to link it to the death of the pedlar was another matter. He decided that another visit to Axmouth was called for soon, whether the missing cog had returned or not.

The solemn days of Easter brought virtually all activity to a stop, as Good Friday was devoted to churchgoing. Matilda had attended an all-night vigil at St Olave's, and next morning John had no option but to accompany her to the cathedral for a special High Mass. After dinner at noon, the exhausted Matilda collapsed into her bed and proclaimed her intention of staying there until late evening, when she would again make her way to her favourite little church in Fore Street. The taverns were closed, but once his wife was sound asleep he whistled to his hound and made his way down to Idle Lane. For once in the year, the inn was strangely silent, the servants having gone home for the day. The front entrance was closed, but he went around to the yard and put his head around the back door, calling out for Nesta. An answering voice came from the loft and, leaving Brutus to nose in the rushes for mice, John climbed the wide ladder and found his mistress waiting for him at the door to her small cubicle, her fists planted on each side of her slim waist.

'I do believe it's the coroner, if my memory serves me right!' she said, though the sarcasm was tempered by the smile on her face.

For answer, he seized her and kissed her almost wildly, and in a trice they were back in her room, collapsing on to the feather mattress that lay on a low plinth on the floor. This time there was no sign of any small devil perching on John's shoulder as they fumbled at each other's clothing and soon – but not too soon – they lay panting and satiated under the sheepskins that served as blankets.

'Now I see why they call it "good" Friday,' he

murmured irreverently as their pulses gradually slowed down.

Nesta pinched his thigh as she cuddled closely against him. 'Don't be blasphemous, John,' she said in semi-serious concern. 'You'll go to hell for saying things like that.'

'I want to be with all my old friends, for I'm damned sure they'll not be in heaven,' he growled into her ear. 'And at least I'll get away from my wife, for with all the praying and bobbing up and down that she does, she must have assured herself a place alongside St Peter.'

He said this partly to tease Nesta, for he knew she was a devout woman with a strong belief in the faith, even if she was not a fanatical churchgoer. In the villages, attendance at Mass was virtually obligatory, with a parish priest ready to chase up and castigate those who fell by the wayside – but in a city like Exeter, full of churches with no strict parish system, it was virtually impossible to keep track of backsliders.

'But surely you must be a believer and not a heretic, John?' she demanded, rising up on one elbow, deliciously exposing her bosom.

De Wolfe, becoming somewhat philosophical in the afterglow of lovemaking, considered this for a moment. Everyone was brought up from infancy to revere the faith, attend church and never to question the dictats of the priests, who were powerful figures with all the weapons of eternal damnation at their disposal. Apart from a few madmen, no one disputed the teachings of the Church, which pervaded everyone's lives. John accepted that he was no exception; he had never once even thought of denying the creed or wondering what proof there was of God, the devil and all the saints and angels. Yet he was supremely uninterested in the whole business, being at the opposite pole from Matilda, who lived and breathed her religious faith. If there was one area that he occasionally wondered about, it was the ritual of the Church, rather than the underlying concept of God and all His works. If Christ was a lowly carpenter, preaching poverty and humility, why did bishops and archbishops and the Pope need to further His mission by wearing outrageously ornate garments and parade around swinging incense? Even when these faintly sacrilegious thoughts came to him, he afforded them no importance. He was in general an unimaginative man, preferring the concrete evidence of his own eyes and ears. To him, life consisted of eating, sleeping, fighting, doing his duty to his king – and bedding a woman when the opportunity presented.

Nesta's question was still unanswered, but she stayed propped up waiting for it, her hazel eyes fixed worriedly upon his.

'No, I'm no heretic, my love,' he said slowly. 'I just don't care much about it all, to tell the truth. What is to be, will be!'

With this fatalistic rejoinder, he slid his arms around her and drew her down under the covers again.

CHAPTER SIX

In which the Keeper makes himself unpopular

The Saturday of the Easter festival was a neutral sort of day, between the tragic sadness of Good Friday's Crucifixion and the triumphant drama of the Sabbath's Risen Lord. People went about their business to some extent, as food had to be bought from the stalls, bread had to be baked, animals had to be fed and meals prepared.

For one man – and his much less enthusiastic clerk – the day was to prove considerably more active. Sir Luke de Casewold, Keeper of the King's Peace for Axminster and a wide area around it, decided that he would pursue his suspicions about Axmouth by checking on the activities of the officials there and the contents of the barns and storehouses along the estuary.

He rose early and left his house in Axminster to rouse Hugh Bogge from his nearby cottage. They collected their horses from his stable and covered the five miles to Axmouth in less than an hour. There were six vessels moored along the bank below the village and several more were to be seen on the opposite side at Seaton. Where possible, the shipmasters had arranged their voyages so that they would spend Easter in port, but the Keeper soon discovered that *The Tiger* was not one of them.

'We'll call on that rascally tally-man first,' announced Luke, trotting his mare to a cottage halfway between the village gate and the sea. It stood between two large thatched sheds with high doors like hay-barns, though these were firmly closed with long bars across the front, each secured with a massive iron padlock.

A crude fence around the croft hemmed in two goats, a sow, several chickens and two small children contentedly playing in the mud. De Casewold dismounted and stood at the wicker hurdle that served as a gate and yelled for the Customs official.

'John Capie! I need to talk to you. Get yourself out here!'

A woman's head poked out through the open doorway, then was quickly withdrawn after she had screeched at the infants to come inside. As they scuttled to obey, a man appeared, looking dishevelled and obviously not long risen from his bed. He was about thirty, thin and with a long sallow face, with hollow cheeks and an unshaven spread of black stubble around his jaw. His hair, which looked as if a tempest had just blown through it, was of the same dark colour, and he futilely ran a hand through it to try to tame it into submission. He wore the same short dun-coloured tunic and green breeches that Luke had seen on him at his last visit.

Capie peered sleepily at the visitor and groaned as soon as he recognised who it was. 'God's guts, Keeper, don't you know it's Easter?' he complained.

'The king's business must be attended to every day, Capie,' he said pompously. 'I need to talk to you – right now!'

The tally-man looked anxiously over his shoulder at the open door, from where children's cries and his wife's exasperated scolding could be heard.

'Not in there. It's bloody chaos with those brats,' he muttered. Scratching himself under both armpits, he came to the hurdle and lifted it out of the way, then replaced it quickly as the goats tried to escape.

'Come over here, if you must,' he suggested grudgingly and led the way over towards the nearest storehouse. He leant on one of the large doors and scowled at Luke de Casewold and his clerk. 'So what is it you want to know so urgently that brings you here to disturb me on this day?'

The Keeper glared at him for speaking rudely to a royal officer. 'I want to know if you have had a hand in any irregular dealings in this port, Capie. I strongly suspect that much of the cargo that goes both inwards and out of here escapes the tax due to the royal Exchequer!'

The tally-man folded his arms and glowered back obstinately. 'I do my best, but I can't be expected to watch every crate and keg that is landed or loaded! This wharf extends for almost three furlongs, and you can see for yourself how many vessels might be here at any one time.'

He flung up an arm to encompass the line of cogs leaning against the river bank. 'If the king or his damned ministers want to collect every half-penny of Customs dues, then they had better employ a couple more tally-men, for I can't cope with it all!'

His aggrieved tone sounded more than a little false to Luke, as Capie had never complained to him or the sheriff about getting additional help. However, the Keeper was craftily working around to a more sinister problem than Customs evasion and adopted a more conciliatory approach.

'That may well be true, Capie, so tell me how you go about your work. That ship there, for instance: how would you deal with that when she arrives?' He pointed to the nearest cog, which seemed deserted at the moment.

Mollified, John Capie explained that as soon as a new

arrival moored herself to the stout tree-trunks buried along the bank, he would question the shipmaster as to the name of the vessel, where she had come from and what the nature of the cargo was. Being unable to read or write, he would remember this and hasten up to the portreeve's house to tell him of the new arrival, while the ship prepared to unload her contents on to the quayside. Capie would then return and, with a selection of knotted strings and hazel rods that he notched with a knife, would keep count of the items that were carried down the gangplank.

'But how do you know which goods belong to which string or tally-stick?' demanded Hugh Bogge.

'The cords are of different colours and the tops of the sticks are marked with my own code,' snapped Capie. 'A notch for cloth bales, half a ring for wine kegs and so on. I go back to Elias Palmer as soon as the hold is empty and he writes it all down on his parchments.'

'What if there are two or more cogs unloading at the same time?' objected Luke. 'You can't keep all that in your head.'

'Mother of God, isn't that what I just complained about?' exclaimed the tally-man. 'I try to keep them separate by forbidding the shipmaster to start un-loading until I've dealt with the previous vessel, but half the time they take no notice, as they either want to get to the nearest alehouse or catch the next tide to get back out to sea.'

The clerk pushed himself back into the discussion. 'What about goods that are being taken out of the port?' he asked.

John Capie shrugged. 'Not so important, as far as I'm concerned. Wool is the main problem, since our beloved king put a tax on its export. We don't get much tin through here these days; all the refined metal goes out through Exeter or Topsham, as the second smeltings and the assays are done there.'

The Keeper came back into the dialogue. 'So you tally up the bales of wool and report the number to the portreeve, is that how it works?'

'Yes. Elias is the linchpin of the system, being the only one who can write, other than the priests.'

Luke noticed his use of the plural. 'Priests? Is there more than one, then?'

The Customs man stared at him. 'Only old Henry of Cumba actually lives here – but the cellarer's man from the priory is here every week, keeping a very close eye on what's due to Loders.' The priory was just beyond Bridport, some ten miles over the border in Dorset.

'And what *is* due to them?' demanded de Casewold.

John Capie looked at him as if he was a backward child. 'What's due? Jesus, they own the bloody manor, don't they! They claim a fifth of everything that is collected for the king, to go into the coffers of the prior.'

'Are you saying that they rob the royal Exchequer of a fifth of the king's dues?' squawked the Keeper indignantly.

Again Capie gave him a look that he usually reserved for the village idiot. 'Of course not! The king's tax is used as a measure – and then a fifth of that is added on for Loders.'

Hugh Bogge muttered something under his breath, which his master failed to catch. It was just as well, as it was a seditious comment about government and ecclesiastical extortion.

'So how is this money collected?' Luke wished to know.

The tally-man shrugged again. 'Don't know; nothing to do with me! I think Elias sends a list up to the sheriff, who collects it as part of the county farm from all the merchants who import and export.'

The 'farm' was the six-monthly accumulation of taxes from every part of Devon, which the sheriff had to take to Winchester in person, in bags of coin in the panniers of packhorses. Here it was paid into the Exchequer, which got its name from the chequered cloth on the treasury clerks' table that was used to facilitate counting the silver pennies that were the only form of currency. The size of the farm was set annually by the Curia Regis for each county – and if the sheriff could collect more than that, he was entitled to keep the difference, which made the post of sheriff so much sought after by barons and even bishops. Some even held multiple shrievalties in several counties at once. However, after the depredations of his predecessor, Richard de Revelle, old Henry de Furnellis was hard pressed to collect the minimum required.

'So it's all down to Elias Palmer as to how much he enters in his accounts,' said the Keeper, cynicism oozing from his voice. 'You can't read, so you've no idea what he's writing down in his accounts.'

'Not my problem, sir! I'm paid a pittance to record as much as I can manage – what happens after that is none of my business, and I don't want it to be.'

De Casewold changed the subject somewhat, waving a hand at the locked doors behind the tally-man. 'So what exactly is kept in these sheds?' he demanded.

Capie moved away from the doors and looked at the barn-like structures as if he had never noticed them before. 'In here? Why, the goods that have either been unloaded and not yet been delivered to the owners – or the stuff that is waiting for the cog that is to carry them abroad.'

Luke de Casewold looked dubious at the explanation. 'A complicated task, sorting all that. Who is responsible for it?'

'The portreeve, of course. No one else can check the goods against the manifest lists, for only he can read them. Tally-sticks and knotted cords are no good for identifying a pile of kegs or bales.'

The Keeper felt that Elias Palmer was in a position to make or break the administration of Axmouth, as he seemed in a position to control every aspect of the trade there.

'I want to have a look in there, so open them up for me!' he snapped.

Capie shook his head obstinately. 'Can't be done, Keeper. I don't have a key. Only the portreeve and the bailiff can unlock them.'

Luke puffed out his cheeks and blew in annoyance, feeling that he was being deliberately frustrated in his search for the truth.

'Then I'll go up and get them to show me what's in there,' he promised, but turned the subject once again. 'Now then, Capie, I want an honest answer and be sure that if I find you are lying, you'll end up in chains before the courts. Do you know anything about goods coming in here as the spoils of piracy out at sea?' He glared at the tally-man and rattled his sword in its scabbard to emphasise his threat.

John Capie stared sullenly into the middle distance and shuffled his dirty shoes on the ground. 'I know nothing of such things!' he protested. 'How could I know? I just count items of cargo as they get carried off the cogs. Where they came from is not within my knowledge.'

His words and demeanour were totally unconvincing, and de Casewold leant towards the man and breathed his foul breath into his face as he spoke. 'Come, Capie, you are the man most involved with these ships and their crews! If anyone heard any gossip about certain vessels pillaging others, it would be you!'

The tally-man suddenly backed away, holding up his palms as if warding off the devil himself. 'I know nothing of such matters, Keeper! Don't ask me. I don't want to get involved in any gossip. I'm a simple man who does a job and just wants to live quietly with my family!'

'You sound afraid, John Capie!' exclaimed Luke. 'Has someone been threatening you if you speak out?'

The tally-man stumbled back even further. 'I don't know what goes on out at sea – and I don't want to know! Go and ask someone else, if you must, but leave me out of it, d'you hear!' The last words had risen into a screech as Capie turned and lurched back to his cottage without so much as a backward glance.

'There's a man with something to hide,' observed Hugh Bogge as they watched him hurry into his cottage and quickly shut the door, which screeched as the wood scraped the uneven threshold.

'I'll have him eventually,' crowed de Casewold vindictively. 'But I want to see what's in these storehouses, so we'll tackle the bailiff and Elias next.'

Entering the harbour gate, they passed the church, where a bell was tolling mournfully for some service, a trickle of villagers gravitating to it through the churchyard. Further up the main street they entered the garden of the bailiff's house and through a wide-open shutter saw him and the portreeve bent over a table. The Keeper went to it and called through the window-opening.

'Edward Northcote! I need to talk to you – and to your portreeve.'

The two men inside swung around and groaned when they saw who it was. 'What in God's name do you want, Casewold?' bellowed the bailiff.

'To ask you some questions – and to inspect those warehouses on the wharf.'

'Go to hell, you interfering busybody!' roared Northcote, coming across to the window-opening and thrusting his large, flushed face right into that of the Keeper. 'It's Easter and we have better things to do than waste time with you.'

Behind him, the portreeve nodded nervous agreement but said nothing.

'Have a care, Northcote. I am a king's officer!' threatened Luke. 'I can have you attached to the next county court – or have you dragged off to Axminster gaol.'

'Indeed! And who is going to do that?' sneered the bailiff, his anger rapidly coming to the boil. 'Is that fat clerk of yours going to haul me off by the scruff of the neck? Or are you going to prod me with your little sword all the way to Axminster?'

'Perhaps not – but a sheriff's *posse* might!' retorted the indignant Keeper.

'Don't talk such bloody nonsense, man!' was the scathing reply. 'You are a damned nuisance, but what is it you want to ask?'

Slightly mollified by Northcote's grudging agreement, Luke leant his hands on the sill of the window. 'Several matters, bailiff. Do you know when *The Tiger* is due to return?'

'No, I don't. What about you, Elias – you're the harbour master?'

The skinny portreeve shook his grey head. 'Shouldn't be too long; it was supposed to be a quick voyage over to Normandy. But I can't tell when she's due; she may have sunk for all I know!'

'Or been scuttled by pirates!' snapped de Casewold. 'That was the other thing I need to know. I suspect that goods seized with the blood of innocent shipmen have passed through this port. Do you know anything of that, eh?'

Edward Northcote prodded the Keeper in the chest with a large forefinger, hard enough to make him step back a pace. 'Oh yes, I forgot. We had a few bloodstained casks in last week! And the portreeve here saw several bales of Flemish cloth smeared with gore, didn't you, Elias?'

The heavy sarcasm served only to inflame de Casewold's own temper, and he banged his fist angrily on one of the shutters hinged back against the wall.

'Don't you mock me, damn you! I am charged with keeping the king's peace, and murder, theft and piracy rank high amongst felonies! I want to see what's inside those sheds on the wharf and to check the contents with the lists that I am told the portreeve holds. My clerk is quite capable of verifying that all is in order – or if it is not!'

The bailiff's florid face, with its rim of black beard stretching from ear to ear, again jutted towards the Keeper. 'I open those doors only for the merchants to whom the goods belong – and to the shipmen and porters who have to load and unload them.'

'Or the prior's emissary, the cellarer's man from Loders,' added Elias Palmer. 'He has a legitimate right to check that the priory is getting its full commission in return for the ships and merchants having the use of its port.'

'Well, I have even more of a legitimate right,' shouted Luke. 'The right of a king to send his officers to investigate the activities of his subjects!'

For answer, Edward Northcote leant out of his window and seized a shutter in each of his large hands. As he began pulling them shut, forcing the Keeper to stand back to avoid being crushed, he made a final suggestion.

'Come back next week, when the quayside is working again – and maybe we'll let you have a glimpse inside.'

With that, he slammed the hinged boards shut and dropped an iron bar across the inside, leaving a fuming de Casewold isolated outside.

As he moved back to the table with Elias, he muttered to him in angry tones. 'We'll have to keep a close eye on that nosy bastard!'

The Easter period passed, with John de Wolfe making several duty visits to both the cathedral and St Olave's Church, accompanying Matilda in her ceaseless devotional perambulations. The Monday was a holiday, celebrated more in the rural areas than in the city, though apprentices and many servants were given a day's respite from their usual work.

The following day there was an unusual call for the coroner's services, which took him at an early hour down to Topsham, the small port fives miles downstream on the estuary of the Exe. He left Thomas behind to say his Masses in the cathedral and, with Gwyn, followed the bailiff of the Exminster Hundred who had called them out. John knew him quite well, as that hundred included his brother's other manor of Holcombe, where Hilda's father was the reeve, as well as Dawlish itself.

They crossed with their horses on the small rope ferry and landed on the marshy area on the other side of the Exe. Riding down alongside the river, they came to the tiny fishing hamlet of Starcross, where they climbed aboard a small fishing boat that went down with the ebbing tide the last half-mile towards the mouth of the river. Here a long tongue of sand stuck out eastwards from the huge area of dunes and scrubland that was Dawlish Warren.

On the wide beach in the lee of this tongue, they saw a group of men standing around a large grey object, and when they came close enough to jump out and wade ashore they saw it was a small whale.

'It was still alive last night, moving its fins a little,' said the bailiff.

As they reached the scene, Gwyn, a former fisherman from Polruan in Cornwall, shook his head sadly. 'Poor thing's stone dead now. Once they get beached, they've not much chance.'

A whale was one of the two 'royal fish', the other being the sturgeon, which by right belonged to the Crown, and one of the coroner's duties was investigating catches and strandings, so that the fish – or more usually its monetary value – could be seized for the king. Half a dozen men and a couple of women and children were standing around, fascinated by the dead animal. About twenty feet long, it lay motionless on the sand, left high and dry by the receding tide.

'It's been swimming up and down for two days,' volunteered one of the younger fishermen. 'Seemed too stupid to know how to get back out to sea around the sand-spit.'

An older one shook his head. 'I've seen a few strandings in my time. Reckon they are usually sick and come close inshore, then are too weak to find their way out again.'

'What's to be done about it, Crowner?' asked the bailiff, a practical man. A whale, even a small one like this, was worth a considerable sum, as the fat rendered down from the blubber was first-class lamp oil, as well as being used for other purposes. If taken fresh, the meat was palatable enough for hungry villagers, and even parts of the skeleton could be used for various purposes.

'It belongs to King Richard,' said de Wolfe. 'Though I doubt we could get it to him in Normandy before it stinks!' he added with an attempt at levity.

'I heard tell that the head goes to the king and the tail to the queen,' countered the bailiff. 'But it sounds a fairy tale to me.'

De Wolfe shrugged. 'I've never heard that before,' he admitted. 'But true or false, I have to dispose of all this beast as soon as possible, before it starts to become foul.'

He looked at the dozen or so people gathered around, some staring expectantly at the dead monster. 'Can you deal with it here? Remove the flesh and the grease?'

The bailiff called over an elderly man, still powerful in the limbs. It was the reeve from Dawlish, whom John knew by sight. After greeting him, the man said that he could soon organise a party to flesh the whale and boil the blubber in pans over fires lit on the beach, taking as much of the meat as they could back to the nearby villages. After discussing the details, the coroner came to a rapid decision.

'In that case, I declare that the whale is seized as the king's property, but that the beast is released to the hundred in the sum of three marks. That will have to be confirmed – or even altered – when presented to the judges at the next Eyre.'

The bailiff nodded his agreement, as though three marks was four hundred and eighty silver pennies, the value of a large quantity of whale oil, plus the meat and whalebone, made it a worthwhile bargain, especially as the money did not have to be paid until demanded at the next Eyre in Exeter, which might be many months away – or even a year or two, if the judges were delayed.

The business being rapidly concluded, John and his officer declined the offer to be rowed back upstream and walked along the beach to fetch their horses. Gwyn knew only too well what was coming next.

'As we are so near Dawlish, it seems a pity not to call there and see if our shipmasters have any news.' John almost convinced himself that this was his only motive. Grinning under his luxuriant moustache, Gwyn hoisted himself on to his brown mare and they trotted off across the sandy scrubland towards the port, only two miles distant.

Almost as if fate was conspiring to assist John's conscience, when they arrived at the small town Gwyn saw at once that another of the cogs belonging to de Wolfe's partnership was beached in the inlet. This was the *St Peter*, whose shipmaster was Angerus de Wile. When they hailed a young lad sitting alone on the tilted deck, they learnt that his captain was in the nearest tavern with the ship's mate.

Gwyn was, of course, delighted with the news and almost fell from his horse in his haste to reach the alehouse for some refreshment. Inside the low tap-room of the Ship Inn, they found a group of sailors standing around a large upturned barrel, drinking their ale and cider. One was the shipmaster, Angerus, who looked startled to see one of his employers appear so unexpectedly but rallied and introduced his crew to Gwyn and the coroner.

'We made port only on the last tide, sir!' he ex-plained. 'So ale was the first necessity after a trip up from Dartmouth.'

He called for drinks for the new arrivals, as de Wolfe explained what had brought them to the neighbour-hood. 'I came hoping to see you or Roger Watts again, to see if I could get any more news of what may have been going on in Axmouth.'

Angerus de Wile, a stringy man approaching thirty, had a prominent projecting lower jaw that made him look a little like a pugnacious bulldog. He had not yet had time to speak to his older colleague, Roger Watts, so did not know of John's previous visit to seek infor-mation about smuggling and piracy. When the coroner explained, there were murmurs from his shipmates and Angerus put them into words.

'Crowner, it's damned strange that you should be asking about this, for not more than a month ago we picked up a man floating on some wreckage, nearer the French coast than ours. He was half-drowned and had a great slash across his head. Poor fellow died before we could land him in Rouen, but he was the only survivor – if you can call it that – of a pirate attack.'

The ale-jugs arrived and John waited impatiently while thirsts were quenched. 'Did he tell you anything?' he demanded.

'The man could hardly speak – and that not for long until his wits failed completely. A Fleming he was, crewing a Dunkerque ship, carrying cloth and wine out of the Rhine, bound for Southampton.'

He stopped for a swallow and his ship's mate, a rotund older man, took up the tale. 'Hard to understand, he was, what with the foreign language and his weakness – but it seems that a faster cog had appeared in mid-Channel and boarded them, killing the crew, then scuttling the vessel after ransacking her.'

Angerus nodded. 'This fellow was struck with a sword and thrown overboard but managed to cling on to dunnage boards that floated free when the ship went down. The pirates sailed off without noticing that he wasn't yet a corpse.'

'Did he say what vessel attacked them?' asked Gwyn, wiping ale from his moustache with the back of his hand.

To de Wolfe's great chagrin, Angerus shook his head. 'It was just another cog. He couldn't read, even if he had the time and wits to see a name on the bow. But he said the assailants shouted in English, he was definite on that!'

'Damn it all!' muttered John. 'Have you any ideas where the vessel may have come from?'

The shipmaster looked around his crew, but they all shook their heads dolefully. 'Could be any port along the south coast – or even up the east or west, come to that,' said the mate. 'The worst bastards are those in Lyme, though maybe blaming them first has become a habit.'

'You've never been attacked yourself?' asked de Wolfe.

'No, thank Mary Mother of God!' said the shipmaster fervently, crossing himself. 'But Gilbert here had a narrow escape some years ago.' He prodded his mate in the ribs. 'Tell the coroner what happened.'

The fat man, who had features like a pickled walnut,

banged his pot down on the barrel as he prepared to tell his story for the hundredth time.

'Coming over from Barfleur we were, in a cog belonging to a Dartmouth owner. This vessel comes beating up behind us, too close to be normal, and eventually we decided the bastard was trying to board us!' He cowered down and put his hand to shade his eyes in a dramatic reconstruction of the event. 'Our master was a cunning devil, thank Christ, for at the next tack he foxed the other one by going in the opposite direction. We were faster downwind than the pirate and gained on him so that after an hour he gave up and sailed away. Made us a day late getting into the Dart, but saved our necks, no doubt.'

'Did you recognise the other cog?' demanded Gwyn.

'It was English, no doubt of that, not a Frenchie,' replied Gilbert. 'The cut of the rigging could be nothing else.'

'Any idea where she came from?' asked John.

'Not then, but a funny thing, a year later I saw a vessel berthed in Dover that I swear was the same one. I even went snooping around her and was told she had changed hands several times.You mentioned Axmouth just now, Crowner – well, the owner before the last one had bought her there.'

De Wolfe and Gwyn exchanged glances, eyebrows raised. 'I wonder who had sold her there?' mused John.

'Doesn't necessarily signify that she came out of Axmouth at the time she tried to board Gilbert's vessel,' cautioned Angerus. 'She might have been sold before then.'

'Did you get the name of the cog?' snapped the coroner.

'I can't read, but the lad I questioned said it was the *Apostle Thomas*.'

Most ships had names with religious connotations, as

tokens of protection from the perils of the deep, but Gwyn pointed out that they changed these as often as women changed their kirtles. 'Could have been a totally different name when she was sold from Axmouth,' he grunted.

Some more discussion produced nothing of help to the coroner, except that Angerus de Wile was of the opinion that Martin Rof, the shipmaster of *The Tiger* at Axmouth, was 'a hard bastard', to quote him exactly. 'I've heard that he has flogged men in his crew to within an inch of their death,' he said sourly. 'That's no way to get your men to work properly!' There were growls of assent from those around the barrel.

'Could it have been his ship that chased you?' de Wolfe asked Gilbert.

The mate shook his head. 'Impossible to say. I don't know what Rof's cog looks like – and they never got close enough to see faces, thank Jesus.'

'Where are you and Roger Watts taking your vessels next?' asked de Wolfe. Hugh de Relaga and his clerks were the ones who ran the practical side of their business, and John was content to sit back and receive a bag of money at regular intervals.

'Now that April's here, we can start sailing long distance,' answered de Wile. 'Both of us are taking the cogs round to Exeter next week to load. I'm taking finished cloth down to St-Malo, and Roger is hauling tin over to Honfleur for the king's army, then up to Antwerp for more cloth.'

It was an open secret that Richard the Lionheart, hard-pressed for money to pay his troops, was diluting the silver coinage with Dartmoor tin.

Soon, John became restless and, muttering something about conferring with his partner about how the business was progressing, left Gwyn to continue drinking with his sailor friends, all of them following his departure with knowing grins.

At the imposing house behind the main street, John found Hilda on her doorstep, just returning from an errand of mercy. Some months earlier, assassins had slain the whole crew of one of their ships. Since then, Hilda had made it her business to see that the bereaved families of the shipmen lacked none of the necessities of life, and she had just been taking some child's clothing and a few pennies to one of the widows. Her face lit up when she saw John coming along the lane, and when her maid Alice opened the front door she ushered him inside, offering her cheek for a chaste kiss as soon as they were off the street. Though she was now an eligible widow, he was a married man and she did not want to provide scandal for anyone who might be peeping in the street.

'You look well, Hilda,' offered John gallantly as they followed Alice up the stairway to the solar. She did indeed, he thought, seeing her in more formal attire than on his previous visit, a light green mantle over her cream kirtle and a snowy linen cover-chief and wimple framing her beautiful face.

The maid took her cloak and they sat opposite each other, Hilda sending Alice for the inevitable wine and pastries. In spite of John's claim to a business visit, he disposed of his conversation in the tavern in a few sentences and settled down to enjoy her company, free from any need to interrogate or make plans.

They reminisced about their childhood and adolescence in Holcombe, their families and their youthful escapades, Hilda coming near to blushes as they skirted the memories of amorous adventures in hay-barns and woods. These had gone on intermittently for years after John had taken up the sword, until his long absences had caused her to seek a husband in Thorgils – and even a few times after that. When alone with a pretty woman, the coroner was a different man from the stern, almost grim law officer that most people knew.

A dozen years seemed to drop away from him in her company. His back straightened, his features lightened and an almost roguish smile crept across his usually taciturn face. As with Nesta, and several other ladies who had now faded into his past, the presence of an attractive woman like Hilda seemed to act as a catalyst, softening his habitually severe manner.

After Alice had brought the refreshments, Hilda waved her away, needing no chaperone in the privacy of her own home, and John's personal devil had a fine time, dancing merrily on his shoulder as the pair leant towards each other, chatting and smiling. With an effort, de Wolfe kept his distance, though every fibre in his body yearned to seize her and smother her in kisses!

Hilda knew this only too well and had difficulty in keeping her own instincts in check, especially as after so many months her lonely bed had become increasingly hard to bear. But she knew of John's long-standing liaison with Nesta, and her innate sense of propriety made her suppress her longing – and dampen down any bursting of passion on his part.

His only chance to relieve his feelings came as they eventually parted, when a goodbye embrace somehow turned into a bear-like hug and a prolonged kiss that left her breathless.

As they left the solar, his arm around her waist, they saw Alice sitting on the lower step of the stairs, gazing up with an impish expression identical to that on the face of his shoulder-devil.

Two days later the coroner's team rode once again to Axmouth. The previous evening a carter had left a message at the castle gatehouse from Luke de Casewold, to the effect that the cog *The Tiger* had arrived that day. As she was likely to sail again very soon, the coroner should make all haste to get down to the harbour, where the

Keeper would meet him by noon on Thursday. In fact, he was waiting for them at the crossroads outside the village when they trotted in from Colyford, with the clerk Hugh Bogge alongside his master.

The group walked their horses down to the upper gate of Axmouth, Luke telling the coroner that Martin Rof had unloaded his vessel the previous day and was now taking on wool for Calais.

'I've already had words with him, but the bloody man will say almost nothing, except to tell me to mind my own business,' complained the Keeper. 'But I have threatened the bailiff here that unless he allows me a view of one of those storehouses, I will petition the sheriff for a troop of men-at-arms to come down and force it open.'

De Wolfe thought that the chances of Henry de Furnellis agreeing to that were remote, but Luke's next words surprised him.

'After that threat, Edward Northcote has agreed to let me see inside one of them, which he says contains goods belonging to Robert de Helion, the Exeter merchant. I'm going in there this afternoon, if you want to see for yourself.'

As they went down the main street towards the gate to the wharf, the village seemed almost deserted, though they received a few scowls and stares from people standing at their doorways to watch them go by. There was no sign of the bailiff or portreeve as they passed their houses, but when they came out on to the bank of the estuary there was much more activity. Four cogs were tied up along the wharf, the furthest being *The Tiger*, identified by an animal head crudely painted in yellow on each side of the prow. Men were carrying large bales across the gangplank, bringing them from an open warehouse on the other side of the road, beneath the slope of the hill behind.

'That's the shed I am going to inspect,' said de

Casewold proudly, as if he had beaten the bailiff and portreeve into submission over the issue. He marched across the track to the large open doors, where the Customs tally-man, John Capie, was standing with notched sticks and knotted cords in his hands.

'I demand to see inside this building,' bleated Luke, as if he expected yet another angry refusal. The tally-man shrugged and waved a handul of cords towards the entrance. 'Help yourself – best hurry or it'll be empty, the rate these lads are loading the ship.'

Somewhat deflated, de Casewold strutted into the storehouse like a bantam cockerel, staring around him pugnaciously. On the left of the large shed there were a score of big bales of wool, trussed in cord, but most of the space had already been emptied. On the opposite side of the doorway a large bay held more bales, but to one side was a pile of kegs and bundles reaching to twice the height of a man. Hugh Bogge and Thomas, the only literate members, wandered over and read out some of the crude lettering burnt into some of the kegs with a hot iron.

'Wine from Anjou, Bordeaux and the Loire,' announced Thomas. 'And other barrels seem to have dried fruit.'

'What's in those other bales, the ones wrapped in hessian?' demanded the Keeper.

'They are full of finished cloth, good English wool coming back from the weavers in Flanders.'

The voice came from behind them and, turning, they saw that the bailiff, Edward Northcote, was standing there, with Elias Palmer and another man.

'And it all belongs to my master, Robert de Helion,' snapped the stranger, a thickset man of about forty, with a pale, puckered scar running from eyebrow to chin down his leathery face.

'Who might you be?' demanded John de Wolfe, glaring at the newcomer.

'I am Henry Crik, one of Sir Robert's agents. Why are you nosing into his property?'

The coroner took a long step towards Crik. 'Watch your tongue, agent! I am on the king's business and I need give you no excuses!'

Henry Crik flushed, and the scar looked whiter by contrast. 'This is private property and you have no right to look here.'

John moved even nearer and looked down into the agent's face, almost nose to nose. 'I will look up your arse if I so choose, Crik! Obstruct me and you'll find yourself answering my questions in the undercroft of Exeter Castle!'

The man seemed to get the message and stepped back, muttering under his breath. The coroner turned to the bailiff and pointed to the pile of merchandise.

'How do I know that all this is legitimate import – and has been tallied for Customs duty?'

Northcote shrugged and waved a hand at Elias Palmer. 'Ask the portreeve. He keeps all the records. And the tally-man – it's his job to check it all.' He bellowed for John Capie at the top of his voice, and the skinny official hurried in. 'When did this lot arrive?' demanded Northcote. 'Tell the coroner what you know about it.'

'It has been here a sennight, sir. Came in from Caen, off-loaded from the cog *St Benedict*. I checked it all and gave the tallies to the portreeve, as usual.'

Luke de Casewold bobbed around to Elias. 'Can you confirm that, portreeve?' he snapped.

Elias looked back at him calmly. 'No doubt I could, if I had my manifests with me. They are in my house, if you wish to check them.'

De Wolfe had the distinct feeling that if they were checked they would be in perfect order – and he further suspected that they had been allowed into this particular shed because the contents were quite legitimate. He further had the suspicion that Elias was crafty enough to be able to produce parchments to legitimise anything that became the subject of investigation.

'When will this stuff be moved?' he asked Henry Crik. 'Does it all go to your master in Exeter?'

The agent shook his head sullenly, chastened by meeting a stronger will than his own. 'Some will end up there, but much will be taken to various places. That is why I am here, to leave instructions for the carters to take these and other goods to different destinations – Bridport, Taunton and even Dorchester.'

De Wolfe suddenly felt that he was wasting his time here. If the damned Keeper wanted to persist in hounding down those who might be fiddling the Customs duty, that was his affair, but the coroner's business was murder.

'Gwyn, Thomas! Come with me, we need to talk to this ship master.'

He marched out with his officer and clerk in tow, and after a brief hesitation Luke followed him across the road to the large cog that was sitting upright on the mud that was revealed at low tide. Men were still humping bales aboard and others were packing them tightly in the single hold. De Wolfe stalked to the edge of the river and looked across at the stern of the vessel, where a raised platform carried the steering oar and roofed over a shallow shelter where the master and mate slept, the rest of the crew cowering under a similar structure forming the forecastle.

Cupping his hands around his mouth, he yelled at the top of his voice, 'Martin Rof! Are you there?'

A figure emerged from the aftercastle and stared around to see where the shout came from. He was a burly man, broad and tall, with close-cropped fair hair and a ragged beard and moustache of the same yellow hue. Dressed in a short tunic of faded blue serge, he had breeches that ended above his ankles, his bare feet splayed out on the deck.

'Who wants him?' he demanded when he identified the caller amongst the group on the bank.

'Sir John de Wolfe, the king's coroner! Come on down here. I want to talk to you and I'm not clambering along that bloody plank.'

For a moment Thomas thought that Rof was going to refuse, but the coroner's tone was one that offered no compromise. The rough-looking sea-captain jumped down to the main deck and padded down the gangway to where they were waiting.

'What the hell do you want? I'm a busy man. I want to sail on the next tide.'

'That depends on what you have to tell me about the death of Simon Makerel. You may be sailing a horse to Rougemont Castle,' snapped John, repeating the threat he had made to Henry Crik.

'Simon Makerel? What in the Virgin's name do I know about him?' snarled the shipmaster. 'The bloody boy left my vessel at the end of the voyage, so how should I know what happened to him?'

'Did anything occur on that voyage that might have led to his murder?'

Martin Rof turned to spit contemptuously into the river mud. 'I don't know what goes on in the forecastle, man! Maybe one of the crew had some sport with the pretty lad – how would I know? He left the ship with his voyage money and was due back two days later, but he never showed up. We had to find another shipman to take his place . . . not that he was much bloody use, anyway.'

'What d'you mean, not much use?' snapped de Wolfe.

'He was not cut out to be a sailor! I heard tell he wanted to be a flaming priest! Soft he was, seasick half the time and too afraid to climb his own height up the rigging! Just as well he never came back, he was a dead weight.'

'He was soon dead, right enough,' retorted de Wolfe. 'Strangled and buried! Now, let's have it straight, did anything happen on that trip to make him a target for some killer? We know he was upset and acting strangely when he got home to Seaton after leaving this vessel.'

Martin shrugged indifferently. 'I told you, I'm a shipmaster, not a bloody nursemaid! I don't know – nor do I care – what goes on amongst the crew.'

John made one last effort to get some information. 'Where did you come from on that voyage?'

Rof's pale blue eyes glared at the coroner. 'What's that got to do with anything? We took wool out of here to Dunkerque, then called at Barfleur on the way home to pick up some wine, though we had a very light load returning – didn't earn us much money. Satisfied?'

De Wolfe was far from satisfied, but short of getting Martin Rof put to the torture under the keep of Rougemont there was little more he could do. He made a final effort. 'What about your crew? Are these the same ones who sailed with Makerel that time?'

'They are indeed!' boomed the captain. 'You can ask them the same silly bloody questions if you like,' he sneered. He turned and yelled at his men in a voice like thunder, calling each by name. Half a dozen came to the bulwarks or stopped carrying bales up the plank to listen to what their master had to say.

'Tell the crowner here what he wants to know, lads,' he said in a jeering voice. 'Did any of you upset young Simon? Maybe somebody bent the ship's boy over the rail for bit of fun, eh?'

Their coarse laughter was cut off by de Wolfe's voice, which easily matched Rof's for volume and carried a sting like a whiplash. 'Enough of that, damn you all! This is serious – a young lad came to a shameful death! Now, do any of you have any knowledge of what may have happened to him, either before or after he left this ship?'

There was a silence, in which each man looked at his fellow and shook his head. They were a ruffianly bunch, even for shipmen, and John could sense straight away that even if they had anything to tell, he would never hear it from them. With a gesture of disgust, he turned away, with a valedictory threat. 'If I find that you are concealing anything from me, it will be the worse for you. So think on that!'

He stalked away and, feeling the need for some sustenance, led the way to the Harbour Inn, just inside the lower gate, opposite the church. A surly innkeeper sold them some indifferent ale and cider and put two loaves, butter and cheese on a table, along with a wooden board carrying a half-eaten leg of mutton. De Wolfe had the distinct impression that the king's law officers were unwelcome in Axmouth.

The five men sat around the food in the dingy tap-room, ignored by the half-dozen others who crouched on stools or leant against the lime-washed walls. They hacked at the bread and meat with their eating knives and discussed in low voices their lack of progress.

'Now that we are here, I'm going across to Seaton to see if that widow has any further idea what was ailing her son before he died,' said John. 'Thomas, you can tackle that parish priest over there once again. Someone must know something, for Christ Jesu's sake!' His voice betrayed his exasperation at the wall of silence that seemed to surround this village.

'Looking in that warehouse got you no further,' observed Gwyn to Luke de Casewold. He was fond of baiting the choleric Keeper, who he thought was a rash idiot.

'I doubt that anything in the other buildings would tell us anything either,' replied Luke. 'False listings are easy to make and I suspect that the portreeve is an expert at deception. Looking at a pile of goods tells us nothing, it seems. All of it may have been pillaged out at sea and brought in in the guise of legitimate cargo.'

As they finished the last of the food, de Wolfe asked the Keeper what he intended to do next, now that all his avenues of enquiry seemed to have run dry.

'That pedlar who was killed – he must have fallen foul of an illicit load of goods,' exclaimed de Casewold. 'They have to move all their loot out of this village or it is worth nothing to them, so I'm going to lie in wait and see what trundles out of this cursed place at dead of night – and where it ends up.'

The coroner was worried that the fellow might rashly stick his nose into a wasps' nest and come to serious harm.

'Have a care, de Casewold! Someone has already seen off a shipman and a pedlar, with little compunction. Why don't I suggest to the sheriff that he sends a few men-at-arms to back you up?'

Luke made a deprecating gesture. 'I can spy out the situation first, Sir John. Then if I detect a pattern, maybe your idea might be the answer. Set up an ambush with king's men and catch the bastards in the act!'

Their uninspiring meal over, de Wolfe gave the sullen landlord a couple of pennies and they left the alehouse, where Luke and his clerk took themselves off up the valley towards Axminster. John and his companions made their way to a rickety wooden jetty just outside the wharf gate and spent another half-penny on a ferry-ride across to Seaton. The tide had just turned, and the old man who rowed the flat-bottomed boat had to pull manfully to broach the incoming flood. On the other side of the wide estuary, the village of Seaton stretched down to a stony beach, where fishing boats were pulled up on the pebbles. Thomas went off to the whitewashed church to seek the priest, while Gwyn asked directions to the cottage of Widow Makerel.

This turned out to be a small hut near the strand, with a roof of flat stones to ward off the winds that swept in from the sea. Behind, they could see the chalk cliffs of Beer, riddled with quarry caves from which came the white stone that formed much of Exeter's cathedral.

In the cottage's single room they found Edith Makerel gutting some fish that a neighbour had given her, while the fat girl who had been Simon's betrothed was carrying in wood for the fire that glowed in a pit in the middle of the room. Against one wall a young man lolled on a bench, which together with a table and a couple of stools formed the only furniture in the house, the corner beds being bags of hessian stuffed with ferns and feathers.

The family looked anxious when the two large men appeared but hospitably offered them the bench, the man who was Simon's elder brother moving off to make way for them.

John politely accepted some ale, and the thin brew was poured by the girl into two misshapen mugs of coarse earthenware.

'I dislike disturbing you and reminding you of your great sorrow, mistress,' he said in a voice that was unusually soft and gentle for him. 'But we must get to the bottom of this tragedy, one way or another. I wondered if you have any fresh recollections of what may have been troubling your son when he came home from the sea?'

Edith Makerel, a gaunt woman dressed in a black kirtle with a crumpled linen apron over it, dropped on to a stool and began nervously twisting the cloth belt of her apron. 'Thinking back on it, sir, I am more convinced than ever that it was the pangs of conscience that preyed on his mind. Something he had done or even witnessed, was my guess – though he would not admit it, even to me, his mother.'

De Wolfe listened gravely, quite willing to believe that a woman's intuition was to be relied upon, especially when it concerned her son. 'Have you no idea what this thing might have been? Did he have the marks of a fight or of some injury he could have sustained?'

The widow shook her head sadly. 'He would say nothing, Crowner. He just sat and stared at the fire, seeming mostly bereft of speech. Not like him at all; he was usually a pleasant, cheerful lad. It was going on that damned ship that ruined him.' Edith sounded bitter, as well she might be.

John questioned both the dumpy girl, whose name was Edna, and the elder brother, but they had nothing to add, just confirming the mother's opinion.

'Was there anything else that was out of the ordinary?' asked John, desperate to avoid the usual blank wall that seemed to face him when he made enquiries into this case.

'He seemed to have more money that usual,' said Edith Makerel slowly. 'He gave me ten pence and told me to buy some good food. On his first voyage, he came back with only a shilling for all those days at sea.'

The girl and the brother confirmed that Simon seemed to have more money. 'He gave me six pence and told me to buy a new shift,' said Edna with a tearful sniff. 'He said the coins might as well be put to some use, as he couldn't give them back. It seemed an odd thing to say.'

'He brought nothing back with him from the voyage?' asked Gwyn. 'No trinkets or a flask of brandy-wine or suchlike?'

There were puzzled shakes of the head, and soon John realised once more that they had exhausted what little there was to be learnt. They left the sad little family and went out into the spring sunshine, as the weather had improved again.

'We'd better wait for the little fellow,' said Gwyn. 'Let's hope he has better luck with the priest.'

They walked down to the beach and squatted on the pebbles, watching the gulls wheeling over the small boats pulled up on the stones, where men were stacking fish into wicker baskets, ready for carting to markets as far away as Exeter and Yeovil. A small island of sand and stones projected from the sea just in front of them, looking like another whale about to surface.

'We've not learnt much about this lad's death in two weeks,' complained Gwyn, throwing a flat stone to skim across the calm sea before them.

John rubbed his bristly chin, which was again overdue for a shave. 'He comes back from his sea trip different from the one before, as then he seemed quite happy,' recounted the coroner. 'But this time he is anxious, worried and depressed, as if something lies heavy on his conscience.'

'And he has considerably more money than before,' added Gwyn. 'So what was different about the second voyage?'

There was a long silence, then de Wolfe offered his opinion. 'I reckon he witnessed something violent or shocking. And that something was lucrative, as even though he was a lowly ship's boy he gets a hand-out as a part-share in whatever happened.'

Gwyn threw another stone and a seagull rose, screaming indignantly. 'And though smuggling might pay well, it's hardly likely to upset him – so what else is most likely?'

The two old friends looked at each other as they sat on the pebbles.

'Piracy!' snapped John. 'He must have seen some bloody deeds, and a sensitive lad, aiming for the cloister, might well be shocked and revolted.'

His officer nodded his agreement but still had some doubts. 'But why strangle him much later onshore? If he had kicked up a fuss at the killing of another crew, they could have just slit his throat and chucked him overboard. I'm sure that bunch of ruffians on *The Tiger* would do that without a second thought.'

The coroner climbed to his feet. 'There must be a reason, but we just don't know what it is – yet! Let's find this damned clerk of ours and see what he has to offer.'

CHAPTER SEVEN

In which Crowner John defeats an ambush

What Thomas de Peyne learnt was repeated that evening over supper at the house in Martin's Lane. John had to be circumspect in what topics he launched with Matilda, as some sent her into a rage, such as any mention of the Bush Inn or Dawlish. Even a mention of Gwyn or Thomas provoked heavy sarcasm, as she considered one to be a Celtic savage and the other a pervert, even though the little priest had long been restored to grace. Many other subjects failed to stir her from her almost permanent mood of sullen depression, but he could usually depend upon tales concerning the Church or the aristocracy to spark her attention. He had previously related to her the mystery of the seaman's death in Axmouth, without getting much response, but now he added what had been obtained from Father Matthew, the parish priest of Seaton. He refrained from telling her that it was Thomas who had interviewed the incumbent and craftily embroidered his tale with a description of the church.

'For such a small and mean village, the church is surprisingly neat,' he observed as he cut some slices from a boiled fowl with his dagger and slid them on to her trencher of yesterday's bread. 'Built of stone, quite small, but a bell-cote at one end and a little porch on the south.'

Matilda stopped chewing for a moment and nodded at him. 'Size is not everything, even in a church. It is the quality of the priest that matters. At my St Olave's, which is tiny, we are blessed with a saint in the shape of Julian Fulk.'

Fulk was her hero in a cassock, and if John had not known her better he might have suspected that she had amorous designs on Julian Fulk. As far as he was concerned, Fulk was short, fat and oily. He had once even been a suspect in a series of murders, and John regretted that he had not turned out to be the culprit. However, he stifled the thought and carried on with his tale.

'This Father Matthew, who seemed an upright and venerable man, did his best to help us over the killing, but of course his vow of silence concerning confessions severely limited what he could tell us.'

Matilda visibly bristled. 'I should think so, indeed! I trust you did not badger the man to break his faith . . . the confessional is inviolate, John!'

'I am well aware of that, wife,' said de Wolfe in his most placatory tone. 'But there is surely a difference between what is said with the intention of it being within the doctrines of the Church and other comments made outwith that rigid rule.'

Matilda glared at him suspiciously. 'What d'you mean by that?'

'Well, a man confessing his sins to a priest is one thing. But if the same man casually tells the priest that he has bought a pound of pork for his dinner, then the priest would hardly refuse to repeat that to someone else on the grounds that it was a sacred secret!'

'I think you are being facetious, husband! Trust you to try to poke fun at the Holy Church. And what sense does this make to your story?'

'The good man admitted that the dead youth had come to speak to him on two occasions after he had returned from his voyage. As you clearly say, he could tell us nothing of the nature of his discourse with the lad, but he told us that Simon was very distressed and fearful for his immortal soul.'

'That doesn't help you much,' grunted Matilda, who had hoped for something more dramatic.

'No, but though the priest could not tell us the substance of the ship boy's anguish, he said that Simon's concern was his dilemma about disclosing it to the authorities outside the confessional. It also seemed a dilemma to the good father as well!'

Matilda scowled down at her chicken. 'I'm not sure that this priest should have told you as much as he did, John. He seems to have steered very close to breaking his vow of secrecy.'

John struggled to keep his impatience in check. 'Look, if what happened was what I think, then there are about six murders as well as the slaying of the young man to be accounted for! Should one solitary priest stand between these heinous crimes and the retribution of the law?'

He had picked the wrong person to whom that question should have been posed. Matilda flared up like a pitch-brand thrust into the fire. 'Of course he should! God is the final judge, not a bunch of barons or Chancery clerks at the Eyre of Assize! Where would we be if it was common knowledge that a priest would go running to the sheriff or coroner with every bit of tittle-tattle heard in the confessional?'

Her husband muttered something under his breath and concentrated on his food, abandoning any further attempt to hold a conversation. He kept it in his head, however, and aired it again later, when he took Brutus for his constitutional down to Idle Lane. When he repeated the story to Nesta, she asked him what he made of the Seaton cleric's response to his questions.

'The fellow was worried himself, that was clear,' said John. 'I felt that he was wrestling with his own conscience, as he knew something that would explain Simon Makerel's murder – and possibly other deaths. Even more, he knew that his silence might lead to similar tragedies in the future, but his vow of silence was too powerful for him to tell me. All he could do was hint.'

The red-headed innkeeper looked up at him with her big hazel eyes. 'And what do you think happened, Sir Coroner?' she asked.

'I think this Simon was so shocked by what he had witnessed on his last voyage in *The Tiger* that he was trying to nerve himself to tell someone, such as the Keeper of the Peace. But someone learnt of his indecision and decided to silence him before he could give them away.'

'And the shocking thing he witnessed?' persisted the Welshwoman.

'Piracy, of course! The seizing of a ship and the murder of her crew. That was why Simon had more money than usual. It was a forward payment in anticipation of the profits – and a sweetener to the crew to keep their mouths shut.'

Nesta reached across her lover to refill his ale-mug from a jar on the table. 'But this is all supposition, John. You have no proof of it?'

He shook his head. 'Nor likely to get any, but it seems the only explanation of what happened. Why else would some dull lad get himself strangled, a lad who has been to his priest to seek solace and advice? If only the bloody clergy would weigh up human life more sensibly against their so-called religious morals, then justice would be better served!'

Nesta smiled at him. 'You are beginning to sound more like Gwyn every day! They'll have you for

blasphemy or heresy if you sound off like that too
often!'

De Wolfe shook his head impatiently. 'It riles me
to think that this Father Matthew holds the key to the
mystery in his head, yet because of some edict centuries
ago from some bloody Pope, he can't tell me!'

His mistress put a consoling hand on his arm. 'Why
don't you talk to your good friend, the archdeacon.
Maybe he can get this priest to relax his silence?'

John shook his head. 'The tradition is too well
ingrained in the Church. A mere archdeacon would
have no power, nor even a bishop. But I have to speak
to John de Alençon soon on another matter, so
perhaps I'll raise it with him.'

That 'other matter' was one that caused the little
devil from Dawlish to peep over his shoulder unbidden.

Though most activities came to a halt on the Sabbath,
certain of the more unscrupulous members of the
population were willing to forgo their day of rest, given
that the rewards were sufficient to make it worth their
while. So it was that at dead of night a certain ox-cart
creaked its way along the lonely track that ran from
Honiton towards Ilminster. The moon appeared fitfully
through broken cloud, but at the speed the beasts
walked there was little danger of the cart going off the
highway, especially as the ruts of hardened mud kept
the big wooden wheels on the track.

On the driving-board, two men sat hunched, silent
and sleepy. The one on the right held the reins, though
they had little function, as the pair of oxen plodded
on regardless of human intervention. Behind them,
the canvas hood was squared off over a framework
of hazel rods to leave a roomy interior. Part of their
original cargo had been off-loaded at Honiton, and the
rest was destined for Ilminster, a few miles further
on. They passed through the usual varied countryside,

dimly seen in the moonlight. Where there were hamlets, strip-fields ran off away from the road. Then common land and waste alternated with long stretches of woodland, where the forest had not yet been assarted to increase the acreage of cultivated ground. The road undulated like the country it passed through, but there were no steep hills to challenge the oxen.

There was no other traffic, every God-fearing person being sound asleep. With no monastery or cathedral within many miles, even the midnight office of Matins was lacking, as parish priests kept to their beds until dawn, many of them having done a hard day's work in the fields alongside their parishioners.

The only accompaniment to the creaking of the axle-pins was the hoot of an owl, the distant bark of a dog-fox and the occasional snuffle of a badger at the side of the track. They passed the village of Rawridge, but if any of the inhabitants were still awake they took care not to peer out at the trundling cart but pulled their sheepskins over their heads and pretended that they were deaf.

Yet a mile further on, the dozing driver and his companion were suddenly confronted by someone who was well and truly awake. In the road ahead, a dim light was waving, and as the patient oxen slowed to a halt a voice rang out in the still night air.

'Halt, in the name of the king!' The feeble candle-glow from the horn lantern reflected off the steel blade of a sword held by the man who had shouted, and it dimly revealed another figure standing behind him wielding a pike.

'Can't be another thieving pedlar!' muttered the driver to his mate. Aloud, he demanded to know who was holding them up. 'If you are seeking to rob us, you'll have to answer to the bailiff of Axmouth – and the Prior of Loders.'

The two men standing in the middle of the track

approached, and as they did so the moon slid out from behind a cloud and gave a far better light than the lantern.

'I am the Keeper of the Peace for this Hundred, fellow,' snapped Luke de Casewold. 'I want to know what you are doing hauling a cart around the king's highway at this hour of the morning?'

'There's no law against that, is there?' growled the driver truculently. 'This isn't a borough or city with a curfew.'

The Keeper brandished his long sword. 'Get down from there! I want to know who you are and what you have in that wagon. Quickly now!' He motioned to Hugh Bogge to go around to the tailboard of the cart. 'See what they have in the back. Here, take the lantern!'

The driver, a thickset man with a face like one of his oxen, made no move to climb down, and his companion, an equally ruffianly fellow, also ignored the law officer's demand.

'We are just delivering goods from Axmouth,' growled the carter. 'One of the wheel bearings cracked in Honiton and we wasted hours finding a blacksmith. I have to deliver the rest of the goods to Ilminster by morning, so we had no choice but to travel all night.'

De Casewold cackled derisively. 'Don't give me that, you liar! Do you crack your wheel bearings regularly, then? Several times now I've seen a cart like this on the roads late at night.'

The driver looked at his companion and shrugged. 'We've done our best,' he muttered cryptically and began to climb down from the driving-board.

There was a cry from the back as Bogge unlashed the cords holding down the tail-flap and the Keeper hurried around to him, followed closely by the two men. Luke found his clerk holding up his lantern and staring aghast into the back of the wagon. Two men, brandishing long daggers and heavy cudgels, were advancing towards them past a pile of kegs and bales. As they stepped back, the law officer and his clerk found that the driver and his mate were blocking their retreat, both now having wicked-looking knives in their hands.

It was Tuesday before the bodies were found. A mile outside the hamlet of Rawridge was a large area of common land, rising to the edge of dark forest. Soon after dawn, a shepherd had rounded up several score of his flock to check on new lambs that were appearing late in the season. His two black bitches had done their work, and the sheep were safely inside a crude pound with a hurdle across the entrance.

An old man of almost sixty, he squatted with his back against the dry-stone wall and pulled a hunk of bread and a piece of cheese from a cloth pouch on the belt that clinched his ragged tunic. His dogs lay nearby, watching him intently with their pink tongues hanging out, until he shared the scraps with them. Then, with an effort, he hauled himself to his feet and forced his aching joints to take him up towards the trees, where a clear spring bubbled out of the hillside. As he bent to scoop water to his lips with his cupped hands, one of the bitches ran off into the woodland. When he called sharply to her to come, she stood uncertainly, whining and looking back at him.

Alfred knew every nuance of his dogs' behaviour, probably better than he could read his wife's moods. He realised that something was worrying the animal, especially when the other bitch ran after her and began snuffling in the scatter of last autumn's leaves. Ambling after them, content that his sheep were safe for the moment, he pushed through the sprouting brambles and nettles along the tree-line to where the dogs were keening.

It was obvious at first sight what was upsetting them. The beech and oak leaves had been disturbed, older black mould from below being mixed with the paler leaves. The younger dog had been scratching at the pile, and a human hand projected like a claw.

Alfred was in a dilemma, as he knew a little about the rules announced by the manor-bailiff a year or two ago concerning dead bodies. He was now the 'First Finder', and his instincts were to turn around and forget all about it, as any involvement with the law was bad news. He stood for a few minutes staring at the hand, which was undoubtedly attached to a corpse beneath. Then a combination of a sense of duty, a fear of retribution and a touch of pride at being the centre of attention for a short while decided him that he had better do something about this. Gingerly, he kicked away some of the soggy leaves and exposed an arm, which was blood-stained above the wrist. As a shepherd, he was well used to gory dead animals, such as sheep ravaged by foxes and the occasional wolf, as well as to slaughter-time and the pig-killings. He gripped the dead hand and pulled vigorously, when a shoulder and a head surfaced above the leaf mould. Hardened as he was, the sight of a gaping cut throat that had nearly severed the head was something of a shock, especially when the disturbance of the corpse had caused a leg to appear at the other side of the heap of leaves.

Dropping the wrist, he backed away, muttering little-used prayers under his breath and making the sign of the cross. Then, whistling at his dogs, he began hurrying back down the common, intent on fetching his manor-reeve as soon as possible.

By mid-afternoon the coroner was approaching the scene with his officer and clerk, brought urgently from Exeter by the news that a king's law officer and his clerk had been foully slain. They had been summoned

by the bailiff of Honiton, after the manor-reeve from
Rawridge had brought him the news.

'I went straight up to this vill, Sir John, to check for
myself,' he reported as they rode the last half-mile to
Rawridge. 'I recognised the poor souls straight away.
I knew the Keeper fairly well. Though to tell the truth
he was something of a nuisance, he should not have
come to an end like that.'

'And the other one? That was his clerk, Bogge?'
growled de Wolfe.

'It was indeed. A harmless fellow, he put up with the
Keeper's odd ways well enough.'

They passed the village, away to their left, and continued for almost a mile, before leaving the Ilminster
road and climbing across the common land to where a
group of men were standing, where the grass gave way
to forest. One was the manor-reeve, another the old
shepherd who was now firmly the First Finder, whether
he liked it or not. The rest were villagers, including the
parish priest, a fat Irishman who was mumbling prayers
over the corpses. Inevitably, Thomas de Peyne soon
joined him, adding his supplications in much better
Latin, though averting his squeamish eyes from the
carnage as he chanted.

There was little they could do at the scene, except to
have the bodies pulled clear of the forest floor, where
most of the leaf mulch and twigs could be brushed off,
so that the full extent of the injuries could be seen.

'Right mess they are in, poor devils,' grunted
Gwyn, bending over the familiar figures as they lay
grotesquely twisted on the coarse grass.

Hugh Bogge had been beaten about the head so
severely that his face was hardly recognisable. However,
his death was due to several deep stab wounds in the
neck and upper chest, soaking his tunic with blood,
much of which had dried to a brown crust. Luke de
Casewold had even more horrific injuries, in that his

head was almost detached from his neck by a single massive cut that completely severed his windpipe and gullet and bit deeply into the joints between the bones of his spine.

'That's no dagger wound; that must have been a sword!' said John decisively.

'Perhaps this was the one?' said the bailiff, who had been kicking about in the base of the hollow where the bodies had been concealed. He held up a yard-long sword with a hilt wound with silver wire and a pommel engraved with concentric circles.

'That's the Keeper's own weapon!' growled Gwyn. 'I remember seeing it at his side.'

John shook his head sadly. 'That's the ultimate sorrow, to be slain by your own sword,' he said. 'Yet he was a former campaigner; he knew well enough how to defend himself. What in hell happened here?'

The bailiff looked around the long sloping land-scape, falling away down to the road a furlong distant. 'But did it happen here? Or were the cadavers just dumped here as a hiding place?'

The shepherd piped up, nervous in the presence of these stern men from Exeter. 'If my bitches had not nosed them out, they may have lain here for years without being found.'

The coroner followed the bailiff's eyes down to the track between Honiton and Ilminster. 'That's where it happened, without doubt. Somewhere along that road.' He turned to the reeve and the handful of men from the village.

'You may have heard of a similar death near Honiton quite recently, when a man was killed and hidden away.'

There were nods and grunts and throat-clearings. 'That pedlar fellow, the drunk Setricus,' muttered the reeve.

'Is there any way of telling when these poor sinners

went to the Lord?' asked the priest in a broad Irish accent.

Gwyn was scathing about the religious euphemism. 'D'you mean when did they have their throats cut and their heads beaten in?' He looked at de Wolfe for his opinion.

'The bodies are not at all corrupt, even though the weather is fairly warm,' mused the coroner. 'They still have their death stiffness, so I suspect their deaths were not before the weekend.' He glowered around the ring of faces. 'Have any of you noticed any strangers passing through your village in recent days?'

The reeve shook his head. 'That is an impossible question, with respect, sir. The main highway there passes from Exeter to Ilminster and beyond to Yeovil and even London! And our village is not right on the road, which skirts it to the south. What chance have we of keeping tally of traffic?'

'What about at night? I have my reasons for asking that.'

A few shifty looks were exchanged between the men. 'We keep ourselves to ourselves, sir, when it comes to night-riders,' said the reeve. 'And hard work by day means sound sleep at night.'

De Wolfe saw that it was pointless to pursue the issue. Both from fear and self-interest, the villagers were not going to divulge anything they might know about villains abroad at the dead of night. He looked down at the pathetic remains of the law officer and his clerk. 'We must move these bodies to the church with all the decency they deserve. They undoubtedly came to their death while doing their duty, which was the king's business. They must be treated with the respect that their office requires.'

The parish priest wrung his hands. 'I will say a Mass over them directly. I hear they come from Axminster, so will they be returned there for burial?'

John shrugged. 'Sir Luke is a widower, but I have no knowledge of other family. Nor do I know who will mourn his clerk, but no doubt enquiries can be made. Meanwhile, I must hold an inquest, which will be later this afternoon.'

He turned to Gwyn, to give him the expected instructions for arranging for a jury to hear the case, futile though he expected the proceedings to be. As the day was advancing, they set the time for the inquest at two hours hence. John knew that they could not get back to the city before dusk and decided to spend the night in Honiton and ride back home in the morning.

'While you and Thomas arrange for the removal of the corpses and organise the inquest, I will have a look at the road, to see if there is any sign of where this outrage took place.'

He took the bailiff, a stolid, sensible man of about his own age and they strode back down to the road, where a couple of lads were minding the horses. Mounting up, John slowly walked his rounsey eastwards in the direction of distant Ilminster, scanning the track and the verges as he went.

'What are we looking for, Crowner?' asked the bailiff. 'This road has been well used for a couple of days since, if you are right about when the men were killed.'

De Wolfe agreed with him but said that he would ride half a mile further. 'I want to check if there are any signs of a fight, such as blood or crushing of the undergrowth at the verge. They are hardly likely to have moved two heavy bodies further than necessary,' he said. 'Though of course it is quite likely that they had a cart.'

Eventually, they turned back and retraced their route, passing the sad procession of the two bodies laid on a handcart brought from the village. A few hundred paces beyond this, John abruptly reined in his horse and slid from the saddle. When the bailiff joined him, he was studying the mud of the road. It had not rained for several days and the ruts had dried into firm ridges, though they were still damp. At the place which he was inspecting, a number of these ridges had been crushed in a confused pattern and, looking four paces to the right, he saw that the weeds and spiky new grass of the verge were flattened. There were many other places where this had happened, and animals like foxes and badgers could have been responsible as they trampled their runs into the woods – but when he looked he saw brown staining on some of the vegetation. Kicking the undergrowth aside with his foot, he came across a drying pool of blood and some fragments of flesh, already buzzing with flies and other insects.

'This is where it happened!' he said grimly as the bailiff joined him.

By now the cortege with its handcart had caught up with them, and all the locals were staring in ghoulish fascination at the gory vestiges of the slaying.

'Doesn't help in saying who did it,' grunted Gwyn, who was walking with the cart, his mare following behind in the care of a small boy from the village.

John rubbed his stubble, his usual aid to deep thought. 'It suggests that a wagon was involved. Why else would a fatal attack occur just here? There is no cover for an outlaw ambush, and the place where the bodies were hidden is a good half-mile away, a long distance to carry them without transport.'

'So you need to find a cart with bloodstains, if the bodies were carried on it,' suggested Thomas.

'A bucket of water and a broom would soon get rid of those,' said Gwyn pessimistically. 'And which cart are we going to look at, anyway?'

An hour later they began the short inquest, which was like the previous ones in this area – indecisive and uninformative. The proceedings were held in the churchyard of St Mary the Virgin, a plain building of pebbled stone set on a hillside. A ring of old yews suggested that the site was ancient long before the church was built. The two bodies were now decently covered with some sacks from the adjacent tithe barn. As befitted his rank, Sir Luke de Casewold lay on the parish bier, a wooden stretcher with legs, which was usually hung from ropes slung over the rafters at the back of the church. His clerk, Hugh Bogge, had to make do with a wattle hurdle laid on the ground alongside.

Gwyn had dragooned a dozen men as a jury, including all those who had been up at the place where the corpses were discovered, together with a few who had gravitated to the churchyard to see what was going on.

The routine was gone through, with evidence of identity from both Gwyn and the bailiff of the Budleigh Hundred, who knew the dead men in life. Presentment of Englishry was obviously impossible, as the Keeper was a Norman knight and Bogge was certainly no Saxon. The imposition of a murdrum fine on the hundred was inevitable, but by the time the justices considered it de Wolfe fervently hoped that the culprits would be found. The old shepherd haltingly said his piece and seemed relieved that he would not be clapped into gaol or be amerced for being the First Finder.

There was no other evidence and all the coroner could do, after the jury had satisfied their morbid curiosity by peering at the wounds as they filed past the bodies, was to declare that the two victims had been murdered by persons unknown and that the inquest would be adjourned *sine die* when hopefully further evidence would be available.

Thomas recorded the proceedings, but these were so sparse that they hardly covered half a leaf of parchment, a palimpsest made by erasing previous writing by scraping and chalking. By then, evening was upon them and, with instructions to the bailiff to send messages to Axminster to convey the sad tidings to the relatives and arrange for the bodies to be collected, the coroner and his officer and clerk set off on the five-mile journey back to Honiton, where they could find a tavern that would provide a meal and a pallet in the loft for the night.

After they had supped the thin potage and eaten a mutton pie with boiled leeks and cabbage, the three investigators sat around a small glowing firepit in the middle of the taproom for a survey of the day's events. As darkness fell outside, Gwyn drank cider, John had a quart of ale and Thomas sipped a cup of indifferent wine with an expression that suggested it was a cough linctus from the village apothecary.

'This has been a sad day for the king's peace in this county,' said de Wolfe in a mournful voice that held an undertone of anger. 'The man was a fool in some respects, but his loyalties were in the right place.'

Gwyn sucked his moustache dry, then replied. 'It galls me to think that there are bastards at large in this area who seem to act as they think fit, then crush anyone who gets in their way!'

Thomas took another cautious sip of his red wine. 'I've not been privy to all that you have seen in Axmouth. Are we thinking all these deaths – the ship's boy, the pedlar and now the Keeper and his clerk – are all part of the same conspiracy – whatever that might be?'

The coroner glowered into the fire and nodded. 'I am convinced they are, Thomas. The lad was eliminated because his conscience was driving him towards betraying the wanton savagery of pirates. But as to who did it, we have no idea yet.'

'What about the pedlar and the Keeper?' asked Gwyn. 'A knight and one very little above a beggar – why should their deaths be linked?'

'Because they both showed too much interest in what was being carted about the countryside,' replied de Wolfe. 'A pity there are so many damned carters about these days, otherwise we could lean on a few of them and see what they have to say.'

Gwyn grunted dismissively. 'If their mouths are as tight as these folk in Axmouth, we'd learn nothing at all!' he growled.

The coroner's trio left Honiton early in the morning, but not so early that they missed breaking their fast. At the inn, they were given oatmeal gruel sweetened with honey, one of Thomas's favourites. Gwyn had already eaten enough for a horse before they were given a couple of eggs and slices of salt bacon fried in pork dripping. A loaf of fresh rye bread with butter and cheese was washed down with weak ale, the whole meal being sufficient to get the Cornishman to Exeter before he needed refuelling again.

They set off along the high road and rode in silence for a while. Though de Wolfe had found the Keeper an irritating person, he was saddened by his violent death and felt a glowering anger that a royal law officer had been so mistreated when he was doing his duty, however unwisely he went about it.

Typically for April, the weather was changeable and today there was a brisk wind pushing heavy grey clouds rapidly across the sky from the west. Occasional spats of rain came down, not enough to dampen them significantly, though Thomas pulled his black mantle closer about him as he trotted along in the wake of the two bigger horses. He was thinking holy thoughts, mainly about when he could save enough from his small stipend to afford a new copy of the Vulgate of St Jerome, his old one being so used that the pages were frayed and the binding falling apart.

A couple of miles out of Honiton, the road went

through an arm of the forest, dense trees, now breaking into leaf, crowding close on either side of the track. As it curved to the left, Gwyn's keen hearing picked out some distant commotion ahead of them.

'Some trouble brewing, by the sounds of it,' he grunted and touched his mare's flanks with his heels to speed her up. John followed suit, leaving Thomas behind but soon able to hear shouts and yells in the distance. As they rounded the bend they saw a mêlée in front of them, and both coroner and his officer kicked their mounts into a canter, hoisting out their swords as they went. As they approached, de Wolfe saw that three men were trying to fight off half a dozen ruffians but were losing the battle. Two other persons were lying on the ground, and a pair of mules and several horses were loose, nervously trying to escape into the trees. One of the defenders had a sword but seemed to be using it clumsily left-handed, his other arm hanging at his side. The other two had staves and were swinging them at assailants armed with clubs and a short pike.

With loud roars, the coroner and his officer thundered down at the tumult, and suddenly the attackers became aware of two large horses bearing down on them, one of them a massive destrier. Each carried a large man waving a wicked-looking broadsword, screaming imprecations that suggested that they were only too happy to use their blades to sever heads from bodies!

The half-dozen outlaws abruptly abandoned their attack and ran for the shelter of the forest, three to each side of the track. Gwyn galloped after one trio and caught the laggard such a blow with his sword that he virtually severed his arm at the shoulder, the other two melting into the trees. On the opposite side, John ran down one man, who vanished under the huge hairy feet of Odin, but again the other two disappeared into the dense forest, where de Wolfe felt disinclined to follow.

The two law officers wheeled back to the road and slid from their mounts to see what damage had been done to the travellers, just as Thomas clopped up on his palfrey. He went straight to the man with the sword, who had sunk to the ground, groaning and clasping his injured right arm. Blood was trickling from the cuff of his leather jerkin, dripping off his fingers on to the earth. As Gwyn and de Wolfe went to look at the two other inert figures lying in the road, the little priest supported the injured man and tried to see what damage had been done.

'One of the swine cut me with a pike,' muttered the victim, a dark-haired man of about thirty. He was pale and sweating with shock, as one of the two other defenders came to his side, the other one limping across to where the coroner and Gwyn were attending to the fallen pair. This new arrival had a livid bruise across his face and forehead where he had been struck by some blunt weapon, but seemed otherwise unhurt.

'Owain, how are you faring?' he asked solicitously, dropping on one knee alongside Thomas.

'We had best get his arm out of that sleeve and see what needs to be done,' suggested Thomas, and with the bruised man giving a running commentary of thanks for their timely rescue they gently pulled Owain's jerkin half-off, to expose a long but seemingly shallow cut running down the forearm.

As Thomas squeezed the upper arm to stanch the flow, the older man produced a relatively clean linen cloth from his pouch and wrapped it tightly around the slashed arm. 'That's better, friends. I feel halfway to being recovered already!' said Owain. 'Thank God the cut looks less serious than I feared. I need that arm to make my living!'

His colour had certainly improved, and Thomas had

a chance to look around to see what was happening to the other victims. For the first time he realised that the two fallen men were priests, rather corpulent men in black cassocks and cloaks. Presumably, they were the ones who had been riding the mules, which were now being rounded up by the second defender. The three horses, reassured by the presence of the impassive Odin and Gwyn's brown mare, were unconcernedly cropping the new grass of the verge.

'Bloody outlaws! Every bastard one of them should be rounded up and hanged!' swore the man attending to Owain. He was a florid, middle-aged man in good-quality clothes, and Thomas marked him down as a merchant, like the other man who had coaxed the mules back into the road.

'We must get you into Exeter and have you treated at St John's Priory,' said Thomas to the younger man with the slashed arm. 'Can you get to your feet now?'

With help from the other two, Owain got up and, with his damaged arm cradled against his chest, was able to walk to the edge of the road, where he sat on a fallen log. By now, the two priests had begun to groan and move, both having suffered blows to the head by the staves of the ruffians who had attacked them. A few minutes later they had crawled to a sitting position, though one vomited copiously into the grass before squatting with his bruised head in his hands.

Gwyn ambled over to look at the outlaw that he had struck with his sword, but the man was stone dead, lying in a great pool of sticky blood that had gushed from a large artery, severed under his collarbone. 'One less for the gallows!' observed Gwyn cheerfully. 'What about the other one, Crowner?'

At the opposite side of the track, de Wolfe found that the scoundrel that Odin had trodden on was equally dead, his chest and head almost flattened by the iron-shod hooves of the old warhorse.

One of the merchants had a wineskin on his saddle and this helped to restore everyone's spirits, as explanations were offered while the two priests recovered their wits. Owain's wound seemed to have stopped bleeding, thanks to a tightly twisted kerchief bound around his upper arm.

The two older men were merchants from Bristol, travelling to Exeter to arrange purchases of wool. 'I thought that riding in a company of five men would be enough to keep us safe from trail-bastons like those,' grunted one under his breath. 'I forgot that two were damned priests who would not have so much as a club to defend themselves with!'

These holy men were canons from Wells, going to Exeter Cathedral on some ecclesiastical errand. Owain was also going to the same great church, but on quite different business.

'I am a stonemason and especially a stone carver,' he explained. 'That's why I am so concerned about my arm – it had to be the right one, too, the one I use most to earn my living.'

Gwyn and John de Wolfe soon realised that he was a Welshman and began speaking to him in their common Celtic language. His full name was Owain ap Gronow and he came from Chepstow on the Welsh border, though his work often took him to Gloucester Cathedral. He had been recommended from there to the Chapter in Exeter, who needed some expert carving done on a new shrine.

'As long as the wound does not suppurate, it should heal well,' advised John, who had seen every possible injury during twenty years on battlefields from Ireland to the Holy Land. 'We'll get you to Brother Saulf at St John's in the city; he's a wonder with such problems. You'll be carving again in a fortnight!'

After half an hour order was restored and their journey was ready to be started again. The two canons, still shaky but anxious to get to the safety of Exeter, were hauled up on to their mules, and Owain was lifted up behind Gwyn on his mare, as his arm was too fragile to control the reins. With his rounsey on a halter behind one of the merchants, they set off on the remaining seven miles to the city, leaving the two slain outlaws to rot away in the bushes at the side of the road.

By early afternoon the party had reached Exeter, and the injured stonemason had been delivered into the care of the healing monks at St John's Priory, while the travelling priests were settled in the cathedral Close. The coroner had called on his friend John de Alençon to explain what had happened, and with his nephew Thomas's fussy assistance the archdeacon had personally arranged for the assaulted canons to be accommodated in the guest rooms attached to the bishop's palace on the south side of the great church.

When all this was done, John went wearily back to his house, still aching from the effects of the long ride. Not unsurprisingly, his wife was absent, and as Mary bustled around to get him some food she told him that her mistress had left the previous day and had not returned.

'She said she was going to seek God, so I suppose she's gone as usual to pray at St Olave's.' Her brow furrowed. 'Though she wore her oldest kirtle and cloak, which is odd, as she always dresses up for the priest's benefit. And she must have gone to stay with someone overnight.'

'God must be bloody fed up with listening to her, day after day!' grumbled John irreverently. 'What does she find to say to Him all the time?'

'Praying for forgiveness for you – and for her brother, Sir Coroner!' replied the maid tartly as she put a wooden bowl of steaming potage in front of him.

He sat on the only stool in the small shed that she

called home, where the cooking was done as well. Mary called him 'Sir Coroner' only when she was annoyed with his behaviour, though he failed to see what he had done this time to deserve her sarcasm. She held a flat pan containing beef dripping over the fire to fry two eggs and some pieces of salt bacon. As she slid these on to a thick slice of bread in lieu of a platter and laid them on the small table, Mary elaborated on her criticisms.

'You'll lose her one of these days, mark my words. There's only so much a woman can take from the men around her.'

Normally, a servant being this outspoken would receive a buffet from her master, but John had a respect and affection for his maid that were not wholly due to their former intimacy in the back of the wash-shed. As he ate, he grunted his excuses. 'She's hardly been a good wife to me, Mary. Without you, I'd have starved and gone around in dirty rags. All she cares about is her damned devotions and her snobbish friends at the cathedral and St Olave's.'

Mary shook her head sadly. 'She's changed lately. I can see it in her face and her very movements. You are a trial to her, with your well-known infidelities, but I think it is her brother who has driven her to this state of despair.'

Richard de Revelle's sister had previously worshipped her elder brother, but had been progressively disenchanted as his bad behaviour was exposed – mainly by her own husband, which made matters worse. His expulsion from his post as sheriff, followed by an ignominious episode in which he had been publicly shamed in an ordeal by battle,* seemed to have driven Matilda into a descending spiral of depression and despair.

* see *The Noble Outlaw.*

'So where has she gone, d'you think?' he demanded between mouthfuls of food and cider.

Mary shrugged and stood over him with arms crossed over her bosom in a faintly defiant attitude. 'You tell me, sir! I doubt she's gone to her brother's house, though I hear that he is back from his manor and is in his fine town house in Northgate Street.'

'Could she be at her cousin's place in Fore Street?' he hazarded.

'I doubt she would have left all her fine clothes behind, if she went there. The mistress is too fond of showing off to her "poor relative", as she calls her!' she added sarcastically.

He rubbed the platter clean with a piece of bread, then stopped with it halfway to his mouth as a sudden thought struck him. 'Surely she hasn't gone back to Polsloe?' he exclaimed. 'She did that last year but soon found the food and raiment not at all to her liking.'

Again Mary shrugged. 'That was last year; she's more desperate now.'

John sighed as he finished his food and drink. 'If you say de Revelle is back at his town house, I'd best go around there and see if Matilda is with him – or whether he knows anything of her.'

A few minutes later he was loping through the busy streets of Exeter, shouldering aside porters struggling under huge bales of wool and dodging men wheeling barrows full of firewood. Swineherds drove fat pigs towards the Shambles for street slaughter, and the raucous voices of stallholders rang out from the booths that lined the roads, selling everything from sausages to shovels. On street corners, barbers shouted invitations for shaves and haircutting – and at Carfoix, the central crossing of the main roads, a villainous-looking fellow waved a pair of pincers, offering to pull any painful teeth. The whole motley throng was part of this vibrant city, thriving on its exports of tin, cloth and wool – even the beggars and vagrants seemed more prosperous than in other towns.

De Wolfe was oblivious to these familiar scenes, his mind full of his own problems, foremost amongst them now being the whereabouts of his wife. Though he could not abide the woman, he was responsible for her well-being and could not ignore the fact that she had disappeared.

His brother-in-law, though he had two large manors in the far west and in the east of the county, had recently bought a house near the North Gate, allegedly for convenience in dealing with various business ventures in the city, one of which was a college in Smythen Street. When his steward ushered John into the solar at the rear of his hall, he was far from pleased to see him. Relations between them, which had always been cool, had hardened into thick ice since Richard had been publicly shamed over the most recent of his misdoings. Yet the coroner's visit seemed not un-expected, as Richard's first words confirmed.

'I suppose you've come enquiring after your grossly misused wife?' he snapped, his pointed beard quivering with indignation.

De Wolfe was in no mood for verbal battles with a man he despised, and he managed to subdue an angry reply. 'I suspect that of late I contributed only a small part to your sister's unhappiness. She is not at home, so do you know where she is?'

'She called yesterday to bid me farewell, as she is entering a nunnery. You have driven her to take the veil, damn you!'

John was only partly surprised, though he thought that her previous attempt to cut herself off from the world had disenchanted her with the idea.

'I presume she has gone to Polsloe again?' he said evenly.

Richard nodded sullenly, piqued that he had not

provoked the coroner into a rage. 'She said she never wanted to lay eyes on you again, John!' Then he added in a rare fit of frankness, 'Nor upon me, either!'

There seemed nothing else to say, and de Wolfe turned on his heel and left the house without another word. As he strode back along Northgate Street, his mind was in turmoil, trying to sort out the implications of this news. Would she stay there this time, he wondered? And if so, what was to become of his marriage? Could he get an annulment, given that his friend the archdeacon was dubious about the prospects of success? And if he did, would he be free to marry Nesta? And would she really want him, with her ingrained conviction that a knight and an alehouse keeper were socially incompatible? Could he remain the king's coroner if he did – or even stay on in Exeter? And then what of Gwyn and Thomas, to say nothing of his house, his maid, his horse and his hound?

He growled imprecations under his breath at these troublesome diversions from the need to carry out his coroner's duties and tried to work out a plan of action. Though his first impulse was to ride the short distance to the Priory of St Katherine at Polsloe, as his mind cooled down while he walked through the lanes back to Rougemont he decided to let Matilda stew for a day. If she could walk out on him without a word or so much as a message left behind, then to hell with the woman – why should he scuttle after her like some pageboy or house-lackey? Instead, he directed his feet towards Rougemont and clattered up the wooden stairs into the keep to see the sheriff. He decided not to mention the problem with his wife for the time being, but to try to work out something in relation to the 'Axmouth problem', as he now called it in his mind.

A few moments later, with the inevitable cup of wine in his hand, he sprawled in a leather-backed chair in

Henry's chamber, facing the sheriff who sat behind his cluttered table.

'I will have to see Hubert Walter again, face to face,' he rumbled. 'These outrages have gone on long enough. We cannot have our law officers slain with impunity under our very noses! That way lies anarchy, just as it was years ago in the time of Stephen and Matilda.'

The mention of the last name made him wonder if all Matildas were awkward, aggressive women like his wife, for the old Empress was certainly cast in that mould.

De Furnellis's doleful face, lined and drooping like that of an aged hound, stared at the coroner over the brim of his cup. 'The Justiciar? You'll have to go a long way to find him, John, if you need to confront him quickly.'

'How do you know?' asked de Wolfe suspiciously.

'I had a royal herald here yesterday, dropping off dispatches about the new rate for the county farm for the next half-year.' Henry sounded sour, so John guessed that the Exchequer were again increasing the tax revenue to satisfy the Curia Regis's demand for yet more money to support the king's campaign against Philip of France. 'The herald mentioned that Hubert Walter had sailed from Portsmouth last week for Honfleur and was not expected back in Winchester or London for a month. It seems he has gone to attend Richard at Rouen – perhaps to tell him that he has squeezed all the money out of England that she possesses!'

John banged his empty cup down on the table in annoyance. 'I can't wait another bloody month just to be able to talk to him! I'll have to go there myself and speak to the king if necessary.'

Henry smiled benignly at his friend's impatience. 'You do that, John. The king is beholden to you for your long and faithful service to him – and encouraging you to hang a few tax-dodging bastards will help his budget, so he should be eager to listen to you!'

John was not so sure about his faithful service, as his conscience still plagued him about his failure to prevent the Lionheart's capture in Austria. But perhaps a visit to Rouen might be the chance to exorcise this particular demon. As he contemplated crossing the Channel, a different demon crept back on to his shoulder. If he was to sail for Normandy, then it made sense to use one of his own ships in which to travel, as the three vessels of their wool partnership made frequent crossings. And to arrange this, he would need to go down to Dawlish again to confer with the shipmasters – and as a matter of courtesy to call upon Hilda for her agreement, as three of the vessels had belonged to her, after Thorgils had died. This of course was a blatant fabrication of his mind, as legally the ships were as much his as Hilda's or de Relaga's, but it suited him to manufacture a semi-legitimate excuse for him to visit the blonde beauty once again.

De Furnellis leant back in his chair and fixed John with his blue eyes.

'Why don't you try sterner tactics with these fellows down in Axmouth? Do it on my behalf – take Ralph Morin and a troop of soldiers from the garrison with you. Demand to see what's in those barns, and if anyone tries to stop you arrest them and drag 'em back here in chains!'

The coroner was mildly surprised at the sheriff's sudden change of attitude, so different from his usual inertia at doing anything active. Perhaps the murder of one of his Keepers of the Peace had hardened his attitude.

'Do you think that would do any good?' he asked doubtfully.

Henry shrugged. 'What's to lose, apart from another

few hours in the saddle? Put the fear of God into the
sods, make them show you all they have hidden away
and demand to see the tallies of what they are supposed
to have. Take your Thomas with you; he can check any
documents they may produce.'

He took another swig of his wine and wiped his
moustache with his fingers. 'See if that creepy little
fellow Capie is as corrupt as most of the Customs clerks.
After all, I pay his salary from the county funds; I've got
every right to check up on him. Take Sergeant Gabriel
and as many men as you need.'

They discussed more details of this pre-emptive raid,
and after emptying the wine jug de Wolfe went on his
way, now more content that he at least had some sort of
plan of campaign about the Axmouth problem.

He was less sure about a plan of campaign in relation
to his tangled personal affairs, but philosophically
decided to allow fate to take its course.

That evening John was at his customary place in the
Bush with Gwyn sitting across the table, each enjoying
a restful quart of Nesta's best ale. As usual, Thomas
was off at his literary tasks in the scriptorium of the
cathedral. Nesta had been seeing to some kitchen crisis
but was now sitting alongside John to hear his story
about the murdered Keeper of the Peace and the outlaws' ambush on the Honiton road. Once again, he had
decided to keep the news about Matilda to himself
until he had a better idea of her intentions.

'A Welshman, you say?' she asked, when he related
the tale of the stonemason's wound. 'Then he's almost
a neighbour to my family, if he's from Cas-Gwent!'
This was the Welsh name for Chepstow, a Saxon title
meaning a market town, though the Norman owners
now called it Striguil.

'He's now under the tender care of Brother Saulf in
St John's,' said de Wolfe. This was a small priory just

inside the East Gate, which had a few sick beds that were all Exeter could offer in the way of a hospital. 'He says that the spear wound is not deep and hasn't damaged anything vital, as long as the flesh doesn't turn rotten.'

Nesta, ever sympathetic to people's misfortunes, especially if they were Welsh, began worrying about the man even though she had never met him nor even heard of him until ten minutes earlier.

'So far from home and no doubt concerned about his livelihood, if that's his working arm,' she fretted. 'How long will he be in St John's?'

'If he does well, no more than a few days, according to the monk,' said Gwyn. 'I'll call in tomorrow and see him. He may like to hear a word of his own language, though he speaks English well enough, after working so much in Gloucester.'

The landlady nodded her auburn head. 'I'll slip up there, too. He may not understand your uncouth Cornish accent!' she teased. 'I'll take him something decent to eat, too.'

The conversation drifted to other matters, and John related how he had been to see the sheriff earlier that day, to tell him of the death of Luke de Casewold, who was one of de Furnellis's law officers, though even Henry seemed vague about what the functions of these peacekeepers were supposed to be.

'I told him that he must report this killing as soon as he can to Winchester or London. The Chief Justiciar appointed these men, so he must be told that one has been slain, even if only to replace him.'

'And seek out those who did it,' grunted Gwyn. 'Otherwise the swine will think they can get away with anything.'

'What's this all about, anyway?' demanded Nesta. 'Is it connected with these misdoings in Axmouth?'

John nodded, waving his pot at Edwin for a refill.

'I'm sure it is. There's organised corruption going on from that port, but so far it's been impossible to get any proof. Everyone clams up like a limpet when you try to talk to them. I sometimes think the whole village is part of a big conspiracy.'

'Is this bailiff at the root of it, d'you think?'

John shrugged. 'He's a nasty, overbearing bully, but I can't bring him back in chains for that. There's nothing to show he had anything to do with the Keeper's death – neither is there for the portreeve, Elias Palmer, though he's such a poor apology for a man that I can't see him slaying so much as a cat, let alone killing de Casewold.'

'So what do we do next, Crowner?' asked Gwyn in his slow Cornish voice.

John sighed and held up his palms. 'The sheriff is all for sending us down there with Ralph Morin, Gabriel and a bunch of their men-at-arms. We are to shake the place up and see what falls out, but I suspect that those bastards are too clever to leave any loose ends.'

'And if that doesn't work?' asked Nesta.

'Then all I can think of is acting like a mole-catcher. If you can't see anything on the surface, you set a trap!'

CHAPTER EIGHT

In which Crowner John goes to a nunnery

Soon after dawn next day, John borrowed a rounsey from the livery stables opposite, not wanting to saddle up his big destrier Odin for such a brief journey. On the lighter horse, he covered the mile or two to Polsloe in a short time and soon arrived at the small gatehouse in the long wall that enclosed the compound. The porter emerged from his hut at the side and grudgingly agreed to inform the prioress of his desire to speak to her. John had been here several times before and accepted that casual male callers were not easily admitted to this nest of women. He waited just inside the gate, allowing his horse to crop the grass that extended around the wide compound, the priory itself being little more than a few stone buildings set in the centre.

A few moments later the stocky gatekeeper returned, shaking his head. 'The prioress says that the lady has left instructions that she does not want to see anyone, especially you!'

De Wolfe glared at him, almost speechless. 'What the hell d'you mean, man? She's my wife, for God's sake!'

With the smug expression of a man who knows he has the whip hand, the porter shrugged. 'I'm only passing on the message, sir. There's no point in waiting here.'

'I demand to speak to the prioress,' fumed John. 'Do you want me to go in there waving a sword?'

The servant began to look apprehensive, as this fearsome dark man, almost a foot taller than himself, looked as if he was quite capable of carrying out his threat. Thankfully, the tension was broken by the appearance of someone else on the front steps of the building as another tall dark figure hurried down the path towards them. It was Dame Madge, the most senior of the nine sisters, skilled in the ailments of women, who had helped the coroner several times in the past over matters of ravishment and miscarriage. She dismissed the gatekeeper with a flick of her hand as she came up to de Wolfe.

'Sir John, no doubt you have come to seek news of Matilda?' she asked.

'I was away at my duties and returned home to find her gone, with no explanation whatsoever.'

The gaunt Benedictine fixed him with her deep-set eyes. 'She is in a very disturbed state, sir. Your wife requires peace and tranquillity for a time, to restore her humours. She wishes to cut herself off from the turmoil of the world until she decides what she wishes to do with the remainder of her life.'

John always felt slightly intimidated by this formidable woman, and his anger evaporated quickly. 'But we went through all this last year, sister!' he pleaded. 'Matilda came here intending to take her vows but soon decided against it. Is this just another fit of pique, directed against me?'

Dame Madge looked at him sorrowfully. 'Not only against you, sir, but from my conversations with her it seems that this time her brother is also a major offender. I cannot tell you what she will eventually decide, but she is certainly greatly troubled in her spirit and soul. We cannot do other than to offer her sanctuary for a time.'

John knew that his wife was a generous benefactor to the religious establishments that she patronised – and having a significant personal income from rents and other interests bequeathed to her by her father, she was able to encourage places like Polsloe to give her shelter when required. He sighed as he accepted the delays that seemed inevitable in getting this matter settled. 'So what shall I do, ma'am? Just wait until she deigns to speak to me?'

'Perhaps she never will,' replied the dame dispassionately. 'In the mood she is in at present, she may never again show her face to the outside world.' She bowed her head and, with a final benediction for God to preserve him, wished him good morning, then walked slowly back to the priory.

John retrieved his horse and trotted away, once again weighing up the chances of this setting him free from seventeen years of loveless marriage. He soon covered the short distance along a tree-lined track to the village of St Sidwell's, just outside the East Gate, where Gwyn lived in a miserable rented hut with his wife and two children. Having just left one priory with a healing mission, he now made his way to the other, a small establishment of the Benedictine Black Monks, who catered for the sick poor of the city. It lay in a side lane behind the gate, a simple range of rooms, the 'hospital' being a single large chamber with whitewashed walls. A row of five straw-stuffed mattresses lay along each side of the room, with a few open window-slits high above. On the blank end wall hung a large wooden cross in full view of every patient, emphasising that the main healer here was the Almighty, aided a little by the devoted staff. The most senior of these was Brother Saulf, a tall Saxon whose fair hair was shaved into a circular tonsure. He had been an apothecary's apprentice in London before entering holy orders and, together with his fellow monks, dispensed simple medical care to those who could not afford to pay one of the three professional apothecaries in the city. As with Dame Madge, de Wolfe had built up a good working relationship with Brother Saulf, after a number of incidents when he had had to call upon his expertise.

Though perhaps the Welsh stone carver was not that impoverished, the urgency of the situation and the monks' inability ever to turn away the suffering allowed him to be cared for – and John would quietly ensure that a generous donation would be made to the priory funds from his own purse.

When he entered the sick chamber, he was surprised to see a group of figures hovering over the pallet where Owain ap Gronow lay. One was Saulf, but the others were Archdeacon John de Alençon, Gwyn and Nesta, the last with a basket over her arm. When he walked past the half-dozen other patients to reach them, he found the Welshman beaming up at him, apparently in good spirits. He had one arm swathed in linen, supported by a leather thong around his neck, but apart from one bloodshot eye and some bruises on his face and neck Owain seemed alert and lively.

'I came to see the poor fellow as I feel a little responsible for his condition,' said the archdeacon, his bright eyes twinkling under the wiry grey hair that surrounded his bald crown. 'After all, it was I who prevailed upon my fellow archdeacon in Gloucester to send us the best craftsman they had to work on some of the statues on the cathedral shrines.'

'And that I'll start doing as soon as I can use this arm, sir,' promised the mason, smiling up at the Good Samaritans who had rescued him. 'No doubt my return to health will be greatly hastened by the good food that this kind lady has brought!' He tapped Nesta's basket with his free hand and she smiled down at him and almost clucked like a hen with a lame chick.

The archdeacon soon took his leave and walked out

accompanied by Brother Saulf, leaving the others to revert to speaking in the Celtic tongue, though Owain's English was excellent, albeit with a strong Gwent accent like Nesta's.

'Are you recovering well, lad?' asked John, calling him that though Owain was probably thirty years of age. He was a good-looking fellow, with dark curly hair and a pleasant face, in spite of the battering it had received.

'I am, sir, and have to thank you for my life,' replied the craftsman humbly. 'I will always be indebted to you and Gwyn here for that – and for sending me this beautiful Welshwoman who comes from within five miles of my own home!'

A little warning bell sounded in John's head. Was this new fellow, though amiable and respectful, going to be another threat like the man last year who had seduced her while working in the Bush? Certainly, by the look on her pretty face she was hugely enjoying compliments from a good-looking fellow countryman who came from her own doorstep.

Gwyn, who was hardly a sensitive soul, missed any such nuances and stood grinning down at the stone-mason, a jar of rough cider in his hand as his own gift to aid Owain's convalescence. 'Get this down you, boy, it will strengthen your arm when you have to chisel a new nose on to St Boniface!'

Nesta launched into some typically Welsh genealogical enquiries, discovering that her second cousin was married to a brother-in-law of Owain's uncle. When they had finished the first round of exploring their relations, John broke in to ask the injured man where he would be staying when he was discharged from the hospital.

'I had no plans, Sir John, not having been to Exeter before this,' replied Owain. 'If it had not been for this affair putting me on my back here, I suppose I would have just taken a bed in the first inn that I came upon.'

Inevitably, both Gwyn and Nesta hastened to recommend the Bush, somewhat to John's discomfiture.

'Perhaps the archdeacon has already somewhere arranged in the cathedral precinct,' he offered rather lamely, as John de Alençon had not mentioned anything of the sort.

'Nonsense, John, he must stay in Idle Lane!' said Nesta firmly. 'It is convenient for the cathedral, and I can offer Owain a comfortable mattress in the loft.'

The thought sprang into de Wolfe's mind that it should be laid as far as possible from her bedroom, then he chided himself for such uncharitable thoughts about a man who was probably a paragon of virtue and good behaviour.

'Best bed and board in Exeter – in all Devon, come to that!' boomed Gwyn. 'The cleanest tavern in the city and she brews better ale than they make in heaven!'

John gave up the unequal struggle but hoped that chiselling faces on the cathedral saints would not take very long and that Owain could soon ride off home to Wales. After a few more minutes of amiable conversation, he managed to prise Gwyn away, but Nesta stayed behind, deeply immersed in reminiscences about their part of Gwent and exploring innumerable distant relations.

'Seems a pleasant enough fellow, that Owain,' commented the Cornishman blithely as they strode away towards the castle, up the hill on the other side of High Street.

'Lucky he's not a dead pleasant fellow,' grunted John. 'If we hadn't come across them yesterday, those bastard outlaws would have slain the lot of them.'

Something in his tone stirred a chord in Gwyn's usually insensitive mind, and it gradually dawned on him that his master was already wary of Nesta's obvious delight in finding such a kindred soul to assuage her *hiraeth*, a Welsh word meaning a longing for home. Wisely, he let the topic drop and reverted to their present problems. 'What did the sheriff say about the happenings over in the east of the county?'

As they climbed the short but steep slope through the outer bailey to the gatehouse, John related what Henry de Furnellis had suggested.

'We are to take Ralph Morin and a troop of men-at-arms down to Axmouth and give the place a good going-over!' he said with some satisfaction in his voice. 'I doubt it will yield much, but at least it will show those crafty swine that we mean business and that we are keeping a close eye on them.'

His officer was delighted at the prospect of some action, as since John had given up campaigning abroad he missed the excitement of battle. Though the coroner's business had occasionally provoked an odd fight or two, he found life rather staid and the prospect of some violence cheered him considerably.

'When are we going down there?' he demanded, feeling the hilt of his old sword in anticipation.

'In a few days' time, but first I need to go down to Dawlish,' replied John.

Gwyn's bushy eyebrows rose in surprise. 'Is Widow Thorgils in need of some help?' he asked, his face a mask of false innocence.

De Wolfe scowled at his old friend. 'Why should you think it was anything to do with Hilda?' he demanded. 'I have to see either Roger Watts or Angerus de Wile. We are going to Normandy very soon and I need to arrange a passage for us on one of their cogs.'

Gwyn's face lit up even more than with the prospect of a fracas in Axmouth. 'Normandy! That'll be like old times – but why?'

John explained that he needed to see the Chief Justiciar and possibly the king himself over the murder of the Keeper and the probability of piracy in the Channel.

'Are we taking the little runt?' asked Gwyn, referring to their erudite clerk Thomas.

John pondered for a moment as they reached the drawbridge and acknowledged the salute of the soldier on guard under the archway. 'I think we had better drag him along, though the poor devil will probably fare worse on a ship than on the back of a horse. But there may be documents to read or to be written – and he might be useful at the court, which is a nest of priests and clerks in holy orders.'

They made their way up the narrow staircase built into the thickness of the wall and found the said Thomas already busy at his parchments, where John gave him the news that he would soon be suffering a sea voyage. The clerk's apprehension at having to cross the Channel was tempered by the prospect of seeing the royal court and meeting the Archbishop of Canterbury – and even perhaps the king himself.

Twittering with excitement, he forced himself back to his pen and ink, while Gwyn and the coroner went in search of Ralph Morin, the castle constable, to confer with him about the form of their punitive expedition to Axmouth.

Before the planned foray upon the warehouses along the estuary of the Axe, John de Wolfe had one more journey to make in the opposite direction. This time he left Gwyn behind, partly to avoid the knowing grins that the ginger giant would undoubtedly give him when John sidled off into Dawlish's back street.

The morning after their visit to St John's Hospital, he rode alone down to the West Gate and across the ford, taking Odin down the sea road towards Kenton. It was a fine morning and he was in no hurry, so he let the big stallion set his own pace, a stately trot that he could keep up for hours. In this mostly open country, the flat moors that bordered the estuary gave little cover for trail-bastons, so the risk from attack was small, even though he was alone.

He had time to ruminate again on his personal problems, which seemed to be getting more complicated with each passing day. There had been no word from Polsloe, though as it was only yesterday that he was there, he hardly expected any news yet about Matilda. From past experience, he knew she was likely to let him stew for some time before letting him know whether or not she intended to stay in the priory or whether she was just making another gesture to upset him.

As to Nesta, he felt a niggle of anxiety both about her feelings and his own. She had been his mistress for two years now, and though at first he had continued his sporadic affairs with other women, gradually he had become more faithful as his feelings for her deepened. There had been Hilda, of course, his first true love, but even after her husband had been killed and he had no need to cuckold him, his attachment to Nesta had prevented him from bedding her, strong though the temptation had been. There had been yet another lady, a young widow from Sidmouth, but she had found a new husband and was now placed beyond his reach. As he trotted along on the destrier's back, he recalled the strains that had been put on his relationship with Nesta, not only when she became pregnant and lost the babe but also when she had succumbed to an affair with a bold young man who had come to work for her at the Bush. Now there was another bold young man in the offing, one moreover who had a strong emotional appeal for Nesta, both linguistically and geographically. Though John loved her in his own odd way and thought that she loved him, he knew they could never marry, even if he were free of Matilda. He was willing to take Nesta away and live with her as his leman, but he knew that she would never agree to it, feeling that the social gulf between them would still remain unbridgeable.

As he passed through Kenton and saw Dawlish on the horizon, he felt a guilty pleasure at seeing Hilda again, as well as unease at the knowledge that he was being mentally, if not physically, unfaithful to Nesta. It confused him, for he was not a subtle man and had a strong need for passion and lust. Years ago, he would not have given a second thought to running several women at the same time, especially as most men of his acquaintance had one or more mistresses.

'Ah, to hell with it!' he suddenly shouted at a surprised coney scurrying into the undergrowth at the side of the track. 'I'm a knight and a king's officer. Why should I be fretting myself over a handful of women?'

He gave Odin a touch of his heels and the big beast lumbered along a little more quickly, hastening the moment when his master's life would become even more complicated. When they reached the village, slumbering under a warm spring sun, John looked keenly at the vessels in the mouth of the small river, as he had done in years past to see if Thorgils the Boatman was at home. This time he wanted to see if any of the three ships belonging to their partnership was beached there. He spotted the *St Peter*, whose shipmaster was usually Angerus de Wile. A crewman working on the rigging shouted to him that de Wile was in the nearest alehouse, the one usually frequented by Gwyn when he waited for de Wolfe to pay his call on Hilda. John found the lanky mariner leaning against a windowsill with a hunk of bread and cheese and a pint of ale. Ordering the same for himself from the slattern, as well as a refill for Angerus, he explained what he wanted.

'A passage across to any port within riding distance

of Rouen for my clerk, my officer and myself. Are any of our ships going that way soon?'

The captain, whose undershot jaw always gave him an aggressive appearance, explained that the sailing schedules were arranged by Hugh de Relaga and his clerks, back in their office in Exeter, but he understood that one cog was due to sail for Calais very soon.

'It's the *Mary and Child Jesus*, going on her first voyage since she was repaired. Roger Watts is taking her, so no doubt he will be willing to drop you at Honfleur.'

'Do you know when she is sailing and from where?' asked John.

'They are taking wool as usual from Exeter. Probably early next week, but you will have to ask the portreeve exactly when they leave. It will depend partly on the weather and the tides.'

The *Mary and Child Jesus* was the vessel that had been wrecked on the west Devon coast last autumn, after all the crew, including Hilda's husband, had been slain.* The cog had been salvaged and refitted and this was to be her first trip of the new season.

They finished their victuals and talked about the new venture. According to Angerus, the endeavour was doing well, as other merchants were paying them to take their own materials across and to import finished cloth and other goods on the homeward journeys. John enquired about any reports of further acts of piracy out at sea, but the shipmaster had heard of no recent events.

'There is talk of Moorish galleys back in the Irish Sea, but no ships have been lost along this coast recently.'

After they had talked a little longer, John arranged with the ostler behind the inn to feed and water Odin and left him there while he walked the few hundred

* See *The Elixir of Death.*

paces to Hilda's fine dwelling. Feeling the same tickle of excitement that he used to experience when he used to come when her husband was away on a voyage, he banged on the door and went through the usual routine with her young maid. Alice, with a covert smirk at the appearance of this impressive man, whom she knew was so attracted to her mistress, took him up to the solar, where Hilda expressed her delight at the unexpected visit. Pastries and wine were ordered, and as soon as the maid had delivered them she was dismissed, with no pretence at keeping her as a chaperone.

'What brings you this time, John, welcome as you always are? I trust it is not only ships and trade that lead you to call upon me!'

John took her hands and pulled her close to him. 'I confess that I have been talking to Angerus de Wile, but that was just an excuse to come to see you.'

Hilda drew back gently. 'Do you need an excuse to visit me, John?' she said softly.

He looked at her lovely face, her sweep of golden hair and the slim body in its sheath of pale blue linen. With a groan, he slid his arms around her and kissed her passionately, almost roughly. Those familiar lips responded eagerly and her hands reached up around his neck, holding his head in an almost desperate embrace. When they came up for air, one of his hands found her breast, and as they writhed against each other their lips and tongues joined together once more. Just as John was scanning the floor from the corner of his eye, looking for a place to lay her down, Hilda broke free and stepped back gasping, her hands up in defence.

'No, John! This is not right. Please, consider what we are doing!'

Aroused and frustrated, he stood breathing heavily, his empty arms still held out for her. Slowly, they drooped, as he gained control of himself.

'Hilda, why not? We both lost our virginity together so long ago. We are very special to each other, are we not?'

The elegant woman backed away and felt for a chair behind her, her eyes still upon his. 'We are indeed, John! There is no other man in the world like you, but we cannot hurt others to satisfy our own cravings. Sit down, I beg you.'

Reluctantly, he lowered himself on to a padded stool and crouched with his hands on his knees, regarding her intently. He had come very near ravishment and his heart was still pounding in his chest like a water-hammer in a forge. With an effort, Hilda fought to bring her own feelings under control and, to cover her agitation, turned to pour some wine that Alice had provided in a jug.

'Take this and behave yourself, dear man,' she said with an attempt at levity as she handed him a pewter cup. 'We are no longer a wayward lass and a wild young lad frisking in the tithe barn at Holcombe!'

Simmering down, he grinned sheepishly. 'It is your fault, Hilda, for being so damned lovely. What man could resist being inflamed by you? You should veil your face to avoid temptation, like the Saracen women do in Outremer.'

As the emotional temperature dropped, Hilda wisely cooled it even further by enquiring about John's wife and mistress. He told her about the latest machinations of Matilda and her retreat into Polsloe once again.

'If only I knew whether she was serious this time – or just provoking me,' he glowered. 'It may be possible to get the marriage annulled if she actually takes her vows, though that will take a year or two and possibly an appeal to Rome.'

Hilda gazed at him steadily, her blue eyes fixed on his. 'And if that comes to pass, will you then marry your Nesta?'

He shook his head decisively. 'She never would do that, I know. She is very devout in her own way and thinks that the wedding bond is for life. Apart from which, she considers herself a lowly foreign Welsh-woman, an ale-wife in a different world from a knighted Norman law officer!' he added cynically.

Hilda shrugged. 'And what am I, John, but the Saxon daughter of a village reeve? Until your brother gave him his freedom, my father was a serf, toiling in the fields.'

De Wolfe snorted. 'You are a queen amongst women, Hilda, wherever you came from. And now you are also a rich woman, with a fine house and a partner in a thriving business!'

She smiled sadly, offering him more wine. 'And a lonely woman, John! I admit I miss Thorgils, even though he was at sea for more than half the year.'

De Wolfe was not sure how to take this. Was it a hint that she needed his company more often? But after her pulling him up short a few moments ago, it seemed hardly likely that she was now encouraging him. Confused, he did not know whether to voice his concerns to Hilda about Nesta and the new arrival on the scene, the stone carver from Gwent. Then he decided that he was being a fool – all he had seen was his unfailingly kind mistress bringing a wounded fellow countryman a basket of food and some consoling conversation. It was ridiculous, he thought, for him to make that into a potentially amorous affair and to mislead Hilda into thinking that he was on the road to breaking off his long-standing liaison with Nesta.

With an effort, they managed to bring their con-versation down to more mundane matters, and John told her about the problems he had in Axmouth and the murder of the Keeper of the Peace. 'It affects us in a way,' he added. 'Our new venture with the ships could be in jeopardy if piracy threatens more vessels plying across the Channel.' He told her of his plans to raid Axmouth and then go across to Rouen to seek the support of Hubert Walter and perhaps even the king, in dealing with the growing problem of seaborne murder and theft.

'Be careful, John. The back of a horse is a safer place than the sea,' she warned, mindful of the loss of Thorgils.

'Roger Watts will look after me,' he reassured her. 'And I'll have Gwyn with me to guard my back as usual.'

Abruptly, he stood up to take his leave and remove himself from further temptation. Hilda rose with him. Tall as he was, her slender figure came to his chin as he held her gently and gave her a single chaste kiss on the forehead. 'I'll see you when I return from France,' he promised.

Impulsively, she reached up to give him a quick but fervent kiss on the lips and then stepped back to avoid provoking his desire. 'Take care, John. I will pray for you.'

She saw him to the head of the staircase, where the child Alice was sitting on the bottom step, as if ready to rush to her mistress's defence if this tall dark man should fall upon her.

He strode out into the street, still feeling the softness of her mouth on his and the feel of her body under his hand. She was lonely, she said ... He feared that soon she might seek someone else to assuage that loneliness, but what could he do about it?

CHAPTER NINE

In which the coroner goes on campaign

That evening in the Bush, Nesta was full of her latest visit that day to the priory to see Owain ap Gronow. As John sat with Gwyn and Thomas at his table near the firepit, she prattled on about the Welshman, especially the increasing number of acquaintances and distant relatives that they shared. She spoke in English in deference to Thomas, and the others began to appreciate the homesickness that she must be feeling. The previous year, John had taken her on a short trip back to Gwent, but it seemed that this had heightened her longing, rather than having relieved it. Nesta had first come to Exeter with her husband Meredydd, but when he died she had been left isolated in a foreign city.

'Is he recovering well?' asked Thomas solicitously.

'Very well indeed. Brother Saulf said that he can leave the day after tomorrow. I will put a mattress filled with new straw for him up in the loft.'

'A wonder you don't fill it with swans' down!' said John. He tried to make it sound jocular, but there was an undercurrent of sarcasm in the remark, which passed over Nesta's head.

'And the first night, I'll make him some good Welsh *cawl* to build up his strength after his injuries.'

She looked flushed with excitement this evening, but John was somewhat reassured, as she was more like a little girl with a new toy rather than a woman with a potential new lover. Cuddling up to his side on the bench and reaching over to take a sip from his ale-pot, she seemed happy and affectionate.

Soon, Thomas changed the subject to that of Matilda, as John had confided in his friends about his latest problem. 'Is there any news of your wife, sir?'

De Wolfe shook his head. 'She's keeping me in suspense again, damn her! Every time I go back to the house, I half-expect to find her sitting there as if nothing had happened, just as she did last year.'

As usual, the kind-hearted Nesta came to her defence. 'The poor lady must be in very low spirits, bless her. That business with her brother must have been hard to take – and you don't exactly make her life any easier, John,' she added caustically.

He ignored the barbed remark, which was not the first in that vein. 'If she doesn't make up her mind one way or the other very soon, she'll find me gone. Gwyn, Thomas and I are sailing across the seas on Monday, if the weather allows.'

This was the first Nesta had heard of the voyage and, after he had explained all about it, she affected an indignation that John suspected was not all play-acting. 'Not only does the royal coroner neglect his wife but he leaves his lover to fend for herself as well! Will you be back this year, do you think?' she added sarcastically.

He grinned sheepishly. 'Within a couple of weeks, God willing. It's the king's business; I have to go.'

'Well, when you return, don't be surprised if I've run off with the baker or the butcher – or even that nice Welsh stonemason!'

Her tone was light, but John wondered why she had so readily added on the last part. It must have been lying sleeping in her mind, he thought sourly. Yet the pretty redhead prattled on about the lavish present she expected him to bring her from France, and her manner with him seemed as relaxed and skittish as always. After Gwyn had lumbered away to a game of dice with the soldiers in Rougemont and Thomas had slid away to his shared lodging in Priest Street, John stayed to enjoy a supper of boiled mutton, leeks and beans, before enjoying a different experience up in the little room in the loft.

With Matilda away, he stayed the entire night and, in spite of his earlier concerns about Nesta, found her to be even more enthusiastic than usual about their love-making. His own responses were similarly uninhibited and afterwards, as he lay staring up into the darkness of the roof beams, he wondered if the frustration he had experienced with Hilda had sharpened his senses. But in that case, he thought darkly, might something similar have stimulated Nesta?

Then he thought of the very public ward in St John's and the fact that the stone carver had one arm in a sling. Reassured, he rolled over to put an arm around Nesta's bare shoulders and was soon asleep.

In Axmouth two days later, it was as if history had slipped backwards two or three centuries to the dark days of the Viking raids, except that this incursion came from the land rather than the sea. The leader of the marauding band was a massive man with a forked beard and, though his round iron helmet had no horns attached, he could have been taken for some Norse chieftain, with his chain-mail hauberk, massive broadsword and a spiked mace at his saddlebow. He was in fact Ralph Morin, the constable of Exeter Castle, and he led a score of mounted men-at-arms in full campaign order. Ralph was well aware that he was unlikely to have to fight a pitched battle with the villagers of Axmouth, but he wanted to show that the authorities took this seriously – as well as a welcome chance to give these idle soldiers a work-out, as few had raised a weapon in anger for years.

As the troop came down the road towards the landward gate, their harnesses jingling, Morin turned in his saddle to look at the pair behind him. John de Wolfe was riding alongside Gwyn and, behind them, Sergeant Gabriel kept company with Thomas de Peyne.

'Where do you want to start, John?' demanded the constable.

The coroner, who wore a helmet and sword but no armour, pointed ahead. 'Get Gabriel to take your men down to the wharves alongside the river, beyond the further gate. Make sure no one goes in or out of the storehouses, for these crafty bastards might well hide something if they're not watched like hawks.'

They entered the top of the main street of the large village, ignoring the surprised inhabitants who gaped at this sudden appearance of such a show of force. As the grizzled sergeant carried on with his troop down towards the seaward end, the coroner and the constable, with Gwyn and the clerk behind them, peeled off and dismounted outside the house of Edward Northcote. Disturbed by the noise, Northcote emerged from his door, followed by Elias Palmer and a florid-faced man in a brown robe, a shaven tonsure marking him as a cleric, presumably in one of the lower orders.

'What in hell's going on?' demanded the bailiff angrily. 'Have the French landed that you need to bring half the army down here?'

Though Northcote was a big man, Ralph Morin dwarfed him, looking even more threatening in his armour. He thrust a parchment under Northcote's nose, a sheet with an impressive red seal dangling from it. Neither could read it, but the bailiff angrily passed it to the portreeve.

'What's this about, Elias?' he snapped. The skinny

official rapidly scanned the words. 'It's a warrant from Henry de Furnellis, demanding in the name of the king that all stocks and wares and any documents relating to trade in Axmouth be made available for inspection by the sheriff's representatives, namely Sir John de Wolfe, coroner, and Ralph Morin, castellan.'

Edward Northcote grabbed the parchment from Elias and waved it aloft. 'Holy Mary, do you mean to say you brought half the garrison down here just to go rooting through our store-sheds?' he jeered at the top of his voice. 'Are you all mad up in Exeter, that you waste your time and disturb hard-working folk with your nonsense?'

De Wolfe stepped forward to confront the bailiff. 'The sooner we start, the sooner we can leave you to your important work,' he said sarcastically. 'Let your man Elias Palmer here show us his lists and manifests of what should be in the warehouses. We have brought my clerk here, who can read what is necessary.'

'He's not the only one here who is literate, Crowner, so don't judge all men by yourself.' This scathing remark came from the fat-faced man in the monkish robe.

'And who the hell might you be?' growled the coroner, resenting someone who made public jibes about his lack of education.

'I am Brother Absalom, the assistant cellarer of the Priory of Loders. I am charged by the prior with supervising his interests in this manor, which belongs to the priory.' He swelled up visibly with self-importance, reminding John of one of the bullfrogs that he had seen on his foreign travels. 'In fact, I consider your presence here and this note from the sheriff to be illegal,' he continued. 'This village and port belong to a French religious house and as such is outside the jurisdiction of the civil authorities!'

John moved closer and poked the clerk in the chest

with a long finger. 'In relation to your cure of souls here, I agree with you, brother,' he grated. 'But if your religious house chooses to indulge in trade and reap the benefits of that, then you are subject to all the laws and practices of England.' He paused to give the lay brother another jab in the chest.

'Furthermore, we are seeking a murderer and have good reason to suspect that illegal acts against both property and persons may have been committed or fomented here. So just keep your monastic comments to youself and stay out of our way!'

The prior's man went even redder in the face and began protesting, but John ignored him and turned to Edward Northcote and his shadow, Elias Palmer. 'I hope you are not going to be difficult over this, or we will have to take you back to Rougemont to question you further in less salubrious surroundings,' he threatened. 'Thomas, go with the portreeve and see that he gives you the right documents relating to the current imports and exports.'

As his clerk followed the reluctant Elias back into the bailiff's dwelling, Northcote's anger seemed to have subsided to a puzzled concern. 'Crowner, I don't understand this! Why this overstated show of force? True, there may be some small irregularities in the way the goods are tallied for the king's Customs levy, but that is a minor matter, mainly due to the inefficiency of John Capie. But a troop of armed soldiers and threats of arrest – that seems excessive.'

There was a certain tinge of sincerity in his voice that puzzled John. Could this man be a villain and a possible murderer?

'There is more to it than that, bailiff. We have a ship's boy cruelly slain and his body buried, then we have one of the king's law officers murdered. The last death, and certainly the killing of a pedlar, have fingers pointing at Axmouth.'

Edward Northcote bridled at this. 'That's sheer supposition, Crowner! You have no proof whatsoever that our village is concerned in any of that – apart from the dead boy, which I firmly maintain was some drunken dispute between shipmen, notorious for their drunken violence.'

De Wolfe glowered at the indignant bailiff. 'Be that as it may, we need to check your records against what is found in your sheds.'

Northcote glared back at him, but it was the monkish fellow from Loders who broke in. 'I can see that it might be within your remit to investigate these deaths, but what possible right can a coroner have to come poking his nose into matters of commerce?'

'The right of a king's law officer to pursue whatever task is allotted to him!' snapped de Wolfe. 'A coroner can be given a commission by the king or his agents to look into anything in the realm. And I have been commanded by the sheriff – who represents the king in this county of Devon – to investigate certain serious allegations concerning the conduct of the port of Axmouth.'

As if to highlight his words, he turned back to North-cote. 'Is that vessel *The Tiger* in the harbour at present?'

The bailiff shook his head. 'No, she left the river a couple of days ago, bound for Ouistreham in Normandy with wool. Should be home next week, bringing fine Caen stone back to build some church.'

De Wolfe was disappointed as he wondered, though without much foundation, whether each return of *The Tiger* might coincide with illicit goods appearing in the quayside barns. His suspicion of that vessel was based mainly on the fact that the dead Simon had been a crew member and had been so agitated on his return from his last voyage – as well as a personal dislike of her shipmaster, Martin Rof.

Soon, Thomas came out of the house with the

portreeve, who clutched a bundle of parchments under his arm. 'What do you want done with these?' he demanded querulously.

'We'll all take a walk down to the quayside and check what's in the sheds against those documents of yours,' said the coroner, already starting to lope towards the gate.

'They'll not be up to date,' called Elias from behind him. 'There are two cogs unloading there today, and John Capie won't have brought me his tallies for them yet.'

He shuffled along behind, followed by the bailiff and Absalom, Ralph Morin bringing up the rear. When they reached the spot on the river bank where two vessels were berthed, they found that Gabriel had stopped the men from unloading while the inventory of the big sheds across the road was being made.

'You are interfering with our work, Crowner,' croaked Elias Palmer. 'We still have to pay these men and now they are all sitting on their backsides while you waste our time.'

A couple of men-at-arms were stationed at the doors of each of the four warehouses, one of which was open, with a disgruntled John Capie standing with a bundle of tallies in his hand. 'This new stuff is cloth from Cologne and some dried fruit and wine from Barfleur,' he protested.

'It's what else might be in these storehouses than concerns me,' snapped de Wolfe. 'I want everything checked against those lists that the portreeve is holding so close to his chest.'

Two hours later, de Wolfe was even more disappointed, as the laborious business of identifying every item in the cavernous barns with the sheets of parchment that Elias had produced had revealed nothing that could be construed as illegal or even suspicious. It was true that many of the casks and crates had little or no markings upon them, and the bales of wool waiting to be shipped out had nothing on them but splashes of different-coloured dyes to denote the place of origin, according to a list that the portreeve held. But overall the total number of different classes of merchandise corresponded with the manifests. There were some errors, but with such a random method as Capie's knots and sticks it was to be expected that there were a few discrepancies.

By early afternoon the coroner and constable had to admit defeat, in that they had found no evidence of malpractice in Axmouth. The bailiff and the brother from Loders had stood around during the search in bored resentment, and when finally the search was called off they were full of righteous indignation.

'Now that you have wasted half our day and slowed the discharge of the cargo from those two vessels, perhaps you will go away and leave us in peace!' snorted Edward Northcote.

'The prior will hear of this, you may be assured of that!' brayed Absalom. 'I have no doubt that he will complain to the bishop about this intrusion.'

'What the devil has the bishop got to do with anything?' countered Morin. 'He's no say in the enforcement of the law in this county.'

'Then I'll complain to the Archbishop of Canterbury.'

De Wolfe leered at him, grateful for even a small victory. 'Then I'll be happy to convey your complaints to him personally, for I'm about to sail to Normandy to see him!'

Rightly suspecting that they would now receive little hospitality in Axmouth, the party saddled up and left the village, stopping instead a few miles along the homeward road for refreshment. At a roadside clearing near Colyford, the men-at-arms dismounted from their short-legged moorland horses and sprawled amongst the weeds to pass around skins of ale and cider and eat the bread and meat they had brought in their saddle-pouches. Leaving the sergeant to keep order, their leaders rode on the quarter-mile into the village and used the solitary tavern to assuage their hunger and thirst.

De Wolfe ordered bread, cheese and cold mutton for the four of them, and while the ale-wife went off to prepare the food they sat hunched on a couple of benches drinking the thin brew and discussing the fiasco in Axmouth.

'You are sure those lists corresponded to what was in the barns?' grumbled the constable, less aware than John how meticulous Thomas de Peyne was in such matters. The little clerk stoutly defended himself and pointed out a gaping flaw in their attempt to unmask any evildoing.

'The manifests of Elias were well written and convincing, and I had no problem in matching the items with the goods,' he said. 'But of course we have no way of knowing how true those lists were!'

De Wolfe peered at his clerk from under his black brows. He had every respect for Thomas's perspicacity but did not follow his train of thought here. 'What d'you mean, not true?'

'Well, the lists could just as well have been written to deliberately conform with what's in the sheds at any time. That doesn't mean that the stuff came off a particular ship and was checked in by John Capie. If the bailiff and the portreeve and anyone else down there feared that they might be challenged – as indeed we did this morning – then they could fabricate those lists as often as necessary, so that everything would appear to be in order.'

Gwyn tried to follow the sharp little clerk's argument, but failed. 'What the hell d'you mean, Thomas? I don't understand.'

His small friend gave him a pitying look, but explained again. 'Look, say a pirate ship comes in with stolen goods. The stuff is unloaded into the sheds and straightway a list is made of it, falsely attributing its ownership to various merchants. As I'm sure they shift the material out very quickly, probably inside a day or two, then it would be virtually impossible to verify any one crate or barrel to some alleged importer in Yeovil or Dorchester. And one bale of wool looks the same as another, and the few markings they have could easily be faked.'

De Wolfe nodded his understanding. 'So for all we know, some of that stuff we've been handling today might have been pillaged. And there's no way of tracing it back to its alleged owners in time. No way can we go haring around England asking merchants if they had a particular keg of Loire wine through Axmouth last month.'

As the woman brought them their food, Ralph Morin summed up their day's efforts. 'So we've been wasting our damned time, have we?'

'Not entirely, I hope,' replied the coroner, spearing a slice of cold meat with his eating knife. 'We've certainly made it clear to them that the law is breathing down their neck, but we're not going to get them hanged by looking at sheets of parchment and sniffing around their warehouses. They've got to be caught red-handed.'

Thomas watched with trepidation as the gap widened between the ship's side and the edge of the stone quay. Though he had been to sea only once before on a short journey between Portsmouth and the Isle of Wight, that had been more than sufficient to convince him that he was not cut out to be a sailor. He stood with the coroner and Gwyn on the raised part of the stern deck as the *Mary and Child Jesus* drifted slowly away from the wharf below Exeter's encircling wall. This rampart came across from the West Gate to the relatively new Watergate, punched through the wall in response to Exeter's burgeoning trade, which needed better access to its port. As they moved smoothly out, the city hovered above them, sloping up to Rougemont at the furthest and highest point. They passed a section of wall that climbed steeply up to the South Gate, and in minutes they were abeam of low cliffs that lined the eastern side of the Exe.

The shipmaster, Roger Watts, had waited until the morning flood tide was just at its highest before casting off, so that they could drift down on the ebb to the beginning of the estuary at Topsham and then catch some wind to help them the next few miles to the open sea. Thomas would have a couple of hours' respite on the smooth waters before he began wishing he was dead for the two- or three-day haul across the unforgiving waters between England and Normandy.

While de Wolfe was indifferent to sea voyages, having crossed many times to Ireland, France and various parts of the Mediterranean, Gwyn was in his element. Trading on his past life as a boy helping his fisherman father in Polruan, he set himself up as an authority on everything maritime and now gazed critically as two youths set the single sail to catch enough wind to give them steerage way in the narrow river. He found nothing to complain about, nor in the way that Roger Watts was handling the steering oar behind them, so he turned to John for a chat.

'Still no news of your goodwife, Crowner?' He could not stomach the woman, who treated him like dirt when she deigned to notice his existence, but he thought it politic to ask.

'Not a word!' growled de Wolfe. 'I'm letting her stew until we get back. No doubt she'll be at home by then.'

Thomas, who felt greatly relieved that the cog was not

yet rolling or pitching, offered some of his unfailing charity. 'No doubt the peace and quiet of Polsloe will calm her disturbed spirits after the upsetting times she has suffered lately, and I pray that she will return refreshed.'

John grunted in appreciation of his clerk's kind thoughts, but privately doubted that Thomas's prayers would improve Matilda's temper.

They stood for a while as they passed the small Priory of St James, with the poles of fish-traps protruding from the water. John remembered being called out the previous year, when a sturgeon was caught there and he had to confiscate its value for the king. The weather was holding well, and Roger Watts called to them from his steering position to forecast a rapid voyage.

'There's a fresh westerly wind which will blow us briskly up-Channel once we get out past Dawlish Warren,' he hollered. 'As long as it doesn't turn into a gale, that is!' he added, to Thomas's horror.

The mention of Dawlish once again set the wheels of John's mind in motion. The memory of that recent kiss and what might have come of it, had not Hilda exercised enough self-control for both of them, was branded into his soul and clashed with his guilt over Nesta, which in turn led paradoxically to his jealous concerns about leaving her for a couple of weeks in the company of the Welsh stonemason. As they glided down the river towards Topsham, his wandering mind was also triggered by the shipmaster's mention of Dawlish to the fact that this very ship under his feet was the scene of Thorgils' violent death and hence the cause of Hilda's widowhood. Though the vessel had been extensively refitted since then, his ready guilt sent his eyes searching the deck planking for non-existent bloodstains.

Shaking the mood off, he forced himself to watch the passing landscape, and when the busy little port of

Topsham had slid by he waited for Exmouth to appear
on the port side, just as they entered the open sea.
On the opposite bow, he recalled the spot where he
had come down to see the beached whale, and beyond
it in the distance he could just make out the village of
Dawlish, where the delectable Hilda was no doubt
spending her lonely life in her solar in Thorgils' fine
house.

Moments later he felt the first lurch as the cog
crossed the sand bar at the narrow mouth of the
estuary and rose to the first wave of the western ocean
as it swept along the coast into Lyme Bay. Immediately,
there was a groan from Thomas and a guffaw of merri-
ment from the unsympathetic Gwyn, who stood on the
deck with feet planted apart, like a rock glued to the
planks. 'Time for some food, little fellow!' he cackled.
'No doubt the ship's boy can fry you some fat pork on
that fire he has in the forecastle.'

The poor clerk tottered to the side and, with one
hand clutching his floppy broad-brimmed hat and the
other clamped to the rail, endlessly began reciting his
Hail Marys, with frequent pleas to God Almighty and
all His assorted saints to deliver him from the perils of
the sea.

Someone in heaven must have paid attention to the
clerk's supplications, for Thomas's ordeal was shorter
than he feared, due to the unfailingly favourable wind.
Also, after the first of the three-day voyage, he discovered that he did not feel so bad as he expected and
was even able to keep down some food and drink,
though not in the quantities that the five-man crew and
the two other passengers seemed to consume with such
obscene gusto. The cooking was done on a small wood-
fire, safely walled in with stones on a large slab of slate
in a cubbyhole under the rising bow, where the crew
slept in turns when not on watch. The passengers had
a low hutch near the stern, large enough for them to

squat in or lie down on straw-filled mattresses laid on the deck-boards.

De Wolfe and his officer spent much of the time on the afterdeck with Roger Watts or whoever was manning the steering oar. John wondered many times if they might be attacked by the pirates they sought, but for three days they never glimpsed so much as a distant sail, until they were within a few miles of the coast of Normandy. He was somewhat disappointed, but also recognised that two men and a timid priest would have been of little use in supporting the small crew against a gang of determined pillagers.

Their shipmaster, with twenty years of familiarity with these waters, made landfall within a dozen miles of Honfleur, a port on the southern side of the mouth of the Seine, encircled by low hills. When they sailed into the small harbour at the entrance of a stream, he put them ashore in the curragh, a small boat shaped like an elongated coracle, made from hides stretched over a light wicker framework that was kept lashed upside down over the hatch. Promising to be back at the same spot in seven days' time, unless the weather was against him, Roger Watts left straight away to catch the wind and tide for his onward journey.

As it was now late afternoon, the coroner decided to spend the night in Honfleur and, equipped with a parchment carrying the sheriff's seal which declared the king's coroner to be on official business, claimed a night's lodging for them in the small castle which protected the port. Advice from the commander led them next morning to requisition horses to take them to Rouen, rather than attempt to be ferried up the winding loops of the Seine on a small boat, as beyond the reach of the tides, progress would be slow and subject to the vagaries of the wind and current. The journey was about forty miles and obviously could not be covered within a day, especially given Thomas's poor horsemanship. They set off on an overcast morning and plodded the well-beaten track all day until they reached the village of Bourg-Achard, slightly over halfway. An uncomfortable night was spent in the only tavern, which housed a particularly savage species of bedbug, and they were only too ready to leave at dawn for the second leg of the journey. By afternoon they had reached the Seine opposite the city of Rouen, which was on the northern bank, but as there was no bridge over the wide river they had to wait for a ferry to take them and their horses across.

A disappointment awaited them at the castle when they reached the imposing structure at the centre of the bustling city, the capital of Normandy and effectively the seat of the King of England more than London or Winchester. After negotiating his way past several clerks and secretaries by the exhibition of Henry de Furnellis's warrant, de Wolfe reached one senior enough to tell him that the Chief Justiciar was not in the city but had left two days before to be with the king at some outpost about twenty miles up the Seine, at a place called Andeli. Again they were too late to set off that day but enjoyed better hospitality than the previous night, John having a bed in the knights' quarters, while Gwyn was happy to eat, drink and play dice in the garrison barracks. Thomas, ever keen to savour the religious life of new places, went to pray at the ancient church of St-Oeun and was invited by fellow priests to eat and sleep in their dorter, though much of his night was taken up with attendance at Matins and Prime.

The horses they had borrowed at Honfleur had also rested and fed well, and by the eighth hour they were again on the road running along the north bank of the Seine. The whole area showed the intense military activity that was now almost permanent, since King Richard had sailed from Portsmouth with his army and fleet of a hundred ships almost two years earlier.

Obsessed with regaining the territory that he had lost to Philip of France, largely through the treachery and incompetence of his brother John, the Lionheart had ranged up and down the length of France, steadily pushing back Philip's borders.

There had been some reversals, such as the attack on Dieppe, where Philip himself had led three hundred of his knights to ransack the town and burn ships in the harbour, but generally Richard's unceasing efforts were succeeding. As the coroner's trio rode southwards, they passed wagons full of equipment and supplies, much of it paid for by the taxes extorted from England. Troops of soldiers marched in both directions, many of them Welsh mercenaries who were the mainstay of the army, especially the archers. Others were foreigners, including some dreaded 'Brabancons', little better than bandits – and John had heard that the king had even employed some Saracens, so impressed had he been with their wild courage in Palestine.

'Where are we going to find Hubert Walter?' asked Gwyn when they were a dozen miles out of Rouen. 'If I remember him aright from the Holy Land, he may well be huddled in some tent with the common men-at-arms.'

'They said in Rouen that this place Andeli is little more than a village, so someone there will surely direct us to the King of England.'

And so it proved to be, when they reached a picturesque hamlet at the apex of a huge bend in the river, where white chalk cliffs broke through dense trees along the north bank. Men-at-arms were camping out at various spots, sitting around cooking fires or tending to their equipment. Mounted heralds and knights rode past between the village and a high eminence to the south, where a craggy ridge of cliff stood high above the river.

'That's where he'll be,' announced John confidently, and as they climbed a track busy with military traffic his guess was soon confirmed. Along a neck of land three hundred feet above the water below, they saw a collection of tents and pavilions bedecked with flags and banners and surrounded by the more mundane paraphernalia of an army camp. Sentries were posted at intervals along the approaches, but John's impressive appearance, aided by a display of the heavy red seal dangling from the sheriff's parchment, got them waved through each checkpoint. Several older men even recognised him as 'Black John' from the years he had spent campaigning under the Lionheart and his father, the equally fearsome King Henry. At the centre of the circle of canvas pavilions, the largest flew a red banner with three golden lions, and nearby was another with the episcopal flag of Canterbury.

'Best leave our mounts over there,' suggested Gwyn as they approached, pointing at makeshift stables of hurdles and poles, where a score of tethered horses were being fed and watered. Alongside, two farriers were shoeing other horses, and another pair of armourers were sharpening weapons on grindstones being turned by young boys. Though a truce with the French had been in force since January, it was a fragile peace, and the activity in the camp was a reminder that the potential front line was only a few miles down the road to the Vexin and Paris.

De Wolfe sought out the camp marshal, who turned out to be a grizzled old knight from Sussex, with whom he had campaigned in Ireland years before. After a few nostalgic reminders, the marshal, who was responsible for the organisation of the camp, arranged for the care of their horses, then took them to a mess tent, where to Gwyn's delight food and ale were in abundance. When they had eaten and John and the old campaigner had indulged in a few more reminiscences, the coroner explained why they had come chasing Hubert Walter across the Channel. 'I need to speak to him urgently, before he goes rushing off somewhere else. I don't have the time to go chasing him down to Aquitaine or Gascony!'

The marshal promised to send one of the clerks from the archbishop's ménage over to see him, and then stamped away to find a page who would guide de Wolfe to one of the larger tents where a number of knights were billeted.

'Your officer here can find a place with the sergeants,' he added, but then looked doubtfully at Thomas. 'I'm not sure what to do with a priest. Perhaps the archbishop's clerk can fix him up with the other shaven pates!'

Both John and Gwyn felt totally at home in this busy place, so redolent of the atmosphere and memories of the two decades in which they had fought their way around much of the known world. It was less attractive to the timid Thomas, though he relished the thought of being attached, albeit temporarily, to the retinue of the Primate of England, even though this particular archbishop was more of an administrator and soldier than a Vicar of God. As they waited for someone to fetch them, Gwyn stared around him with a frown. 'What in hell is our king doing here, camped on a bloody cliff miles from anywhere?'

De Wolfe looked into the distance with a practised military eye, scanning the great curve of the river as it flowed past the foot of the cliffs.

'Richard does nothing without a purpose, Gwyn. He's the best soldier the world has known since Alexander, so they say. I'll wager he's going to fortify this place to block the Seine against Philip Augustus.'

Eventually, a fat clerk came from the archbishop's tent and settled the three visitors in their various lodgings for the coming night. When John explained that he needed to see Hubert Walter about the murder of one of his new law officers, the cleric, who was a canon from St Albans, took the matter with the seriousness that it deserved.

'His Grace is fully occupied this evening, Sir John. He has many matters of grave importance concerning the financing of the campaign to discuss with the king and several of his major barons. But I am sure he will see you in the morning.'

Thankful for the prospect of a good night's rest after their continuous journeying for almost a week, John had another good meal in the early evening. Then he spent an hour or two spinning yarns of days gone by with several older warriors in the knights' quarters, before wrapping himself in his cloak and sleeping soundly on a hessian bag of hay purloined by a page from the stables. Gwyn had a similar orgy of reminiscence with the more senior men-at-arms, several of whom he had met in previous campaigns. As for Thomas, he was delighted to curl up in a corner of the administrator's marquee and eavesdrop on the conversations of several canons and archdeacons from Normandy and Poitou.

The morning was blasted alive by trumpets soon after dawn, and there was an hour of sleepy activity as fires were revived, food cooked and animals fed by the couple of hundred occupants of the clifftop camp. The fat canon, reluctantly seconded from the main court at Rouen, appeared at about the seventh hour and summoned de Wolfe to Hubert Walter's accommodation, a trio of connected tents and a circular canvas pavilion. He took Gwyn and Thomas with him, ignoring the disapproving expression of the canon at the sight of the big untidy Cornishman with wild red hair and drooping moustaches.

The Chief Justiciar was sitting in a folding chair behind a trestle table piled with parchments. A thin chaplain stood protectively behind him, and two clerks worked at a longer table on the far side of the tent. Hubert was a wiry man of medium height, his face lined and leathery, though he had not been on a field of battle since leaving Palestine several years earlier. Only his shaven tonsure betrayed him as a priest, as he wore a leather jerkin over a brown tunic, beneath which protruded legs encased in serge breeches, like any other fighting man. The sole token of his ecclesiastical rank was a small gold cross on a chain around his neck and the large ring of office on his finger.

When John entered, he rose with a smile of genuine pleasure and gestured to a clerk to bring the coroner a stool, which was set for him on the other side of the table. Gwyn and Thomas stood discreetly a few paces behind him, in respectful silence in the presence of this powerful man who virtually ruled England in the king's absence. It was conventional for all those who approached the Primate to kiss his ring, but in these military surroundings he made no move to offer his hand.

'Well, Black John, what brings you all this way? You only visit me when you want something!'

The tone was amiable, almost affectionate, as the two men had known and respected each other for some years, especially during the last Crusade. As John's shadow, Gwyn was also well known to Hubert, but de Wolfe went out of his way to introduce Thomas as his invaluable clerk, which made the little priest squirm with embarrassed pleasure to be noticed by the head of the English Church.

'How is that damned brother-in-law of yours behaving himself?' demanded Hubert, for the last time John had petitioned him was in relation to Richard de Revelle's latest misdemeanours and subsequent disgrace, which had been the cause of Matilda's final lapse into depression.

'He seems to have run out of escapades at the moment, as Prince John also seems to be keeping a low profile these days,' replied the coroner. 'For once, I have come to seek your advice and help on other matters – and indeed to bring you news of a disturbing breach of the law.'

For the next few minutes de Wolfe set out in his blunt fashion a catalogue of the events in east Devon, including the probability of Customs evasion and piracy, culminating in the murder of one of the Justiciar's new Keepers of the Peace.

'The man was one of your appointees, my lord, and, though a rather rash and impetuous fellow, did not deserve such a death, when he was only doing his duty on behalf of our king.'

Even with all the cares and responsibilities that were heaped upon him daily, Hubert Walter looked genuinely concerned at John's news. 'I never met de Casewold, though I recall his name amongst the lists of knights appointed to be Keepers last year,' he said grimly. 'He must be the first to be killed in the course of his duty. They were not intended to be physical enforcers of the law but rather to ensure that crimes were not ignored or tolerated, but always brought to justice.'

For a while they spoke of the significance of the death and the need to appoint a successor, as well as to increase the number of Keepers. The original plan was to install four in each county, but so far the total was far short of that target.

'And you think his killing was linked to this business in Axmouth?' The Justiciar sat with his hands planted firmly on the table, looking intently at de Wolfe.

'I do indeed, as he told me he was intent on tracking illicit goods coming out of that port,' answered John. 'Though we have so far failed to prove it, as I am sure they falsify their records, I'm convinced that they both evade the Customs duty on a large scale and also dispose of loot gained by piracy in the Channel, which is my main concern.'

He recounted the disappearance of a number of merchant vessels and the conviction of local shipmen that at least some of these were being deliberately pillaged, then sunk with all their crew.

'I have heard that the king has begun to build up a navy, based on his new harbour at Portsmouth. Surely one vital task for them would be to rid the seas of these murderous swine who prey on their fellow seamen?'

Hubert nodded slowly. 'It is true that King Richard has a great interest in creating a seaborne army and has already commissioned a number of ships. They are really merchant cogs with built-up castles at bow and stern and manned by fighting men and archers. But they are meant to be a support to his army, fighting the French both at sea and in attacks on their ports.'

'But surely some could patrol the south coast to discourage these vultures who prey on our ships?' growled de Wolfe.

Hubert lifted his hands in supplication. 'Money, John, it is always money! Each month our monarch demands more and expects me to find it every time. Ships are expensive, and to build more at present is beyond our means.' He waved an arm to encompass everything around them. 'Why do you think we are camped on this bloody hill, when we could be more comfortable back in Rouen's citadel? Because the king has now decided to build the strongest fortress in Europe here, mainly to spite Philip Augustus!' He shook his head in mock despair. 'And where am I going to get the money? By squeezing the barons and bishops even harder, on both sides of the Channel – and by grinding more taxes from every family in Richard's possessions. No wonder I am the most unpopular man in England!'

De Wolfe nodded sagely, pleased that his forecast about this site was correct. 'It is certainly a perfect place to dominate the Seine and the surrounding countryside,' he said admiringly.

The Justiciar smiled wryly. 'The problem is that we do not own the land here. It is part of a manor belonging to the Archbishop of Rouen, who has taken great exception to Richard's plans. He has placed Normandy under a religious interdict over the issue and appealed to the Pope, but no doubt we can buy him off, if only we can raise the money.'

'But you are not actually fighting at the moment?' asked John.

'No. Both sides are having a respite after a treaty signed at Louviers in January, in which Richard ceded the Vexin to Philip but recovered other lands previously lost. But it can't last and that's why I'm here, God help me! The king summoned me from Winchester to demand more money and troops, as he intends to break the treaty before long and recover the Vexin. In fact, building a castle here is in direct defiance of that treaty, and I'm sure our royal master is doing it to provoke Philip back into conflict.' The Vexin was a small county north-west of Paris, over which the two kings had long been wrangling like a pair of dogs with a bone.

They talked for a while longer, but de Wolfe was getting the sense that, though Hubert Walter was sympathetic to his problems, he was already too over-stretched financially to be able to do much to help him. They continued talking about ways to police the Devon ports more effectively, but there was no way in which Hubert could commit more troops to that far west province, given the desperate need for every available man to rally to the royal standard in France. Neither did there seem much hope of diverting part of the small navy to patrol the coast to discourage piracy.

He was beginning to despair at the largely wasted journey they had made when a diversion occurred, one that was of great significance to the coroner's trio – and one that was to change the life of the coroner himself. There was a trumpet blast and then a commotion outside. A moment later a tall figure marched into Hubert's pavilion, followed by a trio of barons and scurrying pages and squires. Over six feet in height with broad shoulders and perhaps a little too much weight around his chest and belly for a man of thirty-eight, Richard Coeur de Lion had a mane of reddish-gold hair, which though shaved up at the back and sides was thick and wavy. Dressed in most un kingly garments – a white linen shirt open at the neck and a pair of thick woollen hose pushed into riding boots – he radiated a regal presence that was like a blast of hot wind gusting into the tent. Supremely confident to the point of arrogance, he exuded energy, enthusiasm and impatience in equal degrees. He marched into the centre of the space and stood with his long arms akimbo, his big fists jammed on to his broad leather belt.

'By God's guts, it's true! I had heard that Black John was here!'

A startled de Wolfe dropped to one knee and bowed his head before his king, as did Gwyn and Thomas behind him, but Richard bellowed for them to rise and then, as John clambered to his feet, grabbed him and briefly hugged him to his chest. 'And Gwyn, you old rogue, still drinking and wenching, no doubt!' He gave the beaming Cornishman an affectionate punch on the arm. Loyally, the coroner dragged the bemused little priest forward. 'And this is my clerk, Thomas de Peyne, who has done great service in your name, sire. He reads and writes like Aristotle. I would be lost without him.'

The Lionheart, who unusually for a king was highly literate himself, rested a hand on the speechless clerk's shoulder. 'You must be either an angel or a martyr, Thomas, to endure the moods of this terrible master!'

Hubert Walter came around his table and joined the group in the middle of the floor, surrounded by the deferential circle of retainers, one of whom was William Marshal, Earl of Pembroke, another of John's old campaign comrades.

'Sire, de Wolfe has travelled from Devon with various tidings, seeking help about various transgressions of the law. One of the new Keepers of the Peace which you suggested we appointed in the counties has been murdered, amongst other problems.'

He briefly outlined what de Wolfe had told him, and Richard listened intently, with the concentration of a man who could hold a dozen problems in his mind at a time and deliver almost instant solutions with supreme confidence.

'He must have more help, Hubert! More men-at-arms in Exeter, more Keepers, and this piracy must be combated by my new navy.'

The Justiciar was used to Richard's snap judgements, which were often not backed up by resources. There was no point in arguing about it and pointing out that if the king was willing to dispatch soldiers and ships – and the money to pay for them – from Normandy to distant Devonshire, then his wishes could be carried out.

Hubert nodded blandly. 'I will see what can be done, sire. Meanwhile, we have much to discuss concerning the state of your Exchequer.'

His broad hint that he needed to clear the tent to get down again to the reasons for his being here was interrupted by two breathless pages hurrying in with trays of wine. One bent his knee to the king and offered a large silver chalice, then passed around to give the barons and senior clerics pewter goblets. One of these came to de Wolfe, though the lesser mortals were ignored until Richard yelled at a page to give wine to Gwyn and Thomas.

'These are our guests, who have braved the seas to visit me,' he boomed in his deep voice. 'They serve Sir John here, who did his best to save me from those bastards in Austria a few years back!'

De Wolfe's conscience forced him to speak, his voice hoarse with rare emotion. He dropped again to one knee before his king. 'I failed you then, sire, and the memory has plagued me ever since. I ask for your forgiveness, as I should have been there to prevent you from being taken.'

Richard put a hand under the coroner's armpit and hauled him to his feet. 'For Christ's sake, John, you have nothing with which to reproach yourself! If anyone was at fault, it was me! Fool that I was, I should not have flashed my coins so freely in that bloody tavern and should have hidden those gold rings from my fingers – no wonder it was obvious that I was no ordinary traveller!'

'But I should have stayed at your side and fought for you, not left you alone, sire!'

The king gave him a playful but heavy punch on the shoulder. 'What could you have done, except shed your blood uselessly on the ground? That pox-ridden mayor burst in with a score of soldiers – even I was not going to take on that many.'

Hubert Walter was becoming restive at the thought of all the work that needed to be done, and with a heavy sigh of resignation the king abandoned his reminiscences.

'Get you gone, John de Wolfe, and rest your mind easy! You have always been a staunch and loyal support to me and you have nothing whatsoever to regret. I wish that every man in my service was as steadfast as you.'

With this tribute ringing in his ears, the coroner and

everyone else bowed their heads as the Lionheart stalked out to return to his own pavilion, followed by the Justiciar, his clerks and the whole retinue of major players.

His conscience cleared for the first time in four years, John felt light-headed at the praise that Christendom's greatest monarch had just laid upon him. As they walked back to the mess tent, his feet hardly seemed to touch the ground and even the imperturbable Gwyn was grinning from ear to ear at the reflected glory that he had shared. As for Thomas, he felt drunk with elation, a sensation he had never experienced before. To actually be in the presence of Richard Coeur de Lion was awesome in itself, but for the great man to speak directly to him in such an amiable fashion was like a dream. Once again he felt a deep affection for the coroner for so pointedly bringing him and his talents to the notice of both the archbishop and the king.

In the mess tent, where some were still breaking their fast and others just quenching their thirsts, Gwyn collected a couple of jars of ale and a mug of cider for Thomas. Both beverages were there in abundance, as an army marching on its stomach needs more than just solid food.

'So what do you think of that, young Thomas?' asked his master as they squatted on the straw-strewn ground.

'I can die content, Crowner, after having met our king and the archbishop. Thank you, sir, for your kind words that brought me to their attention.'

'You were damned fortunate to catch Richard in a good mood, Thomas!' cackled Gwyn. 'He can be terrifying when he is out of sorts or in a temper!'

Inquisitive as ever, the clerk wanted to know more about the dramatic capture of the Lionheart on the way home from the Crusade. 'Is it true that you and Gwyn were part of his bodyguard?' he prompted.

'We were almost all that was left of it at the end!' grunted Gwyn, but it was de Wolfe who took up the tale, his recent euphoria making him unusually talkative.

'As Richard had fallen out with almost every monarch in Europe, it was difficult to find a safe way back to England from Palestine. Philip, Henry and Count Raymond blocked any chance of getting through France, Italy or Germany, and the ocean beyond the Pillars of Hercules was too dangerous in winter. So he decided to sail up the Adriatic and head for the lands of his brother-in-law, Henry the Lion, in north-east Germany or perhaps visit King Bela in Hungary.'

De Wolfe stopped to drink some ale, his mind far away in the winter at the end of December 1192. 'At Corfu we left the great ship that had brought us from Jaffa and took two galleys up the coast of Dalmatia and Istria, taking only a few of the knights and nobles with us. A storm drove us ashore in the wrong place, near Aquileia,* but we bought horses and began riding through hostile country. Some bastard spy of Count Meinhard of Gotz spotted us and a host pursued us and captured eight of our knights, but the rest of us eluded them and we eventually reached Friesach in the Bishopric of Salzburg, where another six of our company were seized.'

He shook his head sadly at the memory. 'Now only three of us were left with the king, myself, Gwyn and a knight, William L'Etang.'

Gwyn leant forward and added more to the tale. 'But we rode like hell, hoping to get across into the safe territory of Hungary. But not knowing exactly where we were, we strayed into Austria and when cold and hunger drove us each night to seek shelter we ended up in the early evening at an inn at a village called Erdberg.'

* Near Trieste.

De Wolfe waved his empty pot at a page and while waiting for a refill continued Gwyn's account.

'It was snowing and we couldn't understand a bloody word of their lingo, but it seemed the alehouse had no food for us. We needed fresh horses for next day, as ours were exhausted with the pace we kept up in the mountains, so L'Etang went out seeking food in the village, and Gwyn and I scoured the place trying to buy three decent mounts.'

Thomas was agog with the excitement of this royal drama. 'And the king was left alone in the tavern?'

John nodded as the servant brought a jug to fill his tankard. 'We heard later that he was unwise enough to offer the landlord too much money if he would find victuals for us – and probably let him see the gold in his purse. That, with the heavy gold rings that Richard wore, made the bastard suspicious, as this was the land of Leopold of Austria and the village was actually within the city limits of Vienna. The mayor turned up with a heavy guard and seized the king. We got back just in time to see him being hustled away. They took him to a castle on a crag above the Danube – Durnstein, I think it was called – where he was shut in a cell for months.'

'So what happened to you?' asked Thomas, his mouth agape with fascination at this saga.

'There was nothing we could do, so we melted away into the countryside and within a few days managed to ride the few miles east into Hungary, where we told our story and were received sympathetically. We were taken down to Zara on the Adriatic and eventually back to Corfu, where we met up with a Templar ship that took us to Malta and then back to Plymouth, when the sailing season began again in the spring.'

The story told, each man fell into a reverie, John and Gwyn thinking back to those momentous days and Thomas's fertile imagination reconstructing the adventure in his mind.

Eventually, Gwyn stirred himself to get some bread, cheese and more ale and when he returned asked what they were going to do next.

'There seems little that Hubert Walter will or can do for us,' he muttered. 'But at least we have made the position clear to him. The king has ordered him to put anything we need at our disposal, but that is an empty command if there is nothing to back it up.'

'Maybe one or two ships from Portsmouth may be told to keep an eye out for piracy,' said Thomas hopefully.

'The chances of one such vessel coming across an attack in progress along several hundred miles of coast line are about as likely as you getting married, little man!' scoffed Gwyn.

'Gwyn is right about that,' agreed de Wolfe. 'But there may be a way of reducing the odds, and I intend to put it into practice as soon as we get home.' He rose to his feet as he spoke. 'And get home we must, as soon as possible. The *Mary and Child Jesus* is due back in Honfleur in three days from now, God and the weather willing, which will give us time for an easy ride back there if we leave today.'

They agreed to saddle up after noontime dinner and ride back to Rouen to spend the night in the citadel. Until the food was ready, John and Gwyn went off for a walk around the rocky promontory to see where the Lionheart was intending to build his massive fortress to defy Philip Augustus. John had learnt from his old friend the marshal that the king intended to add insult to injury by calling it 'Château Gaillard', which roughly meant 'Saucy Castle'.

Thomas had gone off to a pavilion set up by the camp chaplains as a place of worship where Mass was celebrated twice each day, so the coroner and his officer were surprised to see him hurrying after them only a few minutes after they had parted. The clerk panted up to them as they stood in the coarse grass on a ledge high above the Seine.

'Crowner, you are wanted back in the camp at once,' he gasped. 'The Justiciar's clerk came looking for you and told me to find you. You must go to the king's pavilion at once!'

'Did he say for what reason?' demanded John, already moving towards the camp.

With Gwyn trundling along in the rear, Thomas was fairly dancing with excitement. 'He said the archbishop and the king wished to speak to you, master! Maybe they have come to some decision about our problems in Axmouth?'

But for once the clever little priest was wrong. When de Wolfe emerged from the royal tent half an hour later, his long, usually sallow face was flushed and his mind was racing to encompass the significance of what he had been told when in the royal presence.

CHAPTER TEN

In which Crowner John imparts momentous news

Though Gwyn was phlegmatically patient about learning whatever had been discussed or commanded in the king's quarters, Thomas was almost bursting with curiosity, for the coroner's grave demeanour since he had returned was such that obviously something of great significance had occurred. He could hardly ask his master outright what had taken place, and his hints were ignored by a very silent and thoughtful de Wolfe as they packed their few belongings into their saddlebags and set off back down the hill to Andeli and then along the river track towards Rouen.

After an hour's trotting, during which time the coroner had not said a word, he slowed his rounsey to a walking pace and motioned to the others to come up alongside him.

'This is something which concerns you both – or may well do, for it will be your choice as to how you wish to act.'

The clerk felt a chill run up his spine, for his devotion to the coroner was profound and this sounded ominously like the possibility of the end of their association. 'Is it bad news, Crowner?' he asked tremulously.

De Wolfe stared blankly at the dusty track ahead of

them. 'It depends on how you look at it, Thomas. The king wishes me to leave Exeter and go to London, certainly for a year and possibly longer.'

This stirred Gwyn into speech. 'But you are the coroner for Devon! Why does he want you to give that up? What will you do in London?'

'The same task, but in a different guise. It would mean travelling all over England, though London would be the base.'

'I don't understand, sir!' said Thomas, miserable at the thought of losing his master and his job.

John took pity on the sadness in the faithful little clerk's voice and began to explain. 'Coroners have jurisdiction over fixed areas, which are the counties of England – and Normandy, come to that. A problem has arisen in that the king's court is always on the move and if some untoward event occurs, such as a murder, then before the local coroner and sheriff have a chance to sort it out, the whole entourage has moved on out of their jurisdiction.'

Gwyn looked at him blankly. 'What has that got to do with us – or, rather, you, Crowner?'

'Here in Normandy, the king has appointed a knight as his own coroner, to deal with all cases amongst the hundreds of people who cluster around him to form his court. When he moves, as he does incessantly, the coroner moves with him, as does "the Verge" a twelve-mile zone around the court within which the coroner's power is paramount. Now the king and Hubert Walter want to set up the same system in England.'

'But the king is not in England,' objected Thomas reasonably.

'Not at the moment, but he will be one day. And in any case there is a large court based on London and Winchester consisting of his barons, judges, clerks and God knows how many hangers-on that perambulate up and down the country. Hubert Walter is at the head of it, but there is a flock of bishops and earls and dukes, all with their chaplains and knights and squires and pages, to say nothing of the scores of lesser servants they gather around them. Add to that the foreign emissaries and ambassadors that plague them, then you have a crowd the size of a small town.'

It was true that the wanderings of a king or even a prominent baron or bishop was a massive and cumbersome operation, with carts and wagons to transport their wives and families, their arms, documents and even furniture, as they moved from city to city or manor to manor. The descent of a monarch or baron upon a local lord could be a financial disaster for him, as he would be expected to house and feed his unwanted guests for as long as they deigned to stay.

'And now King Richard wants you to be the first court coroner,' said the perceptive Thomas.

'I was the first Devon coroner and it seems he and the Justiciar have been content with my performance of my duties, so they wish me to move to London.' John modestly omitted the fulsome praise that the king had heaped upon him, partly to soften the command, for that was what it amounted to, rather than a request.

'And you agreed?' asked Gwyn bluntly. He was very unsure where this left him and Thomas.

De Wolfe grinned wryly. 'One does not agree or disagree with a king, especially when that king is Richard Coeur de Lion!' he replied. 'I swore fealty to his father when I was knighted and that allegiance applies equally to the son. If he says I must go to London, then to London I will go.'

There was silence for another score of hoof-beats on the hard earth until Thomas ventured the big question. 'And what of us, Sir John?'

That question was not fully answered until the *Mary and Child Jesus* was once more gliding up on the flood tide of the River Exe towards the quayside she had left over two weeks earlier.

'We have a month yet before I ride for London,' said John as they watched the twin towers of the cathedral slowly rise above the high banks. 'Hubert wants this Axmouth problem dealt with before I leave.'

'This whole idea was the Justiciar's, I suspect,' growled Gwyn.

John nodded. 'The king is usually led by him in matters concerning the government of England, for Richard is too absorbed by his problems across the Channel. This idea of a "Coroner of the Verge" is but an experiment of Hubert's. If it proves to be unnecessary, he will abandon it after a year and I'll come back to Devon.'

During the long journey back from Rouen, they had agreed that Gwyn and Thomas would accompany him to his new appointment. Gwyn was married with two children, but as he had spent much of the past twenty years away on campaigns with de Wolfe, being absent in London would be no great hardship, especially as John had promised that he could ride home every three months for a visit. Thomas, who was Hampshire born, had no ties to the West Country and was quite content to go to the great city, especially as there would be frequent opportunities to visit the twin capital of Winchester, where he had been a minor canon until his fall from grace several years earlier. His concern had been that he would lose his ecclesiastical sinecure in Exeter, but Hubert Walter had assured John that he would find some similar post for him in London.

With his officer and clerk, if not exactly enthusiastic, at least resigned to the move, it was John himself who faced the greatest dilemma. He had a house, a wife, a partnership, a maid, a dog and a mistress in Exeter, not to mention the attractions of a beautiful former lover in Dawlish. There was no question of his refusing the king's command, but what in hell was he to do about his private life?

As Roger Watts coaxed the prow of the cog around to put the larboard side to the bank, the crew broke into an unmelodious version of the hymn 'Praise to the Good Christ and the Kind Virgin', the traditional seaman's chant sung all over Europe in thanks for a safe end to a voyage. Soon, the coroner's trio felt the strange sensation of solid ground under their feet, and with an agreement with Gwyn to meet in the Bush at dusk they parted at the Watergate to go their various ways. John walked up through the town, quieter at this time in the mid-afternoon, but to him still bustling compared with the solitude of the ship, which with unhelpful winds had taken five days to get from Honfleur. He reached his house in Martin's Lane, and as he pushed open the heavy street door he wondered if he would miss its dour familiarity when he left Exeter. Inside, he listened for voices, but there was only silence. Raising the latch of the inner door to the hall, he peered around the draught screens and saw that it was empty and that the fire was unlit. Even though it was now late April, Mary usually kept logs burning for another month.

John went back into the vestibule and was rewarded by the sound of padding feet as Brutus came around the corner from the passage at the side of the house and advanced on him, tail swishing and head low to the ground in affectionate greeting.

Fondling his big head, he looked up and saw Mary standing at the corner, regarding him with a mixture of relief and anxiety. 'You're back from your gallivanting, then?' she said pertly, then came nearer and planted a kiss on his cheek. 'There's food and drink in my kitchen. You look as if you need it – and a good wash and a shave!'

She fried him onions with 'chitterlings' – sausages

made from a pig's intestine stuffed with chopped pork and offal – followed by bread slathered in beef dripping. Washed down with rough cider, it was a welcome change from the endless thin stew boiled in a cauldron on the rolling ship. As he ate, seated on a stool in her hut, she stood against the doorpost watching him with concern.

'Well, woman, tell me all about it,' he said eventually. 'I can see she's not here. Is there any news of her yet?'

Mary shook her thick dark hair, free of the headscarf she wore outside the house. 'Not a word from her directly, no! But her cousin in Fore Street sent a servant to collect all her clothes, which it seems your wife has said she can have. They are much of a size, so she can get them altered to fit.'

The cook-maid said this with an air of defiance, as if it proved her own conviction that her mistress would never return. 'And a groom from Polsloe came with orders to take her chest from the solar back to the priory.'

This was Matilda's strongbox, in which she kept her brooches and rings, as well as the money which arrived each quarter-day from the lawyer who doled out instalments of the bequest from her dead father. It certainly looked as if his wife was taking this escape into a nunnery more seriously than she had last time.

Suddenly, Mary's bravado evaporated and she came to kneel at John's side, her hand gripping his arm.

'What's to become of me, John? I've been alone in this house for over two weeks. The mistress will never come home now, and that Lucille has gone to serve her brother's wife. Am I to be thrown out into the street if you sell this house and go elsewhere?'

Strong woman though she was, she was near to tears and de Wolfe slid a comforting arm around her. 'You'll never want for a place, Mary! There are big changes coming in my life, but you must never fear for your future. For now, keep on as you are, feeding me and my old hound. In a month or so I may be going up to London for a long while. But Thomas and Gwyn will be with me, and it may be that you too might follow us there, if you so wished.'

He explained what had gone on in Normandy, and she listened in wonderment at the possibility of going to the country's new capital, having hardly been outside Exeter in her life.

'But what of the mistress?' she asked, concerned even though Matilda had always treated her with near contempt.

John shrugged. 'It's up to her. She's my wife, but if she prefers to spend the rest of her life on her knees in that dismal priory, the choice is hers.'

When he had finished eating he took Mary's advice, and in a leather bucket of warm water that she heated for him he washed his face and upper half, using a lump of soap made from goat tallow, soda and beech-ash. Then he scraped his black stubble with a small knife he kept honed to the best edge he could manage and put on a clean grey tunic that the maid had washed for him while he was away.

Feeling uncomfortably clean, he made his way up to the castle, where he went straight to tell his tale to Henry de Furnellis. The old sheriff was most concerned at the prospect of losing de Wolfe to London, and John suspected that part of his anxiety was that he might have to exert himself more if his active colleague went away.

'So who is going to take your place?' he demanded. 'Was Hubert as quick to suggest a replacement as he was to snatch you away?'

'He did mention Sir Richard de Revelle as a possibility,' said John with a straight face.

The sheriff looked apoplectic for a moment until he

realised that his friend was being facetious. 'Don't make that sort of joke, John, please!' he growled. 'Many a word spoken in jest has a nasty habit of coming true!'

De Wolfe grinned and shook his head. 'Don't fret, Henry, the Justiciar would cut out his own tongue rather than recommend my dear brother-in-law for any position other than hanging from a gallows-tree! But he did have a suggestion which is worth considering.'

De Furnellis looked at John suspiciously. 'Who would that be, then?'

'Someone we both admire for his courage. Sir Nicholas de Arundell, who we helped not long ago.'

The sheriff's bushy eyebrows rose. 'Nick o' the Moors? Yes, I suppose he'd do well, a brave knight and a Crusader like yourself. That's if he wants the job?'

De Arundell was lord of the small manor of Hempston Arundell near Totnes, and John had been instrumental in restoring him to his lands at the same time that Matilda's brother fell into worse disgrace than usual.*

'Well, you'll soon find out if he'll take it, Henry, for the Justiciar wants you to approach him about it. And if it fails, find someone else suitable, for I'll be off in a few weeks, as soon as we get this Axmouth problem settled.'

This led him to describe his talks with Hubert Walter and the king himself, which prompted the sheriff to offer an opinion similar to his own.

'Plenty of good wishes, but damn-all action! Typical of politicians – all wind and no water.'

John felt himself trying to defend the archbishop. 'He's desperate for money; the king's French campaigns take every penny Hubert can raise. I doubt they could afford to divert even a single ship from the

---

* See *The Noble Outlaw*.

Portsmouth fleet to run up and down the coast to seek pirates.'

De Furnellis nodded his reluctant acceptance of the realities of life 'I suppose it would be a hell of a coincidence if a naval ship happened upon a pirate in the act of pillaging another vessel. So what do we do about it?'

John leant across the table and began to outline the plan that he had in mind.

That evening, just as the sun was setting on a fine late-April day, the coroner strode down Smythen Street and turned into Idle Lane. The Bush Inn stood before him, its new thatch glowing in the evening light, but he viewed it with some foreboding. More than a fortnight had passed since he had seen Nesta, and, as with his wife, his frequent and often prolonged absences were always a source of irritation and recrimination to his mistress. This time there was the added spectre of a handsome young Welshman to be reckoned with. John had no doubt that Nesta would have imported Owain from St John's Hospital to stay at the Bush, as she had promised.

He pushed open the door and ducked his head under the lintel to enter the room, which occupied the whole ground floor. The atmosphere was clearer than usual, as in this weather only a small fire glowed in the central pit and there was little eye-stinging smoke to filter out under the eaves. The remaining odour was the usual mixture of spilt ale, cooking and sweat, as Nesta forbade the usual pissing into the rushes that covered the floor but drove her patrons out to perform against the fence in the back yard.

Gwyn was already seated at the table near the firepit and John settled on the bench opposite, where Edwin immediately brought him a jar of ale. Even allowing for his ghastly blind eye, the old potman looked more

shifty than usual and hurried away without waiting
to gossip.

'What's wrong with him tonight?' grunted de Wolfe.
'And where's Nesta?'

The Cornishman looked slightly uncomfortable.
'Edwin says they are in the brew-shed, seeing to the
latest tub of mash.'

John looked at him suspiciously. 'What d'you mean –
"they"?'

Gwyn stared down into his half-empty quart pot.
'Seems young Owain is making himself helpful, now
that his wound is all but healed.' He looked up and saw
with relief that the back door had opened. 'Here they
are now, coming back in.'

Nesta made her way across the crowded bar-room
and stood at the end of the trestle table, looking down
at de Wolfe. Her face was slightly flushed, but he
thought she looked prettier than ever.

'John, welcome back! How is Cathay or Egypt or
wherever kept you away for so long?'

Her tone was light and accompanied by a smile, but
he caught its undercurrent of sarcasm. Reaching up,
he grasped her arm and pulled her down on the
bench alongside him. Was it his fancy or did he sense a
certain resistance to this familiar act? He slipped an
arm around her shoulders and bent to kiss her. Nesta
offered her cheek willingly enough, but not her lips.

'Two weeks and she's forgotten me already?' he
said in a semi-bantering fashion to Gwyn. 'Maybe she
doesn't recognise me with this fresh shave and a clean
tunic?'

His officer grinned weakly, for old Edwin had been
whispering in his ear before John had arrived and he
was uneasy. History seemed to be repeating itself, he
thought.

De Wolfe was conscious of someone hovering at the
side of him and looked up to see Owain ap Gronow

standing there, looking far too handsome for his liking. He wore a sleeveless leather tunic belted over a shirt and on his bare right arm there was a linen bandage. The craftsman flexed this arm before John's eyes and beamed guilelessly at the coroner.

'Sir John, welcome back! I am almost healed and have been carving stone for almost a week now. I give thanks to God every night for you rescuing me from those villians on the high road.'

Nesta waved him down to sit alongside Gwyn, though John would have preferred to have had Nesta to himself, as he knew that his officer would soon take the hint and leave. 'I am glad to hear that there were no ill effects upon your work with a hammer and chisel,' he said rather grudgingly. 'So when will your labours be finished, so that you can return home?'

The open-faced Welshman seem to read no hidden meaning in John's words.

'It will be a number of weeks yet, for there is much to do. Though the present cathedral was begun only eighty years ago, some of the carvings have already suffered badly from weather, wear and tear.'

He looked across at Nesta with a smile. 'Yet I am so comfortable in this lodging that I feel no longing yet to return to Wales. Everyone is so kind and hospitable to me, I feel quite at home here.'

This was not what de Wolfe wanted to hear and he looked down at Nesta and gave her a proprietary hug to emphasise their relationship.

Gwyn, looking increasingly uneasy, clambered to his feet and tapped Owain on the shoulder. 'Let's leave these lovebirds to themselves. We'll go up to the Crown Inn in Fore Street and I'll buy you a quart or two. It's poor ale, but afterwards you'll appreciate the brew in the Bush all the more.'

Though the stonemason seemed reluctant to leave, Gwyn hauled him out.

When they had vanished, John turned again to his mistress. 'And what have you been doing while I've been risking my life on the high seas?' His manner was bantering, but she sensed the suspicion in his voice.

'What I always do, John. Chase my servants, cook a little, clean a little – and worry about where you are, if you are alive, dead or in some other woman's arms!'

She, too, strained to be light-hearted, but they both knew they were trying to disguise their real concerns, feeling more like two swordsmen feinting and parrying before the fight began in earnest.

'What of this Welshman – he seems to have settled in very well?' He just managed to stop himself say 'too well'.

'He is a nice man, John. Pleasant and honest and full of gratitude for what we have done for him – especially you and Gwyn.'

De Wolfe gave one of his grunts, his stock response when he could think of nothing useful to say.

'But you, John! Tell me all your news. Did you see the Justiciar?'

His tale was greatly enhanced in her ears when he described meeting not only Hubert Walter but King Richard himself. Nesta seemed delighted when he told her of the absolution that the Lionheart had given him over the Vienna fiasco, as she had long known of John's recriminations about his failure to protect his sovereign. He also recounted the weak promises that he had received about helping to rid the coast of piracy and the crimes in and around Axmouth, but something made him delay telling Nesta about the royal command to leave Devon for London. Intuitively, he knew that this was not the right moment to break the news, and he reminded himself to warn Gwyn and Thomas to keep quiet about it for the time being.

Inevitably, the next question was about Matilda, but

it transpired that Nesta knew just as much – or as little – as John did himself.

'I met your maid Mary at the butcher's stall some days ago and she told me that there was little news of Matilda, apart from the fact that she had removed her clothes and money chest from the house,' she said. 'Your wife seems really serious about withdrawing from the world, John. What have you done to her this time?'

Like Mary, there was a censorious edge to her voice. All these women stuck together like glue, he thought sourly.

'Nothing new, *cariad*,' he said aloud. 'You know well enough that she's known of our affair for several years, so there was no novelty there to drive her away. It was her brother's behaviour that tipped her over the edge, just as it did a year ago. She thought so highly of him for so long that to find yet again that he was a grasping, cheating villain and then a coward into the bargain was the straw that broke the camel's back.'

She pressed herself a little more closely against his side and put a hand on his arm. 'So what's to become of you, John? And what's to become of us?'

He sighed and held up his hands, palms upward. 'I still need to talk to my good friend John de Alençon about the possibility of an annulment if Matilda does indeed stay in that priory. But I am not hopeful that the marriage bonds can be broken.'

Nesta moved away from him a little and looked up into his face, her big eyes serious. 'It would make no difference, John. We can never be wed to each other, you know that. We have ploughed that furrow so often.'

De Wolfe did not answer her directly. Instead, he reached for her hand and held it between his long fingers. 'If I were to go away for good, leaving Exeter and indeed Devon itself, would you come with me?'

She looked at him in surprise. 'Why do you say these foolish things, John? You are the king's coroner here.

You have a grand position, a house and a wife. You cannot just leave!'

Her instant dismissal of the possibility made him drop the subject. He had hoped that she might say that she would follow him to the ends of the earth, but although Nesta had always been the more romantic and sentimental of them tonight she clung to practicalities. After a long silence, she excused herself to attend to her supervision of the two cook-maids out in the kitchen-shed and John was left alone to his ale and his worries.

When she came back, he broached a familiar topic. 'With Matilda away, I am alone in the house,' he began. 'My bed is cold and lonely, so I thought I might seek a night's lodging here.' He looked meaningfully at the wide ladder that climbed to the loft and Nesta's small bedchamber. He tried to ignore the fact that a certain Welsh artisan would be occupying a palliasse on the other side of the thin partition.

However, his concerns were irrelevant, as Nesta, with a sudden flushing of her cheeks, shook her head. 'The phase of the moon is against us tonight, John, if you know what I mean.'

He knew well enough what she meant, but after some rapid calculation in his mind he wondered if she was telling the truth or whether she needed to seek an apothecary.

CHAPTER ELEVEN

In which Crowner John devises a plan

Next day John broke his usual routine by avoiding his chamber in Rougemont's gatehouse and, instead, again rode a borrowed rounsey up to Polsloe. This time he was more forthright with the taciturn porter and demanded that he would go and ask Dame Madge if she would speak to him. He lingered on the porch of the priory building for a few moments, until the gaunt sister appeared. The angular Benedictine was dressed in her usual black habit and veil, with a white coif and wimple framing her long face. Her front was protected by a white apron carrying some smears that looked suspiciously like fresh blood. Ignoring the scowls of the gatekeeper, who was peremptorily dismissed by the nun, John followed her into a vestibule where there were a couple of benches against a bare wall, a staircase going up to the prioress's parlour above and a corridor disappearing into the recesses of the ground floor. Sitting down together, he began without any preamble.

'I have been abroad for several weeks, sister, and need to know what the situation is with my wife. I know that she has already disposed of her personal belongings and had her money chest brought here. Am I never to see her or speak to her again?'

Dame Madge looked at him sympathetically. 'You

239

have not been a good husband, Sir John, as everyone in the county is aware,' she said with a wry smile. 'But I also realise that our sister Matilda cannot have been the easiest person in the world to get along with. Her arrival here once more is the culmination of years of disappointment and anguish, which has come to a head mainly because of the well-known behaviour of her brother – though you are by no means exonerated because of that!' she added sternly.

'But can I see her and discuss this with her?' pleaded de Wolfe. 'She did this once before and caused me great concern – then calmly returned home as if nothing had happened!'

The nun shook her head emphatically. 'If it were up to me, you could certainly visit her. But she has given strict instructions that she will see no one from outside this house. I, and indeed the prioress, must abide by that decision.'

Frustrated, John cast about for some other means of communicating with Matilda, if only to get some clue as to her intentions. 'If I were to get a letter written to her, could someone here read it to her?' he asked earnestly. He thought that Thomas could write something at his dictation and one of the literate sisters here could give her the gist of its contents.

Dame Madge shrugged her bony shoulders. 'You are welcome to send one, Crowner – but whether she will be willing to receive it will be up to her.'

John made one last attempt. 'How long would it be before she makes a final decision about taking the veil?' he asked. 'I am soon leaving Exeter for London on the king's business, possibly for a long time. I need to know what to do about my personal affairs: for example, do I keep my house here, if she is never to emerge from Polsloe?'

The nun sighed. 'I see that you have many problems, too. All I can promise is that I will tell Matilda what you have said, and if she has any change of heart I will send you a message.'

There was little more to be gained by staying, and with thanks to the helpful old sister he trotted back to the city little the wiser for his visit. His first stop was the castle gatehouse, where he had his second breakfast with Gwyn and Thomas, sharing a fresh loaf and a slab of hard cheese, washed down with ale and cider.

He interrogated his clerk about one pressing problem. 'Thomas, I asked you some time ago to discover if any of your religious books in the cathedral library – or if any of your clerical friends – had any notion about a marriage being annulled if one partner entered a religious order. Did you learn anything of that matter?'

The little clerk shook his head sadly. 'I pored over every text of canon law that I could find, Crowner. But I found nothing helpful, nor did my acquaintances in the cathedral have any better information to offer. Everything that was written about the dissolution of a marriage confirmed that it is almost impossible to achieve, except on grounds of consanguinity or impotence.'

He looked crestfallen at being unable to help his master in his hour of need.

De Wolfe grunted. 'Neither of those last grounds could be invoked, not after seventeen years of marriage! Could not a Papal Legate or even the Pope himself grant a dissolution, if he was pressed?'

Thomas grimaced. 'I fear such elevated manoeuvres are reserved for kings and princes, sir! I doubt if anyone less could achieve it, especially given such a long-standing bonding as you have enjoyed.' He used the last word with no suggestion of irony and went on to offer some more advice.

'My uncle, the archdeacon, might have the final word on this matter. He is the most learned man in this diocese, and I am sure that his opinion would be beyond dispute.'

De Wolfe nodded, and when he had thrown down the last of his ale he rose to his feet. 'I have asked him before, Thomas, and he had the same pessimistic view as yourself. But I will make one final appeal to him.'

He reached for his cloak, as it had begun to rain outside and spots were flying in through the open window-slits on the back of a brisk wind. 'I am going to see the sheriff again now. If he agrees with what I have in mind, we will all need to meet again this afternoon. There will be much to discuss.'

After a long discussion with Henry de Furnellis, John waylaid his friend, John de Alençon, as he returned from the cathedral to his house in Canon's Row for his dinner. Just before noon, when there was a break in the incessant devotions held in the huge church of St Mary and St Peter, the priests spread out across the precinct and the lower town to take their main meal of the day. The Archdeacon of Exeter, one of the four in the diocese, had a dwelling halfway along the road that formed the north side of the Close, a narrow but substantial house, one of a dozen that accommodated senior clerics. The coroner, who lived but a few hundred paces away, ambushed him as he walked from the small door in the North Tower and was promptly invited for a cup of wine. De Alençon was a very austere man, unlike some of his fellow canons, who indulged in a luxurious lifestyle. His house was simply furnished and he ate sparingly, which explained his thin body and hollow cheeks. However, he had a weakness for fine wines, and the one he gave to de Wolfe when they were seated in his spartan study was a choice red from Anjou. After they had sampled it and made appropriate comments about its excellence, de Wolfe came straight to the point.

'You may have heard about my wife leaving me again, John,' he began. 'Gossip travels with the speed of lightning in this city, and I know that the Close is by no means immune from its spread. I have asked you before and, now that the problem is more urgent, I must seek your opinion again. If Matilda does take her vows in that Benedictine house, how would that affect the legality of our marriage?'

The grey-haired priest smiled sadly at his friend over the rim of his pewter goblet. 'I know that my sharp-brained nephew has been researching this problem in the library. I, too, have made what enquiries I could since we last spoke of the matter. There is little more I can tell you, except to reinforce my opinion that you would not be free to marry again.'

De Wolfe stared glumly into his own cup. 'I had heard that men who enter some religious orders were looked upon as dead. Surely a corpse cannot remain married?'

The archdeacon shook his head. 'That is rare and usually concerns old men who have no living wife. But in any event that applies only to their secular existence – their loss of civil rights and ability to interact with the world. Marriage is a contract before God Almighty – do not the vows say that those whom God has joined together let no man put asunder?'

'But annulment does happen sometimes?' said the coroner, clutching at the last few straws.

'If a man and his wife *both* enter religious orders, then to all intents and purposes the marriage ceases to exist – but even that is in the eyes of men, not God. The cases where rulers and princes obtain annulments for political purposes are usually founded on often dubious claims of consanguinity. The Holy Father in Rome is usually involved in their granting, and it would be blasphemous of me to even hint at the wisdom of some of those decisions.'

'There is nothing else that could be used? What if one of the pair went mad?'

De Alençon shook his head again. 'Only if it was evident at the very outset, usually before consummation. And the madness would have to be extreme. It has been said that if magic was involved in the obtaining of a wife or husband, then that might be considered as grounds by Rome, but I doubt that you could persuade anyone that Matilda's behaviour has been either lunatic or involved sorcery!'

They talked for a few more minutes, but it was evident that Thomas's careful research was confirmed by the archdeacon's own knowledge. Despondent but unsurprised, de Wolfe let his friend get on with his dinner, while he himself went back to Martin's Lane and Mary's salt fish and boiled beans.

Two hours after noon the coroner collected his officer and clerk from the gatehouse and led them across the now muddy inner ward of Rougemont to the keep, where they filed into the sheriff's chamber.

They found Henry already closeted with Ralph Morin, the castle constable, and Gabriel, the sergeant of Rougemont's men-at-arms. They sat on stools around the sheriff's desk in a conspiratorial huddle.

'I've told the sentry outside to let no one in on any account,' boomed Morin. 'We don't want our discussion bandied abroad.'

De Furnellis bobbed his head, the loose skin under his sagging neck making him look more like an old bloodhound than ever. 'The coroner has a plan to flush out these pirates, if they do exist,' he began. 'So, de Wolfe, let us hear what you propose.'

John dragged his stool a little nearer to the table. 'Our attempt to catch them unawares at Axmouth by searching their storehouses went astray, as the sods were too clever for us,' he began. 'I'm convinced that some of the goods they have there and which they transport away to sell as soon as possible are the spoils of callous theft and murder on the high seas. But we have to catch them at it; that's the only way we'll ever defeat this barbarous trade.'

Morin voiced the obvious objection. 'That may well be, John, but the chances of being in the right place at the right time to see them pillaging some vessel are so slight as to be useless! The Channel is a huge area and, even if we knew where they hoped to strike, how could we get there?'

De Wolfe's long saturnine face managed to produce a cunning smile. 'Exactly the problem, Ralph! The only way to be there when it happens is to be the intended victims ourselves.'

The furrowed brows of his listeners showed that they did not follow his reasoning, so he explained his plan. 'We have to offer a very tempting target, one they can hardly resist,' he growled. 'If it was known that a ship full of treasure was setting sail on a certain day, then such a prize would surely be hard to ignore!'

The sheriff sighed. 'Come on, John, let's hear about it, you devious devil!'

'There are precious few treasure ships sailing out of these ports,' objected Ralph. 'Why should they believe that any particular cog was worth the risk?'

The sharp-minded Thomas already saw the way his master's mind was working. 'Silver – that would be a temptation. Though tin is the main metal sent from these harbours, there is a fair bit of silver mined alongside it.'

He was right, as the panning of the hundreds of streams on Dartmoor, and now increasingly the digging deep into the banks to follow lodes, was producing enough silver to keep a mint going in Exeter.

'But we don't export silver from here,' grunted

Gwyn. 'Surely there's only enough of it to make our own coinage.'

John shook his head emphatically. 'There is silver going away, but not in ships from these ports. King Richard has to pay his troops in Normandy and some Cornish and Dartmoor silver is taken up to Winchester and then across the Channel by shorter and safer sea routes.'

Henry de Furnellis nodded. 'The Exchequer sends an escort down for it every now and then. Between you and me, lately some of the so-called silver coinage sent to the Lionheart's army has had a fair proportion of Dartmoor tin in it, as Hubert Walter is running desperately low in funds.'

The constable tugged at the twin forks of his beard as he digested the argument. 'So you are going to load a vessel with silver and hope that this will attract the attentions of anyone bent on piracy?' he asked.

De Wolfe gave one of his lopsided grins. 'Not silver, but a few boxes full of stones! This ruse depends totally on our spreading false information, which is the main object of our meeting today – and why not a word must get out about the deception.'

As light dawned upon his audience, he elaborated on his plan. 'We can use one of our partnership cogs, perhaps the *St Radegund*, as she is the largest. We need room in the hold to hide at least a dozen of Gabriel's best soldiers to create an ambush if these bastards do set upon the vessel.'

'So why do we need boxes of stones, if the whole affair is a sham?' grunted Gwyn.

'Something heavy has to be seen being carried aboard at Exeter or Topsham, for we want it to appear as if our story is true. A story that must seem like a secret, that is carefully leaked well in advance.'

Thomas bobbed his scraggy head in understanding. 'It will take some cunning, to spread the rumour without giving the game away,' he observed. 'How do we set about that, for not a word of the real truth must escape from this room?'

De Wolfe looked around at the faces seeking his leadership. 'We need to start with the alleged treasure itself, arriving in Exeter soon. I think five hundred pounds' worth would be a credible but attractive prize to tempt anyone.'

The constable whistled at the amount. He was unable to read or write, but he was no sluggard when it came to calculating money. 'That's a hundred and twenty thousand silver pennies! We'll need half a dozen boxes of stones on packhorses or in a cart to shift that lot!'

'With a strong escort of your men, Ralph,' agreed John. 'They can be said to have come from the Bristol mint, so you could send out your men to, say, Taunton to fetch them from the castle there. We could send empty boxes up there beforehand, concealed in a wagon, and you can bring them back heavy with rocks.'

'And make sure that plenty of people see them arriving as a badly kept secret,' added Henry, who was warming to the deception.

'But we need more leakage than that and at an earlier stage,' warned the coroner. 'We have to make sure that the news filters through as far as Axmouth and soon enough for them to decide to act and get a ship ready to intercept the treasure vessel.'

'But subtly enough not to make them suspicious that this is a trap,' cautioned Thomas, as far-sighted as usual.

For the next hour they hammered out the details of the plot. Each was given his allotted task, and eventually they left feeling like arch conspirators in some ancient Roman intrigue.

CHAPTER TWELVE

*In which the coroner visits a
different priory*

After his cool reception at the Bush the previous evening, de Wolfe decided to give it a miss that night and sat gloomily drinking alone at his own fireside, before taking himself early to bed in the lonely solar built above the back yard. He tossed and turned on the big hessian bag stuffed with feathers that lay on a low plinth on the floor, restless under the woollen blankets that now replaced the winter bearskin. It would be wrong to say that he missed Matilda's company there, but he had become used to her lumpy body breathing heavily on the other side of the bed, with the occasional strangled snore.

He went over his plan to try to entice pirates into his trap but was realistic enough to know that it had a slim chance of success. Even if the news of the 'treasure' reached Axmouth, would they want to act on it? Perhaps they would suspect a trick and, even if they did decide to attack, they would have to know exactly when the *St Radegund* left harbour to have any chance of intercepting her. This could not be done within sight of land, so they would have to identify the cog and then follow her for at least some hours. And what if some other pirate beat them to it? If the news was disseminated as well as John hoped, maybe privateers well known to operate out of Lyme or even Dartmouth might decide to try their luck against a hoard of silver.

Obviously, it did not matter greatly which pirates were ambushed, but John felt a particular need to squash whatever was going on in Axmouth. From piracy, the turmoil in his mind moved on to Matilda and her apparent implacable resolve to remain in Polsloe. He felt that part of her motive was to spite and punish him, but he had to admit that she had always inclined towards the religious life. Soon after their wedding, she had admitted to him that she had never wanted marriage. She had yearned as a girl to take the veil, but her forceful parents had insisted that she make a socially acceptable marriage and her heartfelt inclinations to the Church had been denied. There was now nothing he could do about it, and he accepted philosophically the disappointment of the archdeacon's final opinion concerning the impossibility of an annulment. They were saddled with each other until death parted them, so taking a new wife was probably denied him for ever.

From here his thoughts wandered on to the linked problems of Nesta and the royal command to leave Exeter. Here, he felt confused and uncertain, as there were too many unknowns for him to see any clear pathway through the maze of possibilities. He loved Nesta, but did she still love him? Was her fondness for him cooling, given her oft-repeated conviction that they could never live together? Was this new factor, the Welshman, a real threat or just a product of his own latent jealousy? And hovering on the margins of his consciousness was the slim figure of his childhood sweetheart and first lover, the elegant Hilda. He was almost afraid to think of her, for fear that he would admit to himself how much he desired her, even though he loved Nesta.

John knew he would soon have to go down to

Dawlish to talk to one of his shipmasters about using the *St Radegund* for his trap – and he knew that, when he did, the temptation to visit Hilda again would be irresistible.

He hauled his naked body over in the bed with a groan, his head swirling with all these imponderables. As he tried to sleep, his final debate with himself was about moving to London. Would this really be just a trial period or would he never live in Devon again? His mother, sister and brother were not many miles away in Stoke, so how many times would he see them again in this life? In spite of his reassurances to Mary, would he keep his house here? His partnership in the wool trade was no problem – Hugh de Relaga would continue to administer that, as he had done all along – and it seemed that Gwyn and Thomas were resigned to going with him. But what of Nesta – and even Hilda, he dared think? How much of his familiar life would survive the desires of his king? John de Wolfe was a doer, not a thinker, and the effort of juggling these sudden complications in his life made his head ache. Mercifully, sleep eventually overtook him, and in spite of all the problems it was a dreamless coma until the first light of dawn crept through the cracks in the shutters.

Next morning saw a number of new cases that needed the coroner's attention, a welcome diversion from his worries. An alleged rape in St Sidwell's, a man stabbed to death in a brawl in the Saracen Inn, the lowest drinking house in the city, and a rotten body fished out of the river at Exe Island occupied the coroner's trio until the evening.

However, with nothing remaining to be dealt with the following day, in the early morning de Wolfe and his staff were once more in the saddle, a place never much appreciated by Thomas. John had decided that

they needed at least a week or two to set up their trap
and allow the rumours to be spread around Devon. In
the meantime he decided to visit the Prior of Loders,
the manor-lord of Axmouth. After meeting Brother
Absalom, John was suspicious about his activities on
the Axmouth scene. He claimed to be the assistant to
the priory cellarer, the obedientiary responsible for the
material needs of a religious house. John had taken an
instant dislike to the man. Though such aversions were
nothing new for de Wolfe, he wanted to see Loders for
himself and gauge how Absalom fitted into the picture.

So once again they were traversing the east of the
county, taking the whole morning to reach Axmouth,
where they received a frosty reception. The surly
landlord of the Harbour Inn grudgingly provided poor
rye-and-barley bread with cheese that tasted as if it had
been buried in the village midden for a week.

'My mare passes better ale than this stuff,' growled
Gwyn, grimacing over his jug. Thomas, who refused
anything other than a slice of bread, asked his master
why they had called yet again at Axmouth. 'We seem to
learn less at each visit, Crowner,' he complained.

'As we are on the way to Loders, we might as well
show our faces here, to show them that we have them
under our eye,' replied de Wolfe. 'If I could only catch
them out in even one misdemeanour, we could drag
them back to Rougemont and shake them a little to
see what fell out.'

With this ominous threat, which was largely wishful
thinking, they left their poor meal and walked their
mounts along the river's edge towards the sea, looking
at the vessels tied up there. It was low tide, and five
cogs were sitting on the stony mud, leaning against the
bank. Three of them were loading wool, a line of men
carrying bales on their backs from the warehouses
opposite, to trot up the tilted gangplanks.

'That *Tiger* is not here again,' growled Gwyn as they

reached the end of the line of ships. 'Her master seems to be avoiding us, though I suppose that's just chance.'

The coroner was also sorry that Martin Rof, the villainous captain, was not around to be questioned – not that he was likely to admit anything useful.

'Still, we can drop a few hints about our six cases of silver, as long as it's done casually,' he suggested. 'Thomas, you work your charms on that old priest – he looks as if he enjoys a gossip. I'd better not raise the subject myself, but you, Gwyn, could let something slip to that tally-man, what's his name, Capie?'

They ambled their horses back through the lower gate into the village and tied them up at the rail outside the bailiff's dwelling. While his two assistants went off about their business, de Wolfe strode up the path and banged on the door, which was ajar. Without waiting for a reply, he pushed it open and walked in, to find Edward Northcote bending over a table where Elias Palmer was wielding a quill pen over a roll of parchment. Both men turned to face the coroner, but their greeting was anything but welcoming.

'We heard that you and your men had ridden through our village,' snapped Northcote. 'What do you want with us this time?'

Though there was an undercurrent of insolence in his voice, it was muted.

'I want nothing particular, but wish to keep an eye on this manor,' growled de Wolfe. 'I would remind you that a young man was cruelly murdered here and no progress has been made in finding his killer. Neither has your attitude helped my investigation.'

'We have nothing to tell you, Crowner,' replied the bailiff stubbornly. 'You seem unwilling to accept that it was but some violent act of drunken shipmen.'

De Wolfe scowled at the man. 'I have information that suggests otherwise. There is also the matter of the deaths of a Keeper of the Peace and of a pedlar, both of which have features that point in this direction.'

'I don't know what you are talking about, sir!' said Northcote doggedly.

John glowered at him, then shifted his gaze to Elias. 'What is that you are writing, portreeve?' he asked suspiciously.

'Merely a list of the cargo taken from one of those cogs down at the quayside. I am entering the items that John Capie has recorded on his tallies.' He pointed to a collection of knotted cords and notched sticks that lay on the table.

Knowing that he was unable to challenge what Elias said, John wished that Thomas was here to check on the document. Frustrated, he changed the subject. 'I see that ship on which the dead boy Simon sailed is not in the harbour?'

'*The Tiger*? No, she sailed some days ago for Barfleur. Martin Rof will bring her back in a few days' time,' volunteered the portreeve, whose attitude was less resentful than that of the bailiff.

De Wolfe felt that he was uneasy and slightly apprehensive when in the presence of the coroner. 'Has that monkish fellow from Loders been here recently?' demanded de Wolfe, determined to keep the pressure up and convince the Axmouth people that he was watching every move they made.

'Of course. He is the prior's envoy here, he comes once a week,' said Northcote stiffly. 'I don't know what you could want with him, but if you had come yesterday you would have seen him here.'

'No matter. I will be at the priory this afternoon. I can discuss his functions with the prior,' said John smugly and was gratified to see the other two exchange worried glances.

John gave a final suspicious glare at Northcote and Elias and made his way back to his horse. As he waited for his assistants, he looked past the cottages on the other side of the village street to the wide expanse of the estuary, where a stiff onshore breeze was skipping wavelets far up the valley towards Colyford. Beyond the water, the countryside was a patchwork of bright green pastures, brown strip-fields and darker forest, all sloping up inland towards Axminster and Honiton. Above the village, the high ridge south of Hawkesdown Hill was covered in dense woodland running out towards the cliff at the end of the headland at the open sea. It was a pleasant place, and he hoped that soon any evil that lurked there would be driven out. He also realised with a pang of nostalgia that he would miss this Devon countryside when he moved to London.

When Gwyn and then Thomas reappeared, they said little until they were well clear of the village, heading inland for a short way until they turned up at Boshill Cross on to the steep track over the ridge towards Lyme.

Thomas was the first to report. 'I managed to insinuate to Father Henry that you had come back today because you were concerned about piracy in the area, given that a cargo of coin was soon to sail, taking the army's pay to Rouen. I swore him to secrecy, which means that he will blab every word about before supper!'

Gwyn guffawed at his little friend's duplicity. 'I was a bit less forthright with John Capie. I dropped into the conversation something about my going up to Taunton with some troops to collect something valuable that was soon being shipped out of Exeter.'

John nodded his approval. 'We need to put similar hints about the city when we get back. Gwyn, you can do it in the alehouses and again Thomas can seed it amongst the clergy. God knows, they are the biggest gossips in England!'

The Priory of Loders was just beyond the small town of Bridport in Dorset. As the town was not on the actual coast, its name came from the use of the word 'port' for a market, and it was here that de Wolfe decided to stop for the night, as the day was now well advanced and he did not think that they would be all that welcome as guests at Loders. They found a moderately respectable-looking tavern and the coroner bought them all a penny-worth of bed and board, which consisted of supper and a straw-filled sack in a barn-like room behind the alehouse, where they lay wrapped in their riding cloaks.

In spite of the austere accommodation, John slept like a baby, unlike his tossing and turning of the previous night. He woke refreshed, ready for his breakfast of thin oatmeal gruel and a couple of butter-fried eggs on a thick slab of coarse bread.

The rest of the journey was short, a mere few miles further east before they reached the small priory, whose Benedictine mother house was in Montebourg in Normandy, just south of Cherbourg.

As in Polsloe, they had to negotiate with a surly gatekeeper to get into the walled compound, leaving Thomas to wonder how the traditional hospitality to travellers was dispensed, when it seemed so difficult to get inside. Services were still in progress in the priory church, and inevitably Thomas de Peyne vanished inside like a homing pigeon, eager to attend the devotions. The indifferent coroner and his covertly agnostic officer stayed out in the precinct, sprawled on the grass in the spring sunshine, for the weather had improved markedly. There was nothing they could do until the inhabitants of the priory finished the offices of Terce, Sext and Nones, at about the tenth hour. Then a score of monkish figures streamed out of the church, and Thomas came towards them accompanied by a thin priest, whom he introduced as the prior's chaplain and secretary.

'Prior Robert will see you in his parlour in a few

moments,' announced the chaplain in a sepulchral voice.

'You won't want me,' said Gwyn gruffly, subsiding again on the greensward, confirming his antipathy to those who practised religion. John had never discovered what had caused his attitude, which was potentially dangerous in a society dominated by the Church. He would never have got away with it in a village, but the relative anonymity of a city and the army had allowed his phobia to be ignored.

De Wolfe beckoned to his clerk, who accompanied him with alacrity as they followed the chaplain across to a side door of the main building, which led to the prior's residence. They climbed a stone staircase and were ushered into a room that was sparsely furnished with a table, a few stools and a large wooden crucifix hanging on a whitewashed wall. It looked as if Prior Robert of Montebourg was as ascetic as John's friend the archdeacon, and if he was profiting in any way from sharp practices in Axmouth then certainly it was not being spent on lavish living.

Robert was a small man of late middle age, with a rim of grey hair around his shaven tonsure. He had a brooding look, with deep-set eyes and a sharply hooked nose. The black robe of the Benedictine combined with the bare, gloomy appearance of his room oppressed John and made him wish he was still out on the sunlit lawn with Gwyn.

Robert waved a hand at a stool and invited the coroner to sit. His voice was deeper and more melodious than might be expected from a small and rotund body. His chaplain stood behind him and, taking his cue from that, Thomas placed himself at his master's shoulder.

'You are the king's coroner for Devon, I understand?' said Robert. 'I am intrigued as to why you should venture into Dorset to seek out a humble prior.'

'It concerns Axmouth, father, which is within my jurisdiction. I know that the manor and church have belonged to your house since William de Redvers granted it very many years ago.' John had gleaned this information from his knowledgeable clerk.

Robert looked mildly surprised. 'It is indeed one of the manors that we hold on behalf of the Abbey of Montebourg. What interest can that be to a law officer?'

'There have been some disturbing occurrences there recently. A young shipman was murdered and his body buried in the village – and I have reason to suspect that the administration of the port is irregular, to say the least. It may be frankly criminal.'

The prior's sparse eyebrows lifted. 'I find that hard to credit, Sir John! I have heard nothing of any of this. But then I leave all such business to my cellarer, whose duty it is to deal with all the material aspects of our life here.'

'You do not supervise their work or check the revenues that the port generates?' said John. He failed to keep his voice free from criticism.

Robert shook his head. 'I am more concerned with the religious life of this establishment. Naturally, I scan the accounts every quarter-day and remit part of the income to Montebourg when the abbot sends his emissaries across at intervals. But my cellarer, Brother Philip, has been carrying out his duties faithfully for twenty years and more. As they say, why keep a dog and bark yourself?'

De Wolfe thought this relaxed attitude was an invitation to abuse of the system, but he kept his opinion to himself. 'It seems that your cellarer does not deal directly with affairs in Axmouth but leaves them to an assistant. Are you content with such an arrangement?'

'Of course! Brother Absalom is a trusted lay brother. True, he is in lower orders, but Philip has high regard for his efficiency, which he has been displaying these past five years.'

'And you have no doubts as to his integrity, for he must be responsible for considerable sums of money which are due to the priory from all the activity at the port down there?'

De Wolfe was starting to tread on sensitive ground with his implied criticisms, for the prior was beginning to look irritated.

'Indeed, I trust all my staff implicitly!' he replied crossly. 'Axmouth has a bailiff and a portreeve and we keep in touch through Absalom. There has never been any suggestion of malpractice. The cellarer receives their monthly accounts and checks them – and as I said, I look over them myself several times a year. I cannot see what you are hoping to gain by these questions, sir!'

De Wolfe was inclined to agree with him, as he saw the futility of trying to learn anything from Robert of Montebourg. The prior seemed indifferent to the secular side of his responsibilities, content to leave it all to subordinates, especially where Axmouth was concerned. Presumably, as long as the manor turned in a reasonable income, much of it remitted to the mother house in Normandy, no one bothered to check on the reality of the accounts brought up by Absalom. It seemed unlikely that the actual cellarer, Brother Philip, was involved in anything shady, as he was an ordained monk of long standing with no reason to need personal wealth. But Absalom could be party to a conspiracy down in Axmouth, as a lay brother could walk away from a religious establishment at any time and enjoy any wealth that he had managed to accrue by fair means or foul.

John decided it was wasting everyone's time to prolong this meeting and stood up to take his leave. 'I thank you for your frankness, prior. Perhaps you would allow me to have a few words with your cellarer and his assistant, now that we have come all this distance?'

Robert readily agreed, glad to see this law officer go on his way. He instructed his secretary to take them to Brother Philip, and a few minutes later they found themselves in a small room on the ground floor, adjacent to a series of chambers filled with a jumble of food, grain, furniture and all the oddments that were needed to keep the priory supplied with worldly goods.

The cellarer was a stout man, getting towards the end of his active life, and John suspected that Brother Philip rarely left his chair in the office, except to eat, sleep and worship.

The conversation with the prior was repeated almost word for word, and it was obvious to the coroner that the cellarer left almost everything to his lay assistant, especially over dealings with Axmouth. He even admitted that he had not visited the village for the past two years, being satisfied with scanning the parchment lists that Absalom brought up after his frequent trips.

'Is your valuable assistant here?' asked John with unintended irony.

The cellarer reached out across his cluttered table and picked up a brass bell of quite substantial size. 'He is usually within earshot of this!' he exclaimed and shook the ivory stem vigorously. The clangour made John wince and the noise must have been heard all over the priory. A few moments later the flopping of sandals was heard on the flagstones of the corridor and Brother Absalom appeared. When he saw the coroner and his clerk, he stopped dead in the doorway and stared, obviously taken aback.

'What are you doing here?' he asked suspiciously, ignoring any pretence at greeting or deferring to John's rank.

'We came to speak to your prior and the cellarer, but as you are now here we may as well have a word with you.' De Wolfe's tone was dismissive, as if he thought the man of little account.

'What about? If it's that nonsense in Axmouth, there's nothing to tell. You saw for yourself that everything there is in order.'

'We saw some documents that tallied with the goods in the storehouses, but that's not necessarily the true state of affairs,' growled the coroner.

Absalom shrugged indifferently. 'They were good enough for me – and my cellarer and Prior Robert.'

Brother Philip looked anxiously from one face to the other. 'What's all this about? I know of no irregularities in this regard.'

John marked him down as a placid fellow looking forward to a quiet life in retirement in the priory and not wanting any trouble to rock his comfortable existence.

'These law officers have some strange notion that there is vice and corruption in our manor of Axmouth, Brother Philip. It has all arisen because of some drunken brawl amongst shipmen there, which ended in an unfortunate death. God knows why the coroner wants to blame the one on the other.'

'You forget the deaths of a Keeper of the King's Peace soon afterwards,' grated de Wolfe. 'And the killing of a pedlar nearby.'

'Nearby? They both died up towards Honiton. What has that to do with our manor?' Absalom's voice was strident with indignation, and John was hard put to decide whether it was feigned or real.

The cellarer lumbered to his feet, intent on defending his assistant. 'This is the first I've heard of all this; it is in a different county from Dorset. But I can assure you that the trading at Axmouth is conducted in the best traditions of both legality and honesty,' he said pompously. 'The dues we receive from the goods passing through the harbour are substantial and are very welcome in this house and in Normandy. If you have evidence that it is otherwise, then of course you must present it to us and we shall take action.'

This took the wind out of the coroner's sails, as he knew that there was nothing concrete that he could use to accuse anyone. After some minutes of acrimonious exchange, he admitted defeat and he beckoned Thomas to leave, offering a final veiled threat as they went.

'I would counsel you to impress on your assistant here that in future he had better be very careful in his dealings with the folk in Axmouth,' he boomed. 'The place is under close scrutiny by the sheriff and other officers, and any felonious behaviour is likely to end on the gallows!'

With this largely empty threat, they left to seek Gwyn and the horses. Absalom watched their departure through the shutters of a window in the cellarium, biting his lip in concern at this tenacious knight who seemed determined to catch them out in something.

The Sabbath passed and the new week brought a little activity to an otherwise quiet period for the county coroner. He had had no whisper of news from Polsloe and felt that yet another visit to pester Dame Madge or the prioress would be a waste of time, as they had promised to let him know if Matilda changed her mind about wishing to speak to him. He had asked Thomas to pen a short letter to his wife, the message being a rather formal request for her to let him know her intentions. He had sent it by a messenger and at least the boy had said that the sealed parchment had not been rejected at the priory, though no reply had been forthcoming.

The situation at the Bush remained cool but improved somewhat over the course of the next few days. Nesta's excuse about the 'time of the moon' held sway for a couple more nights, and John returned to his lonely bed in Martin's Lane, causing a few puzzled glances from Mary, who had thought that her master would have been taking full advantage of his wife's absence.

Owain ap Gronow was not much in evidence in the tavern during the evenings that de Wolfe took his place by the firepit. John saw him a few times and received a pleasant smile and greeting, but he got the impression that the stonemason was being tactful and was keeping out of the way.

On Sunday night the pretty Welshwoman was more like her old self and *cwched* up comfortably against John's shoulder as he sat on his bench behind the wattle screen. That night they made the journey together up the loft ladder to her box-like room and made love in a gentle rather than passionate way. But afterwards she began crying softly into her pillow and refused to say what was wrong, even when he pleaded with her to tell him. All she would say between her tears was ... 'It's us, John. Just us! What's to become of us?'

When he awoke the next morning she had already risen, although it was so very early. Recalling the previous evening, he climbed sadly into his clothes and went down to the empty taproom. He found her in the cook-shed, busy making him a breakfast of honeyed gruel, pork sausages and fried onions. She smiled at him wanly and avoided him while she chivvied her two servants about domestic trifles. Eventually, she came and sat with him while he finished with barley bread and cheese. There seemed little new to say, so he filled the time by telling her of their plot to try to trap the pirates with a tale of a treasure ship. Though the true plan was a deadly secret, he knew he could trust her and, with the large number of patrons that passed through the Bush, her help in seeding the rumour would be of great use. Nesta also seemed relieved at having something to discuss apart from themselves and their intractable problems.

When he got up to Rougemont that Monday morning, Gwyn was ready for him with news of a fresh case.

'On the bloody horses again, I'm afraid,' he observed amiably. 'A fellow has turned up with news of a killing which needs our attention. Says he's the manor-reeve from Ottery St Mary. They've found a man there stabbed at the side of the road.'

This large village was about ten miles from Exeter in the direction of Honiton but was not on the main Roman road that led eastwards.

'Where is he now?' demanded de Wolfe.

'Gone for some bread and ale after his ride, but he'll come back here soon,' said the Cornishman. When the reeve arrived at the guardroom below the coroner's stark chamber, John went down to speak to him. Walter Spere, a thin man with a mournful face, wore a serge jerkin and canvas breeches, with a thin cloak thrown over his shoulders. On his head was a pointed woollen cap, the end flopped over to one side.

'The cadaver was found by a cowman early today, sir, though he was stone cold and probably died last night,' he began in a quavering voice.

'Where was this?' demanded John.

'On the verge of the road, about a mile this side of the church.'

Thomas, who was lurking behind, could not resist airing his knowledge. 'The church and manor of Ottery St Mary have long belonged to Rouen Cathedral, being a gift from Edward the Confessor, of blessed memory.' He crossed himself devoutly, but de Wolfe was more interested in murder than history.

'And he has been deliberately slain, you claim?'

Walter nodded vigorously. 'Covered in blood, he was! Stabbed in the back, by the looks of it.'

'Any idea who he is?'

'No, sir, but he's not from the village, that's for sure. He has good clothes and boots and a fine sword, so he's probably a merchant or even a knight.'

De Wolfe cleared his throat noisily as he came to a quick decision. 'We'd better ride back with you and see what this is about. Gwyn, go and organise the horses – but Thomas, you may as well stay here and attend to your other duties, as I want to get back as soon as I can.'

Thankful to be spared, the clerk took no offence at this implied hint about his poor performance on a horse and before long he watched the three men ride off down Castle Hill. They left through the South Gate and turned up Magdalen Street to ride into the countryside past the gallows, which was bare of customers that day. The coroner and his officer rode their larger horses side by side, followed by Walter Spere on a rounsey. They rode in silence, as no one had anything to say.

An hour and a half later they were well on their way to Ottery and entering a strip of forest-lined track that John remembered as stretching for at least a couple of furlongs, the tall trees reaching right to the edge of the road. Suddenly, they realised that the regular rhythm of the three horses had changed and, looking around, were mystified to see the reeve cantering off to the left and vanishing down a narrow path between the trees. In seconds, he had completely disappeared and even his hoof-beats were silenced on the soft ground of the forest floor.

'Where the hell has that bloody man gone?' demanded Gwyn in surprise. 'Shall I follow him?'

'No, stay where you are!' snapped de Wolfe, drawing his sword from its sheath at the side of his saddle. 'I don't like the feel of this.'

They sat and listened to the silence of the deep woodland, broken only by the croak of a magpie. Gwyn reached for the ball mace that hung from his saddle-bow. This had a short handle with a chain carrying a wicked-looking iron ball studded with spikes. 'Is this another ambush like the one that injured the stone-mason?' he grunted, looking around suspiciously.

'But why be set up by a manor-reeve?' growled John. 'If indeed he is a reeve. And why try to rob us? We are not rich merchants or priests with fat purses.'

'Do we go on or turn back?' asked his officer.

The coroner glowered around, seeing only an empty road in front and behind them. 'We may as well carry on, now that we've come this far.'

They kicked their horses into motion and began trotting down the centre of the track, their heads swinging from side to side as they scanned the green wall of forest. Suddenly, Gwyn caught something out of the corner of his eye, a shadowy movement just within the tree-line on his left. Automatically, he gave a warning shout and swung his big brown mare around to face the possible threat. Almost simultaneously, he heard the unmistakable 'twang' of a released crossbow and half-expected to feel the impact of a bolt in his chest. But he was not the target, for alongside him there was a 'clang' as the missile struck something metallic.

John had heard the sound of the crossbow discharge at the same second as Gwyn and had instinctively ducked, as well as digging his spurs into Odin's flanks. But before the great stallion had been able to acceler-ate, the bolt had crossed the short distance from the trees and struck the upraised blade of John's sword, just above the cross-guard. It jerked his hand sideways and skittered away to land on the road.

The two seasoned warriors automatically took evasive action, bending low over their saddles and diverging from each other as they prodded their horses into maximum effort. As they pounded up the road, another bolt from the opposite side of the road flew harmlessly past Odin's rump, then they were well out of range, given the time needed to crank back a crossbow for reloading. However, they did not stop until they had emerged from the wooded stretch and were safely alongside open strip-fields.

'The bastards!' fumed Gwyn. 'Are we going to go in and flush them out?'

John examined the dimple and scratch on his sword-blade, which had probably saved his life, as he had been holding the weapon upright in front of his chest. 'No, I'm not mixing with bowmen hiding behind trees! Anyway, they'll have long gone now, having failed.'

'That sod of a reeve or whoever he was led us nicely into a trap!' snarled Gwyn, his usual good temper evaporated by the churlish trick that had been played upon them. 'But what was it all about?'

De Wolfe, although as experienced in battle as any man, was shaken by the unexpected ambush. 'There's a pattern to this, Gwyn! Murdering a Keeper and now trying to assassinate a coroner, both of them king's officers! And in this same part of the county, too.'

'You think it's connected with Axmouth?' asked the Cornishman dubiously.

'What else? We went and shook up the bailiff and portreeve a few days ago and then went and caused trouble at Loders. They are getting worried and want to get rid of me.'

'Maybe it's just as well we are leaving for London!' jested Gwyn, his good nature recovering. 'Otherwise we'll be looking over our shoulders all the time.'

'Not if our plan with the non-existent silver works,' said John grimly. 'I'll see those swine dancing by their necks before we quit Devon!'

*

Later that day de Wolfe related to the sheriff what had happened, but decided not to tell Nesta that he had probably escaped death by only an inch. Henry de Furnellis was outraged at this second attack on a royal law officer and seemed as frustrated as John that they had no proof of who might be responsible. De Wolfe had ridden with Gwyn the remaining distance to Ottery St Mary and discovered that they knew nothing about any corpse. The real manor-reeve turned out to be an amiable, fat fellow, utterly unlike the silent man who had impersonated him. No one in the village recognised John's description of such an unremarkable man, and it was obvious that he could have come from anywhere in the east of the county. The two archers hidden in the woods could have been anyone, as they remained hidden from view.

Tired from a day in the saddle and the stress of the sudden attack, John decided not to visit the Bush that evening, though part of him welcomed the excuse to escape Nesta's emotional mood, as women in tears frightened him more than facing a troop of cavalry. Next day he had to attend the fortnightly county court in the bleak Shire Hall in the inner ward of Rougemont. With Thomas prompting him from his parchments, he made several declarations of 'exigent', outlawing men who had failed to answer to their bail on four previous occasions. There were two confessions to read out from men who had turned 'approvers', trying to save their necks by denouncing their accomplices in cases of robbery, and he successfully persuaded an indignant leather merchant to take his 'appeal' against a fraudulent supplier of hides to the next Eyre, rather than challenge the man to trial by combat, which he was almost certain to lose.

The proceedings were finished by dinner-time, with the sheriff sending three men to be hanged for thefts of items worth more than twelve pence and another for clipping coinage, a felony classed as treason and always punishable by death. Though the efforts of the Chief Justiciar to wean major cases from the local manor, hundred and county courts into the royal courts was slowly succeeding, the old Saxon system was proving hard to eradicate. One problem was that the visits of the king's justices to hear cases at the Eyres were so infrequent that the population preferred the quicker summary justice of the local courts. It was true that to speed up the process, more frequent visits of lesser judges, the Commissioners of Gaol Delivery, had been established, but still the old ways proved most popular with the people.

De Wolfe discussed some of this with Henry de Furnellis when they met that afternoon in the keep, but the main business was to harden up their plans to sail the decoy ship to try to attract the pirates. The coroner had learnt from his partner Hugh de Relaga that the *St Radegund* was due to be back in Topsham within the next week, weather permitting.

'Her master, Roger Watts, is then due for a voyage off, to spend time at home, so we can use Angerus de Wile for our purposes,' said John.

'Assuming he's willing to put his life at risk,' reminded Ralph Morin, who was also present. 'You had better go and talk to him and explain what's required.'

John readily agreed, very conscious that the ship-master lived in Dawlish.

'We had better arrange for this collection of the fake treasure boxes from Taunton,' declared the sheriff. 'You and Gabriel had better go up with the empty ones and fill them full of stones yourselves. The fewer people who know the truth of this, the better.'

The castle constable agreed and added: 'The return journey to Exeter with an escort of men-at-arms needs to be as public as possible. We can store the boxes here in Rougemont until they are due to be taken down to Topsham.'

The finer details were thrashed out until all that remained was for John to get the cooperation of the *St Radegund*'s master. The crew need not be told anything until the contingent of soldiers arrived to be hidden below deck.

'Amongst whom will be myself!' boomed Ralph.

'As will be I and Gwyn of Polruan,' added John grimly. 'Though I think I'll leave my little clerk at home for this particular adventure!'

CHAPTER THIRTEEN

In which the coroner goes to sea

Angerus de Wile lived in a low cottage facing the beach in Dawlish, one of an irregular row of small huts and bigger crofts that housed sailors and fishermen as well as a few traders and craftsmen. As a shipmaster sharing in the profits of each voyage, he was richer than most of his neighbours, but his dwelling was still very modest. The walls were oak frames filled in with cob plastered over wattle panels, and the roof was made of thick stone tiles, as thatch or wooden shingles would not stand the winds that constantly threatened the shore.

His wife had died in childbirth four years earlier, and his eldest daughter, now aged nine, looked after the other two children and kept house while their father was away at sea. John de Wolfe thought that the girl did a good job, as when he came to see Angerus a few days after the conference in Rougemont, he found the little house warm and comfortable. There were clean rushes on the floor and a savoury smell came from a small cauldron hanging on a trivet over the firepit. Unusually for Devon, there was a crude box-bed against the wall, a cave-like cupboard where Angerus slept when he was home, the three children sleeping on hay bags laid on its roof.

De Wolfe, who today had left both Thomas and

Gwyn behind in Exeter, accepted some hot broth that the daughter ladled from the pot, followed by a cup of good wine that Angerus had brought from his last trip to Bordeaux. Seated on stools around the fire, he explained the situation and asked the shipmaster if he was willing to take the *St Radegund* out, given the possible risks. Though the man was virtually his servant, in that he now worked for the partnership, John made it clear that he was asking for a volunteer and that he was free to refuse if he so wished.

The shipmaster sat for a while, staring into the small glowing fire. His lower jaw, which stuck out so that his teeth markedly overlapped the upper set, made him look like an angry dog about to attack a tethered bull or bear.

'I'll take the ship and be glad to do so, Sir John!' he said eventually. 'It was sodding pirates of some sort who so cruelly slew Thorgils, my master and friend! It would be some measure of revenge if I could help you.'

John looked at his daughter and then at the two younger children, sitting wide-eyed watching them from the bed.

'You have a family to think of, Angerus – but with a dozen armed men on board, as well as myself, the constable and doughty Gwyn, there should be no great risk to you or your crew.'

De Wile looked across at his children, who were obviously well loved and well cared for. 'They have been brave since their mother died, Christ bless her soul! I'm sure if the worst happened, Mistress Hilda would see them cared for, as she has done for the families of Thorgils' crew.'

They talked for a while longer about the details of the proposed voyage and agreed that Angerus would sail the cog out of Topsham in ten days' time.

'It may well be that we'll see no sign of any attackers,' warned de Wolfe. 'Or it's just possible that some other privateers will take the bait, like those said to be working out of Lyme.'

Angerus shrugged. 'The sea's a big place, Crowner! You could hide a thousand ships just in the Channel, so the chances of them coming across us once out of sight of land are very slim, unless they know exactly when we left harbour.'

'That's just what we have been trying to achieve, and will do so again in the next few days, now that we have a date. You can tell your men that you have a cargo of silver coin for the king's troops, but for God's sake don't mention the soldiers until they actually turn up at the moment you're ready to cast off your mooring ropes.'

When he rose to leave, John made a point of going to each of the children to press a penny into each hand, as he ruffled their hair affectionately. Though he was not used to children, he sometimes had a yearning for some of his own when he saw a contented family like Angerus's. As he walked back along the strand to the tavern where he had left Odin to be fed and watered, he wondered if things would have been different if he had sired a few on Matilda, though she had never expressed the slightest interest in motherhood, preferring the sisterhood of the Church and apparently yearning only to be a bride of Christ. He was now forty-one years of age and life was slipping by at an astonishing rate, but he knew he still had the potential to be a father – all he needed was the mother!

The thought quickened his steps until he told himself sternly not to be such a damned fool, as an image of Nesta floated into his mind. Doggedly, he walked on and after checking at the alehouse to see that his stallion had been properly cared for, he turned up the side street and loped towards Hilda's grand house, its stone walls and two front pillars marking it out from every other dwelling in the village.

As he approached the heavy door, he felt excited at what had almost happened the last time he came here. He rubbed at his chin to see how much stubble had grown and even ran his fingers through his thick black hair in an attempt to tame it. Flinging the sides of his riding cloak over each shoulder, he tightened his broad leather belt another notch and adjusted the sheath of his short sword at his side. Then he pounded on the door with his fist and waited impatiently for Alice to open it and let him stalk up the stairs to the blonde beauty in her solar.

The oak boards creaked open and the maid looked out timidly.

'Alice, I'm here again to see your mistress!' he announced almost gaily, putting one foot over the threshold.

The young girl stared at him, this great man dressed in black and grey. 'But she's not here, sir. She's gone to Holcombe to stay with her family for a week.'

Deflated and feeling slightly foolish, de Wolfe backed down the steps and trudged moodily back to the waiting Odin.

The next ten days seemed to pass unusually quickly for John. There were a number of new deaths that needed investigation, one in Totnes which occupied two of those days, much of it in travelling. There were no more arrows fired at him, and with no possible means of investigating the failed assassination he had to write it off to experience. He was convinced that, like the killing of the Keeper, it was an attempt to extinguish his interest in Axmouth.

The false 'treasure' was duly brought to Rougemont by an armed party and locked in the sheriff's inner room. Both Gwyn and Thomas reported that the city was rife with gossip about the thousands of silver pennies destined for the king's troops in Normandy.

It was not the first such happening, as genuine exports from the Exeter mint had been made at intervals, albeit recently debased by the covert addition of tin. However, the large amount involved in this new consignment and the fact that it had been brought down from the Bristol mint made it a talking point in the taverns and churches of the city. John's two spies also confirmed that the place and date of its departure were widely known amongst the populace.

'If this doesn't reach the ears of those who would like to steal it, then we'll have to admit defeat,' said the sheriff resignedly as he bumped his shins on the six boxes of stones that cluttered his quarters.

During those days de Wolfe's relations with Nesta had improved, and he had spent several nights with her in the Bush, though he still felt awkward knowing that Owain ap Gronow was lying only a few paces away.

One day he again went down to Dawlish, as he felt he could not commandeer a ship and her crew that used to belong to Hilda without the courtesy of getting her approval. If nothing else, the potential danger to the master and crew made it imperative that Hilda was brought into the secret, as he knew that the welfare of their families was close to her heart. Following the *rapprochement* with Nesta, he decided to take Hugh de Relaga down to Dawlish with him, as the gaudy portreeve was not only the third member of their wool-exporting consortium but would serve as an effective chaperone, as John felt that he might not be able to trust himself to behave if temptation became too great! The meeting was decorous and friendly, and John had no opportunity to be alone with Hilda, much as he chafed against his own decision to avoid temptation. Hilda readily agreed to using the cog as a decoy, as since Thorgils had been killed her anger still burnt against those who so treacherously slew shipmen on the high seas.

The circle of people made privy to the ambush plot was widening, but John felt that he could trust all of them not to divulge the secret until the moment that the *St Radegund* actually sailed. The troop of men-at-arms that would hide on the ship would not march aboard until the very last minute, when it would be too late for any spy to get a message to Axmouth to prevent a privateer from leaving to intercept the treasure ship. John still did not exclude the owner of *The Tiger* from being party to the murderous trade, and his servants in Exeter would be well aware of the departure of the vessel.

It was Gwyn, with his knowledge of the sea, who pointed out that any pirate ship would have to leave Axmouth at about the same time as the *St Radegund* sailed from Topsham, otherwise it would have to wait twelve hours for the next tide to be able to float off and leave the estuary of the Axe, by which time the treasure ship would have vanished over the horizon.

A few days before Angerus de Wile was due to take his ship to sea, John asked Thomas to scribe another short letter to his wife. He decided that though his wife's continued absence was something that he was getting used to – and which he was now quite content to be a permanent situation – he was bound as an honourable knight to try all means to persuade her either to return to him or at least to give some clue as to her intentions.

'I have to let her know that I have been called to London,' he growled to his clerk. 'Perhaps the knowledge that the king himself wants me to become coroner to the royal court will change her mind about staying in Polsloe.'

Thomas was quite ready to believe that Matilda's snobbery and ambitions of social elevation would entice her away from the desire to take her vows of chastity and obedience. His master's thoughts were similar, but John felt that his duty as a husband and a Norman gentleman obliged him to take the risk. The letter was duly delivered to Dame Madge but, contrary to John's fearful expectations, no reply had materialised by the time he left on the *St Radegund.*

On the evening before the departure from Topsham, he went down to the tavern in Idle Lane to tell Nesta that all was set for the following day. He waited until one of Nesta's maids had brought him a thick trencher of bread carrying a meaty pork knuckle surrounded by fried onions – and Edwin had refilled his quart pot with best ale. With the auburn-haired Welshwoman sitting opposite to make sure he ate every morsel, he gave all the details of the trap they were hoping to set for the pirates. She had done well in carefully seeding the news of the 'treasure ship' amongst her patrons. As many of these were merchants or carters who travelled the roads of Devon and the nearby counties, he knew that the gossip machine would have spread the news from the Bush far and wide.

When he had finished his meal, they talked for a time and he found her in a pensive, reminiscent mood. She spoke of the stressful times of the past two years, of the burning of the inn when she had almost lost her life and of the miscarriage she had suffered. John knew from her mood that there would be no climbing the ladder to the loft that night. Before he left, she had a caution, born out of her regard for him.

'Be careful tomorrow, John. You can be too reckless sometimes – you are not indestructible!'

She bent and gave him a quick kiss on the lips, then walked quickly to the ladder and climbed it without a backward glance.

Soon after dawn next day a cavalcade left Rougemont and proceeded through the city to the South Gate, drawing a lot of attention from the people clustered around the food stalls lining the main streets. The statuesque figure of Ralph Morin led the procession, erect on his big horse, followed by the coroner and his officer riding side by side on a pair of rounseys from the castle stables. Three packhorses came next, each with a pair of money chests hung over their backs, flanked by ten mounted soldiers. The rear was brought up by Sergeant Gabriel and another man-at-arms. All the escort wore round iron helmets with a nose-guard and jerkins of thick boiled leather. The only exception was the constable, who had a full-length hauberk of chain mail. All carried swords hanging from their belts, supported by diagonal baldrics over their right shoulders, and long sheathed daggers at their backs. This formidable group took the road south alongside the river, which led to Topsham, five miles away. They reached the port where the river became a wider estuary an hour before high water, and the boxes were quickly unloaded from the pack animals and stowed in the hold of the *St Radegund*, watched by a curious crowd on the quayside. Though the inhabitants of Topsham were used to ships and cargo coming and going every day of their lives, to see such a strong escort of armed soldiers was a novelty – and the novelty was increased when they saw the troop filing aboard the vessel, instead of going back to Exeter once the chests had been safely delivered. The crew of the cog were also mystified, as for the sake of secrecy Angerus de Wile had not yet told them the true purpose of this voyage.

His mate, an old sailor named Alphegus, voiced their concerns. 'We can't house and feed this lot all the way to Honfleur!' he exclaimed, as under Gabriel's direction the soldiers clambered down ladders into the hold and out of sight. He was already puzzled, as the ship had loaded no other cargo for the alleged voyage to Normandy.

De Wile placed an arm reassuringly around the

old sea dog's shoulders. 'Don't worry about feeding them, Alphegus – they've got rations for a day in their pouches. We should only be out for a couple of tides!'

With the other five crew clustered around, he at last explained what they were doing. Though the coroner had been a little concerned at virtually tricking the crew into this venture, they were quite happy to go along with it, partly because they felt safe enough with eighteen armed men aboard and also because they wanted to see revenge wreaked on those who had caused the deaths of fellow mariners.

At high water they cast off and the ebb tide and light breeze took them down towards the open sea, where they turned south-east and began to cross the wide expanse of Lyme Bay. Until another vessel came in sight – if it ever did – there was no need for the men to be concealed, though all but de Wolfe, Morin and Gwyn did stay in the hold, most of them playing dice on top of the boxes of spurious silver.

The offshore wind was light and mainly northerly, unlike the last time John ventured to sea a few weeks before. Then the strong south-westerly hurried them up-Channel, but this much slower progress suited their purpose better, as it gave them more time to be exposed to any rogue ship searching for them. To increase their lingering even more, Angerus deliberately failed to make the best use of the yard-sheets and steering oar, so that they meandered away from the mouth of the Exe, slowly increasing their distance from the land. It was fairly hazy, and by noon the coast of Devon and Dorset was just a misty blur on the northern horizon. De Wolfe was beginning to fear that the whole venture was going to be a complete failure and a waste of several weeks of careful preparation.

'Where are we now?' he asked the shipmaster, who was standing alongside Alphegus, who manned the steering oar.

'About level with the Axe, Sir John,' replied the ship-master. 'But a long way out. There would be no point in trying to flaunt ourselves as a possible victim within clear sight of the shore.'

Half an hour later that landfall had melted into the mist, though east and west, where the haze was thinner, Portland Bill and Start Point could just be glimpsed. The sea was calm, with just a slight swell passing under the ungainly hull – which was just as well, as the effectiveness of some of the men-at-arms would have been badly blunted by seasickness.

Those on deck stared into the distance until their eyes watered, feeling increasingly disappointed as the time went by.

'Can we turn around and go back for a while, to give them a better chance of seeing us?' demanded Ralph Morin, utterly ignorant of the ways of the sea.

The shipmaster shook his head. 'Not against this wind – and anyway it would be obvious that we were heading in the wrong direction for the treasure ship.'

One of the crew had clambered up the rigging and sat perilously on the centre of the yard that supported the single large sail. A few minutes later he gave a yell and called down to those on the afterdeck.

There's a sail away to the nor'-east. Coming out of the haze in this direction.'

There was a buzz of excitement, which was taken up by the soldiers in the hold, who were getting bored even with their gaming.

'How far away?' yelled Angerus, turning his pugnacious face upwards to the lookout.

'About five miles, I reckon.'

The master turned to the coroner and constable. 'Too far yet to see who it is. Might be a legitimate trader out of Lyme or Axmouth. I'll just keep on this course and see what they do.'

Morin motioned towards the hold. 'We'd better

get out of sight soon and just leave the crew on deck.'

They went to one of the short ladders that were propped against the inner edge of the hatch-coaming and went down to join their men. The hold was normally closed by a series of heavy planks across the opening and covered with a canvas sheet. Now, only a few of these boards were in place and the cover loosely draped across them.

Half an hour later Angerus came to the edge of the hold and called down. 'That vessel is coming straight for us, about two miles away. We are out of sight of land altogether now.'

'Can you see what ship it is?' asked de Wolfe.

'Not yet, just another cog, but she's going to cross our path soon, though I'm not making my best speed.'

'Perhaps you better had,' suggested Gwyn. 'If she *is* a pirate, her master will be suspicious if you don't try to get clear.'

There was some shouting and creaking of ropes and spars as Angerus went through the motions of getting a fraction better performance out of the *St Radegund*.

After another half-hour, de Wile called out again, sounding anxious. 'I'm sure it's *The Tiger* – she's closing on us fast. Another few minutes and she'll be here!'

Ralph Morin climbed partway up the ladder and peered over the hatch-coaming. 'You'd better act scared, Angerus,' he ordered. 'Get your men to run around and point. We'll stay quiet down here until they actually start to board, then you cross to t'other side of the vessel and keep out of the way!'

He motioned to the others in the hold to keep quiet, as sounds travel far across water on a calm day. They all drew their swords and a few had maces or long knives in their other hands, ready for action.

John felt the frisson of excitement that always pervaded him just before a fight. Gwyn was grinning broadly at the prospect, slipping his left wrist through the leather loop of his fearsome ball and chain.

In a few minutes they heard their own crew shouting defiance that held a fearful tremor that was not all feigned. Almost at once, a more distant yelling began and they heard the creaking and splashing of another vessel as she came at them from astern with her port side towards their bow, then a lurch and grinding as she slid along their hull, deliberately smashing the steering oar to disable them.

There was a rattling as several grappling hooks were thrown over their side and the *St Radegund* lurched again as the two cogs locked together. All this was accompanied by bloodthirsty yelling from the crew of *The Tiger*, as they began to clamber over the gunwales.

'Right, men, get up and kill the bastards!' roared the constable. As the troop commander, he was in charge, but John and Gwyn were alongside at two of the other ladders, leading some of the men-at-arms up on to the deck. Angerus and his crew had wisely taken Ralph's advice and were running down the port side towards the bow, leaving the waist of the vessel free for the attackers to board. Five or six men were clambering down from the rail, waving knives and swords, as Morin and the others suddenly materialised in front of them.

Their shocked surprise was almost ludicrous as they saw more than a dozen armed soldiers swarm out of the hatch and advance upon them with raised weapons.

'Back, get back aboard!' screamed the first man across the gunwale, but it was too late. John saw that the leader was Martin Rof, and he ran at him with a roar, his own sword upraised. The master of *The Tiger* was no coward and parried John's blow with a clash of metal, as Gwyn and Morin forced other men back against the thick wooden bulwark that ran around the deck.

There was a cacophony of screaming and yelling and

the sound of weapon on weapon. Morin had engaged the mate of *The Tiger*, a huge man with a bald head, who was wielding a dagger and a short stabbing spear. The constable was thankful that he had worn the heavy hauberk, as the mate's pike had a longer reach than Ralph's sword and was bruising his chest and belly with every jab. Gwyn had felled another ruffian with the first swing of his ball-mace and was chasing another back over the rail, while John was dealing with the shipmaster. Martin Rof was swinging his sword desperately as he backed to the gunwale, obviously seeking to get back to his own ship, but John used his yard of steel two-handed and battered down Rof's defence by sheer force. The last swing caught the bearded shipmaster across the forearm, and with a scream he dropped his sword and dagger to clutch his wounded limb, blood pumping from between his fingers.

He tried to get up on to the rail, but de Wolfe grabbed him by the neck of his tunic and pulled him to the deck, where a kick in the head kept him down. When John looked around, the battle was over, and indeed several of the soldiers had not struck a blow, as they so outnumbered the half-dozen who had clambered aboard. Gwyn stood over a dead man, and Ralph had soon overcome the bald mate by chopping his spear-shaft through with a mighty swing of his broadsword. However, the man had leapt back aboard *The Tiger*, where those of the crew who had not climbed across were desperately hacking through the ropes from the grapnels, allowing the vessels to drift apart.

'The sods are getting away!' roared Gwyn, leaping up on to the rail.

Fearful that he would jump across and be left alone on the other ship, de Wolfe yelled at him to stop, but Gwyn's innate good sense overcame his fighting spirit and he contented himself with hurling insults and abuse at the rapidly retreating vessel. He was joined by the crew of the *St Radegund* who ran back from the safety of the port side to jeer across the widening strip of water at the shocked remnants of the pirate gang.

'The swine have made off, Crowner!' said the ship-master angrily.

'Not all of them, Angerus,' replied de Wolfe, pulling off his iron helmet to wipe his brow. 'We've got two of them dead here and another three captive, including their leader.'

Martin Rof lay groaning in the scuppers, still bleeding on to the deck. Ralph Morin, wincing at the bruises that were forming on his own belly, prodded Rof with his boot. 'Better not let him die, I suppose! We may need his confession to nail those others in Axmouth.'

As their blood-lust subsided, the defenders took stock of the situation, while the crew went to haul out their spare steering oar to replace the one that had been shattered. None of the men-at-arms had suffered so much as a scratch, so complete had been the surprise they sprang on the pirates – it was only their constable who had sustained a few bruises.

'Where can *The Tiger* go now?' asked Ralph, looking across at the receding cog as the remnants of her crew struggled to regain control.

'Not back to Axmouth, that's for sure,' replied de Wolfe. 'Every man of her crew who survived must live there, and we could soon find them and hang the lot if they try to go home.'

'Perhaps they'll join the other rogues in Lyme or Dartmouth,' suggested Ralph. 'Or even take the cog over to Flanders or Brittany, though I doubt they've got the brains to do that, without their master here.'

'*The Tiger* belongs to that merchant in Exeter,' observed Gwyn. 'He'll not take kindly to losing a valuable vessel. I should think they'll beach it somewhere and vanish into the woods.'

They went to look at the men they had vanquished

and confirmed that two were dead, including the one whose head Gwyn had crushed. These they tipped over-board without ceremony, and John decided that, being miles out to sea, they were not within his jurisdiction and he needed to hold no inquests upon them.

Two other seamen had deep sword wounds, one in the neck and the other in the chest. They had both lost a lot of blood and he suspected that they would both eventually die, especially if suppuration set in. Martin Rof had started to recover from the kick in the head and his arm seemed to have stopped bleeding. A rough bandage was wrapped around it by one of the ship's crew, and to be on the safe side John got Gwyn to lash his ankles together to prevent him from getting up.

By now, Angerus had shipped the new oar and had got the vessel under way again. 'Where are we bound, Sir John?' he asked. 'The Axe or the Exe?'

John looked at the castle constable. 'I suppose we had better get back to Topsham or Exeter?'

Morin stuck out his forked beard like the prow of a ship and nodded. 'Not much point in confronting the Axmouth villains with only these few men. We need to go down there with a large sheriff's posse – and the sheriff himself, if we can get him away from his clerks.'

The shipmaster brought the *St Radegund* about and they began clawing their way back westwards.

'The wind has moved more southerly, so with luck we'll just catch the evening tide to get upriver,' observed Angerus. 'Otherwise we'll have empty bellies by the morning if we have to stay out here all night.'

As they crawled across Lyme Bay, John went to the three wounded men lying with their backs up against the bulwarks. 'You'll all hang for this, of course,' he observed pleasantly. He opened his hand and showed them some pebbles that he had taken from the 'treasure' boxes.

284

'There's the silver you're going to die for! As you've nothing left to lose, except your lives, you may as well tell us what's been going on in Axmouth. Confession is good for your souls and, though you'll get a priest before the end, you can tell me as well.'

The one with the neck wound, a young man of about eighteen, began to cry, but Martin Rof summoned up enough strength to spit at the coroner. 'Go to hell, damn you!' he growled.

'I think you'll be there well before me, captain!' retorted the coroner. 'Now, who killed that poor lad Simon Makerel – and why?'

Martin turned his head away contemptuously, but the youngest man was desperate to grasp at anything that might save him from the gallows. 'It was him, sir, the shipmaster here! I saw him do it, as did half the crew. He caught the boy outside the tavern and dragged him around to the yard, where he strangled him with a length of rope.'

'You're a bloody liar! Keep your mouth shut!' snarled Rof.

'Tell me more about it, boy,' commanded the coroner.

'He was going to tell the Keeper about it, poor lad,' John told the sheriff later that evening. They had just caught the tide and decided to ride it all the way up to Exeter, rather than stop at Topsham. The prisoners had been taken up to Rougemont, using the soldiers from the ship as escort. The two badly wounded men were carried on litters, but Martin Rof's ankles were freed, so that he could walk. All three were locked in the foul cells in the prison below the keep, then John, Gwyn and Ralph Morin went up to eat in the hall above. Henry de Furnellis came out to keep them company and sat with a quart of ale while they made up for their sparse rations that day with food from the castle kitchens. He was regaled with their account of the dramatic scene out in Lyme Bay.

'This Simon Makerel was so conscience-stricken about the killing of the entire crew of that cog they pillaged that he decided to tell the Keeper of the Peace about it, after first confessing to his parish priest in Seaton,' explained de Wolfe. 'Unfortunately, he also disclosed his anguish to the young fellow we have down in the cells, who in turn was worried that he would suffer himself if Simon split on them. So he told the mate, that bald-headed swine who gave you those belly bruises, Ralph!'

'But the mate didn't kill the boy,' said Henry.

'No, he went straight to Martin Rof with the news, and the shipmaster waylaid Makerel in the village that same night and strangled him like a chicken, in front of some of the crew as a warning. He got the mate to bury him behind that bush, but unfortunately for them he was found quite quickly, thanks to the priest's dead dog.'

'Have you got that confession in writing?' asked the constable.

'I'll get Thomas to take it in the morning. I don't think the man will die for a day or two. I suppose I'd better ask Brother Saulf to have a look at their wounds tomorrow, just for the sake of Christian charity, but it seems a waste of time as they are going to hang anyway.'

As John tipped his wooden bowl to his lips to drain the last of the mutton stew, de Furnellis turned to Ralph. 'What are we going to do about Axmouth now? Unless this man Rof confesses, we really have no proof that the people onshore are involved.'

'But they must be, if we now know that *The Tiger* and her crew – which all belong to Axmouth – were taking stolen goods back there,' protested de Wolfe.

De Furnellis still looked worried. 'I'll wager they'll say they thought the stuff was legitimate cargo from abroad. We need to get these three men to confess as much as possible, especially the shipmaster.'

'The young one would turn approver, given half a chance,' replied John. 'But I'm not sure he knows much; he's little more than a ship's boy.'

Ralph Morin was more blunt in his approach. 'Turn Stigand loose on them, that'll loosen their tongues,' he growled.

Stigand was the grossly obese moron who acted as gaoler and occasional torturer down in the undercroft. He carried out the various 'ordeals', such as walking barefoot over nine red-hot ploughshares or picking a stone from the bottom of a barrel of boiling water, to distinguish innocence from guilt. In addition, he always relished the chance of applying a little torture to extract confessions. The previous sheriff, John's brother-in-law Richard de Revelle, was quite willing to give Stigand his head if it meant solving a case more quickly, but Henry de Furnellis was usually loath to use him unless all else had failed.

'Let's see how much we can get out of them tomorrow,' he advised. 'Then we have to decide what to do about Axmouth. You think that cog won't have sailed back there?'

John and Morin shook their heads. 'There's nothing there for them now, except their families. And I'll wager that the bailiff and the portreeve would give them short shrift, wanting to distance themselves as much as possible from Martin Rof and his pirates, now that they have been exposed.'

Gwyn had been silent while his superiors were speaking, but now he raised a matter that had so far not been mentioned.

'What about the owner of *The Tiger*?' he asked. 'How could he not know that the cog was being used illegally? If she was out at sea robbing other ships, she couldn't be doing her normal trading work. And with a hold full of stolen cargo, there would be no room for her own legitimate goods.'

There was a pause while the other three considered this new angle. 'You've certainly got a point there, Gwyn,' muttered Ralph. 'It depends, I think, on how closely this Exeter merchant, whatever his name is, keeps an eye on the comings and goings of his ship.'

'Robert de Helion is his name,' supplied de Wolfe. 'It seems this agent of his, Henry Crik, handles all the details. I know de Helion owns a number of ships, so maybe he doesn't keep a close watch on them all, as long as his money keeps coming in.'

The sheriff nodded. 'That would be easy enough, topping up any loss of charter fees from the proceeds of piracy. So maybe we need a stern word or two with this Henry Crik, as well as with his master in the city.'

It was getting late and soon the coroner decided to go home, weary with the excitements of the long day and the sea air. Gwyn insisted on walking back with him to Martin's Lane, mindful of the arrow that had just missed his master and the darkness of the city streets, lit only by occasional pitch flares around the castle and the cathedral Close.

They arrived at his door without mishap and Gwyn turned to go back to Rougemont, where he would bed down with his soldier friends.

'Let's hope those pirates don't die before the morning,' he said cheerfully. 'Stigand would be so disappointed.'

CHAPTER FOURTEEN

In which Crowner John goes campaigning

When John went to the castle gaol next morning, he found the new prisoners alive, but only just, as far as one was concerned. The man with the chest wound was gasping for breath, and the hole between his ribs where a sword had entered was bubbling a mixture of blood and air at every laboured movement of his chest. Though he was inevitably going to be hanged, John could not see him suffer this much, especially lying in a filthy cell.

The prison was in the undercroft, partly below ground so that the main floor of the keep was raised above it for purposes of defence. It was a dank, dark cavern, the arches vaulting the roof green with mould. Half the place was for rough storage, divided from the other part by a rusted iron grille, in which was a gate that led to a dozen foul cells. They held only a stone slab for a bed and a dirty bucket on the rat-infested straw that covered the earthen floor.

When Gwyn and Thomas accompanied the coroner to the gaol, Stigand opened up the gate for them and waddled ahead to unlock the cell. He wore a filthy tunic, covered by a long leather apron spattered with stains, some of which appeared to be dried blood.

'He'll be dead by morning, Crowner,' he advised confidently as he threw open the blackened door to reveal the prisoner lying on the slab. He was panting for breath and his lips were almost violet in colour. 'A punctured lung, no doubt about it,' he added with the confidence of a physician.

John tried to speak to the dying man, but he was unresponsive.

'You'll get nothing from him in this world, sir,' grunted the gaoler. 'But the other two should last until they swing.'

John, who like everyone else loathed Stigand, scowled at him. 'Nevertheless, I'll get Brother Saulf up here to look at him and if he so recommends we'll have him carried down to St John's. Now, let's have a look at the others.'

He left the cell and went next door where Martin Rof was sitting on his slab, contemplating the insect life that crawled in the dirty straw. He had rags wrapped around his arm but seemed alert and truculent.

'It's the bloody Crowner, by Christ! I need you visiting me like a dose of the pox!'

Gwyn gave him a clout across the ear which knocked him sideways on to his bed. 'Keep a civil tongue in your head when talking to a king's officer, damn you!' he growled.

The shipmaster pulled himself up and glowered at the men in his cell. 'My tongue has nothing more to say to him,' he sneered.

De Wolfe towered over him, though Gwyn stood ready to intervene if the man became violent. 'You're going to hang, so you may as well tell me. Who else is involved in your pirate venture? Is the owner of the vessel in on this?'

'Sod off! I'll not betray my friends,' answered Rof defiantly.

'We'll find out soon enough, whether you tell us

or not. I'm just curious as to whether your master, Robert de Helion, was party to the misuse of his cog?'

This seemed to touch a sensitive chord. 'He had nothing to do with it. He's a good man, so don't go persecuting him.'

John was satisfied with the reply, in that if he could confirm that the ship owner was ignorant of the situation, then this agent Henry Crik must be implicated. He put this to Martin Rof, but got only a mouthful of abuse in response. The same happened when he tried to discover if the bailiff and the portreeve were part of the criminal conspiracy in Axmouth.

'What about the prior's man, this Brother Absalom?'

Rof raised a dirty, blood-streaked face, his dishevelled dark hair sprouting stalks of straw from the floor. 'That slimy toad? I wouldn't know, but if he was I'll bet the prior is getting a cut!'

He refused to answer anything else, apart from offering a string of blasphemies, and for the time being John gave up his questioning.

'Perhaps a few days in that hellhole will soften him up,' suggested Gwyn as they moved to the next dismal room, where the young man with the neck injury was curled upon his stone bench, sobbing into his hands. A soiled cloth was wound beneath his chin, bloodstained at the edges. As soon as Stigand turned the rusty key, he pulled himself up, then sank to his knees in front of John as the coroner entered the cell.

'Mercy, sir, save me! I don't want to hang!' he sobbed. 'I didn't want to be a pirate; I was just part of the crew. I had no choice!'

'You were one of the first over the rail, waving your sword!' snapped de Wolfe. 'You didn't seem so reluctant then, did you?'

The young man raised his terrified face to the coroner, his hands held up clenched in supplication. 'I'll turn approver, sir; I'll testify against the others!'

'We've got to catch the buggers first,' grunted Gwyn practically.

'And I don't think we need an approver, thank you,' added John. 'We've plenty of eyewitnesses, including myself.'

The sailor burst into tears and sank to the floor, face buried in the filthy straw.

'But you can tell me who onshore was involved, as your captain seems to have lost the power of speech in that regard!'

The man looked up with a flicker of hope in his face, and John felt somewhat false, as he knew that whatever he was told this lad would inevitably be pushed off a gallows ladder with a rope around his injured neck.

'What do you want to know, sir?' he gabbled.

'When pillaged goods were taken back to Axmouth, who dealt with them?'

'They were unloaded and put in the warehouses, sir, the same as any other cargo.'

'But did anyone come to check what was there? The bailiff or the portreeve?'

The sailor grimaced with pain as he tried to shake his head. 'Never saw either of them down on the quay. Only Henry, the agent for some noble merchant here in Exeter – and of course John Capie, he was always hanging around.'

It was soon apparent that the seaman knew nothing more of use and they left, with John promising to ask the monk from the hospital to look at his neck when he came to see the dying man. With the lad's plaintive supplications following them down to the gate, de Wolfe and Gwyn left the prison, leaving Thomas behind to write down the confession that the young man had made, especially his oath that Martin Rof had strangled Simon Makerel.

'Where are we going now?' asked Gwyn as they

strode out of the castle down into the quieter lanes near St John's Hospital.

'Someone had better tell Robert de Helion that he's lost a ship from his fleet!' said John. 'And see what he has to say about his agent.'

The august, rather supercilious merchant-knight was aghast when John informed him that one of his cogs had been involved in piracy and was now in the hands of criminals, but God knows where!

John was inclined to think that his shock and indignation were genuine, unless he was as good an actor as he was a businessman.

'Are you saying that I may have lost my vessel altogether?' he cried in distress. 'That cog cost me five hundred marks to have built!'

John shrugged; he had more pressing problems than the price of a rich man's property.

'She may turn up, Sir Robert – who knows? The crew may abandon the vessel and leave her on some beach when they flee to become outlaws. Or perhaps they will sail to Brittany or Flanders and try to sell her there,' he added mischievously.

De Helion groaned. 'That idiot Henry Crik, he should have known that something like this might happen. I'll have the miserable fool flayed alive!'

'It seems likely that your agent was party to this evil trade,' said the coroner. 'I presume you had no suspicions of his involvement?'

There was a veiled hint here that de Helion himself might not be lily white, and he rose to the bait in a temper. 'Sir John, I trust you are not suggesting that I have any complicity in this? I assure you that there has not been the slightest breath of corruption coming from Axmouth, which is but a small part of my commercial interests. *The Tiger*'s voyages have always turned in a reasonable profit, according to the records that Crik brings to my clerks here.'

He shouted for his chief clerk, and soon a bent elderly man hobbled in, looking too threadbare to have made any money from piracy. His master interrogated him about the accounts and the records relating to Axmouth, but the cowed old fellow could say nothing but that everything had always seemed to be in order.

'Yet if the documents were falsified, would you be any the wiser?' asked John. '*The Tiger* no doubt spent most of her time on legitimate voyages – but if she returned earlier than expected, who was to know in Exeter that she might make an extra short foray out into the Channel to seize a passing ship?'

De Helion huffed and puffed but had to admit that this was a possibility. He even added that *The Tiger* might have come across a victim when returning from a normal voyage, especially if she was coming home light or with only a part-cargo, so that there was still room in her hold for pillaged goods.

'That swine Martin Rof is the man behind all this!' he raved. 'I met him but once, when I took him into my service as a shipmaster, and I took a dislike to him then. But I admit that I have had no complaints about his seamanship – indeed, he seems to have made a very successful pirate!'

Neither the merchant nor his chief clerk seemed to know where Henry Crik was at that moment, so soon the coroner left him still bellowing about the loss of his ship and ordering his old clerk to send messengers out along the southern coast in both directions, to see if she had turned up anywhere.

'Where are we going to seek this fellow Crik?' asked Gwyn as they walked back to Rougemont. 'He must surely be the key to this mystery.'

'The only mystery is who is involved in this scandal and who is not!' replied de Wolfe. 'De Helion was trying to include the Prior of Loders in the conspiracy, but I doubt that is the case.'

'I wouldn't trust any bloody priest,' muttered the Cornishman, half to himself, but aloud he said: 'Do you think Axmouth have heard of the loss of their *Tiger*, for she can never go back there, unless de Helion finds her abandoned somewhere.'

'I doubt the news has travelled that fast yet, unless someone guessed why the *St Radegund* came back to harbour the same day that she left,' answered de Wolfe. 'But no doubt someone will take the news to Axmouth within a day or two. The men-at-arms are bound to boast of their success in the alehouses here, so carters and pedlars are sure to spread the news far and wide.'

'What will that bailiff and portreeve do about it when they hear?' mused Gwyn. 'D'you think they'll make a run for it, if they have been involved?'

The coroner pondered this as he stalked alongside his officer across High Street and up the track that led into the outer ward of the castle. 'I doubt it. Those who are guilty will brazen it out for as long as they can. Otherwise, they can only turn outlaw, and I can't see them doing that readily, after the nice comfortable life they've had stealing so much from the king and the merchants.'

Back in their upper chamber in the gatehouse, they found Thomas at his usual task of neatly scribing the various parchment rolls that the coroner would have to present to the Justices in Eyre, when they eventually came to Exeter. As they sat down to their ritual second breakfast of bread, cheese, ale and Thomas's cider, de Wolfe fretted over what should be done next.

'We cannot delay too long in getting the sheriff's posse down to Axmouth. Even though I suspect they will play the innocent and blame everything on Martin

Rof and his crew, one of them will surely break and admit to something.'

'We'll get nothing from that Rof fellow unless we let Stigand loose on him with a branding iron – or make him submit to the Ordeal,' boomed Gwyn.

Thomas crossed himself, as he scorned such a barbaric attitude. 'The Church is becoming more concerned about the correctness of the Ordeal,' he said primly. 'The Holy Father is likely to forbid it before long, on the grounds that it smacks of un-christian paganism and magic.'

His ginger friend hooted with scorn. 'Not that it's painful, cruel and humiliating, eh? Just that it's unchristian!'

John raised a hand to stop their frequent bickering. 'At least we have the seaman's confession that clears up the death of that poor lad Simon. Now, I can complete the inquest on him, and Martin Rof will hang for the crime in due course. But we have nothing more to point to how the Keeper or that pedlar came to their deaths.'

'It will all come together in the end,' said Thomas hopefully. 'Someone will speak unwisely out of fear or conscience.'

After dictating some more case summaries to Thomas, de Wolfe tried again to study his lessons in reading and writing, which recently he had sadly neglected. Then he ate his dinner in the hall of the keep, and the afternoon was spent discussing the new situation with Henry de Furnellis and Ralph Morin and organising another military expedition to Axmouth the next day. The sheriff felt that action was needed without delay, hopefully before the news of *The Tiger*'s rout arrived in the village. Henry was afraid that either the culprits would run or at least destroy any remaining evidence of their activities. 'And they'll have a chance to dream up some excuses, if we leave it too long,' he added.

The constable went off to organise another troop of soldiers, as to call the force a 'posse' was not quite accurate, for a *posse comitatus* was a band of freemen conscripted by the sheriff 'to maintain the peace of the county and to pursue felons'. They agreed to ride out at dawn next day, led by the sheriff and coroner, hoping to catch any malefactors unawares.

De Furnellis pointed out that seizing Henry Crik was a priority and, assuming that he dwelt in Exeter, he sent several of his clerks scurrying into the city to discover where he lived. Within an hour one of them was back, reporting that though Crik, a widower, lived in St Mary Arches Lane with a leman, he was not at home. His woman said that he had left in a hurry early that morning but would not tell her where he was going.

'Blast the fellow!' cursed de Wolfe. 'He must have heard about the return of the *St Radegund* and taken off to Axmouth to warn them.'

When he returned to his house in Martin's Lane, he was struck by the empty feel of the hall, which was not a very welcoming chamber at the best of times. Now, it seemed even more cold and silent and the two vacant monks' chairs that sat near the huge hearth were a pathetic reminder of the state of affairs.

When he went around to the back yard, there was a similar sombre atmosphere, as Lucille's hutch under the solar was deserted and Mary was sitting listlessly in her kitchen-hut, absently stroking Brutus's head. Even the hound seemed melancholy.

The cook-maid raised a doleful face to her master. 'How long is this going to go on, Sir Crowner?' she asked listlessly. 'The mistress has gone, the maid has gone, I have almost nothing to occupy me, as you are away half the time and I have no one to feed except myself and the dog. You don't need a house or a maid.'

He bent to kiss her cheek and to try to reassure her

that eventually all would turn out well. 'Someone will have to look after me in London, and I'm sure it won't be my wife, whether she comes with me or not. You may depend that once I get settled there I will send for you, Mary. I will keep this house for at least a year, in case I have to return. If Matilda does decide to leave Polsloe, then she may wish to come back to live here.'

Mary brightened at his assurances and busied herself fetching him some of her own-brewed ale and heating up some mutton stew, as his dinner at Rougemont had been an uninspiring platter of tough pork, cabbage and last season's beans. He squatted on a stool to eat and told her of the events of the past two days, to which she listened with rapt attention.

'But if this monster of a shipmaster won't speak, how can you be sure who is guilty and who is innocent?' she asked.

She had touched on the very matter that concerned de Wolfe, and he hoped that the next day would see some breakthrough in that problem.

'The sheriff is pinning his hopes on this agent, Henry Crik,' he replied. 'If the fellow is found in Axmouth, then he has some explaining to do as to why he ran there as soon as he heard of the failure of *The Tiger*'s attack.'

Mary was not so convinced. 'Won't he just say that he was going to the port anyway, in the pursuit of his usual business?'

John finished the last mouthful and washed it down with a draught of ale. 'We'll just have to see what happens tomorrow. For all we know the whole lot may have fled, though I doubt they'll give up so easily.'

'Might they not make a fight of it?' asked Mary, looking worried for John's safety. 'The prosperity of the whole village must depend on the success of the harbour and its trade, so would they not try to protect the men who run it?'

'We're taking a dozen experienced men-at-arms, the same ones who overcame the pirates,' he assured her, but she still looked dubious.

'Even a dozen soldiers would fare badly against a hundred angry villagers armed with scythes and pitchforks!' she said stoutly.

John grinned and hugged her around the shoulders. 'Don't dream up a civil war, Mary! If it eases your concern for me, I'll wear my coat of mail tomorrow – but I draw the line at taking my old shield from the wall!'

Later that evening he walked down towards the Bush, passing through the cathedral Close, where the usual collection of urchins and youths were throwing a ball made of rags bound with cord. A few drunks and beggars slumped between the grave-mounds, but the fine spring evening had also brought out a few families, who were ambling along the main paths, enjoying the fresh air that was a welcome change from the cramped, odorous accommodation that many of the city dwellers had to endure.

When John came out of the Bear Gate passage into Southgate Street, the stall-keepers were packing up their wares as the evening waned. Crossing into the small lanes that led down towards the river, he passed wives gossiping outside their huts and cottages, their shrieking children still playing in the dirt of the road, dodging the occasional handcart or packhorse going down to the quayside through the Watergate. He wondered if he would miss all these familiar scenes when he went to London, until he reminded himself that one town was much like the next, only there would be far more of it in the case of the capital.

When he reached Idle Lane, he also wondered what sort of reception he would get from his mistress, having been away for a day or so. He once again found Nesta in a quiet mood, amiable but somehow distant. She sat

with him and listened attentively to his detailed story of
the ambush of the pirate ship the previous day and the
foray that was planned on Axmouth in the morning.
Once again, she cautioned him about his own safety.

'Be careful, John, if you are going with a troop of
soldiers to fight!' she warned with a worried look.
'You are not so young as you were and, though I have
no doubt about your courage, your eyes may not be so
keen and your sword-arm might not be as brisk as they
once were.'

He bridled a little at this. 'I downed the pirate
captain at my first stroke yesterday!' he protested. 'I am
not yet a feeble old man in his dotage – as I could prove
to you up in the loft tonight.'

Nesta smiled wanly at him. 'Perhaps not tonight,
John. I feel tired and out of sorts this evening. Maybe
there is a thunderstorm brewing – it affects me that
way.'

John recalled a blue sky free from a single cloud as
he walked down to the tavern. This time the moon
could not be blamed for her indisposition, and again a
niggle of concern slid into his mind. He looked around
the crowded taproom, but he saw no sign of the Welsh
stonemason.

'Are you perhaps sickening for something, *cariad*?'
he asked in their habitual Welsh. She shook her head.
'No, John, just a headache and a passing lowering of
the spirits.'

De Wolfe recalled that when she had been pregnant
the previous year, she had been in a strange state of
mind – indeed, it was only Thomas's intervention that
had saved her from doing away with herself. John
did some rapid calculation in his head and decided
that this was unlikely to be the problem now, unless
he himself was responsible.

They talked on quietly for a while, and Nesta spoke
of the journey they had made some months earlier,

when she had accompanied him back to Wales for a short visit. He had been on the king's business but had left her in Gwent to visit her family, whom she had not seen for several years. Now, she spoke longingly of her mother, who lived not many miles from Chepstow, wondering about her health, as she was advancing in years. John was on the point of promising her another such pilgrimage when he realised that soon he would be two hundred miles away in London.

He had still not told Nesta of his new appointment, being held back by some ill-formed fear of her reaction, but now he saw that he could delay no longer. Bolstering his courage, he reached to take her hand.

'Nesta, my love, I have something to tell you. This came about when I was with the king in Normandy.'

She looked at him almost fearfully, her big eyes wide in her heart-shaped face. 'I feel that this is news that will alter our lives, John!' she said. Like the mother she pined for, she was blessed – or perhaps cursed – with a certain clairvoyance, which had led her near mortal trouble in the past.

Still holding her hand, he slowly and clearly told her of the Lionheart's summons to London, an order that could not be disobeyed. 'I must go within a few weeks, *cariad*, as soon as this Axmouth problem is dealt with. I have sent news of it to Matilda, and she has not replied in any shape or form. So the way is clear for you to come to London with me – it will solve our eternal problem, as we could start afresh in a great city where no one knows or cares about us!'

When he had finished, he wondered if her famous temper, which went with her red hair, would explode over him. He did not know what to expect by way of her reaction. Would it be joy, confusion, hysterics or anger? What ensued was none of these, but a calm appraising look that unnerved him.

'Why did you not tell me this before, John?' she asked, her hazel eyes upon him.

'I lacked the courage until now. But tomorrow, though the danger is slight, I will again be handling a sword and, as you keep telling me, maybe I am getting too slow to keep out of trouble, so I felt I should unburden myself to you tonight.'

'And what of us? What of me? I have this alehouse, which is my life.'

'You must come to London with me, my love. We have spoken of leaving many times. This is a chance to make a clean break.'

Nesta looked at him dispassionately. 'There is the small matter of your wife, John. Will you just abandon her?'

John made an impatient gesture. 'I have told her what is to happen. She has made no response. It is now up to her to do what she wants.'

'And the Bush? What of my home and my livelihood?'

'We can arrange for someone to run it for a year, until we see what is to happen. I told you, this is for a trial period – for all I know, I will be back here in a twelvemonth.'

He half-turned and gripped her by her upper arms. 'Nesta, this is the opportunity we have been waiting for! London is a huge place; no one knows us there. Gwyn and Thomas will be with me, there will be new friends to make, new sights to enjoy! It will be exciting, moving from place to place when the court travels to the country. Sometimes we will be near Wales, and you can visit your family there.'

The mention of Wales caused a shadow to pass over her face, but John was too intent on persuasion to notice. 'All we have meant to each other over these past few years cannot be lost to us now, *cariad*! But I have no choice but to go where my king commands.'

She was silent for a moment, the colour drained from her face. 'This is a great shock, John. I had not expected anything like this. I must think deeply about what you ask.'

He pulled her gently against his chest, ignoring the covert glances of others in the taproom. 'Nesta, come with me to a new life! It is the chance we have sought for so long.'

She pulled away and sat looking down at her hands folded in her lap. Then she looked up into his eyes. 'Go to your battle tomorrow, John, and may God preserve you. When you come back, I will give you my answer.'

Sir John de Wolfe went to battle soon after dawn reddened the eastern sky. The jingling of harness, the scraping of impatient hooves and the snorting of horses marked the second armed contingent that week to assemble in the inner courtyard. The same men-at-arms who had sailed on the *St Radegund* were there, plus a few reinforcements. The sheriff felt obliged to accompany them and wore an old and slightly rusted hauberk that had not seen service for a decade, since he had given up campaigning.

John's similar long coat of mail, slit at the back and front for riding, was in better condition, as the previous evening Gwyn had insisted on giving it a rub-down with sand and wet rags. Ralph Morin, who had plenty of manual labour in Rougemont for such tasks, had armour whose links glittered in the morning light. The mounted soldiers, as well as Gwyn, wore thick jerkins of boiled leather, with metal plates on the shoulders – and all wore the usual basin-shaped helmets. The only one with nothing but a faded black robe was Thomas, who rode uneasily in the centre of the troop. He had protested when John ordered him to join the expedition, but the coroner was adamant that he might need someone to write down any confessions that might be made – and promised the very nervous priest that he would be kept well out of any violence until all conflict had finished.

They left at a steady trot in good weather, and even Thomas on his borrowed rounsey managed to keep up with them. They stopped at Sidford to rest the horses and eat their rations, but by noon they had covered the twenty miles to the Axe valley. The last stretch of the journey was down from the bridge over the river at Boshill Cross, upstream of the inland end of the estuary. The troop went more cautiously now, riding in pairs with the sheriff and constable at the head. A couple of furlongs from Axmouth, they kept their promise to Thomas and left him hidden behind a hazel thicket at the side of the track, where he squatted uneasily with his writing bag of parchments, pens and ink beside him. They continued down the road, the wooded slopes of Hawkesdown Hill rising steeply to their left, until the few outer cottages and then the north wall of the village came in sight. The gate was firmly closed, and Henry de Furnellis raised his gloved hand to bring them to a halt a hundred paces away.

'Never seen that shut before,' growled Ralph Morin. 'Is it for our benefit, I wonder?'

'It's hardly Dover Castle!' said the sheriff cynically. 'So what's the point?'

The wall seemed more suited for keeping out livestock than resisting a siege, for it was a dry-stone wall little more than the height of a man, though it ran from the edge of the high ground inland to the edge of the estuary, where piles driven into the mud extended a fence a little way out into the water. The gate was of stout oak, about the same height as the wall and wide enough for a cart to pass through.

'Do we shout, knock or smash it open?' asked Morin. 'They obviously knew we were coming – probably had spies posted on the road.'

'I'll go and look,' volunteered Gwyn, slipping from his saddle.

'Have a care – remember those arrows last week,' warned de Wolfe as his officer ambled towards the gate. The expedition watched as the big Cornishman picked up a rock from the side of the road and used it to pound on the gate. 'God blast you, open this bloody door!' he yelled in a voice that could probably be heard over in Seaton.

There was no response, even after Gwyn had hammered on the unyielding panels a few more times.

Impatiently, the constable nudged his horse's belly to walk it towards the gate, where from his elevated position he could see over the top. The main street stretched before him, houses on either side, with the church and the gate to the quayside in the distance.

'Half the damned village is standing in the road!' he shouted over his shoulder. Turning back, he bellowed over the gate at the few dozen men and a handful of women who were staring at the head that had appeared above the wall.

'The sheriff is here and he commands you in the name of the king to open this gate!'

There was some shuffling and gesturing amongst the throng, who stood some distance away, outside the house of the bailiff. A few defiant shouts were thrown at him, but no one approached to unbar the gate.

'Are they armed?' called de Wolfe, starting to move his own horse up to the barrier.

'A few sticks and cudgels, but nothing more,' said Ralph, wheeling his horse away and coming back to meet the others, who were now moving closer to the gate.

'I'll soon get us in there!' growled Gwyn, spitting on his hands. Reaching up, he seized the top of the gate and with a mighty heave pulled himself up until he could tilt his belly across the top. Though he was a big, heavy man, he had such strength in his arms that he could lift his bulk sufficiently to straddle the top and pull his legs over, to drop to the ground on the other side. There was an outburst of angry shouts from the crowd down the road, but still no one approached.

Gwyn pushed up the long bar from its iron sockets on the back of the gate and threw it aside, then hauled the gate wide open. Led by the sheriff, the troop trotted through and advanced on the throng further down the track.

As they approached, some of them scattered, but others stood their ground and jeered truculently as the king's men bore down on them. John saw that Edward Northcote stood by the fence around his cottage, with Elias Palmer and John Capie by his side. Further away, the old priest, Henry of Cumba, leant on his stick alongside some of the less demonstrative of his parishioners.

'Why have you broken into our village, uninvited?' demanded the bailiff. 'This is Church land. You know well enough that it belongs to the Priory of Loders.'

'It is not Church land, as you call it,' snapped de Furnellis. 'It is a manor ceded to an alien house. Which is irrelevant, anyway, as in murder or treason the king's writ runs everywhere, apart from the temporary respite of sanctuary.'

Before Northcote could argue, the coroner broke in. 'Why did you bar the gate against us? A futile gesture, as you see, but it points towards your guilt before we even ask a single question!'

'Guilt about what?' demanded Northcote.

'Don't play the innocent with me, man,' snapped the sheriff. Henry was getting too old and intolerant to bandy words and came straight to the point. 'You know damned well that *The Tiger* and her crew were caught red-handed in an act of piracy. Martin Rof is in gaol and will be hanged – he should be hanged twice, once for being a pirate and again for strangling that lad Simon Makerel.'

'What has that to do with me?' shouted Northcote angrily. 'I know nothing of piracy. What Rof or anyone else is up to in secret is their affair, not mine.'

'Tell that to the king's justices when you are arraigned before them,' suggested de Wolfe. 'For I don't believe that anything can happen in Axmouth without your knowledge – and probably your permission.'

As they were speaking, the soldiers had spread out so that they were partly surrounding the villagers, many of whom had already slipped furtively away to their homes.

'You were warned about our coming, no doubt,' snapped the sheriff. 'And you were told of the rout of *The Tiger*, almost certainly by Henry Crik. Where is he?'

'How should I know? He is Sir Robert de Helion's man, not mine.'

'Right, then we'll do this the hard way,' said de Furnellis grimly. He muttered to the constable and Morin sent Sergeant Gabriel and most of the men-at-arms hurrying off to search every house. There was an outcry from some of the villagers, but they were pushed aside as a wholesale hunt went on in the two-score dwellings of the village, as well as in their storehouses and stables. While this was going on, the bailiff, the silent portreeve and the Customs man Capie were taken into Northcote's house and stood between two soldiers while they were questioned further. Stolidly, they denied all knowledge of any piracy or illegal disposal of pillaged goods, claiming that all the cargo that was landed from every vessel was properly accounted for.

'If Martin Rof was stealing from other ships, then he must have disposed of the cargo at other ports,' said Elias, speaking at last in a quavering voice. 'Maybe

Lyme or Dartmouth – they are not particular there where their stuff comes from.'

At that moment there was a scuffle outside and Gabriel entered with two soldiers pushing a couple of men before him. 'We found these hiding in the wash-house behind the portreeve's house,' said the sergeant. The two fugitives were Henry Crik and Brother Absalom, both putting on a great show of indignation, which was cut short by the sheriff.

'Why did you hide yourselves away, eh? What have you got to hide?'

The lay brother from Loders angrily tried to shake off the hand of a trooper who was grasping his arm. 'We fled because we heard that soldiers were descending on the village,' he snarled. 'Knowing of the ways of crude fighting men, we feared for our life and limb!'

'I know nothing of what goes on here. I am a servant of a respectable merchant,' cried the agent.

'Crik, you are a liar and a thief – and possibly a murderer!' said de Wolfe. 'I accuse you of disposing of stolen goods obtained through piracy. I suspect you are one of the main plotters, along with these other men.'

The agent strenuously denied the accusations and defied the coroner to offer any proof.

'What about you, Brother Absalom?' cut in the sheriff. 'As someone who looks after the priory's interests, I fail to see how you could be unaware of what's been going on here.'

The cellarer's man looked sullenly at de Furnellis. 'I am in holy orders and I decline to answer any questions whatsoever. If you have questions, address them to the prior, for I'll say nothing at all, except to deny these scandalous accusations.'

The interrogation continued but was met with total denial by the four men.

John turned to John Capie, who had been skulking

in a corner trying to look inconspicuous. 'You, what do you know about any of this?' he growled.

The excise man turned up his hands. 'I told you last time, Crowner, all I do is count what comes in and goes out of the ships' holds. Where it comes from and where it goes is beyond me. My job is just to make tallies and give them to the portreeve.'

The bailiff drew himself up haughtily, having recovered all his considerable confidence. 'Once again, you law officers have unjustifiably disrupted and insulted our village! If you have no further business here, leave us to get on with our labours.'

Henry de Furnellis gave a cynical laugh. 'Yes, we'll be going, when it suits us. And all of you will be going with us, back to the prison in the undercroft of Exeter Castle! If you persist in lying, then you will have to be persuaded.'

There was a hubbub of anguish and protest, especially from Absalom. 'You cannot touch me, I claim Benefit of Clergy. I can say the "neck verse" to prove my status as a clerk! You have no jurisdiction over me!'

De Wolfe thought that he was probably right, but he decided to turn the screw a little tighter. 'Yes, in the fullness of time you can claim to be tried by your ecclesiastical courts under canon law – though as you belong to a foreign alien order and do not come under the rule of a bishop, even that claim might fail. But you cannot evade my questioning or my accusing you.'

'And if you don't like it, appeal to the Pope!' added de Furnellis mischievously. 'You might get a reply within a year or so!' He turned to leave the house, ordering Morin to place a guard upon the suspects until they were ready to leave for Exeter. Outside, Thomas de Peyne had just arrived, having satisfied himself that a pitched battle was not taking place in the village.

'Is there anything you require of me yet, Crowner?' he asked timidly.

'Unfortunately not, Thomas. These bastards have decided to keep their mouths clamped shut and may need some persuasion to open them.'

The clerk shuddered at the implications and crossed himself nervously.

'Keep the men searching until they have covered every inch,' ordered the sheriff. 'I think we had better look again in those warehouses on the quayside that you described to me, John.'

Demanding the keys from Capie, they set off towards the edge of the estuary beyond the church, where two cogs were visible against the bank.

'Had we better mount a guard on those, in case anyone tries to slip away by sea?' asked the constable.

Gwyn grinned and shook his head. 'No need. The tide is out – a vessel would need wheels to get away in the next eight hours!'

One cog was empty, having already discharged her cargo, and the other was half-loaded with wool, so no suspicion attached to either ship. In the warehouses, there was a collection of goods ranging from tuns of wine to bales of Flemish cloth, from cubes of fine Caen stone to baskets of tin ingots. Outside were stacks of trimmed limestone from the nearby quarries at Beer. But without a genuine manifest of what should be present, it was impossible to say whether or not it was all legal.

On the way back to the centre of the village, they met Sergeant Gabriel coming towards them. 'Found something odd in one of the barns, sheriff,' he reported, his grizzled face alight with satisfaction. 'Hidden behind a stack of straw that looked as if it had been piled there deliberately.'

They followed him into the eastern part of Axmouth, where part of the village was tucked into the neck of a small valley cutting up through the hillside. Amongst the crofts and huts were a few barns, in one of which two soldiers stood sentinel over a four-wheeled ox-cart. It had a canvas hood and stood almost totally concealed behind a mound of oat straw that reached nearly to the roof. The drawshaft lay empty on the ground, and there was no sign of the two beasts that would have pulled it.

'Who does this barn belong to?' demanded the sheriff.

Gabriel hurried outside and returned in a moment with an old man he found hiding behind the fence of the nearest house. Pulling him by the scruff of his woollen blouse, he dragged him before the sheriff and coroner.

'Is this place yours?' he barked. 'And what is this wagon doing here?'

The terrified villager immediately disowned both. 'The barn belongs to the manor, sir. Mostly hay, straw and turnips are stored here.'

'Do you store wagons here as well?' demanded the coroner, but the sarcasm was lost on the old fellow.

'It belongs to some of the carters who take the cargoes inland, sir. Nothing to do with me!'

'And where would these carters be now?' boomed Ralph Morin, jabbing his beard almost in the man's face.

'They usually lodge in the tavern, sir. There are a number of them. They come and go, as they are not Axmouth men.'

The constable ordered his sergeant to search the Harbour Inn and if they were not there to seek them in the village. Once out of earshot, Gabriel began muttering that he didn't know how to tell a carter from a wheelwright, but he set his men to find them by some means.

The wagon was empty apart from a single crossbow bolt lying on the floor behind the driving-board. Gwyn picked it up and showed it to de Wolfe, with a quizzical look on his face. John nodded his understanding, but neither could attach any real significance to the find.

'There are crossbows aplenty around the country, Gwyn. This may be nothing to do with the ones that were fired at us.'

When they went outside again, John noticed Thomas in deep conversation with Henry of Cumba, the old parish priest, but they did not approach him and, together with the sheriff and constable, he began walking back to the bailiff's house, annoyed and frustrated that they had been unable to get any confessions from their suspects.

'There seems nothing for it but to drag these bloody men back to Exeter and see if a few days of Stigand's hospitality might loosen their tongues,' observed de Furnellis gloomily.

'What about this blasted monk from Loders?' asked Ralph. 'There'll be hell to pay when his prior finds out we've dragged off one of his staff.'

'I don't give a damn about that,' replied Henry stubbornly. 'This is a task specifically ordered by the Chief Justiciar and with the consent of the king himself, more or less. I've weathered far worse than the anger of some Benedictine.'

As they reached the main track, John became aware of his clerk padding behind him and making some patently false coughing sounds to attract his attention. 'What is is, Thomas? Have you a frog in your throat?'

The priest adopted a conspiratorial manner and came so close that John could see the habitual dewdrop on the tip of his sharp nose. His voice was little more than a whisper. 'Henry the priest has been talking to me, master. I think you should hear what he has to say.'

Henry of Cumba was standing behind Thomas, looking very worried and almost guilty.

'Does he want to confess to being a pirate, too?' demanded John.

'It may well be a confession, but not of the sort you mean, Crowner,' replied the clerk. 'He says he wishes to speak to you and the sheriff, but wants to do so in the sanctity of his own church.'

De Wolfe frowned at this play-acting. 'Can't he just come out with it here?'

Thomas shook his head. 'I think you should indulge him, sir. It might be important.'

The coroner stepped across to where the sheriff was talking to Ralph Morin and Gwyn and told him what his clerk had said. De Furnellis shrugged and agreed to humour the two priests, as there seemed nothing to lose by it.

The constable said that he would go with Gwyn and see if there was any sign of the missing carters. As the tavern was directly opposite the church, they all walked down the village street, leaving the indignant prisoners held in the bailiff's house guarded by half a dozen soldiers.

John, Henry and the two priests turned into the churchyard alongside a double-stone stile, which was used for resting coffins upon before burial. The church of St Michael was a fairly new structure, built about fifty years earlier. It was a substantial building with a nave and chancel, having a squat tower and a striking arched doorway carved in zigzag patterns. The subdued parish priest led the way into the cool nave, which was set with columns on either side. Here, Henry of Cumba spoke for the first time.

'We should all pray to the Almighty for mercy and forgiveness – especially me!' To suit his words, he dropped prone on the floor at the entrance to the chancel, arms spread out as in a crucifixion, and began muttering in Latin into the flagstoned step.

Thomas also fell to his knees and with hands clasped towards the altar began declaiming aloud in Latin. The two law officers bobbed their heads, dropped to one knee and crossed themselves as a token to their faith and waited for the two black-robed figures to climb to their feet.

As with all churches, there were no seats on the packed-earth floor of the nave, but the parish priest led them to the stone ledge that ran around the church, used by the aged and infirm who 'went to the wall' when necessary. They sat in a row and waited to hear what Henry of Cumba had to say.

'I have prayed to God for guidance and His consent – or at least to avoid His wrath,' began the priest.

He fell silent, and Thomas had to prompt him. 'Tell us about Seaton, Henry.'

'When I heard that my fellow priest across the river had felt obliged to tell something of what that poor lad Simon had confessed, I went to see this brother in God. We spoke long and earnestly about the sanctity of the confessional, when the substance concerns the very lives of our flock.'

'Have you learnt something here about the crimes that have been perpetrated?' grated the sheriff, somewhat insensitively given the obvious temerity and reluctance of his namesake to speak, but Henry appeared not to hear de Furnellis's words.

'We tried to separate that which is given in formal confessional for the seeking of absolution for sins and purification of the soul – from what might be said to a parish priest as a personal friend and counsellor. We came to the conclusion that it was difficult and sometimes impossible.'

Thomas took it upon himself to try to interpret this philosophical dilemma. 'You are unsure what you may tell others of what you learn from your parishioners, is that it?'

Henry nodded. 'We also decided that the division between the two was not a fixed point but moved according to the seriousness of the matter concerned.

A confession about lewd thoughts or pilfering apples was not in the same class as murder or putting lives at risk.'

De Wolfe was becoming impatient with this priestly long-windedness. 'So what is it that you feel able to tell us, Father Henry – if anything?'

The sheriff chipped in again. 'Remember, many lives have been lost, and if it were not for our subterfuge this week another full ship's crew would have been slaughtered!'

The parish priest looked doleful and chastened. 'I realise that – I have heard today that that evil ship-master is now known to have strangled the unfortunate lad whose body I found. It was that and the knowledge that the same man intended the deaths of those shipmen this week that has decided me to speak.'

Thank God for that, thought John, and he meant it literally. 'Tell us what you know! It may save more lives. Do you know who killed the Keeper of the Peace and the pedlar?'

Henry looked at his fellow priest, Thomas de Peyne, and the little man nodded reassuringly for him to continue.

'This was not heard in this church as a confession, so I feel free to repeat it, even though I suppose it was meant as a confidential whisper. One of the villagers, admittedly a little free with his tongue from drink, told me that he had heard someone boasting in the tavern across there that they had "seen off" a drunken pedlar who was poking his nose into business that did not concern him.'

The sheriff roused himself and leant across, his bloodhound features only inches from the priest's. 'Ha! And who was that someone?'

The other Henry hesitated, then took the plunge. 'It was one of the carters who take goods inland some-where. That's their wagon in the barn.'

The sheriff and coroner exchanged a look of triumph. Though the chain of confession was tortuous, they were getting somewhere at last.

'And what else do you know, father?' asked John encouragingly. 'Tell us anything that you feel is not sacred to your confessional. It may save more lives.'

'No more confessions, but now that I have started I can tell you that with my own eyes and ears I know that the portreeve and that man from Exeter have been up to no good in respect of the goods that pass through this harbour. And I suspect that that surly wretch from the priory is mixed up with them, too.'

'What have you seen, brother?' asked Thomas, trying keep up the momentum now that the old priest's tongue had been loosened.

'Elias sometimes seems to forget that I can read as well as himself. I have been in that chamber where they scribe all their records many times – in fact, I slid back in there deliberately not long ago when no one was there.'

'You checked the records, you mean?' asked John. 'But we have done that endlessly and have no means of telling whether they are true or false.'

Henry tapped the side of his nose. Now that he had committed himself to his saga of disclosures, he almost seemed to be enjoying it. 'You had no means of checking against John Capie's tallies, did you? I went out of my way to ask Capie to explain how he did it with his sticks and his cords – just as a matter of idle curiosity, you understand? Then when I saw them on Elias's table, along with what Elias had listed in his rolls, I saw that there were numerous omissions in that day's entries.'

'Do you mean in respect of the Customs dues on the wool?' asked de Furnellis.

The priest was scathing in his dismissal of the sheriff's suggestion. 'No, not that! Everyone knows that the wool tax is fiddled all the time; John Capie and the bailiff see to that. I mean the alleged imports of wine, and cloth and fruits – sometimes even tin and marble!'

'Why didn't you tell us this before?' snapped the sheriff.

The old priest stared at the floor. 'I have to live here, my son. I am old and have not much longer to endure this world, but there is nowhere else I can go.' He faced the altar and crossed himself, Thomas following suit. 'I turned a blind eye, God forgive me, until that lad was strangled and I saw his young body in the pit I meant for my dog. Then the Keeper was slain and that drunken hawker. My conscience began to overwhelm me, and now that you king's men have descended upon us and will carry off those who would have wreaked vengeance on me if I had betrayed them I cannot hold my tongue any longer.'

He sank to his knees and began to pray again. It seemed that he had said all he was going to divulge.

'Stay with him, Thomas,' murmured de Wolfe. 'When he is ready, take down every word he said and see if you can get more detail.'

They left the two clerics talking to their Maker and left the church, going directly across the track to the thatched building opposite. As they entered the Harbour Inn, they saw the surly landlord hurrying out of the back door to see what was going on in the yard behind, beyond which was the barn where the coroner had lodged on a previous visit. As they followed him, they heard shouting and scuffling and found Ralph Morin and Gwyn coming across the yard, helping two soldiers to subdue two scruffy men who were turning and twisting in their grip.

'Found these two sods hiding together in the privy,' announced Gwyn with a great grin on his face. 'We thought of pushing them down the hole, but I thought you might want to speak to them first!'

The sheriff grabbed the innkeeper by the shoulder. 'Who are these men?' he demanded.

'Two of the carters who serve this port,' replied the man, deciding that telling the truth was the best course of action today.

'No, we're bloody not!' yelled one of them, a squat, black-haired man with a face ravaged by cowpox. 'Just travellers, passing through.'

'Just passing through the privy, is that it?' said de Wolfe sarcastically. 'Which of you killed the pedlar, or did you do it between you? We know all about it, so don't waste my time by lying.'

The reaction was surprising and satisfying to the law officers. Though the pox-ridden fellow again started to rave denials, the other, younger man, thin and fair-haired, tried to fall to his knees but was jerked up by his captors. He began wailing and sobbing, his eyes rolling wildly. 'It wasn't me, it was Dolwin who killed him!' he screeched, jerking his head towards his companion. 'And it was him who did for that bloody Keeper! I had nothing to do with it!'

Dolwin almost burst a blood vessel trying to struggle from the grasp of Gwyn and a burly man-at-arms to get at the man who was betraying him. A stream of blasphemies accompanied a promise to 'tear his lying tongue from his head', but Gwyn silenced him with a punch to the belly that doubled him up.

'Do you know the names of these men?' demanded the sheriff of the tavern keeper, who decided that cooperation was now the safest policy.

'That one with the scars is Dolwin Veg – and the skinny fellow is Adam Grendel. Both of them are carters, working for the manor.'

Henry de Furnellis, beginning to feel his age after all the activity of the day, sat himself on a tree-stump and pointed at the two captives. 'Right, we need to hear a little more of their tale,' he said amiably. 'Ralph, get them tied to those fence posts over there. We'll wait until Sir John's clerk is free to take down some confessions. Meanwhile, landlord, we'll all have a jar of ale to revive us after all these exertions!'

CHAPTER FIFTEEN

In which Crowner John receives a shock

Though John had always considered that Henry de Furnellis made an unenthusiastic, even indolent sheriff, he seemed to have found a new source of energy and even ruthlessness over the Axmouth situation.

The two carters had been interrogated while roped to the tavern fence. Though the truculent Dolwin Veg had only spat curses at his captors and threats of horrible mutilation at his partner, words had tumbled from Adam Grendel and were duly scribed on to parchment by Thomas de Peyne. Afterwards, the two men were locked into one of the storehouses on the quayside, and soon the other suspects in Northcote's house were herded down to join them. Their protests were bitter and vociferous, but the sheriff blithely ignored them and promised that this accommodation was better by far than that which they would soon enjoy in Exeter Castle. Some bread, cheese and ale were left with them and the doors locked again. Sergeant Gabriel and another soldier were left on guard outside, with instructions to eavesdrop in case any useful information was bandied about during the arguing and recriminations that inevitably must take place.

The search of the village revealed no other fugitives hiding away nor any further evidence that would help the law officers. It was now late afternoon and there was no prospect of getting back to Exeter before dusk, as they intended to use the ox-cart to transport the seven prisoners to Rougemont.

'We'll stay the night in the alehouse,' decided de Furnellis. 'The men-at-arms can forage for themselves in the village and bed down in a couple of the barns.'

Seeing the way that the village had been stripped of its leading inhabitants, the landlord became more cooperative, especially after the sheriff hinted that people who gave shelter to a couple of murderers might themselves be in trouble. He found potage, cold pork, boiled beans, bread and cheese for them, together with a passable ale and some rough cider, which Henry, Ralph and the coroner's trio ate around a rough trestle in the main room. The tavern was larger than the Bush but had the same low walls of mortared stones supporting the high trucks and rafters which held up the thatch. As they ate and drank they discussed what they had learnt so far.

'Those two swine we caught here killed the pedlar and the Keeper,' said Morin. 'But was it on the orders of someone else?'

'I suspect that killing Setricus was on the spur of the moment,' declared de Wolfe. 'They had already caught him spying on their wagon at dead of night and then later trying to steal something from the back of it. They had to get rid of him for their own safety.'

The sheriff spat a piece of pork gristle into the rushes on the floor, where a pregnant bitch immediately slunk up and seized it. 'But surely the killing of our poor Luke de Casewold and his clerk was done in cold blood,' he said.

De Wolfe tore off a piece of barley bread to wrap around a slice of the tough meat. 'I don't know about that. It depends on what that foolish Keeper was up to. He told me he was going to haunt the roads at night to catch them shifting stolen goods. Maybe they caught him red-handed?'

'Or perhaps they set a trap for him, as we did for Martin Rof?' hazarded Ralph. 'If he was making a dangerous nuisance of himself, then the ringleaders may have decided to get rid of him.'

'But who are the ringleaders?' grunted Gwyn. 'I'm confused as to who's guilty of what!'

'Henry Crik is certainly one of them, for the younger carter admitted that they got their orders from him as to where to drop off their goods,' said Thomas, timidly joining the conversation.

The sheriff agreed. 'He may be the centre of this conspiracy, as being a merchant's agent he would travel the county and could find customers who wanted cheap goods. Then he organised these carters to deliver what was ordered at the right places.'

'The portreeve is also a leading figure in this,' said John. 'It was his falsification of Capie's tallies that allowed the documents to appear legitimate, if they were questioned – as we did and the Prior of Loders does at intervals, so he claims.'

'What about John Capie – is he a criminal as well?' grunted Ralph.

'He probably knew what was going on. I fail to see how he could not,' replied Henry. 'But he's small fry compared with the others, though I'm sure he fiddles the wool tax for a cut from the exporters.'

De Wolfe wondered if his own partner Hugh de Relaga or his minions took part in this sort of evasion – then decided he did not wish to know.

'Edward Northcote – he's the problem, I feel,' said Ralph. 'Is he or is he not involved in piracy and theft?'

There was a pause, broken only by sounds of chewing and Gwyn slurping his ale. 'I just don't know,' said John eventually. 'It's hard to see that a bailiff of a place like this doesn't know everything that goes on here. But no one has put the finger on him so far.'

'We'll see who cracks first after we get them back to Rougemont,' said de Furnellis grimly. 'A spell in the undercroft should loosen a tongue or two!'

The journey back to Exeter next day was painfully slow, as the two oxen moved at a snail's pace. The sheriff and constable left most of the troop of soldiers behind and trotted away over the horizon with a couple of men, but John de Wolfe, who was in no particular hurry, stayed with the caravan. This suited Thomas, to whom horse-riding at anything more than walking pace was a miserable experience. They trudged all day across the southern part of Devon, the cries and curses from inside the covered cart becoming less shrill as no one took any notice of them. The prisoners' wrists were tied together and the ropes passed from one to the other, so there was no possibility of escape. The most vociferous was Brother Absalom, who called down vengeance from everyone above, from God Himself to the cherubims and seraphims.

By early evening the cart had reached the castle, and the passengers were given over into the care of the evil guardian of the undercroft. Gabriel had reported that when they had been locked in the barn at Axmouth, his efforts to hear anything incriminating had been frustrated by Henry Crik, who had ordered everyone to shut up and say nothing, as it was obvious to him that they were being spied upon. The sheriff agreed with de Wolfe that it was probably a waste of time to have someone listening all night in Rougemont, especially as they were all in different cells.

John took Odin back to his stable and went thankfully to his own door across the lane. He was weary and anxious, but at least the last traces of the boil on his buttock had disappeared, so the long ride had not been too uncomfortable. As he had not returned the previous night, Mary had no idea when to expect him, but he soon had a cup of wine in his hand and a promise of food within the hour. He sank gratefully into the chair near his hearth, with Brutus at his feet, though given his absence and the mild weather Mary had not lit a fire in the empty grate.

'No message from my wife?' he called at her departing figure as she went back towards the cook-shed.

'Nothing at all, Sir Coroner,' she replied. 'She's keeping you dangling, right enough!'

He sat with the pewter cup in his hand and sipped the good red wine of Aquitaine as he pondered the situation. 'Bloody woman!' he muttered to his dog. 'She's doing this on purpose, to make my life difficult. She knows now that I'm leaving for London, but how can I go not knowing what she's intending to do?' Brutus looked up at him, head on one side, but the hound had no suggestions to offer.

John sipped again and thought of Nesta. He had posed the big question to her, but she had given no answer, either. Could he just ride away to Westminster or wherever and leave her behind? She had promised him an answer when he returned, but he was almost afraid to hear it. However, the nettle must be grasped, and as soon as Mary had fed him he would go down to Idle Lane and hear her decision. He felt like someone arraigned at the Eyre of Assize, waiting for the justices to deliver a verdict that could send him to the gallows!

Mary had no chance to go out to buy fresh food at that time of the evening, so she raided her stores and found three smoked herrings hanging from a nail in the rafters of her cook-shed. She grilled these on skewers over her firepit and served them with boiled cabbage and fried onions. After two decades of eating whatever could be found during campaigns in forest, desert and ravaged countryside, John ate anything that was put before him and made no comment about this peculiar combination. Too early in the season for fresh fruit, it was followed by a bowl of nuts and raisins and a small loaf of fine wheaten bread, a change from the usual coarse ones made from barley or rye.

By now, dusk was falling, and when he had finished his solitary meal he plucked up his courage and whistled for Brutus to make the customary walk down to the Bush. As he went, he again thought of the familiarity of the route and the fact that within weeks it would be just a memory.

As he passed through the twilit lanes, men touched fingers to their foreheads and women bobbed their heads respectfully. The tall, slightly hunched figure dressed in black was a familiar sight to most people in the city, loping along with his dog at his side. They knew him for a stern but fair and honest man, which was more than could be said for many in similar positions of power and influence. Those who had already heard that he was leaving for London wondered if his successor would be as well respected as Sir John de Wolfe.

As he approached the door of the Bush, he took a deep breath and marched in, this time without hesitation, resigned to getting this over with as soon as possible. It was gloomy inside, as, like Martin's Lane, the fire was only a heap of dead ash and the sole illumination came from the flickering tallow dips in their niches around the walls. Though the shutters on the few narrow window-holes were open, the final pale light of the western sky did little to dispel the shadows, and at first he had to strain his eyes to seek out the trim figure of his mistress.

Nesta was standing by the barrels of ale, racked on wedges near the back door, dipping a jug into a large crock of cider. As soon as she saw him, she thrust it into Edwin's hand and hurried across towards him as he stood near his table. On the way, she snatched her shawl from a peg on the wall and somewhat to his surprise threw it over her head and shoulders. When she reached him, she slipped her arm through his and pulled him towards the door.

'John, let's walk. I am glad to see you safe. I was worried about you.'

Bemused, he let himself be taken out into Idle Lane, where Nesta guided his steps to Smythen Street, the dog loping along behind them.

'Where are we going, *cariad*?' he asked.

'Let's walk a while. I have a fancy to see the last of the daylight from the city wall,' she replied firmly.

This was not what he expected, and he didn't know whether it boded good or ill for him. They walked steadily down towards Stepcote Hill, where the steep lane was terraced to give a foothold. As they passed the church of St Mary Steps, he attempted to broach the big question.

'Nesta, have you thought of what I said last time?' he asked anxiously.

'I have thought of little else, John – but wait until we are there.'

She pointed to the jagged top of the town wall, silhouetted against the fading light. Across the road from the church, narrow steps were built into the stonework to reach the walkway fifteen feet above. Holding up the hem of her long kirtle with one hand, she climbed up and, when they reached the parapet, set off slowly towards the Watergate away to their left. After a few hundred paces, they reached the nearest of the twin towers that straddled the gateway below. Turning so that her back was against the stonework, she held out her hands and grasped his own.

'John, I cannot come with you to London,' she said simply.

De Wolfe tried to ignore the sudden void in his

chest. 'Why not, my love?' he asked, hoping that she wished to be persuaded.

'Because I am soon to be married,' she murmured, her eyes cast down as she spoke.

He dropped her hands as if they had become red hot. 'Married? How can you become married?'

This was the last thing he expected. After her fling with a servant in the tavern last year, he might have expected another affair with the good-looking Welshman. Yes, that was within his expectations. But married!

She raised her face and they stared at each other. 'Is it so extraordinary, John? I can never become your wife, we both know that. Am I to remain your leman for the rest of my widowed life, seeing you when it suits you? A lonely foreigner in a strange country for ever?'

'This is that Owain, no doubt?' he muttered grimly, already wondering whether he should seek out the stonemason and kill him.

'Of course it is Owain,' she answered. 'A good man, kind, and of my own age and kin. He has asked me to marry him and I have said that I will – and go home to Wales with him.'

'Have you lain with him?' he rasped.

Nesta stiffened a little and stared at him defiantly. 'How is that any of your business, John? You are not my husband,' she said crisply. 'But if you must know, I have not! He is a man of honour and is content to wait until the Church has bound us together.'

De Wolfe, for all his stern, stolid nature, crumpled at this. He pulled her to him, and his hand pressed her head against his chest.

'Nesta, Nesta! Does this have to be? I thought you loved me?'

'Of course I love you, John! But now I also love Owain, and he I can have, unlike you.'

'How can you love us both?'

327

She looked up at him in reproof. 'You should know that, sir! I have always felt that I have shared you with Hilda of Dawlish.'

It was something of a shock for him to realise that she was right. He had never suspected that she knew of his real feelings for the blonde Saxon.

'Is there nothing that I can say or promise that might change your mind?'

She shook her head, still close to his body. 'You cannot marry me or take me home to Gwent, John.'

There was iron determination in her voice that told him that nothing he could say would alter her decision. At that moment he knew that his life was going to change far more than just a move to London. His mind capitulated and his practical nature straightway began to make plans.

'Sit here, my love. We must make sense of this thing,' he said gently, guiding her to one of the stone blocks that sat behind the crenellations of the wall. Down below, Brutus had run along keeping pace with them and was now sitting looking up, whimpering slightly as he sensed that something disturbing was going on.

'Nothing will divert you from this course?' he began.

She shook her head again. 'God knows I have agonised over it long enough, but this is my last chance. I want to go home and I want to be with this good man. Do not hate him for it, John. He truly loves me and will be kind to me.'

'I should break every bone in his body, Nesta – and chastise myself as well, for it was I who was foolish enough to bring him to you!' He said this without bitterness, as a kind of calm had descended upon him. 'But what are we to do about . . . everything?' he asked helplessly.

She reached out and held his hand again, as they sat side by side on the cold stone. 'You have been so good to me, John. When Meredydd died, you saved the Bush and saved me. And again after the fire, you had the inn rebuilt. I can never repay you enough.'

He gave one of his throat clearings to cover his emotion. 'It was nothing, for I loved you, Nesta. But what are we going to do now?'

'You are going to London, I am going to Wales. The Bush is rightly yours, you must do as you think fit. Sell it and recover what you have spent on it.'

He pulled her head towards him. The shawl had slipped off and her auburn hair flowed over his shoulder. 'Nonsense! The Bush belongs to you. That loan I made when your husband died has been repaid, thanks to the skill you showed in running the place so successfully.'

'You paid for the repairs when it was burnt, John!'

'The profit from a few cargoes of wool soon covered that. No, it is yours, for you will need money to start your new life.'

'Owain is a master mason, he has a house in Chepstow and can support a wife with ease.'

John did not miss the tinge of pride in her voice and knew that the situation was irrevocable now. 'Money never comes amiss, but we will see. Maybe I already have the germ of an idea,' he said.

Now that the die was cast, he became the practical man of action that had ensured his survival as a warrior and his success as a law officer. Shocked though he had been, he already felt an unexpected sense of lightening and freedom, like lizards he had seen in the desert, which shrugged off their old skin and started life afresh. Standing up, he held out his hands to the woman he still loved but could not have.

'Come, let's go back to the Bush. I had better meet this Owain again and congratulate him – the swine!'

Next morning de Wolfe carried on with his usual routine, going up to the gatehouse of the castle to decide on the day's tasks with his clerk and officer. When Mary had put his breakfast before him in the cook-shed, he had decided not to tell her about Nesta until he had worked out a plan of action. As he spooned down his oatmeal gruel sweetened with honey, he recalled with some surprise that he had slept like a log, after fearing that sorrow and recrimination over Nesta would keep him awake all night.

Now, he was sitting behind his table in the bleak chamber at Rougemont, with Thomas scratching away on his rolls with a goose quill and Gwyn perched on his window-ledge, picking his teeth with a splinter of wood. 'When the cathedral bells ring for Prime, we are to meet the sheriff and Ralph Morin in the undercroft to see what we get from those bastards locked up there,' he announced. 'In the meantime I have some grave news to tell you.'

His tone made Gwyn throw down his toothpick and Thomas laid his pen aside, as both men stared expectantly at their master.

'Nesta is to be married to that stonemason and is going back to live with him in Wales,' he announced flatly.

The reaction of the two men was very different. Thomas adored Nesta, who had been kindness itself to him during his many and various problems. He was devastated and his eyes immediately filled up.

'Nesta leaving us?' he gasped. 'May Christ Jesus make her happy, but, oh, how I will miss her!' He crossed himself repeatedly and sniffed back his tears.

Gwyn, on the other hand, scowled ferociously and offered to go down and strangle Owain ap Gronow. When de Wolfe had explained a little more and made it clear that he had become resigned to the situation, Gwyn asked the obvious question. 'But what about the Bush?' he demanded. 'What will happen to that when we go to London?'

John, who had thought long and hard about it before going to bed the previous night, had a proposition to make.

'Gwyn, you are fonder than most men of good food and good ale. How would you like to be the new owner of the Bush?'

The big Cornishman stared at him, uncomprehending. 'Me? How could I buy the Bush? I've not two pennies to rattle together!'

'I'll buy it for you, Gwyn,' growled John. 'Nesta is going. Though she wants to give me the place, I'll buy it from her, then pass it over to you.'

His officer looked at the coroner as if he had taken leave of his senses — which perhaps he had.

'But I'm coming to London with you!' he protested. 'How can I become an alehouse keeper in Exeter?'

John was unperturbed. 'You live in a hovel in St Sidwell's, renting a shack from some grasping landlord. You have said many times that you wish you could move your goodwife and children into somewhere better, so now's your chance!'

'You mean put them in the Bush?' asked Gwyn incredulously.

'Why not? I know your wife is a capable, strong-willed woman and a good cook. She could run the inn as well as Nesta, for there's old Edwin and the two maids to do much of the work.'

Gwyn floundered for something to say. 'But why me? Why give a valuable property to a drunken old soldier like me?'

'An old drunk you may be, but you've served me for twenty years and saved my life more times than I can count on my fingers. It's time you had something to rely on for your old age.'

'I can't just take it, Crowner. How can I? It's not proper.'

John turned up his hands. 'I don't want to see the

331

Bush fall into disrepute and end up a foul den like the bloody Saracen. If it eases your conscience, I'll keep the freehold myself and give you a rent-free lease for your lifetime, allowing you to keep any profit you make. That should see your wife and family secure.'

Thomas, who had been listening to this exchange with delight, offered his help. 'I can draw up a deed to that effect, master. Nesta told me that she has a parchment which her husband Meredydd obtained when he bought it, confirming his title to the land in Idle Lane. We just need to set out the new arrangement, everyone puts their mark upon it and have it entered in the burgess court to make it all legal!'

It took another half-hour of argument and discussion to convince Gwyn that de Wolfe was deadly serious in his intentions.

'Will your wife agree to this?' asked Thomas solicitously. 'It is she who will have the burden of the place, if we are gallivanting off to London.'

Gwyn, finally reconciled to the idea, began to revel in its implications. 'Free food and ale for life!' he chortled. 'Of course Avisa will agree. Anything that gets her and the boys out of that hovel in St Sidwell's will be like a gift from heaven! She has a sister in Milk Street, with a great lump of a daughter, who can help her when needs be.'

John, who was trying to submerge his sadness in boundless activity, stood up and announced that he was going over to talk to the sheriff. 'Then we have work to do in Stigand's cesspit,' he reminded them. 'Gwyn, you go home and talk to your wife about my proposition. I have no wish to force this upon you, but I see nothing but advantage for everyone.'

His officer could walk through the East Gate back to St Sidwell's in a few minutes and be back well before the bells rang for Prime at about the ninth hour. Gwyn clumped off down the stairs, whistling cheerfully, and left Thomas and the coroner looking at each other.

'That was a very kind and generous act you did for him, sir,' offered the clerk, a rather bold speech for him to make to his master, but he was full of admiration for John's generosity.

'He has been my best and sometimes only friend for almost half my life, Thomas. It is time I did something in return.' He looked keenly at the little priest. 'And I will not forget you, when the time comes.'

Thomas looked acutely embarrassed. 'You have already saved my sanity and my very life by your kindness in taking me as your clerk when I was destitute, sir. And my needs as a priest are small. There is nothing I desire, other than to be able to serve you.'

John grunted and rumbled a little at this close shave with emotion and after a few nods at his clerk vanished down the stairs.

De Wolfe spent some time with Henry de Furnellis discussing the events of the previous two days and trying to make sense of what they knew of the suspects incarcerated below their feet. John told the sheriff nothing about the recent developments in his private life, feeling that they had better settle their official problems first.

'What about this damned lay brother from Loders?' grumbled Henry 'Someone must have informed his prior by now. We'll soon have an army of monks besieging us to get him released.'

'I suppose we can't be as hard with him as the others, if the need arises,' said John. 'It depends on what we can learn from them as to his involvement. If he's clean, which I doubt, then we'll have to let him go.'

'I'll wager my money on this agent Crik,' mused de Furnellis. 'He had the best opportunity to set up this conspiracy, being the agent for *The Tiger* and having contacts for getting rid of the stolen goods.'

'If that's so, he and Martin Rof must be close accomplices. They are the two who need to be squeezed the hardest.'

The distant bells sounded from the cathedral, and they made their way out of the sheriff's chamber into the hall and then down the wooden stairs to the inner ward. As they turned into the low doorway of the undercroft, John asked the sheriff what had happened to the two shipmen from *The Tiger*.

'The one your monk took away to St John's died, as they expected. The other one seems to have survived – at least until we hang him.'

A group of people were already waiting for them in the dank, dismal cellar. Only feeble light came through the doorway and from a couple of slits in the walls opposite the grating leading to the cells. As his eyes became accustomed to the gloom, John saw that Gabriel and half a dozen of his men-at-arms were lined up, with Ralph Morin, Gwyn and a reluctant Thomas standing behind them. There were another two persons whom he failed to recognise for a moment, then realised that they were Robert de Helion and his wizened chief clerk.

Henry de Furnellis marched over to the merchant, who stood with a rich red cloak pulled closely about him in the clammy cold of the undercroft.

'I'm not sure that you have the right to be here, de Helion,' he said. 'This is king's business and we have to seek the truth from the prisoners by whatever means proves necessary.'

'I'm a knight like you and de Wolfe here,' responded the ship owner tartly. He was not used to being told what he could and could not do. 'I've done my share of fighting and seen plenty of violence, so don't concern yourself with my feelings. I heard that my servant Crik had been caught up in your snare and I also want to know if any of these people know where my ship has got to.'

The sheriff nodded. 'Very well, but your agent seems to be the most suspect of the lot, apart from your shipmaster.'

'If Crik was involved, then he must be punished,' countered Robert.

'If Crik's involved, he'll be hanged,' was the sheriff's laconic response.

The corpulent gaoler came out through the rusted gate in the row of iron bars that went from floor to roof in the centre of the undercroft. Stigand waddled up to the sheriff, jangling a ring on which were a collection of keys. 'Do you want them brought out yet, sir?' he said thickly, his round, waxy face with the hooded eyes reminding de Wolfe of a large toad.

'Yes, let's get on with it,' grunted Henry and motioned to Gabriel.

The soldiers filed through the gate after the sergeant, and after a great deal of clanging, scuffling and a barrage of shouting and cursing the prisoners were led out in a line. They were in a sorry state, dirty, dishevelled, their clothes soiled and scattered with stalks of filthy straw. Several faces showed numerous recent bites from lice and other vermin. All wore leg-irons to prevent them from running away, but their hands were free, which they used to shake furiously at their captors as they raised a cacophony of protests and demands to be freed.

De Furnellis stood this for a moment or two, then bellowed for silence. He was only partially successful, and after a moment Morin signalled to his sergeant, who walked along the line of prisoners with a short staff, whacking the shins of the noisiest offenders until they subsided into sullen silence. The last one to obey was Henry Crik, who seeing Robert de Helion shrieked out for him to save him. He got no response from a stony-faced de Helion, and another crack from Gabriel's stick shut him up.

'As you are so talkative, Crik, we'll start with you first,' said the sheriff.

John again marvelled at the new-found energy that the old knight was displaying, after months of letting the coroner do most of his work.

The agent was jerked forward by two of the soldiers and stood before de Furnellis, who looked him up and down before starting his inquisition.

'Tell us how you and Martin Rof worked this criminal conspiracy, which has cost the lives of many innocent seamen,' he began sternly.

'I've nothing to say, for I am innocent,' growled Crik sullenly.

The sheriff repeated the question in various ways several times; Crik either ignored him or snarled that he had nothing to say. Eventually, de Furnellis gestured to the soldiers, who held Crik by the arms and led him across to an alcove beneath an arch a few yards away. The sides of the undercroft were formed by these stone arches, green with slime and mould. Most of the alcoves were used for the storage of building materials and old timber, though one held the squalid living quarters of Stigand. The area that Crik now faced was empty apart from an unlit charcoal brazier, but had four rings set into slabs in the damp earthen floor, positioned in a square. Everyone listened as the sheriff began to speak again.

'Henry Crik, I declare you wilfully "mute of malice". The law has prescribed a treatment for this sad condition, the *peine forte et dure*.' He waved a hand at the gaoler. 'Show him the plates, Stigand.'

The obese man went to the side of the alcove and, wheezing with the effort, picked up a heavy iron plate about eighteen inches square. He took it over to the sheriff, and de Furnellis hit the rusty metal with the hilt of his dagger, producing a dull thud.

'To encourage your memory to return and to loosen your tongue, we can tie you down to these rings and place this plate upon your chest. If you still feel unable to tell me what I wish to know, then Stigand here can fetch another – and another. We have no shortage of iron, I assure you.'

'You can't do this to me, it's not allowed!' howled Crik, turning pale with fright.

De Furnellis made a show of turning around and staring about the undercroft. 'Can you see anyone here who says I can't? I am the sheriff of this county and there is no one this side of Winchester who can prevent me.'

Crik made one more attempt to call his bluff, but at a sign from the crafty old sheriff Stigand dropped the plate with a clang and went to pick up some lengths of rope, which he began to thread through the rings on the floor. Sweating, Henry Crik began to weigh up which form of death he must choose. He, like most people, knew exactly what the *peine forte et dure* meant – increasing pressure on the chest, inability to breathe, blueness of the face and lips, burst blood vessels in the face and eyes – and eventually a horrible death from asphyxia.

If he confessed, he would be convicted and hanged – but because of the tardiness of the courts, that might be some time away, and many prisoners escaped, either by bribing the gaolers or escaping to claim sanctuary or to vanish into the forest to become outlaws. As his guards jerked him towards the rings, he suddenly broke and screamed out that he would talk.

'Too late, Crik. I can't deprive my gaoler of his sport. He might lose his touch if he fails to get enough practice.'

The wily sheriff had no intention of torturing the

man, but he knew that an extra dose of terror would ensure that Crik did not change his mind.

Just as Stigand held up a rope to tie around the screaming man's wrists, the other Henry clapped his palms together to halt the charade.

'Give him once last chance, then. Crik, I want everything you know, or you'll be tied down on that floor!'

It took the rest of the day to squeeze the truth from the crowd of suspects and for Thomas to write down all the facts and confessions on his rolls. Once Crik had broken and implicated others, it was just a matter of time and threats to extract the truth about the long-running conspiracy in Axmouth.

The proceedings were interrupted in the afternoon by the arrival of the Prior of Loders with his chaplain and cellarer. They had ridden as fast as their horses could travel to bring them to the rescue of their brother Absalom. Behind him was Archdeacon John de Alençon, whom the prior had roused out of the cathedral before coming to the castle. Robert of Montebourg was in a state of high indignation at the arrest of his servant, and when he saw him in such a bedraggled state, shackled like a common criminal, he became incandescent with rage.

'Release him at once, sir! He is a cleric, albeit in lower orders, but still immune from the secular power! What are you thinking of, treating him like a felon!'

Henry de Furnellis was unmoved. 'Because he *is* a felon, prior! He has admitted it from his own mouth, and you are welcome to read the confession that Brother Thomas here has written for consideration by the king's justices.'

The prior angrily scanned the parchment that Thomas handed to him, then deflated like a pricked pig's bladder. He strode over to the hapless lay brother and glared at him. 'Is this true, Absalom? Have you been deceiving me?'

The man's sullen scowl and his silence were enough for the prior. He gave Absalom a resounding slap across the face and marched back to confront the sheriff. 'Nevertheless, it is not seemly that one of the priory's brothers should be held in this place. I want him released into my custody,' he demanded.

'And that would be the last we or the court would see of him, eh?' said de Furnellis stubbornly. 'He is party to piracy and murder. He must be called to account, like the others.'

As it seemed an impasse, John de Alençon stepped forward to intervene. 'I see both points of view, gentlemen. I suggest that this clerk is transferred to the custody of our cathedral proctors. We have secure cells in the cathedral Close and robust men to guard them, until the bishop and the prior come to some agreement as to how the matter should be resolved.'

Rather grudgingly, the sheriff agreed, and two soldiers unshackled Absalom and took him stumbling out after the churchmen.

De Furnellis turned back to the line of prisoners, now wilting badly after their long ordeal. 'Right, now let's hear from you, Martin Rof – unless you want a hundredweight of iron to keep your chest warm!'

With Henry de Furnellis in such an unusually bullish mood, John had been more than content to stay in the background. He felt somehow remote from what was going on, his mind full of images of Nesta. The years they had had together now seemed like some dream, already fading but shot through with clear images of times they had made love or had sat together in the warm fug of the Bush's taproom, as well as the several crises that had bonded them even closer. As he stood in the dank undercroft, the yells from the prisoners and the bark of the sheriff's voice faded in and out as he recalled learning that Nesta was with child, then the loss of the babe, her attempt at drowning herself – and the time when she came near to being hanged as a witch, let alone her close escape from death when the Bush was set on fire.

The many hours and the frequent nights that he had spent in her little cubicle screened off from the public loft wafted in and out of his consciousness as he stood alongside Gwyn in Stigand's domain, half-listening to the cries, the pleas and the protests of the men from Axmouth.

The sheriff's voice snapped him out of his reverie and he pulled himself together, chiding his own inattention at such an important point in their investigation.

'The bastards are contradicting themselves and starting to accuse each other, John, which is just what we need. But I'm getting confused about who did what, so I hope your clerk is making more sense of it than I am!'

Poor Thomas, now seated on a box dragged from one of the alcoves, was sitting where he could get enough light from the doorway to write on the parchment resting on a board across his knees. A pot of home-made ink rested precariously on one corner, and he was scribbling away as fast as he could.

'Are you getting the gist of this down, Thomas?' said de Wolfe, leaning over his shoulder. He saw an irregular series of marks, which although he could not read looked different from his clerk's usually immaculate script.

'It is my own method of making brief notes, master,' answered the harassed Thomas. 'Everyone is speaking too quickly for me to record it verbatim; it is not like dictation. But afterwards I will transcribe it into a fair copy for you – and presumably the Justices in Eyre.'

'Well said, Thomas!' cut in the sheriff. 'This is getting

so damned complicated that I suggest we should keep the sods locked up and push the whole problem over to the king's judges or the Commissioners, when they next come to the city.'

When all the half-dozen prisoners had been interrogated and shouted at sufficiently, they were forcibly herded back into the cells. The law officers and their assistants adjourned to the hall upstairs for some refreshment and to discuss what they had learnt. The sheriff commandeered one of the long tables, clearing off the people who had been sitting there, and the castle constable yelled at some servants to bring them food and drink.

'So what did we manage to squeeze out of those lying swine?' asked John, determined now to give his full attention to the matters in hand.

Thomas spread his tattered palimpsests on the table and scratched his shaven crown with the end of his quill as he began deciphering the shorthand he had scribbled down.

'We know that Martin Rof strangled Simon Makerel, as the young shipman admitted that he had seen him do it. Whether or not the other conspirators like the bailiff and portreeve sanctioned it, is not clear.'

'What else have you got written down, Thomas?' asked John.

The clerk shuffled his parchments on the table. 'The carter Adam Grendel blamed Dolwin Veg for killing the pedlar who had spotted them delivering at dead of night – and for the death of the Keeper and his clerk, though it seems that both Grendel and some others were involved. It seems that they had a sideline as paid assassins as well as running an ox-cart.'

'Remind me of what Henry Crik had to say,' grunted the sheriff. 'He was the real breakthrough, of course. The threat to crush his chest certainly made him talkative.'

Thomas found the correct page and studied it short-sightedly, running his finger along his hieroglyphics. 'He says that Martin Rof and the portreeve were the ones who first decided to start indulging in piracy, about two years ago. The evasion of Customs duty had been going on much longer, though it got more lucrative when the King's Council brought in the wool tax and increased the other import duties. As they had had such success with that misdemeanour, they thought they could make even more profit from stolen goods brought in by *The Tiger*.'

'And Henry Crik got involved because he was the cog's agent and they also needed him to help find buyers for the illicit goods,' added the sheriff.

John rubbed a hand over his black stubble, often an indication that he was puzzled. 'So how did this bloody lay brother from Loders come into it?'

'Crik says that he soon tumbled as to what was going on and demanded a share in the racket, or he would denounce them to the cellarer and prior. Absalom denied it all, of course, but Crik says that he was keen to put a nice nest egg aside and then vanish from the priory to live comfortably far away.'

The food and ale had arrived and they broke off to cut fresh bread, hack hunks of cheese and chew some hot meat pastries that the castle cooks had provided. Then Henry de Furnellis returned to the main issues.

'So we have Elias Palmer, Martin Rof, Henry Crik and Brother Absalom certainly guilty of either murder, piracy or evasion of Customs dues. Then these two carters killed the pedlar and the Keeper, according to both Crik and Grendel, who tries to shift the blame on to the other carter, Dolwin Veg.'

'And I suspect they attempted the murder of Gwyn and myself,' growled de Wolfe. 'They are most likely the bastards who laid an ambush for us with crossbows, when we were getting too close to their misdoings. The business with the false call to a corpse in Ottery St Mary was too clever for those dullards. No doubt the Axmouth gang set it up, with some stranger paid to impersonate the Ottery reeve.'

The sheriff put his tankard down on the table with a bang.

'What about the bailiff, this Edward Northcote? And that John Capie, the fellow the county employs as a Customs collector, God preserve us? What are they guilty of?'

The little clerk thumbed nervously through his notes. 'No one has actually said that either of them were involved in the piracy and the selling of the stolen goods, sir. But everyone seems to accept that the whole village knew about evading the taxes, so they must have been aware of that, for Capie was the man responsible for counting the stuff.'

John strove to keep his mind on the problem. 'I'll wager the bailiff knew every damned thing that went on in that village. He may not have taken an active part in the piracy nor perhaps shared in the loot. But there's no way that he wouldn't have known about it, and at the very least he must have turned a blind eye.'

Henry tossed the crust of a pastry to a thin cat that was slinking from under the table. 'Well, as I said earlier, I'm going to dump the problem in the lap of the king's court. The Commissioners of Gaol Delivery are due here next month, so let them sort it out! The villains from Axmouth can rot down the cells until then – and I'm letting the Church decide what they want to do with that fellow from Loders.'

John thought rather sourly that the sheriff's recent revival of enthusiasm had suddenly petered out, but in a couple of weeks he would be in London, so it would not be his problem.

What was his problem was managing the upheaval in

343

his private life, and the sooner he got down to dealing with it, the better.

De Wolfe had expected that having to go down to the Bush again would be an ordeal, but somewhat to his surprise he found that a certain calmness had entered his soul. That evening he walked Brutus around the Close for a while, not to disappoint him, but then returned him to Mary and set out alone for Idle Lane.

He entered the taproom without hesitation and strode across to his table, as he had done for several years. Gwyn was already there, as arranged earlier, a bowl of fish soup and a hunk of bread before him. As John sat down, Edwin came across as usual and placed a pot of ale in front of him but hovered about, an uneasy look on his aged face.

'Hear you're off to London, cap'n,' he said rather nervously. 'We'll all miss you greatly.' He hesitated for a moment. 'And we'll be lost without Mistress Nesta, too.' He swung away quickly, as if he feared a tear would appear in his one good eye.

John took a deep swallow of the ale, thinking that he had better make the most of it, as it was unlikely that he would get such a good brew in London. He glanced around at the score of men drinking in the room and knew from the way they studiously tried not to look in his direction that the news was already all over the city ... 'the ale-wife's getting married and the crowner's leaving town!'

A few moments later he broke off talking to Gwyn as he saw Nesta coming down the ladder from the loft. At the same time Owain ap Gronow appeared through the back door, carrying a large pitcher of cider which he placed alongside the ale barrels. An illogical feeling of relief flooded John's mind when he saw that the Welshman had not been up with Nesta in her tiny bedroom, until he realised that it was now none of his business.

He stood up and stalked across the taproom to where the pair were now standing together, apparently discussing the ale and cider. When Owain saw John advancing upon him, he stiffened and looked as if he was expecting an assault upon his person, but John held out his hand and gave a twisted grin.

'By rights, lad, I should give you a beating – but I'll settle for congratulations!' He gripped the mason's upper arm in a gesture of acceptance, and Owain smiled in relief as Nesta watched warily.

'I don't know what to say, Crowner!' Owain blurted out in Welsh. 'Nothing can be adequate after what you've done for me. Saved my life, then led me to the best woman in the world.'

Again, John smiled crookedly 'I'll not argue with the last part, though perhaps I should have let those outlaws cut your throat!'

He turned to Nesta. 'We have important business to talk about, *cariad*. It now concerns your future husband, so let's all go and sit down with Gwyn, for he's involved as well.'

Mystified, Nesta did as she was bid, and as she sat down Gwyn noticed with a sigh of sadness for times past that she placed herself on the bench opposite de Wolfe with Owain close alongside her. John leant forward and the others did the same, not wanting their business to be heard by the other patrons.

'Nesta, you had the silly notion of *giving* the Bush to me when you left for Gwent, but that just cannot be! I will purchase it from you and there will be no arguments.'

He overrode the start of her protests. 'It is true that I helped you when Meredydd died, but you have repaid that to me from the success you made of running the inn. It is also true that I paid to repair the building after it burnt down, but in recent years Exeter has burgeoned with its trade. Now, property is worth more, so unless you object to the price I will repay you what Meredydd paid four years ago.'

With flushed cheeks, she again started to reject his offer as too generous, but he would have none of it. 'Look on it as a dowry or a wedding gift, Nesta. Perhaps you might wish to open a tavern in Chepstow – it would be a sin if the world was deprived of the best ale in Christendom!'

Then he went on to explain his plan to give the tenancy of the Bush to Gwyn, the place to be run by his wife Avisa in his absence. Gwyn, after his initial bewilderment at his master's generosity, had taken enthusiastically to the idea. He had already told John that Avisa was delighted with the proposal, a dream come true to get out of the squalor of their hut in St Sidwell's and have a bigger home and a business to run.

Now knowing that her good friend Gwyn was to be the beneficiary, Nesta soon came round to accepting John's stratagems. She knew Avisa as a strong, sensible and capable woman and was sure that she would make a success of running the inn. It was also a relief to Nesta to know that the Bush would be in friendly hands, instead of being taken by a stranger who might let the place degenerate, like some of the other drinking dens in the city.

At first, Owain was a little insulted that John felt that his bride might need her own money, when he, a master craftsman, could easily support her. However, Nesta's new-found enthusiasm soon weaned him around to the good sense of the scheme. It was not long before Nesta was plotting with Gwyn to have another partition in the loft to act as a sleeping place for the two boys, an almost unheard-of luxury in all but the most affluent homes. They talked for a time, and as they drank each other's health in her best brew, all trace of awkwardness between them faded away.

De Wolfe looked at the two younger people across the table and saw that they were genuinely fond of each other. He knew how much Nesta yearned for her homeland and her family and resignedly accepted that this had to be the best solution. John accepted that he could never marry her and that as they grew older the division between them would grow more obvious. However, after an hour or so, sadness began to creep over him again as he saw how his visits to the Bush would never be the same again – and in fact would soon cease altogether except on occasional visits to Exeter.

The sight of Nesta sitting so close to her new man at what had always been 'their table' eventually drove him away, and after a warm kiss on the cheek from her, he stalked out into the night. Gwyn thought of going after him, but in a rare moment of sensitivity he decided to let him go alone. Five minutes later, he slid away himself and went to the Crown Inn in High Street for a final quart before the East Gate was closed at the evening curfew. Then he went home to Avisa to confirm to her that her new life would soon be a reality, but at the same time he wondered what the future had in store for him.

Two weeks later, on a bright morning in early May, a farewell party assembled in Idle Lane, outside the front door of the Bush.

A score of the inn's regular patrons formed a large half-circle, inside which Edwin and the two maids were going round with jugs of ale, topping up the pots and cups with which the crowd was toasting the health and happiness of Nesta and Owain.

The stonemason was already seated on his horse, a grey mare which had been recovered after his ambush and housed ever since in the farrier's stable in Martin's Lane. Owain looked flushed and slightly embarrassed at the unexpected celebration that was attending their departure, but happy that he was going home with such a comely bride-to-be.

Gabriel, a frequent customer of the tavern, held the bridle of Nesta's mount, a sleek rounsey that de Wolfe had bought her for the journey. Brought up outside a small village in Gwent, she was an expert rider, having sat bareback on Welsh mountain ponies since she was old enough to walk. Now, she stood for the last time with Gwyn, Thomas and John, in a tight little group alongside her saddle. The little clerk was openly crying, as she hugged him close and gave him kisses on both cheeks.

'May Jesus and his Blessed Mother keep you safe and happy, Nesta,' he gulped, pressing into her hand a parting gift. It was a small ivory crucifix, one of his few prized possessions. She kissed him again, tears in her own eyes, then moved into the bear-like hug of Gwyn, another of her devoted admirers. He kissed her enthusiastically on the lips, his great moustaches tickling her face and neck.

'Look after yourself, good girl!' he boomed in his version of Welsh. He gave her a small eating knife, in a wooden sheath that he had carved himself. 'If that bloody man doesn't treat you well, stick this into him!' he added with a great laugh that softened his advice.

Lastly, Nesta moved to John, standing silently near her horse's rump. Crying unashamedly now, she reached up and put her arms around his neck to kiss him farewell, oblivious of her husband-to-be sitting on his horse a few yards away.

The kiss lingered, then her face moved to his shoulder as she whispered into his ear. 'I will always love you, *cariad* – but this has to be the best way!'

All he could manage when she slipped out of his

arms was a rasping noise in his throat as he watched her through a blur as she went to Gwyn, who lifted her on to her side-saddle as if she were a doll.

'We must be off!' called Owain, raising his hand in the air. 'Or we'll miss our company at the East Gate.' They had arranged to travel as far as Taunton with a group of merchants and pilgrims for safety against the threat of robbers on the highways.

With a noisy chorus of well-wishing, the circle opened to let them through and the two riders clopped away, their few possessions, mainly clothes and Owain's tools, packed securely behind the high cantles of their saddles. With final shouts and waves, they reached the junction with Priest Street. As they turned, John's eyes were fixed on the figure of his lover, her green cloak flowing over the palfrey's back, the linen of her cover-chief bright in the morning sun. His last sight of Nesta was of her raising a hand to her lips and throwing a kiss to him – then she was gone.

As the throng broke up, many of them vanishing back into the tavern where Gwyn's wife bustled around to serve them, John felt as if all his blood had been sucked out of his body. He went to the wall of the Bush and slumped down on the bench, a plank laid across two logs. Gwyn came and sat on one side and Thomas on the other.

'That's that, then,' he muttered. 'She's gone and may God take good care of her!'

Gwyn did his best to console him, in his bluff and hearty manner. 'We'll see her again, never fear, Crowner! By what you told me, this new job of ours will take us all over the country. William the Marshal's castle of Chepstow is bound to be visited sooner or later – and the other Welsh Marches, like Hereford, are not far distant.'

'That young man Owain is a good and devout fellow,

master,' said Thomas through his sniffles. 'He will be kind and gentle with her, never fear.'

De Wolfe was grateful for his faithful servants' efforts to raise his spirits, but he wanted to be alone for a while, to come to terms with this wrench in the ordered pattern of his existence. He stood up and stretched his back and his arms, as if he had just awoken from a deep sleep.

'I think I'll walk Odin back up to the farrier and then pester Mary for an early dinner,' he said slowly. 'Maybe there'll be some message from my wife, for we have only two days now before we leave for London.'

His words had an immediate effect on Thomas, who went pale and smote his forehead with a hand. 'Forgive me, sir, I quite forgot, with all this sad excitement of Nesta leaving.' He scrabbled in the pouch on the belt of his shabby cassock and produced a small square of parchment. 'This was brought to me after early Mass by a servant from Polsloe. It is a note written by Sister Madge.'

De Wolfe snatched it from him, then handed it back. 'Read it for me, Thomas, I beg you!' he commanded.

'It says: *Written at Matilda de Wolfe's behest. She wishes to inform her husband that she needs more time to contemplate her future life and to arrive at a decision between her earnest desire to remain in the company of God or to return to the state of matrimony, whether in London or elsewhere.*'

Thomas handed the parchment back to John with an apologetic look. 'That's all it says, master, I'm afraid.' He backed away when he saw the thunderous look on the coroner's face as he leapt up from the bench.

'The bloody woman!' he roared. 'She's doing this on purpose, keeping me dangling on a string! Why the hell can't she make her mind up one way or the other?'

He pushed Thomas aside and strode towards the side of the Bush, where Odin was tethered to a rail, contentedly cropping at the rough grass. His officer and clerk followed him, bemused at his sudden change in mood. John grabbed the reins to untie them, then put a foot in a stirrup. As he swung himself up on to the destrier's back, he let rip another blast of invective.

'She's torn between God and the prospect of being wife of the Coroner to the Royal Court, that's what it is!' he shouted angrily. Pulling Odin's head around, he touched his flank with his heels.

'Are you going up to Polsloe, Crowner?' called Gwyn.

De Wolfe looked down from the stallion's back. 'No, I'm bloody well not!' he shouted. 'I'm off to Dawlish, where I have unfinished business!'

POCKET
BOOKS

THE AWFUL SECRET
Bernard Knight

Intrigued and irritated by the presence of a
mysterious figure who is watching him, John's
henchman Gwyn finally manages to catch up
with the man, and no one is more surprised than
John at the identity of his stalker . . . Gilbert de
Rideford claims to be in possession of an awful
secret and needs John and Gwyn's help to escape
from a secretive order of warrior monks. As John
is drawn deeper into a world of religious intrigue
and dangerous politics, he realises that he must
take Gilbert much more seriously than he had
first thought . . .

PRICE £6.99
ISBN 0 7434 9208 0

POCKET
BOOKS

THE SANCTUARY SEEKER

Bernard Knight

November, 1194 AD. Appointed by Richard the Lionheart as the first coroner for the county of Devon, Sir John de Wolfe, an ex-crusader rides out to the lonely moorland village of Widecombe to hold an inquest on an unidentified body.

But on his return to Exeter the coroner is incensed to find that his own brother-in-law, Sheriff Richard de Revelle, is intent on thwarting the murder investigation, particularly when it emerges that the dead man is a Crusader, and a member of one of Devon's finest and most honourable families . . .

PRICE £6.99
ISBN 0 7434 9205 6

POCKET
BOOKS

CROWNER'S QUEST

Bernard Knight

Christmas Eve, 1194. Sir John de Wolfe gratefully escapes a party given by his wife Matilda, to examine the body of a canon who has been found hanged. Suicide is suspected, but it is soon apparent that there is more to this case than meets the eye.

As usual, John's investigations are hampered by his brother-in-law, Sheriff Richard de Revelle. But when a local lord is killed, John begins to suspect that the cases are linked and Sir Richard's reasons for delaying the investigation may be more sinister than the usual petty vengeance.

PRICE £6.99
ISBN 0 7434 9207 2

POCKET BOOKS

This book and other **Pocket** titles are available from your book shop or can be ordered direct from the publisher.

☐ 0 7434 9205 6	**The Sanctuary Seeker**	**Bernard Knight**	£6.99
☐ 0 7434 9206 4	**The Poisoned Chalice**	**Bernard Knight**	£6.99
☐ 0 7434 9207 2	**Crowner's Quest**	**Bernard Knight**	£6.99
☐ 0 7434 9208 9	**The Awful Secret**	**Bernard Knight**	£6.99
☐ 0 671 02966 5	**The Tinner's Corpse**	**Bernard Knight**	£6.99
☐ 0 671 02967 3	**The Grim Reaper**	**Bernard Knight**	£6.99
☐ 0 7434 4990 8	**Fear in the Forest**	**Bernard Knight**	£6.99
☐ 0 7434 4989 4	**The Witch Hunter**	**Bernard Knight**	£6.99

Please send cheque or postal order for the value of the book, free postage and packing within the UK; OVERSEAS including Republic of Ireland £2 per book.

OR: Please debit this amount from my:

VISA/ACCESS/MASTERCARD ....

CARD NO..

EXPIRY DATE...

AMOUNT £ ....

NAME...

ADDRESS..

....

SIGNATURE..

www.simonsays.co.uk

Send orders to: SIMON & SCHUSTER CASH SALES
PO Box 29, Douglas, Isle of Man, IM99 1BQ
Tel: 01624 677237, Fax 01624 670923
E-mail: bookshop@enterprise,net
Please allow 14 days for delivery. Prices and availability subject to
change without notice.